Praise for *No Clock in the Forest*, Book I o.

"This is a romance in the best sense of that old word: a tale of strange adventures and a struggle between good and evil in a world where we are never very far from beauty or terror. It invites comparison with both Lewis and Tolkien because they are all drawing water from the same deep spring."

—Loren Wilkinson, *Earthkeeping*

"*No Clock in the Forest* takes its place in the long tradition of fantasy writing—but with a difference. Willis weds to the world of faerie a precise and intimate knowledge of the wilderness and perhaps has invented a new and timely sub-genre: the eco-fantasy."

—Daniel Taylor, *Tell Me a Story: The Life-Shaping Power of Our Stories*

"This is a work of both careful craftsmanship and rich imagination. Willis takes his readers into a wilderness where nothing is predictable. He leads them to wisdom and joy. Then he returns them to their everyday world renewed and changed."

—John Leax, *Grace Is Where I Live*

"*No Clock in the Forest* makes the Pacific Northwest feel a little like Narnia. Willis has produced moral fiction that doesn't moralize, touching issues both timeless and timely."

—David C. Downing, *Looking for the King: An Inklings Novel*

THE ALPINE TALES

The
ALPINE
TALES

No Clock in the Forest

The Stolen River

The Silver Spire

The White Fawn of Otium

PAUL J. WILLIS

WordFarm
SEATTLE, WASHINGTON

WordFarm
2816 East Spring Street
Seattle, WA 98122
www.wordfarm.net
info@wordfarm.net

Cover Image: iStockphoto
Cover Design: Andrew Craft
Illustrations: Laurie Vette

Book text is set in 12 point Monotype Centaur.

USA ISBN-13: 978-1-60226-006-1
USA ISBN-10: 1-60226-006-0
Printed in the United States of America
First Edition: 2010

Library of Congress Cataloging-in-Publication Data

Willis, Paul J., 1955-
The Alpine tales / Paul J. Willis. -- 1st ed.
    p. cm.
ISBN-13: 978-1-60226-006-1 (pbk.)
ISBN-10: 1-60226-006-0 (pbk.)
1. Wilderness areas--Fiction. 2. Ecology--Fiction. 3. Fantasy fiction, American. I. Willis, Paul J., 1955- No clock in the forest. II. Willis, Paul J., 1955- Stolen river. III. Willis, Paul J., 1955- Silver spire IV. Willis, Paul J., 1955- White fawn of Otium. V. Title.
PS3573.I456555A79 2010
813'.54--dc22

                                                                2009049236

P 10 9 8 7 6 5 4 3 2
Y 16 15 14 13 12 11

for Sharon

beauty as well as bread

Contents

✳

BOOK III: WINTER

The Silver Spire

BOOK IV: SPRING
The White Fawn of Otium

Preface

✳

I feel perhaps that I owe the reader some explanation of the history of these four tales. The first two, *No Clock in the Forest* and *The Stolen River*, were published and then republished in earlier versions some years ago. The second pair, *The Silver Spire* and *The White Fawn of Otium*, were then composed and laid to rest in a cabinet for Horace's nine years and more. It was the generous suggestion of one experienced editor that all four tales be combined in a single volume. "Readers of fantasy," he said, "like to get lost in long books." This notion gradually took hold, and eventually a willing publisher came forward.

What remained was to revise the whole quartet in ways that had suggested themselves over the years. But it seemed like such old work, the odd remains of a younger self. I was not even sure that I could re-inhabit it. But I found to my relief and delight that I was able to enter these stories once again and make them into a firmer whole.

Those readers who have met with previous incarnations of the first two tales will not have to suffer through radical alterations of plot. My changes have been almost entirely stylistic. I think it was Mark Twain who said that the difference between the right word and the almost right word is the difference between lightning and a lightning bug. Though I cannot promise a splendid alpine thunderstorm on every page, at least I may have gotten rid of some of the more obnoxious mosquitoes.

Paul J. Willis
Santa Barbara, California
October 2010

What did you go out into the wilderness to behold?

—Luke 7:24

BOOK I: SUMMER

No Clock in the Forest

❋

Rosalind: I pray you, what is't a' clock?
Orlando: You should ask me what time o' day;
there's no clock in the forest.

—Shakespeare, *As You Like It*

Chapter I
A Serious Ax

✳

As Garth drove through the last of the clearcuts, William leaned his head against the window of the car. He felt his skull rattle faintly and saw his own eyes in the outside mirror, moveably framed by fields of stumps all silvered and shattered and shifting by in a roadside dance of death. When he sat up straight he saw a fresh round chin, plopped in the mirror like a scoop-and-a-half of vanilla ice cream. He tensed his jaw and jutted it slightly. The effect was heroic; the effort, however, hard to sustain.

Beyond William's reflection, the road passed into the forest and left the stumps behind. The amber signs that marked each curve began to hide in the reach of red cedar. At every turn the highway vanished, swallowed up in the greenest of worlds, an asphalt snake consumed by the garden. Garth slowed down as if to relish such a thought.

"Have you seen," he said, "how the sword fern come to the road right here?" He held the arc of the steering wheel as if it were a single frond, pendant with morning dew. He held it gently, so the dew would glisten where it was and not drip into his lap.

William turned and grunted. He saw the long white hair, the long white beard, thick like the lichen on the trees passing by. Why, he wondered, had he ever agreed to climb a mountain with Garth?

Climbing mountains was nothing new to William. Far from it. By the count that he kept on the green-glow screen of his home computer, he had conquered sixty-six of them. No one else of his acquaintance yet owned a computer, and few that he knew had anything like his growing alpine resume. In spite of his somewhat flabby physique, he thought of himself as fairly accomplished, decently skilled, a real mountaineer. In short, the standard routes were beneath him now. What mattered were Serious Climbs. A Serious Climb held objective danger. It required boldness and commitment. It took fury in the heart and courage in a rucksack; it met the mountain on its very own terms. If William completed enough of these routes (or knocked them off, as he put it), he might one day be referred to as a Serious Climber. It would be whispered quietly, behind his back, at the University Alpine Club. In years ahead he would flip through slides of his latest expeditions. The clubroom would be dark with awe. "Baltistani tea is bloody wretched," he would say. "It's all we had for a week in the blizzard at Camp IV." Afterwards, total strangers would ask what kind of mittens he had worn on the summit day.

As of yet, given his job in instructional technology, he had not found time for the far-off ranges of the world on the weekends. So he sought his manhood in the local hills, and found his partners, such as they were, at the Alpine Club meetings on Tuesday nights. But on the last Tuesday night, Garth had found him. The aging professor had marked him from across the room, edged to his side, taken his arm, and politely proposed they attempt the South Queen. For a moment, William was ecstatic. The northeast face was a climb he coveted. But the southwest slope was what Garth had in mind, which confirmed what everyone said of the man—that he only did walk-ups. This made Garth the worst sort of partner for an aspiring Serious Climber. So that should have been the end of it. William tried to edge away, but the old man held him with a glittering eye.

"Will you go?" said Garth.

"I will," said William. He answered with the surreal and sacred surprise of a bridegroom at a wedding ceremony.

So on this particular Saturday morning, Garth and William were trailhead bound, one watching ferns, the other regretting a weekend lost. William sighed, tuned in static on the radio, tuned it out, pushed up his sleeves, pushed them down, peeled his thumbnails, wished them back, and bent down to untie and retie his boots. That completed, he fished his ice ax from the seat behind him and held it on display. It was the mountaineer's tool, his rod and his staff, his terrible swift sword. And since this his ax was newly purchased, it was more than worth discussing.

"New ax?" said Garth.

"New ax," said William. He drew a large breath before telling its secrets. "Seventy-centimeter. It's got a chrome-moly head, drooped pick, razor-cup adze, *plus*, a laminated aluminum graphite and fiberglass shaft—so it won't vibrate. *And*, the angle on the pick is adjustable." This he demonstrated, ratcheting the head of the ax in all directions. "The coating on the shaft is electrostatically applied—won't chip off like regular paint. Got it 35 percent off, too—at that warehouse place on Apple Street."

Garth checked the rearview mirror. "Old one break?"

"Uh—no," said William. "But this one handles lots better."

"Of course," said Garth.

William twisted around and put the ax away. He saw Garth's wooden ax on the back seat too. It was nearly as long as an antique alpenstock, and battered enough to have been one. No ice tool, that—merely a cane for hobbling up snowfields. He knelt backwards on the seat and ran his hand along the shaft. The wood was dark, smoky, smooth. In places he saw knots and whorls, obvious weak spots. One short fall on a boot-ax belay would snap it like a twig.

"How strong is yours?" he asked.

"As strong as you trust it will be," said Garth. For William it would not be strong.

He tried to guess the wood. Not laminated bamboo, certainly. Maybe ash, or hickory. He asked the old man.

"From the original," said Garth.

"Original what?"

"The original grove," Garth said. "The forest primeval."

William was not familiar with this kind. "But how well does the shaft take the shock on ice? Does it make your hand shiver?"

"Sometimes," said Garth, "it makes my hands tremble."

"I thought so," said William. He was pleased to have guessed the flaw.

He examined the head of the ice ax now, stroking the smooth and tarnished arc. He brushed the edge of the adze, the edge of the pick, both blunt with age. He stopped. Blunt were they? He drew back his fingertips, strangely numb. His own red blood was beading there. How could it? He brought his fingers to his lips and sucked them clean and held the taste within his mouth. The taste made him shudder. He checked beside himself—Garth had not seen. Now his other hand traced the ax head, looking for the manufacturer's imprint. The metal was smooth. It bore no stamp.

"Where'd you buy this?" he asked.

"It was a gift," said Garth.

Maybe the shaft had a logo. William brushed his fingers down the wood once more. They stopped on a pattern of grooves so obvious that he blinked. Minutes ago the wood had been quite plain. He was sure of it. He doubled over the back of his seat to peer more closely. The car rounded a steep curve, and his head swarmed with motion sickness. But on the shaft, unmistakably, were hand-carved letters in an antique script. With a little scrutiny he traced three words: *CAST ME AWAY. Good idea*, he thought. He turned the shaft over. On the other side were three words more, carved in the same script: *TAKE ME UP.* That gave him pause. How could a person do both? He gripped the shaft tightly, and trembled.

"Would you like to use it?" said Garth.

William dropped the ax as if it were the known instrument of a bizarre cult murder. He turned back around in the seat, his chin exhibiting new shades of pallor. "No," he said finally. "Thanks, but no. It's a little too long for serious ice." He had not meant to say *serious*—using the word for oneself was not done.

"It may be what you need," said Garth. "It's a serious ax." He left it at that.

So did William.

In a short while, Garth pulled into a shady turnout beneath a small waterfall. He switched off the key, and the motor shuddered three times—a repeated death rattle or, perhaps, the violent exorcising of a stubborn demon. The car gave up its ghost—or stood quietly cleansed—and the two men stiffly got out. The air was cool on the small of their backs, where their shirts had come untucked. Beside them, a neatly cut trail broke into the forest, not quite wide enough for two. A brown wood sign announced the itinerary:

Lost Creek Meadows 7
Obsidian Trail 8

Garth slipped away to the base of the fall and stood beneath a dogwood tree. Its blossoms were starting to wilt. The fading flowers trembled in a fine cool spray, and the spray fell softly on his beard. He paused to see the white foam splash, the black stones glisten. Then he knelt at the water's edge, and his knees sank deep in the mossy bank as he reached his lips to the stream. It was very good. He drank for the taste of melting snows and decaying cedars and settling must of fallen needles, for the fading damp and duff and detritus that made the water sweet. It was a taste far to be desired above the inside of an automobile, or for that matter, above the inside of the finest book. After his drink Garth stayed to consider the toil and spin of the waterfall, and lingered long.

Meanwhile William redeemed the time by donning his armor. Soon he towered beside the professor in full array: his feet were shod with white polyurethane, his shins were greaved with blue polypropylene, his loins were girded with beige polyester. His chest was mailed with a thoroughly waterproof, thoroughly breathable, thoroughly crimson parka. And his shoulders were hung with a marvelous burden, likewise crimson, looming behind him like a burning chest of drawers.

A concealed pocket behind his scalp held secret tools of navigation: a carefully folded contour map entitled "South Queen," laminated with clear contact paper to make it rainproof; the *Climber's Guide to the Three Queens*, second edition, in which every route he had mastered was duly checked and dated; a liquid-filled compass, magnifying glass attached; and a small altimeter. The altimeter was unreliable, but it did offer a number whenever it was consulted. William prized his digital watch for the same reason, even though it unaccountably stopped at times.

Three accessory pockets festooned each side of the pack. One side held a plastic liter bottle that fizzed to capacity with miracle electrolytes; tropical chocolate bars, guaranteed not to melt; and a compact camera, used only to record, and occasionally to contrive, the serious nature of William's exploits. The film in the camera had already been exposed six times to the downward plummet of an ice couloir, lost below in a foggy abyss.

In the other set of pockets lay a tube of Western Cwm Cream ("as used by the the conquerors of Mount Everest"); a mint-green stick of protective lip balm ("specially prepared to screen out dangerous high-altitude rays"); a small hand mirror, to ensure proper application of both; a bottle of liquid amber soap ("Absolutely Biodegradable"); a plastic vial of insect repellent ("New! Improved! Stops Bugs Dead!"); a chartreuse toothbrush, part of the handle sawn off to save weight; a can of foot powder ("GETS THE ROT OUT!"); and a small cylinder of toilet paper—in the bathroom of his tiny apartment he carefully set aside each roll before it was completely used up.

This side of his pack was also home to exactly half of the Ten Essentials. Here lay a pair of prescription glacier goggles in a crushproof lavender case; a lithium-cell headlamp—The WonderBright; a waterproof box of waterproof matches; a silver whistle—The Acme Thunderer; and a red pocketknife, itself an arsenal. Folded into its recesses were tweezers, scissors, leather punch, awl, screwdrivers (flat-blade and Phillips), cutting blades (short and long), toothpick, file, miniature crosscut saw, can opener, bottle opener, corkscrew, and magnifying glass. The magnifying glass troubled William, because he already had one on his compass. He often wondered whether he should vandalize his pocketknife to eliminate this redundancy.

And in the womb of William's pack? At the bottom, tightly curled like a slumbering fetus, a lime-green sleeping bag, quilted with down and laced with synthetic fibers. There, too, a canary-yellow air mattress. And beside it a bundle of fiberglass reeds, tightly wrapped in a purple shroud. Unleashed, they collected themselves like Ezekiel's bones to frame the flesh of a nylon geodesic dome.

Further inhabitants: a sackful of stove in bottles and tubes, a nesting set of aluminum pots, foil packets of freeze-dried delights, booties and gaiters and stockings and mittens, caps and cagoules and bandanas and—suffice it to say that these were a few of his favorite things.

Crushing it all was a 150-foot rattlesnake coil. No rope was needed for the snowfield they planned to climb, but William had packed it in the wan hope that Garth might be persuaded to try something More Interesting. Ice screws and pitons, chocks and carabiners, harness and helmet were stashed here too—just in case. William's versatile ice ax was strapped to attention on the back of his pack, its inverted head pillowed on a pair of black crampons. And that was all.

"Ready?" said William.

Garth left the waterfall and donned his own pack. It hung loosely on his shoulders, a weathered canvas bag of tricks. His coat was faded, a dubious gray. His pants were tattered khaki.

"As I'll ever be," said Garth. He waved his ax as if to say, *After you.*

For the load that he carried, William took off with amazing strides. And his tongue kept pace with his feet. This was the maiden voyage of a new hip-belt suspension system—an ingenious concoction of snaps and buckles and Velcro straps—and William extolled its features for at least a full mile. As he talked, his palms cut diagrams in air, and he stared at them as if they would vanish if once he looked away. But since his student walked behind him, walled off from the ersatz blackboard, it did not really matter if the drawings were erased.

And Garth was looking elsewhere. His eyes kept track of the wandering stream beside the trail—purling in roots of red cedar, fanning over smooth

logs, stopping in dark pools. In one dark pool—*there!*—flashed the orange belly
of a newt.

Where the forest was thick, sword fern overhung the water. Where the forest was thin, the bracken foamed waist-high. Here they walked by faith, by a
miraculous parting of pale green seas, and faith crushed the fiddleheads underfoot like so many sunken chariots. Shafts of sunlight, roiling with pollen, shed
blessings on the ferny deep. The sunlight pierced an understory of vine maple,
first to catch autumn fire. Slide alder grew in shadowy thickets, good reason for
a trail. And dogwoods—one here, one there—dropped yellowing blossoms on
the path.

Over the maple, the alder, the dogwood, sometimes shutting them off in
darkness, great hemlocks and great cedars rose, giants on the earth. The cedar
trunks were red and shaggy. Cobwebs hung in fire-scarred hollows, safety nets
for cones and dust and dead leaf sprays. The hemlock trunks were gray and
even, bearded with pale lichen. The huge trees groaned aloud at times, travailing
in a heavy staccato—not any one tree, but all.

Yet the topmost branches held echoes of wind—soft, distant, the muted
empyrean roar of a sea shell. From this verge of heaven, nudged by the breeze,
hemlock cones leapt down to earth, littering the path, so small an incarna-
tion of so great a tree. The cones fell almost soundlessly, touching the ground
like shy-blown kisses. They slipped through William's diagrams as if through
airy nothing.

William quit his lecture at last when the path upended itself in switchbacks
over a valley step. Here he found comfort in merely breathing. He let his diagrams dissolve, and fell to watching the manly rhythm of his polyurethane
boots. Sometimes, in mid-stride, they clicked together like a gumball machine.

And so miles passed, hours passed. The two men watered the path with the
sweat of their brows, anointing change in the green world about them. Cedars
and hemlocks slipped away. Douglas fir appeared, then vanished. True firs raised
their straight-brushed steeples, sticky with cones that squirrels sever. Cones like
gently curved bananas hung from statuesque white pine. Then mountain hemlocks, shorter than their lowland cousins, drooped their limp crowns, each one
crooked like the hat of a witch. Last of all grew whitebark pine, wind-raked
clumps of rubbery twigs, refuge in a storm.

Ferns gave way to mops of bear grass. Mossy earth dried up in dust. Then
came a snowpatch, hollow and arched like the shell of a tortoise. The surface

was scalloped, stained with needles. William broke through into meltwater pools, and Garth followed after, wetting his cracked leather boots. It was then that his nose caught the first sweet sting of alpine slopes. Here was manna at their feet, hinting a promised land.

And before very long it was upon them. The forest simply ended, and they stood on the verge of a vast meadow parkland. Except for islands of hemlock and whitebark, all was treeless, open to the bright sky. The land lay green, lavish and undulating, dotted with ponds and ahum with mosquitoes. All of this, paradise enough, was but a velvet footstool to the raised splendor of the South Queen, her train of snowfields sweeping gently on the right; on the left, the austere profile of her face. They lifted their eyes to her fullness, her presence, as if nothing else mattered.

"Ah," sighed Garth. His burden slipped unbidden from his shoulders.

"*Ah!*" cried William. "*Aiee!*" He slapped a mosquito on his temple and missed another on his forearm. Then he reached one hand behind his shoulder. There, his wrist painfully bent, he unzipped the waiting pocket in his pack and seized upon the vial within. He had what he wanted. It pooled yellow in his palms. The bitter poison stung his eyes and crept between his lips.

Chapter 2
Watermelon Snow

❋

A COLD FOG CAME UPON THE MEADOWS THAT NIGHT, and dawn did not turn it away. By mid-morning the fog still hung white and thick, bending down the grasses under wet frost. Somewhere in the blank swirl, a pika squeaked. Elsewhere, a marmot whistled. And from the cluttered depths of William's pack came the delighted squeals of a pair of ground squirrels, feasting on the forgotten remains of a chocolate bar that would not melt. Periodically the squirrels issued out from the pack to parade their success around the camp with toilet-paper confetti.

Such joy was only possible because the master was away. For at this moment, high on the mountain, William was trudging in wet soft snow, stepping where Garth had stepped. The mountainside was foggy too. The snow gave the fog an opaque radiance, and the tinted goggles that William wore did little to help him see. Garth, however, was noticing things. He had first pointed out an invisible pair of rosy finches. Then, he had bid William kneel before a spider in a suncup. Now, Garth stopped so abruptly that William bumped into the back of him.

"Have you seen," he said, "how the algae bloom?" He pointed to the pink sides of a suncup, blood-red at the bottom. "Watermelon snow, it's called. Even tastes like watermelon. Try some."

He scooped and offered a mittenful. William took it with the strange reluctance of a grown man accepting a candy cane from a department-store Santa Claus.

"Not too nourishing for us, but the ice worms thrive on it. Tiny ones, no bigger than the hairs on your chest."

William looked down and mentally X-rayed his red parka. He had always been aware of the lack of any real hair on his chest. He rarely took his shirt off, even on the hottest days.

"You seldom see them," said Garth. "In fact, I've only seen them once in my life. It was a very sunny day, late afternoon on the Center Queen. Suddenly, where minutes before there had been only snow, the glacier was wriggling with thousands of ice worms, bursting forth like upstart flies from the mud of the Nile. Spontaneous generation."

Before Garth finished speaking, a group of ravens swirled from the fog. They brayed in William's ear and vanished, still clamoring, a cloud of witnesses. One returned and, passing closer, chuckled aloud. William had never heard a raven chuckle. What was the joke? What did ice worms have to do with the mud of the Nile?

They switched the lead. William plodded up into the fog, not at all sure where snow and sky met, for each shone white, dazzling, effulgent. The harder William strained his eyes, the more he saw merely the tiny flashes, the hallucinogenic explosions that his eyes created to fill the void. Mentally he marked a spot for each foot to rest, but the foot would find purchase while still in mid-air—a miracle of levitation. He walked as if on a dark stairway. But it was not dark—his feet were groping in glorious light.

Fortunately, Garth had climbed the route before and was sure of the way. Occasionally he tapped William on the shoulder and pointed his ice ax through the fog. At these moments they exchanged the ritual hope that the summit would break above the clouds, but William told himself he did not really care. A real mountaineer, a Serious Climber, did not come for the view. The important thing was to complete the climb, and to do so with daring efficiency.

It was nearly mid-day when a breeze met their faces. The summit was nigh. Ragged red rocks thrust out of the snow like half-sown dragon teeth, shredding the fog. The snowfield channeled upward in all directions, but the way was clear—earlier climbers had left a dirty trough behind. This they followed through the rocks to a cinder path at snow's end. The cinder path, in a very few steps, led them at last to a cast-iron box stamped with the logo of their alpine club. It lay at their feet between two basalt horns like a toppled tombstone. William and Garth each grabbed the side of a horn and leaned over the brink of the northeast face into the wind. They saw nothing.

"We're here," said Garth.

William did not reply. He knelt by the iron box and twirled the wing nuts that clamped it shut. They squeaked in the wind, as did the hinges when he opened the lid. He reached inside and plucked a battered ledger from a nest of four pencil stubs, two dried pens, one flattened tube of zinc oxide, innumerable moleskin scraps, a calling card for Inevitable Life Insurance, and choice droppings of an alpine rodent.

Still kneeling on the cinders, William opened the ledger. The last entry was two days old:

> *Praise the Lord Jesus! He helped me every step of the way! Thank you God for your fantastic creation! He's my Redeemer—he saved my soul! Christ is King!*

The preceding passage bore the same date:

> *No shit, it's cold up here! How the hell do I get down?!*

On the opposite page, a group from You-Can-Do-It Expeditions had left their mark:

> *MY FIRST CLIMB!! I CAN'T BELIEVE I DID THE WHOLE THING!!*
> *Sweet. But don't look down.*
> *This is my second time. A real breeze (ha-ha).*
> *I love you, Scotty, wherever you are!*
> *I never thought I'd make it, but Savidge wouldn't let me quit, so I really didn't have much choice, did I?*
> *I'm going to come back and bring Harvey, my dog.*
> *Hey, I climbed the little sucker!*
> *I would like to dedicate this climb to Linda, who had to stay in camp today because she was throwing up. She's been such an inspiration to us all.*

William turned back a few pages, forcing them against the wind.

> *NE face—definitely grade IV. The bergschrund is a bitch this time of year. Heavy stonefall in the hourglass. Very hard ice. 12 hrs. from Lira Col.*

William took note. He had a special place in his home computer for these tidbits.

Then a nearby entry in delicate script caught his eye:

So fully cosmic to partake of the oneness of earth and this universe, united at this lonely apex by our individual souls encompassing the goodness of all terrestrial forces indivisible with sun and moon, triumphant in our eternal bonds, freed by the all-loving sasquatch mother of mankind and every creature gathered in eternal celebration of the energy of our togetherness and aloneness, ebbing and flowing in one wind, one tide, one womb of the universal cosmos.

William turned back to the most recent entry and selected a pencil stub from the box. He did not care for effusion, but he did enjoy a public record of his achievements. "William Arthur, #67," he wrote. His signature surprised him—a childish leaden scrawl. He was colder than he knew.

An involuntary shiver stood him up, and he gave the ledger and pencil stub to Garth. "Here," he said, and pretended to stare off the northeast face while looking out of the corner of his eye to see what Garth would write. "Garth Foster," he saw. And then, "Get their glad tidings." Glad tidings? What tidings? Whose tidings? Where gotten? People must say what they mean. It was one thing to be unclear by accident, but another—an unforgivable thing—to be so by intent.

Meanwhile, the breeze poured through him and seized his bladder with a chill. He descended several steps farther than he needed to and turned his back on Garth and the wind. There he assumed the time-honored stance, and there he began to find relief. And there, *in medias res*, a shift in the wind left relief unconsummated.

No little shift. A gust of cinders raked his teeth and filled his ears. He staggered back and barely managed to zip himself up. His parka billowed out behind him like a sail. He spun around, and the crimson sail reversed itself to swelling pregnancy. His cap! It flew into the fog before him. He reached for it much too late, and his reach gave the wind the advantage it needed. It pounced and knocked him to his knees, bellowing triumph. Such wind as this, so fierce, so sudden, he could not remember.

He crouched in the cinders and shut his eyes, groveling before the summit as if in abject worship. What of Garth? He peeked upwards. All he could see was boiling fog. He had once read of a man who was literally blown from a mountaintop in a freak storm. Maybe Garth could hang on to one of the summit horns.

The wind blasted a rift in the fog, and William looked. The old man was still there, his coat snapping like a flag. He was not crouching on the ground like William. He was not clutching at the lava horns. He was, to William's astonishment, standing fully upright between the two rocks, straddling the iron box with his feet. He was chesting the storm, welcoming it with arms outstretched as if it blew some preternatural energy into his heart. The antique ax sailed high in his hand. The wind tore at the old man's beard, parting it like an angry sea, and his long white hair was streaming behind him. Garth was speaking, but not to William. Great guttural chords and rumbling diphthongs rolled into the storm, louder than the wind itself. The words, if that is what they were, sounded long and deep, old and strong. They rode upon the wind, and spurred it, called it into being.

William listened, prostrate in the cinders. The wind searched him to an aching core, and he clenched and shivered with bony cold, remembering the time that a boulder the size of a millstone had flown past his ear on a silent mountainside. That had been just as real, and unreal.

Garth stood unmoved, speaking into the tempest, speaking more urgently now. The wind, if anything, blew more strongly. It whipped his coat about him like an old and tattered robe. William sensed that something was about to happen, and his voice welled up unbidden within him. "No!" he shouted. Without knowing why, he chanted it out: "No! No! No!" The words were high-pitched, puny, the wail of a child. Garth gave no sign of hearing them. His ice ax swung across the clouds, and as it swung, the words and the wind more deeply roared. All at once the fog rushed into the swirling robe. And Garth was gone. For an instant, William saw the ice ax gleaming overhead—alone, disembodied, the thing itself. Then it too disappeared, as if flung far into the fog.

CAST ME AWAY, he remembered.

Immediately the wind expired, the mists hung still, all was bright calm. William slowly raised himself, groping for the violence gone from the air. He looked about fearfully, braced for a blast from any quarter. But none came. He walked unsteadily, like an infant, the few short steps to the summit. There, on the lid of the iron box, a single snowflake softly melted.

Chapter 3
Inches to the Mile

❉

"No toilet paper? None?" Grace was appalled.

The youngest boys were snickering at her. She brutalized them with a glance, then checked the other faces in the circle. The older one with the curly hair—what was his name? Lance. Rhymes with *dance*, with *chance*. She remembered that from the name game they had played. Lance sat perfectly cross-legged, aloof and inscrutable. Grace could not tell what he thought about twelve days without toilet paper, which was too bad. It would be nice to have Lance on her side. The girl in braids beside him looked absolutely serene—as if she never ate anything but yogurt and lentil soup, and freedom from toilet paper would be one more step to complete holiness. The two girls sitting next to her, however, seemed much less destined for ascetic purity. Their faces were blanched with shock. But they were weak. They would go along with using sticks and rocks.

"Snow works best, actually," said the leader. He was a young man with glasses and a wooly red beard.

"What about lava!" screamed the smallest boy. "That would clean you out!" He convulsed with giggles and tipped over backwards in the dirt. Grace noticed that Lance was ignoring him, and again she hoped for an ally. She caught his glance and rolled her eyes toward the little screamer. But Lance looked away, ignoring her too.

A nutcracker screeched in the whitebark pine overhead. *Too bad for you!* it seemed to say. *Too bad for you!* Grace stared up into its hard black eye. She made it relent. The bird flew away across the meadows, diminished itself to a dark silhouette against the cloud-wrapped mountain.

"Bury it at least six inches deep," said the leader. "You should be able to stand on the dirt barefoot when the hole is filled up."

"*Eeeoohh!*" said the two girls next to Grace. They looked down at their new waffle-stompers in disgust, imagining their bare toes mired in their own fresh offal. There were more snickers from across the circle.

"Make sure you're at least a hundred feet away from any lake or stream. And we don't wash our pots in the lakes and streams either."

We? thought Grace.

She slapped a mosquito on her calf, and the sucked blood burst across her carefully shaven skin. She tried to wipe it off, but the blood and mosquito fragments mixed with the dust and damp already there. Mile upon mile they had hiked that day, in filth and in fog. When the fog had lifted, the mosquitoes had descended. Her thighs were swollen white with welts, some of them dug into bloody craters by the tips of her well-filed fingernails. All day they had hiked, bearing hideous burdens. Her shoulders ached from the abuse. And the leader had lied. He had lied about how far it was. At their last rest in the woods he had said there was only a half-mile left. That was hours ago. They had just arrived at this patch of dirt which he called camp.

The mountains did not seem to be Grace's sort of place. She was more of a valley girl, she thought. And now she knew just what she thought: what utter bliss to be back at the trailhead, hopping into a low white sports car. She would not even put her pack in the trunk. *Thump!* It fell from her shoulders and hit the dust, sprawled on its back like a helpless potato bug. *Slam!* The door shut her into a vinyl chamber, spotlessly red, pulsing like a sinewy heart at the urge of a stereo tape deck. The car leapt to the road as with muscled thighs. She rolled down the window and the air poured by, winnowing hapless mosquitoes from her hair. Beside her, raking through the gears around hairpin turns, the wheel firm in his grasp, was Lance.

Rhymes with *trance.*

Grace blushed. She looked at him as if he could have heard. But there was no danger. Lance was listening intently to the red-bearded leader.

"Right," said the leader, "if you want to know how far we've come, look at your map. A couple of you ought to have one. Grace, don't you?"

"I dunno," she said. It was an affront to expect her to keep track of such a thing.

"You ought to know," the leader said firmly. "Each of you should know what you're carrying."

"I have a map," said the girl with braids. She held it out to the leader.

"No, Jennifer, it's for you to look at. Try and figure out how far we've hiked."

With Lance's help, she carefully unfolded the map and laid it out on a poncho in the middle of the circle. A slight breeze overturned it; one of the younger boys grabbed some rocks and plunked them on the edges. The rocks shed grit that rattled on the map.

"All right, how many miles to the inch?" said the boy.

"You mean inches to the mile, stupid." That was his friend.

"One inch to a mile," said Lance. "It says down here."

"Who's got a ruler?" asked one of the more frightened girls.

"No, first we have to find out where we are," said the other.

"We're right here under this tree!" yelled the smallest boy. He giggled uncontrollably. "Don't you know that, stupid?"

The girl became very quiet. Then she gripped the hand of her friend.

"Maybe get where you can see the map, Grace." This was the leader's suggestion.

She was not about to. That leader thought he was the grand wonderful master of ceremonies.

"Did we start here?" said Lance. He pointed to a spot in a sea of green where a black dotted line met a red-and-white striped one.

"What do the rest of you think?" asked the leader.

Everyone shrugged their shoulders, except Grace, who was searching for a mosquito on her forehead. She slapped it dead, then looked the leader bang in the eye.

"Who cares?" she said.

"You'll care," he told her, "when you're lost in the wild."

✳

The mosquitoes went away when the cool darkness came. Grace put her head outside her sleeping bag. At last there was no tiny whining in her ears, no hot-itch needles probing her cheeks. But now she shivered, almost epileptically. She had been advised to wear a wool cap, but she was not wearing one. A wool cap might give her split ends. At the very least it would mat down her hair.

She lay on the verge of a plastic tarp, next to the boy who giggled. Regrettably, Lance was sleeping several bodies away. She would have arranged the bags differently, but had been sent to the creek to wash the supper pot, and come back to find everything laid out. It would have been too bold a move to rearrange the bags. Further, she had been told that the pot was not clean enough—there was still some bulgur burned on the bottom. She had not enjoyed eating the stuff (*vulgar*, she called it—how Lance had downed three bowls of it she never would know); she enjoyed scouring the burnt kernels even less. Grace had stomped away and, in a courageous gesture of civil disobedience, washed the pot right in the creek. But rebellion has its price—the creek water had numbed her hands beyond belief.

As far as she could tell, everyone was asleep but herself. Twice the little giggler had kneed her in the back as he jerked in his slumbers. Both times she repaid him with a kick to the shins, but he did not awaken, and she envied him. Grace felt she might more easily fall asleep on a concrete floor. She had tried every position and found them all wanting. What's more, her new down jacket made an utterly inferior pillow. Bunched one way, it formed a lump no softer than Jacob's stone. Stretched out more evenly, it slumped her head so that she lay with her jaw tilted up like a candidate for artificial respiration. When the down was plumped to the right loft, a zipper or snap invariably stuck in her ear.

At home, Grace's parents had just bought her a waterbed, and she had soon become used to it, the way she became used to all the things they gave her. This mountain trip was also their gift. She had begged to go after seeing the slide show at her high school for You-Can-Do-It Expeditions. She saw golden boys and dark slim girls, arm in arm amid deep purple wildflowers. They went splashing together in the sandy shallows of a hundred sparkling lakes. They sent up silver sprays of snow as they slid down crystal slopes. They cuddled close around night's glowing embers. It was more than a midsummer's dream come true. After her mother had carefully inquired over the phone about the safety record of You-Can-Do-It Expeditions, Grace was given the money to go.

Just yesterday her parents had brought her to the dusty base camp. They stayed long enough to meet her leader, then glided away. When the chrome-spoked wheels had disappeared, the young man with the red beard—so nice at first—began to chide her for not having broken in her boots. Then he rifled through her suitcase and confiscated her nail polish, shampoo, and blush. Before she could object, another car crawled tentatively into sight, anxious parents frozen in the front seat, terror-stricken child in the back. The leader turned with an open smile.

From over the mountain the gibbous moon emerged full in her face. Now she surely would not sleep. She half sat up and watched the silvered bodies beside her, their knees drawn up in fetal slumber. Only Lance lay flat on his back. She thought she could hear the rhythm of his breathing, but lost track of it when the boy beside her abruptly flipped and began to snore, an asthmatic soprano. As a mere matter of routine justice, Grace readied another well-aimed kick. But she paused. Her eyes swept over the brightly lit meadow to the dark forest verge, and there came to her a wonderful notion, poking into the moonlit night like a fiddlehead in the forest.

She would leave.

The audacity of it suited her perfectly. She would flee in the moonlight, escape in the dark, run away in the night—all of those things. *Yes!* she told herself. The plan trembled and grew and luxuriated in the nourishing rays of the gibbous moon. She would walk to the trailhead—downhill, every step—and in the morning hitchhike home. She could tell her parents she had gotten sick, and that the leader had put her on a bus, and that she had had to walk home from the terminal because she couldn't get through on the phone, or because she didn't have any money for the call, or—or—no matter, she could fix that later. But now—now was the appointed time to leave.

Should she wake up Lance? Her gaze rested on his upturned face, curls shining, lips slightly parted. But close beside him, almost touching his ear in the moonlight, was the braided brow of the girl called Jennifer. Grace knew: she would leave alone.

Now she had reason to stay awake, and oddly enough, she yawned. The air began to chill her shoulders. She thought how warmly they might nest back again in her bag. A moment's rest before she set out, the briefest nap—that was all she asked. She would not leave now, but then. She sank back. Her eyelids closed.

Had not some small creature chosen just this moment to traverse the length of her sleeping bag, this story would be much shorter than it is. As it was, Grace sat fully upright and awake and slid on her down jacket. And in one stroke having destroyed her pillow, she had no choice but to go through with her plan. Quietly, she swung her legs out from the bag and hitched up her shorts. Her thighs exploded in myriad goose bumps. A clothing list had required wool pants, but it had not been a requirement to her taste. *Keep moving,* she told herself. *On with the boots. You can do it.* Her fingers stumbled over the laces. Then carefully she stuffed her bag into a tight nylon sack—most of it, anyway. She rolled up her pad in a spongy scroll. In the moonlight it was easy to strap the pad and the bag to the bottom of her pack.

Silently she withdrew from her pack a few issued items: a silver bottle of white gasoline, a bulging sack of freeze-dried carrots, a gleaming helmet, a limp harness, and some sort of ice pick—she hadn't been told what it was. What about the map? She held it in her hand. No, it didn't weigh much. Yes, it might be useful. But, she knew the path, And, she couldn't read it anyway. The map joined the other discards on the ground.

She set her pack against the tree, sat down, wiggled her arms into the straps. Even with the lightened load she stumbled on arising, and lurched back to correct herself. A small branch snapped. The report rang soft as thunder. On cue, the red-bearded leader sat up like Lazarus called from the tomb. Grace froze in the shadow of the tree. The leader groped in a boot for his glasses. Then he groped in another boot—no glasses. He peered at the sleepers beside him. He peered at the branches above him. He peered at the trunk and its moon-shadow. Then he hung his head in his lap and meditatively picked his nose. In a few minutes he lay back down and began breathing heavily.

When the leader was most certainly asleep again, Grace slipped out of the shadow and away from the camp. She stepped softly in the grass, as if stalking a ground squirrel, and at length she found the trail (not right away, because the leader had insisted they camp out of sight from all other wilderness travelers). Her boots shone wet from the dew in the meadow, but now they dulled in little puffs of silver smoke. The path sloped down to the forest edge, easy to see and to follow. She could not get lost.

There is something exhilarating about walking alone and in secret by moonlight. Grace felt giddy and sure and strong, summoned to shout to the stars that shone for her alone and not for sleepers. Over her shoulder the mountain glowed huge and white. Before her the meadows unrolled pale splendor. The night was good and she was in it.

But she entered the forest all too soon. There, the night was not so good. It was like walking into a dark cellar of a strange house, and groping for a light cord that someone has told you is "right there," and not finding it, and brushing against soft dusty sofas, and stepping on piles of boards that rattle, and wondering if some of the boards have nails, and suddenly finding cobwebs in your face that stick on in fragments, and wondering if a spider might have gotten onto your face too. There weren't so many cobwebs in the forest, but there was no hope of a light cord either. The moon did not penetrate the darkness of the canopy, and Grace had neither candle nor flashlight.

She had not walked far when her knees and toes collided with something firm but soft. A little scream escaped her, an exaggerated hiccup. Her legs rubbed up against pulsing fur: a bear. She knew. It must be asleep. It must have fallen asleep on the trail. She had not woken it. Or maybe she had. Maybe she had woken it up, and it was just pretending to be asleep. She stood very still for a long time.

Then, slowly, she inched backwards, taking very short steps. Suddenly her calves touched more soft fur. Despair thrilled her. It was another bear, this one also feigning sleep. They had trapped her. Once again she stood very still. Then she moved her foot sideways. No good—there it touched the bear's paw, outstretched on the ground. She moved her other foot—it met the other paw. She was standing in its arms!

Grace shivered miserably. Maybe—and this was her only hope—maybe she could step over the paw and run away. She lifted her foot and extended it far to the side—slowly, softly, the way she had learned in ballet. *Farther*, she thought. *Farther*. But one extra inch cost Grace her balance. Backwards she tumbled, into the waiting jaws of death. But death only put a splinter in her thumb. The two bears, clever to the last, had transformed themselves to mossy stumps.

She took a deep breath, picked herself up. Her feet shuffled over the soft duff till they found the path from which they had strayed. The trail was firm and good again. She felt relieved, but only a little. She thought of the seven sleepers now, at peace in the bright meadows, and of the empty spot at the edge of the tarp that was hers. For a moment she paused. It was not too late. It was not too far. She could still . . . and she could yet . . . But for some reason—the inertia of pride, perhaps—she continued, barely picking each boot off the path for fear of losing the way again.

She heard things. First the stream came creeping by. The water bubbled darkly, swirling and sucking almost at her feet. It asked for her by name. Then it receded into silence. That was worse, for Grace then feared she was lost. The trail stayed on the bank of the creek the entire way, did it not? A little creature skipped over her tracks and froze her in them. She heard it scour the brush. Then groans and creaks shot overhead, squealing like doors on rusty hinges. These were only trees, she knew, but were the groans too loud, too full, for a windless night in the forest? Down the trail the stream swung near again; the rushing water covered all sounds else. This was not good. It is what you cannot hear that finds you.

And she ran into things. She tripped over roots. She hit her shins on boulders. Sharp dry limbs plucked the down from her jacket. Tendrils of maple reached into her hair. Once she missed a turn on the trail and planted her face in the trunk of a tree. The moon shone into little clearings, but here she waded through bracken fern that kept her steps in darkness. The wet fronds slithered across her thighs, sent rivers of dew to her ankles.

The night stumbled on, fraught with terrors, and at length Grace grew too tired to care. All the horrors of sleeping bears and darkling streams and grasping limbs and slithery things amounted to naught before an almighty yawn. She grew not only tired—she grew cross, and said a great many things to the red-bearded leader in her mind. "If I hit my shin just one more time," she threatened him, "I'll quit. I will." No sooner had the thought been formed than she caught her shin on the corner of a rock. She half-pronounced a fearful curse and sat down. She meant to keep her promise—at least until daylight.

Grace knew she was somewhere between four miles and four yards from the highway. That would have to do. She dragged out her sleeping bag, threw it on the trail, and crawled inside, head downhill. Her boots were still on, and her sleeping pad stayed strapped to her pack. A tangle of roots brought their knees to her spine, but Grace hardly noticed. Soon she was snoring as prettily as the boy she had left in the meadow.

The night was far gone. One short hour brought early light, and two hours more saw the sun shine into the low forest valley. But neither dawn nor sunrise awakened Grace. The light lay dappling over her eyelids, and she slept on.

What waked her was a voice. "Who do you think you are?" it said.

Chapter 4
A Gentle Wight

✳

GRACE OPENED HER EYES TO SEE THE VOICE. Overhead hung a twisted face, round and pale like the full moon. *The man in the moon,* she thought. His lips were pursed, his eyes hollow, his jowls unshaven. Grace closed her eyes again. She would pretend to be asleep, like a tree stump.

It didn't work.

"You heard me," said the face. "Who are you?"

"Me?" said Grace. "I'm just—out walking."

"Had me fooled," said the face. "I would have said you were out sleeping."

"Well, I was," she said. "Walking, that is. Also sleeping."

"On trails, though? Do you always sleep on trails?" he asked. His voice was sharp.

"I do when I'm tired," she yawned. She sized him up and found him lacking. The face was determined but slightly bloated—it wanted to belong, but it didn't.

"Listen," she said. "How far is the trailhead from here?"

An arm appeared and waved in a circle. "This is it," said the bristly face.

Languidly, Grace raised herself on one elbow and looked down the path. Not twenty steps away, it plunged into another field of bracken. Nearby, the stream cascaded down a mossy falls. Grace strained her eyes for the white sports car of her dreams, or at least for smooth pavement. She saw only ferns, waving in the sun, and beyond the ferns, thickets of alder.

"Where's the road?" she asked.

"I wish I knew," said the face, only now it was an entire man in a torn red parka that rustled and squeaked like aluminum foil.

"So it's down the trail a ways?" she pressed.

"What trail is that?" said the man.

"Why, the trail we're on—what else?"

He wagged his head. "Sorry," he told her. "No more trail." By the way that he spoke, Grace knew that at least for her sake he was not sorry at all. "This," he announced, sweeping both arms, "is the end."

"But there's no road," Grace insisted.

"Precisely," said the man. "There is no road." He stood back with arms folded, pleased, it seemed, with the novel concept of a roadless trailhead.

Grace decided to drop it. She must have come down the wrong trail in the dark. She got out of her sleeping bag and made a show of poking around in her pack. She knew just what she wanted from the man.

"Could you spare a little breakfast?" she asked. "I seem to have eaten most of my food." She smiled her breezy smile.

Without answering, the man turned and walked to the clearing. Grace followed, dragging her pack and sleeping bag behind her. The man was right; the trail simply ended in the ferns. They waded into full sunshine and stopped next to a tall red pack. The ferns beside it were crushed into a bathtub of green, at the bottom of which stretched a lime-green sleeping bag. The man pulled a plastic bag from the pack and gave to her a chipmunk's portion of store-bought granola.

Suddenly he swore aloud. More granola was dribbling out of a freshly chewed hole in the plastic. "This needs to last," he explained.

"That all you have?" she asked.

"Pretty much. Unless . . ." His voice trailed off. His eye came to rest on a weathered canvas packsack strapped atop his own. Here was a place he seemed to have overlooked. He unstrapped the packsack, untied the drawstring, and thrust in his arm. He groped in every corner. There—he had something. He brought up the booty—a fist-sized globe, wrapped in a piece of paper. He quickly shed the wrapping and held up an apple, red and shining.

"Want a bite?" he asked. Before she could answer he took one himself. His teeth sank deep. His eyes lit up with pain and surprise. He plucked the apple from his mouth and roared. "It broke my bloody tooth!" he cried, and looked at the apple as if it had bitten him.

"What's this?" he said. His fingers dug through the juicy pulp and extracted a dripping key. He held it up and let the apple drop in the ferns (where Grace snatched it). They looked at the key together. It had two flat teeth, a cylindrical shaft, an ornate ring on the end. There were a few spots of orange rust. Grace had seen no key like it. She wondered what it opened.

"Did it really break your tooth?" she asked.

The man checked with his thumb. "Maybe not," he said. "Feels like it should have." He laughed abruptly and shoved the key in his pocket. *That was that,* he seemed to say. *No use troubling about it.*

His eyes then fell on the crumpled paper in his hand. He smoothed it out and inspected both sides. Something snagged his interest. He held the paper up close to his face and moved his lips silently. "It's some kind of poem," he said aloud. His voice held a trace of disgust. He shoved the paper at Grace. "Here," he said. "You like poetry?"

She shrugged her shoulders. "A little," she mumbled. She wiped the granola crumbs from her palms and took the paper. She would humor the man for a few more minutes, and then leave. Her mistake, however, was to glance at the script.

All at once her lips faltered, her fingers trembled. She knew whose writing it was that she held—knew it better almost than her own. The carefully etched hand echoed from a myriad of birthday letters and lengthy notes composed upon "special occasions"—The Hoary Marmot Holiday, The Trilium Tragoo, The Feast of Free Waters. (There were many others, and even in her youngest years she had half an idea they were improvised for her sake.) All of the letters, once cherished, now discarded, concluded in the same way: "Your affectionate uncle . . ."

The paper grew hot and slippery in her hands. She was afraid the stranger would change his mind and take it back, and that made the poem quite hard to read:

> A gentle wight for gentle ladies three
> Aduentured through a verdant wood newgrowne,
> Through wildernesse that mote a wastlond bee,
> Vnless he greete the greenwood for his owne,
> Vnless he know the leaf as ice and stone.
> Faine needs he find a maid of faerie eyne
> To spie the shielde vpon the second throne,
> To limn therein the ledgers ancient line—
> Lest Beast and woman darke the northerne morning shyne.

Grace read the stanza three times over, swiftly moving her lips. It was just like him: beasts and thrones and fairies—the sort of thing he always had written her. She tried to feel scornful. It didn't work.

The man began to eye her suspiciously. He looked as if he wondered why he had been so generous with the paper. "What does it say?" he demanded, and snatched it away. He read the poem again, brows knit. "What nonsense," he announced, and stuffed the paper in a little compartment at the top of his pack.

Grace folded her arms fiercely. She was angry—and curious. "That your pack?" she asked, pointing to the canvas heap now tossed in the ferns.

"My friend's," said the man. He did not sound very convincing.

"So where's your friend?"

"My friend? He—uh—went down the other side of the mountain. I was going to meet him there."

She gave a dissatisfied nod. What would her uncle be doing up here with such a fool as this? She, for one, could do without him. She stepped to the waterfall and drank deeply, suddenly admiring the taste of melting snows and decaying cedars. Then she returned. Her plans were made: another getaway.

"Thank you for breakfast," she said politely. "Very kind of you."

The man was recoiling the intestines of his pack. He didn't answer. Perhaps he, in turn, could do without her.

"I really must go now," said Grace. "This isn't the trail I wanted at all."

The man still took no notice. He couldn't get his air mattress to fit.

There was room in Grace's pack for her sleeping bag, so she threw it inside instead of strapping it on the bottom. "Goodbye," she said, sorting her arms through the shoulder straps. Her voice quavered a little.

He barely looked up. "See you," he grumbled, and waved her off. The man returned to the bowels of his pack, and Grace strode into the trees.

She was reasonably sure she had missed a trail junction in the dark. The path they had taken the day before began at a road, not a patch of ferns. And it followed a creek the entire way. Had she followed that same creek all night long? She must have changed creeks somewhere. But then she would be on the left bank instead of the right bank, for she had crossed no bridges. Yet that would only be true going downstream. Going upstream, the near bank of the old creek would match the right bank of the new creek. And the bank closest to her now was on the right. Although, if she were standing in the water it would be on the left, which would make it the left bank. Facing downstream, however, it would still be the right bank, which proved—what? She had forgotten. She had taken the wrong path. She would leave it at that. Meanwhile, best to watch out for the red-bearded leader, in case he came looking for her.

Her head felt light from little sleep. But as she walked, her limbs awoke to the morning. The forest was a green and gentle place by day. The stream, so evil-sounding in the dark, now purled at her feet. One bird chanted a single note that calmly echoed through the trees. A chipmunk raced beneath her feet and down the path, tail erect. Grace laughed at him. "Why run?" she called. "I won't hurt you." The chipmunk eyed her for just a moment, then dashed into a green-shine patch of thick salal.

She stooped to see where it had gone, and saw a bed of twinflowers. Each pair of blossoms hung shyly downcast, a lavender inch from the ground. She touched one softly, and thought to wonder what it was. And there were more. She saw white pointed petals of delicate queen's cup, six to the lily. She saw tiny coolwort, dappling the ground like forest sunlight. She saw pink-striped candy flowers, cupping the dew. On she sauntered, her eyes alerted. There, in the shadows, the red-pulp explosion of coralroot. And there, in the ferns, the tight orange ball of a tiger lily. Here, thigh-high, the chalk-green stalks of pearly everlasting. And here, head-high, the thrust of corn lily, crowned with clusters of green and white blossoms. Though Grace did not know any names for these flowers, they looked as lovely, and smelled as sweet, without them even so.

She took thought, as she walked, of her uncle's poem. It was curious—a poem like that in a place like this. Could she recite it? She tried, stumbled, stopped. This brought panic. She resolved to write down what she could. You-Can-Do-It Expeditions had required her to bring pen and notebook. She still had them, hopefully. Forty feet above the path she spied a cedar of gigantic girth. She clambered to it and parked her pack on the backside of the trunk, out of sight from the trail. The pen and paper were there in her pack, sticky beneath the mangled apple. She sat down to record.

First she repeated the lines to herself—*A gentle wight for gentle ladies three*—stroking her hair when memory failed. Then she rushed to put down each word before it left her mind. Before long, she was fairly sure she had it. She understood the poem no better after writing it out. But it felt more familiar now. Her own fingers had stroked the words into being—they were partly hers. And insofar as the words belonged to her uncle, they were the closest friends she had.

Not so very long ago, Grace and Garth had been quite inseparable. He an old bachelor, she his only niece—that explained it for most people. And worried some—Grace's mother in particular. But as Grace well knew, their bond was wholly innocent. It was not about bodies; it was about books.

Grace recalled his knotty hand that led her up the dark stairs to the crack of light beneath the door. Even before it opened she could smell the books inside. They circled the room on tall oak shelves. Most of them had thick brown covers and barrel-ribbed spines, all faded and scuffed like the old green carpet on the floor. When she sat on his lap and he opened one up, the musty smell grew sweeter, and she put her nose in the very crease to breathe the odor in. The pages were yellowed, especially at the edges, where she liked to run her fingers on the rough-cut paper. The print was very black, but sometimes the letter in the northwest corner of the page was a brilliant red, and ten times the normal size. Tiny men and women, wearing sheets that did not stay on well, sat on these letters, and vines and flowers curled as on a trellis.

Uncle Garth would read aloud. Sometimes Grace listened, and sometimes she just smelled, and sometimes she rubbed the ragged edges of the paper. But with each ponderous turn of the page, she always hunted for the big red letter. Once she saw a purple one, squealed, pounced on it. She often wondered what it would be like to wear flowers and sheets and sit on a letter in one of her uncle's books.

Uncle Garth read well. When the story had a dragon in it, his voice rumbled, and she felt his stomach shudder. When there were fairies, she felt tiny moths that tickled her tongue. She had wanted to know how he did it, how he made the voices exactly right. One day she asked.

"Ho ho!" he laughed, and she felt his stomach shudder in his dragon voice. He bent his face very close. "You can too," he whispered. "Just you and I, niece. It's who we are. And a wonderful thing." She never forgot it, even though she wasn't sure exactly what he meant.

Although they lived in the same town in the valley, Grace received many letters from her uncle and very dutifully answered them. He was careful to begin the first word after "My Dearest Grace" with a large red capital, all bestrewn with marmots and wild strawberry vines. Grace always began her reply with the same red letter, carefully copied from the one he had drawn. He began with a different one each time, so that in just a few years they had run through the entire alphabet. X had been a problem, of course, but he had addressed the subject of xylophones, and she Xmas (which was cheating, a little).

When Grace entered junior high school she left off copying the large red letters. Her replies became more brief, more general, more delayed. In the eighth grade, she moved with her parents to another city and began to subscribe to a magazine that advertised lip gloss and eye shadow on almost every page. It was then that she quit answering her uncle's letters altogether, and before very long she only heard from him on birthdays. And since her parents did not like to visit Garth, she was happily spared the awkwardness of seeing him.

Now, however, Grace missed her uncle. She sighed as she looked at the poem on her lap. And then a pleasant thought occurred. If she could not find her way to the road, perhaps she could find her Uncle Garth. The wilderness surely was not that large. She just might run into him.

Just then she heard footsteps—footsteps thumping the hollow earth on the trail below. Might it be? Even now? She peeked around the trunk, flattening her cheek to the cinnamon bark. Hope sprang, only to be sprung: Garth it was not. Instead she saw the red-bearded leader, with Lance on his heels. They marched quickly, bearing only rucksacks. Their eyes swished back and forth, looking for someone.

Grace ducked behind the tree and pressed her back against the trunk. She sat holding her knees to her chin. Her head felt light again. When the footsteps were passing directly beneath her, it was Lance's voice that she heard. "Hey, like—can we stop for a minute?"

The footsteps ceased. "Sure," said the leader.

Twigs began to snap. It took just a few seconds for Grace to realize that hers was the largest tree by the trail. She braced herself. The first thing she saw when he rounded the trunk was his belt hanging loose. On impulse she grabbed it and hauled him down beside her before he could say, "No kidding?"—which he said a little later.

"One word and you've had it," she hissed. She was not at all sure what it was that he would have.

"No kidding?" he said. His eyes bulged out like toadstools.

"I mean it," she whispered. They regarded each other warily, deadlocked in threat and surprise. This status quo might well have persisted had they not heard the sound of another pair of footsteps on the trail. The footsteps stopped directly below them.

"Howdy." That was the leader, pretending to be Wyatt Earp.

There was no reply.

"Say, maybe you could help me out. Have you seen a girl on the trail, sixteen or so? Long brown hair, sort of tanned, orange pack?"

Sort of tanned? Grace wondered. *Sort of?*

A pause, then a voice. "What's the name?" She knew the voice: it belonged to the man from the end of the trail.

"Grace. Grace Foster. I know, it's a funny name."

What's so funny about it? Grace wanted to know.

There was another pause down on the trail.

"No," came the voice finally. "Haven't seen her."

"I don't believe it," Grace whispered to herself. Then she included Lance. "I don't believe it," she said aloud. "Bizarre."

"Who is?" said Lance.

"Quiet!" she ordered. "They'll hear you."

"No more than they'll hear you," he replied.

That took her aback. The only defiant person she liked was herself.

"What are you doing here?" Lance pressed. "Why'd you leave? Couldn't take it? Home to mama?"

Grace shrugged her shoulders.

He leaned towards her. "We were supposed to go climbing today. Why did you ruin it?" The anguish in his voice carried well beyond the tree.

"Everything coming out alright up there?" called the leader. He cackled wickedly.

Grace recovered herself and nodded towards the laughter. "So," she said, "you call that a good time?" She paused dramatically.

Lance seemed to think it over. There was something curious in the way he looked at her.

"You like this boot-camp business, Lance? You call this trip fun?"

Lance seemed to think about it some more. It appeared that rhetorical questions posed a special challenge for him. That, and the sound of his name on female lips. "Uh, I—"

She cut him off with a fierce whisper. "Listen, you don't think it takes a little *machisma* to hike all night?" She paused to gauge the effect of her question. "Don't give me this bit about 'home to mama.' I can be tough when I want to be tough. See, I've been up here lots of times. All by myself. But if you think I'm going to follow some red-bearded turkey around in the woods for a week and a half, you can guess again."

This came off well. Lance looked impressed. "So you're planning to get away?" he asked blandly.

"No doubt about it," she affirmed. She felt more doubtful every minute.

There was a long pause.

"Well," he said, "I think I know why you left. That guy—he, like, never tells you anything you want to know, and he tells you lots of stuff you don't want to know." Here Lance pulled from his pocket a small roll of toilet paper. "But he doesn't know everything."

Grace could not help smiling.

"And those other ones." He rolled his eyes. "Two of them—those two boys—aren't even supposed to be on this trip. They're too young—they're junior high. Their parents talked somebody into letting them come."

"I thought so," said Grace.

"And that one girl," said Lance. "She's like, so *mellow*." He lingered on the word derisively. "It just kills me. This morning she asked what my sign was. She says she's a *Libra*."

They shared a good sneer.

"And those other two girls," Grace went on. "Did you hear them last night? They asked him five times if there were any bears."

They both snickered as if to say, *Imagine. Afraid of bears!*

Then another silence ensued. They had run out of persons to critique, except for each other, and there would be plenty of time for that, perhaps.

"Would you mind," began Lance, "if, um . . ." His whisper had grown throaty. "I mean, would you mind if I like, went with you?"

Grace tried to appear indifferent. "I don't know," she pondered aloud. "You got a map? Did you bring any food?"

"Both right here," he said eagerly. He pointed at the rucksack on his back.

She still looked dubious. "Can you make yourself useful? Clean my boots? Cook supper? Light my pipe?"

"No way!" said Lance. He began to laugh.

"What, Lance?" called the leader.

"Nothing!" he shouted. "Down in a minute. I'm looking for some smooth stones."

"So was David," said Grace, unable to suppress herself.

"David who?" said Lance.

"Douglas fir cones!" shouted the leader. "They're good when they're wet."

Lance peeked around the tree trunk. "The other guy's gone," he whispered.

"We should be too," Grace said. "Help me with the pack."

Lance hoisted it up. Grace slid her arms through the straps as if slipping into coat sleeves.

"We've got to crawl for a while," she told him. "Don't break any sticks."

Hunched over like two slavish courtiers groveling towards an Oriental despot, they left the trunk of the cedar tree and inched away into the woods. It was hard to crawl noiselessly—the bushes around them rattled like tambourines.

In a short while they heard a voice: "Lance! Lance, where are you? Lance?"

They looked behind them. The cedar tree was no longer visible.

"Let's walk," said Lance. "If we run he might hear us."

They rose and tiptoed through mats of salal, holding their breath, pantomiming agility. The calling voice echoed more faintly as they went, and soon they heard it not at all. That was sweetest silence.

And so they walked till they came to a stream, deep in the forest. The water looked a very dark green in the shade. The stream was not so swift or so deep that they could not cross, but they felt safe for the time being, not to mention clever, so they took off their packs on the mossy bank and drank their fill. The water was strangely tepid. Chins dripping, they scooted back and sat side by side in the sloping moss. Grace pulled out the disemboweled apple, took a bite, and offered it to Lance. He ate the rest.

In the quiet, she knew: there was no leader, no group, no stranger on the trail—just the two of them. The nakedness of it began to sink in. The silence turned shy. The dark current slid quietly past, and a black whirlpool eddied at their feet. A toad she had not seen beside them plopped into the water.

Lance seemed to gather his courage. He looked Grace full in the face. She looked away. Then, his hand began creeping along the moss—secretly, behind her back—like a large but discreet spider. Before it reached her she sat up straight and put her hands in her lap.

"What stream is this?" she urgently asked. "Look at your map! Who's got a map? Everybody should know what they have!"

They both laughed, but not spontaneously. Lance reached dutifully into his rucksack, unfolded the square green map with white borders. Some of the folds were starting to tear, and the borders were already smudged. He only had to consult it briefly.

"This should be Lira Creek."

"How do you know?"

"It's the next one north of the stream by the trail. We've contoured almost a mile."

She grabbed his hand and saved him all his sneaking effort. "Lance, the trail you came down today—is it the very same one we hiked up yesterday?"

"Of course."

"You're sure?"

"I'm sure. There's no other trail, not below the meadows anyway."

Grace looked slack-jawed at the dark eddy. "Bizarre," she said.

"Who is?" said Lance.

Chapter 5
Her Sparkling Eyes

✳

IT TOOK MUCH EXPLAINING ON GRACE'S PART, but Lance finally believed her, or at least said he did—to preserve the savor of their new acquaintance. He foresaw them wandering arm in arm through forests and sunsets, their lips shyly meeting in the glimmering twilight, and not so shyly meeting after dark. Let the highway be gone. Her earnestness on this point scared him a little, but only enough to tinge infatuation with the exotic. He would go along with her plans—until the gorp ran out, anyway.

Her plans were to find Garth.

"Where did the guy say he was going to meet him?" asked Lance. He was picking the chocolate chips from his stash. Most of them were already gone. All he could find were peanuts and raisins.

"On the other side of the mountain," said Grace.

"Which one? There's three of 'em, y' know." He held up three raisins by way of illustration.

"He didn't say," she answered quietly.

"That's easy then," he said. "We just hop on over to the other side of *the* mountain and chance upon your long-lost uncle." He laughed.

Grace did not. She used the moment to ponder his possible imperfections. "Well, which mountain does the trail go to?" she asked.

Lance checked the map. "South Queen." Why hadn't he thought of that?

"There you go," said Grace. She blessed him with a satisfied smile. "And there *we* go. Let's find a way to the other side of the South Queen. And who knows? Maybe there are roads on that side. If we don't find my uncle I bet we can still get out of this place."

This sounded plausible to Lance, so together they consulted the map. Or, rather, Lance consulted the map and Grace looked vaguely over his shoulder.

"Lira Creek ought to do it," he said. "It'll take us to the saddle between the South and Center Queen. From there we pop over the other side."

Grace, who saw only a morass of squiggly lines, readily agreed.

By now it was early afternoon. They got up stiffly, put on their packs, and peered at the dark forest. It looked nothing at all like the green piece of paper they had spread on the moss. The map had been so cozy. You slid your finger across the paper and you were there. Standing up in the forest was different. The problem was, you *were* there.

Lance had his own way of coping: he gallantly offered to take Grace's pack. Grace replied that she could carry her own pack quite well, thank you, to which Lance responded that he was just as capable and more than willing, to which Grace answered that if she wanted him to take her pack she would ask, to which Lance replied that she didn't have to be so touchy, at which point Grace asked who was being touchy.

In this harmony of spirit they set out. And to their surprise, the forest quickly opened on a bright clearing. The sunlight raised their eyes and hopes. Over the treetops they spied the summit of the South Queen herself. It seemed quite close—a little walking, a little effort, and they would be past it.

Lance was first to notice the bushes hung with purple-blue berries. The berries filled the clearing. He stooped and picked one. It was the size of a pea.

"Think it's poisonous?" he asked.

She didn't know.

He placed it on his tongue.

"Good," he said. "Awesome!" It dawned on him there were more to be had. "Look at this mother! No. Here! Boatloads of 'em!"

They were huckleberries, and before long they were cascading one after the other into his mouth. Like a faithful retriever he passed his better prizes on to Grace, but she let them slip through her fingers when he wasn't looking, which was most of the time. She had noticed the spreading purple stain that graced his lips and tongue. The effect was not handsome.

When Lance had gorged his fill they again set out. The stream led them into the forest once more, and soon they came to a desperate thicket of slide alder. The alder trunks shot everywhere in slippery layers, ready to slap, to trap, to crush the unwary—an arboreal Slough of Despond. Fools rush in, and so did Grace and Lance. Grace bravely barked her shins and knees in all the same places that she had the night before—which might have been tolerable if she were getting somewhere. But no sooner did her foot cross one small trunk than another knocked her back. Pairs of branches closed on her waist like wooden scissors. Other times they pinned her pack frame firmly in place.

It was time to get serious. She lashed, she cursed, she trampled, she swore, she heroically unleashed a branch directly into Lance's face. It caught him with a vicious swat. He stifled a response, but reflected that the magic moments they so recently had shared were perhaps forever ended. He saw that Grace's tangled hair had filled with twigs and leaves. Greasy locks lay plastered on her sweat-streaked forehead. It came as a revelation: she was not that beautiful after all.

After an hour of this pastime, the thicket was as thick as ever. Every so often Grace asked if this were the best way, and Lance replied each time that they could go back the way they had come if she wanted, and each time Grace declined.

But at last, when the alder had whipped their patience to a raw and bleeding spectacle, the thicket vanished. Before them, the creek ran languidly between dark pools set in a wide space of moss. Neither Grace nor Lance had ever seen moss so soft, so smooth, so green, so inviting. Spaced across the carpeted expanse, like potted palms in a hotel lobby, grew head-high plants with huge green leaves. They had stumbled on paradise.

"We're finally out of that stuff," said Grace. She looked at Lance in a way that held him fully responsible for *that stuff*.

"Don't blame me," he said.

"Who's blaming you?"

She was being unfair, and she knew it. But, brushing the leaves and twigs from her arms, she set off in a high huff. Her feet hit the moss—and sank like millstones. Wet black ooze poured over her boot-tops. She mentioned this to Lance: "*Laaance!*"

For his part, Lance had never seen anything quite so amusing. He laughed drunkenly on the dry shore.

The muck clung cold and thick around her ankles. She pulled up hard on her right foot. It slowly surfaced, then plucked free with a loud black suck. The wet ooze gushed and gurgled in the footstep. Her foot now hovered in air, dripping its mantle of sludge on the moss. For a moment Grace felt the domestic horror of turning around in a living room to see the mud she had tracked on the rug. But her problems were much deeper. In regards to her left leg, about knee-deep.

"Help me!" she wailed. "I mean it, Lance."

Lance lost control. Laughter convulsed him like a demon.

Grace grabbed wildly at the stalk of a nearby plant—one of the many so tastefully spaced across the green. It happened to be devil's club; her hand closed tight upon hundreds of needles. "*Aiee!*" she said, and drew back her hand. The flesh was all prickled with hair-like spines. They burned without mercy. Her palm began throbbing in red and white splotches. Meanwhile, she had planted her right foot beneath the moss again, and now both legs were stuck fast.

Lance roared, thoroughly entertained.

"You pig!" she shouted. "You filthy pig! Get me out of here!"

Because her back was toward him, she had to twist around awkwardly to deliver her withering stare. And, more intent on executing this gaze of revenge than on keeping her balance, she collapsed in the mire with an ungainly shriek. Lance stopped laughing.

"So you finally realize this is serious," said Grace. She was reclining in the ooze at his feet.

There was no reply.

"Here's my hand," she offered.

No hand was extended in return.

She saw then that Lance was not looking at her. He was watching something across the bog. His mouth hung open. Grace turned and looked too. And gasped.

Wending across the mossy expanse were four pair of marmots, harnessed in a column to a small barge. To Grace, who had never before seen a live marmot, they looked a little like cats—or perhaps beavers. Unlike Grace, they were light enough, apparently, to stay atop the moss. In the front of the barge a single silvered marmot was standing upright, holding the reins between his paws. Behind him, seated on a high-backed chair, was the most imposing woman Grace had ever seen. The woman wore a long gown of the brightest red. Her raven hair swept both bare shoulders. She held her head high, and rested her hands on the arms of the chair with great composure. The skin of her face was white and firm, and her eyes were green and dark and direct. The barge was slowly winding towards Lance and Grace; the eyes of the lady were fixed upon them with cool interest. Soon the team of marmots drew up beside them and stopped at the edge of the bog.

"Stuck, I see," the woman announced. Her voice rang high overhead in the boughs of fir. "Perhaps the young man could be of assistance." Lance was skewered with a commanding stare.

He looked back dumbly, his mouth still open.

"Hop to it, boy," she said. "Stop your flycatching."

As if in a trance, Lance reached down to Grace's hand. He began to pull. It took both of his hands and both of hers before she moved at all. The bog around her shuddered like pudding; her legs began to wrench free like mixing spoons caked in the bottom of a bowl. Lance strained, his teeth clenched manfully. When least expected, her feet slipped out with a *pop* and both of them tumbled onto the bank. The bog regurgitated noisily in her footsteps.

"Splendid, young man. Splendid," said the lady.

Lance's face showed a shy tinge of heroism, but Grace looked down at her filthy legs in distress. "My boots are gone," she cried. "I've lost my boots." She had only a very muddy pair of wool socks on her feet.

"So you have," said the woman. "And you are right—they really are lost."

Lance sat panting while Grace looked the woman in the eye. It scared her, but she had to try. She encountered flint hardness; the power there astonished her. The woman was eagerly looking for something.

"Let me introduce myself, weary travelers," said the woman. "I am Lady Lira, and my doorstep is near at hand. My house lies open to succor those who must cross these wastes. So allow me to beseech you. Look about—the day is far gone. Surely you are tired and in need of rest. Warm baths, hot meat, a pillow for your heads—will these not help you on your way?"

Grace, coated like a tar baby, heard the word *baths*. Lance, his chocolate chips depleted, heard the word *meat*.

"I get so few visitors in these desolate parts, and seldom does such a strong young man come to my door, or such a clever young lady with sparkling eyes."

Lance blushed, and Grace, though she recognized flattery when she heard it, visibly glowed. If anyone else had talked this way, Grace would have laughed aloud. But Lady Lira had bizarre authority.

"You will come then," she said. "Here, there is room on the barge at my feet—and my marmots are more than strong enough to carry us all."

Lance and Grace exchanged a glance, not to consult but to share their awe. *Marmots*, thought Grace. She tasted the word.

"Don't be frightened," said Lady Lira. "I won't eat you." She laughed at the notion. *Preposterous*, she seemed to say.

Lance slipped nervously onto the barge and crouched at her feet. He did not need to crouch, but it felt appropriate. Grace still hung back. On second thought she did not like the reference to her sparkling eyes.

"Is the young lady bashful?" said Lady Lira. "I have extra shoes at home. You are welcome to any pair you like. Come now. Be bold like your companion."

Lance, who looked anything but bold, blushed once more. He could not keep his eyes off of her.

"It's not that," Grace lied. "It's just that I don't want to get any mud on your beautiful dress."

"Oh!" trilled Lady Lira. "Take no thought for that. I have so many more at home, and one for you too, after your bath."

Grace was just vain enough to picture herself in Lady Lira's shoes, and in her gown too, sweeping through forests and sunsets in bare-shouldered glory. She would be stunning. So she stepped onto the barge, stood before the chair, and shrugged her pack onto the deck. It lay upside down in its own filth, helpless as a potato bug.

"That's it, dear. Now we must all become better acquainted. I have told you my name. I pray you tell me yours."

"I'm Lance," said Lance. It was the first he had spoken.

"Grace," said Grace.

"Splendid," said Lady Lira. "Now we are properly introduced."

She looked past them now to the marmot before her. All this time he had quietly stood at the helm of the barge. Grace, in fact, had already felt the urge to stroke his head.

"James," said Lady Lira, "home." The marmot jiggled the reins before him, and the barge slid away across the moss, slowly weaving through spiny clumps of devil's club.

The leaves of poison slipping by made Grace remember her hands were still on fire. She was cold and muddy. And she couldn't help feeling a little frightened of Lady Lira. But at the same time she laughed inside that anyone would have a driver—a furry one, no less—to whom she would say, "Home, James."

Chapter 6
Want to See My Blister?

❋

He should have known. Something in her eyes. *Foster. Grace Foster.* Was she granddaughter, cousin, niece to the old man? The moment William heard her name he knew he must find Grace in the wilderness. So he told the red-bearded one he had not seen her, and went his way. The red-bearded fellow presumably went his.

Yesterevening still grew on him. Flinging the pack off, trampling the ferns, snatching the fronds till his palms ran green. Then rioting in the underbrush, crashing in the alder, tearing limb from limb until darkness came. Given a machete, William would have put a whole trail crew to shame. But there was no trail to be cleared—not even a deer path. That was the big surprise.

And the dreams he had had, there in that misplaced field of ferns. Ravens hurtling, ice worms wriggling, axes swinging in radiant fog. Then a dark forest tide had swept out before him, sucking at his knees. It regathered itself in a great green wave, piling up against the horizon, heap upon heap. He turned and ran for the mountaintop, but a terrible rainbow crowned the summit, an emerald rainbow too stunning to look upon. So he turned again to the mounting wave. It smashed in upon him, tumbling him down into deep green chaos; then he awoke, sodden with dew, the scent of fern like oil on his brow, and a waning moon in the fronds overhead.

In the morning Grace had come and gone. Why had he been so smug with her? Why had he bullied her off? He could not say. He only knew he was lonely when she left.

William, in fact, had never felt so small in the forest. At all other times, the woods were but a thin strip of green between a parked car and a mountaintop, easily crossed in a scramble to a high camp, easily recrossed in a dash to a hot shower. He had always ignored it without effort. But now the forest was large enough to ignore him. A tide pool had spread itself into an ocean, not something to splash through but something to drown in. Unfathomed acres pressed in on his shoulders. He hardly could bear it. Which is why he had come back up the trail. He had to escape the forest in the way that a child must escape a dark closet. The weight of darkness suffocates, and so can the green weight of glory.

Of course, he had also come back up the trail because high in the meadows was a junction. At the end of another trail, perhaps, he would find a road. But that he doubted. Garth's windspoken disappearance howled in his mind. The man—gone. The road—gone. The forest—here and everywhere. It was all too strange and tied together. He had a key; he had a poem. The key might unlock something; so might the poem. But the poem itself needed unlocking. He wished for someone who could read it better than he. This much he had known by the time that he met the young man with the red beard.

Now he knew more. He knew he needed Grace. So William walked on, at each bend hoping to catch a glimpse of the girl with the orange pack. But Grace eluded him.

And gradually, weary of crisis, his mind took rest in the ordinary. Today was Monday, and he should have been at work. On Mondays, William enjoyed telling people at the office about his weekends. He especially liked to tell his supervisor. He would wander to her door and slouch against the frame with a mug of coffee in hand. His slouch showed how fatigued he must be, and displayed the casual indifference of an outdoorsman toward the confines of a mere office building.

On the Monday before, his supervisor had smiled and said, "How was your weekend, William?"

"Pretty good," he had answered. "I went to the mountains."

"Oh? Where?"

"You ever been up around Jackass Lake?"

"Jackass Lake," she told herself. She looked for the lake in the intimate glow of her fingernail polish. "Is that the one you drive by on the pass?"

"No," he replied. "You can't drive to it. You have to hike in."

"Oh my," she said. "So you walked the whole way. How far was it?"

"To the lake, you mean? About four miles is all."

"Four miles is quite a bit for an old lady like me!" She laughed explosively. "Was the fishing good?"

"No," said William. "I mean, I don't know. I didn't go fishing."

"*Mmm,*" she replied. Her eyes began scanning the green-glow screen of her computer.

"I was doing a little climbing," William added.

She looked back up and William saw her eyes widen. "Oh, that's right," she gushed. "I'd forgotten. You're our mountain climber! You be careful up there, William."

"It's very safe, really, if you know what you're doing," William said. He scuffed his toe against the doorframe modestly.

Now, as he walked through the forest, William's hand still gripped his coffee cup. The other hand made casual gestures. Sometimes his shoulders shrugged beneath the red tower of his pack, and sometimes his lips moved silently. It was more pleasant on a Monday to talk in the office than to walk in the mountains.

At length the trail broke into the meadow. The gleaming South Queen hove upwards once more. He stopped. Still he had not found Grace. He glanced at his watch and found it had halted at the eleventh hour—about the time they had summitted the day before.

Out of habit, he looked up and raked the peak with a hungry eye. The easy snowfields they had climbed were on the right. On the left, more to William's taste, a glacier tumbled down steep blue steps, each step splintered in jagged seracs. A lava headwall, bright red, rose above the cirque of the glacier. William could not tell for sure, but he thought he saw a ribbon of ice that split the headwall clear to the summit. Would it go? He eyed the tiny summit horns, and locked his gaze in the gunsight between them. Even as he watched, a white cloud tip poked into the slot.

"Quiet!" said a voice. William heard giggles in the grass behind him.

"Look at that pack!" said another.

William turned around. Just off the trail were two young boys, lying on their stomachs before a small burrow.

"Shut up! Shut up!" said one to the other. "He hears us, he sees us, he's coming."

They sat up as William approached. He asked if they had seen Grace. They hadn't, not since yesterday anyhow.

"Hey mister," said one, "you ever climbed that mountain?"

"Yesterday," said William.

The boys exchanged looks of wonder.

"How hard is it?" said the boy. He was wiggling his legs and picking at the grass.

The other boy cut in before William could answer. "Did he say we were gonna climb it? He didn't say for sure, did he?"

"I bet we will," said the first. "He'll probably make us do it."

"Looks scary to me," said the second.

"You chicken?" said the first.

"You said it looked scary yourself a minute ago," said the second.

"Like yeah," said the first boy scornfully.

The second boy appealed to William. "How scary is it?" The boy was pale and thin, and wore black-framed glasses that made him appear like a gangly raccoon. The other boy had swirls of freckles across his face, and red hair, cowlicked. They looked intently at William. A black wet nose poked out from the burrow behind them.

"It's not hard if you go up on the right," said William. He set his pack down to rest.

"I bet that's how we'll go," said the boy with the cowlick.

"Yeah," said the pale one, "but what's easy for him might not be so easy for us."

"Hey," said the first boy to William. "You ever caught a marmot?"

"No," said William. He saw the nose withdraw into the burrow.

"There's one in here," said the boy. "We're gonna catch him when he comes out."

They all looked at the hole.

"Hey mister," said the freckled one, "want to see my blister?"

"You should see his blister," said the other. "Big as a half dollar."

The first boy took off his boot and peeled away several socks. The sock closest to the skin was bloody at the heel. Underneath was a glistening red sore. He twisted his foot so that William could see it in full. "Bet you never saw one that big," he said.

"Look out!" said the raccoon-faced boy. A silver blur charged out of the den. The boy lunged. He knocked it against his friend's bare foot and tried to hold its furry sides. "I got him!—I think. Gimme some help, Arnie!"

Arnie grabbed his foot and screamed. "He bit me! He bit me! Ronald, he bit me! My blister, it hurts! It hurts! It hurts!"

The marmot shrieked like an escaped balloon and shot into a lush patch of purple lupine. There at a distance it sat up and whistled, one blast after another. Each series faded like a disappearing train.

"You can't believe how it hurts!" said Arnie. He held up his heel to solicit belief anyway. William stepped nearer to look. Blood welled out of two incised holes in the round red blister.

William's stomach began to tremble. "Best to let it bleed out," he told him.

Arnie looked pale between his freckles. "Who's got the first-aid kit?" he asked.

"How should I know?" said Ronald. He maneuvered in for a closer look. "Wow," he said reverently.

The boys, mesmerized, watched the blood drip. It fell from the heel and hung on separate blades of grass—wet, shining, a crimson dew upon the meadow. They were watching so closely that they merely heard a grassy thud.

Ronald glanced up. The man in red was stretched on the ground, his head softly pillowed in a blazing clump of Indian paintbrush.

How peaceful he looked.

Chapter 7
Tincture of Benzoin

✳

RONALD AND ARNIE NO SOONER SAW THE MAN PROSTRATE than they made bloody tracks to their camp across the meadow. Now more than ever they needed the first-aid kit. Surely it contained some potion to revive the faint or to raise the dead. Once in camp they tossed through mounds of sleeping bags and piles of nylon clothing. They ransacked a row of slump-sided packs leaned up against a log.

"It's in a red stuff sack, right?" said Ronald.

"Hey," said Arnie. "Where's the first-aid kit?"

He was addressing three girls lying on foam pads behind the log. They all wore shorts—and tee-shirts that were rolled up to their navels. Each played shepherdess to an enormous flock of mosquitoes.

"Got him!" said one girl, slapping her stomach.

"You've got it?" said Ronald.

"Got what?"

"Forget it," said Arnie. "Here it is."

He leaned over the log and snatched a red bag from beside the girls' heads. It was open, and scissors and moleskin poured into the dust unnoticed. Arnie and Ronald stirred through the remaining contents. A roll of dirty white tape first caught their eye, and they decided to bandage Arnie's heel before looking any further. The tape, however, was impossible to sever. Each strip wrinkled to a gummy knot as they tried to tear it from the roll. The scissors, of course, lay safely hidden behind the log.

"Forget it," said Arnie. "It probably needs to air out anyway."

They recognized everything else in the kit except a sticky brown bottle labeled *Tincture of Benzoin*. Ronald held it up between them. Nothing else looked potent enough to arouse the stranger. But even as Ronald held the bottle aloft, the sun disappeared and the meadow darkened round about them. The tiny white cloud at the tip of the mountain had spread like ripples on a blackening pond. Whitebark pine twigs started to quiver. The girls arose, picked up their pads, and climbed back over the log into camp. They rolled down their tee-shirts and joined the boys in staring at the sky.

"Think it'll rain?" said Ronald. His voice was reverential. Indoors, the question would have sounded idle.

Just then a thunderclap sounded on high. The three girls screamed in unison, then tittered nervously. Ronald and Arnie kept silence, but old fear bellowed in their hearts. Then came a second blast, avalanching into the meadows like a bursting glacier.

Just that spring, Ronald had completed an earth science project on "What Makes Thunder?" It had won second prize in the eighth-grade science fair. The thunder itself was represented by the red letters B-O-O-M!! which he'd painted on the posterboard at the end of a series of diagrams. But now the thunder was gray, and hollow, and full of might. It echoed terribly between the mountains, and each rolling echo tumbled Ronald's poster across the treetops, shredding it upon silver snags, hurling the title into the air: "What Makes Thunder?"

"It's raining, it's raining!" shouted the girls. Fat drops kicked up the dust at their feet.

"Who's got the tent?" the oldest girl said.

"We don't have a tent," said Ronald. "We have a rainfly." He quailed inside. He knew that the green nylon bundle in his pack was called a rainfly, but he had no idea how to set it up.

The rain came more earnestly, and the wind moaned.

"Put your ponchos on first," he told everyone. "Then help me set up the fly."

The words amazed him. He had never taken charge of a crisis in his life. The girls immediately donned their ponchos, and this amazed him more. People were doing things merely because he had told them to. He usually just did whatever Arnie suggested. But now Arnie was silent, stooped over, looking at his bloody heel. Arnie had not put on his poncho. Ronald found the poncho and threw it over him.

"You okay, Arnie?"

"I'm okay," he said quietly.

Ronald did not put on his own poncho. There was not time. He began to unwind a small rope from around the rainfly. The girls huddled in a row before him, cowled like wizards in their blue rain robes. Once the fly was unfolded, an intestinal mass of white cord emerged. Ronald knelt down like a diviner examining the entrails of a sacrificed animal. He found many separate cords all snarled together. Each was attached to a different point on the edge of the fly.

"Let's get these lines untangled," said Ronald.

"*B-O-O-M!!*" went the thunder.

Obediently, the three girls knelt with him to unravel the great knot.

"Hey, don't. Don't pull that one."

"Wait a sec—I'm trying to get this end through."

"Here, let go."

"There, I got it."

"You just made it worse!"

"No, get that part."

"Stop! Look what you just did."

"What'd I do?"

Ronald grew scared. He could command ponchos into place, but he could not command the cord to disentangle. His shirt stuck wet on his back. He shivered.

Fortunately, nature and genius intervened.

"It's hailing!" screamed the girls. The meadow around them filled with a white hiss. Pellets sprang from the rainfly and rolled into the fold, piling up in little drifts.

"Let's just get it over us," one girl said. At once they abandoned the knot and crawled under the fly, using their heads and shoulders for tent poles. Arnie, still staring at his heel, had to be pulled inside. They sat cross-legged atop wet sleeping bags, facing each other in a tight circle. The hail seemed to bang on the fly even harder. But they had fenced it out, and blew their steamy breath into one another's faces.

Ronald was scrunched up against the oldest girl with long braids—the one who had gotten them under the fly. Her hand rested carelessly on his knee. He had never in his life been so close to a girl, but it seemed best to pretend that he had. His glasses had fogged up completely.

"Are you warm enough?" she asked him.

"Sure," said Ronald. His teeth began to chatter.

"Here," she said. "I've got an extra sweater in my pack."

As it happened, her pack was under the fly behind her, and she quickly gave the sweater to Ronald. It was pink, but he put it on. Under the fly it looked a little greenish, and that was some comfort. He wished he could remember her name.

Meanwhile, the girl turned her attention to Arnie. "How are you doing?" she asked.

"Fine," he said.

"Let me see your heel." She had noticed, though no one had told her.

Arnie stuck his heel in her lap, exposing the bitten blister.

"Gross!" said the other two girls.

Arnie looked numbly at the first-aid kit still clutched in his hand. He passed it over on demand. The girl washed his wound with a clear solution, then bandaged it with gauze and tape. The tape tore cleanly along her fingernails.

Ronald was just beginning to feel the warmth of wet wool, wet nylon, wet bodies stirred together. Then he remembered. "There's a man," he blurted. "Out on the meadow. He's unconscious or something. He's not moving." He wondered how he had forgotten.

"Are you kidding?" said the girl.

"He's not kidding," said Arnie. Now that his heel was bandaged he felt like talking again. He told them the whole story. When he had finished, they heard the hail beat the fly and felt it hit their heads. It made their silence loud.

"We should—go help him, shouldn't we?" said the girl. The prospect was fearful.

"We were going to bring him some—some . . ."

"Tincture of benzoin," said Ronald.

"I think that's what my mother uses when she gets dizzy," said another of the girls. "She puts it in her ear with an eyedropper."

"I don't think we have an eyedropper," said Ronald. He had an eye for detail.

"I think we should check on him anyway," said the first girl. She squeezed Ronald's knee for the second time. "Why don't you come with me? No use everybody going."

Ronald was electrified. Never before had he been asked out. "Sure," he said. His voice was breathless.

The girl grabbed the first-aid kit with one hand and Ronald's arm with the other. Together they peeled off their side of the fly and stood up in the hail. It did not feel as terrifying as it had sounded. The slick green fly, draped over the others, quivered on the ground like a lump of lime gelatin.

"Which way?" she asked.

Ronald found his poncho and dutifully led her toward the trail. They walked silently for a hundred yards, drenching their knees and calves in the grass. The hail ricocheted off their shoulders. Then, curiously, they stepped out of the hail as if through a curtain. Around them the air hung still. Beside them the hail fell hissing. They could have been standing by a waterfall.

"How funny," said the girl.

"The sun!" said Ronald.

Suddenly its beams were pouring under the clouds. The meadow glowed an astonishing green. For an instant the curtain of hail shone white beside them, transfigured to a brighter splendor. Then it simply melted from the sky, and the black clouds glistened in a new stillness. In the stillness they heard toads and frogs—croaking, croaking at the death of the hail,

As if there were no such cold thing.

"A rainbow!" said the girl.

It arched from a snowfield, crossed the sky, and dropped into the dripping forest. The mountain hemlocks bloomed like roses, like daffodils, like violets. This end of the rainbow was not far away; it touched where the trail emerged from the forest. The boy and the girl hurried on toward the rainbow's end and breathed the wet air, new-bathed with light. They strained to gather in the rainbow—all of it, all at once.

They were almost to the forest when Ronald held up his hand and stopped. "He was right here. There's the marmot hole." He pointed at it.

"The same one?"

"Yep." He paused. "Pretty sure."

"Well he's not here now," she observed.

A horrible thought struck Ronald. What if the man had been dragged away and eaten by marmots? It would not do to alarm the girl. He put a brave face on it: "I bet he just fainted and the hail woke him up and he hiked off. It's not like he was hurt or anything."

The girl pondered his theory. "I hope none of those marmots started gnawing on him," she said.

"Marmots?" he replied. "They only eat grass and stuff. Don't be silly."

The girl nodded slowly. Then, case dismissed, she changed the subject.

"What's your name?" she asked. "I know we told each other our names at the base camp when we started, but I forgot yours."

"My name?" said Ronald. The request thrilled him. "My name is Ronald." He tried to pronounce it in an important way.

"My name's Jennifer," said the girl. "I'm telling you because I think you're afraid to ask."

"Me?" said Ronald. "I was just going to ask."

"Well, now you know."

"Yep," he said, "now I know."

What Ronald did not know, however, was what else to say. He searched the sky and found that the rainbow had faded. He searched the meadow and found it suddenly unremarkable. He searched his mind for a suitable topic of conversation, even for a suitable phrase unrelated to a definite topic. None came. Their man was gone, the storm over; their mission completed, the crisis passed. What was left to them in common? Jennifer stood with her head cocked to one side, apparently inclined to let him suffer. The awkward moment broadened to a painful silence, it deepened to an abyss of despair. With all of his heart, Ronald wished he could crawl into the burrow at his feet and escape the face of the earth—better the bloody fangs of a herbivore than the fatal poison of shame.

Then, from an unexpected quarter, rescue arrived. Out of the trees trod their red-bearded leader, his boots and legs bespattered with mud. Ronald ran to him in joy, and Jennifer came close behind.

"Did you find her?" he asked.

"Did you find her?" she echoed.

"Where's Lance?" they both said.

The leader eyed them mournfully, as if he were not happy to see them but knew that he must. His face was scratched, his beard full of twigs. "We found her," he assured them. "Everything's fine. Grace got lost in the woods last night and sprained her ankle pretty bad. I had Lance drive her down to the nearest clinic. We'll have to continue without them for a while."

He paused. "Any of the rest of you planning to run off on me?"

They shook their heads obediently.

"Why did she leave?" asked Jennifer. "Did she say?"

"Why did Lance have to go?" asked Ronald. "Why didn't you go?"

"Well, somebody's got to lead this expedition," he snorted. He ignored Jennifer's question with one of his own: "So, staying out of trouble? I'll bet you guys figured out how to set up the rainfly in a hurry!" He laughed very loudly, as if it were a joke they were not supposed to get.

"We're doing fine," said Jennifer.

"Great," said Ronald.

On the way back to camp the two of them stayed well behind the leader. Jennifer tugged on Ronald's poncho and cupped her hand to his ear. "I'm glad she's gone," she whispered. "She was sort of a bitch."

Chapter 8
Land of Shadows

✳

WHENCE THESE RED-BEARDED LIES?

Whither William's body?

First, the beguiled instructor. When Lance did not return from behind the cedar tree, our leader went to check on him. Finding the spot empty, he wildly tore at the bark with his nails and beat upon his breast, cursing the day he had first signed on with You-Can-Do-It Expeditions. He called and called out Lance's name and searched and searched the nearby woods, but all for naught. He had no birds in hand, and two in the bush.

Were the two birds together, and taking flight to the trailhead? He feared so, and this was bitter for him. No one, ever before, had escaped from one of his expeditions. It was enough to make him wonder if the forest were enchanted. But the woods seemed as unenchanted as ever. They were simply his workplace, where he made people hoist heavy packs and back down cliffs and get up early in the morning. He had loved the wilderness once, and he thought he still did, but more and more he merely loved new ways to teach ice-ax technique, new "initiative tests" for the uninitiated, new rules of "minimum impact" to impose with maximum vigilance. More than he loved wilderness, he loved the idea of himself as a wilderness leader. That is why it hurt to see his leadership refused.

So, feeling disconsolate, he returned to the trail and hiked the remaining distance to the road. For him the road was once the outer boundary of adventure. But it, too, was part of his workplace now. It was the place where he met and disposed of his charges. Road or trail—it felt the same to him.

At the highway he saw no sign of Lance or Grace. But sitting by the fall was a stout, bald man with a snow-white beard. He offered the leader a cup of cold water. "Drink up," the old man told him. He did. It tasted more delicious than water ever had.

He asked the man how long he had been there.

"All my life, feels like." The old man guffawed.

Had he seen a girl and a boy hike out?

"Seems to me just half an hour ago," he said. "No sooner hit the pavement than they're waggling their thumbs, and wasn't five minutes got a ride down the mountain."

He asked what they looked like.

"The young fella—curly in the head, wearin' a rucksack. She had a full pack—orange, I think. Nice legs but chewed up by the skeeters." He guffawed again.

Was the old man going out?

"Outgoing anyways."

Would he deliver a note to the You-Can-Do-It base camp down the road?

"I'll get it to the right place," he said.

So, the leader wrote a note for the chief instructor, explaining that two wayward students had escaped his strict supervision. He signed the note with his name, Park Savidge, and entrusted it with the white-bearded, bald old man. Then he began the long walk back to the meadows—long enough to concoct the tale he told to Ronald and Jennifer. To the chief instructor he had to tell as much as half the bitter truth; he wished to save face with those left in his power.

❋

Now William, collapsed in the paintbrush. There he lay. Ants soon fell to exploring his armpits, and two mosquitoes delicately pierced his nose and drank their fill, gorging their pinstriped abdomens almost to the bursting point. They reeled away in sodden flight, and William awoke. His nose was throbbing, large as an apple. He felt for the escaped culprits, then dove his hands for the armpit ants. He looked about at the empty meadow, at the empty burrow. Ah, he remembered. Yes, he was shaky still. But, best to leave before rescue came. So he lurched to his feet, lifted his pack, and set out once again.

His trail climbed half-a-mile higher in the meadows, at times disappearing under suncupped snowbanks. At the very foot of the South Queen the path reached a junction. Here he had camped with Garth. When he got there this time, the sky had darkened. He could turn left, and traverse high meadows to the Center Queen, or turn right, and dip into a web of wooded canyons to the south. He stood and pondered. Before he could decide, a thunderclap split the

air, and he flinched. More thunder exploded. And more. Suddenly th
gained cosmic proportions. How to decide? William had had enough of forests.
He turned left.

As soon as he did so, a spate of rain thumped his chest. Thunder burst, the
ground shook. Marmots mingled desperate whistles with wailing winds. All at
once—and he had no idea why—William felt every inch a hero. His crimson
coat flapped bravely about him, his bitten nose throbbed wildly in the rain. He
strode the high trail like a giant in a tempest, not even bothering to walk around
the swelling puddles of snowmelt. Rain became hail, and he firmly crushed the
little balls of ice beneath his feet. The path, a gleaming white ribbon in the grass,
uncoiled before his every step.

Thus he braved the elements till, having forgotten to don his gaiters, his socks
and boots filled up with hailstones. That was cold. Also, a widening rip in the
nape of his hood had invited the hail onto his neck. Ice was dripping down his
back, and that was very cold. William fell to unheroic bouts of shivering. He
searched the land for shelter.

To his left, the meadow gave onto a rocky plateau, flecked with shining obsidian. The plateau halted at a lava rim and dropped away to the forest. To his right,
the meadow rose through lava bluffs to moraines of glistening rubble. In the
nearest outcrop, partially screened by a clump of trees, he spied a shadowed hollow beneath an overhang—perhaps a cave, at least a sheltered nook. It was worth
checking into. He left the trail and drenched his sagging socks in the grass. His
boots made sloshing, sucking noises, easily heard above wind and hail.

He reached the base of the overhang and pulled back branches of scrubby
hemlock to get a closer look. It was a cave indeed—a lava tube, from the looks
of it—a hollow conduit through which magma had once poured from mountain depths. He squirmed through the screen of snapping twigs and crouched
in the tunnel entrance. It was dry, even quiet—he had left the hail behind. Off
came the pack, off came the boots. There were little lava spikes on the floor, but
he did not care. He unrolled his canary-yellow air mattress and unleashed his
sleeping bag in a shivering frenzy. There. Inside its crumpled folds he found a
dank and hazy warmth.

The hail ceased, the sun shone, the rainbow bent across his threshold. But
William did not know. He lay surrounded by steaming clothes, snoring in the
cave mouth, tucked away in a land of shadows.

Chapter 9
Baths for the Guests

❋

GRACE WAS IN HEAVEN. The smoking water lapped to her chin, and she lay half-floating in sponged indolence. The bath was huge. The basin itself was inlaid with tile, all a green mosaic save one red dragon couched on the bottom. The head of the dragon lay under Grace's heels, and out of its mouth boiled an underwater fountain that soothed her feet. Above her toes the water poured out through a notch in the brim. Thence it was channeled across the floor to a hole in the wall. All of the mud had sloughed off and poured out long ago. The water was clean now, and so was Grace. But she made no plans to get out. There was no better place to think.

Lady Lira's home was cavernous. After traveling some distance across the green bog, they had come in the barge to a tall lava cliff. Here the bog ended. Or here it began, rather, for out of a cave flowed a murky sludge, the undistinguished headwaters of Lira Creek. Grace feared they would enter the cave itself. But at the very last instant James pulled on the reins, and the barge veered left alongside the cliff. They slipped quietly beneath the face, so close to it that ferns on the cliffside trailed their fronds in Grace's hair. A vault of conchoidal obsidian passed, smooth and black, glinting like glass. Then they skirted the base of a fall that shot from a hole in the rock. The waterfall steamed; it sent hot spray upon their cheeks. And then the barge stopped. They were next to a rock landing that jutted out from a wooden door. There were window niches in the cliff above.

Grace had studied the door in the rock. It seemed an odd place to live. It seemed a strange sort of woman who lived here—dressed to kill and enthroned, imperious, on a marmot-drawn bogsled. Perhaps Lady Lira was merely eccentric. Perhaps she was the ranger's wife, and this was how she coped with boredom. Perhaps—but here Grace's hypotheses were shattered in thunder. Echoes crossed the hollow sky. The air thickened in new darkness.

"Quickly now," said Lady Lira. "Inside before it rains. Hurry—James will get your packs." She swept them over the landing and through the door, from gloom into gloom.

Inside was no ranger station. They traversed a dim passage and stopped on the edge of a great hall, carved deep in the rock. Its ceiling was lost in shadows. Long red hangings draped the walls, and torches sputtered in brackets. At the far end was a long table set crosswise. Behind it, two doors framed a huge lava fireplace. A glaring fire burned there now—Grace saw the table in silhouette against it.

She and Lance were standing on flagstones in the entry passageway, but a thick green carpet spread out at their feet. In the center of the carpet was the immense woven figure of a red dragon. The creature was really too bloated for a dragon, but Grace knew no better name for it.

Lady Lira appeared from behind them. "Welcome home," she announced. Her voice echoed to the dark ceiling. Immediately a pair of marmots bounded towards them over the carpet.

"Baths for the guests!" she ordered.

The marmot next to Grace stood quickly up on his hind feet. He had silvered shoulders and a dusky face—and so looked a little like an overweight Siamese cat. But his buck teeth belonged to a beaver, and his thick red tail to a raccoon. The marmot pointed his nose in the air and squinted up at Grace. He squinted as if he had just woken up and could not find his glasses. Then he put his black-webbed paws on his belly and nodded politely. When Grace nodded back, the marmot collapsed on all four paws and darted off to a staircase. He dragged his tail like a limp rag, and at every step his shoulders quivered in furry rolls of fat. Grace followed, amused, and found her bath.

She lay there yet. The water soothed her swollen hand—the one poisoned by the devil's club. It gave her good enough reason to linger, and turned her thoughts to Lance. She saw him howling on the bank, his mouth a blackened cove in his face, his lips a purple stain. Had he lifted a finger to help her? He had not—not until ordered by Lady Lira. She saw him crouching on the barge, blushing obsequiously, gazing at the woman, adoring her bare shoulders. Just hours ago, Grace had thought him emphatically cute. The memory of it brought wonder and disgust. So easily did one day turn the shadow of her judgment; so easily falls the son of the morning.

Right then, right there, Grace decided she could find her uncle on her own. There was firmness, there was satisfaction in her resolve. She raised her fist and thumped it squarely down in the bath—and shot a geyser into her eye. It did not faze her. She was invincible.

At this crux of glory her marmot reappeared. He stood upright in the doorway with a bundle in his paws. "Monsieur marmot," she asked, "can you help me find my uncle?" He walked unsteadily to the basin and held his burden up to Grace: on top, a red towel; underneath, a folded gray gown. But this trick of balance was too much to ask of a marmot. He swayed, he toppled, he crashed to the floor, and the laundry with him. Then up he shrieked, and he whistled out the door on all four feet.

Grace rose laughing from the water. "He just—he just—fell—over!" she sputtered. It put her in real merriment, enough to make her sides ache.

She stepped out and retrieved the towel and, having dried herself, put on the gray gown. A full-length mirror gave the proper prospect. At first Grace admired what she saw in the glass. But then a smile crossed the reflection of her face. The mirror, no less than the marmot, had awakened her sense of the true ridiculous. Her image presented but a flimsy imitation of Lady Lira's grandeur. *Let the woman deck herself out*, she thought. *No need to pay her the homage of an ape.*

The dress fell in a rumpled heap. Grace plucked her muddy shorts from a bench and plunged them in the bath. Her sweater went in too. She could wear them wet, dry them by the fire. So she scrubbed them off, wrung them out, put them on, and stepped into the cold upstairs hallway. Her marmot awaited her there.

"Do you know," she asked, "how cute you are?" She tried to stroke his silver back, but he ran down the passage to another door, where he stood up and nodded. Grace followed and looked in. She saw her pack leaning against a small bed that was built into a casement window. A single candle burned on the window ledge. Outside, in bog and forest, it was nearly dark.

Then the marmot brushed her legs and led her downstairs to the green carpet in the cavernous hall. Her bare feet sank softly in the carpet. It was like walking in a thick lawn, newly mown. She was sorry it ended before they got to the table and the fire.

Lance was already standing by the fireplace—the mantle was higher than his head. He wore a billowy white shirt, provided no doubt by Lady Lira. He looked at the fire. He looked at the ceiling. He did not look at Grace.

"Greetings, Prince Charming."

"Please," said Lance.

"So where's your shining armor? There are dragons, you know—deeds to be done. What about that big fat sucker right on the rug? Now *there's* a menace."

Lance sulked and scowled and scuffed the hearth.

Grace was content to let him be. She stood as close to the fire as she dared and felt her clothes dissolve in steam. Her marmot was gone. She wished him back to rub against her legs. When her front became hot she put her back to the fire; when her back became hot she turned around again. After turning several times, she realized her mind was more at ease when she faced the hall with her back to the fire. The room had the large hollowness of a deserted coliseum, the emptiness of a theater when the audience has left. The absence of all who might fill the great hall was in itself a discomfiting presence. So Grace kept watch and saw the shadows flicker on the carpet. That was best.

She was thus absorbed when the doors flew open on either side of the fireplace. She whirled. Lady Lira swept from the left door, trailing a long green gown. A column of marmots bearing cups and plates and food and drink trooped in from the right. What timing! What effect! Grace looked at Lance. He was trying his best to appear very calm. His arms hung down like fire pokers.

"Welcome again, my guests," said Lady Lira. "I trust you have bathed well." She spoke so loudly that Grace checked again to make certain that they were the only ones there.

The woman looked at them carefully. "Young man, your shirt well becomes you. But Grace, did I not send you better clothes? Did that clumsy marmot drop them?"

"Oh, no," said Grace. "He brought the gown, Lady Lira. I just feel more comfortable in—in shorts."

Lance failed to control a snicker.

Lady Lira dug hard at Grace with her eyes. Each eyebrow arched like the back of a cat. "Of course," she purred. "Whatever is most comfortable for you."

The marmots, meanwhile, laid out the supper by mounting the benches and raising each dish to the table. Four places were set, a pair on each side, directly before the fire. Two of the marmots ushered Lance and Grace to the seats nearest the hearth. Lady Lira walked around the table and assumed a place across from Lance. Grace wondered whom the fourth setting was for. Then James the marmot popped up next to his mistress. He stood gravely upright on the bench with no apparent difficulty. Grace noticed that his mantle of fur was hoarier than that of the other marmots.

The plates and utensils gleamed like silver, because they were. Heaping dishes of savory meat and bread and greens were waiting for them in the glare of the fire. James the marmot filled their cups with something very steamy and red.

They fell to—Grace with care, Lance with abandon. He only regretted there was no ketchup, and said so. But even *sans* ketchup his plate was soon empty, and Lady Lira quickly passed the meat to him again. "You eat no more than a pika," she scolded.

Grace had never tasted flesh so sweet and so tender. Just like Lance she wanted more. But she was too sleepy. The hot bath, the warm fire, the steaming food— not to mention the miles of trail, salal, and alder—all of these conspired against her in a yawn. Her head began to nod. She jerked it to attention—a reflex nurtured in lectures and sermons of days gone by. It would not do to fall asleep at the table. But could she hope to last until Lance had finished? He had started now on a third helping. She watched his plate doggedly. When it was clean, Lance looked up eagerly. Grace heard Lady Lira's voice as if from very far away.

"Dessert will taste much better," she said, "if we renew our appetites with the tales of your adventures. You have surely seen much that bears the telling. And perhaps, in knowing the end of your journey, I may be of greater assistance."

"What's for dessert?" asked Lance.

"You shall soon know," said Lady Lira. "But I long to hear of your travels."

Lance discerned he must sing for the rest of his supper. So he plunged in. "We were on a You-Can-Do-It Expedition, see, where you do climbing and stuff. Except our leader and the others, they were definite losers. So Grace, she split the first night and went back to the road, except it wasn't there, or she got lost, or something. Then the leader took me to look for her and I like accidentally found her behind this tree. So we took off and decided to find her uncle. Which is where we were going when she fell in the mud. And then you showed up. Where's dessert?"

"And where is Grace's uncle?" asked Lady Lira.

"Other side of the South Queen—we think." He looked to Grace for corroboration. She was propped on her elbows and breathing rhythmically.

"How did you know that?" said Lady Lira. Then she seemed to catch herself. "Perhaps we should let the young lady retire, and save the dessert for tomorrow. The chocolate will easily keep."

"Oh, no," said Lance in a panic. "I can tell you. It's this guy she met at the trailhead. He's the one that said the road was gone. He said he went climbing with Grace's uncle and was gonna pick him up on the other side of the mountain. He had a poem that her uncle wrote. She recognized the writing."

"How lovely," said Lady Lira. "I'm so fond of poetry. What was the poem about?"

"Beats me," said Lance. "She never said." He looked over his shoulder at the wooden door whence dinner had emerged on the pitter-patter of furry feet.

Lady Lira scrutinized Grace, who was slumbering sweetly, her face in her palms. Then the woman leaned across the table toward Lance. Her long dark hair brushed over her shoulders, her low-cut gown revealed uncharted territories. "Perhaps," she said softly, "someone as clever as—"

But here Grace's elbows caved in. She crashed to her plate and the whole table rattled. Grace looked up in stupid wonder. Her cheeks were dripping with grease. What place was this? What companions were these? She saw a fleshy boy whose eyes burned with longing. She saw a dark-haired woman whose eyes burned with knowledge. She saw a stone-faced rodent whose eyes had burned to ashes. The eyes were upon her in a large, dark cavern. And she feared them all.

Chapter 10
Devour This Day

✳

SHE AWOKE IN A SEA OF SOFT GREEN LIGHT. It was morning, and Grace was still in the house of Lady Lira. Her shoulders ached as she turned. At home, turning in bed set off undulating tides that rocked her back to sleep. But this bed was firm, like a beach. She was not at home.

Beyond the window were many fir trees, row on row, festooned with chartreuse lichen. The trees kept the shores of the mossy bog. Nearer at hand, the window ledge outside the glass bore ranks of pale green fruiting cups. They stood on end like trumpets waiting to sound the judgment. She put her nose on a single pane and, straining her eyes, could barely glimpse the landing below. Alongside it, the barge was waiting. Eight small marmots were slumped in the traces.

Grace turned over once again and looked about the bedroom. There was a stone fireplace, two straight-backed chairs, a green hearth-rug. This rug too had a swollen red dragon in the center. Grace studied its fatness with disinterest and closed her eyes to sleep.

Then, without warning, the door to the bedroom opened wide and in came Lance, still wearing the billowy shirt that Lady Lira had given him. Apparently, it had not occurred to him to knock.

"Breakfast is over," he announced. "Thought I'd tell ya." He looked at the dragon. He looked at the fireplace. He did not look at Grace.

Grace, meanwhile, had pulled the covers tight to her lips. "Okay by me," she said. "Not hungry."

"The bacon, I tell ya—fantastic bacon."

"Mm," said Grace, and planted a rancid pause.

Lance looked past her out the window. "Awesome place, huh?"

"Awesome," she echoed.

"Be kinda fun to stay here awhile, no?"

"No doubt," said she.

"Lady Lira says if I want I can go with her and catch marmots today. She trains them and everything."

"Amazing," said Grace.

"Sounds pretty great if you ask me, hunting marmots."

"A fine time, indeed," she answered.

Lance sensed something amiss. "Grace," he requested, "will you shove it?"

"Sorry, Lance. I'm not the pushy type."

"Don't you like it here?" he demanded. "She seems a little strange, yeah, but once you get to know her—"

"Like you have?"

"Well, yeah—sort of. We had a nice talk at breakfast, anyway." He paused. "Listen. She says it's impossible to find your uncle. Too dangerous. If you go over the pass like we wanted to, you hit these big mother glaciers with humungous cracks in the ice. You slip right in and nobody ever finds you. And if you go around the mountain instead, you hit these river gorges with no bridges or nothing. Really big cliffs, and the water is too deep to cross. You drown for sure if you try. Lady Lira says we can stay here a few days and then she'll take us out to the road when she's got time. Sounds like a plan, doesn't it?"

"A most sensible plan, Lance."

"You serious?"

She thought it over. She was none too good at walking on bogs. They would leave as they had come—in Lady Lira's barge and at Lady Lira's pleasure.

"Serious," she said.

"Good," he replied. "Glad you agree."

He looked to the floor in a way that imported a weighty transition. "Besides," he added, "are you for sure positive it was your uncle's writing you saw? People's handwriting can look real similar, you know."

"True," said Grace.

"So it might not have been his."

"Possibly not," she said.

"What did it say, anyway? You never told me. I guess I'm sorta curious."

"The poem?" she asked.

"Yeah, what's in it?"

She drew a deep breath and knotted her forehead as if making up her mind.

Then she exhaled with considerable calm. "Sorry if I forgot to let you in on it," she said. "Because you do deserve to know. Here, I'll get you some paper and something to write with—and you can copy it down if you want. I just have it in my head." She drew pen and notebook from the pack by her bed and tore out a sheet for him. "Okay. Pull up a chair. Ready?"

"Ready," said Lance.

Grace sat up straight and cleared her throat. "Listen carefully. All right? Here goes:

'Twas brillig, and—"

"'Twas what?"

"*Brillig.* You know—one of those Old English words for *stormy.* Shakespeare uses it all the time."

"*Mm,*" he said. He got it partway written before the pen punched through the paper in his lap.

"'Twas brillig, and the slithy toves—"

"Wait a minute. *Toves?*"

"Right. They're a really yummy sort of mushroom."

"How do you spell it?"

"Just like it sounds: *T-O-A-F-Z.*"

Lance labored the letters into print.

"'Twas brillig, and the slithy toves—"

"I though you said *slimy* toafz."

"No, no, no. *Slithy.* Where do you go to school, anyway?"

He lit up. "West Central. Undefeated the last two years in—"

"Here," cut in Grace. "You just listen and I'll write it down for you when I finish."

He gladly surrendered the paper and pen.

"'Twas brillig, and the slithy toves
Did gyre and gimble in the wabe:

All mimsy were the borogoves,
And the mome raths outgrabe."

"The what-raths?" he asked.
"I'll write it down for you," she said.

"'Beware the Jabberwock, my son!
The jaws that bite, the claws that catch!
Beware the Jubjub bird, and shun
The frumious Bandersnatch!'

"He took his vorpal sword in hand:
Long time the manxome foe he sought——"

At this point memory failed. Grace broke off.

"Is that all?" said Lance. "Sounds to me like it's just getting started."

"No, that's the end," she insisted. "It's sort of an *avant-garde* poem. You're not supposed to live happily ever after."

"Oh," said Lance. He got up from the chair and paced the rug while Grace wrote out the poem on her bed. She gave it to him and he shoved it in his voluminous shirt.

"Sure you don't want to go marmot hunting?" he asked.

"I never said I didn't," said Grace. "But now that you mention it, I'm sure that I don't."

"See ya then. Gotta go. Leaving pretty soon. Back tonight, I guess." He said all this from the door.

"While you're out in the woods," said Grace, "pick me some toves for supper, will you?"

"Sure," said Lance. "I bet there's lots of 'em."

"Thanks," said Grace. "Thanks a lot."

"That's my name," he smiled.

"What's your name?"

"Lott."

"Sure. Thanks a lot, Lancelot."

"Not Lance E. Lott. Lance *Q*. Lott."

"*Q*? As in Quincy? Quentin? Quizzler? Quark?"

Lance bristled. "Quercus," he said.

"Quercus," she replied.

When Lance was gone, Grace paged to the real poem in her notebook.

> *A gentle wight for gentle ladies three*
> *Aduentured through a verdant wood newgrowne,*
> *Through wildernesse that mote a wastlond bee,*
> *Vnless he greete the greenwood for his owne,*
> *Vnless he know the leaf as ice and stone.*
> *Faine needs he find a maid of faerie eyne*
> *To spie the shielde vpon the second throne,*
> *To limn therein the ledgers ancient line—*
> *Lest Beast and woman darke the northerne morning shyne.*

She pondered the words—but not for long, for the door swung open once more. Anyone entering could have seen her cram the notebook in her pack—anyone, that is, save a marmot balancing a tray of toast and eggs and tea and bacon on his head—which is who it was. She looked at him with amused relief. Was it "her" marmot? She thought so—he seemed younger than James, and smaller than the marmots in the traces outside. Now he walked precariously across the floor and slid the tray onto her bed.

"You're so cute!" she gushed. "I can't stand it."

He toppled backwards as if overcome by the compliment. Grace laughed until her bed shook half the tea from its cup. The marmot took his cue. He sulked to the door, tail dragging.

"Wait," she called. "Come back, slithy marmot."

He looked at her in a mimsy way.

"Come here. I want to pet you."

The marmot considered for a marmot moment, then nosed his way back and lithely sprang to the foot of the bed. Grace leaned forward and gently touched his wet nose. He quivered but did not move away.

"You're a good fellow," she told him. "Remember that."

She sat back and ate her breakfast and watched her marmot. Unlike any dog or cat she had known, he did not come snooping across the covers to sniff at her food. After a while he did not even watch her plate—instead he gazed out the window. Grace mopped up the last bit of eggs and looked out too. She saw what he saw: Lady Lira, James, and Lance gliding away on the marmot-drawn sled. It made silent sweeping turns around the clumps of devil's club.

"Do you wish you were going too?" she asked the marmot. He looked at her blankly. From out the window she thought she heard—she might have heard—the snap of a whip.

Breakfast done, she helped the marmot carry the dishes down the stairs and across the hall, now faintly sunlit and very dusty and not nearly as foreboding as the night before. When they got to the table, two marmots pattered from the door on the right and took their dishes. Then they were left in the dim hall alone—no place, Grace decided, to spend the day. She recrossed the carpet and traversed the passage to the entryway. The marmot followed after.

The door was unlocked, but she needed her shoulder to shove it open—it was that heavy. Outside, her feet slapped cool on the stone landing. The air was fresh but mosquito-laden, humming like a pitch pipe blown in anger. On the mossy cliff above, she could see the niche of her bedroom window. At the top of the cliff was poised a patch of blue sky, far away.

She sat down on the edge of the landing and watched a mosquito drill her knee. She let it drink deep and fly away, let the white welt burn and rise in her skin. The others she would kill. Her toes fell to dabbling on the surface of the bog. It shook like gelatin, rippled like a waterbed. In time the marmot crept beside her and let her stroke his neck. His hair was full and coarse. While her one hand nurtured, the other dealt doom, and a score of mosquitoes breathed their last in swift and bloody explosions.

"It's going to be a long day," she sighed.

Heeding the prophecy, the marmot circled behind her back and curled up to sleep. She too lay back, pillowed her head on the obliging marmot, and shut her eyes. For a while her hands reflexively swatted all comers. But soon they lay at peace in her lap, and her feet sank quietly through the moss and disappeared in ooze.

And so she slept, and the day wore on, and mosquitoes fed in armies upon her offered flesh. When at last she awoke, the sun flamed red in the trees. It felt late. Her face was swollen, her back was aching, her feet were frigid. The patient marmot had not moved; he still lay under her head.

Grace sat up and shivered. "Wake up," she told the marmot. He uncurled himself and stretched like a cat. Grace sucked her feet from out of the bog, got up, staggered to the door, and pried it open with both heels planted. The marmot slipped in. After wiping the mud from her feet, she followed.

The great hall was silent and chilly—no one had started a fire. From a few, high, recessed windows, dusty red sunbeams angled to the carpet. One burned the dragon in the center.

Grace shivered again, and ran upstairs for her down jacket. The bedroom was eerie. Instead of the soft green light of morning, an orange glare filled the chamber. Grace plucked the jacket from her pack. On impulse, she snatched her notebook too. She tore out the poem and put it in her pocket, then fled downstairs to the marmot.

Together they sat at the empty table. The jacket helped, but her feet were still cold. She tried to slip them under the marmot; the marmot sidled away. So, naturally, she thought of the shoes that Lady Lira had promised her. Had the woman forgotten? She looked at the door on the left of the fireplace. It was only a few steps away. Perhaps Lady Lira would not mind. It would take but a minute to find a pair—just an *old* pair. But then—was she the type of person to go picking through someone else's wardrobe? She was not. Lady Lira should soon be home. She could wait that long.

Grace tucked her feet beneath her knees, Indian-fashion, and resolved to sit patiently. But her feet got no warmer, and not too many minutes later the door got the better of her. She arose and stole past the hearth on tiptoe, making no sound. But she was not brave enough. An accomplice was needed. "Come on," she whispered, and the marmot obligingly padded behind her.

Grace pushed open the wooden door and peered inside. She saw a modest-sized room, candlelit but deserted. Shadows flickered on the ropy lava ceiling. She slipped in and held the door open for the marmot. He hesitated on the threshold, his silver fur quaking. "We're just going to find a couple shoes, that's all," said Grace. The marmot entered, froze, then shot beneath a four-poster bed that filled one side of the room.

"What a chicken," she murmured, and let the door close. She saw a red dragon on the green bed quilt, another on a carpet at her feet. An oval table with two chairs stood opposite the bed. It held two smoothly burning candles and a very large letter opener. She saw neither closets nor bureaus nor any stray shoes. (This was not like Grace's room at home, where shoes were scattered like mushrooms in a forest.) But the corners of the chamber were very dark. Perhaps there was a wardrobe in the shadows by the bed.

She stepped towards the darkness. The silence was stifling. She wanted to tell the marmot to come out from hiding. But she didn't tell him anything.

There! Something moved. It was across the bed, at eye level. Grace stood very still and looked at the shadows. Whatever it was had stopped. Then she saw them: two bright eyes, marking her intently. She met the gaze and glimpsed and guessed the outline of a face. She could not bear it long. She opened her mouth to speak, perchance to scream—and so did the other.

And then she knew. "It's just a mirror!" laughed Grace, her fears relieved. Her reflection laughed nervously with her.

Grace made her way around the bed and stood before a full-length glass in the shadows. "I look awful," she whispered. Her long brown hair was tangled. Her nose was sunburnt and peeling. Her face and arms and legs were bruised and scratched and mosquito-ravaged. She had never looked like this before. Quietly she gazed, mentally repairing her image.

Then she saw something more. The corner of the mirror reflected two pin-points of candlelight. They had softly burned there all along. Now, however, they blazed more intently. She was sure of it. She looked behind her at the candles on the table. They burned as smoothly as before. She looked again at the tapers in the mirror. They were two eyes now, glowing in darkness, hovering at the shoulder of her double in the glass. She wheeled around—there was no one in the room. Then she faced the mirror again. The two eyes were there still, resolute, and brighter if anything. Now, around them—was it?—a face was gathering substance there. A moan escaped her. It was a man's face, an old man's face, an old man's face with a wealth of white hair and an aged beard. In short, it was her uncle's face.

"Uncle Garth?" she whispered.

A hand in the mirror touched her shoulder, or its reflection, anyway. Did she not feel it? The man in the mirror called to her as if she were far away. "Grace," he said. She was glad and ashamed to hear him call her name. "Come," he told her, and the hand in the mirror tugged gently on her shoulder as if trying to turn her around.

Her reflection did not budge. She wanted to ask her uncle where he was, and where she was, and how she could find him. This she was about to do when she heard a voice at the door.

"James! This way."

Uncle Garth faded like morning mist. For one terrible moment, Grace stood before the mirror and watched only her own eyes, transfixed by her widening pupils. Then two furry paws grasped her ankles, and she dropped to the floor and slipped under the bed. As she did so, Lady Lira entered the room.

"James!"

Grace's breath revolved in shallow pats. Her marmot quivered beneath her arm. His whiskers tickled her nose. She would sneeze, she knew it.

"James!"

The voice was next to the table now. Lady Lira seemed impatient. Two pair of paws came through the door. Grace could just see them through the fringe of the quilt.

"What?" said a voice. Apparently, the marmot himself had spoken. Grace was too frightened to wonder at it.

"Sit down, James."

"What?" James must have been somewhat deaf, for Grace could hear Lady Lira quite clearly.

"Sit down, worthless marmot, and hear better. Your hide will make a tender morsel yet."

"No—I mean yes," he said briskly.

Grace heard two chairs scuff the carpet. She felt bacon rising in her gorge. It was stuffy under the bed.

"He didn't have the nerve," hissed Lady Lira. "The sentimental ass. He's giving it up—letting someone else do his dirty work. Well—it has taken him years enough to make up his mind. You, James—"

"What?"

"You—just a puppy when he first had the chance. How long I have waited! And now his chance is squandered. The fool! He thinks the ax can pass to another beneath my very nose—and I won't find it first? Hah! Once cast away, it belongs to who can snatch it. And if I can't, James—if I can't, I'll snatch the ones it's meant for.

"And such weaklings! It was always his way. I could hardly fear them even with the ax in their hands. It is almost an insult—sending filthy little children to spy on my doorstep. I nearly had them murdered in their beds last night—a pity I needed to find out more. As it is, the young prince of the feast has used up his tenure. Poem indeed! I doubt the ax is meant for that clodpoll. Even so, it was wise of you, James, to suggest we put him out of the way. I am glad we have done it."

Grace felt her stomach shudder again, harder this time.

"Thank you," said James.

"Now, the girl," said Lady Lira.

To Grace it sounded as if the woman had turned to face the bed.

"A most wary, spiteful creature. Blood kin to him—I knew it from the moment I first saw her eyes. She may not know what she is about, but she will help him just the same. That's his way—very unfair, too. She knows enough to fear me, though, and that's too much.

"Where is the little witch? Sleeping, no doubt, if she drank the drowsy potion in her tea. Check her room, James."

"What?"

"Check her room, I say—and her pack, too. Take anything that's written. And when you find her, bring her downstairs to the fire," she added. "Perhaps we can find ways—wonderful ways—to prompt a poetry recital."

Lady Lira began a drawn-out laugh, and James padded to the door.

"We have her sure," the woman cackled. "There's no way out save through the looking glass, and she'll need more than fairy blood to discover that."

James left, and Lady Lira's feet approached the bed. Her slippered heels stepped around to the mirror and came to rest just inches from where Grace lay hidden. She could easily have bitten them, and almost wanted to. Part of her was calm enough to wonder if the woman saw anything more than her own reflection in the mirror. There was no way of knowing.

Then Lady Lira began to speak. No, she was not speaking, really, but chanting—chanting in a solemn voice:

> "You will be fed,
> You must be fed,
> You shall be fed.
> Devour, devour, devour this day
>   your daily bread.
> Devour this day your daily bread."

Grace nearly vomited. The marmot beneath her arm grew stiff as stone. Lady Lira repeated the chant in deadly earnest:

> "You will be fed,
> You must be fed,

You shall be fed.
Devour, devour, devour this day
your daily bread.
Devour this day your daily bread."

It sounded nothing like her, and everything like her. She went on, turning and returning the words, gathering an intensity of pledge and prayer and promise. It seemed to Grace that the mirror must shatter.

But then, as abruptly as she had begun, Lady Lira broke off and paced away. The door opened and closed as she quit the room.

Grace lay more still than ever. She thought of her future. Any minute now, Lady Lira would find she was not upstairs. Then they would check on the front landing. Then they would check in the kitchen. Then they would check here. Beyond that, she refused to think.

Her hand crept from beneath the bed and grasped the bottom corner of the mirror. She pulled gently, and the mirror swung open like the front of a medicine cabinet. Out poked her head, in she looked. A single candle burned beside a bath. Steaming water purled over the lip, just as it did upstairs. Beyond the bath was an open wardrobe. Gowns of all colors were waiting in glory, and rows of shoes beneath them. Next to the wardrobe was another door.

Grace smothered the marmot to her breast and crawled behind the mirror. Then she pulled it shut behind her—it closed without a click. She stood up, trembling. The door beside the wardrobe beckoned. She crossed the room, turned the knob—and stood on the threshold of darkness. It seemed to be a tunnel, a passage. There was no telling where it might lead. There was no time to guess.

She grabbed the burning candle and stepped inside. Her feet came down on tiny things unutterably sharp. She jumped back. The candlelight showed spikes of lava, crowding the floor of the passage. It was time to get the shoes she had come for. She turned to the wardrobe and chose what looked sturdy—a tough leather pair, boots really, with thongs that wrapped to the knee. She fumbled with the thongs while the marmot looked on. "Don't wait for me," she whispered. But he did anyway. When her shoes were fastened she picked up the candle again and ushered him on ahead through the door. It closed behind them soundlessly.

Once in the tunnel, Grace discovered that even with her leather boots the lava spikes were sharp. She walked as if she were plagued with blisters, holding the candle unsteadily aloft. The marmot, though, had no such problem. He romped as if through grassy meadows, staying just at the edge of the candle's pooled light.

For many steps the way continued straight and level. Then it split in two. One fork led onward, the other up and left. The marmot stopped, stood up on his hind legs, sniffed the air. Then he bundled up the left-hand passage, and Grace followed. The new way angled steeply upward and kept on bending left. Grace clutched at the wall to balance her steps. The going was even slower.

At any moment she expected to hear the echo behind her of a door unlatching and Lady Lira's "There they are!" that would unleash a horde of marmots, ripe to devour their daily bread. But instead, after many steps, she felt a hint of a breeze in her face; the candle began to sputter.

"I think we're almost out," she whispered. And then they were out, for needles and branches were scratching her face, and through them she saw the twilight sky. She ducked low to get through, and something met her elbow. She thought it was the marmot at first. But it was not the marmot. Whatever it was was leaning against the entrance of the cave. She needed several moments to see what it used to be. For the pack was partly burnt, partly shredded in strips that hung from the metal frame. She quickly stepped back; her feet touched a soft lumpish shape on the floor. Her hand jumped, and the candle erased itself in the breeze. In spite of herself, she bent down and groped in the dark: more tattered nylon—caked with something. And then she felt the grasp of a mitten.

"*Eeow!*" she screamed.

In that same instant a glow appeared far down the tunnel, and with the glow came the echo of a cry: "After her!"

Grace and her marmot burst through the branches like wood grouse flushed from cover. The stars arose to the very occasion, and girl and marmot wildly ran in their broken beams, through stones, through grass, through dewy night.

Chapter 11
One Lavender Shooting Star

❈

HER VOICE AWAKENED HIM. "You're not so hurt as I'd thought," she said.

I'm not? he wondered. William lay stiffly on a sweet-smelling pallet of grass. Above him he saw wooden beams, around him walls of stone. The woman was rubbing his hairless chest with something moist and cool. William lifted his head and caught sight of himself. He gawked. His chest was raked in a musical score of scabby lines. He raised his shoulders, but this hurt him sorely. So he let the woman push him back. Now he recalled it: a roar in the night, a blast of breath, a slicing of flesh. And now the coolness, and a woman's hands.

"Must've been a bear," he mumbled.

"A bear," she said, considering. Through a window came the doubting notes of a mountain chickadee—one high, two low, in a minor key, the unsure announcement of morning come. Pieces of sunshine came in at the door and roamed the woman's hair. It was brown, like her smock. Her eyes were very green, and her nose was splendidly sunburnt.

"Here," she said. "Now that you've awakened I will answer your questions."

"But I haven't asked any," William shot back.

"All the more reason to have them," she replied.

Why was he so obstinate? That was one question, anyway.

"First," she said, "my name is Lady Demaris."

"*Lady* Demaris?" he queried. "Not *Ms.*?"

"*Ms.*" She tasted the word. For a moment her fingers lay still on his chest. "No, I should think I am Lady Demaris."

"I'm William," he volunteered.

"Thank you," she told him. "Last night, William, my herdsman found you in a cave, about three miles off. He heard you shouting and discovered you alone—a bit mauled, as you see. Luckily, it was only toying with you."

"The bear?" he asked.

She was silent for a moment. "It was not a bear," she said quietly. "You might as well know. You were found at the door of the Lava Beast."

The Lava Beast. The words burned his chest and darkened his mind. William had never heard the name, but he felt, inexplicably, that he knew the creature. "I see," he said, and nodded.

"You are fortunate," she continued. "A little deeper and he would have torn your heart." She began to knead his sternum softly. William could feel his intact ventricles flutter against her fingertips.

It dawned on him what he ought to say. "I must thank you," he told her. Then he added, "What's that ointment you've got there?"

"Something," she said, "to make you whole. But this afternoon, when you are ready, find Colin outside. He is the one to thank."

He grunted, the way he did to reward a woman for a job well done. Then he lay silent, and relished the cool massage. At the other end of the room he could see a sleeping loft. Underneath was a rough wooden table with stools. On the wall nearby hung cups, pots, and a large wooden pail. The pail was by the door that was letting in the sun.

"You live up here, Lady Demaris?"

"This is my home, yes."

"Year round? Even in winter?"

"Even in winter."

"Amazing," he said. "So what do you do?"

"I care for the place."

"This cabin? That doesn't take much, does it?"

"No," she said. "But I mean the whole place." She took one hand from off his chest and waved it toward the door.

"So you own a few acres up here—a little inholding?"

"I own none of it. All that lies beneath the Queens, I care for."

"But this is wilderness," said William. "No one needs to take care of it. You just leave it alone. That's what makes it wilderness."

"Ah," she said, "but that's the problem." Her voice and her green eyes dropped. "There are those who will not leave it alone."

Her answer made him cross. "Lady Demaris," he said, "do you think there is such a thing as too much wilderness?"

She made no reply.

"I mean," he continued, "lately I've seen more trees than I ever cared to."

She removed her hands, and his wounds stung deep. Her eyes met his in a pitying way, and he shrank beneath the load of condescension that he felt. He much preferred Rational Discussion to Knowing Looks.

But he backed down a little. "So tell me, what are you doing these days—to care for the place?"

"Right now," she said, "it's the marmots."

"The marmots," he repeated sagely.

"Yes. They normally go where they will, but lately they've been preyed upon. You see, Lady Lira, my sister—" Here she broke off and bit her lip. "My sister seizes them almost daily. Some she trains for her service. A few she completely corrupts to her will. But most of them she feeds—to the Lava Beast himself."

William felt again the dark hush of the name.

"Once we cared for the forests together, but now she serves . . . him. It is very sad to me. Perhaps you cannot understand it all."

William attempted a skeptical nod, but it came off with reverence.

"Colin and I watch the marmots in the meadows now, to keep them from my sister. We are never completely successful—there are just the two of us here. I imagine the Lava Beast did not eat you because he had devoured his fill for the day. Whatever we can save from Lady Lira and the Lava Beast we do—that is part of why Colin saved you. Perhaps right now—in caring for you, William—I am caring for this place. I do not know. It may happen you will be of great help someday."

This was unsettling. William did not like the way she had slipped in his first name. But he decided to humor her. Or was he curious?

"Why does the Lava Beast need your sister?" he asked. "Can't he catch his own marmots?"

"The Lava Beast," said Lady Demaris, "is a creature of darkness. Even the pure cold starlight of winter is noxious to him. He never ventures from his caves, and no marmot is foolish enough to venture in. So, he relies on his devoted ones to appease his appetite."

"What does he look like?" said William.

"Some say—" she began, but then she halted. "I do not know. I've never seen him."

William pounced on the admission. "Then how can you be sure there *is* a

Lava Beast?"

She touched his raw and scabby stripes. "By his deeds," she said. "Though seldom seen he makes his mark—in all of us, I'm afraid. He is too often near, and when we doubt his presence, then he is closest."

William felt dishonest for asking. Somehow he was sure of the Lava Beast himself. "So why does your sister work for him?"

"That is a mystery to me. Perhaps it is the lava mansion he gave to her. But it is such a dark and hollow place—I do not understand why she wanted it. Perhaps it is the clothes he gave her, and the servants. I do not know. Her gowns are splendid now, but her skin is pale as death. And the servants—I cannot tell why she needs them. Maybe she tired of bringing the water up from the stream to our cottage."

Here she looked at the wooden pail hung up by the door. She put her hands in her lap and sat very still. "But she does not just 'work for him,' as you say. She is part of him now. It is as if he has eaten her too."

"So why don't you stop her?" he asked.

"It is not that easily done. She will not listen to me now—I have little power against her. She is very strong, and has many marmots to enforce her will. And even if I were able, I know I could not harm her. She is still my sister.

"But there is a weapon by which the servants of the Lava Beast are felled," she continued. "Some say it will wound the head of the Lava Beast himself. Once, I think, it was a great sword, and before that, a rod in the desert. But now it is an ice ax."

William narrowed his eyes.

"The ax belongs to an old man now. He often walks this way. Other servants of the Beast he has felled in his time, but now he is loath to wield the ax."

"Too old?" said William.

"No, he is not feeble. It is just that—" She stopped for a moment. Her green eyes glistened. "You see—he loved my sister. Before she chose the Lava Beast, she was nearly wedded to Garth."

William started, but Lady Demaris did not seem to notice.

"It is hard to believe now," she continued. "Morning by morning they strolled in the meadows hand in hand. He made songs for her, put lupines in her hair, found for her the first of wild strawberries to appear. On summer eves they raced to the golden snows of the Center Queen. There they slid down reckless slopes, clasped together, shadowed in spray, shouting aloft to the first-formed stars. No one knew two better lovers.

"Then, on the midsummer morning of their wedding day, Garth came to the cottage to wake his bride. The sun had cleared the Center Queen, the meadow shone with dew. Behind him tumbled troops of marmots, all wearing garlands of bluebells and buttercups. Colin came romping and singing among them, and all the marmots were whistling in time. Ah, I remember they made such joy! 'Come out!' they sang. 'Come out, sweet Lira! Today you'll be married, be married today!' I opened wide the door to them, and led Garth to the loft to wake his bride."

Lady Demaris and William looked up at the loft.

"And it was empty. Sometime before dawn she had slipped away. And I, up early, gathering herbs and flowers, had not seen."

Lady Demaris shook her head. "No, he will not use the ax anymore. It is time—past time—he surrendered it to another."

This brought on a thoughtful silence. She gazed at William in a way that guessed at future possibilities.

"Don't look at me," he croaked.

Lady Demaris stood up and smiled, still gazing at him. For a moment her hair shone bravely in the sunlight from the doorway. Then she turned, slipped the wooden bucket off the wall, and vanished outside.

William gazed after her. He had seen it in her eyes. She thought him heir apparent to the tool and trade of her unfinished business. He would tell her nothing—not a thing—to strengthen his claim to that inheritance. He lay his head back on the sweet-smelling grass. His eyes wandered over the rafters. Nothing. He would say nothing. He was sure. He kept repeating it, rafter by rafter. *Nothing. Nothing.*

Then he slept.

When William awoke, the room was still and noonlike. He heard no birds. One fly buzzed his head like a chainsaw. He sat up slowly, expecting very great pain in his chest—but it barely ached. His wounds, in fact, were already whitening into scars. He touched them. Where was their sting?

Lady Demaris appeared in the doorway. "How do you feel?" she asked.

"Tell me," said William. "What's in that ointment?"

"Oh. Many good things," she laughed. "But how are you feeling?"

"Like what things?"

She whimsically tilted her head in the air. "Let's see. North-facing moss from a thousand-year cedar, timberline dew from a midsummer morning, stamens of arnica, gloss from a marigold, hoarfrost and ice worms and snow watermelons. Tender tips of staghorn lichen, buckwheat pollen, sap from a whitebark, fiddle-head hearts that are cut in the moonlight—and one lavender shooting star. It has to be northward pointing, too, and that sort is hard to come by." She smiled, obviously proud of her recipe.

William shook his head.

"There's lunch on the step," she said, pointing behind her—"if you feel up to it."

William shambled to the door and sat down on the step. He found a loaf of hot bread and a pitcher of water—also a salad of much that was green but nothing that was lettuce. He ate it anyway. He was no vegetarian (more a chocolaterian) but it went down well. He turned to Lady Demaris in the cottage behind him: "What's in the salad?"

She slyly tilted her head again.

"Never mind," said William quickly.

The sun shone squarely on his white and hairless chest. It was a good feeling, a new feeling. He wondered why he had always hid in polypropylene. He drank huge gulps of water, and some of it dripped from his chin to his belly. There was a slight breeze, and it cooled his wet flesh wonderfully.

He looked out from the step to a brook that splashed down a grassy ravine and entered the forest below. Above, it gushed from glaciers that tongued their way from the Center Queen to the meadows. He lifted his eyes to the mountain. It was perfect in symmetry—one vast shimmering dome. The ice shone white, silvery white in the noonday sun. To the left, behind a grove in the meadows, he saw the North Queen too. Like the South it rose in lava cliffs, crossed by amber and burgundy bands. Unlike the South Queen, its summit mounted above the cliffs to a snowy crater ring. This made the North Queen highest of all.

His lunch finished, William rose to wander down the brook. He wore no boots, and his toes sank softly in the grass. This was new. Down by the water the lupine grew thick and covered his feet completely. The hot sun probed his shoulders now, and so did the mosquitoes. Should he return for a shirt? Or shoes? His feet voted otherwise. Damn the mosquitoes—half speed ahead! So on he sauntered through bits of meadow and streamside gardens and groves of fir and hemlock. He felt brave and soft and careless. He had never walked in alpine parkland just to walk. Always he had been madly en route to a summit or a car. He was somewhere he had never been.

By and by, along the stream, he came upon a field of marmots snuffling in the flowers. He walked in among them, and none seemed to care. The marmots neither ran nor piped nor even looked at him. Across their pasture, under a stand of mountain hemlock, a young man lay on his side in the shade. The youth was singing softly, and William drew near to listen. This much he heard:

> "Beneath a forest shade I watch
> My marmots feed beneath the sun;
> Upon the dawn they come to me
> And go when day is done.
> When day is done I lay me down to sleep,
> And Rosamond my thoughts like marmots keep.
>
> "Beneath a forest shade I hear
> The brook new-shed from mountain snows;
> In morning it runs shallowly,
> At noon it overflows.
> At noon I lay me down beside the stream,
> And Rosamond then overflows my dream.
>
> "Beneath a forest shade I touch
> The lupine one and two and ten;
> The sunrise brings new drops of dew,
> And sunset brings again.
> The sunset brings to me the parting hour,
> When lupine fade but Rosamond may flower."

The young man sighed and dug his toes in the grass. Then he turned on his back and looked upwards through the branches. William stood by, too far away to introduce himself and too close to blend with the scenery. He could not tell whether the young man saw him.

Finally he called out in a yoo-hoo sort of voice, "Hello! Are you Colin?"

"I am," said the youth, still contemplating the branches. "And you, old man—how are you feeling?"

"Very well," said William, "thanks to you, I think."

Colin abandoned his arboreal vision. He leapt to his feet, ran to William, slapped him on the back. "Glad to hear it!" he told him. He inspected William's scars with approval, then invited him into the shade. "It's a little hot just now," he said.

They sat down together. It was cool in the shade, and William sprouted a harvest of goose bumps. Colin put his hand on William's knee. "On a day like today," he confided, "'tis right for a contest."

"A contest?" said William.

"A singing match," said Colin.

"I don't sing so well," William said. "I can't even read music."

"I don't read music either," said Colin. "I sing it. You must try—the time and the place require you."

"Require me?" said William.

"First we must think what to sing of. Ah! It is clear. I shall sing of Rosamond and you of your own love. Line for line, thus: I sing one line, and you answer with your own."

William looked reluctant.

"What's the matter?" said Colin. "Have you no lady love?"

"Well, no. I'm too busy with computers."

"Aha! The lovely Computressa—you cannot keep her name from your lips."

"No! Not her. I mean, not them."

"There is no lady in your life, then? None whom you seek? None?"

"Not really. Except, well, right now I'm looking for a girl named Grace. Have you seen her?"

"No. Sing of her heavenly beauty, though, and she will grow nearer to your heart. But lovely as she is, she cannot compare to my Rosamond—the nonpareil, the inexpressive she."

"But—"

"Say no more," Colin assured him. "I know your concerns. We have need of referees for our contest. Luckily they are close at hand. Marmots have a very fine ear for music. All of them whistle in perfect pitch. Ho! Over here, you rascals! You must judge our singing match!"

Ten of the closest marmots galloped to the shade and stood in a line, testing the air with their whiskers. "Ready?" said Colin. They all looked it. So he began to sing:

"I saw a fair young mountain maid
Holay, holay, holay-o . . ."

He paused, and the jury of marmots turned their heads toward William, who sang nothing.

"Here," said Colin gallantly, "I'll assist you. Now you must sing something like this:

A-walking in the forest glade
Upon the first of May-o.

See? That's not so hard."

William started to shiver. The shade was green ice.

Colin began again:

"Her hair it shone the finest gold
Amidst the morning ray-o . . ."

The marmots looked at William.

"What?" said Colin. "Still stumped, my friend? Think what you wish to praise about your Grace. What is it that delights you most? What of her lovely hair?"

"Her hair?" said William. "I've never seen it combed. It was dirty."

"Her eyes, then," said Colin.

"Her eyes," echoed William. "Her eyes have a certain—it's hard to . . . Wait a minute, what have you got me—"

Just here William was cut short. Urgent whistling shot from afar. At once their jury joined the call and blasted in a chorus. Colin jumped to his feet. "Trouble," he said. He grabbed his staff, and barefoot sped across the grass and into a grove of trees.

This left William alone in a sea of piping marmots. He stumbled out into the sun and looked on every side. *Go!* said the whistling marmots. *Go somewhere!* Knowing no better direction, William ran where Colin had. But halfway to the grove of trees he stepped in a hole and landed flat on his chest—so flat that he had the wind knocked out of him. Face down in the lupine, biting the earth, he fought to breathe.

The whistling redoubled behind him. At first, paralyzed as he was, he could not look. Then he turned his green-stained face—and marveled. The jury of marmots he'd left behind were bundled together in a net, bumping in tow behind the strides of a woman dressed all in green. A silvery marmot trotted at her side. She had to be the sister, strange and estranged, of Lady Demaris.

William rose and shouted at her, "What are you doing! Hey! Hey!" He wanted to thunder an ultimatum but could not find the words. His voice was quivering badly.

The woman turned her head and laughed at him. Her eyes pierced his and he shivered in their shade. Then she spoke something to the marmot beside her, and strode on.

Immediately the marmot rushed him. It glowered and hissed and bared its teeth. William froze, then sprinted in terror. If a peaceable marmot could slash one's heel, what could a rampaging marmot inflict? It was wonderful, how William sped. He leapt, he ran, he flew half-crazed. He stepped in no holes and tripped on no logs. It was terrible, how William felt. He sweat, he bled, he panted, he foamed. He crashed through trees and coated himself with twigs and needles and cones and lichen. Finally, his lungs afire, he came upon Colin in a faraway clearing and collapsed at his feet, groveling in asthmatic frenzy.

"Don't let him—" he gasped. "A ferocious, the most ferocious, you ever saw."

Colin looked puzzled. "You must have outrun him, old man."

William looked fearfully behind. The groves and the grass were at peace.

"I think I know the one you mean," said Colin. "A big hoary fellow that she keeps with her. Did you see the woman, too?"

William nodded. "A netful," he panted. "She took a whole netful. Tried to stop her. Sorry."

"Blast her name!" cried Colin. "I've been decoyed! All that was here was a young boy tangled in his own net." He pointed to the net lying empty on the grass. "I made *him* black and blue for his trouble—before he ran off. But what's the good?"

"I tried," said William meekly.

"No, not your fault, man. She does have a fierce marmot or two. Nothing you could do without a staff of your own."

This made William feel better.

"Beastly business," Colin muttered.

✱

In the evening the marmots dispersed to their burrows. William and Colin walked upstream, and the dew brushed cool on their feet. The creek was full, the mosquitoes at rest. A chickadee called that day was done, then proved it so with silence. At a bend in the stream they saw the cottage. Its windows were faintly lit. Above, out of the darkening meadows, the Center Queen rose all tinted with pink.

William let Colin go ahead. He stood very still in a cloak that he had borrowed from Colin and rested his eyes on the peak in the alpenglow. There were no Good Routes there, nothing to interest a Serious Climber—only solace for a serious mind. His gaze descended to the dampening meadows, and then to the curtained hemlocks at his side. The trees and the grass were pleasant to his eye. It was the first time. Slowly, he turned and looked upon ridge after ridge of soft dark fir, fading to a pale green glow where the sun had set. *Was there such a thing,* he wondered, *as too much?*

Lady Demaris had supper on the table, and when William arrived they sat and ate. She nodded sadly as Colin explained how Lady Lira had done it again. A single candle burned in their midst. It flickered pensively.

"The boy," she mused. "He is new—a fledgling servant of the Lava Beast. His skill will increase. It will go the harder for us."

There was a long silence. The candle shadows ebbed and flowed. William felt the urge to speak.

"I could stay and help," he said to his own surprise. "I mean, I would, if you need me to. That is, if I wouldn't be in the way." He nervously scratched the new whiskers on his chin.

Colin beamed. "Good show, man. You'll make a brave song yet."

Lady Demaris still looked thoughtful. She took a scrap of paper out of her smock and smoothed it on the table. "The last time Garth was here," she said, "he left this with me." She pushed the paper across the table to William. "Read it," she told him.

He knew the writing. He slowly read the lines aloud:

> *"Out of the jaws, out of the cave,*
> *Is saved the man that us shall save."*

"That man is you," said Lady Demaris.

William was stunned. His plans were crumbling. "I have a poem too," he confessed. "And also a key. They were Garth's." He pulled the key from his pocket and laid it beside the scrap of paper.

Colin whistled. "Now that's doubling the rainbow," he said.

Even Lady Demaris looked surprised. She took the key and studied it closely, holding it up in the candlelight. "This once belonged to my father," she whispered. "He never told us what it opened." She paused. "And the poem?"

"In my pack," said William. He looked around the room. His face fell.

"Sorry, old man," Colin said. "All burnt and shredded, I'm afraid."

"Do you recall it?" asked Lady Demaris. "Any of it?"

"No, not really," he said glumly.

A problematic silence descended. William felt unutterably foolish. "There's someone else," he blurted out. "A girl. She read the poem too."

"The lovely Grace?" asked Colin.

"Yes. I met her at the trailhead. She was lost, I think. I found the poem then and showed it to her. Then she left, and later I met someone looking for her—he told me her name: Grace Foster. For her name's sake I thought she might be some relation to Garth. And from then on I wanted her to help me. But I don't know where she is now. I haven't been able to find her."

Lady Demaris nodded. "Garth has a niece," she said. "He often speaks of her. But in recent years she has made him sad. From what he has told me, I never expected to see her here. But changes are afoot. Perhaps she has come to the mountains at last. Let's hope she comes to us before she comes to Lady Lira. Meanwhile, you must wait for her, William."

"And I for my Rosamond," sighed Colin.

Lady Demaris laughed merrily. "Your Rosamond has her own good creatures to tend just now. You too must be patient."

She turned to William again. "So tell us: how did you come by the key and the poem?"

William gazed at the candle and drew a deep breath. The others settled on their stools. It was the moment most savored of any tale—the moment before it begins, when anything is possible and nothing yet precluded. It was in this moment, as William searched for words to start, that suddenly the door beside them shook with clamor. They all jumped, and William uttered a little shriek. Someone outside was desperately knocking. Before they could move, the door flew open, and in staggered Grace, her wild breath abounding.

Chapter 12
Will You Help Us?

❅

GRACE COLLAPSED IN THE OPEN DOOR, too winded even to ask who lived there. Seconds later a small marmot shot across the threshold and quivered in her lap. It too was spent. They sat with heads bowed, weary refugees, mother and child.

Lady Demaris was first to rise. She filled a cup with cold water and stooped over the girl. "Drink this, child," she said. "You are welcome here."

Without looking up, Grace took the cup with shaking hands and drained it, gasping. Some of the water fell into her lungs. She coughed violently. The time came to stop but the spasm went on. The marmot jumped away.

"That's her," said William softly. "That's Grace."

"Lovely indeed," Colin said. "She's had a scare, I think."

At length her coughing departed. Grace felt less exhausted now, but her breath still came hard. She gripped the doorpost and peered outside. The meadow was in starlight. She saw no one out there. Even so, she leapt to her feet and slammed the door.

"Who is chasing you, dear?" asked Lady Demaris.

Somehow Grace did not mind being "dear" to this woman. She risked the truth in reply. "Lady Lira," she panted.

"Beastly woman," muttered Colin.

"Rest yourself, Grace," said Lady Demaris. "You are safe here. She cannot come in this house anymore." She paused. "Do you recognize any of us?"

Grace wondered that the woman knew her name. Then she saw the man from the trailhead, and pointed at him silently.

"Do you remember me, Grace?" he said.

She nodded.

"I'm William—I didn't tell you last time. This is Lady Demaris. And Colin—

he lives here too."

Grace nodded to each of them. To her surprise, she even smiled at Lady Demaris, who seated her at the table. The marmot hopped in her lap again.

"I ran into someone looking for you," William explained. "That's how we know your name. We've been hoping you'd come."

That she was expected here, in this strange cottage, seemed very eerie to Grace. "Where's my uncle?" she blurted out. She had not planned to say this.

"I don't know," said William. "I just know where I saw him last. Maybe Lady Demaris has an idea."

Lady Demaris shook her head. "Your uncle will find you when the time is right," she said. "In the meantime, will you help us?"

From anyone else the question would have been untimely. But from Lady Demaris it was the warmest of invitations. Still, Grace wondered, could she trust these strangers? She thought it over. The man from the trailhead, so rude before, now seemed merely nervous, almost considerate. Lady Demaris was motherly enough, and Colin, she had noticed, was no friend of Lady Lira's. It occurred to Grace that she had to trust someone in these mountains, someone beyond the warm marmot in her lap.

The others remained silent. It had taken William all day to choose; Grace had only minutes. She looked up. "I will help you," she said quietly. Her choice had melted into place before she knew she had made it.

"A brave girl!" cried Colin.

Grace was released like a hemlock that springs from the snowpack in May. It flings the ice clods aside and rocks in the sun. Just so, she basked in the welcome of the three faces.

Lady Demaris put hot buttered bread and a bowl of stew before her. Grace ate all of it, except for some morsels she slipped to her marmot. Then she asked what was in the the stew, and William found this funny. He laughed very hard, and Grace laughed with him—she didn't know why. They laughed much longer than the joke was worth, then laughed because they were still laughing, at which point Colin and Lady Demaris laughed too, and the end did not come quickly.

At last—when they could manage it—Lady Demaris served tea all around. At the second cup she touched Grace's arm and said, "Now, child, can you tell us how you came here?"

Grace was only too ready. She scrunched up on her elbows to begin. "It all started," she said, "when I signed up for a trip with You-Can-Do-It Expeditions."

"You can do it?" said Colin. "You can do *what?*"

"I don't know," said Grace. "I didn't stay long enough to find out."

"Let her tell her story," said Lady Demaris.

Grace went on. They listened patiently until she came to writing down Garth's poem.

"Do you still have it?" asked Lady Demaris.

"Right here," said Grace. She pulled the paper from her jacket and waved it in her hand.

"Good girl," said Lady Demaris. "Continue."

They were silent again till she got to the part about Lance going off on the marmot hunt. Then Colin spoke up. "So that's who the little toad was."

"You've seen him?" asked Grace.

"I've laid more than my eyes on him."

"Hush," said Lady Demaris. "We can tell our story later."

But Lady Demaris herself interrupted when Grace told about seeing Garth in the mirror. "You really did see him then? That's good. That's a good sign, dear."

Then Grace told them what Lady Lira had said about snatching an ax—or those it was meant for, and about Lance being "put out of the way." William paled, and Colin slapped the table with last-straw conviction.

Grace realized she had not had time to worry about Lance until now. She turned to Lady Demaris. "What do you think she has done with him?" she asked.

Lady Demaris looked troubled. "Let us hope for the best," she urged.

Grace continued, faltering now, until she reached the shredded pack and the mitten at the end of the tunnel.

"That could have been me," said William. "But it wasn't."

"Who was it, then?" asked Grace.

"No one," he said. "All that I had. My remains."

Grace puzzled over this. Then she told of the cry far back in the tunnel, and of running down a starlit trail that finally led to the cottage.

"That's a good three miles," said Colin. His voice was admiring.

"Again," said Lady Demaris, "welcome, Grace. We are glad you are with us."

William and Colin nodded emphatically.

"Now," she said, "it is your turn, William."

William cleared his throat and promptly set out. For the first time the others heard the full circumstances of Garth's disappearance. Lady Demaris kept nodding as if she had known all along that this was to happen. Even the missing road did not surprise her.

"What did happen to the highway?" William asked her.

"Oh, it comes and it goes," she smiled. "It depends who you are."

This did not satisfy William. But he went on, describing when he came to it what he could recall of his night encounter in the cave. For Grace's sake he explained what Lady Demaris had told him about Lady Lira and the Lava Beast.

"Your sister?" Grace said in astonishment. Then, "Why would he ever want to marry *that* woman?" And, "So *those* are the dragons in her house." And, "He eats marmots?" She held her own marmot close to her cheek. He was now fast asleep.

"You have eaten them too, child, if you dined at my sister's house," said Lady Demaris.

Grace felt her stomach revolt.

"How perfectly awful. I—I didn't mean to."

Colin clapped her on the shoulder. "Take heart," he said. "You couldn't have known."

To change the subject—but not by much—he told her about the afternoon marmot raid.

Grace looked at him sharply. "You beat him?" she demanded.

Colin nodded meekly. "I didn't know," he answered.

"He deserved it," Grace said. But suddenly she began to cry. If only Lance had not been "put out of the way" she could hate him freely.

Lady Demaris leaned over and put her arms around Grace. "Poor fool," she said. "Poor dear fond fool. Have hope." The woman held the girl, the girl held the marmot, and the marmot awoke to hot tears splashing on his back. Colin grew misty-eyed. William stared blankly at the table. Grace wept as long as she had coughed, which was a long time. When her tears had subsided she sniffed several times and recomposed herself, humbled and refreshed.

"Sorry," she said.

"You don't have to be sorry," they all replied at once.

Lady Demaris got more tea for everyone. When she sat down again she pointed to the paper now crushed in Grace's hand. "The poem, child," she said. "I think we should know what your uncle would say to us."

Grace uncrumpled the poem and placed it on the table by William's key and Lady Demaris's slip of rhyme.

Colin saw how long it was and whistled softly. "Now that's genuine poetry."

The stanza was carefully traced in the back-slanting script that some girls favor and no one else can quite make out. Since this was the case, Grace read the poem aloud:

> "*A gentle wight for gentle ladies three*
> *Aduentured through a verdant wood newgrowne,*
> *Through wildernesse that mote a wastlond bee,*
> *Vnless he greete the greenwood for his owne,*
> *Vnless he know the leaf as ice and stone.*
> *Faine needs he find a maid of faerie eyne*
> *To spie the shielde vpon the second throne,*
> *To limn therein the ledgers ancient line—*
> *Lest* Beast *and woman darke the northerne morning shyne.*"

"Nicely read," said Colin.

"What does it mean in English?" William asked.

Colin eyed him suspiciously. "It is in English," he said.

"*Shh*," said Lady Demaris. "Let's see what Grace has to say."

Grace wrinkled her brow and rescanned the poem, musing in silence. Then she had something. "All right. The 'gentle wight,' if I remember correctly, is simply a man—a nice man, maybe, or a man of noble birth, perhaps. He is going on an adventure for the sake of three ladies. But I'm afraid I don't know who these ladies are."

A thought occurred. "You don't have another sister, do you, Lady Demaris?"

"We once did," came the reply, "but she drowned, in a way. It was very peculiar. Perhaps I can tell you more later on."

"I see," Grace said quietly. "Well, that wouldn't fit anyway. Lady Lira couldn't be one of the three, for she is the woman with the beast in the last line—the Lava Beast, most likely. The man must help the ladies by keeping the beast and woman from ruining things, from bringing darkness."

"Why can't the three ladies be our Three Queens?" said Colin.

"Who?" said Grace.

"Our Three Queens—the mountains we live under."

"I suppose they could be," Grace said—"if there are three of them." She herself did not remember if there were three or three hundred.

"I think we've skipped something," said William. "Who is the man?"

The table was still. No one looked up.

William sighed. "I was afraid of that," he said.

"Don't worry," said Grace. "I'm sure you'll make a good wight." She smiled at him hopefully. "And look. It has to be you, William, because what you found at the end of the trail was a 'wood newgrowne.' It is a wilderness, but not a wasteland—apparently there's a difference. But it might become a wasteland if you don't 'greete the greenwood' or 'know the leaf.' What do you suppose that means?"

William looked at the floor.

"William," said Lady Demaris slowly, "do you love this place?"

He stared harder at the floor. He felt cornered. A snarl began to well beneath the scars on his chest. He looked up, ready to say the whole thing was unfair. But when he met Lady Demaris's green eyes he recalled the peak in alpenglow, the cold stream running through lupine thickets, the soft forest fading to the western sea. And he simply said, "It's a good place. It is good."

"Long ago that was spoken," said Lady Demaris. "And at some times, and in some places, we can almost say it still. Would that we could." She sighed. "William, it is left for us to believe those words have found their truth again. Do you understand that?"

"I think so," said William. He understood not at all.

"You see," she said earnestly, "before this you have grasped only part of the good of the mountains, and in grasping only part you have rejected a great deal else that is good. Get their full tidings, William. When we are given something fair, we must accept and care for all of it. Not that we ourselves can remove the curse—we *are* the curse ourselves. But the curse is fading, in us and around us. Our greatest work is to rest in that hope."

She held his eyes for a long time before turning to Grace. "Go on, child," she told her.

"Well," stammered Grace, "the next thing our wight must do is find a girl with fairy eyes, whoever that is." She had half an idea but was not about to volunteer it.

"I think you know," said Lady Demaris. "Your uncle has told me you are like him in many ways. You would not have seen him in the mirror otherwise."

Grace snorted. "Me?" she said. "Do I fly around snatching teeth from under pillows? I'm a girl, not a fairy."

"Most of you is a girl," said Lady Demaris. "But a little bit of you, enough to help us now, is fairy. Anyone who knows can see it in your eyes."

"So they sparkle," said Grace. "Lots of people have eyes that sparkle." She looked to Colin and William for support. They, in turn, looked to the rafters and lent their support to the roof.

"There is no use pretending you are not who you are," said Lady Demaris.

"You can do it," said Colin.

"Don't worry," said William, "I'm sure you'll make a good fairy."

Grace stuck out her lower lip.

"Go ahead with the poem," said Lady Demaris. "You are doing well."

Grace drew herself up. "This fairy," she said in disgust, "is supposed to look at a shield—or something—on 'the second throne'—wherever that is. See—I have no idea where that could be. It can't be me."

"I'd guess 'the second throne' is the summit of the Center Queen," said Colin. "That's not so hard."

"Well I have *no* idea how to get up *there*," wailed Grace. "I've never climbed a mountain in my life. I don't even like stairs."

I know the way," said William calmly.

"Then you don't need me," Grace pouted.

"What does the next line say?" asked Lady Demaris.

She looked. "I think it says there is a book in the throne—that is, on the mountaintop."

"And?" said Lady Demaris.

"And—" She paused. "And that I am to read it." There was defeat in her voice. "But why me? Anyone can read, can't they?"

"There are readers," said Lady Demaris, "and there are readers."

"Okay, okay," said Grace. "So I go up there and read this book. But then what do we do?"

"I don't know," said Lady Demaris, "but you know what to do now."

"What about Lance? We can't just leave him, can we?"

"The surest way to find him, dear, is to follow the poem. You cannot weaken the hold of my sister any other way, I'm afraid."

Grace shrugged her shoulders. She was out of objections. She would not look at William. "So when do we leave?" she finally said, as if any one time were as bad as another.

"You must go before dawn," said Lady Demaris. "My sister knows you are here and will return at sunrise. Meanwhile, she has no doubt left some of her own to watch us. You must try to elude them while it is dark. We must get you ready—it is now past midnight. The moon will soon rise."

Lady Demaris got up from the table and so did everyone else. Grace and William shared a glance. For all their reluctance they now felt slightly important. They stood shyly together while Colin poured out a cascade of gear from the loft: boots and ropes and packs and caps and mittens and knickers and candles and lanterns. For their feet he tossed down iron-clawed creepers that crashed to the floor. Lady Demaris came to Grace with sweaters and coats, saying, "Here, try this on. Perfect fit, dear." At one point she put a small wooden ice ax in her hand and whispered, "My younger sister's. She would have wanted you to have it."

When all was ready, William and Grace were transformed. Grace had exchanged her shorts for green woolen knickers that reached to the top of Lady Lira's boots. A thick olive sweater replaced her jacket, which was now compressed in a canvas rucksack. William wore hobnailed boots that clattered on the floor, and knickers and kneesocks of coarse gray wool. Beside him leaned a drab packsack on a wooden frame. It had neither zippers nor compartments, and smelled distinctly of hot bread.

"One more thing," said Lady Demaris. She fetched from a corner another ice ax, battered and smooth, and handed it to William. "This belonged to my father, Lord Linton, who built this cottage long ago. With this ax he was first to climb all three of our Queens. The shaft was cut from an ash tree many miles to the north, farther north than any other ash tree grows. The tree yet stands, and when the wind blows in that northern vale, the ax still trembles. You will feel it."

William felt it. His hand shook nervously.

"Use my father's ax for now," she said. "There is only one better."

Out one window the quarter moon began to rise, rimmed by the peak of the Center Queen. They blew out the candles and waited in a silvered darkness, hoping that anyone watching the cottage would think they had turned in. The air smelled late in the candle smoke. Everything felt strangely still. Getting ready was easy. Being ready was hard. The quietness held doubts.

Grace began to yawn, and then she felt the wet poke of a marmot nose in her hand. She stroked the marmot's head. "I wish you were going," she whispered.

"He should go," said Lady Demaris. "What you cannot see, he can smell. These days, a good marmot is hard to find."

Grace was glad. "You hear that?" she told the marmot. "You're coming with us." She pressed him against her knees.

Then Lady Demaris opened the door, and the raw cold rushed in.

Chapter 13
Utterly Dark

✳

THE THREE CLIMBED SOFTLY UP MOONLIT MEADOWS. Grace kept close on William's heels, the marmot close on hers. Wet grass wrapped and clung to their feet, and a light breeze cooled their faces. Island clumps of mountain hemlock loomed beside them, passed them by. Each time they brushed these close-knit villages of trees, Grace feared unfriendly eyes in the dark. But neither whistle nor whisper broke the night. They seemed to walk unseen, unsniffed, on their way to the mountain.

In time, the hemlock clumps grew small and sparse, the air more sharp. The dewy grass released their steps and shrank in frosty manicure. There were terraces where quiet streams stopped in shallow silvered pools, tinged with borders of thinnest ice. Deep in their waters, fathoms deep in crystal darkness, shone all the stars of heaven.

Then came piles of stony rubble, snaking into the meadows. The climbers wandered up grassy halls until the grass gave out. They hopped from boulder to boulder then, and stopped at the foot of a steep rock mound. Grace's breath echoed in her ears. Her nose was dripping. If William had not paused just then she would have spoken up.

"Last moraine," he whispered.

Grace looked at the sky. "Doesn't look like any more rain to me," she said.

"No, this," he answered, tapping the rocks with his ice ax. "The glacier piled these boulders here. We've got to climb over to get to the snow. Be very careful. Stay beside me, not behind me—I might kick something loose."

Grace nodded.

"And keep your ice ax away from the rocks. No use battering it up worse than it already is."

Grace winced at the insult, as if the ax were really hers. Before she was ready, William started up and she had to scramble after. It wasn't easy, for very few of the stones stayed put. (Somehow, this seemed to be William's fault.) They clunked and teetered underfoot as if randomly piled one atop the other, which they were. Only the marmot, light on his feet, passed undisturbing and undisturbed. The entire moraine was loose—so loose that with each new step Grace feared she would trigger a massive rockslide. And halfway up, she did. She had no sooner mounted the uptilted edge of a large flat stone than it swung shut like the lid of a trunk. As it scooted away she leapt to the side, trembled, watched. The stone ponderously upended itself, hung for an instant poised in the night, then tumbled on, recruiting whole armies of boulders for the charge. The clatter was immense, like the smashing of giant dishes. Grace saw sparks as rock broke upon rock—and smelt them too. William watched beside her as the noise faded, died in the darkness.

"Do you think they heard?" she asked.

As if in answer, a whistle pierced the night below them. Then came another, faraway, and a third, more distant still. Grace felt with her hand for her own little marmot, worried he might have been caught in the rockfall. He was safe at her side. But his body was quaking beneath her mitten, just as it had beneath the bed of Lady Lira. The whistling repeated itself in the distance; the marmot went absolutely rigid.

"He's frightened," she said. "What he hears, he knows." Her heart sank—in part at the prospect of fewer rest stops.

William shrugged. "Guess we better move on," he replied. He seemed almost happy for the excuse to climb more quickly.

And so they tiptoed up the moraine—like barefoot children on summer asphalt—and this time left each stone in place. From the crest they hopped a short ways down the other side to a long snowshore. The snow was rippled, frozen hard.

William shed his pack. "Out with the irons," he said. "I'll uncoil the rope."

Grace gaped at the rise of glacier ahead. It swept toward them, all of a piece, one vast pouring of ice. It seemed to her like the white train of a wedding gown. But unlike a bridal train, its icy fabric was scissored and torn. Deep crevasses were plentiful, especially higher.

She pointed at them. "How do we get through those?" she asked.

"Mostly we walk around them," he told her. "Sometimes there are bridges of snow."

Grace wondered why bridges of snow should hold when piles of solid rocks did not. William, meanwhile, strapped the iron claws to her feet and tied the end of a rope around her waist. The rope was braided and rough and hairy—she could feel it through her mittens. William was tied to the other end.

"This way I hold you if you fall," he explained.

"What if you fall?" Grace shot back.

"I won't," he assured her. "But if I do, you stop me with your ax."

Grace looked askance at the bladed pick of the ice ax in her hand. "My aim is pretty bad," she said. "Besides that, it would probably hurt." She pictured William safely impaled on the lip of a crevasse.

"Not that way," William replied. "Throw yourself down and dig your ax into the snow. Then the rope stops me." He lay face-down and demonstrated. "You should probably try it," he told her.

Grace watched him grovel in the cold hard snow. It looked very uncomfortable. "I don't think there's time," she said. "Shouldn't we be going, since—in case we're being followed?"

William emitted a dubious grunt, but he gave in and got up. Before setting out he merely made sure that she held the ax head properly: thumb beneath the adze, fingers curled over the pick.

They were not a perfect rope team. Grace followed William by some sixty feet. Though her iron creepers bit firmly into the snow, they weighed her steps down heavily. Her pace soon slackened, and the rope jerked taut on her waist. At just this moment the rope stopped William in mid-stride. He was no more pleased than a dog on a leash, nor Grace than its owner pulled behind. After many such moments, each one suspected the other of venting some hidden spite, and what began by chance proceeded by malice. Without quite intending it, William walked in quick busts to catch her by surprise. Grace, equally crafty, let coils of slack drift out of her hand, then ever so slightly dug in her heels to watch him bounce on the end of his tether. The marmot was lucky. Without a rope, he walked behind them unmolested in natural innocence.

At the first hint of dawn, William stopped at the lip of a real crevasse. They had stepped over a few small cracks in the ice, but this one was larger by far. Grace caught up to him, prepared to deliver her withering stare. But instead she looked down. The ice walls plunged to a cavernous trench. They were white at the top, then faintly blue, then lost in black below. She saw no bottom. One slip and she would be lost to the world. She looked up, awestruck.

William had his pack off, and he gruffly handed her bread and water. She sat down on her rucksack and tried to eat, but had no stomach for it. She shivered a bit, patted her marmot, and told him not to fall in the hole.

William overheard. "A crevasse," he said. "Not a *hole*."

Meanwhile, the dawn gathered around them. The glacier blushed a faint rose tinge that deepened by the minute. They were high enough, and it was light enough, to see to the moraines below, tossed up like earthworks against a siege. Lower still stretched the meadows, waking into color, and in amongst the groves of trees they even saw the dot of a cottage. Then westward surged forest, soft and dark, reaching whole and entire to the morning star, bright beneath the dusky moon. Grace did not know that the normal vista was of patchy brown checkers, tiered with roads. She did not know that shining Venus was often lost in a brown haze. But William knew. And unaware, he blessed all that was below him.

The glacier was fully flushed now, and the summit of the North Queen, visible to one side, burned gold in direct sunlight. They saw it and put on their packs again. Most of the glacier remained to climb.

William led off around the crevasse to where it pinched away. Grace was about to follow when she heard something. It was a faraway tintinnabulation, like a wind chime in a faint breeze. The marmot stopped still, and she heard the tinkling sound again. Then she spied small puffs of gray, floating up from the nearest moraine. Tiny figures scuttled onto the lap of the glacier. One was much larger than the others.

"Look," said Grace. She pointed.

William saw, and groaned. They were not much more than an hour ahead. "Can you go any faster?" he called back.

He set off, and she answered with her feet. The rope quivered more evenly now. Their creepers sliced in better rhythm. Crevasses slipped by, on the right, on the left, some beneath winding bridges of snow. Once Grace leapt from lip to lip, the marmot tucked under her arm. Compared to Lady Lira, she thought, crevasses were friendly.

Soon William led them through upreared towers of banded ice—a maze of seracs. They shone turquoise and gold in the dawn. He wound steeply between them, chopping steps with his adze in close succession. Shavings of ice sprayed out from his ax into morning light. Grace followed quickly, clawing each of her feet into place, and the marmot swiftly bounded behind, dragging his tail up the steps.

From out of the seracs they emerged upon a sloping snowfield. It was dazzling white, and the sky burned blue. Only one more crevasse now crossed their way. The largest yet—the bergschrund. It would require a long end run.

"Can you see them?" called William. He sounded anxious.

Grace looked back, breathing heavily. She could only see the tumble of seracs. As she began to reply she heard a sound, not a jingling of rocks this time but a stifled groaning of ice. Under her feet the glacier shuddered, shifting within. Then down the slope, in slowest motion, a serac the size of a stone mausoleum gave way and exploded across their tracks. Shivering chunks of ice flew up and powdered the air in clouds of crystal. Grace stared agawk at the settling powder.

William came down and put a hand on her shoulder. "That'll hold 'em up," he said. He tried to sound as if falling seracs were something that came his way each morning. But his hand was trembling.

"Should we—be going?" Grace asked.

William nodded solemnly and retraced his steps back up the glacier. When the rope went taut, Grace felt a comfort.

The summit was nigh. They traversed the bergschrund far to the right, then turned the end and marched directly up steep white slopes. Feathers of ice now brushed their boots, and the air stabbed a chill in their lungs. William's face was clammy white. Grace was starting to wobble. Their hearts were racing much faster than their feet. But their axes plunged on, steadily on, as if separately empowered.

Grace believed that just ahead the slope would level out. But *just ahead* was most unjust—it just kept on receding. Her breath came wildly. Her feet splayed here and stumbled there. She bargained with the mountain for fifty more steps, then fifty more. The bargain, she decided, was not worth renewing. So Grace caved in, draping herself on the head of her ax like a towel thrown over the back of a chair.

"Sorry," she wheezed. "Gotta stop."

William looked back. "Almost there," he said weakly. He peered below, and thought he saw movement by the first large crevasse. But he wasn't sure. He gave Grace a minute to recover. Then he pulled gently on the rope. "Not much farther," he called down.

Grace had not really caught her breath but followed anyway, dragging a bit on the end of her leash but too dizzy to care. Then, suddenly, the slope began to ease. In a few steps more it leveled completely. This was the summit. No, this was not the summit. William had not stopped. He was plodding towards a rocky nub in the midst of a snowy plain. The nub was far away. Grace felt cheated, but staggered on. Like a mirage, the rocky nubbin kept its distance. It mocked all notion of progress. She gave up watching the summit rock and fell once more to counting steps. At exactly two hundred she peeked—and regretted it. At two hundred more she looked again, and saw enough to hope by. Six hundred steps and there it was—she'd caught the summit napping. William was to the rock now. He scrambled up and turned to reel her in. Grace stepped from the snow, balanced up beneath him. Her creepers skated on stony ledges, the shaft of her ice ax bumped and banged. At William's feet she dropped the ax. And collapsed.

"Is this it?" she moaned. The marmot was licking her face.

"The very place," he answered proudly. "Too bad my watch is busted—I think we made it in record time." He paused to regard her. "You did all right, you know."

Exhausted as she was, Grace still felt the full force of this compliment. She lifted her head. "Thanks," she panted. "Thanks a lot." She thought of her long-lost Lance Q. Lott and began to examine the far-flung view.

William checked her. "The book should be in there," he said. He pointed to a silver box that was right beside them. "Let's take a quick look."

He crouched over the box to unfasten the screw clamps. To his surprise, there were none. He inspected the lid closely. Instead of the stamped logo of his alpine club, it framed a curiously engraved picture. The detail was exquisite. He saw a graceful mountain draped with ice. Below it were tottering moraines, rolling meadows, streams, flowers, marmots playing—even deer standing shyly at the edge of the forest. The entire picture was no larger than a handheld shield, but in whatever place he looked, William could make out as much detail as he liked, down to the whisker of a marmot.

He motioned to Grace, speechless.

She knelt beside him and followed his eyes to the lid of the box. The first thing she saw was a cottage in the meadows. The front door was open to let in the sun. Then she caught her breath. Out of the door in the picture walked a woman. Her face was easy to recognize.

"Look!" said Grace. "It's Lady Demaris!"

William followed her finger. "I don't see her," he said.

"Right there!" Grace insisted. "She's looking up at the mountain now. She seems very worried."

William eyed the girl suspiciously.

"And look here, down the stream," she continued. "It's Colin, tending the marmots. I think he's singing."

William could not see Colin, either. "Are you making this up?" he demanded.

Grace wasn't listening. "And here," she said. "You can see our tracks up the side of the mountain. Right there is where the ice fell over."

Suddenly she began to shake. "And there's Lady Lira," she whispered. "And her marmots. I can see her face—her eyes, even." Grace had to look away. The woman's eyes were fixed on her, cold as malice congealed.

"Where are they?" urged William.

She braced herself for another look. "They're in the ice towers now. She's got one, two, five, six—let me see—ten marmots with her. And in her hand she has—" Grace stopped, barely able to say what she saw—"a dagger."

They looked at one another and William tittered nervously. He would never be able to explain why.

"The book," said Grace. "Maybe we can take it with us down the other side."

"There aren't any screws," William said flatly. He pried at the lid in vain. "I don't know how it opens."

Grace inspected the sides of the box. On the front she saw a keyhole. She pointed silently.

"Worth a try," William agreed. He wished that he had seen it first. He bit off one mitten and snatched the rusty key from his pocket. It fit perfectly. He turned it. As if by magic the lid arose.

Within lay a folio ledger, old and scuffed and leather-bound. The edges of the leaves showed ragged and yellow. Grace very carefully scooped it up, but the book tugged back like a partner on a rope. She felt underneath it. The spine was fastened to the box by a chain—and the box itself was immovably fixed in the summit rock. This book was not for borrowing. She looked up at William.

"We have a while, anyway," he said, shrugging his shoulders. "Read what you can and we'll slide down the backside soon enough."

To Grace this felt like a timed examination, except much worse. A test could sometimes make her ill, and her stomach right now was poised on the verge. She told herself to calm down. She took a deep breath, and the alpine pungency ached in her nostrils. Then, with trembling mitten, she pawed the cover open.

The first thing she saw was a huge single letter—an *L*—at the top of the page. The letter was green, and well adorned with boughs of fir and tumbling marmots. She smiled faintly to herself. But beneath the green *L* stretched a column of stanzas in antique angular script. It was poetry. Her heart dropped. She flipped through page after page—relentless verse, all of it—and hope decayed with each falling leaf. How could she begin to read it all?

Midway through the book, partway down one brittle page, the writing abruptly stopped. She swiftly checked the remaining pages—all were blank. So she glanced back at the final stanza and read the final line:

> *Lest* Beast *and woman darke the northerne morning shyne.*

In quick surprise she skimmed the lines above. To the word it was her uncle's poem, now only part of a poem partly written. But this part she already knew—there was no use dwelling here. So she paged toward the front of the book once more.

"Where do I start?" she whined aloud.

"Beats me," said William. He was nervously checking the snowy plain at the place where their steps met the sky.

In despair, Grace returned to the first page. After she got a start on it, maybe she could skip around.

Here is how the book began:

> *Lo here the mount where Muses faine would dwell,*
> *Forwearied of Parnassus grimie hill,*
> *Forsaking Helicons heat-parchéd well*
> *For fountains of green ice that higher spill.*
> *Lo these the mountains, these my song shall fill*
> *To ouerflowing with deepe historie.*
> *Reeds oaten, trumpets sterne, use that ye will:*
> *Both fitting bee to blazon to the skie*
> *Brave deeds of maids and men lest praise of them may die.*
>
> *Help then, O Muses, here awaited long—*
> *Ye welcome bee farre flown across the seas.*
> *Vnwearied now renew an alpine song,*

Blow forth glad breath and sweete the vernall breeze;
Make autumn gales my falt'ring notes to seize.
Three Queenes here reign your seruice to demand;
Three Queenes require your seruice, ye thrice three,
To sing the heroes in their high command
That laboured haue long time to green a groning land.

Gag me! thought Grace. Gag the Muses! If there's a story, let's get on with it.
She skipped several pages and read on in a hurry:

So he expelléd was from that green world;
To loue and tend vnwilling had he beene.
Mosquitoes now before the portal whirl'd
Hot deadlie needles, guarding all the green.
He once that honor'd euery verdant Queene,
Now hurl'd in dusty exile selfe-impos'd
For plucking that was pleasant to bee seene:
Not keeper he but taker was expos'd
When rounde the trembling fruite his grasping fingers clos'd.

Now out, he best considers his reuenge,
How most to quyte the place he cannot in.
Full sorelie he desireth to auenge
Him that would say his new-wonne knowledge sinne.
For now his eies are open that had been
To wisdom clos'd: that trees may build a towre,
That meadows are most ripe of gold within,
That rivers damm'd churn glorie into power.
The verie grapes that grow, but for him would bee soure.

So pricking too and fro he seeks a waie
The arbor vitae he may haply smite.
From dust to dust he faine would sift the clay;
To life in death fower rivers he would spyte.
But grutching he remaynes vntill the night,
For much he fears the dread mosquitoe sting;

Their fatal poison he can no-wise fight.
The hallow'd ground they adamantly ring;
Full thicke they thirst for blood, full angry they doe sing.

Almost the wight was given to despayr,
When lo, a monstrous forme, by hidden heast,
'Gan suddeinly seepe vp into the ayre
From out the ground in trickling bloodie yeast
That gurgl'd darke—and grisly it increast.
Full gracelesse shape it tooke, of filthie hue,
And fearfull was its name: The Lava Beast.
All bloated was its maw with magma stewe
That dript downe from its iaws, and from its nostrills too.

Addressing then it selfe vnto the man,
It spoke in fire and breathéd smokie ashe:
Ye wish (quoth it) to enter if ye can
Where one surcharg'd of surquedry so rash
Did whip thee hence with cruell mosquitoe lash.
Unfairly is the land lockt vp in paine
Agaynst thy needful use—ye rightly gnash
Thy teeth to lose that ought to be thy gaine.
Thy manhoode bears a slight, thine honor suffers staine.

Now hearken thou to me, areed my words,
For I can ye most excellently ayde
To penetrate yon thicke mosquitoe herds
Unharm'd, unstung, unscath'd, and well ypaide
By vse compleat of all before thee layd.
For nought can yon mosquitoes bear my fire,
And 'fore my smoke they quick disperse and fayd.
All needs ye doen is join ye to mine hire:
Staie fast by me alway, and 'scape the buggy ire.

Fear not (it said), I stronger am then he
That would vpon thee place a feeble hex.

And if he gave it thought he'd certes see
That what he wrought in thee he cannot vex—
Created to subdue: Domini lex!
Subdue? Yea, haue dominion he did say,
Reign lord o'er all the land, tyrannus rex!
What think ye now? Wouldst thou hold all in sway?
Join then thyself to me: I only am the waie.

Right glad the wight receiuéd this aduice;
To all the Beast *did say he well did harke—*
In fine, he made the bargain in a trice.
Vpon his hart the Beast *then sear'd a marke,*
With inly marke his hart made flamy darke—
Not on the foreheade as it has been tolde,
But deepe within a fest'ring smokie spark.
By this the Beast *brought him into his folde:*
Now easie to bee bought, but harder to be solde.

Grace stopped again. William was drumming on the lid of the box.

"So what are we supposed to do?" he asked. "Did you find out?"

"There's a few things here about the Lava Beast," she said, "but nothing really helpful so far. It's a poem that tells a story. I can't begin to read it all."

William sliced at the rock with his heel. They should have been gone by now.

Grace had her own thoughts. "William," she quavered, "when you met the Lava Beast, he didn't talk to you, did he?"

"No ma'am," said William.

"So you never talked to him, either?"

"Are you kidding? I was barely awake. Besides, I was busy—being mauled." He winced at the memory. "Look at that lid again, will you? See if you can spot her."

Grace looked. Lady Lira was through the seracs and striding over the final bergschrund. Fewer marmots were at her side—she must have outdistanced the slower ones.

Grace pointed to the spot on the picture.

"Time to head out," William declared.

Grace closed the book and replaced it flat in the box. She felt as if she were turning in a far-from-finished essay. She reached for the lid reluctantly, and sighed. Then something strange occurred. Till now the marmot had roamed the summit, testing the air with upheld whiskers. But suddenly, he bolted towards them and jumped in the box atop the book.

"Get out, silly marmot," said Grace. "We're leaving."

The marmot would not budge.

"Scat," said William.

The marmot remained. Grace tried to pick him up—he scratched her. William tried to swat him out—he bared his teeth.

"Let's go," said William. "It'll follow us."

"But we can't leave the lid up," said Grace. "I don't think Lady Lira should touch this book."

"Better the book than us," huffed William.

He clambered off the rocks and began tromping east, away from their tracks. Grace watched the rope slither out from her feet. It was almost uncoiled when she heard a sharp whistle. William stopped. Grace saw them first—three silhouettes on the eastern horizon. They all were galloping straight for William. At the very same time, three more marmots emerged on the north.

"Come back!" she shouted.

She reeled him in frantically. He stumbled towards her, a clumsy fish. Now she checked the south—yet three more were over the edge, running her way.

"Hurry!" she called.

Grace hauled him to the rock and he flopped onshore. She glanced behind. A giant of a woman raced over their tracks, taking one step for their two. In her hand she held a dagger aloft, and a single marmot dogged her heels.

William stood panting at Grace's side. He turned slowly around and marked each approaching party. But his eyes returned to the woman. "Looks like we use these bloody axes," he said. He wondered if dispatching a marmot would require a perfect golf swing. He had not golfed in years.

"Untie from the rope," he told Grace. "Stay up on these rocks. Remember you can kick the little buggers with your spikes."

Grace took off her mittens and tried to untie the knot at her waist. Her fingers, however, hung limp on the rope. The marmot began to rub her legs like a cat that wants attention. But Grace kept her eyes on the closing attackers—in a minute or less they would all arrive, and then what? She could see the eyes and teeth of the nearest marmots, the quivering lips of Lady Lira. A black gown swept behind the woman, a black hood cowled her face. Her white hand held the dagger high—a flag and a standard ready to strike.

Grace felt another furry nudge on her leg, and this time she looked down. The marmot had upended the book. He was pawing at something on the bottom of the box. Half-heartedly, Grace looked inside. Where the book had been was another keyhole.

"William," she said. "The key!" She tried to shout it but only whispered.

"*Hmm?*"

"The key!" This was a real shout.

"If you want it," he murmured. His eyes were still on Lady Lira, gliding closer with appalling strength. He held the key out listlessly.

Grace snatched the key and shoved its teeth in the new hole. It smoothly fit and smoothly turned. This time, the entire box unhinged from the rock, swinging up like a thick trap door. Underneath was an open shaft, wide as her shoulders. Steep cut steps—a ladder, almost—led down into darkness.

"In here!" cried Grace. She pressed the key back into his hand and quickly tossed their packs in the hole.

William revolved in a trance. His lower lip was sagging. He gazed at the shaft as if miles away.

Grace dropped in her ice ax next. It clanked and echoed—a noisy penny in a wishing well. The marmot dove in after it. Then, after closing the book inside its box, Grace squirmed down the hatch herself. Her creepers struck sparks on the hard stone steps.

Very slowly, William gathered up the rope and dumped it in on top of her. He looked to the west. Lady Lira's outstretched hand now touched the rocks below him. He looked north and east—the marmots too had left the snow. He turned south—and a rush of fur sprang snarling upon him. His ice ax dipped and swung on the tee, just as he had imagined. He sliced it. One soft thud and the marmot flew in a gentle arc, touching down on the white fairway. William wondered stupidly at the warm blood dripping from his adze.

"Get in here!" hissed a voice from below.

Clutching his ax, he wriggled in waist-deep and with one hand grasped the edge of the box. It swung down sweetly over his head. But just as he released it, a white-hot slash tore into his hand. He squealed in pain. Then the silver shield clicked shut.

It was utterly dark.

Chapter 14
All the Gas

❋

"CAN WE PLEASE STOP?" It was Jennifer who asked. The pack straps cut her shoulders cruelly. Her hands hung numb, the knuckles puffy with pooled blood.

"We just started," Arnie said firmly. "We can't stop yet." He snorted to show it could not be otherwise.

Arnie was hiking in front today, hunkered beneath a burden meet for a camel with gifts from the Queen of Sheba. His pockets were stuffed with obsidian chips, and each hand held two large mushrooms. Jennifer was breathing in gulps at Arnie's heels. Then came Ronald, his nylon glasses slipping down to the end of his nose. Had his nose not turned up at the end like a ski jump, his glasses would have long since fallen to the trail, there to be crushed by the tottering steps of the two girls behind him. They, if possible, slurped the air more raggedly than Jennifer. The girls were passing a paisley bandana back and forth, each, in turn, tragically stroking the sweat from her brow. The gesture came easily at midday—the hour of soap operas now sorely missed.

Trailing the two girls was the red-bearded young man. He had enthroned Arnie as Leader for the Day, which meant that he himself could placidly observe the agony and the anarchy while dawdling in the rear. This was called Non-Directive Leadership. He was quite good at it. At present he had begun to notice that Jennifer would be most delighted to bury her ax the requisite six inches deep in Arnie's skull. This he recognized as Group Process. He would skillfully manage it by refraining from any intervention whatsoever. Only then could the group members reach a Genuine Consensus, preparing themselves not only to function harmoniously at later stages of the expedition, but to mature as assertive yet cooperative individuals in Society at Large. Besides, hiking solo in the rear gave the leader ample time to memorize the immortal ballads of the

North—no small passion of his:

When you're lost in the Wild, and you're scared as a child,
And Death looks you bang in the eye,
And you're sore as a boil, it's according to Hoyle
To cock your revolver and—

"Please, stop," wheezed Jennifer, and suddenly she did. Ronald crashed into the back of her pack, and apologized. But Arnie walked on, determined, a shepherd without his sheep. Soon, however, the silence at his heels grew suspect. He turned around. Some distance behind him, four carcasses were scattered about as if thrown by a seismic blast. Arnie dropped his mushrooms.

"Hey, I didn't say you could stop!"

"Outvoted," said Jennifer. She lay open-mouthed and panting, her wide eyes pinned to the sky as if dazzled by an angel vision.

Arnie appealed to the red-bearded one, who stood a little ways back. "Hey, I never said they could stop. I'm the leader, aren't I?"

The leader nodded vaguely and walked down the trail to relieve himself. Desertion was mounting. Arnie looked to his friend and ally.

"Why'd you quit, Ronald?" he demanded.

Ronald looked at Jennifer. "I don't know. Tired, I guess."

Arnie rejoined them and took off his pack with manly disgust. He stood over his prostrate followers. "What a bunch of woosies!"

No one denied this.

"I'm the one with the heaviest pack," he said, thumbing his chest. "I got all the gorp, all the lunches, the rope, the stove, all of the gas—"

"You've got all the gas all right," said Jennifer.

Ronald thought this uproarious. He laughed in little hiccups.

One of the girls turned to her friend. "Can you get my water out?"

"Mine too," said Jennifer to Ronald.

The plastic bottles were duly extracted, and inspection revealed a dead fly floating inside the first. The two girls shrieked in unison. One held the bottle at arm's length and dumped the water out.

"Afraid of a little fly?" said Arnie.

No one answered him.

Then Ronald asked for some gorp.

"I'm saving it," said Arnie. He got out his map instead and pondered it alone. This seemed like a leaderly thing to do. As it happened, however, his study was repaid.

"Hey!" he announced. "The map shows a cabin just down the trail. I'm serious, look."

No one got up.

"Maybe you could bring the map over here," said Ronald.

Arnie scowled but came over. He spread out the map between Ronald and Jennifer—the other two girls sat apart, brushing their hair. Arnie stubbed down his finger on a tiny black square by a thin dotted line. The square was labeled "Demaris Cabin."

"How far?" said Jennifer.

Arnie seized the reins of leadership. "Maybe a mile. If we leave now we could get there by lunch—have lunch at the cabin."

"But it's time for lunch now."

"I think it'll be worth waiting—lunch at the cabin, you know."

At this point the red-bearded leader returned, and was asked to arbitrate this most crucial of the day's choices. Normally he respected the Group Decision-Making Process, carefully playing the part of a blank wall that impartially rebounds wayward tennis balls. But in this matter, for special reasons, he deigned to intervene.

"How about the cabin?" he said. The leader well knew that whatever he asked was not really a question.

As it turned out, the cabin lay more than a mile away—at least Jennifer said so when they got there. It sat slightly uphill from the trail, in a meadow, next to a stream that leapt down from the Center Queen. The walls were made of blocks of lava fitted together in a crude puzzle. The roof peaked high in bleached and splintered shingles. Some of the shingles littered the beaten ground by the door like broken teeth of a dragon. The door stood ajar, disclosing shade and coolness and mystery. From a pack-laden vantage on the dusty path, it was the door to heaven.

"Can we go in?" asked Arnie. "Does this Demaris guy still live here?"

"Not anymore," said the leader. "Just the backcountry ranger—when she's not on patrol."

The leader routed his groups this way whenever he could. Right now he wished with all his heart that the ranger would be in. As if wishes were binding, there appeared at the door a comely young woman, blonde and sunburnt. He waved to the woman cautiously, hoping he was remembered.

"Hello!" she called. Her voice fell upon them like haloes of spray. "I thought you'd be coming—I have huckleberries for you! Come in, won't you? Come in where it's cool."

The group balked, wonderstruck. Then they advanced very shyly, like squirrels approaching a hand-held peanut. At the ranger's direction they parked their packs against the wall and timidly edged through the door. It was indeed cool inside. She sat them around a rough-hewn table that held a bowl of berries. Arnie snagged the first handful.

"Look at that attic," he said, pointing to a loft. "Do you sleep up there?"

"When it rains," said the ranger. "But I usually sleep outside." She flipped a thick blonde braid behind her and took a seat at the head of the table.

"If I lived here I'd never go outside," said Arnie. "Except when I went climbing."

"So you're a climber?" she said, her green eyes wide with appreciation.

"Yeah. South Queen. Yesterday. Piece o' cake." The report came out in huckleberry fragments.

"How did the rest of you like it?"

"Fun," said Ronald modestly.

"Most of it," said Jennifer.

"Uh-uh, my feet got cold," said one girl.

"Too far," said the other.

"The best part was comin' back," Arnie added. "I just put on my rain pants and sat down and like, I was gone! I'd climb all the way up there just to slide down again. They should build a lift or something."

"They might," said the ranger. She rolled her eyes.

"Really?" said Arnie.

"What do you mean?" said the leader. It was news to him.

"Ah," she replied. She hunched forward. This creased her khaki uniform shirt and set her badge askew. "So you haven't heard. Well. Bring in your lunch, then—I'll tell you."

Jennifer went outside to fetch the lunch from their packs. She found a melting block of cheese and a smashed box of crackers. She could not find Arnie's gorp, and said so.

"Forget it," said Arnie. "Let's just eat. I wanna hear about the chairlift." He took a terrific drag from his water bottle and settled forward on his elbows, a full conspirator with the ranger. She waited for Jennifer and then began.

"Do you remember the creek you hiked up on your first day—Lost Creek?"

They remembered.

"You should see the blister Arnie got there," said Ronald.

"I didn't get no blister," said Arnie.

"That whole drainage—up to the meadows—lies just outside the wilderness boundary," said the ranger.

The leader nodded. He knew that.

"Who's got a knife for the cheese?" said Jennifer.

From under the table the ranger produced a knife with the heft of a dagger.

"Thanks," said Jennifer. "That'll work great."

"Now for years," said the ranger, "they have wanted to build a road and cut the trees along Lost Creek."

"But that's in the courts, isn't it?" said the leader.

"It was," she answered. "But the final appeal was denied last week. They start on the road next summer."

"Who's *they?*" asked Ronald.

The ranger paused. "It's us," she answered. "*They* is us."

"I see," said Ronald vaguely.

"The road will go almost to the meadows beneath the South Queen. They may push it a little farther to accommodate a drive-in campground with a splendid view of the mountain." She looked and smiled at the red-bearded leader. "This," she added a little too brightly, "is but one example of the way in which timber harvesting opens up diverse recreational opportunities."

The leader greatly admired her way of putting things.

"Will the campground have showers?" asked one girl. "That might make it worth coming."

"That's the next part," said the ranger. "The campground may have *hot* showers."

"That would be *so* wonderful," said the other girl. "I haven't had a shower in five days. If my mother saw me now, she'd make me take a bath with the dog in the garage."

"Except the dog wouldn't be able to stand it!" shouted Arnie. He held up his nose between his fingers, coating it generously with cheese.

"What are you getting at?" the leader said.

"Okay," said the ranger. She surveyed her pupils. "Do any of you know how the Three Queens got here?"

Ronald felt a summons to speak the truth. "God made them," he said huskily. He felt his face burn.

"Maybe there weren't enough kings to go around," said Arnie. He sputtered crackers on the table in front of him.

The ranger addressed Ronald: "Yes, but how did he—ah—or what kind of mountains are they?"

Ronald lit up. "They're volcanoes."

"Right," said the ranger. "And what makes volcanoes erupt?"

This put Ronald on home ground. "Gasses inside the earth. They get super-heated under high pressure and force up magma to the surface. That's the quiet kind of eruption. In the violent kind, the gasses themselves explode into the air, spreading huge clouds of ash and cinders."

Jennifer's gaze spilled admiration.

"Good," said the ranger. "Now. These three volcanoes haven't erupted for hundreds of years, but they're still quite active. In fact, if you climb the North Queen you'll find sulfur vents below the summit. They shoot out hot steam and smell like someone who likes baked beans."

She waited for Arnie to stop giggling.

"So even though these peaks are covered with snow, they're actually pretty warm underneath—and all of that heat is a valuable resource. For a long time, people have wanted to drill deep holes in the meadows up here, and to pipe away as much steam and as much hot water as they can find. Most of the places they've wanted to try are inside the wilderness boundary. That means they can't drill there. But the Lost Creek road will pave the way to a corner of the meadows just outside the designated wilderness. When the road is finished the drillers will come. In fact, if it weren't for the lawsuits, they would have come by helicopter long ago.

"Anyway, when they find a little they'll wish for more. So to help things along, they will urge the government to quietly relax a few minor management con-straints upon test drilling in the wilderness itself. The government will eventu-ally agree, for we obviously need to meet our country's energy needs."

"Let's have some of those crackers down here," said Arnie.

"You've *had* yours," hissed Jennifer.

"For several summers, helicopters will visit the timberline meadows, bringing in equipment for more test sites. And once a profitable amount of geothermal energy is discovered, a need for it will suddenly arise. Soon the Three Queens will radiate a full network of pipes, like a giant furnace in the basement of an old house. To construct and maintain these pipelines, roads will be built up virtually every drainage. These roads, of course, will be carefully designed so as not to compromise the wilderness quality of the area."

"How could that be?" asked Ronald.

"She's kidding," Jennifer told him.

"No, good point," said the ranger. "For once the roads and wells and pipelines are in place, perceptive legislators will recognize, in all fairness, that this area is no longer wilderness—that in fact to so call such a place after it has been accessed for our emergency energy needs would be a sham, an embarrassment, a stumbling block to the integrity of the wilderness ideal and to the vitality of the rich frontier heritage so dear to our nation. So, in a bold move to protect the remaining wilderness in our country, the Three Queens will be subject to revisionary legislation that will entail minor boundary adjustments. The summits themselves will of course retain their wilderness character and classification. But the parameters of management flexibility will be happily enlarged for the rest of the region."

"I'm lost," whispered Jennifer.

"Me too," said Ronald.

"So then the ski lifts get built," said the leader.

"Exactly. The southwest slope of the South Queen has the longest potential run in the state. They'll be helicopter skiing right up to the day the lifts and lodge are completed."

Arnie was not listening anymore. He had decided earlier that the ranger had forgotten about the ski lifts. His thoughts were on the gorp in his pack. His pack was in the sun, and the chocolate chips had probably collected at the bottom of the bag in a molten brown syrup.

"From the lodge they will groom a ten-foot-wide trail for the rugged sort who cross-country ski. This very cabin will likely serve as a warming hut at the end of it. There by the door will be a telephone and a pop machine. In that corner, video games."

Arnie heard these magic words. "All right!" he said.

"Skiers will use the trail in the mornings, and snowmobiles in the afternoons. When the snow melts, hikers and motorcycles will trade off in the same courteous manner. But then you will be able to drive directly to the hut, the summer headquarters for the School of Western Alpinism Guide Service. For two hundred dollars, SWAGS will lead you through the pipelines to a summit conquest, then back to the parking lot in time for a getaway to the restaurant of your choice."

"Yum, pizza!" said one girl.

The leader was wondering if he could get a job with the new guide service. The pay sounded excellent. "What else will happen up here?" he asked.

"Well," said the ranger, "all the pipeline roads will provide good timber access too—that goes without saying. But once the boundary adjustments are made, yet another dream will be fulfilled. The deepest canyon beyond the South Queen—Amoenas Gorge—will become the site of a picturesque reservoir. The blessing will be complete: the wilderness shall become a pool of water."

"Can we water-ski up here then?" asked one girl. Without waiting for an answer she turned to her friend. "I got up on one ski last week," she confided. "That's the first thing we'll do when we get back—go water-skiing."

"After we go get pizza, you mean," said the other girl.

"That's for me!" crowed Arnie. "A sixteen-incher! Double cheese and onions and olives and sausage and pepperoni and Canadian bacon and pineapple and green peppers and tomatoes and mushrooms and anchovies and—"

"*You* like anchovies?" The two girls were incredulous.

"Don't you?" said Arnie, equal in his unbelief. Then he appealed to the badge of authority: "Do you like anchovies?"

"Sometimes," said the ranger. She smiled.

Lunch was over, and the lecture with it. "Thank you," said everyone. "Thank you for the huckleberries."

"My pleasure," said the ranger. "Come again."

As the group filed out to their sun-warmed packs, the leader imagined what it would be like to steal a kiss in the shadow of the doorway.

Chapter 15
Down, Most Likely

✳

THE SILVER BOX WAS RINGING, and William's head sang like a clapper in a bell. Grace could hear the ringing too, from the more aesthetic distance of six feet farther down the shaft. Here, wedged upright in a snarl of rope, she was much more attentive to William's creepers resting on her shoulders. Each blow on the box seemed to pound his spikes down deep into her flesh, a yoke of pain she bore in the darkness.

Still, she did not speak, she did not squirm—did nothing to uncharm the shield and bring down ruin on their heads. So might meadow mice quietly crouch in the shadow of a hawk. Eventually the shadow passes, and so, at last, did the clamor overhead. The blows stopped, the din faded, a faint and faraway curse spun aloft. Then, silence rolled down.

Grace listened to the air pour in at her lips. She waited for her eyes to adjust to the dark—for the wall, the rope, her hand to appear. But wait as she would, her eyes beheld nothing at all. She could not call it total darkness, for there was nothing total about it—it was not sum, but lack. It was only dark because the light was missing. The light did not come, and her eyes could not illumine the darkness. They were not the lamp of the body after all.

William, meanwhile, quietly lifted his feet from her shoulders. That felt worse. Now she was alone.

"William?" she whispered. "You still there?"

"I think so," he said. His voice echoed softly.

"She's gone, isn't she?"

"I think so," he repeated.

"When you lifted your feet up I thought you'd left me. Let's stay together, all right?"

"All right," he said.

"You sure you're okay, William? You don't sound so good."

"Just fine," he whispered.

"I can't see anything, can you?"

"Nope."

"Think you could open the lid and peek out? Get some light in here, anyway?"

"Sure," said William, and lifted up his hand. Then he brought it back. "What if they're waiting for us?"

This was a thought.

"Quiet!" she hissed. "Don't talk so loud, then."

She paused. "You think we should go down?"

"Okay."

"Don't say that! Say *yes* or *no*."

She paused again, surprised at her own vehemence. "You think this goes anywhere?"

"Yes."

"Where?"

"Down, most likely."

She breathed disgust. "Do we have a light or anything?"

"Candles," said William. That meant finding their packs, which lay somewhere below them.

"I'll look," said Grace, which obviously she couldn't. She stretched out her foot as if testing the water in a pool. It touched one, two more steps, but no packs.

"William, why don't you go first? Would you? Just for a bit? Until we find our packs?"

"No room," he said.

She pressed the walls around her. A coffin would have been more spacious.

"Okay," she conceded. "I'll go first. But stay behind me, all right? Hang on to the rope or something so you don't lose me."

"Sure," he said.

She slid down one full step, then hesitated. "William?"

"Yes."

"Are you scared?"

There was no response.

"I mean really. Tell me the truth."

Serious Climber though he was, William told the truth. "I'm terrified," he said.

"Good, me too. Let's be scared together, okay? It'll be nicer that way. When I was little, you know, my uncle would read me stories. Sometimes there were parts that got me frightened—and I'd cry. Then he would put down the book and hold me close, and I'd look up and see his eyes, and he'd say, 'I get scared too, Niece.' It hardly seemed possible—that he could be scared—but it always made me feel better."

She paused. "William?"

"Yes?"

"I wish I could see your eyes right now."

He was flattered.

"Did you know my uncle well?" she asked.

"Not very well," he replied.

She thought this over. It seemed a bit odd. "Why do you suppose he picked you, then? For the ax, I mean. If he hardly knew you and all."

"Good question," he said.

Her thoughts began to take her where she did not wish to go.

"Don't you think this whole thing is a little bizarre, William? I mean, sometimes I feel like everything's under control, and that my uncle has it all planned out somehow. But mostly I feel like everything happens by the strangest luck. Like, things turn out, but just barely. Makes you think twice before climbing down a dark tunnel to meet who knows what—the Lava Beast, maybe?"

She shuddered. All of a sudden it seemed so absurd.

"You know what my problem is?" she whined. "My problem is that I'm not very brave. I'm not, and I don't see the point of being here. Why we're supposed to go to all this trouble for the sake of a few marmots is beyond me. Because, I didn't ask to come—this isn't the trip I signed up for, you know. Sometimes I wonder if he thinks this is some kind of a joke, playing around with us like this. I wonder if he is amused. Seriously, I do. I wonder if right now—"

And right then, cutting her off, a peal of laughter sprang from above. William and Grace went utterly limp.

"Ah, Grace," came the voice. "You see the humor of it now! Your dear uncle couldn't go away unnoticed. He had to leave his little posthumous comedy." The voice trailed off into laughter again, and Grace began to whimper.

"Surprised to hear me, dear? It's only fair that if you hide under my bed, I hide next to your bedtime storybook. Did you read pleasant tales? Or did they frighten you, dear—make you cry? Let me comfort you with my eyes, then.

"And William. Brave Sir Terrified William, defender and champion of marmots in distress. Such wisdom in your courage! Such discretion in your valor! Have you found your rusty ice ax, William? Do you think it lies under the mountain? What a pity it is not there.

"But you well know what is there, William. You know what lies in wait below. There is still time. Think on it, William. Show yourself wise. Open the shield while yet you can and come back out from your grave to the living. I have flung my dagger far away in the snow. Open the shield, William, and we shall make peace together. I that am above know how to be gracious; he that is below knows only to devour. Choose, William. Choose, then."

William stood quietly. His hand stung deep where she had slashed it. He did not feel like talking.

"Shy, William?"

He did not answer.

She heaved a piteous sigh. "Have it your way, then," she said. "And never pretend I did not try to help you.

"But Grace, tell me, dear, why did you desert your young friend Lance? He's so lonely without you now. A pity, too, he shall never see you more. Unless, of course, you care to come with me. Then I could send you all back to your homes, just as we'd planned, remember? This whole foolish business would all be over like a dream gone by."

She paused, but Grace did not respond.

"Won't you come, Grace? Do you really wish harm upon your friends? And upon yourself, too? Or perhaps you are planning to desert William as well, somewhere deep in the bowels of the mountain, when convenience offers."

Grace spoke before she knew it. "You deserted my uncle," she said flatly.

"Your uncle was a fool!" shouted Lady Lira. "And so are you both!"

In that instant Grace knew her uncle was not a fool.

"Farewell then," announced the woman. "The light of day bids you farewell."

The shield overhead rang out once more. This time Grace did not stay to listen. She launched her body down the shaft, creepers skating over the steps, striking out sparks like newborn stars. It was not safe, but it was not dull, either. She stopped on a stair that was comfortably wide, her feet punched into the soft underbelly of a packsack.

She turned around. "Come on!" she whispered.

She heard him slowly scrape to her side. There was room for both of them on the stair, and that felt good. She clutched his arm, but said nothing.

Once settled, William leaned forward and groped through the pack with his unhurt hand. On the bottom (of course) was a flint, a lantern, a fistful of candles—Colin's doing. He put all the candles but one in his pocket and readied the one to light. The flint struck, the wick caught, the candle burned in a bloody mitten. He placed it in the lantern, and checkered holes of light and shadow sprayed the lava walls. The tunnel was lit.

There was room to stand up—they could see that now. And they could see a stairway curving downwards, first to Grace's tumbled pack, and then to her fallen ax, and last to a pair of marmot eyes, shining like planets on the edge of twilight. Grace looked at William's ashen face and then at his mitten, all in tatters.

"How did you do that?" she asked. She made him put the lantern down, then held his wrist and peeled away the blood-soaked wool. The back of his hand was grisly to see.

"Does it hurt?"

He nodded.

She bound it with a handkerchief and told him to relax. He sank back placidly. Then she unstrapped his creepers, her creepers, stowed them away. The rope she gathered in a snaky ball and stuffed it in her pack. The bread was in William's. She gave him some but he ate very little. Grace ate much, and the marmot with her. She found a skin of water and drank it half down. William said he was not thirsty. So, she put it away and fastened their packs. In theory, they were ready.

"William?"

"Uh huh."

"Do you think she was telling the truth about the Lava Beast?" She looked down the stairs. "You think he's waiting for us?"

"Could be," he said. His voice was utterly complacent.

She shook him by the shoulders. "What's the matter with you?"

"I'm fine," he said.

"You are not fine. Listen!" She grabbed his collar. "I'm going down these stairs—all right? And you're going with me. If we find a way out, we find a way out. That's all we can do." She remembered something the red-bearded leader had told them. "*Buck up! Do your damnedest!* Okay, William?" She looked him bang in the eye.

"Okay," he replied.

How far they descended she could not tell. The steps curled down, relentlessly left, and the ragged ceiling slipped by. Grace tried to count the steps at first, but always her mind would steal away to the tapping of their axes—tapping, tapping, tapping on the stone in still small echoes.

The marmot flirted in shadows ahead. He slipped beyond the lantern light, a vanished mirage, and softly reappeared. Then he waited, whiskers alert, watching them come—gone when they got there. It was nice to believe he knew where he was going.

Because they didn't. By the time that their third candle had burned low, it seemed to Grace they had dropped too far—farther than they had climbed in the dawn. Her knees had begun to grate inside, as if pieces of lava were scouring the joints. It was warmer now. She was thirsty, too. She wanted to stop.

She noticed then that the marmot himself had come to a halt. He was standing up on his hind feet and squinting back at the lantern. Beyond him the lantern light skipped and flashed. She drew up beside him and saw what it was—a black spread of water. The stairway ended just at the shore, and the walls flung apart in a half-submerged cavern.

She stooped, laid her ax aside, and gently combed the water. It was warm. She touched her fingers to her tongue. And it was wretched. She tried to spit the taste away.

William, meanwhile, sank down wearily on the steps. His eyes were vacant. Grace saw a twig that was caught in his hair and teased it out like a fretful mother. She carelessly tossed the twig in the water, and there it shone like a golden bough. Then it was gone, swept from sight.

"There's a current to it," she said aloud.

"A current to it, do it," her voice echoed back.

This gave her a notion. She lifted high the lantern and peered across the cavern. There, in the shadows, she saw what she was looking for—stairsteps climbing out of the water. There was another side. Perhaps the river could be forded.

She seized her ax and plunged it in. The end of the shaft struck one submerged step, then another. She sank it to the hilt on a third. Then, dropping to her knees, she skated it out as far as she could reach—there did not seem to be a fourth step.

"I think we can wade it," she reported.

"Wade it, aid it," the cave said back.

William looked steadily at the water and said nothing.

Grace did not see further use in consulting him. She stripped off their sweaters and stuffed them tightly in both packs, leaving her own pack partway open.

"You ride in here," she said to the marmot. She scooped him up and settled him inside. His head and forepaws poked out the top. Then she hoisted the pack to her shoulders, which took some straining. She felt the marmot's wet nose on the back of her neck.

William went through the motions of putting on his own pack. "Go steady," Grace told him. "Keep your hand on my waist."

They stood on the shore then—the mother, the marmot, the maimed—ready to test the waters. Carefully holding the lantern aloft, Grace splashed onto the first submerged stair. That was easy. The second stair was knee-deep, and it filled her boots with a thick warm flood. The marmot began to clutch her neck, and William gripped her waist. Still, it was trivial. But the third stair gave the current a voice. It called out softly from her thighs, insisting she turn her steps. She gathered her strength, edged out farther, inched her way against the swell. Another stair would sink her too far. But the going was level—there were no more stairs. With dripping sleeve she plunged her ax to the left, to the right. She found no bottom. A drowned causeway, narrow as their hopes, was all that parted the waters.

"Stay close," she said to William. He stood half-submerged in the wake of her shadow, the shadow of himself.

Grace moved very slowly—one foot, the ax, the other foot, the ax again. It was hard to keep the narrow way. The water moaned around her thighs, pushing her where she dared not step. Before very long she grew weary of denying it, tired of bracing all her body. How easy, how desirable to swerve, to sigh, and then to yield. She almost wished it.

And so it was that the first stair caught her by surprise. When you are contemplating failure, success is a bizarre intrusion. She mounted out of the river's grasp, shedding the tips of its watery fingers. Two more steps and the river was gone and her knickers hung wet on her thighs. William's hand still touched her waist. It was trembling.

"How are you doing?" asked Grace.

"Fine," said William. He shrugged off his pack and it nearly rolled into the water.

"How about you?" she said to the marmot.

In reply, the marmot leapt out from the top of her pack and wandered cautiously into the shadows. She held up the lantern to watch him go. The way ahead looked smooth and stairless, but the candle had burned quite low, and she couldn't see far. The lantern was flickering badly.

"Got another candle?" she asked. He did. She replaced the stub in the lantern box and set the lantern aside.

Her feet were swimming in private ponds, and so were William's. She sat him down and plucked off his boots and poured libations to the river. She wrung his socks out one by one, then dried his feet with the sweater from her pack. On the knuckles of his toes were a few stray wisps of hair.

She had scarcely put William together again when down the tunnel the marmot whistled—shrill urgency that seemed to echo from far away. But even as they turned to look, the marmot was upon them. And he did not stop. He careened from the dark like a rabbit pursued, shot between them, glanced off the lantern, gathered his paws for the final leap and hurled himself into the river. The lantern tumbled after him and smacked the water in a deep dark hiss. Then all was black.

William and Grace sat very still. They were quite confused. But then they felt it—both at once. The air grew heavy, close, and hot. They tasted acrid smoke. The very floor grew warm beneath them. It was silent, it was dark, but it was coming and they knew its name.

William groaned, forlorn and forsaken. His hand and even his chest ached horribly. The darkness thickened. It seemed to pierce him to the heart.

Grace felt trapped and pressed and stifled—the way she had felt beneath the bed while Lady Lira chanted. The same presence was closing now, like slow-moving magma, this time unmediated by mirrors and words and woven symbols. It came slowly, surely, for her alone: the thing itself. The wicked weight was more than she could bear.

It was up to Grace. She planted her ax like a pillar of stone, and slowly she began to rise. Slowly she rose, as if in a dream, as if she were crushed by a murderous burden. She reached for William, caught his arm, decided to press his wounded hand. At first he would not move. But she gripped his wound till it bled once more, and felt him give.

They would have to try. She turned and splashed in heavily: one step, two. The third step seemed to be farther down than it was before—much farther down. When the water closed over their heads, she still had not found it.

Chapter 16
The Sniveling Boy

✳

SHE LET GO OF HER AX FIRST. Then, somewhere inside the warm womb of the current, Grace let go of William's hand. Was it instinct? Ah, but she knew the quality of her own instincts. Lady Lira had been right about her: she was merely a deserter. Now she had proven it clear to the end. Even as her breath grew short, she groped for him in the watery dark. But William was gone.

And then her breath grew very short. Groping still, her hands found the surface and brought it to her mouth. She gulped the darkness—three full breaths—and sank back into the river.

She began to wish things. She wished she had not stopped writing to her uncle. She wished she had not left Lance with Lady Lira. She even wished she had not run away from the red-bearded leader. She pondered her wishes under the water, and warm sorrow bathed her soul. Then, bit by bit, the memory of her sorrows ebbed away.

She mechanically reached for the surface again, and this time did not find it. She panicked, kicked upwards, knifed gasping into air. Unaccountably, the air she inhaled was no longer dark. She could see her hands in a shadowy light. The light was dim, like the first gray of dawn, just enough to hope by. So she worked her arms to stay afloat, to see what she could see. Before very long her shoulders were aching with the effort. She wanted to rest, to sink once more. But that would be the third time.

Meanwhile, the light grew, and her hopes with it. Walls and ceiling reappeared, slipped by. Then, ahead, the water began to glint and flash, as rivers do in the city at night. The pulse of the stream began to languish. It washed her into the glinting water and swept her round a bend. All at once she saw before her an open portal, radiant with a misty light. The light was not like that of the sun—it was harsh like the glare of a fire. Grace wafted through the portal like a freshly fallen leaf. She gently whirled in a vanishing eddy, and then the current was gone. Her feet touched bottom. Her body came to rest.

Where was she? Grace stood in the midst of a vast steaming lake, in a cavern so tall she could not see the roof of it. All about her, just as in Lady Lira's mansion, torches were burning in brackets on the walls, spaced like angels around the shore. The walls of the cavern were far apart, and some of the torches she could not see because of the steam on the water. It swirled about her like morning fog, strangely lit by tongues of fire. All was eerily quiet here save lapping waves and sputtering flames.

Grace stood brooding in the waters, immersed except for her head and shoulders. She listened to the emptiness, and found that because there was nothing to hear she listened all the harder. And then she did hear something—a still small splashing that filled the void. Out of the mists came a little lone creature, paddling towards her like a beaver out of practice. And like a beaver, it held a stick in its teeth as it swam. Before it reached her she knew him well—it was her very wet marmot. In his jaws was her once-lost ice ax.

She took the ice ax from his mouth and touched his sagging whiskers. "Welcome back, little marmot," she said. She gathered him up and he climbed to her shoulder. There he curled around her neck—a dripping marmot stole.

Now they were two. She felt his heart beating on the back of her neck, and bent her cheek to his. The silence returned but was not quite as empty as it had been. And yet, it was empty still. They needed a third.

When the marmot had caught his breath, Grace turned and asked him, "What should we do?" Immediately, the marmot stood up on the top of her shoulder—as if only now he had just remembered what he never should have forgotten. Then, without a word of explanation, he dove into the water and swam away.

"Where are you going?" Grace shouted. This was desertion.

The marmot disappeared in a white cloud of mist, and Grace lunged after him. "Wait up!" she called. Though he swam much faster than Grace could wade, she pressed her thighs against the water and followed in his wake. She guided herself by the sound of his splashing, and at last it stopped beneath a torch on the steam-wrapped shore ahead. She saw him there through the clouds.

And she also saw, as she forced her way, a man that stood in the water beside him. His back was slumped against the wall. His face hung down, shadowed by the torchlight. It had to be William.

Grace plunged to his side and held up his head—and William it was not. For a moment she gaped, adjusting disbelief. Then she kissed him, her own Lance Q. It was a modest kiss, but a sincere one. He slowly opened his weary eyes and fixed her with a faint smile. "About time," he murmured, and he kissed her weakly in return. All this while the marmot paddled at their side, looking back and forth from one to the other.

After more greetings of this sort, Grace stepped back to better appraise him. At once she noticed a thick iron chain that hung from the wall and vanished in the water. "Are you connected to that thing?" she asked.

He was. Lance raised his arms from the water and displayed his shackled wrists. They were bound together in one iron cuff attached to the iron chain. He yanked it a little to prove that it held.

"Not good," said Grace. She grabbed the chain and pulled it herself. It was stuck fast in the wall. But she had an idea in hand—her ax.

"Stand back," she told the marmot. The marmot, however, had disappeared again—which was just as well, since there was nothing for him to stand back on. Grace heaved the ice ax over her head, and with both her hands she brought it smashing against the rock where the chain was fixed. She did not expect much, and not much happened. The adze went glancing off the chain and shot towards Lance and neatly grazed his lips.

"Hey, watch it," he said.

"Sorry," said Grace. She took a firmer grip this time and gathered up her faith. The second blow struck square and solid, where it was meant, and the rock crumbled out from the roots of the chain. But the chain still held. Now, however, she believed it could be broken. One more time she reared the ax and swung it with mind and heart and strength. The dolorous stroke hit hard, hit home, and the chain sprang free from the rock. In fact, that was the least of it. The entire wall came tumbling down in huge cracked chunks that splashed around them, leaving a hole at the waterline that gaped like an open door.

Lance and Grace both gaped in return.

"Some ice pick you got," said Lance.

"It's not mine," said Grace. "I'm borrowing it."

They looked inside the broken wall. It seemed quite hollow. How far it went they could not tell. Grace climbed out of the water first, then pulled Lance up. He sat on the edge, feet in the water, clasping his fettered hands. They were jelly-soft and wrinkled from the wet. Meanwhile Grace stood up on tiptoe and plucked the torch from the bracket in the wall above them. She brought it down and thrust it in; their recess came to light. And it was more than a recess. They were poised on the verge of a prickly passage, rough with lava spikes. It was the sort of tunnel that Grace had seen before.

"Any other ways out of here?" she asked.

Lance shook his head. "Not for us," he replied. His voice wavered. He looked out over the rising steam and then looked back at Grace. "The water goes out through a tunnel to the bog," he said. "We saw the end of the tunnel on our way to her house that first time, remember? Anyway, that's how I was brought in here. On the other side of the lake is a landing—she took me there first, with all the marmots we caught." He shut his eyes and swallowed. "I wish I could forget," he whispered. "Let's go," he pleaded. "Please, let's go." Very quietly, Lance began to cry.

Grace looked down at the weeping boy and softly stroked his hair. She was all for going too—she just wished there were more of them to go.

And then there were more of them—too many more. From far across the lake she heard a terribly familiar voice.

"Stop the barge," it said. "Listen."

"What?" said another.

Why? thought Grace. She crouched on the brink and peered through the fog. Something silent slipped their way. But it wasn't a barge. It was her very own marmot, sleek as an otter, making his return. And that wasn't all. For behind the marmot came William himself, lumbering towards them with ice ax in hand. His hair was plastered on his brow, and his cheeks were wet and pale. He looked to Grace with the dazed expression of one whose mind is changed.

And then he was with her, raising himself from the waters of the lake, and the marmot with him, both man and marmot trying not to make a sound—which is much easier for a marmot. The bandage was gone from William's hand; the gaps in his flesh lay fully exposed.

Grace pressed his fingers and put her mouth to his ear. "I'm sorry," she whispered. "I let go."

He in turn brought his lips to her ear. "I let go too," he told her.

Then William turned his eyes to Lance. He knelt beside him and touched his hands. They were still firmly anchored by the chain in the water. The boy was free but not free, loose but unable to escape. Even if they could lift the chain, it was bound to make much noise.

William inspected all sides of the fetters, running his fingers over the iron as if he were fondling an ax. He found underneath what he had learned to look for—a keyhole. He hoped he had the key to match. He drew it from his pocket, set it in the lock.

But the key would not turn.

There was one thing to do then. He looked at Lance. "Lay your hands on the ledge," he told him. "Close your eyes."

The boy obeyed.

"Hold the chain steady," he told Grace.

She did.

He took careful aim. He would have to split the manacles just between the wrists. The adze sang downward. The iron sounded, pealed like a bell. And the fetters cracked and fell asunder, cloven like firewood.

Lance opened his eyes. There was blood on his hands. Grace, meanwhile, had kept her hold on the loosened chain. Now she lowered it into the water, and let go.

Then came the voice. "James?" it echoed. "It's time we checked on the sniveling boy."

Presumably that's what she did, but the three and the one slipped far away, and no one stayed to greet her.

Chapter 17
Lentil Soup

✳

A SNAP, A CRUMBLING OPENED HER EYES, and firelight churned on the rafters. Grace lay dry and deep in her blankets. They scratched her a little but she did not mind. She had no idea where she was, and she did not mind that either. Two more sleepers, swaddled in wool, were curled against her on either side, and that was enough.

She stretched her arms and brushed her fingers over a wooden floor. It was rough to the touch but soft on her back—as if she were lying on boughs of fir and not on planks of wood. Across the floor was a dark stone wall with a latticed window halfway up it. The window shuddered faintly. Strange as it seemed, snowflakes whirled thickly by, tapping on the glass. The light from the window was gray like winter dusk.

Grace turned from the storm and looked again at the roof beams in the firelight. She watched them for a long time. Then she half rose up to see the fire itself. It blazed at her feet, a generous fire in a fireplace made of round smooth stones improbably stacked like a house of eggs. Over the flames hung a blackened kettle, and stirring the kettle was a long wooden spoon, and holding the spoon was a fat old man who sat on a stool. His nose and cheeks shone red by the flames, and the top of his head shone too—for the man was as bald as his chimney stones. He was eyeing the kettle in a way that said he would love hot soup on a day like this.

Grace raised herself a little more and saw a steaming ball of fur rolled up inside the three stubby legs of the old man's stool. She vaguely recalled, like the memory of a dream, following the marmot through dark blowing snow, over piles of stones that were cold and wet—and soft, somehow, when she fell on them. She had followed him, too, down a rough lava passage, and let him choose the way. Then the walls had turned to ice, glistening and black, devouring the light like greedy mirrors that gave back no reflection. Deep in the ice were buried faces, set in long anguish. Grace had glimpsed them, hurried on. Then the ice was white and turquoise, opaque swirls and mingled veins—bright in the torchlight. Waterfalls crashed in liquid columns; others held silence, frozen in place like pillars of salt. One chamber there was—too splendid to ever forget—where groves of crystals clung to the walls, radiant, delicate, soon dissolved in a single breath. Then had come darkness and driven snow, and this warm place that shut the storm away.

The old man caught her eye and winked. "And a good night's morning to you," he told her. "Can't say you didn't take the best way. Weather like this, why should a body get up? Not sure why I did, anyways. It'll come to me, though." He stopped stirring the kettle and tasted the broth. "Ah, there it came, the *ratio surgendo!*"

Grace looked at him blankly.

"When you eat with the devil you need a long spoon," he said, holding up his own. "You know why?"

"Why?" said Grace.

"So if he doesn't mind his manners you can smack him 'twixt the eyes, and that makes him cross-eyed, a good Christian demon. Then he'll be behaved and say your name before he eats."

"My name?" she said.

"Yes, he'll say Grace."

"When would he say your name?"

"Why, when he wants a second helping. 'Chambers!' he will say. 'Chambers, ho! Another pot of soup!' And so I get my chamber pot and soup him on the head, and beat him out the door with my spoon!" The old man cackled with untold joy, and rapped on the kettle like a drum.

"So your name is Chambers?"

"Sir Chambers, officially," he said, throwing back his shoulders. "It's Chambers to you, though. We met last night or maybe this morning, but you were busy getting acquainted with those blankets. I was hoping you'd come, too—when I saw you yesterday."

Grace looked confused.

Chambers pointed his spoon behind him. "I keep an eye on things in the pond out back. Had a pretty close watch on you most of the time till it clouded up."

Grace still looked bewildered.

"Pond don't work when the sun's not out," he explained.

"You could see us?" Grace said. She remembered seeing others in the lid of the silver box on the mountain. How strange to think she might have been in someone else's picture.

"You was quite a show!" he cackled. "That's one mean woman. Always told your uncle he shouldn't put you up to this. But here you are, still in the flesh, so I guess he was right. Nothing recedes like regress, when you're headed that way."

He spooned out a bowl of soup and set it by her feet. She had to sit all the way up to reach it and drank directly from the bowl, holding it with both hands. The soup was full of tiny beans that warmed her stomach wonderfully.

"You know my uncle?" she asked.

"He knows me," he said. "Haven't seen him lately, though. I imagine you will soon—hard to say. Man pulls a stunt like that and who knows where he's gone to—or his ax, neither."

"How soon is soon?" said Grace. She was anxious. "When do we see him?"

"When it's finished," he said.

"Which is when?"

"It ain't finished till Lira's finished. You help your friend there find the ax. Then let him do the finishing."

"So why didn't Garth just give him the ax?"

"Because it's not just given. It's found, too. You only know how to use the dern thing if you've looked a long time."

"Then I'm afraid I've botched it already," said Grace. "I was supposed to find directions for us in the summit book—but I couldn't read fast enough."

"Don't worry," he said. "You prob'ly found plenty good directions. Not all directions is east, west, north, and south."

He filled himself a bowl of soup and drank it off, coating his hoary mustache green. "I know a little about that book. It takes you back to get you forward. It opens above and it closes below. You start at the middle and belong in the beginning and live in a blank at the end."

"That's right," she said. "The last pages were blank."

"You know my theory?" he asked, licking his mustache white again. He leaned over and whispered it in her ear: "Invisible ink." Then he raised his eyebrows and nodded his chin in a most knowing fashion.

Grace decided on one more try. "Well, you know my theory?" she said in reply. "It's that I'm not even supposed to be here! Lance and I, we ditched our group—I don't know how long ago. But our leader has got to be worried by now—so we have to get back, see? It would be mean not to."

"Your leader?" said Chambers. "The ninny with the red beard? The one that lost the key to his nose, so he always has to pick it?"

She nodded solemnly.

"Ah, then don't worry, Grace. I told him you went home."

"But that's a lie!"

"Is it?"

"Of course. I'm here, not home."

"Well, *semper lentus sed numquam certus* is precisely what your uncle says: always slow but never sure."

"What does that have to do with anything?"

"I'm not sure. But if you want to get picky about it, you could say your home is here and mine is not."

"So where's yours?"

"No place I know—that's the point. But take, say, this little room in the glacier cave just up the hill. Maybe you been to it on your way down here. The chamber's lined with these feathery crystals—no place prettier; no place more like home to me. What I'm never sure about is what to do once I get there. If I go inside, the crystals disappear when I step on 'em. Even breathing makes 'em collapse. But if I stay outside, I can't see 'em all. So usually I go inside. But I can never look it all in. Once I tried to take some crystals with me, but they melted in my hand. Once I carved my initials in the ice, but they melted too. Once I brought some blankets and slept there. Nearly froze. I woke up and thought to myself, *So, I've slept here.* Then I chopped a bench in one wall where I could sit and look, and it didn't look any different from standing up. The next time, I brought some paper and tried to draw it all down, which I couldn't do, so I started writing instead. I wrote a whole list of words: *splendid, dazzling, radiant, delicate, exquisitious.* But the crystals hung there in the cave and the words pooled on the page—they weren't connected. So you see? I'm never quite sure how to make myself at home, even when I think I'm there."

Long before he had finished, Grace figured she was. She sank back in her blankets and resigned herself to many blank pages. "I'm not sure I follow," she murmured. "I guess I'm a little slow."

"It's the soup," replied Chambers. "Lentils make *lentus*."

The window was dark now; the panes were still tapping as Grace fell asleep again.

❋

Her eyes next opened in a shaft of sun. The fire had burned low, and the blankets beside her were broken empty like old cocoons. From an open door a quiet breeze came in and teased her hair. The air was fresh, and the walls and rafters were strangely bright, aglow with more than the morning sun.

She rose and went to the door—and saw why. All about her the land shone white beneath a warm blue sky. Whether the ground was barren or fertile, boulders or bear grass, she could not tell, for all of it was smothered with snow. There were no trees in sight. At her feet a pure white plain descended to a lake. Its waters, dark against dazzling shores, were ruffled by the breath of summer come again. Grace wondered if this were Chambers' pond. Above the lake rose a massive mountain that made it look like a pond indeed. The top of the peak was a broad smooth splendor; below it were cliff bands, reds and yellows, laced to perfection with new-fallen snow; then a sweep of glaciers that for all she knew came clear to the lake. It was a mountain that astonished. She guessed it to be the North Queen, and as she found out later, she was right.

Presently she saw the others. They were walking up from the lake to the cabin with pails of water in their hands. Lance, she noticed, went shirtless. The veins in his arms were sharply etched from the strain and pull of the water buckets. He looked up at Grace when they came near, but not for very long.

For breakfast they sat in the cabin door, eating oatmeal from wooden bowls and saying little. It was too good a morning to spoil with speech. So the wind and the sun conversed alone—and talked the snow away. Drops fell down from the cabin eaves: few, many, many more, joining in a stream. The line of footsteps coming from the lake began to brim like springs. There were trickling sounds of water unseen, and then, in hollows, snow gave way to rivulets, noisily drenched in its own decay.

"Be all gone by afternoon," Chambers said. "Still summer, even though these hills get confused sometimes."

He looked out over his so-called pond, its surface broken by the warm full wind. Then he winked at Grace. "Don't work so good in the breeze, neither," he said, "but I'll keep an eye on it for you. Maybe we can find where you're off to next."

Grace hoped to herself that the wind would hold. She did not feel like being off to anywhere, that day.

She got her wish. Morning melted to afternoon, and they lolled beside the cabin, soaking in the sun, drying their clothes in the breeze. Chambers bandaged William's hand, applying to the wound three drops from a vial he had from Lady Demaris. "Practically neighbors," he said. Then he found three old canvas packs and set about sewing them up. Lance offered to help and stabbed his thumb with the needle six times. Grace volunteered to coach him then, and Chambers and William left them be. She knew little enough about sewing herself. Nevertheless, always slow but never sure, they sat on the doorstep and went to work.

At first they confined their conversation to the wonders of needle and thread. But by the time she had bled her own thumb dry, Grace found the courage to speak her mind, and said she was sorry—she really was sorry—for running out on him just the other day at Lady Lira's house, and that even though she had sort of had to leave, it was the way she had felt that counted, and, well, she hoped he would forgive her, that's all, to which Lance replied that the fault was his, whereupon Grace reclaimed sole credit, whereupon Lance answered firmly that he alone deserved title to guilt, at which Grace insisted that she and she only was ever to blame, to which Lance said, "What*ever*," to which he inadvertently added an exceedingly long and resonant fart. And Grace laughed, and then Lance laughed, and then they both laughed together as new old friends.

When they had got their breath (and cleared the air), they sat quite close and told their tales. Grace went first, and Lance believed her, every word; nothing seemed too awful or too wonderful anymore. Even so, Grace kept one part back, and it was not until Lance had had his turn, and the packs lay beside them against the cabin, long-since sewn up, that she confided her final secret—that, according to Lady Demaris, she was part-fairy. "She says that's why I see certain things."

"No kidding," said Lance. He edged away to regard her from a distance.

"Do you wish I weren't?" she asked, wishing she weren't, and wishing she had kept it to herself.

"Sure—I mean, no—I mean—"

"You do! Admit it! You think I'm something totally bizarre!" she whined.

"Listen to me, Lance. Most of me is normal. It's just a little bit that's different.

It's like I still look the same and everything."

Grace knew she was floundering. She felt her face grow hot, her eyes grow moist. Without really knowing what she did, she jumped to her feet and ran away, out across the plain. The snow had all but melted.

Meanwhile, Chambers had taken William inside, where they pored over wrinkled brown maps. "Don't know where you're going to," he said, "but at least you can get the lay of the land."

The maps showed features that William's did not. Lava caverns and glacier caves and a maze of underground lakes and streams were marked in red and silver and blue. William whistled softly when Chambers traced the length of their subterranean journey. They had surfaced at the snout of the Mirror Glacier, on the north flank of the Center Queen. Chambers' cabin lay just below, on a high broad saddle that separated the Center Queen from the North.

Small green circles marked gathering places, on meadow slopes or in forest glades. Here, explained Chambers, footraces and dances and song contests lasted far into midsummer evenings.

"Song contests?" William said, coloring slightly.

"The same," said Chambers. "Should've seen Colin go to it last time. Nobody better. But if you're still around by the next full moon, maybe you could challenge him."

"Maybe I could," said William.

Purple dots were scattered across the map below timberline. "Huckleberries," Chambers said, patting his rotund belly. "The very best patches. Getting to be the right season for 'em too."

Other spots on the map were marked with crossed ice axes.

"Mines?" asked William.

"No, sir. Battlegrounds. Historic sites. Places where the lackeys of the Lava Beast have had to reckon with the sorry likes of us."

William saw that the crossed axes stretched far westward, into the lowland forests.

"Those are the oldest battles," said Chambers. "Lord knows, few of 'em won, and not enough of 'em fought. The ax doesn't show up all that often—and when it's around, it don't get used enough. We've lost a lot of ground."

He looked up at William, paused and spoke: "If the ax comes to you, William, let it do its work. It never strikes at the wrong time—that's what's good about it. Nobody gets hurt but what's supposed to get hurt."

William turned pale. He would rather no one at all got hurt, especially he himself.

"We're part of a mighty tradition, William, that's got all the appearance of a lost cause. But one comes—maybe soon—who's said he'll destroy the destroyers of the earth. Some say he's a man. Some say he's a lamb. Some say he's a white fawn. Whatever he is, all that we've lost he's already won. Don't ask me how. Just fight the good fight, man. That's all we're asked."

*

Outside the cabin the snow had vanished, and dark green heather stretched away in sodden slopes. The heather blossoms, tiny red and tiny white, tossed lightly in the breeze—the white like shoulders on a blouse, the red like little bells. That was Grace's impression, anyway, and where she knelt she could see them well. She was far from the cabin, out of breath, crying no longer. The snow-soaked heather had cooled her knees and quieted her troubled heart. *Fairies must like heather*, she thought. But her legs were cold—that much she had to admit.

So she got up to walk, and not yet ready to face the others, she headed for the lake. As she walked, the west wind poured across her face, went streaming through her hair. She felt blown into place with the blank blue sky; she felt flung away with the heather. She could not see off the edge of this world to any forest below. Were it not for the lake and the North Queen above it, Grace would have had little sense of walking anywhere at all. The vast sameness, the windy expanse, seemed to mourn its own beauty. For a moment she was part of it.

She reached the darkly lapping lake and looked for her reflection. But the wind confused the waters. *Don't work so good in the breeze*, she thought. That was fine with her, wasn't it?

She saw a path in the heather along the bank. It beckoned her—that is the power of every path—and she followed. She walked it just to walk, or maybe to circle the shore, or maybe to keep warm. Sometimes the path crossed tiny streams that spilled into the lake. Each was only a step across, but she leapt them all with sailing grace, just for the joy of leaping.

She was halfway around when she met with a stream too wide to jump. It was boulder-strewn and milky blue, swift and noisy, cold to the touch. She was not about to wade it. This was far enough. She sat herself down on a rock by the lakeshore, folding her arms around her knees to keep the breeze away. Across the lake and up the slope she could just see the cabin. It seemed very small from where she was, little more than a dot on a map. Above it domed the Center Queen, half-forgotten, less a place than a silvery dream. It was odd for a mountain to still exist, once she had already been there.

While she was gazing, two small figures came down from the cabin—to fetch a pail of water, she supposed. Which two they were she could not tell. Then, from over the western horizon, a single figure came gliding towards them. Was it the third of three, or another? Again she could not say. Those from the cabin reached the shore, and there the other joined them. Perhaps they were talking. But Grace heard only the wind.

When her eyes grew weary of prying from a distance, she fell to watching the lake at her feet. The surface was broken by gold-flecked ripples, and the waters were dark like buried ice—she could not see the bottom. In a way she was glad of it; she would shed no tear if her vision should perish. But in another way she desperately wanted to see whatever there was to see beneath the surface.

And then, she did. The lake at her feet grew suddenly calm, and in the water—not reflected but real in its presence, the lovely face of a very young woman was gazing up at Grace. Her hair was golden, floating and falling, and twined with lavender shooting stars. Her eyes burned green, and her face and throat shone pure as the morning snow. The woman's arms were sapling smooth, and her breasts hovered deep in the icy waters like lilies drowned in crystal black. And fast in the grip of the woman's right hand, slowly rising toward the surface, was an ice ax.

It was unlike any ice ax Grace had seen. The head of the ax shone brilliantly, like Sirius on a winter's eve. The wooden shaft was long and dark, and it shivered with curiously carved designs. Grace did not know which to watch—the woman's eyes or the rising ax. So she watched both, and neither.

The head of the ice ax closed with the surface, then broke the water like a silvery fish. The shaft slid upward, glistening wet, at crooked odds with its lower self till the woman's hand slipped out of the lake and held it completely aloft. The hand inclined the ax towards Grace. It hovered at arm's reach. As if in a trance, Grace put out her trembling hand and closed it around the head of the ax—thumb beneath the adze, fingers around the pick. She had it securely.

Or it had her. For in the moment she grasped it, her arm heaved forward out of the socket. It was like shaking hands with a man who decides to throw you to the ground. But the ax was different—it threw her in the lake. She was yanked from her rock with swiftest ease, and once she was in, the ice ax ripped itself from her hand.

Stunned by the cold, Grace thrashed about till her hands and knees struck bottom. She raised herself on her arms—and stopped. The unfathomed waters were lapping at her elbows. It was that deep, no deeper. There was no ax, no woman. Grace lunged ashore and stood up shaking, clutching herself. At her feet the water chopped and slapped, just as it had before.

She would have to think about this. First, however, she would have to dry out. So she lay down flat on the bare outcrop. There, out of the wind, the sun-warmed rock brought comfort. She wondered if William would have had the strength to wrest the ax away—that is, if it really were there, which it was not, in the end. In the beginning, though, the woman and the ax were more there than anything Grace had ever seen. The burning green eyes, the utter loveliness of the woman's face—Grace could not forget them. She would ask Chambers who it was.

Grace started back when she was warm enough to walk. Her clothes were still wet, but the afternoon was too far gone for the sun to dry them—they would have to be hung by the fire. Three figures remained on the far lakeshore. They turned as Grace approached. She made out William by his up-and-down posture, Lance by his practiced slouch. The third was a woman in a plain gray smock. She guessed, she hoped, and then she knew: it was Lady Demaris. Grace waved her arms and they all waved back. She could not help running the rest of the way.

"Lady Demaris!" she called. "What are you doing here?"

The woman caught Grace in her arms and kissed her on the forehead. "Dear Grace," she said, "I came for news of all of you. I was hoping Sir Chambers might have seen you in his tarn. But here you are, and this whole hour I have been marveling at your adventures."

In her hand she waved a graceful bouquet of larkspur and purple asters. A basket of huckleberries, plump to bursting, lay at her feet. Lance's lips were already dyed a cyanotic blue.

"Have some, Grace," he said.

She ignored him without really meaning to.

"You look wet," said William. "Did you fall in the lake?"

"Not exactly," she answered. "I have to tell you—I think I saw the ax."

"The ax?" said William.

"The *ath?*" said Lance.

She felt the wind dry her lips as she told what she had seen. William looked nervous. "Then maybe we should go back," he stammered. "Maybe I could grab it." A new breeze gusted across the lake, and William's suggestion fell curiously flat on the waters.

"Lady Demaris," said Grace, "do you know who I saw? The woman had green eyes like yours—and like your sister's."

Lady Demaris smiled softly. "That is because she is our sister. You have seen the young and beautiful Stella. But you will not find her here, for though she lives in the waters of a lake, it is not this one."

She paused and sighed. "Years ago, before Lady Lira parted from us, and when our father, Lord Linton, was yet alive, we all four lived in the cottage by the Center Queen. No one delighted to climb with our father more than our sister Stella. From the first day she could wield an ax she followed his steps on every Queen. The North Queen, though, was much her favorite. When Stella grew older—and our father too old—she spent many a summer day alone, toiling up the glaciers of her best-loved mountain. On top is a great snowy cra-ter—look, you can see the edge of it—always filled with a deep blue lake. The lake is said to be so pure that the stars themselves come down to drink. There on the crater rim, late into the summer night, Stella would linger and gaze upon the ice-bright stars drowned fast in the lake. All night she would watch, until Venus alone lay bathing in the dawn.

"One morning, the dawn of deep midsummer, she did not come home from her all-night vigil. We all grew worried, our father especially, and I remember the rattle of his ax on the ice as we hurried up the mountain. All that we found was her small wooden ax, plunged upright on the eastern rim."

"The one you gave me?" asked Grace.

Lady Demaris thought for a moment. "Yes," she said, "the very one."

Then she continued. "We did not know at first where Stella had gone. Only when our father took the key to the summit of the Center Queen, and opened the Shield, and read in the Book, did he find that Stella had given herself to the crater lake, to live beneath its waters with the stars in the night. For all is recorded in the Book of the Queens, and some things are foretold. And each living person may only look once in the Book."

"The book I read?" asked Grace. "Why didn't you tell us this about the key and the book before?"

"Yes," said William, "you yourself said you didn't know what the key unlocked."

"Well!" said Lady Demaris. She laughed merrily and waved them off with her spray of flowers. "You did not expect all the family secrets at once, did you?"

"I guess not," said William. "But do you think we could find your sister on top of the North Queen? Would she give us the ax?"

"Perhaps," laughed Lady Demaris. And then, more seriously, "Very likely." And then, in a grave voice, "Leave at dawn. No earlier, for the night is nearly moonless and the dangers are many. But leave at dawn, before Lady Lira gets wind of your presence. Her eyes are close, and her dagger is near."

"We will," promised William.

"Then farewell," said Lady Demaris abruptly. "I must return home before nightfall. My heart stays with you. May your steps be firm. Give my love to my dear sister, should you be able."

With that she gathered the basket of huckleberries under her arm and strode away down the lakeshore path. The wind had calmed; the lake was still. They watched her depart in the yellowing silence of late afternoon. Before she left the shore, Lady Demaris turned to bid a last goodbye, waving her larkspur and aster bouquet. Grace waved in return, and glanced at the woman's reflection in the water.

Her hand gripped William like the jaws of a weasel: the face in the water was hard and cold. One arm cradled a snarling marmot; the other raised a dagger aloft. A puff of wind erased the image, and the woman turned, with her flowers and her basket, and was gone.

"What's the matter?" said William.

"That's not Lady Demaris," she whispered. "It's Lady Lira."

"Are you sure?" he asked. He fixed his eyes on the vanishing figure.

She was sure.

"Lance, did you see anything strange?" he said.

No answer came from behind them. They turned. Lance lay flat on his back in the heather, his head rolled listlessly to one side. The trickle from his lips shone brightest blue.

Chapter 18
The Sky Below

✳

OUTSIDE THE CABIN THE HEATHER BURNED ORANGE; the sun was aground on the edge of the world, nearly interred in a wilderness sepulcher. Inside the cabin a small fire puttered against the shadows. Lance lay deathly still by the hearth. The others crouched beside him.

"One more huckleberry," Chambers said, "and he'd a been dead for the rest of his life. What a hazard that woman is." He shook his head.

"So he'll make it?" asked William.

"Let's hope so," he answered. "*Numquam certus.*"

Grace looked on Lance as if her eyes could wake what slept there. "He's so pale—he's hardly breathing," she said. "There's nothing we can do?"

"Not here," said Chambers. "Up yonder, maybe." He nodded towards the rose-flushed peak in the window.

"Up there?" she said. "But that was *her* idea. That's right where she wants us. Besides, we can't believe her story, can we? I mean, why would she tell us the truth?"

"Because she had nothing to gain by lying," said Chambers. "I could've set you straight on Stella—it would only have exposed her to tell another tale. When you disguise yourself as an honest woman, honesty is part and parcel of the disguise."

"Then how did she know about the key and the book when Lady Demaris didn't?" asked William.

"She knew by cheating on her father," said Chambers. He sat down thoughtfully on the hearth, then spoke to them with a new directness. "When old Lord Linton left on his last climb of the Center Queen, he made his daughters promise not to follow him. Soul of goodness that she is, Lady Demaris stayed at home—but Lady Lira snuck up to the edge of the summit and saw her father read in the Book. He was sobbing as he read, and looking up, he saw her, and sobbed all the harder. That made Lady Lira ashamed, and she came to him. 'It is not for Stella that I weep,' he told her, 'but for you, my daughter.' Having said this, his heart broke in two, and he died. Lady Lira reached for the Book, but a great wind blew it shut, and the Shield closed over it. She reached for the key in the lock, but it vanished—right in the grasp of her hand, it vanished. All this I saw in my pond."

"And you have seen Stella too?" said Grace.

"Yes," said Chambers, "but only on the morning she failed to return. That's how her sisters know what became of her—I'm the one that told 'em. But today, Lady Lira couldn't stay quiet about the Book. It's on her mind constantly. The Lava Beast, see, wants it destroyed."

William took the key from his pocket and held it up in the firelight. "So she wants this too," he said. He offered the key to Chambers. "Maybe you should keep it."

"Nope," said Chambers—"you'll still be needing it. When you reach the lake atop the North Queen, you must give it to Stella. It's your key to the ax."

"But won't Lady Lira be up there waiting for us?" said Grace.

"Not if you leave tonight," he said. "No reason to wait till dawn—even without much of a moon, it's never really dark on a glacier. She only wanted to delay you. Lady Lira has a nightly appointment to keep: the Lava Beast never likes to miss a meal. But she'll be back in the morning, first thing. You know how fast she is on her feet."

Grace felt an appalling hollowness inside. The firelight on the four stone walls seemed so much better than another icy peak in outer darkness. "Wouldn't it be safer to stay here?" she said. "I mean . . ." Her voice trailed off.

Chambers looked her in the eye. "Lots safer," he replied.

Grace realized then that some things were like this. You didn't so much decide to do them as they decided to be done by you. It was as it had been when she had fallen into the underground river. Once in, she couldn't decide to swim upstream.

She reached down and stroked her marmot. His fur was already warmed by the fire. "I'll go if you go," she whispered.

They packed quickly; the window was already dark. Sir Chambers gave them a frayed rope and some rusty creepers, stiff woolen cloaks, and mittens with holes. He filled their bellies with soup and their packs with provision, and showed them to the door. They were ready that fast.

Grace stood outside shivering in the shady damp, not really listening as the two men plotted the route. She heard a few words like *hourglass, schrund, cornice*— but what she saw through the open door was Lance lying deathly pale by the fire. Then the door closed. They belonged to the stars.

William went first. The heather was uneven, and not yet adjusted to the subtlety of starlight, he stumbled repeatedly in the dark. He knew the climb would take all night, and Grace did not. She was going to ask but saved her breath—silence is swift, and it seemed to her that William was too. She hoped that she could keep the pace—and keep the peace as well. She promised herself she would not get angry. As they passed through the night a breeze still blew, and it brushed her lips like wings of a moth.

The lake slipped by, bristling with broken stars. Halfway around it they found and followed the wrinkled noise of the stream that Grace had found by day. It led their feet on spongy slopes, up, away, till heather disappeared. Moraines arose, darker than sky, and the stream sank into stones. They heard it sound beneath their feet, full of noise, bereft of substance, and kept on following what they heard. By echo of the buried stream they wound a way through walls of rubble, grateful not to climb them.

Then moraines melted away; the hidden gush of the stream fell silent. Stones lay scattered, and under them, like a polished floor half-hidden by marbles, was hard and gleaming ice. Before them now rose the dim white veil of a glacier.

They stopped.

"Tired?" asked William.

"No," said Grace. Oddly enough, she was telling the truth.

William unpacked the rope and the creepers, and they put them on. When all was ready he felt her knot twice over with his fingertips. Then he left, and she heard his ax click against stones on the ice. The sound was fading when the rope tugged hard—it nearly sent her sprawling. *Not so fast!* she almost called. But this time she wanted things to be different. She wanted to keep up with him, to weed the tiny grudge before it flourished in her heart.

So Grace doggedly went to it, stumbling at first, muttering at times; but at length the glacier lost its stone cover, and her feet bit smoothly across the ice. The rope began to glide, a single canoe on glassy waters. And Chambers was right—it is never really dark on a glacier. Even without the light of the moon, their path was strangely luminous. It was especially bright where the ice was covered with skiffs of fresh snow. Up here it had not all melted.

Soon, however, the glacier was torn by a criss-cross snarl of dark crevasses, none of them wide, but all of them unimaginably deep (or so Grace imagined). Most she could stride across, a few she had to hop. But one small step for Grace was a leap of faith for the nerve-wracked marmot, and before very long she stowed him away in the top of her pack.

Beyond this maze the steely ice gave way to the older snow that remained from winter. It steepened quickly, and hid beneath a mantle of the snow freshly fallen. William kicked through the loose layer into the firm, and made a ladder of steps for Grace. Her creepers found good purchase at first, but as the slope grew steeper, the steps grew smaller. Soon she stood on only her toes and hung her heels in space.

Because of the steepness, William had begun to chop the footholds with his ax. Grace waited beneath him in showers of crystals, more at leisure to glance about as each new step was made. The mountainside was high and airy. This made her grateful for the relative darkness; it muffled the distance to the glacier below and obliterated all else—all, that is, save a faint speck of light beneath her heels, hovering like an earthbound star. That, she knew, was the fire-lit window of Chambers' cabin. Should she slip, she might float like a feather to his comforting hearth.

Slowly, unsurely, William lengthened their ladder of steps. The night already seemed far gone. On left and on right the stars had begun to disappear. But it was not the dawn that erased the stars—it was cliffs of rock. The snow that they climbed was pinching down in a narrow funnel, buried from the sky. The walls of the funnel were tall enough to eat the heavens away. It was dark inside.

They were deep in this cleft when something whizzed by Grace's head— something swift, small, like a spring-crazed swallow. Then, gone before it came, something else dove past her ear.

"Quick!" she heard. "Up here."

She had no choice. The rope popped her up like a bucket on a windlass and pulled her under a balcony of snow. It was a sort of cave that she suddenly entered—an overhung crevasse, really. They stood inside on a small ice shelf. Outside, the air screamed softly.

"Steam vents up above," said William. He was matter-of-fact in his explanation. "They warm the snow, and that loosens the rocks. Once we get above this spot, the chute opens up. If we stay to the side we'll miss the worst of it."

Just as he finished, an ugly volley raked the roof. Then it was silent, and the silence lasted for several minutes. Did he dare? William took a deep breath and edged outside. On cue, a single stone shot over his head. He ducked back in.

"This is serious," said Grace.

He looked at her, but could not really see her face in the dark.

"Aren't you scared?" she asked.

"Me?" he replied. The pronoun was alien to his person; it was as if he had specified someone else.

Another precarious calm descended. The longer it lasted, the more fragile it seemed. But they could not get past *seemed*. The problem with fate was its un-guessability. So William stopped guessing and peeked outside. It was still quiet.

He stood out from their shelter and strained his eyes for a way to get over the bergschrund. It belted the waist of their hourglass funnel, splitting the ice from wall to wall. Next to one wall, however, the gap was bridged by a sliver of snow. He carefully traversed to it, staying beneath the bergschrund lip. The bridge was nearly vertical, and so slender that he feared to touch it. But there was no other way.

Before committing himself, he chopped two steps with delicate strokes. Nothing toppled. So he mounted the steps in the way that a cat might hop up on broken glass. Then he chopped two more. And two more. The top of the bridge, he knew, would be the weakest part. He reached it nimbly, poised himself for an uncertain moment, and drove his ice ax over the lip. He felt the shaft sink firm to the hilt. It was blessed assurance.

Grace watched his shadow vanish over the brink, then waited until the rope pulled taut. She was more ready than she knew. With fear-born ease she crawled to the bridge, swam to the top, and flung herself gasping over the lip—gasping because of the furry paws that had her by the throat. It was splendidly done, and she knew it. From there she stumbled up easier ground to where William waited beside the wall, away from the center of the funnel. He was pulling the rope around his ax, which was plunged in the snow by his feet. When she reached his side he dropped the rope and solemnly shook her mitten.

"Hard part's over," he said.

Grace smiled in the dark. They were climbers.

So they climbed on. The slope grew wider, the going more gentle—gentle enough for the marmot to walk on his own four feet. They veered away from the center of the bowl, whence sometimes drifted the whir and clatter of falling rocks—which minutes before could break their bones but now would never hurt them. Grace felt almost smug.

But without warning, her satisfaction wilted in a sulfurous cloud of steam. It hissed at them from vents in the rocks—noxious, defiling, odor most foul. It drilled their skulls like a vengeful dentist who will not let up, no, not even when you are squirming in the chair and tears are raining down your cheeks. Grace squeezed her head between her hands; she marveled at the pain.

And it got worse. New gusts of wind redoubled the fumes, served them up in a cold force-feeding. She choked, she spat, she staggered about in dull, disjointed steps. Grace wanted to stop. She wanted to chop out her grave in the snow.

But gradually Grace found reason to breathe. For bit by bit, like fog in sun, the sulfur was washed from the air. As they climbed higher the wind blew fresh, the steam vents left their hissing behind. As an emblem of hope they saw on their right a crescent moon, newly risen, and on either side the mountain began to curve away in silvered purity—not a concave curve, as in the sulfurous bowl they emerged from, but a perfect convex rounding. This was the final summit cone, higher by far than the sister Queens they dimly saw below them. Far to their right, at the edge of the stars, crept a faint glow—very faint—promising the dawn. Overhead the Dragon threatened, the Dippers poured out blessing.

The snowslope grew a little steeper, though not too steep for the marmot. They switchbacked up in angling symmetry, kicking, breathing, rising in rhythm. Grace felt as if she were climbing on another mountain, somehow separate from the one below shedding rocks and steam. This mountain floated, disembodied, unwilling to mingle its roots with earth. It was a place, she thought, where the stars might dwell. She wanted to climb it world without end, to keep on moving and stay where she was and never reach the top.

So it was all too soon, to Grace's mind, when they crested the crater rim. Here the breeze blew strong across their faces. They stood on the edge of a vast snowy ring, a perfect circle. The summit was everywhere and nowhere, and for this reason the North Queen had never been dear to William's heart. It was one mountain that would not yield the desired feeling of conquest.

Grace stepped towards the inner brink, but William pulled her back. "There are cornices here on the south and the west," he explained. "It's not safe near the edge." Grace did not know what cornices were. They sounded quite sinister.

William led them around the crater to the opposite side—the northern edge—a quarter-mile distant. They swept the rim like the hand of a clock, and when the clock struck twelve they shed their packs, knelt on the verge, and peered inside. Their eyes were watering in the wind, but still they saw. They saw virgin snowslopes drop away, cupped in starlit stasis. And when they looked to the bottom they thought that they saw through a hole in the earth to the sky below—except the sky in the crater was so much purer, so much more abounding in the brightest of stars, that it couldn't have been this world's sky. No, not the sky of this world at all. Grace told herself it was simply a lake. Her eyes knew better.

For a very long time they contemplated the crystal shores, the starry depths, and lost themselves in looking. The dawn began paling the eastern sky, but they did not know it.

William was first to look up. He could see Grace's face in the early light. It shone with its own morning glory.

"See anything?" he asked.

"Stars," she murmured.

He rose to his feet and suggested they go down.

"How?" said Grace. To her it looked steep.

By way of reply he mimed a way to descend steep snow—plunging the heels, locking the knees. She would go first, he said. That way he could stop her on the rope if she slid toward the water.

Grace had her doubts, but she got up anyhow. "Stay here," she told the marmot. And with that she tottered over the brink. Just one step took her out of the wind, into an amphitheater of calm. Nothing appeared save water below, sky above, snow between—a curious three-part universe. For the first time she noticed the lip of the crater across the way and to her right. It was overhung, curled inwards like ocean surf. This, she guessed, was the shape of a cornice, thrust by the wind. As she descended she saw it more clearly, outlined in the dawn.

Her heels sank firmly into the snow. To descend was more like floating than walking. She relaxed in the rhythm, forgot to fear, and soon drew up at the margin of the lake. Fewer stars shone overhead now; the sky was losing its night hue, and the lake was gaining a turquoise glow. The waters spread motionless at her feet.

By the time William joined her, she had stomped out a platform big enough for both of them. William nested the rope in the snow. He didn't want it wet.

"See anything now?" he asked.

Grace looked everywhere. Her toes were growing cold on the platform. "Nothing," she said.

"So now what?"

Grace had an idea. "Remember what Chambers said about the key? About giving it to Stella? Maybe you should toss it in and let her know we're here."

William shrugged his shoulders. *Why not?* he seemed to say. And he bit off one mitten to search his pockets barehanded. He drew out the key and held it aloft as one holds up a glass of wine. Then, plunging his ax well out of the way, he hurled the key in a glittering arc. It met the lake with a comic *bluup!* Ring after ring rippled out from its sinking place. They watched the outer ring grow large, large as the lake itself,

> *As when a stone is into water cast,*
> *One circle doth another circle make,*
> *Till the last circle touch the bank at last.*

And at that very moment, the moment of touching, the crater shook with a sharp report that jolted them to their knees. Their little platform bobbed beneath them.

"We're floating!" cried William.

They were. Their platform had calved off into the lake. Now it was a snowberg, drifting from the bank. Grace's ax was planted beside them, but William's was not. It was not on shore, either.

"No more ax," said William.

Grace said nothing. She trembled on her knees and did not move for fear that their floating island would overturn. The water around them was swimming-pool blue, but it was not for swimming.

And so they wafted out from shore, rocking as in a cradle. By and by they came to rest at the center of the lake, marking the spot where the key had sunk. And there, quietly, not as bursting vision but as simple fact, the lovely face appeared once more, smiling up at Grace.

"She's here," whispered Grace.

William lurched to Grace's side, and the berg tipped hard. They tossed up and down like a tree in the wind and nearly fell in the water.

When the snowberg settled he peered off the edge. "I don't see her," he said. "Did I scare her away?"

"No," replied Grace. "She's smiling again. I think you amuse her."

Grace saw the woman's hair luxuriate in the water. It swayed like tall wild grass in autumn. A circlet on her brow shone not with flowers but with gems—or were they stars? But the eyes, the lips, the lovely breasts: it was the same woman once again.

> And she is known to every star,
> And every wind that blows.

The ancient ice ax rested in her right hand, its silver head burning like winter sun. It was slowly drifting towards the surface.

"Give me your hand," Grace whispered to William. She guided it out over the water, poising his fingers where the ax would emerge.

"When it comes up," she told him, "pull very hard."

"But I don't see it," William said.

Even as he spoke, the gleaming adze broke the surface and his hand recoiled. The dripping head of the ax rose higher; the dark wood slid like a sapling from the earth. *TAKE ME UP*, he read on the shaft. Then—and William saw it—the strong slender hand pushed out of the water, raising the ax aloft in its grip.

"Take it," urged Grace.

William moved with glacial swiftness—which is to say, he did not perceptibly move at all. The arm of the woman inclined the ax until it hovered beside his bare and listless hand. A bead of sweat dripped off one fingertip.

"Take it," said Grace.

And then he did. He gripped the ax and it was his. The woman's hand released the shaft and sank beneath the waters. Grace glimpsed her face for one last time before it disappeared beneath them. At once they started floating back to shore.

"She's pushing us, I think," said Grace.

William hardly noticed. He held the ax at arm's length, possessed by fear and holy disbelief. He looked on nothing else.

Suddenly the air was perplexed with song. Wordless notes, wildly sweet, swirled around them like water round an oar.

"Look!" called Grace. She pointed to the crater rim.

Shining round about its lip, spaced like the stars on Stella's brow, stood brilliant white figures, blazing in the dawn. One light only hung now in the sky, sole director of the song. No other stars remained aloft, unless—but no, they refused to think it—unless the singers on the summit were the stars themselves, come down with wetted fingers to cool the tongue of lowly earth, to grant one brief taste of the music of the spheres. Their harmony whirled like rising steam, it echoed through the crater like swiftly shooting stones, it lapped at their ears like quiet waters.

Once, a long time before, William's mother had awakened him deep in the night and led him by the hand out onto the lawn. The neighbors were standing on their lawns too, bathing their feet in the nighttime dew and looking up at the sky. William looked with them: the heavens were shivering the glory of green. They were rippling, frothing like pools of a waterfall. He saw the green sky part in two, heal together, die to itself once more. "The northern lights," his mother told him. Now, floating on a snowberg, dumbstruck again by a chorus of the skies, William remembered the northern lights and sobbed within himself. The music he heard was the music he had seen.

For Grace it was different. Her memory presented a line from a poem that her uncle had read aloud to her in his musty room at the top of the stairs:

Poor verdant fool! and now green Ice!

For a moment she could see her uncle—really see him. She sat in his scratchy lap once more as he read each word with slow soft pleasure: "Poor verdant fool!" He looked at her as he said it. His eyes held the music that was hidden at the borders of the words. And now, it was this same music, released by the song from the hinting lands of language, that pierced her through.

Before they were aware, the tiny barge moored itself to the bank, filling the gap from whence it came. It fit like a key. Grace and William stepped ashore as if in a dream, gazing upward at the shining ones. The faces burned too brightly to be seen, and William covered his eyes. But Grace was granted—what? a moment's glance? She remembered it so well afterwards that it seemed an hour's contemplation. She saw a glorious woman, and yet no woman, naked and yet fully clothed in a radiance that held every color, green above all—an emerald rainbow. Most astonishing, the woman was looking directly at Grace. Her gaze was not soft and serene, like that of Stella's upturned face, but full of terrible benevolence—the gaze of someone looking down. Grace looked away. It was a fearful thing to be singled out by unknown glory.

And in the instant that Grace averted her eyes, the song ceased. All was calm. They looked again, and the shining figures were no more. And yet, as William and Grace traced the empty rim above them, whitened by the rays of the risen sun, they were certain the song had not really ended, that it had continued and would continue. Just then they wanted nothing else than ears to hear the song once more. But they sensed it would be years before it came to them again. *Even so*, they thought, *come.*

They turned to each other and exhaled the wonder trapped in their lungs. For a bare moment their eyes met. Then William looked to his ax. He held it closer to his side now. He held it thoughtfully. Then, without a word, he trudged up the slope. Grace waited till all of the rope at her feet had ascended like a wisp of light. Then she followed in his steps.

Chapter 19
The Good Fight

✳

WAITING ON THE RIM WAS THE FLAT WHITE LIGHT OF MORNING come, more banal than brilliant. It was windless, almost warm. The marmot lay asleep on Grace's pack—dreaming, perhaps, of distant green meadows. But what fool would go about to expound this dream? Not Grace. And not William, certainly. They surveyed the bowl of late summer snow, the quaint but perfectly natural lake, and wondered if these were places of miracle after all. Where were they when the morning stars sang together?

They did not agree on what to do next. William was for retreating down the other side of the mountain. His instincts told him never to stay on a summit too long. Grace, however, thought they should wait for Lady Lira, who was sure to come. And what, William asked, would they do when she got there? "Heave-ho? Have at her? Chop away as if she was a block of ice?"

Ill at ease, out of sorts, he traced the crater rim. All was blank; and then, all was not. A dark silhouette was emerging on the south, growing like a shadow. They had stayed too long.

"Look who's here," said William softly.

And as Grace turned, a horrible scream rent the crater. Again it sounded, shuddering in air. The marmot awoke. He bristled like a cat. Then the scream mingled with a whistling cacophony of many marmots, all gathered at the feet of the silhouetted woman. It was a battle cry they voiced, a lust-song for blood. To hear it yourself would make you wish you were not there. That was certainly Grace's wish.

As before, the woman and the marmots divided to conquer. She stretched her arm rightward, pointed the way. Instantly, her marmots broke free and galloped the rim towards the rising sun. One marmot only remained at her side. For a moment she stood with her arm still raised. Then she wheeled, and the marmot with her, and began to circle west.

"Grace?" said William. He had untied his knot and was untying hers. "Grace? Take your ax and your marmot and hold off the pack of them if you can. I'll take care of Lady Lira." How easily he had said it. It amazed him.

"Sure," whispered Grace. "I can do it." Her throat was dry. She felt William pat her shoulder in a most awkward way. Beside her the marmot stood ramrod erect, eyes bright. "Well, let's go then," she told him.

And off they ran.

By now the pack of hoary marmots was already close to the eastern rim. They swept along like the second hand of a clock keeping time in a mirror. Grace swept not so smoothly. What adrenalin she had was drained by the altitude. Her lungs burned, her creepers weighed like lead on her feet. Her marmot pranced like a windblown leaf, but Grace could only stumble.

The marmots came swinging around the bend, paws flying, mouths drooling, yellow eyes ablaze. Grace had once seen a painting of a cavalry charge—at Waterloo, she believed—in which horses and riders burst recklessly at her, and every face—even those of the horses—was terribly twisted and savage. If these marmots would pause, just for a moment, she could sketch a picture much like that one—or at least take a photograph. But the marmots did not pause; she would just have to remember. Grace braced herself for the full shock, ready to plow headlong into carnage. She even felt a flicker of bravery. But then she slipped.

She did not slip, really. The spikes on one foot merely snagged a bootlace on the other. All the same she fell down flat—and Stella's ice ax flew from her hands. The airborne shaft, her one last hope, met the charging marmots with no real force. It struck none, but touched them all, harmlessly sliding across their backs like a mother's caress. Grace cringed in the snow and kicked her feet, trying to disentangle her laces. Perforce she awaited nature red in tooth and claw.

They were upon her in an instant, tearing at her cheeks with soft wet noses, slashing her neck with leather-smooth paws. A dozen of them ravaged her spine in a tumbling circus. To a marmot, they were merciless in their affection. It was more than Grace could endure. She rolled to her side and they swarmed in her arms, each one desperately wanting to be petted. And so she petted them, every one, stroking their heads and holding each in turn to her face. Beside them lay her fallen ax—Stella's ax, the one that belonged to the lady in the lake, the one she had left right here on the eastern rim. Grace looked at the ax and wondered at its possible powers.

William, meanwhile, rushed apace to the western front. Lady Lira came striding on in her tireless, efficient way, smiling at him in cruel amusement. Her marmot was running to keep her pace. William ran too, like a lover to his own, and for no good reason. The air was too thin. He wheezed and watched his vision dissolve in gray dotty flashes.

When almost upon her he slowed to recover, and cast a glance across the crater. How was Grace faring? He squinted. *Not well*, he decided. She was down, motionless, buried in marmots. They swarmed her body like ravens at a cache. He stopped. A groan, a curse escaped his lips. He clutched the ax till his fingers trembled and dashed its head against the snow. He was becoming something he never had been—utterly furious. William had been mildly irritated most of his life, but nothing in all his computer-placid days had ever taught him fury.

Lady Lira had stopped. She was waiting for him, jauntily dangling the dagger from her hand, and James too, snarling at her side. Very deliberately, William walked to within ten paces and halted. He eyed them warily. Lady Lira wore a tight-fitting hood, which hid all of her hair. Her dress was thick and black. William had seen the like in old photograph books. Women wore such dresses, years ago, for climbing mountains. William remembered how stern the women had looked in the photographs. Lady Lira looked more than stern. She looked scornful.

"Fool," she said. "You tasted no berries, but today you will feed on these blossoms." She held up her dagger as if it were part of an obscene gesture.

"Look there," she told him, pointing to the far rim. "Look how your Grace makes a meal for my marmots. Such a long climb makes them hungry. And, of course, they themselves need to be fattened.

"Don't you feel sorry for her, William? Don't you feel sorry that you sent her to her death because you wanted to face Lady Lira alone? Send the pawns off to slaughter while kings and queens prove their prowess in single combat—a noble tradition, no?

"And have you now a magic ax from the dead hand of my drowned sister? Fancy, now. Ax or no, I think you do not even have the will to fight. Do you not fear me? Do I not see your hand tremble on the shaft? You have good cause to tremble, William. I shall soon cast your carcass to the lake below to join my sister in a watery grave. Here is my steel, William. Taste it, feed deeply."

She laughed out loud when her taunt was finished. William stood quietly.

"Have you nothing to say?" she asked.

"I—I never liked you," he replied lamely. "All the same, I never thought I'd try to hurt anyone." He contemplated this.

"But look what you've done!" he burst out. "Look what you've done to Lance with your poison! Look what you've done to Grace with your marmots! And the marmots—look what you've done to them for the sake of your filthy Lava Beast!"

He tore open his coat, tore open his shirt and exposed the white scars over his heart: "And look what he did to me!" Then he held up his injured hand and peeled back the mitten: "And look what you did." He spat at her feet.

"Lady Lira," he said, "whether or not this ax be magic, I suggest you look out for it."

He looked at the ax thoughtfully, surprised at his own vehemence. Then he murmured, "And would I gore such a woman as you? And gore such a woman? And gore such . . . ?" He was stammering to himself now—boast had turned soliloquy.

When he realized he had finished, William stepped cautiously forward. Lady Lira's plan, he guessed, was to harry him with her marmot and wait for the time to step in with her dagger. Matched alone against his long-handled ax, she'd have less of a chance.

He was right about her tactics. James leapt forward and sank his teeth so quickly into William's knee that William only gaped. Too late he sawed the air with his foot—the marmot had flashed behind him. He twirled and sliced with a stroke of the adze but James was gone again. And so it went. The wily marmot darted here, darted there, and William tangled limb with limb in trying to get in just one blow. All the while he kept half an eye on Lady Lira, which was half an eye too little. For in the midst of the dance she reached in quickly from the side. One clean slash laid open his forearm. William howled. It was most unfair. The wound bled like a sickly fountain, dyeing the snow scarlet.

So William decided to forget about the marmot. He turned and charged at the black-robed woman. She leapt back lightly to the rim, then leaned forward with her dagger thrust toward him. It looked extraordinarily long. The marmot tore madly at the back of his thighs, leaping from the snow like salmon in whitewater. But William ignored him.

He realized he could wait no longer. With both his hands he heaved the ice ax over his head, poised it to bury the pick in her heart and be done with the bloody business. With all his might he swung the shaft. But he missed his aim, missed it so badly that he wondered if the ax had a mind of its own. For the ax struck nowhere near Lady Lira. Instead it gouged deep in the snow between them—so deep, that it stuck fast. A sword in a stone could not be more fixed.

"Aha!" screamed Lady Lira. "What power in your ice ax now?" She reared back her dagger to deliver the death stroke while William struggled to retrieve his ax. Her arm drove forward. The blow had all but fallen. When suddenly—*pfft!*—a hairline crack split the snow between them, shooting out from the buried ax. The rim released a muffled groan. And Lady Lira was gone. The entire cornice on which she stood had split away at William's feet. His very toes hung over the crater. The ax rested free in his hands.

He watched, amazed, as Lady Lira dropped away, riding the fallen cornice. The snow was intact, the woman on her feet, the dagger still aloft in her grip. But when the cornice hit the edge of the lake, it sent up a towering curtain of spray and broke in a thousand pieces. Lady Lira was jolted into the water. She screamed, she flailed, she tossed her head—which, tightly hooded, to William's addled imagination looked very much like a ripe black olive, bobbing about in a crushed ice cocktail. Her dagger, of no use to her now, flew glittering from her hand. It splashed in the very center of the lake and sank from sight.

"James!" she cried. "Help me, you fool! James!"

"What?" said the marmot. He nervously crept to the broken edge and glowered down at the lake. Then, abruptly, he turned tail and sped away, down the side of the mountain. And William never saw him again.

"Help me!" screeched Lady Lira. "Help! Please!"

William paid her no mind. He turned from the rim and began to stumble dizzily back around the crater. Maybe, he thought, he could still help Grace. His arm left a wandering crimson line that followed in his tracks. The snow was growing dim and splotchy; it danced with pinprick flashes of light. The screaming woman in the lake below seemed far away, a remnant from a dream, a story told by a lost acquaintance.

He was nearly to Grace when the marmots suddenly left their prey and rampaged towards fresh meat. He staggered to a halt, set his feet, drew back his wavering ax to dispatch them. But he had not the strength. The marmots cruelly set upon him and felled him to the snow. Their noses nuzzled without mercy. Their whiskers savagely tickled his face. He closed his eyes and lay in darkness.

He had fought the good fight.

After a time, a gentle hand lifted his head. "William, you all right?" said Grace.

He opened his eyes. Things were clearer—the world had less of dance and flash. The cold snow on his outstretched arm had begun to damp the bleeding.

"You aren't all eaten up, Grace?" He asked it like a little boy.

"Not at all," she said. "I think they like us."

The shrieking below had intensified. "For the love of my sisters, save me! Oh, please!" the woman shouted.

Grace helped William back to his feet. They peered over the rim together. Lady Lira was in the center of the lake now, thrashing to stay afloat. Her skirts were ballooned like a big black lily pad, half-submerged in turquoise waters. Even from a distance, her hooded face looked unutterably forlorn.

Grace felt a twinge of pity. "Can we just let her drown?" she asked. "It seems too awful. Her marmots have changed; maybe she can too."

William delayed an answer. His arm still burned, his head still swam. Charity he could resist.

"How would you get out to the center?" he said.

"We got there before," she replied. "Maybe *we* could get there again."

But even as she spoke, a change came upon the lake. First they noticed a churning of waves—more than the flailing Lady Lira could have stirred up by herself. Then, one by one, the broken bits of snow disappeared from the water. They simply melted away. Steam began to rise from the surface, surging to the rim, blasting them with warmth. Beads of water condensed on their faces. Their parkas became too hot.

Then the turquoise waters stank. The lake began to roil in earnest, like a noxious soup that was almost ready. Lady Lira tossed in the seething. She was barely visible through the steam. Grace caught one clear glimpse of her face. It was dark and contorted, a very emblem of despair. Her cries for help were finished now. All they could hear was a drawn-out wailing, inarticulate, fading fast.

And even this was not the end. Through the mist—did they not see it?—a mottled head thrust up from the water, bloated beyond all size. It carried with it a murky glow that disillumined the crater. Smoldering eyes, yellow like jaundice, seized on their prey. The great jaws opened. There was one brief glimpse of the oozing cavern, haven of all appetite. Then it, too, was swallowed in steam.

In a twinkling of an eye the wailing fell silent. All that was left was an empty simmer.

Chapter 20
Goodbye, Little Marmot

✳

EVEN AS GRACE AND WILLIAM WATCHED, the lake was changed again. The steam blew away, the churning subsided, and all was as it had been before. Pale blue waters, cold and clear, lay quietly at their feet. The broken cornice across the crater remained to remind them. That was all.

William checked the gash in his forearm. But the wound was gone. He rubbed the place. Where once there had been a trenched-in slice there was now not even a scar. Wholeness of flesh—he marveled at it. For the second time that morning, William felt he had waked from a dream.

He turned to Grace, but she was gone. She had drifted from his side to the summit's outer edge, and stood surveying the lands below.

She beckoned him. "What are those?" she called, pointing beneath her.

William joined her and looked out. Dark forest spread from the base of the mountain. By now the sight was familiar. But just a few miles distant the forest expanse was mingled and mangled with huge brown clearings. The whole was like a patchwork quilt in which the brown patches outsized the green ones.

"Clearcuts," he told her.

He pondered this. Lady Lira was gone, the marmots freed, the lake restored, his wound healed—but why had the scars on the land returned? *Scars?* He wondered at his diction.

"I think," he said, "we can go home now, Grace."

"Home," she repeated. "Wherever that is."

She thought it over while William retrieved their packs and rope from the northern rim. But when he returned she was not contemplative—she was enormously hungry. Chambers, they found, had packed away two bottles of soup and a loaf of bread. So they had at it. The soup was tasty, the bread quickly broken. The marmots gathered in a fawning choir and wheedled for every sip and crumb they could possibly get. They got more from Grace than they got from William, but even he was generous.

When the feast was finished they roped together and plunge-stepped off the summit. William knew of another way down, longer but gentler, and Grace was relieved that he did. They descended east towards the climbing sun, and descent was sweet. Their feet floated lightly, free as stray bubbles. Their eyes drank in, not columns of steps, but whole world views in terrestrial flavors. It was effortless return, peace with honor, and after a while Grace found herself wishing they never would get to the bottom.

Did the marmots wish the same? On left, on right, they shot down the slope, careening by like playful otters. Some slid on their bellies, sending up spray; others surfed the snow on their backs and waved their paws in air. Whichever way they went they piped with glee. Whichever way they went they looked uniformly silly. Grace shouted her laughter to let them know. She giggled to see each one.

When crevasses put a halt to their sliding, the marmots found new sport. In twos and in threes they jumped the rope like dolphins leaping a bowsprit. Grace waited her chance, flipped the line, caught one in mid-air. "Got you!" she cried. The unlucky marmot spun down on his back. This made good game. But once the marmots were on to her she couldn't trip a one.

At length the snow gave way to ice, the ice to rubble and rushing waters. Off came the rope, off came the creepers, gladly discarded like chains and shackles. On they descended through braided streams, through dusty moraines, until they came to a meadowland so green, so new after ice and rock that Grace was glad they had got to the bottom after all.

In the middle of the meadows they found a trail traversing south, and William said it would lead them close to Chambers' cabin. So they took it. On flat-packed earth their feet found rest—no rocks, no holes, no half-carved steps. They quietly filed through hemlock groves and lupine gardens, sunlight and shade; and every dip in the winding path immersed their feet in a foaming stream. Grace now knew what she had not known—that walking in such a place is good.

Behind came the marmots, a ludicrous parade of them, nibbling by the way and shoving one another into every stream that offered. Yet every time Grace turned her head, there seemed to be one marmot less—although she could not be sure of it, since she had never counted them all in the first place. But one chance look confirmed her suspicion. Flashing across a grassy knoll below the trail were two silvery marmots, homeward bound.

And so the rest of them departed, singly or in pairs, until one marmot only, the smallest and the plainest, was trotting at her heels. And then he too was gone. She did not hear him leave, but suddenly there came a *peep! peep! peep!* from a rocky outcrop above the trail. She turned and saw him, balanced precariously on his hind legs, waving his paws to keep from falling.

"Goodbye," called Grace. "Goodbye, little marmot." She waved her hand slowly. One, two, three tears ran off her cheeks and fell to the earth.

But she did not have long to be sad. Around a bend in the trail marched Lance himself.

"Hey! hey! hey! hey!" he shouted. Anything but aloof, he clapped William on the shoulder with a healthy swat and gave Grace a hug so unabashed she wondered why this was only the first.

"You're all right!" he exulted. "You look all right, anyway. Me? Sure. Don't worry about me. So what happened? Did you find the ax? Did you give old Lira what she deserved?" He danced on his toes and shadowboxed in air.

"Well," said William, "what she deserved, she may have got." He held out the ax for Lance to see, but Lance hardly gave it a look.

"How was it, Grace? Were you scared?"

"Me!" said Grace. "Of course not."

Then she laughed so long and so hard that she got the hiccups, and every time she hiccupped she laughed again, and everyone with her. They could not help it. Soon all of them collapsed on the grass, holding their sides and pleading with one another to stop; but the slightest word, the least gesture, set them all going again. In the end they lay on their backs exhausted, utterly inert.

"*Ahh*," said William, and he sighed for all.

They remained on their backs and watched the sky and found their breath and felt the turf all cool beneath their shoulders. It was a good place, a quiet place, a place to hear the breeze and touch the sun, to watch lupine bloom and lupine wither, to taste the snow and sniff the rain, and having done all this, to listen to the meadow streams fall down into the forest. It was their place, and not their place, which is why they could stay, and why they had to leave.

At last they sat up, and William asked Lance since when it was he had been so healthy.

"I can't tell you much," said Lance. "This morning I woke up, that's all. The sun was in my eyes and there were ants in my shirt. My stomach was wasted. I was lying on the ground inside this stone foundation that was all sort of overgrown. Sir Chambers wasn't there and neither was his cabin. I guess I was lying in all that was left of it. So I went down to the lake for a drink, and who do you think I met there?"

"Henry the Eighth," said Grace. "No? Prospero, then. Caliban meets Prospero."

"Oh, come on," he told her. "It was your uncle, Grace. I could tell by his eyes. And his beard, too."

"You could tell he was my uncle by his beard?" Grace mocked.

Lance ignored her. "His beard is awesome. I'm gonna grow one exactly like it. Anyway, he just walks up and asks if I want any huckleberries. I go, 'No thanks,' and he laughs like crazy. I thought he would bust.

"Then he tells me who he is and we walk around the lake and he points to some smoke on top of the mountain. He's real serious now and sort of choked up. 'Do you know what that is?' he says, and I say, 'No,' and he says, 'The smoke of her burning. It has to be.' I didn't ask him what he meant. He claimed it was a good sign, but you never would've guessed by the way he looked.

"So we go on a little further around the lake and suddenly he asks me a question. 'Lance,' he says, 'are you afraid of me?' He's sounding pretty stern now. 'I don't think so,' I say. 'Then don't be afraid of Grace,' he says. 'She's been given eyes to see, but she doesn't see anything that isn't really there. She's part fairy. What you need to know is that's nothing too strange.'

"Then he said if he told me about all of *my* own parts, I'd be truly terrified. So I asked him not to. And then he says, 'I will tell you a little. You must fear your own appetite most of all. Much there is that should not be eaten. Satiety brings ruin.'

"When we'd gone about halfway around the lake, he gave me three small biscuits and pointed me over a rise to the trail. He said if I walked this way I would meet you both. So I did, and here I am, and here you are. And here, I saved two of the biscuits for you."

He held them out. Grace took one shyly, William the other.

"Is Garth still at the lake?" she asked. "Did he say he would wait for us?"

"He didn't say," Lance replied.

"Why didn't you ask?" Grace said sharply. And suddenly she was on her feet.

As it happened, Garth was waiting. In late afternoon they left the trail and crested a rolling divide to the west. Heathery slopes fell away at their feet to the lake they had known. The cabin was gone, as Lance had said. But standing in the ruins of its foundation was one man alone, easily marked by the whiteness of his hair.

"Uncle Garth!" called Grace. She flung off her pack and broke like a deer across the heather. It was a long way, but the farther she went, the faster she ran and the higher she leapt the boulders and gullies. And then she was there, gasping for truth, crushing herself in her uncle's arms.

"Poor verdant fool," he said, gathering her in. "You cannot outgrow who you really are. You cannot do it."

She buried her face in his full white beard and never thought to reply.

At last, William and Lance approached with much shuffling of feet, and Garth greeted them both. Grace swung around, still clutching his side like a long-lost daughter, and smiled brokenly, sniffling at odd moments. Lance felt his own eyes begin to brim, though he fought it very hard. But William felt business to attend to.

"Your ice ax," he said, and held it out to Garth.

"Not mine any longer," Garth replied. "So much as any of us ever possessed it, the ax is now yours, William. And when time is full, you too must pass it on."

"But—what shall I do with it?" he asked.

"You might as well ask what it shall do with you," said Garth. "When the time comes, you will know. By now you have learned that much. It is a very old ice ax. Even I know little about it. The shaft was cut from a branch of a tree in the Land of Four Rivers. What sort of tree we do not know, except that it was pleasant to the eye. The metal of the ax seems to be of no one kind: now silver, now iron—for some, in fact, lead. Keep the ax well, William. Use it as you are used by it."

"I will," said William. He looked utterly meek.

Then he remembered something he felt obliged to report. "Her marmot got away," he said. "He wasn't changed like the others. Do you know the one I mean? She called him James."

"I know that one," said Garth. "He is part of her, and he will stay that way, even now that his mistress is gone. As long as he is loose you will have a task at hand.

"But for now," he continued, "come with me, William. It is time at last we returned to the trailhead. If we leave right away we can reach the Demaris Cabin just at nightfall. There is someone there I would like you to meet."

"What about us?" cut in Grace. She drew away, hurt. "Can't Lance and I come too?"

For an answer he pointed to the eastern horizon whence they had come. A swerving line of bright orange packs was dropping from the rise. There were five in all. The packs collided, jolted to a stop, and voices floated across the heather upon the evening air.

"Who's got the map? We gotta make sure this lake is the one."

"Hey, it's right in your hand."

"What are we stopping for? Let's just get there."

"Yeah, my feet hurt."

"That's gotta be it."

"Uh-uh, look. The map shows two lakes. This is the wrong one. I'm positive."

"Who cares? Let's go! It's not gonna stay light forever."

"Okay, forget it then. If we get lost it's not my fault."

"Hah! Nothing's ever your fault."

With that the flaming caterpillar launched itself again. Illogically, circuitously, it found a way to the shore of the lake, and there it made its final collapse.

Please, thought Grace. *Oh, please.* She turned to ask Garth if they really had to. But Garth and William were gone. She saw them striding in the distance over open fields of heather, already small in the westering sun. As if by signal, the two men turned and waved. William swung his ax aloft. It glinted in the light. Garth's white beard shone golden now, like the evening snows upon the mountain.

Grace looked at Lance. They both shrugged. Then, very shyly, she slipped her hand in his. Side by side, they stepped out from the ruined stones and slowly took their way to the lake.

BOOK II: AUTUMN

The Stolen River

✳

It is required
You do awake your faith.
—Shakespeare, *The Winter's Tale*

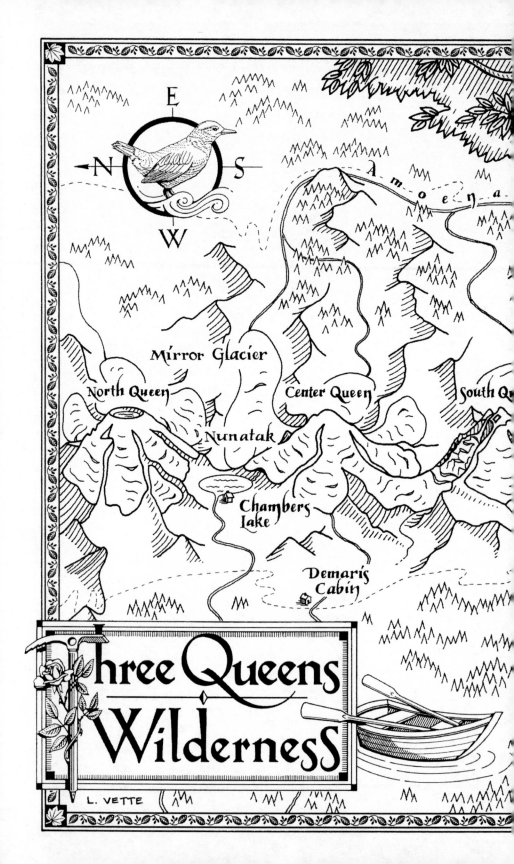

E

N · S

W

Amoena

Mirror Glacier

North Queen

Center Queen

South Q

Nunatak

Chambers
Lake

Demaris
Cabin

Three Queens
Wilderness

L. VETTE

Chapter I
The Nunatak

✳

"READY WITH THE BOOK, JEN? I think I've got this thing." Ronald hovered over a thick yellow tripod, not looking at Jennifer but at a small bubble in a glass rod, part of a head-sized instrument that looked like a green Cyclops. He balanced his arms on either side as if holding the instrument upright by a sorcery of air. Jennifer's father could level a theodolite in two minutes, even on ice, even in a wind. After weeks of practice it still took Ronald fifteen on a calm day.

What concerned him this morning was not the wind, for there was none, but the gray ceiling of lowering clouds. From where they stood on a rocky island dividing the glacier, they could no longer see the summit crest of the Center Queen above the cirque. Ronald knew that the glacier could be wrapped in fog in a matter of hours—minutes even. If he didn't complete his survey by then, he would have to start over another day. This late in the season, there would not be many good days left.

"Let's fake the data," Jennifer said as if reading his thoughts. "This glacier's been moving one foot a day all summer. It's not like it's going to change its ways all of a sudden." She was lounging by a rock cairn on her olive rucksack, her parka hood pulled all the way about her face in the sunless chill.

"But—"

"Oh yes," said Jennifer, jumping up. "It's for *science!*" She threw out her arms like a cheerleader, then regathered herself and demurely held an invisible microphone to her lips. "Ronald Miller, junior researcher, apprentice and pawn to the eminent, learned, world-renowned senior glaciologist, Dr. Geoffrey Howe, PhD, here with us today on this barren nunatak separating the twin lobes of the Mirror Glacier high up in the unexplored reaches of the savage Three Queens Wilderness—here, I say, with his lovely fiancée and assistant, Ms. Jennifer Howe, the beguiling daughter of the aforementioned Dr. Geoffrey. Yes, Ronald Miller, by his exacting persistence, here to discover what no human being has ever found or known before—to probe before our very eyes this mystery of the universe, this question at the center of existence: *Do glaciers really move?*

"And the answer is—*yes!* A foot a day! Every day! All summer long! And the dedicated Mr. Miller is about to prove, after three more hours of freezing his scientific rear (not to mention the derriere of his lovely assistant), that this week too—wonder of wonders—the Mirror Glacier has moved seven feet! Just like each of the *last* ten weeks!" She then began to make trumpet noises, punching the air with both fists to bring in the drums.

Ronald had by now a very silly look on his face, which is just what Jennifer wanted to produce.

When she had finished her instrumental prelude, Ronald swung the blank eye of his green Cyclops to the higher, western lobe of the glacier. If he could sight in each one of the bright orange flags that were spaced in an arc across its width, he might have time to track the flags on the lower—and wider—eastern lobe. Jennifer stood resignedly beside him, holding a pencil and a bright yellow notebook that said on the cover, *Write in the Rain.*

"Okay," said Ronald, squinting through the scope. "First one, horizontal reading: 63 degrees, 24 minutes, 17 seconds."

Jennifer wrote down, "#1H: 63° 24' 17"," and then, "dried peas, bulgur, vanilla pudding." She knew that her father liked this combination, and that Ronald didn't care. She wasn't sure about the others down in the cave and over on the North Queen. Being expedition cook—and logistics coordinator—wasn't easy.

Ronald called out the vertical reading, then shifted the scope slightly. "Number two, horizontal: 66 degrees, 49 minutes—"

"What do you think about Heinz—and Grover and Cheyenne and Marian—think they'll go for dried peas again? And that strange fat fellow, Escee, it's hard to tell what he'd like at all. Roscoe, I know *he* won't eat them, but he won't eat anything. 'Steak,' he says. 'Gimme steak, woman.' And I tell him, 'We just do veggie here, Roscoe—you know that. Same as they did in the Garden of Eden.' And he says, 'Maybe that's why they call it the fortunate fall. *Ha—Ha—Ha—Ha!*'" Jennifer put on a belly laugh to imitate the carnivorous Roscoe.

"Horizontal: 66, 49—"

"Ronald!"

"Jen!"

"I asked you a question, Mr. Science. Now give me some help on the menu. You have no idea how hard it is to think of something every night."

"Dried peas are fine," he said politely. He sighed and looked up. The clouds seemed closer.

She knew she could expect no more, and that she really should not have interrupted, but even so, Ronald drove her a little bit mad.

He located the next three flags, and Jennifer dutifully wrote down the coordinates. She was quiet until he started mumbling he couldn't find the sixth one. "The one below the icefall?" she offered. "Maybe something fell on it. And good riddance. One less piece of worthless data."

"What's that?" said Ronald.

"I said one less piece—"

"No, on the glacier. Something moving."

"Heavens. Run!" Jennifer cried. "Bigfoot! The Abominable Sasquatch! Maybe even a monstrous rosy finch, come to reclaim her rightful realm and peck out the eyes of peeping intruders."

"I think it's a marmot," Ronald said matter-of-factly. "But I've never seen one this high. Look for yourself."

He stepped back, and Jennifer refocused the lens just in time to indeed catch sight of a hoary marmot. It loomed before her, bigger than she thought it should be, then disappeared into a dip of the glacier. For a moment she looked serious. Marmots, she knew, were the largest of North American rodents, but this one seemed much larger still. She was reminded of something rather odd that she had seen the night before, something that she did not care to speak about.

"You see it, then?" Ronald asked.

"Marmot ahoy!" She tossed back her hood. "Mr. Smee! Pipe up the crew! All hands on deck! Double the powder and shorten the fuse! Range 42. Elevation 65. Three degrees west. Steady now . . . steady . . ." She lit the imagined breech of the theodolite and sent the roar of a cannonball echoing across the glacier.

"Blast it all!" she cried, swiveling the scope back into position. "We've missed the scurvy knave again."

"Careful with that," Ronald said quietly. "Don't yank it off level, Jen."

"But here," she said, peering in the glass and stepping back smugly. "We did locate your little flag, still gallantly streaming and all that. Just took a good bomb burst to find it, I guess."

He checked and nodded. "Hey, thanks."

"Hey, it was nothing."

To prove her congeniality she took down the next nine readings in silence. They made an unconsciously heroic pair, standing docilely side by side on a nub of stone and scree and talus halfway up the immense white flanks of a quiet volcano. The scissored bowl of the glacier before them was almost a mile across, extending from the clouds near the summit to the silvered fan of its terminus a good deal below them. There the glacier succumbed and decayed beneath piles of boulders that merged with heather farther down near a large gray lake on a windswept saddle. Beyond the lake another mountain, banded with crumbling lava cliffs, reached into the thick flat clouds.

The glacier behind them was even larger, falling down the northeast flank of the Center Queen to a river valley far below that curved into the east and south. This lobe splintered apart beneath its debris at an elevation where cedar and hemlock lined the banks. From the confusion of its end a shining rush of water emerged and lost itself in the dark forest.

As Ronald worked, measuring a baseline angle to each orange flag till he reached the one almost at his feet, the gray-bellied clouds sagged down from the summit and wisps of fog began to enshroud the nunatak. This last flag was firmly in view, and then it was not. He read off the degrees and minutes and seconds without being exactly sure the sights were fixed on the base of the staff.

"That's it," he said flatly. "We'll have to do the eastern lobe tomorrow." The fog then firmly closed in around them, a sudden and eternal cloak. Normally he would sight in again on the farthest flag to attain closure, checking to see if the instrument had in fact remained level, but of course he could not. This left his data sadly provisional, and left Ronald sadly distressed. What would Dr. Howe say? If he had leveled the theodolite quickly at the start, there might have been time.

"Tomorrow?" said Jennifer. "Tomorrow's Sunday. Tomorrow's our day to hike down to the Demaris Cabin, remember? Gwen and William are expecting us."

"Who?" said Ronald, still peering into the fogbound theodolite.

"Gwen the backcountry ranger? And William the climber guy? Gwen and William Arthur? Our friends?"

"Oh," said Ronald. He looked up vacantly. "Them."

Jennifer narrowed her eyes. "We get one day off a week," she said. "You need to remember how to use it."

Unlike Jennifer, Ronald did not like to argue. He was silent for a lengthy moment, which bothered Jennifer more than anything. Then he said, "The weekly survey's got to be done, Jen. I can't help it. And the ablation stakes across the glacier have to be measured too. There's just one week left before school starts, and still so much left to do. Your father needs me down in the cave, and I told him I'd be ready Monday."

It seemed they had had some version of this exchange all summer. Jennifer looked dispiritedly down through the fog as if for something new to say. And suddenly her eyes widened.

"Well, look who's here," she breathed. "The Grand Pooh Bah of all marmots." She laughed as she said it but felt a hollow shudder inside. Scuttling off the glacier and onto their nunatak forty feet below them, barely visible in the fog, was the oversized marmot they had seen by flag number six on the icefall. It climbed the rubble to where they stood and seated itself upright on a rock as if it were the overseer of their joint enterprise.

"Scat," said Jennifer. "Scram! Beat it! Don't come where you're not wanted. You're interfering with the important work of the GNP, the prestigious Glacier and Nature Project, and are liable to censure for obstructing research, for just being, for using these few moments of life to sit there on that old gray stone. Up! Up! My friend!"

The marmot stayed put, and looked at her with incurious eyes. It was so obese, so absolutely dropsical, that she could have thought it a misshapen bear cub. She wondered how it moved at all.

"Ignore him," said Ronald. "He'll go away." He unscrewed the theodolite from its base, stowed it away, and strapped the legs of the tripod together.

Jennifer looked hard at the marmot. Its eyes seemed dead. "Like yeah," she said. "Like let's ignore the Tibetan Buddha." She pulled her crampons out of her rucksack and plucked off the rubber spiders protecting the prongs. She strapped them on the bottom of her boots and had already tied the rope to her harness when Ronald finally found his crampons underneath the theodolite case. He was so very slow, so excruciatingly deliberate in everything that he did. Each day it seemed to arouse her impatience a little more. She picked up the aluminum shaft of her ice ax and started down to the edge of the glacier they'd just surveyed. She did this to hurry him up, to brood alone, and perhaps to escape the presence of the marmot.

"Don't go on the glacier till I can belay you," Ronald called after her.

Jennifer huffed. It was like being told not to cross the street, something that did not bear repeating. She clashed down stone and scree in her crampons, pulling loops of rope behind her, and stopped beside a pillar of rock at the frozen shore. The fog had thickened, and already Ronald was lost from view.

The snow before her was hard-packed firn, the stubborn remnant of late September. A bit lower, there would be no firn at all, just bare ice littered with rock and grime. Sixty feet down the slope, past a bamboo wand they had left to mark the proper path, lay a gaping bergschrund—a crevasse along the edge of the glacier that separated the moving ice from the more immobile snow by the nunatak. She could not see the crevasse in the fog, but she could hear the lonely gurgle of meltwater trickling away in its icy depths. When Ronald joined her, he would belay the rope from the pillar of rock until she was safely across the schrund on a sunken snowbridge.

When they had come in early July to lay out the flags and survey stations, the crevasse had been merely a hairline crack. Two weeks later Jennifer had punched through to her waist, and Ronald, behind her, had anchored the rope to his ax in the snow as she struggled out, lest the entire roof collapse and she with it. By late August the bergschrund was twelve feet wide and numberless deep, and they crossed on a bridge that week by week sagged lower in the center, so that recently they did not so much balance across it as descend to the middle and climb up the other side.

Ronald crashed down out of the fog and looped a sling on the pedestal. He rubbed her nose with an outstretched finger. "Glob of sunscreen there," he said. "Belay's on."

Chapter 2
Welcome to Our Laboratory

❋

RONALD AND JENNIFER DID NOT DESCEND BELOW THE FOG till the firn gave out and their crampons bit into steely ice near the snout of the glacier. This was fortunate, for the wands they followed out of the cloud had weeks ago melted out and fallen down on the bare ice. Roped together they threaded their way, Jennifer first, down gray frozen ramps past sharp chasms of deep blue—the true color of the heart of a glacier. Finally, a steep incline left them among a wasteland of boulders at glacier's end.

The ice they had left rose up at their backs in a furrowed wall, and the heaps of rocks lay gathered before them into a long ridged mound—a terminal moraine. This moraine was breached by a small stream that issued from the scalloped arch of a cave in the ice. They were taking off crampons and coiling the rope when a tall man in an orange parka stepped out of the cave entrance. He was talking into a radio, and his face beamed with the satisfied intensity of work worth doing. After a brief exchange about something, with someone, he collapsed the antenna and caught their eye.

"Well!" he said, and walked firmly toward them. "You're getting on as a surveyor, Ronald. Finished early this time, eh? Fine, fine." His rather red face bobbed up and down with hearty approval. "Just in time, we can use you in here. Dr. Slupensky has just located a major reservoir under the cirque of the eastern lobe. The largest I've seen—anywhere. We have to sound it, of course, and it's opened a whole new down-glacial system to map before the end of the season."

Ronald started to answer but the man cut him off. "Jennifer, how's my girl?"

"Fine, Dad. Bulgur tonight?" Seeing him, she wished her mother were there to make it.

"It's foggy, Dr. Howe," Ronald got in. "We didn't finish." He didn't say that as far as the data were concerned, they hadn't really gotten started.

Jennifer's father scratched the stubble that silvered his chin. "That so," he said, looking up at the low dark clouds. "Well, it can't be helped. Get in here with us for the afternoon and you can finish topside tomorrow, perhaps."

"Tomorrow?" said Jennifer.

Her father went on, undeflected. "Jennifer, down you go. Be time to think of supper soon, and anyway, I have a message for you to give to our visitor in camp. I came out to raise him on the radio, but he must have forgotten the schedule. Tell him we found the subglacial lake. That'll make him happy."

Before he had finished, Jennifer was returning the wave of two figures who had appeared in the gateway of the moraine. "Gwen!" she shouted. A genuine smile came to her lips. "William!"

"Well," said her father, playing as ever the sanguine host. "Look who's here— our loyal greenclads!" He advanced down the small stream to meet them walking up. The woman wore the khaki shirt and dark green pants of the forest service, not pressed and trim in a rangerly way, but several sizes larger than seemed to be necessary. She had an open face and thick blonde braids that Jennifer envied, given her own thin chestnut hair. Behind her came a strong-built man with a rather humble look on his face that belied the shadow of bristle on his chin. He carried a wooden-shafted ax much longer than the metallic ones resting beside Ronald and Jennifer.

Dr. Howe shook the hands of the new arrivals cordially, still saying, "Well, well." Jennifer caught up to her father and gave both of them hugs, and Ronald did something—not quite a handshake, not quite a hug—awkwardly in between. With friendly vigor they talked about the chances of rain and their states of health and the glacial progress of research. Then Dr. Howe asked, "To what do we owe the honor of your presence? Just visiting, or . . . ?"

"Actually," said the woman named Gwen, "we did notice the helicopter that flew in yesterday afternoon, and since your landing pad was constructed for emergency purposes only, by terms of your special-use permit, we wondered if you had run into trouble. We couldn't get you on the two-way radio, so we thought we'd hike up ourselves and check."

"Yes, yes," said Dr. Howe to the rocks at his feet. "Your concern much appreciated. No mishaps, we're all fine, just the advent of a special visitor, that's all. Our grant sponsor—needed to check on the project and such. A bit in a hurry, no time to walk—I believe, my dear, he worked things out with your district supervisor—a little exception. For science, you know."

There was an awkward pause.

"But no one is authorized to make that exception," Gwen said firmly. William touched her arm in caution, but she went on. "I don't know what the district ranger may have done at the office, but here on site I have to consider that helicopter an illegal intrusion. As you well know, no motorized vehicles or motorized equipment of any kind are allowed within a wilderness area. Federal law. I'm sorry, Dr. Howe, and no offense, but I'll have to find your visitor and write out a violation."

"Great!" said Jennifer. "Just where I'm headed. We can go together." She knew this was an impertinence, but it was the way she really felt, and she thought to interpose a little ease before her father became truly upset.

At present he was sputtering in a gentlemanly sort of way, still the master of ceremonies. "Now, now, now, Gwen dear, you understand I completely admire your adherence to duty—quite exemplary, to be sure—but I don't know if our visitor would take your perfectly justified remonstrances in quite the way you intend them. Escee is very much the important man, not used to much in the way of criticism—I'm not sure it would do to call his attention to his mode of travel just now, what with our research just reaching a critical stage. Perhaps a discreet letter addressed to his secretary—I'll vouch they'd be happy to pay the fine, if there is one for this sort of thing. Just a friendly note of caution—your best interests in mind, of course. I'm sure he'd be willing to put in a little word for you at the district headquarters, and—"

"Dr. Howe!" said Gwen, her face flushed. "Do you realize what you just—"

"Now, now, now, Gwen dear. I know what you're thinking. You're a few years older than Jennifer, and remarkably mature and perceptive, but you're still young, and with a little one on the way, I hear—" he winked and nodded grotesquely at William—"you and William need to be thinking about the future. A backcountry job at a wilderness cabin is all very well for a fit young couple like the two of you, but there are other positions available, promotions to be had, just the thing for a growing family and all that."

Jennifer was acutely embarrassed for her father. By the studied silence in Gwen's face she knew her friend was deeply offended.

"We appreciate your concern, Dr. Howe," William said huskily. He seemed uncertain how to navigate between elder and wife. "But—"

"But we're not for sale," Gwen said acidly.

Dr. Howe looked disconcerted, as if she had deliberately smashed his most expensive theodolite. Then his tension seemed to dissolve. "Of course you're not," he said warmly. "And I never meant to——"

"And where we raise our children is our own business, Dr. Howe. I can think of many less healthy places than right here. In fact, I can't think of a healthier place than right here."

"As you wish, then, as you wish—didn't mean to intrude. Your domestic matters are no affair of mine, you're perfectly right, Gwen dear. Just trying to help."

"Do you want to help me right now, then, by giving me the name of your guest?" She shed her rucksack and fished out an official-looking pad. "In case I can't find him?"

Dr. Howe looked rather flummoxed. "Gwen, dear, if you feel you really need to do this, perhaps you could just leave the papers with us. Be glad to pass them on—at an opportune time."

William looked rather hopefully at Gwen.

"What ho!" said Dr. Howe. "Speak of the devil!" He was looking beyond them down the stream to the gap in the moraine whence Gwen and William had just come. Lumbering towards them over the stones was a bald-headed man in an ill-fitting crimson parka—ill-fitting because of the man's enormous bulk. To Jennifer he looked as if he might have rolled up the hill, and that if he rolled back down his case would be that of Humpty Dumpty's. As he jolted closer over the rocks, the deep tan of his face became apparent, as did the many furrows that began at his eyebrows and climaxed somewhere high atop his bare skull.

"Good afternoon, Escee! We didn't expect you. Welcome to our laboratory." Dr. Howe genially swept his arms in every direction.

The man he called Escee labored toward them without any acknowledgement of this greeting. Before he quite reached where they stood, he collapsed in a decided heap, resting on his ample haunches until the others migrated into his presence. He was wheezing and puffing dramatically.

"That cursed hill. You never told me your cave was on top of a mountain, Howe. Oh, good God for a drink."

Gwen pointed helpfully at the stream, but he didn't seem to notice.

"But now that you're here," said Dr. Howe eagerly—"and what a splendid surprise—we can give you a little tour, Escee."

"Sir," said Gwen, not even waiting to be introduced. "Sir? Are you the one that——"

"Yes, yes," Dr. Howe interrupted. "Precisely the one I've been telling you about. Executive Director of Southland Hydro Replenishment Research, here to visit one of the many projects he and his group are so generously funding. Such a privilege for—"

The man cut him off with a wave of his hand. "Just show me the cave, Howe. And get me a drink."

"I've got something," Ronald volunteered. He jogged up the stones to his pack for a poly bottle of lemonade.

"It's in mine," Jennifer called after him. "In the pocket next to the data book."

Ronald returned with the lemonade and handed it to Escee, who took it without any thanks and made a face as he put the bottle to his lips.

Ronald was worried, but not by the man's response. "Jennifer," he whispered, nudging her aside. "The data book. It wasn't there." It held his entire summer's work, some but not all of it copied into a ledger at basecamp. Just that morning he had found the ledger shredded and chewed—by mice, he supposed.

"Must've dropped it into the schrund," she said. "You know, accidentally." She snickered, then stopped. Her face registered the certain pain of sudden recollection. "Oh, Ronald," she said. "I left it. I know I did. I'm so sorry. It's just that that marmot—" She stopped and they looked at each other intently.

"We're ready, then?" said Dr. Howe. "Ronald, will you join us? And Jennifer, perhaps you could loan your ax and crampons to our—"

"I'm sorry, sir," Ronald mumbled.

"Eh, what's that?"

"I'm sorry, sir, but I can't go. I left the data book on the nunatak. After what happened to the ledger last night, I'd better go get it."

Escee finished the distasteful bottle of lemonade and rolled his eyes. "I see you run a tight ship here, Howe."

Jennifer's father visibly cringed, and Jennifer herself felt a sudden urge to tip the fat man into the stream. She saw Gwen sink onto a nearby boulder, suddenly pale.

"Gwen," she whispered. "You alright? You need to go down?"

"Sick," hissed Gwen. "The whole thing's sick."

Jennifer looked puzzled.

"The baby, I mean—that's all. No, that's not all. I can't stand it."

She stood up uneasily and addressed Escee. "Sir," she said, "if you are the one that flew in on the helicopter yesterday, it is my duty to—" And here, as if it *were* her duty, Gwen suddenly and forcefully threw up on the stones that separated her from the rotund man. A little of it splashed on his boots, and he pulled them away in plain disgust.

William was immediately helping Gwen to sit down again. "Take it easy," he said. "Just rest. We'll get back down nice and slow." To Dr. Howe he said apologetically, "I told her she wasn't up to this."

Jennifer touched William's shoulder. "Let me stay with her," she urged. "I've got to go down anyway, and Ronald needs someone to climb back up the glacier with him." She saw this as a chance for Ronald to spend time with a man she considered a model husband. Besides, she couldn't face the thought of Ronald's resentment quivering at the end of the rope as they climbed the two long hours up to the data book—if indeed it were still there.

William checked Gwen's face. She nodded approval, and he turned to Ronald. "All right with you?"

"Great," said Ronald, but it just sounded like *okay*. He was none too proud of the occasion.

"Well then, Gwen dear, we'll be seeing you," said Dr. Howe, helping Escee to his feet. "Do take care. You've got a little one to think of, you know—don't overdo it." He accepted his daughter's ax and crampons and escorted the unsteady man to the entrance of the cave, where he commenced a lecture on recrystallization of glacial ice to apparently less-than-enraptured ears.

Ronald began uncoiling the rope, and he and William offered their goodbyes to the women—William's heartfelt, Ronald's more tepid.

"Watch out for that man-eating marmot!" called Jennifer. It was a joke that she and Ronald shared from years ago when they had first met. Except now it felt forced.

"The what?" said William. He looked vaguely concerned, and swung the pick of his ax to the ice as if testing its strength after long years of disuse.

Chapter 3
Pluck and Find

※

WITH A LITTLE PERSUADING OF HER FRIEND, Jennifer was able to strap Gwen's rucksack atop her own, and the two headed slowly down the stream. Once they had passed through a maze of moraines, the rocks gave way to a smooth slope of dark green heather, broken by a narrow footpath stooping down in clay steps. The little stream occasionally stopped in milky pools that were edged with the tawny grass of autumn. At one of these pools, perhaps halfway down to the lake below, Gwen asked to rest, and they stretched themselves on the sunburnt stubble, watching the gray-bellied clouds sweep past.

They remained quiet for a long time. Even in her queasiness and exasperation, Gwen had a calm about her that seemed to Jennifer different from her own brooding. She was trying to decide whether to tell Gwen about the dream she had had the night before and what she had seen upon waking from it. She had gotten into her sleeping bag a bit late. The estimable Escee had arrived without warning in late afternoon, and Jennifer at her father's bidding had prepared her best raisin-and-rice casserole, which she served with onion bagels and some carefully saved cream cheese. The visitor ate his entire supper with grotesque scowls and grimaces that he did not even deign to aim in her direction. After cleanup, Jennifer left the cooking tent in a sour mood. In the starlight she strolled away from the camp to the edge of the lake, just where the outlet purled away from the quiet waters. She thought about Ronald, back in camp and still earnestly listening with the others to the talk between her father and the visitor. She thought of returning to college in just a week, and whether she should tell Dr. Hassler what she really thought of his precious English major. (Dr. Hassler's favorite word was *scholarly*, though *squalorly* was the way he said it.) More than anything, however, she thought about her present self, broken like the stars in the water, her summer hopes not at all turning out the bright best way.

She had walked back to her tent, a small dome-like affair, and crawled into her sleeping bag with the door left open, zipped down like a drawbridge to let in the freshness of the night. Immediately she fell asleep, and dreamed herself lost in an angular maze of trimmed hedges, the sort she had once or twice explored in the formal gardens of an old brick mansion she had visited as a girl soon after her mother had died. The hedge in her dream was thick and thorny, and higher than her head, and the path kept turning in sharp corners until she arrived in an opening at the very center of the maze. Here there was a fountain of water, not a spigot on a pipe but a spring bubbling out of the grass. Above the fountain a scarlet rose grew out of the hedge. Beside it stood a splendid woman dressed in red, with raven hair and clear green eyes. She was looking at Jennifer with an intensity that broke all bonds, and pointed to the scarlet rose.

"Pluck and find the goddess within," the woman said in a deep clear voice. "Pluck and find."

Jennifer felt very frightened—the way that she had when her mother had died—but she wanted to do what the woman said. It felt necessary, and daring, and important—the path into her real future. Hardly taking her eyes from the eyes of the woman, she reached her hand to the stem of the rose and inadvertently pricked her finger on a thorn.

"No!" she cried, and found herself wide awake. She felt her finger damp with blood outside her bag, and wondered if she had sliced it with the jag of a broken fingernail or the cusp of a zipper. The moon was up, shining in the open door, and the skin of her tent was all aglow. And there in the doorway, just at her feet, was the bloated marmot.

It sat fully erect, looking at her with dark dull eyes. She tried to scream, but no sound came. The marmot kept watch impassively, billowing mounds of fur and flesh inert in the moonlight, and in a few moments her fear had changed to deep disgust. She coiled her legs and kicked at him with her sleeping bag. And very slowly, as if not at all in response to her movement, he got down on all fours and walked away into the night.

On the glacier that day, she had wanted to tell Ronald, especially when they had seen the marmot out on the ice, and even more when it came to them on the nunatak. But a dream—so silly—he wouldn't have listened. Now as she lay on her back by the stream, nursing her finger between her lips, she wanted even more to tell Gwen. But when she opened her mouth she heard herself asking,

"Gwen, are you happy?"

Gwen turned to look at her curiously. "Sick, yes. Angry, yes. Happy?" She paused. "Yes."

"William is good to you, isn't he? I can tell."

"Well, yes. I think I'd say so. He's learning—and so am I."

"You mean, he wasn't always? Was he—insensitive? At first anyway?"

Gwen laughed weakly. "When we first met he was just bashful, that's all. An old friend brought him by the cabin one evening, after a climb, and they stayed the night. He was so sure we had met before—it embarrassed him to say it. He was even more embarrassed when I assured him we were strangers, but hoped we could be better friends.

"How can I explain? He loved the country, just as I did—not the flag so much as the land itself. He liked what I liked, and asked what he could do to help. I could tell that he liked me, too, but it wasn't just a random crush. I got a lot of guys stopping by back then—you know, You-Can-Do-It Expedition types—I could tell *they* liked me. But William liked what I stood for. He knew. Not for very long, he hadn't, but he knew.

"He had to go the next day, but he kept showing up on the weekends to climb. Funny, every weekend the rest of that summer it rained—hard. We did a lot of talking at the cabin. In early October our friend Garth married us—in the presence of about one hundred marmots. For some reason, they all seemed interested."

"Sometimes they do," Jennifer put in.

"That was—let's see—six years ago now. Our anniversary is in just eight days."

"Six years," said Jennifer. "That's when Ronald and I met. Led, no doubt, by one of your suitors on You-Can-Do-It." She paused and laughed at the possibility. "I think he might have even taken us to your cabin. A woman gave us huckleberries—maybe it was you."

Gwen smiled and shrugged. "Time goes by," she said.

"He—Ronald—was so cute then. Such a nerd, really. Even his name—he always had to go by *Ronald*. He was proud of it. I mean—*Ronald!* He wore these black nylon glasses too, that made him look like Buddy Holly. He was so pathetic I couldn't help liking him, even though he was two years younger—and that matters in high school. We ended up at the same college, where Dad teaches. By then I had taken a couple years off—you know, to travel—but mostly I worked in a health-food store right next to campus. So when Ronald came we were both freshmen. He took all of my father's geology courses in the next two years—even one for graduate students. Meanwhile, I barely got by in Victorian lit and Renaissance poetry. I liked the Thursday readings in the health store better—these *wonderful* women reciting their stuff on, you know, the goddess. The goddess within."

Gwen looked at her quizzically.

"From the heart—so *natural*. But I could never get Ronald to come—he was always in the lab or in the field. Which, well, has been the story, especially since we got engaged in April. My dad thought he was doing us a favor to have me along as part of the research project this summer, since Ronald was coming anyway. But all they let me do is cook, and Ronald's been so—*dedicated* up here. I hardly feel like I exist."

She half sat up and looked moodily out at the lake below and the bright puddle of tents on the shore. "We came here on that expedition six years back—just over that rise from the east. We weren't even sure it was the right lake. Except for Ronald. *He* was sure. At the time I thought it was charming, the way he knew, forging ahead and not listening to anyone."

"William can be like that," said Gwen.

"Charming?"

"No—well, of course that, but—*focused*, I suppose. Like I said, though, he's learning. When you love, he can learn."

It took Jennifer half a second before she realized she had been handed a piece of advice. She resented it, a little.

A raindrop fell, and Gwen suggested they go on. They continued down beside the stream, picking their steps carefully. When the slope eased, they walked in the heather side by side, and Jennifer resumed their talk on safer ground. "The helicopter—that bothers you, doesn't it? And Escee—what a jerk. You've got to keep the rules, because that's your job, but they don't make it easy for you."

"It's more than all that," Gwen said wearily. "You know what your father's research is for, don't you?"

"For *science*," Jennifer announced. "To push back the frontiers of knowledge and benefit the future of all humankind."

"That's all he told you?"

"He didn't have to, I already knew—since I was two, I think."

"Your father," said Gwen, "is interested in much more than how fast these glaciers move and melt, and how much water they discharge. At least, the people who are paying him—Escee, for example—are not interested in these things for their own sakes. But they are the kinds of things one needs to know if one is planning to build a dam downstream—say, across the mouth of the Amoenas Gorge, thirty miles below the glacier."

Jennifer received the information blandly. "Well, yes, I guess they were talking something about that last night. But Amoenas Gorge—that's way out of your district, right? A dam there is not going to interfere with *your* mountains, is it?"

"The gorge is part of the Three Queens Wilderness," Gwen said. "It may be thirty miles downstream, but the river wraps around the peaks so that the dam-site, at Otium, is only a little ways from the South Queen. But that part—the illegality—is literally neither here nor there. If you had once visited, you would feel . . ." She lapsed into silence.

"I'm sure it's very beautiful," Jennifer offered, feeling a bit uncomfortable in the face of Gwen's obvious emotion. When she said this, however, she was think-ing how tired she was of the mountains, and how good it smelled—the herbs, the candles, the aromatic soaps—in the health-food store. Perhaps she would not re-enroll in classes after all.

"It's not a matter of rules," said Gwen. "It's a matter of love."

Once again Jennifer sensed she was being corrected, and did not like it. By now they were getting close to the camp, a scattering of chartreuse tents near the western shore of the lake. The clouds were lower and darker now in the late afternoon; the moraines behind them were lost to view, and the North Queen before them was likewise gone. Their world was merely a bowl of heather slop-ing down to the gray-flung lake.

Jennifer was in no hurry to get back. The thought of preparing another meal in the empty mess tent—prying open the lids of a large stack of tins—made her quite as nauseous in imagination as Gwen was in fact.

"I'm glad we're close," Gwen murmured. "I'm afraid I have to lie down again."

"Then use my tent," Jennifer said. "You know the one. I think I'll take a walk by the lake and then get supper started. There's still time. You rest until the others get back, and then you and William can eat with us."

Gwen agreed, and the two women parted beside the tent at the outskirts of camp. Jennifer left the rucksacks with Gwen, taking only her green cagoule in case the rain should begin in earnest. She began on a path heading counter-clockwise about the lake, and was starting to think she should return to change out of her heavy boots when, for a startling moment, a patch of sunshine swept the lake. An opening of blue appeared overhead—a sucker hole, for almost as soon as it came, it closed. But before the sunshine left the heather, it illuminated something atop a rise set back from the water. It was only a ragged protuber-ance, really, a natural row of stones perhaps, but as she had never explored that spot before, and as the lapping of the water depressed her spirits, just as it had the night before, she sauntered away from the path by the shore to investigate. Some hundred yards brought her to a flat crest, and there on the ground was not simply a row of stones, but an entire enclosure, knee-high, of rocks fitted closely together. It looked for all the world like the old foundation of a cottage or cabin that might have once stood on this heathery knoll above the lake.

Jennifer saw all this in an instant. What drew her attention were not the stone remains, however, but something inside them. Planted erect in the rust-brown grass at the very center of the ruin was an old wooden ice ax, not quite as long as the one that William had carried with him to the glacier.

Jennifer stepped over the stones and onto the grass, and approached the ice ax gingerly as if making her way to a tombstone and fearing to walk atop the dead. When she reached the ax her breath came in a sudden gasp. The shaft was weathered by rain, wind and snow into grainy ridges—but it was not that. The pick and the adze on the head of the ax were spotted with rust—but it was not that. What she saw, hidden from her heretofore since it bloomed on the south-facing side of the shaft, was a red, red rose, perfect in shape, growing out of the ax itself. Its little stem was grafted into the wood of the ax at the top of the shaft just under the pick and adze—not grafted but growing, as if roses naturally came from axes. In spite of the cloudiness of the afternoon the flower was opened in full display, the soft layers of twining petals already dewed by the coming fog.

She knelt in wonder, not daring to touch the ax or its flower, and gazed for a long, long time. The clouds crept down and the fog slipped round her without her even knowing it. A light wind began to blow, ruffling the petals of the rose.

Then she heard a voice—whether in the fog or in her mind or in the memory of her dream she could not tell. But the voice told her, low and deep in full rich tones of womanhood, "Pluck and find the goddess within. Pluck and find."

At the sound of these words there welled up within her distaste for Ronald, disgust with her father, and absolute hatred of Escee. She was also aware of a poisonous envy for William and Gwen. *Pluck and find.* Here was an action, a self, that would satisfy. As if in a trance, Jennifer reached her fingers to the fragile stem. This time there was no thorn. The rose broke easily in her grasp, and she brought it hungrily to her face, crushing it to her nose and lips and closing her eyes in a deep fragrance.

She had only a moment to revel in the sweet sensation before she realized her fingers were wet. She pulled the rose away from her face, opened her eyes, and saw to her astonishment that her hands were dripping with crimson blood. Jennifer dropped the rose in horror and saw that the blood was not confined to her own hands but was also welling from the broken stem and streaking the wooden shaft to the ground.

"Stop!" she cried. "Oh, stop!" She wiped her hands on the dead grass and pressed her palms on the wounded shaft, applying the proper direct pressure as she had been taught in her first-aid classes. But the blood kept rising through her fingers, and the wind blew past her in a mortal sigh. Her hands were crimson once again—and the entire shaft was coated with blood, collecting now in an outspreading stain on the ground that began to envelop the soles of her boots.

"Please, stop!" she cried, but her voice was lost in the rising wind. In desperation she let go the shaft and put her hands to the pick and the adze, gripping them hard against the slipperiness of her flesh. She screamed without words. In one mighty pull the ax was uprooted. And the bleeding stopped.

In that moment the rain began. What Jennifer realized, as she stood there gasping with the ice ax dangling in her hands, was that she heard it beating on a rooftop.

Chapter 4
Snow on Snow

✳

IT TOOK MOST OF RONALD'S CONCENTRATION to follow the cleated holes in the ice that he and Jennifer had punched that morning with their crampons. In the fog there would not be much else to guide him until they got to last year's snow—the softer firn—which still held the wands upright. He was glad that William was well behind him. Ronald didn't feel like talking, and telegraphed as much by the rope that sawed between them across the ice.

He knew William a little bit from their visits to the Demaris Cabin. It was three miles on a faint track down the outlet stream from Chambers Lake, then three miles more on a real trail down gentle switchbacks to where the cabin stood in the meadows and groves of timberline on the western flank of the Center Queen. It was a pleasant enough walk, and a fine thing, near the cabin, to stroll in the shade of real trees after days in the open on ice and heather.

Ronald remembered coming there for the first time six years before as a negligible member of a You-Can-Do-It Expedition, the trip on which he and Jennifer had met. A hailstorm had brought them together beneath an unpitched, crowded fly, and the tyrannies of their red-bearded leader had kept them from drifting apart. He recalled the strange eagerness with which the leader had allowed them to stop at the cabin for lunch, and how hot it was that midsummer day, and how cool it was when the ranger had invited them inside the basalt block walls into dim shade, and how they sat around a roughhewn table and passed a bowl full of huckleberries that she had picked. He remembered too the crush of the berries on his dust-coated teeth, and some of the things that the backcountry ranger had explained to them about the Three Queens Wilderness—plans in the making for a ski resort on the South Queen, for geothermal drilling at timberline throughout the area, for clearcutting and new roads in the forest approaches to the peaks, and for a new dam on the nearby Amoenas Gorge. The ranger had sounded calmly ironic about these things—almost as if she didn't approve of them.

Which had confused Ronald. He had been taught that God had made the world for Adam and Eve to subdue. What good was a wilderness locked up from human use? His geology classes with Dr. Howe had recently made him not so sure that God had created the earth after all, or that there really had been a Garden of Eden, but Ronald kept quiet about these doubts. At any rate, he and his professor were in perfect agreement that the earth was a storehouse of rich resources to be used for the benefit of humankind. Geologists helped to uncover these riches and make them available for all. He thought of himself on this his first research expedition as one of a team of daring philanthropists, as a modern Prometheus of sorts, helping to bring not fire but water.

He had guessed long ago that their purpose in measuring movement and wastage of glaciers on the east side of the Three Queens was to check their potential for water release to a downstream dam. Not only potential, but also reliability. Sometimes scientists came across a glacier that "galloped," and signs were that the eastern lobe of the Mirror Glacier, the major source of the Amoenas River, had moved rather quickly at times in its history—much faster than the rather sedate one-foot-a-day observed by the smaller western lobe. In the ten weeks he had measured it, the eastern lobe had picked up speed to almost five-feet-per-diem. Some glaciers could hit seventy, and when that happened, the ice would literally explode, suddenly discharging giant volumes of water downstream. He had seen slides of Russian scientists fleeing what looked like part eruption and part tidal wave somewhere in the Pamirs. These glacial catastrophes happened much more frequently in volcanic regions, where subglacial warming could lubricate the underside of the glacier ice with unusual amounts of meltwater. The eastern lobe of the Mirror Glacier seemed to be sited on such a hot spot. This would account for the rather constant year-round outflow of water from the terminus. It would also account for the large subglacial reservoir discovered that day, the presence of which might please their visiting grant sponsor if he were ignorant of what it implied about this glacier's destructive potential. In Iceland they had a name for it: glacier burst. *Jokulhlaup*.

The point was, no dam could survive such a high-speed wall of ice and water. But people were eager to build this dam, and Dr. Howe, he could tell, was eager to please both them and their money. It was doubtful whether the good professor, now guiding his visitor through the caves that linked the two lobes, was at this very moment lecturing him on glacier surge and glacier burst. Not that Dr. Howe would suppress the evidence in his report. He simply might omit to interpret it, leaving it to engineers raised in the desert to draw their own desired conclusions from his glacial mass of glacial data.

These suspicions left Ronald with an ethical dilemma. In the last day or so, he had sometimes thought he should take the detestable Escee aside and apprise him of the real possibilities. On the other hand, he knew how rare an occurrence a *jokulhlaup* really was, especially in smaller glaciers in the middle latitudes, a point on which Dr. Howe kept insisting. Five-feet-a-day was not unheard of for an alpine glacier, and the geologic evidence of a glacial catastrophe here in the past was rather vague. And the dam was needed. Great cities far to the south were dying of thirst.

Part of Ronald would have liked to talk about these things with William as they climbed. But he already knew, by a few hints that the other had dropped, that William was definitely not in favor of any dam at all. Telling him about *jokulhlaups* would give him the ammunition he needed to alert the press, hire a lawyer, and stop the project altogether. And William would do it. Hadn't he stopped the ski resort, the geothermal drilling, the illegal clearcutting in just the same way in the past few years? Mild-mannered though he might seem, the man was a formidable archdruid if there ever was one. Quiet enough, pleasant enough, but a dangerous radical nonetheless.

When they first met, earlier in the summer, Ronald had been interested to learn that William was a computer technician before he was married. Ronald had a fascination with computers himself. He looked forward to the moments, perhaps next month, when he would transform the data he had collected this summer into so many bytes of electronic memory. Putting the facts onto the screen was so much more neat, more satisfying, than gathering them on the nunatak. But his first surprise upon meeting William was that he no longer liked to discuss computers—that, in fact, he no longer owned one. So they had found little to talk about, and Ronald had formed a certain basic distrust of the man.

So even if William had not been walking a hundred feet behind him at the end of the rope, hidden by a curtain of fog, Ronald would not have disclosed his mind. He heard only the occasional chink of the spike of William's ax on the ice, and felt hardly a tug on the rope. William knew how to walk on a glacier without pulling his partner about, in spite of Ronald's stopping and starting to search the way. But there, ahead, was the first wand, a green bamboo garden stake with a small orange flag tied round the top. His crampons settled into snow. The way would be easier now. He could see their morning's tracks in the firn, and where he couldn't, it was only a matter of charting his course from wand to wand.

Given the chance, he might have talked with William about the stress vectors of glacier mechanics, about the logistics of planning a survey, about the way in which a theodolite works. Something that would not have occurred to Ronald to share was the state of his feelings for Jennifer, though she too was much on his mind. Was it possible to be so annoyed with someone you were in love with—engaged to even? The thought itself was a deep annoyance, since it violated the defined commitment he thought he had made.

He knew he was what his old friends called a science geek, someone who never went anywhere, not even to a party, without his pocket calculator. Not that he went to many parties of any sort, wild or tame, for he did not drink and was much too inhibited to dance. (He was, after all, the son of a preacher. His father had died in the pulpit he pounded, excoriating the children of Israel who played about the golden calf.) From the day he had met her, Jennifer had touched his soul with a needed warmth and spontaneity, which though he had not been able to share he could at least appreciate. Jennifer loved to perform for him, and did not seem to expect him to be more than a grateful audience. That is, until recently.

As their summer in the mountains had passed, he had sensed her growing impatience with his native passivity. She expressed it in barbs and in outright objections to his dedication to research. Could he help it if Dr. Howe were his major professor? Was it his fault he aspired to become a junior version of her father? The closer he grew to the tutelage of Professor Howe, the farther she removed her affection. By the end of the summer he had figured this out in the form of an equation: as a approaches b . . .

It presented him with yet another personal dilemma, no less ethical perhaps than the choice of whether to blow the whistle on the chance of a *jokulhlaup*. Of course, there was a way of joining the two. He could relieve his conscience with a note to Escee, alienate Dr. Howe forever, and thus win the undying love of his fiancée, who by definition should already be in love with him anyway—whatever *love* was. And if it were an anonymous note, Dr. Howe would never know, though Jennifer could, and—

His thoughts were cut short by a sudden unsettling of snow at his feet. His stomach made a quiet lurch, as when an elevator begins its plunge. He was poised on the glacier—and then he was not. Before he could even think to call out, Ronald found himself dangling at the end of the rope in a blue-lit cavern. Over his head spun a bright round hole in an arched roof of rotten firn. His hand still grasped the head of his ax, which hung comically useless above an abyss where blue walls dropped into darkness.

And comical is the way he felt—not so much frightened as desperately fool-ish. In his mind he heard Jennifer laughing derisively. *Watch your step, Mr. Science!* He reached his ax in front of him. With the tip of the spike at the end of the shaft he could just touch the closest wall. There was no question of climbing out with crampons and ax. He would have to prusik up the rope.

Blocks of snow came cascading onto his shoulders. "You okay, Ronald?" William's face was peering down from the now enlarged hole above.

"Fine," said Ronald. "Just hanging around."

William laughed, not in mockery, but in a way that put Ronald at ease. Suddenly, there was something he liked about this man.

"The rope's fixed," William called down. "I've got it anchored on a snow fluke. Have enough prusiks?"

"Plenty," said Ronald, fingering the loops at his waist.

"I'll back off then," William said—"before I join you."

Ronald had never actually fallen into a crevasse before, but he had practiced getting in and out of them many times. One way of gauging the health and history of a glacier was to rappel into an open crevasse alongside a measuring tape and to note the depth of each layer of accumulation of snow-turned-ice. Each year's layer was separated from the next by a thin brown line, dirt blown up on the old summer surface. It was a little like counting tree rings—or more like bathtub rings. The farther down you went, the closer the rings drew together. Here the firn had compacted itself by its own weight into blue and then into black ice. When he had described this process to Jennifer, she had said:

> "*. . . snow on snow*
> *Snow on snow,*
> *In the bleak mid-winter*
> *Long ago.*"

As Ronald clipped his ax to his harness with a carabiner, he measured the strata on the wall before him with a newly trained eye. The top layer ended just over his head—this year's addition—and the firn below it was a tinge grayer. He counted six bands down into dimness. These were the snows of yesteryear—what Jennifer called a practical answer to an elegiac question.

To business. He wrapped a cord in a sliding prusik knot on the rope, attached a green nylon sling, and secured it around the instep of his left boot, careful not to puncture the sling with the fangs of his crampon. Then he tied another prusik above the first and clipped this second cord to the harness at his waist.

"Climbing!" he called to the empty hole. He stood up on his sling-wrapped foot and watched the prusik tighten on the rope. Then he slid the higher knot up, sat down on it with his full weight, and raised his slung foot once again. By this tedious process, inches at a time, he swung and twirled his way up the rope.

His progress slowed at the very top where the rope lay partially buried in the lip. This hidden crevasse was capped by a roof some three feet thick; when Ronald had fallen through, the rope had cut into the edge of the hole. He tried to shove his prusiks ahead, but they would not follow the rope through the snow.

"Stuck?" said William. He was just out of sight up over the lip. "Excavate a little. I've got the shaft of my ax beneath the rope back here. It won't saw into the snow any farther."

Ronald gingerly unclipped his ax and pawed at the snow above with the adze. Chunks and clods came streaming down against his chest, some falling inside his parka and lodging next to his tender skin.

"Just one thing," said William casually. "Try not to cut the rope."

Ronald imagined the consequences, and took care. A few more minutes of chilling work cleared the way. He edged his prusiks up the trough that he had made until they neared the ax at the surface. Then William reached it down to pull him out the rest of the way. Ronald was glad that William's ice ax was so long. Grasping the head of that dark smooth shaft was like grasping a hand sent down into deep waters.

They sat together back from the hole. Ronald was panting, his body shivering without his permission. He felt wet all over, from sweat or melting snow or both. William put his arm around him, and that was good. Then there was warm lemonade in a bottle, and chocolate to eat, and the world was a better place. The fog all about them was kind comfort, a welcome back to the land of the living.

"You don't find many roofed-up cracks like that in September," William marveled. "Count yourself a discoverer."

Ronald smiled. The fog lifted a tiny bit, and he saw the silhouette of a ribbon-capped wand far off to the right. In his musings he had swerved off route.

"Getting late in the afternoon," William said. "I suppose we could get the data book another day?"

Ronald stiffened. "Oh, no. We're close. I'm all right—really." He stood up and began to untie his prusiks.

William looked at him dubiously, but Ronald insisted.

"Let me go first on the rope at least—the last thing you need is another plunge."

"But I know the way," Ronald said—"at least, when I'm paying attention I do. It gets a bit tricky ahead at the schrund." Ronald wondered whether William admired his pluck or scorned his haste. In reality it was only fear—if he failed to recover his data he might as well hop into the bergschrund sans rope as face Dr. Howe again.

In the end William merely made sure that Ronald had emptied the snow from his clothes, and let him continue. Ronald regained the misplaced wand and, watching closely, found the next, and the next, and the next after that in the darkening clouds. They would need to move quickly on the descent to avoid the coming of rain and night.

When he reached the schrund with its sagging bridge, Ronald brought William up beside him and asked for a belay. William nodded, and sank the shaft of his ax in the firn until only the head was poking out. Then he knelt and braced the head with his boot, wrapping the rope around leather and shaft in an S-shaped curve. Ronald worried a bit about the strength of the wood, but said nothing.

"Belay's on," William said, and worked the rope around boot and ax while Ronald edged his way down the bridge. He experimentally plunged his ax in front of him at arm's length, doubting the firmness of the causeway more than he ever had before. At the lowest point he looked into the chasm on his left. The upper wall, banded white, then gray, then blue, then black, was much higher than the one behind him, and more than slightly overhung. The noise of meltwater rushed to his ears from somewhere very far below. The glacial stream continued, he knew, to where the walls of the schrund pinched together some hundred yards off in impassable chaos. There the meltwater doubtless entered a cave in the ice, perhaps one that Dr. Howe and the others had already mapped with a

Brunton compass.

Ronald turned to the ladder of kicked footsteps that surmounted the upper wall ahead, and slotted his boots, one at a time, in each pocket. If any part of the bridge broke he thought it would be this upper ramp, ready to slough when gravity beckoned. But he reached the top without incident, and called to William that by the time he had run out the rope he would have him on belay. There was no need for William to belay him any longer.

Eighty feet more brought Ronald to the projection of rock at the loose foot of the nunatak. He stopped for a moment at the margin of the snow and peered upward into the fog. It was eerily quiet in an anticlimactic sort of way. He could not see far, certainly not to the top of the nunatak. But then, a gust of wind rearranged the fog, and something emerged—something he did not want to believe.

Halfway up the rock slope, the obese marmot sat on a ledge with a yellow notebook in its paws. Its teeth were tearing slowly at the pages, and its cheeks were just beginning to bulge with masticated theodolite readings. The marmot looked at Ronald impassively with dead black eyes.

"Drop it!" screamed Ronald. Without thinking, he lunged up the slope, clashing at the rocks with his crampons. Strangely, the marmot went on chewing and did not move.

"Give me the book!" Ronald shouted. He was almost up to the marmot now, and leapt forward with arms outstretched as if to seize it by the throat. His hands were just about to close on the book—or on what was left of it, anyhow—when Ronald felt a sharp jerk from behind on the rope that sent him reeling back down the slope. His crampons caught on one another, and he somersaulted down the scree and landed with a jolt against the pillar of rock by the snow.

For a few moments he lay there in a crumpled tangle, cursing his fall and the loss of his data. His nose hurt, and seemed to be bleeding. Then he realized what had happened. In his rush to reclaim his damaged book from the marmot, he had pulled William into the bergschrund, where now, no doubt, he was dangling like a marionette, wondering why Ronald had popped his strings.

"You idiot!" he muttered to himself.

Much more slowly than he would have liked, he rose to his feet, bracing himself against the steady pull of the rope, and slipped a sling around the pillar. He tied a prusik around the rope and clipped it off to the sling with a carabiner.

Then, hands shaking, he untied the slack from his waist and knotted it to the sling with a bowline for good measure. The rope was anchored.

He glanced upward and saw neither book nor marmot. Below him the taut rope disappeared into graying snow and fog. He did not yell, knowing that William would not be able to hear his voice until he got to the very edge. He tied his other prusik to the quivering line, clipped the prusik to his harness, and headed toward the brink, sliding the knot down the rope as he went.

He had not gone far before he saw the marmot again. It was bent over astride the rope just above the lip of the schrund. The book was gone.

Ronald stumbled closer. "Beat it!" he shouted. "I'm warning you!" He waved his ice ax menacingly. When he was almost upon the marmot again he saw exactly what it was doing, and stopped for a moment in sheer despair. Quite deliberately, the bloated creature was gnawing away at the sheath of the rope, worrying the woven strands the way a dog worries a bone.

In a fury Ronald leapt forward and swung his ice ax hard through the air, aiming for its neck with the sharp-edged adze. At the last instant the marmot shot aside. And the adze sliced neatly through the rope, finishing what teeth had begun. As Ronald fell against the pull of his prusik he watched the rope fly over the edge and flicker in the fog like the tongue of a snake.

He lay face down in the cold-churned snow. On his neck he felt the beating of rain.

Chapter 5
Caught Red-Handed

✳

JENNIFER FOUND HERSELF STANDING ON ROUGH-HEWN PLANKS, and wondered where the heather had gone. The ax in her hands was slowly dripping blood on the floor. She was in the center of a fair-sized room amid stone walls and wooden rafters. A generous fireplace stood at one end. Water was streaming down two small windows, and an open door let in the sound of falling rain. She remained as rooted as the ax had been, too frightened to move a single step.

After listening to the rainy silence a long time, Jennifer looked down at the ax and saw that the blood was no longer welling out from the shaft. The rose lay crushed on the floor at her feet. She stooped and took it in her blood-soaked hands. It comforted her that the rose was still there—even though it should not have been there in the first place. *Strange comfort that,* she thought.

Emboldened, she stepped to the open door. The rose was real, the floor was real—and so was the rain as she stood in the doorway. The fog had lifted, and in the light of late afternoon she looked down the same gentle slopes of dark green heather and rusty grass to the slate waters of Chambers Lake. There was nothing for it but to traipse back to camp and consult with Gwen on these odd things.

She was three steps out the door when she took in the western shore of the lake. She stopped, stunned. Where the ungainly clutter of tents had been— summer headquarters of Dr. Howe's prestigious Glacier and Nature Project, the GNP—lay only an empty space of heather. The camp was gone.

Walking towards her, however, from the vacant site were two tall figures, a man and a woman by their gait. Jennifer hoped the woman was Gwen; she could not guess who the man might be. But she also feared it was not Gwen, since so much else was not as it should be. Suddenly, the strange cabin felt more inviting.

She retreated to the shelter of the open doorway, and even glanced about the room for a place to hide. There was a bed, a stool, a rocking chair, and in one corner a small table. A black iron kettle hung in the fireplace, and for moment she thought of curling up inside of it. But without quite choosing to do so, she stayed in the door and gave herself up to meeting whoever was coming this way. For a moment she wondered how Goldilocks felt, but then recalled that Goldilocks had had the good fortune to be asleep when the Three Bears returned home. She put the rose on the doorstep and tried to wipe her hands clean on the wet heather, thinking she would not make such a good impression with blood-soaked paws. But her hands remained red, as if stained with dye.

As the figures approached, Jennifer saw that each was hooded with a brown cloak, their faces so cowled against the rain that she could not see them. They did not appear to have noticed her; by the pointing and nodding of the hoods at each other, the pair appeared deep in conversation. But within just a few steps of the cabin, the larger of the two pulled back his hood and looked straight at Jennifer.

"Well, there you are. Caught red-handed." Then he laughed in a rough but merry sort of way. He had a smooth bald head with a ruff of white hair about his ears, and a large plain face, set off by a ruddy nose.

"For shame, Sir Chambers. 'Tis not a matter for lightness," said the other. This was the woman. She too put back the hood of her cloak, and advanced with grave but gentle eyes. What struck Jennifer immediately was that the eyes were green, like Gwen's. But the woman's hair was a sheaf of brown, not blonde and braided. It was someone else entirely.

"Oh child, child," the woman sighed, and grasped both of her bloodstained hands. Jennifer felt ashamed and accepted all at once.

Then the woman stooped down and took up the mangled rose on the step. She looked at it sorrowfully, and Jennifer wished with all her heart she were back in the cook tent stirring a pot of dried peas and bulgur. From within her cloak the woman took a small glass vial and folded Jennifer's hands around it. Without a word she held the flower over the vial and began to squeeze—hard, the way one squeezes a sponge dry.

The man stepped up and watched closely.

A sweet clear liquid, not at all the color of blood, began to drip into the vial. When the vial was full, the woman opened her hands and they were empty. The rose was gone. She capped the vial with a crystal stopper, and Jennifer offered it back to her.

"It is for you to take," the woman said, "to help the wounded sleep. When it is time to use it, you will know. Keep it till then."

Jennifer nodded timidly. "Can you tell me," she asked, "who you are, and where I am?" The woman seemed to know much. Jennifer realized she badly needed an explanation of her present circumstances. And for some reason she wanted to add, *Can you tell me who I am, as well?*

"Why yes," the man put in. "All this hocus pocus and no proper welcome. Let's go inside out of this rain and introduce ourselves, of course." He ushered them into the darkened cabin in much the same way that Jennifer's father had brought Escee through the door of the mess tent the night before—with the same harmless, officious grandeur.

Then he took Jennifer's hand, and made a small bow. "Sir Chambers," he said, "at your service. You are, at present, a guest in my cabin, on the shores of my lake. Mine in a manner of speaking, of course—can't say that they're mine in any but the loosest proprietary fashion. They might as well be yours, or hers, and in fact they are, and yet none of ours at all. That's what I call a conundrum of ownership. And who, may I please ask, are you?"

I wish I knew, thought Jennifer.

Before she could say, Chambers continued. "Friend or foe, we'll show you kindness, no worry for that. A fire is just what's needed now, and a pot of soup. What say you to lentil soup—or perhaps it's dried peas you like?"

"Shush," said the woman. "You know we have no time for that. Let the girl speak, and we'll be on our way."

"I—I'm Jennifer Howe," said Jennifer. "I'm not sure how—"

"Is it Jennifer Howe or I'm-Not-Sure Howe?" interrupted Sir Chambers. "I'm not sure which, though I'm sure you're not—a witch, that is." He laughed again, in the same hearty way. "But then again, *numquam certus*—I'm never sure, just like you. We've established something in common, you see—perhaps the basis for a lasting acquaintance."

The woman put her hand on his arm and looked at him severely. "Go on, child," she said to Jennifer. "You must bear with us."

Jennifer looked at each of them in turn, feeling more confused than ever. "What I mean—I think—is that I'm not sure how I got here. In this cabin, that is. And I'm sorry about the rose and the ax—they weren't mine to disturb at all. If you'd just take me back to my friends who are camped nearby—at least they were—except I don't know—and—" And here, Jennifer began to cry.

The woman gathered her into her arms. "What's done is done, Jennifer. And all that is done you do not yet know. It cannot be helped but it has been helped. We're here to give you—Sir Chambers and I—some of the help that is already given."

These words struck Jennifer so strangely that she began to stop crying out of sheer curiosity.

"My name is Lady Demaris. Perhaps you have been to my cottage before?"

"*Your* cottage?" Jennifer exclaimed.

"In trust, you understand," Chambers interjected—"as I was explaining."

"But that's where Gwen and William live."

"Precisely the ones we're concerned about now," said Lady Demaris. "From what Sir Chambers has just seen, in a moment of sunshine in his lake, your friend William is in sore need."

"But he's up on the glacier, not in the lake."

"Exactly," said Chambers. "I saw him where he wasn't. And if we don't manage to get to him soon, he won't be at all. So excuse me while I pack a few things for our walk up the hill." With that he lit a couple of candles and began to rummage through a chest and to take down things from a shelf over the fireplace.

Jennifer listened to the rain on the roof. She felt rather dismal about the prospect of hiking back up to the glacier with this odd man in the wet gloom. "What about Ronald?" she plaintively asked.

"The boy who is with him?" said Lady Demaris.

Jennifer nodded.

"It sounds as if that has been your question for a very long time. Perhaps you are the one who can answer it."

Now Jennifer blushed. She could think of nothing to say in reply. She was glad when Chambers was standing with them once again, tin lantern in hand and a canvas rucksack heaped on his back. Jennifer put on her cagoule and wool balaclava without being asked, and tucked the vial in a deep front pocket. She picked up the bloodstained ax again, then quickly offered to put it down.

"For now it is yours," said Lady Demaris. "It was once my sister's, and still is, most so when in other hands. What you have won by violence, take."

Grotesque as the wounded ice ax was, Jennifer was glad to keep it. There is something good about having the head of an ax in your hand when heading into the cold and gloom. With the coming of the rain it was nearly evening.

"You are staying?" said Chambers to Lady Demaris.

"This time, yes. I have a care-swollen mother to visit tonight. Take young Jennifer to the cave. I am bound otherwhere."

"Farewell then," said Chambers stiffly. He seemed to be hiding some disappointment. "Until the Feast of Free Waters, perhaps?"

"Perhaps," echoed Lady Demaris.

Then she took Jennifer in her arms again. "Take courage," she said. "We will see what good may be worked out of evil. Often more than we desire, let alone deserve—any of us. You have only done what we ask or think. I shall see you again, and then perhaps all shall be well—all manner of thing shall be well."

She kissed Jennifer on the forehead, and Jennifer backed into Chambers on the step while mumbling goodbye. Chambers steered her out of the door and into the wet, and they were gone.

Though dusky and damp it was not quite dark, and the light from the lantern which Chambers held was still somewhat superfluous. He led Jennifer at a quick pace on a small path that contoured gently up the hill. When it dipped to meet the stream from the glacier she recognized the grassy bank on which she and Gwen had rested and talked on the way down. *Poor Gwen*, she thought—*quite disappeared.* And yet it seemed that Lady Demaris would find a way to comfort her. And William hurt? She thought of the snowbridge over the bergschrund, and wondered if it had finally collapsed. And if it had, how would Sir Chambers have known about it? She wanted to ask him more concerning what he had seen, but the stream was so loud, and the rain was beating so hard all around them, and they were both so wrapped in cloak and cagoule, that she would have had to be at his shoulder to make herself heard. And the path was so narrow, and the footing so dim, that she had to walk in file behind him.

So she trudged uphill in silence, grateful not to be carrying a pack, but feeling the rain pelt cold and hard on her back and shoulders, and wishing she had sealed the seams of her cagoule more recently, for the water was gradually seeping through. Her boots, too, already damp from a day of use, were saturating her socks to the skin. In the last few weeks, since the softer snow had melted down to firn and ice, she had neglected to waterproof the leather.

By the time they reached the end of the heather and began to stumble through the moraines, the lantern had become of use. The light that shone through the holes in the tin was just enough to speckle the path for each step. It was truly dark. Jennifer stayed on Chambers' heels, not conscious of anything now except where to place her next foot. So it came as a surprise to her when Chambers stopped, and the rain with him. She was not so clumsy as to run into the back of him, but in catching herself she suddenly slipped, and found herself shouldered against a wall of ice. It was strangely quiet except for the hollow splash of the stream that sounded in echoes.

"A fine and private place," said Chambers, "and a dry one too. Watch your step and welcome to Chambers' Chambers, I call 'em. Not that they're mine, you understand."

"I've been here before," Jennifer told him, annoyed by his condescension. "At least right here, at the entrance. My father is mapping these caves. He knows all about them."

"Does he, now," Chambers said, pulling back the hood of his cloak and wrinkling up his massive brow. "What an admirable thing, to know all about them, as you say. I could never claim so much. My aim is merely to know them, and to know myself. Probably the same aspiration. So far, except in perhaps the tiniest moments, I have failed."

Jennifer looked at him curiously.

"But that doesn't mean I can't guide you to the living heart, the center of search, the crystal chamber. I know how to get there, just as your father probably does. The problem is, I never know what to do—or how to be—*once* I get there. I'd love to have his confidence—pack in a ruler, calculate the cubic cubits, and walk away knowing all about it. But I have an idea the beauty of the place, the essence of it, grows out of some immeasurable goodness, and after that, some immeasurable tragedy, and beyond that, I'd like to know."

He was not being comical now. Jennifer could see the earnest sense of quest in his eyes as he looked down the cave and into the shadows beyond the lamplight. Sir Chambers seemed an unlikely candidate for ever finding the goddess within. For a moment she wished he could cross the barrier of gender and so have at least some hope.

"But it's time we were going. There's tragedy enough at hand if my intuition serves me right. You don't have anything for your feet, do you—to keep you up on the ice ahead?"

"No, I'm afraid I gave my crampons away this afternoon."

Chambers took his pack off and fished out two pair of black iron spikes that he called *creepers*. "Strap these on," he said.

As Jennifer did so she noticed that her hands, streaming wet from their hike in the rain, were still blood-red. She wiped them together with no result. Her ice ax, equally washed by the rain, was no cleaner. She stood up to follow Chambers into the cave and tried not to think about it, but of course she did. An unwelcome echo came to her mind:

> *Therein the patient*
> *Must minister to himself.*

She felt the impossibility of cure.

The cave near the entrance was ten feet across and not quite as high. It was floored with rubble, and the walls and ceiling were smoothly scalloped out of clear black ice that shone like obsidian in the light. Jennifer could see starred explosions beneath the surface, the flaws and stresses of a hidden world. They followed the stream up over the stones until it too was flowing on ice, more quietly now, slipping in a sinuous runnel. More than once, Jennifer nearly stepped in the water because she thought it was part of the floor.

Before very long the passage narrowed, then climbed steeply, arcing left. The stream at their side found voice again, the continuous rush of a clear cascade. She found it soothing to pick her way up the ice beside it, sometimes setting the pick of her ax to steady her balance on the ascent. But after a while her calves ached, and she longed for rest.

Just when her legs were beginning to tremble beyond her control, the passage opened into a level chamber, its invisible ceiling supported by pillars of silvered ice. Three separate tunnels, each bringing a small stream, led up and away. But for now they paused.

Chambers held up his spotted lantern alongside the closest pillar, and Jennifer thought she glimpsed a ceiling some thirty feet up. "Moulins," he said. "Water falling from chutes overhead. Up higher they won't be frozen."

The walls of the room were a creamy mixture of blue and white, sometimes mingled in brilliant turquoise. The waterfall pillars were solid, brilliant, statuesque. Jennifer felt as if she had entered an airy, tasteful gallery of sculpture. "Lovely," she said.

Chambers bobbed his head and smiled, as if to hint there was better to come.

He chose the center of the three passages; it wound less steeply than before, back and forth, serpentine fashion, further up and further in. By and by Jennifer heard the crashing of water up ahead, and around a corner, falling to the floor like great shafts of liquid light, were three live moulins, raging and hissing from ceiling to floor. The pair slalomed around them, hooding their faces against the spray, and continued on past further pillars, frozen again. The ice now was white on the ceiling and upper walls, with a wainscoting of pure black. Once more, the passage was narrowing.

Soon they had to walk in the stream single file, turning and slipping between the walls in the smallest places. The water was only ankle deep, but Jennifer's feet became very cold. She began to wonder how it would feel to drop through a hidden moulin underfoot. And when she slithered against the walls of ice she felt they were moving in on her, traveling their daily foot in a moment to catch her completely by surprise.

She was about to insist they turn around when Chambers gained a steep dry passage that left the stream. The walls opened out a bit, and after a few twists and turns, Chambers came to a sudden halt. This time Jennifer did bump into the back of him, and not so much the back of him as into the arm that held the lantern, which crashed to the floor and extinguished itself.

But it did not matter. The chamber in which they found themselves was already illuminated with four tall candles. The walls and ceiling were coated with crystals that reflected the light like the hung glass of fine and feathery chandeliers. In this light she saw much in an instant.

Amidst the candles, bandaged and bleeding and lying on a bed of blankets, was the body of William—or what Jennifer hoped was still William himself. At his side knelt an aged man in a cloak like Chambers', the hood pulled back to make room for a long tangle of white hair. An equally long beard spilled down the front of his robe. And next to this man, soaked and pale and staring right at Jennifer, stood a mournful version of Ronald Miller. He held a bloody ax in his hands. To the wrist they were coated a brilliant red.

Chapter 6
Fire and Ice

✳

"Greetings, brother," Chambers said to the white-haired man. "You are very welcome." He spoke as if it were the other who had just arrived and Chambers who had been there first—which, in his loosely proprietary way, he probably had.

Ignoring Ronald, he approached the prostrate body of William and solemnly asked, "Is the hurt unto death?"

Jennifer sidled up to Ronald and grasped his hand. She felt it shivering in her own, and looked down to see their fingers interlaced in blood. The same blood? *Not likely,* she thought. *And yet, what was?*

"Unto death?" repeated the man. He was tall and sad—his face a crag and his eyes deep-set. "It well may be."

William was breathing raggedly now. He tossed his head from side to side and let out a low moan like a wind far down in the cavern. His temples and forehead were bandaged with a swath of cloth. If the deep bright stain on the cloth told true, they were bleeding still. His side also was terribly wounded. There where William's parka was torn, the sad old man held a thick compress to staunch the welling.

"And you, my daughter," the old man said, fixing his gaze upon Jennifer. "What do you bring in your bloodstained hands?"

Jennifer let go of Ronald and looked at her hands in blank confusion. She brought guilt, perhaps. And she supposed she brought the goddess within. That is, if she had found her yet. But neither seemed to be of much help in the present moment.

"The vial," said Chambers, pointing to the pouch of her cagoule.

Jennifer had forgotten. She found the vial and held it out. "I do bring something," she timidly said. "A gift, I think. It is every drop of a red, red rose that I broke from this ax and that Lady Demaris crushed in her hand. She said it would make the wounded sleep. It's all I have."

Jennifer still held out the vial, but the old man did not reach for it. "The same hands that broke the rose must bring it to his lips," he said. "Step up, daughter, and do not be afraid. You bring help, not harm, now."

Jennifer left Ronald's side and edged behind the aged man to William's up-turned face. They made a symmetrical company then, she at his head, the two white-bearded ones facing each other on either side, and Ronald standing at William's feet. Between each of them, at the corners of the body, the tall white candles burned quietly. The chamber glowed like a holy place, and when Jennifer lifted William's head and put the vial to his lips she felt as if she were following the written rites to a ceremony. She was not taking action so much as perform-ing a role. It was the difference between breaking a rose and being broken by it.

The distillation, sweet and clear, slipped between the swollen lips like a sigh recalled, and William at once lay still and calm, quietly breathing. The old man lifted his hands from the compress and examined the gash in William's side.

"He bleeds no more," the man announced, and all four of them, just like William, visibly relaxed.

"Doesn't she have the touch, though," Chambers said admiringly. And by the way that he said it, turning his head and nodding toward the passage behind him, it was obvious he was not referring to Jennifer. "One fine woman, I always say. Be a lucky man who—"

The other man, looking not at all lucky but still quite lorn, interrupted Chambers as if he had not been speaking at all. "And now," he said, turning to Ronald and then back to Jennifer, "it is time to wash your hands and your axes. Go both of you down the eastern passage till you come to the river, and cleanse yourselves. Then I shall tell you what you shall do."

Jennifer and Ronald each nodded submissively. Jennifer started for the pas-sage at William's feet by which she had come; Ronald, his eyes self-consciously downcast, turned to an exit at William's head.

The old man stopped them. "No—together. The *eastern* passage." He pointed to a tunnel behind him that led away from William's side.

"Oh," they both said. Chambers offered his lantern to Ronald, who accepted it with mumbled thanks. Ronald relit the wick inside with one of the candles burning between them. Holding the lantern at arm's length as if it were a bucket of shame, he shuffled down the corridor with Jennifer close behind him. The way gently descended through clear black walls that gradually opened till Jennifer could comfortably walk at Ronald's side. It was a relief somehow to escape the chamber.

"Who's the old guy?" Jennifer asked. "And what in the name of all that's good are we doing here?"

"Just what I was going to ask you, Jen," Ronald replied in a shivering voice. "Who's the fellow *you* showed up with?"

"I asked first. And tell me, will you, what happened to William? Somehow I feel I had something to do with it. If only I hadn't forgotten the data book. Though that's the least of it, I suppose."

She saw that he was averting his eyes. "Ronald?" She paused. "Did you—were you . . ." She trailed off, not knowing how to put into words the symmetry of guilt that she guessed. By his silence she knew they shared one fault. In the spotty light she slipped her arm about his side and groaned to herself as she felt him quiver.

After a long quiet, peppered by the tapping of their axes on the ice, Ronald said, "Well, it's Garth. That's what he says his name is. And good thing I ran into him too. Otherwise I'd be—listen! Do you hear water, Jen?"

They stopped, and she nodded in affirmation. Round one more bend they came upon the glistening bank of a deep dark stream that crossed their passage from right to left. It was just wider than they could jump—and fortunately they did not need to. Ronald set the lantern between them and knelt on the ice, laying his ax carefully aside. Jennifer knelt and laid her ax aside as well.

They looked at each other for an awkward moment, then plunged in their hands and kept them there, scrubbing them desperately one against the other. Cold pierced flesh like little knives. Jennifer gasped at the steely pain, and tears formed in her eyes and fell. She could of course have removed her hands at any moment, but could not bear the thought of seeing them even partially red again. In time she was sure that her hands were no longer freezing but burning, as they did when she put them in a basin of boiled dishwater before it cooled outside the cook tent. "Fire and ice," she found herself whimpering. "Fire and ice."

After much longer than she thought she could stand it, she raised her arms, and so did Ronald. She looked at her throbbing hands in the lamplight and found them clean, white as the crystals in the chamber behind them. Her tears redoubled, and she saw that Ronald was weeping too, something she had not known him to do. There was no blood left on his hands either. They stiffly intertwined their fingers above the lantern, hardly able to feel the comfort of cold flesh, and waited for warmth and strength to return.

"Now," said Ronald, still sniffling a little, "if you can face doing it all over again, we've got to wash the axes too." He always liked a complete task.

Jennifer shuddered. She'd had enough purging for one day—perhaps enough for a lifetime. On the other hand (though she still wasn't sure she could feel one apart from the other), she couldn't see trudging back up to the chamber with scrubbed palms and bloody axes. It would be like cleaning her father's fish and returning his pocketknife smeared and fouled.

"All right," she said. It was only then, as she grasped her ax and held it out with two hands, as if in offering, that she noticed the ax that Ronald held over the water beside her was not his own. "Whose is that?" Jennifer asked. "It's too long to be yours. Is it William's?"

Ronald nodded and lowered it carefully into the water. "I'll explain," he said. "I had to leave mine on top—for an anchor." But instead of explaining any further he moaned with the force of cold renewed in his fingers—and so did Jennifer, who had settled her ax in the stream as well.

She squeezed her hands back and forth along the shaft, and took special care, and quite literally special pains, to wipe the blood from the pick and the adze on the silvery head. The metal ached even more than the wood, and once again the agony was unbearable. But as she lost the sense of touch from her hands, half afraid she would lose her hold on the ax in her numbness, she felt something odd occurring. The spike of the shaft seemed suddenly blunt. The shaft was becoming thick and round, and its upper end, as she traveled its shape, was growing wide and thin somehow, until there was—it was quite impossible—until there was no head at all. Jennifer lifted her ax from the water, and Ronald did the same with his. She held in her hands, and he held in his, a dripping wooden oar.

Their surprise was so great they forgot the pain of cold in their fingers. Quietly they stood their oars blade-up on the ice and knocked them together—the tips were even. William's ax had been longer than the one that Jennifer had taken, but the only difference between the oars was the color of wood—both clean of blood, but one, William's, dark and smoky like oiled oak, and the other, from the sister of Lady Demaris, clean and white like fresh-split ash. They rose astonished, unable to put words to wonder, and held their dripping oars before them as minutes before they had held their axes. A few drops kissed the lid of the lantern and extinguished themselves in a tiny hiss. The black walls danced in the light, and the deep dark stream flowed quietly on.

Jennifer was about to state the obvious weirdness of what had just happened, and was in fact ransacking her mind for some metamorphic precedent. Ovid, perhaps. But before she could speak, something large came bumping down the stream from the darkness. Ronald encircled her shoulders protectively and held out his oar in a defensive posture, wishing it were still an ax.

The thing came looming into the light—not an animate foe at all, but a large wooden rowboat, square at the stern, arching high to a pointed prow, and almost as wide as the channel itself. Its wooden benches were perfectly empty. As the boat came alongside of them they each leaned out and laid hold of the gunwale. For a moment the current tugged the boat against their grip. Then in tacit agreement they slid it sideways onto shore. The keel caught on the lip of the bank, but when they dropped their oars and put all four of their hands to the task, the boat soon listed full on the ice beside the lantern.

They panted a little, hands on hips, and wondered even more.

"You suppose we should get in?" said Jennifer. "We have oars." Even as she made the suggestion, she recoiled from the idea. Who knew where the stream might take them?

But Ronald seemed to ignore her. "Let's get back to the others," he said.

Jennifer shrugged and picked up the lantern. They had no sooner turned up the passage, however, than they saw Chambers descending towards them, holding out a second lantern he must have taken from his pack. Behind him came Garth with a measured tread, bearing William in his arms. Jennifer had had no idea the old man was so strong.

When Chambers reached them he held out his lantern over the boat and whistled softly. "Why, *Amoenas*," he said, as if addressing a stray cow, "what are you doing busting loose from your moorings like that? Never could keep you in just one place."

"She has only spared you the trouble," said Garth. He approached the boat and carefully laid his burden in it upon the blanket that had swaddled the body in his arms. William's head he neatly pillowed in the prow, and tucked his feet just beneath the rowing bench. The boat was still listing, and Ronald and Jennifer carefully rocked it upright to afford a more decent resting place. They stood on either side of the prow, looking down at William's face. He was still and peaceful, breathing quietly. Chambers unfolded another wool blanket from out of his pack and spread it over the sleeping form, tucking it under the motionless chin in a motherly way that surprised Jennifer very much.

Then Garth, standing grim at the stern of the boat, spoke again. "I send you on a journey, my children, for your cleansing and for his healing. I know that now your hands are clean, and the axes are washed, but these things are but a beginning. From here the stream leads through the dark to the eastern highlands, and thence south and west to Amoenas Gorge, where you will find rest at the Tower of Otium. From Otium it is still many miles to the Western Sea, and there your task will be at an end. At the shore you will meet those to whom you may give the sleeping body of your friend, and they will accomplish the final healing in the course, perhaps, of many years."

Having given this charge, Garth held up his aged hand as if in blessing and benediction, in just the way that Ronald's father used to conclude a very long church service. But the words that he spoke were not familiar from any service Ronald had known:

> *"The tongues of ice and water go with thee,*
> *The arms of the floating maiden support thee,*
> *The song of the ouzel lead thee aright,*
> *And may thy voice find praise with these.*

"Farewell," he said. "Seek thy rest on the restless river."

Chambers tossed his pack in the boat and fixed their lantern to a short post at the back of the stern. At his nod they helped him skid the boat back into the stream, and he held it there while Ronald and Jennifer took off their crampons and clambered in, Jennifer thinking that this could be the stupidest thing she had ever done. But having helped to create this icy labyrinth of sorrow, she felt determined to follow the thread of Garth's directions out of it. She took her seat on a bench by the lantern, facing Ronald, who sat amidships on the rowing bench. His feet straddled the upturned toes of William's boots that poked out from underneath. Chambers was handing him both oars and showing him how to fit them through the oarlocks to row.

"But you won't need them here, where the channel is narrow. Keep them inside the boat just now so they don't get broken. Follow your nose—or William's, maybe—and let Jennifer do your seeing for you. There are plenty more candles in the pack, and blankets too, and a bit to eat if you get hungry. It's a long ways, but the dark and the ice do not last forever. All glaciers have an end, and all rivers their first beginning. The Alpha really is the Omega, when you think about it, though for a while you'll be in between."

Jennifer wanted to ask about this, but already he had pushed them away.

"*Semper lentus!*" Chambers called after them. "*Festina lente!* Don't go too fast if you can help it, and hasten slowly. Those oars may have a bit of magic, but I know for a fact the boat does not. On ice or rock it will stave in before you can say—"

What Chambers could and might have said was lost in an indistinct series of echoes, for the boat had bumped around a turn and cut him away from sight and sound. For just a moment Jennifer saw the glow of his lamp from around the bend, and then they were floating quite alone down a keyhole passage filled with water. She reached her hands to the walls and ceiling and felt them glide beneath her fingers, cold and hard.

Chapter 7
Dark as Obsidian

✳

"SO THEN WHAT HAPPENED?" Jennifer said in an awful whisper. She had already told him her story—about the rose and the cabin and Lady Demaris—and now was hearing his. It was a good time for telling stories, for although they were still in the boat with William, under the surface of the glacier, they were no longer coursing a narrow passage but plowing about on a huge black lake in a large cavern, so tall they could not make out the ceiling. Ronald was rowing as Chambers had shown him, but somewhat haphazardly since there was no real current to follow. He was just beginning to think, in fact, that he might be better off not rowing at all, for if the lake had an outlet, as it no doubt did, the boat would sooner find it by drifting. But just sitting there, oars dripping into unfathomable darkness, felt so forlorn to both of them that he kept rowing to prove to himself that they did exist.

"What happened," said Ronald, "was that I was so overcome after cutting the rope that I just lay there in the snow—in shock, I suppose. Then the rain brought me around. It had started to rain."

"Just then?"

"Just then."

"Oh, Ronald," she moaned. "That's when it started for me too—when the ax bled, and I pulled it out. Don't you see? It was I who really severed the rope—when I severed the rose."

Ronald stopped rowing and touched her shoulders with both wet oars. "Fallacy, Jen: *post hoc ergo propter hoc.* In fact, for all we know the cutting of the rope was not *post hoc* at all. You might as well say that my action caused yours. Or that they occurred simultaneously—and perhaps coincidentally. Hume, you know."

"Whom?"

"Forget it."

"How can I? You can have your *post* and *propter hoc*. But it's obvious to me we're in this together. Linked by fate."

"Fate?"

"Yes. Linked by fate. Torn by passion. Alone with the man she never knew. Together against tempestuous odds on subglacial seas of indifference. Subglacial? No, *subglacial* will never sell. But I can see the cover, can't you? Except that the neckline on this cagoule does not plunge nearly enough—in fact, it doesn't plunge at all. We'll have to fix that. But you with the oars—just perfect—and that little wet curl on your forehead, gleaming in the lantern light. That's it, set the jaw, and—"

"Jen!"

"Well, it's worth considering," she murmured. She was a bit surprised herself at her own intemperate silliness, given the moment. But she supposed it might be good for morale—hers certainly, and Ronald's secretly. And somehow he had set her off.

"You know what I've been thinking?" said Ronald, sounding as if he'd been thinking it for a long time.

"What?" said Jennifer. She set herself for a new romantic revelation or, failing that, some devastating reflection on her character.

"I've been thinking this lake is the same one that Dr. Slupensky discovered today—or yesterday. You know what I mean. Which puts us under the eastern lobe, like Garth said. The crystal chamber must have been beneath the divide, just below the nunatak."

Jennifer nodded distractedly. Their location was not so important to her as it was to him. She could rely on Ronald in any conversation to transform feelings to information.

"So," she said, nudging the tips of William's boots, "what *did* you do? After it started raining and all."

"All I *could* do," Ronald replied. "With the rope cut I couldn't get any closer to the edge of the schrund, since it might collapse at the overhang. So I scrambled up to our pillar of rock, untied what was left of the rope, and brought it back to where I'd been lying in the snow. There I sank my ax to the hilt and tied a bowline around the shaft. I padded the lip the best I could with my rucksack and threw down the rope. I hoped there was enough to reach. And then I rapped in."

"You rappelled? With that marmot around? He could have bitten off your rope too!"

"I thought of that. And I looked for him the best I could. But it was foggy, remember? I had to risk it."

In spite of her retroactive concern, Jennifer found herself admiring him for what he had done. "And?" she said.

"And the rope reached—just. When I got to the bottom I found him bleeding, unconscious, in three inches of running water. I knew I had to get him out of that ice water right away, no matter if his neck was broken, no matter if he was bleeding to death, because he'd die of hypothermia first. It was roomy down there—maybe eighty feet down—and I dragged him up on a dry shelf under the wall. There were a few drips from the cornice above, but he was out of the stream, and out of the rain. I stuffed my parka beneath his shoulders to insulate him from the cold, and tried to stop the blood from his side. It didn't work—you saw my hands. As far as I could tell there were no bones broken—a miracle, considering—but not much help if he didn't stop bleeding.

"In my mind I was trying to work out how I could strap him to my back and prusik up the rope—though as long as it rained he would stay more sheltered there in the crevasse. But if I could stop the bleeding I knew that I might have to leave to get help. So I was thinking these things, holding my hands against his side, when the rope that was hanging from my ax suddenly came down in a heap."

"You mean, the marmot chomped it?"

"I mean, the rope fell in a heap in the running water below our ledge. That's all I could directly observe. Marmot or no, same result."

Jennifer wondered what drove him to be so distressingly factual. "It must have been the marmot," she complained. "What else could it be?"

"A bad knot, a sharp edge of ice—who knows? But yes, the marmot is a distinct possibility, given its recent strange behavior."

"So you walked."

"I walked. But first I waited. The cave at the closed-off end of the schrund looked none too inviting. I hadn't been in the system before, and anyway, I didn't have a light. My headlamp was up in my pack, eighty feet of overhung ice away. It was getting dark as night came on, and the rain wasn't stopping."

"Sounds like you in a heap of trouble, boy," Jennifer said.

Ronald looked hurt, and stilled the oars. She knew he would need some coaxing to continue, and asked herself why she didn't keep still and let Ronald be Ronald. "Hey," she said feebly, "a joke. I'm sorry."

"Anyhow," Ronald went on quietly, "that's when Garth showed up. At first he was just a light down the tunnel as I looked in from the ice shelf. I called out as loud as I could, hoping it was your dad, or Slupensky, or someone else on the cave survey. But the light just kept on floating toward me, and no one called back. When it reached the open air of the schrund, still at a distance, I made out a single figure, in a poncho or something, and walking as if out for a stroll. When he got to us I saw he was wearing a long wool cloak and a long white beard. He was no one I had ever seen.

"I said, 'Hey, we're in trouble.' He simply took my hands from William's side and held them in his own. He didn't say anything—he just looked at me—and Jen, his eyes were unspeakably sad."

Jennifer nodded, a bit surprised at his sudden passion.

"I suppose they were dark anyway, but in the evening rain at the shadowy bottom of that crevasse, his eyes were dark as obsidian." His voice faltered.

"Obsidian?"

"Yes," he said. "Obsidian."

She blessed the hour he had met this man who had dislocated him into poetry.

"There's not much more to it, really. He told me his name after a while, and said to me, 'What has come to be has been appointed, but woe to him who severs the heart.' He sounded sorry and matter-of-fact—not at all judgmental, if you know what I mean."

"I do know what you mean," said Jennifer. "Lady Demaris spoke like that. They're serious, aren't they? But I don't think they're out to get us. They know how to be angry without being mad. Like Mom was."

Ronald paused. Jennifer sensed he was wishing he could say the same for his dead father. That they were each partly orphaned was the secret they were still learning to touch upon.

"Anyhow," he continued, "Garth untied the rope and lifted William into his arms. Then he nodded to William's ax and simply said, 'You'll be needing that.' I hadn't noticed the ax since I'd come down the rope. It was stuck in the ice spike-first in the stream. I yanked on it but it didn't come out. Then I yanked harder. 'On your knees first,' Garth told me. 'Then it will come.' I kneeled down in the same stream William had just fallen into, and the ax came out—just like that."

"I suppose it might," Jennifer mused.

"Then I coiled up the two wet ropes—or the two parts of the wet rope—and followed Garth down the—what's that?"

"Down the *what's that?*"

"No, listen. Don't you hear it?"

Jennifer strained her ears past the echo of their dying voices and heard the rush of water ahead. "One of those moulins," she said. "A little shower out of the ceiling. Please to row around it, James."

"It's much louder than that," said Ronald, holding the oars erect in the air like rabbit ears at full attention. "And it's getting louder. Which means—"

He placed the oars back in the water and tried to reverse their course. Jennifer watched him strain and grimace.

"Which means there's a current all of a sudden. I can't stop us, Jen."

By a quickening of air in her face, Jennifer felt their new momentum. The noise ahead was no longer an echo. It was gathering to a greatness of sound.

"Hold up the light!" Ronald shouted.

Jennifer's feet jumped at the sound of his voice. She reached for the lantern and snatched it up so quickly that the flame snuffed out. Ronald shouted something else but now it felt too dark to hear. The sound of rushing water ahead redoubled and redoubled again, filling her ears like the terrible sound of glaciers calving into the ocean, something she had once seen and heard with her father on a large ship in the north. It seemed to her that the Mirror Glacier was destroying itself, falling in upon the lake in bergs and slabs and monstrous pieces.

When the sound could not possibly get any louder, the boat tipped forward. Jennifer suddenly lurched from her seat and bruised her face on William's boots. She felt the boat hurtling downward, the splash of water and hiss of air against her back. Her stomach was caught up into her throat, and she waited, and waited, and waited for the impact—the moment when they would hit bottom and smash into splinters of wood and bone. No one, she thought, would ever find them, much less recognize them, and this prospect turned her fear forlorn. She had read of a man discovered at the foot of a glacier some four thousand years after he had fallen into a crevasse. But she would not have even that immortality. She would merely be rolled round in a glacial river with rocks and stones and trees.

But the obliterating impact never came. First the boat tipped left as if banking a curve on a bobsled run, and then suddenly right, so sharply that Jennifer grabbed the bench above her head—and was horrified to discover that Ronald was no longer on it. He must have gone overboard. Lying in the loud and rushing dark, shifting this way and that as the boat plunged its course, she tried to imagine how and where she might search for him.

How long she raced down the black whitewater she did not know. After a while she gave up her anxieties—for herself, at least. It was no use cringing at every turn when nothing happened, and keeping herself at a pitch of fright was too exhausting. Little by little the noise and velocity seemed to lessen, and at length she realized she was holding the bench above her head much harder than she needed to. She found that she was quite wet, and that next to her ear there seemed to be water sloshing about in the bottom of the boat. Then the roar of the water outside the boat subsided to a gentle murmur, echoing like a dark caress. She lifted her head, slow and cautious in case the ceiling were low here, and righted herself on her knees in the bilge. Her hands were clasped on the bench as in prayer when the boat turned a corner into thin gray light. The stream was broad and the ceiling high over steely swirls. And there in the bow was Ronald—*was Ronald*, her only love—thrown on his back like a bug, lying askew atop the waterlogged body of William and gripping both sides of the boat for life.

Then the cave was gone, passed like a dream, and raindrops fell on her upturned face.

Chapter 8
Old Growth

❋

"WHAT ARE YOU DOING DOWN THERE?" asked Jennifer. "Niagara Falls on the River Styx and you decide to take a nap."

Ronald rose up out of the bow as if he were William's departing spirit. He slowly took his seat amidships by the oars, and Jennifer, still down on her knees, clasped him tightly about the waist. "You okay?" she asked more gently. "I thought you were gone."

Ronald was still too stunned to reply, and perhaps too shy, but he welcomed the touch of her arms about him as he welcomed the touch of sky and rain. He sat quietly looking at clouds and trees and sand and river revealed in light. The river was broad, a milky gray, and calm but swift between sandy flats. He had seen this spot a dozen times from the nunatak high up on the mountain, but never before had he been here where the Amoenas River shot out from the Mirror Glacier at this low elevation into the forest. The stone-mottled walls of the glacier behind them were fast retreating, and the nunatak was lost in clouds. Even the giant cedar trees that anchored the shore were wrapped in mist, huddled and dark except for the flame of vine maple that sometimes ignited beneath them.

"Hello," said Jennifer, suddenly releasing him. "We can't let William just wallow about in the water down there. We've got ourselves a regular lake. What do you say we row to shore and find a way to dry out a bit? I'm not any too warm myself—and neither are you, by the feel of you, Ronald. We're much too wet and cold to be safe. Hypothermia, you know—killer of the disprepared."

Ronald agreed, and pulled at the oars till they reached an eddy by a small creek on the left-hand bank. Both of them splashed into the shallows, and with some straining they pulled the boat up onto the sand and lifted William out of the bow. He felt dangerously sodden in their arms, so Ronald dragged him heels-down toward the edge of the wood while Jennifer gathered the blankets and lantern and looked for a way to secure the boat. There was nothing at hand to tie it to, and she couldn't push it any farther from the river herself, so after tipping the water out she simply left it where it was. Then she stuffed everything into the generous pack and plodded up the beach after Ronald.

It was still raining.

She caught up to him at the edge of the trees, and lifted William's sandy heels over the brush and into the quiet, the rainless hush of the old-growth forest. Here cedars grew that were girthed like ancient temple pillars. High above, thick branches wove a canopy to protect them from the worst of the wet. On the forest floor grew clumps of fern but little else. Unobstructed, they hauled William across the duff until they came to a fire-scarred hollow within the base of a particularly large red cedar some ways into the wood.

Once inside they found the hollow really to be a snug dry room, large enough for all of them to stretch out in comfort. They laid William down on his wet wool blanket until Jennifer found two drier ones in the very bottom of Chambers' pack. There was also bread, and a bottle of soup inside the blankets—and just as important, candles and flint. Ronald collected an armload of branches and just at the entrance started a fire from dry shavings and dead twigs that Jennifer had gathered from within the room. They shed boots and socks, and found various blackened knots and niches from which to hang steaming sweaters and parkas. Then they sat on their blankets next to the fire and felt their fingers and toes come to life.

Jennifer broke off half a loaf, and it tasted rough and sweet in their mouths. The soup they kept at the edge of the fire, and when it was as hot again as it had been in Chambers' kettle, they drank huge portions down in turn, and felt as warmed within as without. Jennifer had a wonderful feeling of safety, and of home. She wondered if it would be like this should they really marry.

But when they had grown quite comfortable, they realized they had forgotten to tend to William's welfare. "He's not just a dead body, you know," Jennifer scolded.

Ronald removed the boots and socks and loosened the clothing to let it dry. He checked the wounds and found no discharge. William still breathed peacefully, apparently in a deep sleep.

"Do we save some for him?" Jennifer said, holding out the soup and bread.

"Maybe," said Ronald, "but not now. If he sleeps for a week, I think we should let him."

"A week!" said Jennifer. "We'll be rowing this river for a week?"

"Well," said Ronald, "it's a day or two to the gorge, anyhow, if it is the same one I've seen on the map. I don't know exactly where in the gorge this Tower of Otium will be—where Garth says that we are to rest. And how long it will take to get to the sea is anyone's guess. You've been on top of the North Queen, right? That's the highest, and you can just glimpse the ocean from there, a glimmer of it anyway, when there's no slash burning and the air is clear. It's a ways, Jennifer."

He paused for a moment. "Finishing the survey might have been easier," he said darkly.

This stung in her ears. It was as if to say, *If you hadn't forgotten the data book, Jennifer, we'd never be on this wretched trip.* But that was the marmot's fault, when you thought about it, as was William's fall in the schrund. Though Ronald didn't have to go lunging after the book in the first place. And it *was* rather clumsy of him to slice the rope. All she'd done was to pick a beautiful and unusual flower—something anyone might have wanted to do. And a good thing too, for without the elixir that Lady Demaris had squeezed from the rose, William might have been dead by now. Jennifer realized that she was really the heroine in this mess that Ronald had created. But she would remain tolerant and not allow herself to gloat or to take offense.

"You'd like to finish the survey, wouldn't you, Ronald?" It was an echoing tactic she had learned in a psychology class.

"Well, of course," he faltered.

"For science?"

"For science."

"Gwen says it's just for the dam."

"Well," said Ronald, "not *just* for the dam."

"But we wouldn't be here if it weren't for the dam, would we, Ronald? I mean, that's where the money comes from, right?"

"I suppose. In this case, anyway."

"But that's the way it always is, isn't it? Science is knowledge. Knowledge is power. That's Francis Bacon, that much—I had to suffer through his *Essays* with Dr. Hassler. But power pollutes. Power destroys. Power is always power against. In our world, on merry middle earth, science is the slut of industry. Either that, or the whore of war."

"Jen!" He would have been much less offended if she had slandered some person in particular.

For Jennifer's part, she was sorry she had spoken, but as she was playing the heroine, she could not bring herself to apologize.

Ronald drew a deep breath. "Speaking of science—"

"Which we were," Jennifer affirmed.

"Speaking of science," he began again, "I should mention something I just saw—or didn't see. The little stream where we pulled out the boat—that's the one that comes off the saddle near Chambers Lake. There should be a stream gauge—a little orange tower—just above it on the river. It's the one that Roscoe has to hike down to once a week. I've never been with him, but I know what it looks like and where it is. And it's not there."

"Washed away?"

"Possibly, but there hasn't been any flooding to speak of. This is the first hard rain of the season, and glacier release has been pretty even except for the normal fluctuations of day and night."

"So what you're saying is that we've got—"

"—an anomaly, Jen. And I've got half a mind to hike back up to the saddle from here and report it—in camp." As he said the word he remembered that he would be more likely to find a cabin. And if anyone were there at all, they would probably send him right back here with Jennifer to continue their appointed task. If he ever hoped to finish his survey, he first had to begin their quest.

He did not correct himself out loud, but merely lapsed into forlorn silence. "What time is it anyway?" he finally complained. "I left my watch in my ruck-sack."

"Don't ask me," said Jennifer, looking about the inner walls of the burnt trunk as if for a clue. "There's no clock in the forest. In fact, I don't know if it's morning or afternoon, do you? No matter, though." She stood up and struck a thespian pose, arms outspread in front of the fire. "'I like this place,'" she declaimed, "'and willingly could waste my time in it.'"

"You what?" said Ronald. "*This* place?"

"Shakespeare," she said. "The Forest of Arden. Almost as good as Shelley. Mary, that is. Although Frankenstein—his monster, I mean—spends more time cruising around on a glacier than he does holed up in the forest."

"I'd like to check on that stream gauge," said Ronald.

"That's fine, Frankenstein." She sat back down.

He peered past the fire and held his hand out the entrance. "I think it's stopped. At least it's not raining as hard as it was. I'll run down to the river for just a bit and come right back."

"If you want," said Jennifer. "Just don't fall in or anything." She heard much more concern in her voice than she thought she had intended, and realized it was as much for herself as it was for him. She did not relish the prospect of being left by herself in the wilderness. It is one thing to feel the solace of open spaces on alpine slopes, and quite another to be tucked deep down in a dripping forest by the icy surge of a glacial stream. She felt entangled and enfolded here, far back in the sinister ply of the non-human. This was the forest not as she liked it but as it was.

She felt almost ashamed of these darkwood thoughts, but in the moments that Ronald put on his boots and recollected his sweater and parka, she had to admit these *were* her thoughts. Too embarrassed to give or receive a parting kiss for such a brief errand, she watched him step around the fire and over the rich rust floor of the forest, out through a corridor of trees till he merged with the gloom. She caught one last glimpse of his innocent head in a crimson explosion of vine maple, and then he was gone, perhaps crossing the sand to the river's edge. She watched the spot in the vine maple for a sentimental length of time, then sighed and added more wood to the fire.

She turned to William and tried to breathe as slowly and calmly as he did. "I love him, you know. Every bit as much as Gwen loves you." At the thought of Gwen she allowed herself to cry softly, and wondered where her friend might be and what she could know of all that had happened. "You have to get better," she instructed him. "You're going to be a father soon, and I don't think you'll want to sleep through *that*. You'd be the first, anyhow."

She fell to musing by the fire, shifted her boots away from the flames, and curled up on top of her blanket and under Ronald's. Staying up all night in a glacier cave had not improved her wakefulness, and though she wished to wait for Ronald's return before falling asleep, she proved herself no different from any one of the ten virgins waiting for the bridegroom in the parable, and drifted off.

When Jennifer awoke, the fire had collapsed in embers and the forest was very nearly dark. She heard the breath of William beside her, as dead and calm as air from a bellows—and no other breath besides.

"Ronald," she whispered.

She sat up. "Ronald!"

No one.

Just to be sure, she stoked the fire and found in the glancing light of the flames that Ronald certainly was not there. She had no idea how long she'd slept, and two ideas, both unthinkable, about his absence—accident and outright desertion. And a third idea—murder most foul—when she considered that loathsome marmot.

Jennifer knew from experience that out in the open next to the river it would still be light. Hastily, she threw a few more boughs on the fire to ensure a beacon for her return and set off in her newly dried boots and socks. She felt the air quiet and cool about her face, a presence between the living columns of bark and heartwood. In a few moments she reached a thicket of vine maple, struggled through it, and found herself on the sand near the river—not too near, for the beach was wide, testimony to the glacier's power of swift release. The roar of the river was thick and steady upon her ears, and the clouds swayed low, blowing eastward.

On her left she heard the thin rush of the tributary that came from the saddle, and she followed it in the failing light to the corner of shore where brook met river. There were bootprints here, partly melted by the rain. For a moment her gaze was distracted by a parting of the clouds upstream that framed the face of the evening star in the twilight sky. Then, in an instant, she took in what wasn't there—no boat, and no fresh tracks leading back to the forest.

"Ronald!" she cried. The name was swallowed by the sound of the river. Even as she watched, the water scooped the sand from her feet and hurried on.

Chapter 9
The Ouzel Aright

✳

WHEN RONALD STEPPED OUT OF THE WOODS to the sand sometime that morning or afternoon, he glanced upshore and down through the misty rain for the orange-towered gauge he knew in his heart he would not see. Only as an afterthought, as he came close to the river's edge, did he think to check on Chambers' boat. He reached the water a bit upcurrent from where they had left it, and sure enough, when he looked downstream, there it was beached on the spit of sand that brought the creek and river together. The boat looked secure for the time being, but was perilously close to the water. Though the glacier would not release its afternoon melt, the new rainfall might cause the river to rise even so, and Ronald determined to pull the boat farther onto the shore if he could.

For a moment he wondered at Jennifer for leaving it so close to the water, but part of him realized that *he* had left the boat as well, so he excused her at least to the level of complicity. He was deep in this disposition of blame, and perhaps forty yards away from the boat, when it inexplicably started to give—not the boat but the shore, and not inexplicably, given the glimpse he suddenly had of a mountainous marmot trenching the sand from under the stern. It fixed him with an ashen eye and tore at the sand undergirding the boat with doglike fervor.

For a moment Ronald stood still in surprise. Then he flew at the boat and the marmot with all the strength and speed he could summon—and partway there tripped over a rock, swan-dived onto the ground, and choked on the loss of his own wind. From his prone and breathless vantage point he watched as the boat sank away with the sand and slowly slipped out into the water. For a moment it hovered near the shore, and then the current caught the prow and gently whirled it past the mouth of the small creek. The marmot stood on the broken bank and glared at Ronald as if to say, *I dare you to act.* Then it splashed through the tributary and swung across the beach to the trees. For a fat marmot, it could gallop like a buffalo.

Ronald took the dare and stood up. He was still gasping from his fall. But he stumbled ahead, splashed through the creek behind the marmot and, feeling the return of his breath, paused to consider whether he should go after the boat, the marmot, or Jennifer. Revenge, and the marmot, was his first impulse; and then solace, and Jennifer. Heroism, and certain drowning, was not really a live option, until suddenly the boat strayed into a shoreside eddy, underneath a half-buried log that was not so very far downstream, and began to loop in a lazy twirl tantalizingly close to the sand.

That made up his mind, and he dashed down the sand, socks squishing inside his boots, carefully leaping the snags and boulders in his path. He reached the log and the lucky eddy just as the boat swung past his reach. He stood on tiptoe, waiting for it to orbit again, but this time the boat slipped back into the waiting current, bouncing stern then prow against the log and then sailing down the river again in midstream. He had no intention of diving in after it—but what happened once might happen again, so he hurried down the sandy shore, hoping the boat would meet again with a helpful eddy or obstruction.

It easily outdistanced him on the swift strong current, and soon disappeared around a bend in the barren drizzle. He stopped in momentary despair, but then considered he could not know what lay around the bend in the river unless he went to see. And so he did, keeping up a dogged spirit, and rounded the bend in time to watch the boat fade away around the next one. But that bend too might render serendipities, and so he continued, and continued, and continued, till he did not see the boat anymore, and was wetter from perspiration within his parka than from the fading drizzle without. After a while he lost the strength and urgency to trot along, and settled into a fatalistic walk, telling himself at every turn to give it up and go back to Jennifer, but somehow not doing so. The body has its own inertia, even when the mind has other plans. And so it was that Ronald kept walking, long after he had given up on reason and hope.

What stopped him finally, long after the rain had ceased, was the thunder of rapids that came to him from a rocky defile just ahead. The beach was pinched off on either side by mossy bluffs, bright green and water-slick, that crowded in against the river and shot it through a boiling slot. The river water, to this point a milky gray with the glacier flour of ice-ground stone, was thrown into raging columns of white that slammed into a fern-decked wall and exploded off in a sudden turn. Ronald walked to the end of the sand and looked down the Charybdis of whitewater to where it smashed into the Scylla of the ferny wall. The boat, of course, was nowhere in sight, and he reasonably concluded it was shivered into wet chips like slurry in a pulpwood mill. For a moment he was grateful the marmot had launched the boat as it had. There was no way they could have survived the rapid, and the current above it was so swift that they may not have been able to beach the boat before being swallowed down this throat of unbearably dark white noise.

He stood mesmerized at the head of the rapid for quite some time, wondering what he might do next. There was no scrambling over the mossy bluffs—they were too steep and slippery. And having come this far in pursuit of the boat, he didn't much relish the idea of returning to Jennifer empty-handed. He had reached an impasse of mind and place.

Eventually he found himself watching a slate-gray bird—a water ouzel—dipping about where the last smooth stretch of river current plunged into the violence of the narrows. Heedless of the chaos—or perhaps heeding it most of all—the ouzel hopped and flung itself this way and that, sometimes diving beneath the water to re-emerge, unscathed and unruffled, at the very edge of the white upheaval. The more he watched, the more Ronald wondered that the bird was so well able to thrive on the boundary of death. *Be careful!* he wanted to call out, and each time the ouzel disappeared, he sympathetically held his breath until it resurfaced. As if conscious of this sympathy, each time it popped back out of the water the bird was a little closer to Ronald. And then it was perched on the shore at his feet, shaking itself in a fit of flutter. Ronald now saw it was smaller than a robin, larger than a sparrow, a plump bird with a stubby tail.

"So you're safe, are you?" he said aloud. "I'm glad for that." He surprised himself with his sentimentality. At least that's what he would have called it before.

The ouzel looked at him steadily, dipping on its legs like a nervous courtier making a series of awkward bows. "*Bzeet!*" it said.

"Aren't you cold?" Ronald asked. "It's drier out of the water, you know."

As if taking his suggestion, the ouzel bounced past Ronald's feet and stopped on the other side of him. Then it hopped farther, closer to the forest, and halted and looked and hopped again. At the very edge of the big trees—hemlocks, not cedars—and up against the mossy wall, it paused and eyed him once more, dipping and bowing as politely as ever. Then it disappeared into the dark green world.

Ronald stood looking after it, wishing somehow the bird were back. Suddenly it was, watching him from beneath the fronds of sword fern at the forest edge. "*Bzeet-bzeet-bzeet!*" Then it darted back into the woods.

In his mind there echoed Garth's voice of commission:

The song of the ouzel lead thee aright.

The words seemed alarmingly slight things to trust. But he sensed that he might, and the possibility filled him with strange exhilaration. He paused, and then, still doubting himself, he followed the bird into the trees. Waist-deep in ferns, he did not see its shape at first. The ground was steep here, hard against the rising bluff, and he had to peer upward to catch sight of the ouzel again, resting against the firm gray trunk of a stolid hemlock. It paused there as if waiting for him, and when he caught up, the bird took off again.

And so they pursued the journey in stages, the ouzel darting effortlessly, and Ronald pulling himself upward, staining his hands with fistfuls of fern. After a while the hill began to ease to an angle of something closer to human repose. Ronald was able to make his way unaided by ferns, though still crouching on all fours. The duff in his hands was deep and rich, musty with the millennia of hemlock which had given their lives, their fallen bodies, for each succeeding generation. The air was quiet away from the river, and unexpectedly, Ronald felt a sense of home, deep beneath the giant trees and lacy needles, somewhere lost in a dim, damp canyon, pawing the earth like a lumbering bear. He had known such surprising contentment before—the sheer pleasure at times of standing on the nunatak amidst the swell and spill of ice. It was a pleasure unrelated to whether he completed the survey of the day or not. It was the simple happiness of belonging, of being there, a participant in something ancient, more grand and good than he could imagine. And now in the forest it was like this too.

But the feeling was fleeting, impermanent as an ouzel at rest. Soon the slope eased even more, and Ronald was able to pick his way along upright. When the ground became nearly level he suddenly lost sight of the ouzel and crashed through the ferns in a panic. Then, quite simply, he found himself standing on a comfortable trail leading left and right, parallel to the river below. And just to the right of him, bobbing obediently, the ouzel waited on the path. Then it turned eastward, downstream, and Ronald followed.

He was delighted of course to find a trail, but dismayed to be going still farther from Jennifer. It seemed dimmer in the forest than when he had entered, and he sensed that evening was coming on. And why, he wondered, was he trusting a bird? But he went on in spite of himself, thinking the trail might very well lead back to the river below the rapid. It was perhaps too late to return anyway, and this might be his last chance to find the boat, should it still exist.

As he had hoped, the trail after coursing level began to descend and finally to switchback down through the forest. The ouzel fluttered faithfully on, and as the woods began to grow truly dusky Ronald started to hear the river once again. Then he could see it, just to the right of him through the trees, under limbed curtains of pale green lichen, and he plowed through the ferns again until he regained the familiar flood-bared sandy shore.

The river and riverside looked quite empty under the deepening evening clouds. He felt all alone, and more than foolish, and suddenly realized he no longer had a clue as to where the ouzel might be. For all he knew it was still on the trail. He turned to enter the woods again, tired beyond discouragement, and knew he must find a place to rest. He had just touched the edge of the ferns when the bird alighted on his sleeve and announced itself. *"Bzeet-bzeet!"* Just as quickly it hopped away down the beach.

"You again," Ronald said, feigning exasperation. But what he felt was relief and wonder—relief that the bird had come again, and wonder that it came to him as friend to friend. He summoned the strength to follow the ouzel once more, wondering how far it would lead him.

Not far. In less than a minute the ouzel stopped in a natural cove, split off by a rock from the river, and came to rest on the silhouette of Chambers' boat, calmly afloat and completely intact on still waters. Ronald ran up and burst into tears. It was so unlike him, and he did not care.

He carefully reached to the prow from the sand and pulled it ashore, all the lovely, smooth-knit heft of its marvelous entirety. He dragged it well up onto the beach and smiled at the bird in the gathering dark. The ouzel only bowed, of course. Ronald pulled the boat all the way to the forest edge and, with his last strength, tipped it over against a log well-banked with ferns.

He looked upstream to the parted clouds and the evening star. "Good night," he said, and crawled inside.

Chapter 10
Subjected in Hope

*

It was dark when Jennifer listlessly returned to the forest. It seemed clear that Ronald had deserted her. But how? And why? How estranged he must have felt to abandon her in so desperate a way. She reviewed in her mind each playful insult that had passed her lips in his company, and regretted them all. It was her fault.

And then it was not her fault—it was his. No sooner did Jennifer slap face-first into something solid and wooden in the dark than she became victim in love as well. How stupid of her to promise herself to a man hardly human, a robotic piece of empiricism who was only happy when scoping out little orange flags on a glacier but incapable of admiring the view, natural or feminine, outside a theodolite. *Good riddance,* she thought.

And yet, how lonely and sorry she was!

And so she accused and repented by turns, paying very little attention really to where she was walking, letting the dim broad trunks slip by, and sometimes tripping over a root or mashing into a clump of fern or devil's club, the sting of which only served to re-arouse her feelings of fury, should they have temporarily abated. Not taking care where she went, it soon followed, when she stopped to think, that she did not know where she had come. In the back of her mind she supposed she had been looking for the fire at the door of the tree, but she saw none now, and realized she had been on the beach quite long enough for the flames to have burned very low. Her sense of duty for William's care began to displace her penitent and outraged sense of romantic loss, and she stood in one place for a long time, gathering her breath and thoughts. She listened for the voice of the river, but it was faraway and indistinct, no closer before her than behind.

She stumbled this way and that for a while, hoping to catch sight of the embers. She even called out William's name before she remembered how ineffectual that would be. But her aimless sorties were no use. She was lost, and would stay so till morning. Not knowing what else to do, she burrowed into the damp and duff against the roots of a great cedar and, covering herself with bark and ferns, curled up with her hood round her face to try to get some sleep.

Which she didn't, of course, not at least till the night was far gone. For hours she listened to small things scurrying past her ears. Little bugs crawled onto her face from time to time, and once, she thought, something wet and soft like a toad landed on her forehead. Her bones ached with cold and fatigue, and her stomach gouged itself with hunger. *So much for being one with the earth,* she told herself.

Somewhere towards morning a breeze must have sprung up overhead, for the tree beside her began to groan as if in sadness. She must have been listening to the sound of it when she fell asleep, for in her dreams the tree began to speak with her—except it wasn't the tree exactly, nor a disembodied tongue neither, but the arboreal essence of it, a walking thing, tall and lean and incredibly mournful, standing before her with bark-browed eyes. Its feet were crumbling into the earth, falling apart in shreds and chunks like frostbitten flesh.

"What think you of this bondage to decay, daughter?" He must have seen a look of confusion on Jennifer's face, for he sighed and continued, "I am hoping you may be revealed as such—as daughter to the Most High. Consider the cedar along with the lily—consider us well. Subjected to futility, you may think. But also, remember, subjected in hope. The river gives its life for me, and I shall give my life for the river. Gladly I shall lay it down, just as the fawn has laid down his since before the roots of time."

It shifted on its own roots as if to scrutinize her better. "Do not fear. I and all my brothers are with you, insofar as you become your liberty. The freedom of the river is yours, and the freedom you gain shall be the river's. Until then we groan, my daughter. There are pangs of birth too deep for words." And then the wind seemed to blow through his topmost branches, and he groaned indeed, a drawn-out sigh like the pitiful whine of a big, sad dog in his sleep. "Take care," he said. "Take joy. Farewell." And with these last words he clapped his hands, and a rain of bark broke off from his arms and fell to earth.

She awoke, it was dark. Jennifer had the strangest feeling that a huge branch had crashed to the ground from high overhead, but there would be no way of knowing for sure, even in the light of morning. She shivered, cold and sore in her nest, and pondered the figure in her dream. She had read of the spirits of trees before: dryads in Ovid (though these were female, as she remembered), and gentle emanations of the goddess herself in the poetry of the health-food store. But this tree seemed neither god nor goddess. He appeared rather grand, to be sure, but only in a decrepit sort of way. He was hoping for something and hoping in something—her, in a way, but mostly something beyond her.

She turned and returned her troubled thoughts until she slept and dreamed again. This time she was walking in the forest, the same one in which she lay. It was morning. Shafts of sunlight played upon the rain-fresh floor, and she quickly found the hollow tree. The fire was out but wisps of smoke still rose from the embers. She stepped around them to the door, hoping to find William at least and perhaps even Ronald. But what she saw was the mounded bulk of the hoary marmot, gnawing at something. She heard the click of teeth on bone. Instinctively she shouted and gave it a vicious kick, but the marmot hardly gave way. It looked up and glared, and flashed its incisors, and she kicked it again, and again, and again, and finally it galloped into the forest. In the place where it had done its work were the grisly remains of William's feet, the heel of each one quite chewed off and bleeding, bleeding into the ground. As if he had not bled enough.

She woke up weeping, pale sunlight in her face. Her body was shivering all over from cold, or grief, or perhaps both. In that moment she longed for her mother, the touch of her hand on her waking brow, the word of welcome to the day. But her mother was no more. *In bondage to decay. Subjected to futility.* She repeated the dryad's phrases in her mind.

"Still asleep, dear?"

Jennifer rose as if from the grave, bark and fern sliding off her soiled cagoule as she sat up. Standing beside her, stranger than dream, was the smock-clad figure of Lady Demaris.

"There, you are awake," she said.

"Am I?" said Jennifer.

Lady Demaris stooped beside her and brushed the tears from her cheeks. "Very much so, child," she said. "There is much to be sad about, I know. But I come now with bread for your journey and words of cheer."

"Where's Ronald?" she asked plaintively.

"Ronald shall return, my dear, and you must return him to your love. William must away and you both must find him, but first press on to the Tower of Otium. Where the water is white, you are most in the arms of my good sister. Trust her care."

"The sister with the ax, the one you gave me?"

"Yes, that sister."

"Why not you, Lady Demaris? Why don't you stay and take care of us?"

Lady Demaris paused to consider, then shook her head. "Just now I must take my leave. Do not fear, Jennifer. We shall meet again at the Western Strand, or even at the tower itself, when all is well."

She offered her hand, and Jennifer clasped it and arose, brushing off the beard of earth that clung so closely. She was about to ask Lady Demaris to repeat and explain everything that she had said, but the woman pulled her quickly in tow through forest and sunlight, over the ferny banks and gardens, past red-pulp explosions of coral root, all as fresh as in her dream. Soon they came to the hollow tree, guarded by its wisp of smoke, and Lady Demaris gestured within like the angel at the empty tomb. And it was empty. Jennifer stooped and looked inside and quickly saw that William was minus not only his heels but also, as it were, himself. There were the blankets, there was the pack. There, even, were his boots and socks.

"Where have you taken him?" Jennifer demanded.

"Child," Lady Demaris replied, "it is not I that would take him, but would keep him." She gently touched Jennifer's elbow and turned her around. "Look there," she said, and pointed to the churn of duff on the forest floor. "Those are the tracks of many horses that belong to the servants of the great El Ai. He himself is slave to the spirit of my sad sister, the Lady Lira—worshiped now in that desert kingdom as Lady Lyra, we are told. For her revenge and for his need, the need of El Ai, the marmot has come and the body is taken."

"The body?" said Jennifer. "You mean—"

"Until his deliverance, until his revealing, William is hardly anything else."

"I—I'm so sorry. I know last night I should have . . ." She trailed off.

"Should have. Should have," Lady Demaris said. There was a trace of bitterness in her serenity. "To know only *should have* is to be in bondage."

"To decay?" added Jennifer.

"Yes," she answered. Lady Demaris stroked Jennifer's brow. "But we are subjected in hope, child."

There it was. Just as the crumbling dryad had said.

"Now gather your things," Lady Demaris said briskly. "I will set you on your way."

Jennifer folded the blankets and boots into the pack, and Lady Demaris handed her new loaves of bread. They broke one together and ate in quiet, listening to the varied shrill of a hermit thrush.

Jennifer found herself studying the gentle face, the strong green eyes, the rich brown hair with admiration. "Lady Demaris," she finally said. "Are you—a goddess?"

Lady Demaris laughed like a spring in an alpine meadow, tossing her head in genuine merriment. "If I am," she said, "it is only with a very small *g*. It is he that made us, and not we ourselves. And not *he*, perhaps, not really a man—or even a fawn. But, oh dear, not woman neither. Male nor female—something, someone much better than that. Something, someone closer to us than the air in our lungs or the blood in our veins. I consist in him—or her, if you will—but I am not he, and she is not I. You just might meet him here; she is completely in this place, but not of it, not at all."

"At the Tower of Otium—there perhaps?"

"You can look, my daughter. He blows with the wind. And with her, sometimes, so do I—for I did not think to see you so soon. It is important to find him where we are found."

Lady Demaris turned her head. "But see who comes to find you now, seeking for the woman within and the woman without."

Jennifer looked and saw Ronald striding far off in the trees. He did not yet see them. She called his name and jumped up and ran to where he was. His face was pale and his hair a damp mess. She felt a terrible need to recover and take care of him, and when she reached him they fell into an awkward embrace, each one mumbling apologies.

"But come here, look," Jennifer said, pulling him by the arm to the tree. "Look who's here, and look who isn't."

But there by the tree where sparrows hopped among the crumbs, it was all *isn't*.

"But she was just here," Jennifer complained.

"Who?" asked Ronald.

Chapter 11
How Green They Were

*

IT WAS JUST MID-MORNING, AND CLOUDY AGAIN, when Jennifer and Ronald arrived back at his hermitage under the overturned boat. Their trail, which passed quite close to the tree from which William was taken, had been full of hoofprints pointed downstream.

"Well," said Ronald, pushing over the boat, "at least they spared us one problem. We could never have brought him all the way down the trail ourselves. Think about it. We might have constructed a stretcher of sorts, but that would have taken at least four people to carry. A blessing in disguise, as my father used to say."

"If we get him back, that is," said Jennifer. Ronald's assessment struck her as the least bit callous. She had been more than relieved that the boat was found, that Ronald was safe, and that she herself was unforsaken, and had smothered him all the way down the trail with tears and heartfelt resolutions, but now that they stood by the boat once more on the wide and sandy bank of the river, she felt the irritability of fear, wondering what the journey might bring. She had never rowed a river before, and to her knowledge neither had Ronald. They had friends at school who invited them from time to time on rafting trips, but she always had to work at the store, and Ronald always chose to study. Over the summer they had learned their way around on a glacier, but when their axes had changed themselves into oars she knew they were launched into unknown waters. And there was no choosing. With William or now without, their charge was to float to the Tower of Otium. After hearing from Ronald about the rapid their boat had navigated without them, she hoped they would be alive when they got there.

But what she voiced was a milder fear. "This Tower of Otium—do you think we'll know it when we see it?"

"Beats me," said Ronald, shrugging his shoulders. "It's in the gorge some-where."

That word *gorge* did not set well with Jennifer. She imagined black walls rising sheer from miles of boiling cataracts, with no way out but down and through, and that way quite impossible. "Well," she said simply, "I imagine we'll find it."

She helped him pull the boat to the cove where he had caught it the evening before. With William gone, they stowed the pack in the bow for ballast. Ronald offered her the oars, but she declined and took her seat in the stern again. Ronald sat down facing her, then changed his mind and turned completely around on the bench.

"I want to see what's coming," he said. "You bail." He pointed to a wooden bucket wedged underneath her seat. "When the water comes in, you scoop it out. I'm afraid you'll be as busy as I am." With that he stroked them out of the cove and into the current, and with face set downstream he poised the oars for what might come.

And to their delight, what came first was the water ouzel, skimming across the water from shore to alight on the tip of the bow, dipping and bobbing like the moveable figurehead that it was.

"Is that—" said Jennifer, and Ronald nodded vigorously, as if asking her to please be quiet.

"He's so cute!" she gushed.

But before she could satisfy her interest, a steady roar began to gather in her ears. Half rising to peer downstream, Ronald began to pull on the oars to slow them down. The boat suddenly turned at an angle, and Jennifer saw the river ahead crushing itself on a pile of snags and logs midstream. Around it the water churned white and dropped away on either side.

"Left!" she called, thinking she saw safe passage there. "No, right!"

Ronald was trying, she could tell, to gauge the same choices. But each side pounded a terrifying violence, and it was not yet possible to look over the brink in either direction. They would have to commit themselves very soon, for Ronald could not stay them completely, and if they kept on course they would smash into the pile of debris. It seemed a forlorn way to go, twisted under a snarl of timber on a cold and lonely stretch of river. But then, she reflected, most ways probably were. She would have to accept the end she got.

It was then that the ouzel abandoned ship, flirting across the gathering noise until it reached the end of a snag on the right-hand side of the logjam. It bobbed there as if nodding to them, then dove out of sight down into the turbulence.

"Ronald!" she called, and pointed where the bird had gone. She felt the boat turn after it and wished that she could somehow help as Ronald flailed at the oars. She could tell he wasn't sure whether he should push with the current or pull against it. The choice soon became academic. Very swiftly, they bore down on the pile of logs and veered right on a cushion of water around the snag where the ouzel had paused. Then the boat simply dropped, as if the river had given way. The bow plunged into a kettle of foam and then nosed its way—sedately, she thought, for the raging and plowing of water all about them—past a fall-decked tier of logs on each side. Then they swirled in a boiling eddy and the bow swung under one edge of a curtain of water. It stopped and staggered beneath the influx.

"Bail!" screamed Ronald, and he pulled the left-hand oar from its lock and jammed the blade against the log that hung over the bow. Even as he strained against the face of the fall she felt the foam flood over her boots. She scooped the water but it deepened by the instant. The boat was not moving.

And then it was, inching out from under the fall in response to Ronald's might and main. Then they were free, and the boat drifted down the frothy wake quite nearly submerged. Jennifer redoubled her efforts with the bailing bucket and hoped against hope she could clear the boat before another rapid sank them. Ronald, of course, was rowing for shore, but he might as well have been sailing an anvil until, after a good ten minutes, Jennifer had managed to empty out much of the water. He reached a sandspit next to a tributary stream and ground the boat out of the river.

Jennifer, exhausted, slumped in the stern, her boots still resting in the ice-cold bilge. "That ouzel of yours," she panted. "I don't know."

Ronald was silent. "When you were bailing," he quietly said, "I looked back. The other side was worse, Jen—a sheer drop, onto more sharp snags. I think he brought us the right way. Maybe with practice we'll get better." He smiled sheepishly.

"You really are trusting that bird, aren't you?" As she said it the ouzel reappeared, landing on the bucket in her hands. It looked at her and sang out a melodic triumph: "*Bzeet! Bzeet! Bzeet-bzeet-bzeet!*"

"Now that you mention it," Ronald said, "yes."

The rest of the day went according to the pattern they had now established—

not at all a smooth pattern but soon enough a predictable one. The ouzel rode bobbing atop the prow as they coursed the current of milky gray past sand, past snags, past thickets of browning and yellowing alder, past aching crimson of vine maple and towering stands of cedar and hemlock, and over this living, changing shore the full-bellied clouds that hung dark and low and always threatened to rain but didn't. Then a roar up ahead, gathering to a solemn greatness, not thunder in the sky but thunder in the waters, and then the sight of a logjam, or a fern-decked gorge, or a maze of boulders suffused in white, and off the ouzel would scoot from the bow to mark safe passage, and Ronald would pull against the current until he saw where the bird had gone. Then the release to the chosen path, the whirling through foam past snags and rocks, and the boiling of eddies, the sudden slap of spray from the bow that caught them hard and open-mouthed, the tug of water in the bailing bucket that made Jennifer's arms and shoulders ache, and then, if they were frightened and wet enough, and if Ronald were able, a brief landing to put things to rights and to reconsider where they had been. Sometimes they had to wring out their clothes, and more than once they were thrown from their benches and almost toppled overboard. But the path of the ouzel proved always just safe enough, and by late afternoon, shivering and wet, they had covered many miles of river.

The shore had grown more generally rocky, and the cedar and hemlock now hugged the river in dark comfort, spreading their boughs out over the boat and knuckling their roots down into the water. The river itself had changed its gray to a green translucence, and bore on its surface the scarlet leaves of the vine maple and the pale yellow of fading alder, whirling downstream like Pharaoh's horsemen caught unawares in the closing sea.

They had beached themselves in a tiny cove and were even thinking of making camp when a shaft of sunlight pierced the clouds and bathed them in its sudden warmth. All of a sudden their shady nook hard under the trees looked, yes, adequate—a bearable place to spend the night—but the sun on the water brought promise of better haven down the river and, without their knowing it, convinced them their bones held strength and succor for one more go. Ronald felt a second wind, a fullness of being, the way he did when the fog cleared away from the nunatak some afternoons and left the ice in sudden splendor.

Jennifer, feeling the same quickened hope, clambered back into the boat and struck a pose that included Ronald as her fellow mariner. "'That which we are, we are!'" she cried.

"One equal temper of heroic hearts
Made weak by time and fate, but strong in will
To strive, to seek, to find, and not to yield."

She held up her hand as if raising a sword, and the ouzel promptly landed on it and left in her grip a pile of droppings. She flung him off. "To your post!" she ordered, wiping her palm. "Thirty lashes for the scurvy lookout."

Ronald laughed for the first time since—well, in a long time—and Jennifer marveled at their delight. They very easily could have been drowned twenty times over that day, and there was no guarantee they would not succeed on this the twenty-first attempt. Yet they went, finally, in howling good humor, and all she knew was that it felt right. So what if Ulysses sank to his death in his old age somewhere past the Straits of Gibraltar? He and his men knew life's full joys before they got there, and that was enough. As she looked with pride at Ronald guiding the boat with the oars, dipping them no less deftly now than the ouzel flew and dipped itself, she gloried in the strength of their weakness and glimpsed an end to their momentary light affliction. *Subjected in hope. Perhaps this is what it means,* she thought.

The river had now turned back to the west. From ahead of them, the sunbeam multiplied itself into a sudden sheet of light, shining under the edge of the clouds and setting the river all aglint as if the water were streaked with fire from within. The mossy shore gained definition, a brighter green, and each lichened tree trunk slipping by now stood apart in the thisness of its new creation. In Jennifer's eyes each plank of their boat showed grainy luster, the ouzel fairly shone on the bow, and Ronald's neck and jacketed shoulders belonged to the gods.

Jennifer was so caught up in her vision of light that she scarcely heard the approaching rapid. She felt Ronald pull hard against the current before she saw why—the thundering line of standing waves that reached entire from shore to shore. Instinctively she looked for the ouzel to dart ahead, marking the way they had come to trust. But strangely enough, the bird remained still—as still as an ouzel can be, anyway—bobbing its respects on the bow.

Ronald could not hold them long, and they took the first wave head on, shipping a huge cold wall of water and plowing through to a bigger ahead. The ouzel had bounced itself high in the air to avoid the splash, but alighted now on

Ronald's shoulder as if to say, *Your guess is as good as mine.*

The second wave sent Ronald tumbling backwards into Jennifer's lap, and would have sent her overboard had Ronald not already landed right on top of her. Once over the wave they both pitched forward, tangled together between the benches and half submerged in the water sloshing about on the boards. All that Jennifer could see were the handles of the oars tearing back and forth—that, and the courteous ouzel, perched again on Ronald's shoulder and looking at her hard in the eye. Her body felt a shock, and a sheet of spray, as if they had staved themselves on a rock, and then the boat whirled about, and the light turned, and finally the ouzel flew off.

In that moment Jennifer felt the entire boat grow suddenly weightless, lifted it seemed from the pounding of water. Then she knew a soft sinking sensation, which ought to have grown faster but didn't. The oars were still, and the air was full of spray, and brightness, and profound calm. With utmost caution, Jennifer disentangled herself from Ronald's arms and met his eyes in fear and wonder. They both peeked over the gunwale at once.

What Jennifer saw should have frightened her to the utmost, but for some reason—perhaps it was the placid steadiness of their boat—she felt instead a quiet exhilaration. Far below them was spread a more beautiful valley than she had ever imagined. The river looped and meandered through meadows grown white and rust and yellow with autumn. Here and there, groves of cedar and hemlock stood, the shade and repose of Elysian Fields, of wilderness open and at rest. Containing the valley were walls of granite, pearl and gray. They rose tall and sheer and unbroken, smoothed by the brilliance of evening light.

She was so taken by this grand place, so willing to waste her time in it, that for a moment she hardly noted the improbability of their airy vantage point. The boat had left the rapid behind and was falling, slowly, light as a leaf, down the face of the highest fall she had ever seen. And she could not see this one well. The top was already indistinct, materializing out of sky, and the bottom was still so far below she could not yet hear the thunder of it. They were caught, somehow, safe in the middle, the boat resting fully upright and drifting down the face of the fall as if held by the strands of a parachute.

But there was no chute, and truth to tell, Ronald was much more disturbed by this than Jennifer could be, feeling as she always did that the universe of its very nature had to be stocked with sacred surprises to be what it was. They both, however, peered over the side to see what might be holding them. Ronald said later that he thought he saw something like a giant swan, white as the spray of the waterfall and bearing the boat upon its back. But he couldn't be sure—the light of the sun was full in his eyes, and the spray all around them was more than dazzling, like a whole forest of chandeliers all swaying and exchanging places.

Jennifer later said it was not anything like a swan at all. What she saw was a woman reclining outstretched on her back, supporting the boat with clean white arms. The skin of the woman was pure as the stars, and her eyes were green as the dogwood in spring, green like the eyes of Lady Demaris—and like the eyes of the dream woman who told her to find the goddess within. For a moment, she thought, the woman looked at her calmly and smiled. Her hair floated round her, bound at the brows by a circlet of flowers. It was blonde, and full, and the face that it framed held more contentment than Jennifer thought possible. Whatever those green eyes saw in the world, Jennifer wanted to see as well.

She looked much longer than she had intended. For suddenly the woman vanished in a rush of white, and the boat was bobbing in the thunder and foam of a giant plunge pool among the rocks, and the waterfall stood like a curtain behind them, erasing the world of miracle.

Her eyes found Ronald's once again. She had never noticed how green they were.

Chapter 12
Against the Stars

✳

THAT NIGHT THEY CAMPED BY A CEDAR GROVE on the edge of a meadow, almost surrounded by a wide and glassy loop of river. When they had drawn the boat up onto the grass the top of the waterfall high above shone golden in the dwindling light, and the sound of it was a pleasant pulse, as constant and quiet as the beating of their hearts.

They spoke sparingly as they sat on their blankets next to the fire that Ronald had made. The sky had cleared and the stars were coming one by one, and too much talk would only retard their shy appearing—or so felt Jennifer. She was drowsy and dry before the fire, filled again with Chambers' wonderful soup and bread. Her flesh and bones felt the memory of churning water as one might feel the aftermath of a good massage. She laid her head on Ronald's shoulder, interested more than anything in a night of rest. The sky grew dark and the full moon bloomed like a silver rose at the top of the fall, quieting the meadow about them and making the stone cliffs pale and perfect, filling the gorge with a lake of light.

On the edge of sleep, Jennifer found herself murmuring her version of an old poem:

> *"Earth has not anything to show more fair:*
> *Dull would he be of soul who could pass by*
> *A sight so touching in its majesty:*
> *This Valley now doth like a garment wear*
> *The beauty of the evening; silent, bare—"*

"If it's wearing a garment," Ronald interrupted matter-of-factly, "then how can it be bare?"

"Ronald!" She raised her head and looked at him reproachfully. Then she sank back onto his shoulder and let her eyes rove across the contours of cliff above them in the moonlight.

He followed her gaze. "Well," he said, breaking the silence, "whatever a person's preference might be, you have to admit it's a perfect place for a reservoir. Pipe it south and they'll never have to worry about a drought again. The wilderness shall become a pool of water—that's how my father would have put it."

Jennifer leaned away again, now rudely and fully awake. "The dam?" she said. "Here?" She had forgotten where it would be.

"Not here, exactly. Perhaps downstream where the canyon narrows. But the enclosure is so symmetrical that I imagine the water will rise almost to the top of the falls."

"But here?"

"Jen, it just goes down to the ocean otherwise. Use it or lose it. And they *need* the water, after all."

She drew herself up. "*They* again. *They need.* O reason not the need," she hissed. "Gwen told me all about it."

"What's there to tell? It's no secret or anything." Ronald was whining.

"What's there to tell? What's there to tell?" She looked all about them and held out her arms in best stage style:

> "*For this, for every thing, we are out of tune;*
> *It moves us not—Great God! I'd rather be*
> *A Pagan suckled in a creed outworn.*"

"A what?" he asked.

"And not *Great God* neither, but the great earth goddess mother of us all. You wouldn't understand and you've never understood. You'd dam the stars with your precious theodolite if you could, and drain their light for some dark use of the distant future. And why? Why? Tell me, Mr. Science. I'm dying to know."

A silence followed. Jennifer could tell that she had pushed Ronald to the brink. His lips worked, and several times he started to speak. But when he finally opened his mouth, what came out was not speech but song—an old song they had both known since childhood:

"Tell me why the stars do shine,
Tell me why the ivy twines,
Tell me why the sky's so blue,
And I will tell you why I love you."

Jennifer smiled in spite of herself, pleased to hear his hesitant voice. Then she joined in on the reply, a verse she had specially composed for him:

"Nuclear fusion makes the stars to shine,
Photosynthesis makes the ivy twine,
Solar refraction makes the sky so blue,
And hormone secretion is why I love you."

Their two voices lit up the sky, and he put his arm around her when they came to the end. Then it was silent again, and they lay back to watch the stars. How could she be cross with him after all? And yet, she could be. Hormone secretion indeed.

"Shall we sleep by the fire?" he murmured in her ear.

Jennifer hesitated briefly. Then she removed his arm which clung so closely. Into his ear she said in return:

"Nay, good Lysander. For my sake, my dear,
Lie further off yet; do not lie so near."

Ronald looked confused for a moment, then seemed to catch her drift. "Of course," he mumbled apologetically. He gathered his coat and shuffled off into the darkness.

Jennifer remained by the fire, conscious of Ronald curling up in the shadow of the wood behind her, and conscious of her cruelty. All for the sake of a larger and better cause than romance. He would have to learn. She wrapped herself in her two wool blankets (Ronald had one, but she had William's in addition) and lay by the flames, watching them fade as the sparks flew upward and coursed the night like rising stars. Then she was no longer watching the fire, but merely feeling its warmth on her face. And soon she dissolved into embers of sleep.

Jennifer had hardly left her waking self when she saw she was back on a twisting path in the noontime sun among tall, trimmed hedges. Once again she found her way to the bubbling spring at the center of the maze. And standing beside it, larger than dream, was the splendid woman with long dark hair, piercing her with emerald eyes. Next to her the rose grew showy and red, reflected in the fountain beneath it and filling the air with rich fragrance.

"Pluck and find," the woman urged. There was deep-throated elegance to her voice. "Pluck and find the goddess within."

But I tried that, Jennifer wanted to say. She could not get the words out.

As if to tutor her in the method, the woman reached and crushed the flower in her hand, then scattered the petals in Jennifer's hair and suddenly caught her about the waist. *Caught her up* was more like it, for Jennifer found herself rising quickly into the air with the arms of the woman tight about her. The day was gone and there were stars, and when she looked down she did not see the shrubs and flowers of a formal garden but the moonlit floor of Amoenas Gorge. Directly beneath her she saw herself sleeping, a homely dishrag of a girl, sprawled in her blankets beside the fire. She felt a sudden superiority, an elevation, the surprising knowledge that she could at will transcend herself and no longer succumb to the thoughtless oppression of professors in fact and professors in training. Fathers and fiancés alike could never know her hidden life, her inner richness, her secret vantage point within from which she could grace them from time to time with bittersweet drops of condescension.

As she thought these things her sleeping figure grew smaller and smaller, and Jennifer felt the woman's arms slip slowly away until she was merely touching her hand, mounting the sky with the sureness of her own new power. Far from being alarmed, she exulted, watching the moonlit walls slip by in the night that glowed for her alone and not for sleepers. Soon they cleared the top of the gorge, and she saw in a breath the loom and shine of all Three Queens—South, Center, and North—startling and soft like a heaving sea that bares its bosom to the moon. And still they climbed, swirling now in a cold clear breeze that came and went in delicious rhythm,

> *The winds that will be howling at all hours,*
> *And are up-gathered now like sleeping flowers.*

The woman took her higher yet, past the craters and crags at the top of the Queens, till they seemed almost among the stars, and she gestured with her hand that was not touching Jennifer's, sweeping over all that was below them, and all that was around them, as if it say, *This too is yours, if you now possess it. All earth and sky and the stars besides—these are your footstool. Pluck and find the goddess within.*

"Yes," said Jennifer. "Yes. Yes!" And she removed her hand from the touch of the woman as if to claim her rightful place.

In that very instant she began to fall. Not a gentle descent, as she had known in the arms of the other strong woman with the same green eyes, not the drifting down the face of the fall, but a stark plunge, an accelerating drop that lifted her stomach into her throat and kept it there, each moment worse than the last.

She looked for the woman but could not see her. The stars fell away, the shining bulk of the Queens rushed past, the forest resurged to the rim of the gorge, and the gorge itself opened to meet her with terrible alacrity. There below by the river their fire appeared, and the sleeping form of her lonely self, and she wondered if she would fall on top of her—that girl—and which one would be crushed by the impact. The self became larger, and next to the head of the sleeping girl she suddenly saw the shape of a marmot, a very large one, crouched at her side and speaking obscenities into her ear. How she knew this from such a height she wasn't sure, but she supposed she was in both places at once, and so could hear.

The marmot and girl were coming up fast. She tried to scream—to warn *her* anyway if not *him* (for such a creature had to be male)—but no sound came. Instead she heard Ronald shout something confused: "Hey! You! Hey! Beat it!" He ran up from the river swinging his oar, and the marmot fled, and Jennifer blessed him from barely on high. Then the ground and the campfire rose in a rush, and before she could even properly cringe she quite literally came to herself, lying quietly by the fire and watching Ronald stand panting above her.

All that moved was the trembling oar, held high in his hands against the stars.

Chapter 13
Soft as Willows

✳

"SO HE REALLY WAS THERE?" Jennifer asked it not quite as a question. The sun was high and she and Ronald were drifting down the quiet river, watching the pearl-gray cliffs slide past. Jennifer was at the oars, facing Ronald for comfort and letting him direct their course when the need arose. She was not bothering to row very often, and Ronald sat languidly erect in the stern, alert and at ease, trailing one loose hand in the water and holding the other under his chin. Their boots were off, and the wood of the boat was warm beneath their toes in the open but cool and mysterious under the arms of alder and cedar. The water was clearer here in the canyon—glacial milk become glacial wine—and here and there swam muscled salmon, sleek and red like the leaves of autumn, carving their way upstream from the sea to spawn at the foot of the great falls.

All morning long, Jennifer had been on the verge of telling Ronald about her dream—about all her dreams. But she had held back, perhaps because a dream loses so much of itself when put into words; and out of pride, or privacy, or even the spell of the dreams themselves, she wanted to keep them only hers. Some part of her reflected, though, on how little they shared if she refused to navigate her dreams with him. These visions were like burdens to be borne—or, when she thought of the dryad, like a mystery to be proclaimed. They startled and scared her, and Ronald might share their pain and proof—but she knew what he was more likely to do.

Not laugh, exactly. Ronald never laughed at such things. He would merely look down and lapse into silence, abstaining from any reassurance of voice or vote. But she needed talk, and if not about the things that mattered, then about those that nearly did. And when she thought about it, the marmot mattered as much as her dreams, seeing it was in them—and out of them too—both at once, just as she had been in the night. So she asked about him one more time.

"It was there," said Ronald, "until it left. That is, till I chased it off. But I wish I had gotten one good crack. I'd like to have flattened the thing with my oar. I could have, too." He lifted his fingers away from the lips of a curious salmon. "I mean, what was he doing? Eating your ear? Did you feel his teeth? Good thing I was up, checking the boat. I didn't want him tampering with *that*, not like last time, and then I saw him tampering with *you*. I wouldn't have looked, but you shouted something—I could hear you from down by the river. It sounded something like *Less! Less!* Were you dreaming then? Talking in your sleep? Do you remember saying something like that?"

She shrugged her shoulders.

"Well," he said, "with a marmot like that sitting next to your ear, you're bound to have a nightmare or two. But he's gone for now." He paused to think out his next words. "In the future, I think, it will be my duty to sleep closer by." And he spoke it as if it were indeed his solemn duty. Jennifer felt charmed and amused and even grateful, all at once.

Just at noon they passed a fall on the northern rim, a free-floating ribbon that trailed from the snows of the South Queen, for here the river wrapped itself around the peaks on its doubled way to the Western Sea. Soon afterwards they pulled out onto a pleasant lea to eat the remainder of Chambers' bread. Jennifer found some wild onions, and so they had sandwiches after a fashion, and when they were done they took separate ways to bathe themselves in the heat of the day.

Ronald went upstream, barefoot in the dry grass, until he reached the creek that rushed from the base of the fall. Their own waterfall—the one they had so preternaturally descended—was now lost to view in these lower windings of the canyon. Each turn had brought new lawns, new groves, new stunning prospects of granite prows and shields and awnings mellow with the light of autumn. He was beginning to think that all of this might not look so fine when it was submerged by a reservoir. But he doubted he'd ever tell Jennifer that.

For a while he sat beneath the cedars that grew hard by and watched the side-stream purl over the mossy roots and mingle its life with the life of the river. It was a large creek, large enough for a few of the salmon that thronged the river to leap their way up it in quest of an end and a beginning. In the creek and in the river they flowed like blood against the current. *The water and the blood*, his father would say. He thought of William's terrible wounds at the very source, the staining of meltwater in the crevasse, and how fragile a rope was—how fragile a life—how easily cut by steel and ice. He thought of the blood that had steeped his hands, and the purifying ache of the subglacial stream, of the body borne in the bottom of the boat, and the losing of it. His father's voice returned again: *They have taken the Lord out of the tomb, and we do not know where they have laid him.*

And then he thought, as he always did without knowing it, of Jennifer, and why he loved her, a question incapable of solution. He remembered their going out into the hail in a thunderstorm, long ago on their You-Can-Do-It Expedition. They were looking for someone—a man who had fainted—but he remembered they'd found a rainbow instead at the end of the hail, and wet grass about their knees. He remembered how good and new it had felt to be with her, even though he hadn't known the words to say. Then as now, she was as cruel as she was kind, not losing the chance to embarrass him in his speechlessness. He told himself he did not mind, but wondered now if perhaps he did, and entertained for a brief moment the possibility of his protest.

In the midst of these considerations, he heard a sudden *bzeet! bzeet!* and saw the dark brown shape of an ouzel skimming down the creek through the trees. It came to a bobbing rest on a stone and looked him quickly up and down.

"Hello," said Ronald placidly. "You again." He wondered if it were another ouzel, but decided to believe it was not. The bird flew away back up the stream through the tunnel of trees. It paused for a moment amidst a small rapid, looked back, and then flew further upstream and was gone from sight.

Out of curiosity and acquired habit, Ronald followed, clambering over roots and logs and finding in places a path on the very edge of the creek. Before very long—for the floor of the gorge was rather narrow—he reached a misty amphitheater deep in a cleft of the granite wall and stood on the brink of a foaming pool, all turquoise and green, stirred by the touch of a feathery fall that might as well have dropped from the sky for all that Ronald could see the top of it, high above on the rim of the gorge. The amphitheater was tufted green with spray-laden moss and nodding ferns, and the white of the water was rich against it. The beat of the fall was strangely muted, and by the way that the ouzel, which he now saw, was flitting about and even through it, Ronald saw that the curtain of water was thin enough that he might have hopes of swimming out to it safely enough and combining his bath with a bracing shower.

He was just about to remove his clothes and enter the water when he saw that someone had beaten him to it. From behind a boulder far to his right an unclad figure suddenly dove into the pool and struck out with a whoop of delight for the fall itself. Once there, the figure sank in the foam and turmoil of the water for quite some time—so long that Ronald began to fear he had witnessed a drowning—but then the person popped up with a shaking of hair and more whoops and shouts and swam splashing back to the waterfall to resubmerge himself again. *Himself,* for by the sound of the voice, Ronald was sure it was a man. Even so, he still felt like a peeping intruder, and decided to descend from the pool until the swimmer had finished his frolic.

He turned and left, unseen he hoped, and after a wait of perhaps ten minutes reascended to his vantage point beside the pool. The swimmer was gone. Not knowing quite what else to do, he cautiously approached the boulder from whence the bather had first emerged. Partway there, he noticed above him a trail winding improbably down a series of ledges on one side of the amphitheater, a trail which reached the bottom of the cliff just on the other side of the boulder. He was about to step around the stone when he heard a voice, a young man's voice, speaking not to him exactly but not entirely to itself. He could not make out what the voice was saying above the noise of the waterfall. And then it paused, and Ronald was sure that the speaker had heard him, so he came a step closer to reveal himself and get the suspense over with.

But before the man came into view the voice began once again, and Ronald stopped, and this time he heard what it said:

> "Your heart is made a waterfall, and I
> Would gladly slip away across the brink
> To plunge the waiting pool amidst the sigh
> Of green bright bubbles rising as I sink
> Down to a floor with granite pebbles lined,
> Each shining gently in a wat'ry light.
> Deep currents soft as willows will I find
> That silent swirl me round and lift my sight
> Unto a canopy of spreading foam
> Far tingling overhead in brilliant shade.
> So quietly I float and wafting roam,
> Till slowly toward the surface wreaths I fade:
>   But there you meet me in a lacy roar,
>   And plunge me to your green bright depths once more."

Though Ronald had heard a number of poems from Jennifer's lips, it can be truthfully said that this was really the first poem he had ever *listened to* in his life. It excited in him a longing he could not begin to understand, and he stood with his hand on the moss of the rock with his legs all atremble, anxious to meet the man who spoke and to know the world as he knew it, but also anxious to hear more from his place of hiding. Caught between these two impulses, Ronald leaned closer so as not to lose a further word. Unfortunately, he leaned too far and came stumbling and tripping out from the boulder in an awkward attempt to right himself, falling at last at the outstretched feet of a young man wearing loose brown knickers who looked as surprised as Ronald was embarrassed.

"What's here?" said the man with strange good humor. "A little eavesdropper. An appreciator of *fine* poetry. Well, what's your business? Speak up." The young man, bare-chested, was resting on his elbows. He spoke from behind a full blonde beard.

"I—I was just going swimming," Ronald said. "That's all. But I decided to wait my turn. And then I heard you, and wanted to listen. I thought you would stop if you knew I was here."

"Hah! Not likely," the young man laughed. "That I would ever stop, I mean. Though I did stop here at the foot of the trail, and as for the swim, I do recommend it. But how came you here, strange one? You're a long ways from El Ai, though I hear that some of your sort are in these parts nowadays."

"El Ai?" said Ronald. "You mean down south? No, I mean, I live near here, at least for the summer. Chambers Lake."

The man raised a thick blonde eyebrow.

"But Jennifer and I, we came in a boat. We're going to the Tower of Otium, though we're not quite sure where it is. Do you, perhaps?"

"And why might you be headed that way?"

"I don't know," Ronald confessed. "To be completely honest I have no rational idea."

The man relaxed. "Ah! Well that's the best sort of journey. But who told you to go there—or that it *was* there?"

"A very old man," Ronald replied. "His name is Garth."

At the mention of this name, the young man suddenly rose to his feet. "And mine's Colin." He put out his hand as if in salute.

Ronald took it hesitantly. "Ronald," he said.

"I'm going to the Tower of Otium myself," Colin said. He crushed Ronald's one hand in both of his. "You're almost there. I'll show you the way."

Ronald felt grateful, as if he had been struggling for days with a task in the laboratory and Dr. Howe had suddenly appeared to competently put it to rights.

"But first," said Colin, "you really do need a swim."

The ouzel skimmed across the pool and came to rest on Colin's shoulder, bobbing in complete agreement.

Chapter 14
Afternoon Prayers

✳

As for Jennifer, when Ronald had left she stretched herself on the sandy shore of a quiet cove. She was on a bend of the river just downstream from where they had left their lunch and their boat. The cove was shaded by willow and alder rustling in a whisper of wind, but the sun shone warm on the sand where she lay, and she lingered there, not yet undressing to bathe. The unhurried quiet, the shy sublimity of the place, had a calming effect upon her spirit.

She looked over the water and past a grove to the rise of stone across the gorge and felt safe in its massive shelter. There was a rightness to its presence, and also to hers at the base of it; by being here she somehow undergirded its grandeur. She thought of the great gray flanks of granite as motherly in some distant way, something that could nurture her if she chose to let it, and something that she in turn could care for in age and time. And she thought again of her own mother, so calm in the midst of her father's perpetual agitation, and wondered if she felt her nurture even still.

She let her eyes drop back to the water and remembered the verse her mother had taught her:

> *Dark brown is the river,*
> *Golden is the sand.*
> *It flows along forever,*
> *With trees on either hand.*

But this river of course was green, not brown, green as a lucent apple kiss unwrapped in her hand and almost placed upon her tongue. She begged her mother to buy that kind when they went to the store. But her mother was gone, and *ubi sunt*—where were the kisses of yesteryear? Dissolved in the surge and shine of the river. Somewhere, there, she longed for an answer, a glimpse that would make her less forlorn.

And then it came, a stirring of the waters. As if in answer to her desires, she saw something that caught her breath. Some things, rather. Not things, but faces. They emerged from the river in the same inevitable way that Proteus was supposed to rise up out of the sea—dozens of them, as numerous as the burning salmon. For there in the cove the water was filled with the visages of strong young women. They emerged together like riverine mermaids come up for air, their long hair spreading about their shoulders like sunburnt lily pads in the green water. They looked perfectly human, and yet—well—too *damp* to be made of human flesh. Jennifer thought of the woman who had held their boat in the waterfall, and wondered if these were anything like her, and whether that woman might be here among them. The faces were half-turned from her; she quickly searched the pale wet profiles but did not find the face she remembered. Each one, however, held a restless beauty all her own, looking as if fully at ease in the river yet eager to roam and course with the current, impatient to remain for long.

Their appearing took only the merest instant. For as Jennifer gathered these impressions, before she could even move or speak, the women in the water began to sing. First one poured out a single wordless quavering note, more like a flute than a human voice, and then another, in harmony, and yet another, adding to the diapason, until each joined each to create a chord so perfect and so various that the music of creation could not have been more pleasing to the ear.

And then there were words, a proclamation in unison that found its way into Jennifer's heart and promised to stay. The song was haunting, simple, edged with irrepressible joy:

> *"Sing ye trees and sing ye mountains*
> *Sing ye earth and sing ye sky*
> *Sing for mercy, sing for justice*
> *Sing for love that never dies.*
>
> *"Gentle sisters, raise your voices*
> *Sing out clear and sing out high*
> *Sing for courage, sing for beauty*

Sing for love that never dies."

The song was repeated, and then became antiphonal, echoing from one high wall and then the other. And then it renewed itself in a round, circling back on its end and beginning until all parts could be heard at once, until the song had no more first and no more last but was simply always, all at once. And then, suddenly, Jennifer realized the words had resolved themselves again to wordless notes, perfect meaning in pure sound, and she was not sure but that trees and mountains, sky and earth, had not joined the singers and answered the song by becoming part of it in that moment. She wanted to sing the words herself, and include herself in all that mattered. But something kept her, the same thing perhaps that finally kept her from sharing her dreams; and the notes ghosted away to an echo, and the beautiful faces, full of such purity and such longing, sank back in the water, each

> *like a creature native and indued*
> *Unto that element.*

And Jennifer kept silence, grateful for what she had seen and heard and nursing regret that she alone of all creation had failed to participate.

"Yes," said a voice behind her. "The afternoon prayers are often the best."

Jennifer quickly swung about and half sat up. Standing there was a short blonde woman, pert and lively, and not much older than Jennifer herself. She wore a clean white blouse with an apron over a dusky skirt, and like Jennifer was barefoot, except somehow magnificently so, as if shoes were things she never touched on principle.

"I come here each day just this time; at morning and evening they come to me in the cove at the tower. Perhaps you would like to hear them there—and sing, too, when you're given the courage?" Her face held a modest trace of humor, as if someday Jennifer might catch on.

"But who are they? And who are you?" asked Jennifer. She rather liked the woman already but it seemed to her the invitation was a bit familiar, coming as it did from a stranger.

"To make the last first, I am Rosamond," the woman said with an impish smile. "And these, of course, are the naiads—the ones, at least, who live here in Amoenas Gorge."

And so they might be, Jennifer thought. Naiads to wet the ancient lips of the tormented dryad of her dreams. Ovid again. And yet, she sensed, something other and greater than Ovid.

"This was to be my last day to hear them alone. Though as it turns out, I have heard them with you, my sister. And gladly too—I think that it is better that way—to prepare myself for companionship, for the sharing of joys. You are welcome here, and I must know you." Rosamond extended her hands.

"I'm Jennifer," said Jennifer shyly. She felt meek as she touched the young woman's fingers.

"You marvel at me," Rosamond said, and she laughed like the ripple of the Amoenas. "Please, do not. You have the pleasure of coming here on the evening of my wedding day. My attendants are poor and few. In fact, you have seen them all in the water. Not poor in spirit, for they see their author as we but hope to. But I was so much wishing for someone to come to be my bridesmaid. And see, Jennifer, you have been sent."

"Sent?"

"Yes. Sent by the love that died and never dies, the love that I shall become a part of in one small way, that always yearns to be part of us."

"Well, I *was* sent, though I suppose it was my fault that he had to send me— Garth, I mean. The old man. He was the one who told us to come."

"And Garth shall be here," she interjected, "at noon tomorrow to perform the ceremony."

Somehow Jennifer wasn't surprised. They were all deliciously entangled, this community that roamed within the wilderness. She was relieved to know that Garth was coming. Maybe he would know what to do, how they might rescue the sleeping William.

But surprised or not, she wanted to know how Rosamond knew the strange old man. She was about to ask when Rosamond, looking up the shore, gave a start, and blushed, and opened her mouth but said nothing at all.

Jennifer got up off the sand and saw coming toward them a blonde-bearded man who was running his course with evident joy. He was young, and handsome, his shoulders draped with a roughspun shirt that could not hide the strength beneath it. Behind him, walking at some shy distance, was her own Ronald, glasses off and hair plastered wet to his scalp. The young bearded man came sprinting up and with scarcely a glance at Jennifer took the speechless Rosamond firmly and fully into his arms. For a moment, as she watched them kiss, Jennifer felt a twinge of jealousy—Ronald had never arrived like this.

But then Ronald did arrive, and quietly took her hand in his, and Jennifer found new hope in the present. The two of them stood patiently by the embracing couple without feeling any of the embarrassment they supposed they should. The love they saw was the love they might share.

"They're getting married," Jennifer whispered.

"I know," said Ronald. He seemed as proud of the fact as she did.

Then they were all four introducing each other, and all at once, so that Rosamond made them start all over until their names were justly distributed.

"Well then," said Colin at last, "if I've heard correctly, we're all headed for Otium?"

"Of course," said Rosamond. "Colin to come live with me and be my love, and Ronald and Jennifer to be each other's and our own." She swept her arms along the shore, inviting them to follow her down a faint path in the sunburnt grass. "There are many rooms in my father's house."

"No need to walk," Ronald said. "We have a boat that will carry two—and two besides."

"Then both may go!" Colin shouted. "Both pairs of us." Then he began to sing, laughing Ronald into confusion.

Rosamond readily consented, the more so when they all noticed a mass of thunderheads rising above the gorge downstream in the deepening heat of the afternoon. "If we put ourselves to it, we may yet prevent the storm," she said.

"But you can't prevent a storm," said Ronald.

"She means we'll get there first," whispered Jennifer, digging her thumbnail into his palm.

They sauntered back to the boat, and before they got there the pile of cloud had shrouded and stolen the warmth of the sun. Colin took the oars in hand, and Ronald and Jennifer squeezed together in the stern while Rosamond sat half-turned in the bow, a much more pleasing ornament than the plain gray ouzel had been thus far. Speaking of which, it was no surprise to Jennifer that the ouzel itself came skimming downstream as they launched off, coming to rest in Rosamond's extended hand.

Colin rowed with sure strong strokes, pushing them ahead of the current at cunning and delightful speed. The borders of alder, of willow, of dogwood now, slipped by with the cedars on either hand, giving way to new meadow vistas of rock walls purple with thickening light. Deer lifted their antlers from the grass and watched them go, sniffing the air as if sensing the approach of the storm.

On the boat, the four of them held their tongues in quiet, listening. What little breeze there was had ceased, and the only sound was the dip and plunge and creak of the oars, and the scattering of drops from the blades. The sky darkened, and darkened, and around a bend the wind returned, this time in erratic puffs, disturbing the surface of the river first here, then there, in gentle gusts.

Jennifer quickly dug their coats from the pack at her feet. Colin, straining gloriously, said no when she offered one, so she passed it up to Rosamond and wrapped the other about both Ronald and herself. She felt wonderfully cozy, the way she once had years ago sitting next to him under a slick green fly they had failed to erect in a hailstorm. The fly had enclosed them side-by-side in the warmth of wool and huddling bodies. She looked at him now and wondered if he remembered that moment, if his mind could blend that time with this.

She caught his eyes as if to ask, and thunder crashed like the noise and collapse of exfoliating sheets of granite. The wind gathered strength and direction, blowing upriver into their faces, and soon the air flung drops of rain, falling at first like scattered pebbles. Then the sky shot aching white, and the thunder exploded in full strength, reverberating across the gorge.

Colin swept them round a bend, and there before them, lit up in a mask of light, a huge stone pinnacle rose up out of the midst of the river. Jennifer got just a glimpse before the rain came down in earnest. The skirts of the rock descended to the river in tiers of forest and meadow, and facing upstream on the topmost tier was a generous cottage built against the side of the tower. Above the cottage the rock rose smooth and sheer and gray, narrowing to a tiny summit as high, it seemed, as the walls of the gorge on either side.

Jennifer took in just this much before sheets of rain filled the sky. The wind soon gave them a thorough perpendicular drenching, and she felt the water begin to collect in the bottom of the boat. She peeked at Colin, who was pushing the bow through wind-stung whitecaps, and saw that he wore a smile of pleasure. He winked at her and shouted, heartily, "Perhaps you could use that bucket of yours?" Before she could move, Ronald found it under their seat and began to bail with a will.

The thunder now came without interruption. In a separate moment of sky-forked brightness, Jennifer saw through the pelting rain that they had almost reached the tip of the island. Instead of landing them there, however, Colin pulled the boat to the right, and she watched the island begin to slip by with the sudden worry that perhaps this was not the Tower of Otium after all—or, worse, that Colin and Rosamond meant to take them somewhere else, that they were not at all the friends they seemed. She looked at them with suspicious eyes, and put her hand on Ronald's knee.

Then all at once the rain was shut out, and Jennifer saw they were passing under a low stone bridge, a natural arch, that connected the island to the shore. The storm was suddenly distant and hollow, more echo than force. When they floated back into the rain again it seemed less insistent, and Jennifer could see ahead down a long steep valley more like a *V* than the *U*-shaped canyon behind the arch. At the end of the valley, where it turned beneath a generous flank of virgin forest, sunlight shone, the end of storm, and beyond it she saw ridge after ridge of soft dark fir that reached, perhaps, to the shore of the sea.

They had drifted almost past the island, and Jennifer's worry was beginning to increase, when Colin tucked them behind a sandbar and into an eddy with a few smart strokes, and then rowed the boat sedately back to a shady cove at the foot of the tower. The rain stopped as they ran aground beneath the arms of a giant alder, and the thunder grumbled at half strength, retreating reluctantly somewhere farther up the gorge.

"Welcome!" said Rosamond, leaping from the bow. She helped Ronald with one hand and assisted Jennifer with the other, and they stood on the sand without letting go, the three of them laughing because they were so thoroughly wet, though Jennifer thought perhaps that wasn't quite the reason. It was more the laughter of climbing partners on a snowy summit, of old friends at the front door, of children allowed an extra hour of freedom on a summer evening. And Jennifer knew she could trust these people after all.

Colin hauled the boat ashore, and then joined their hands in a perfect circle. The westering sun broke under the clouds and illuminated his wet blonde beard, and the tower behind them glistened like silver in rain-slick polish. The ouzel reappeared in their midst, *bzeet*-ing and bobbing. Across the cove and down the valley a rainbow shone in the new-washed sky, resting its promise in rivers and mountains without end.

Chapter 15
Come Out, Dear Sister

✳

"YOUR FATHER'S HOUSE DID YOU SAY THIS WAS?" Jennifer was sitting back from the modest table that was scattered over with empty plates, once again looking out from the main room of the cottage. The shutters of the generous windows were opened upon a grassy terrace that dropped away through arbors and groves to the placid river that stretched upstream between the walls of the lower gorge, tinted with rose in the gentle dusk.

This was precisely the stretch of water they had navigated in sheets of rain through which she had gotten her first glimpse of the Tower of Otium. After landing in the cove behind the tower, they had circled back on a path that climbed through yellowing dogwood to mossy ledges, each affording pleasant prospects that begged for at least a day, an autumn, a life, of slow contented contemplation. Then they had rounded an outcrop and found themselves before the cottage, built against the base of the tower and in this season amber with meadow to the door. A spring bubbled out from under the tower next to the cottage, and rushed away in a clear-flowing stream across the terrace and down to the river. It made Jennifer think of the fountain beneath the rose in her dream, and made this dwelling more strangely precious in her mind.

And so Rosamond had lifted the latch and welcomed them into this common room, low-roofed with beams. There was a fireplace where Rosamond cooked at one end, the table at which they now sat in the middle, and another fireplace ringed with cushions on which they might recline at the other. Rosamond had taken Jennifer into a bedroom and helped her select a dry smock to wear, green like the river, and Colin must have found clothes for Ronald, for by the time that Jennifer re-emerged both fires were lit and the two young men were standing about in gray knickers and clean white shirts. Then had come soup and warm buttered bread, and crumbs and laughter, and the scooting back of heavy chairs.

"Indeed," said Rosamond. "My late loved father the Lord Amoenas, brother to the renowned Lord Linton of the western meadows, built this cottage for my mother after meeting and marrying her by the great falls at the head of the gorge. Here I was born and here I grew in the care of my father after my mother burst smilingly in the labor of bearing a mortal such as I."

"Your mother—?"

"Well, *dissolved* is more like it—released to her native element."

"You mean—?"

"Yes. My father was an earthborn man, but my mother was the most beautiful of the mountain naiads. Though I have more of my father in me, and am well content to live warm and dry in the cottage he built, I serve as protectress if not companion to my cousins."

"Naiads?" said Ronald. He sounded a good bit over his head.

Jennifer thought how she might explain, and realized she couldn't. "You know—water nymphs. The river when it sings."

Colin clapped Ronald on the back and said, "You'll catch on, lad. It's nothing too difficult."

"Why, yes," said Rosamond. "Lord Linton, my uncle, was married to an oread princess—"

"Oread?" said Ronald.

"A mountain nymph," Jennifer whispered. "At least I think so."

"And Colin himself is dryad on his father's side," Rosamond continued. "Cedar, I think. Or was it—"

"Oak," said Colin. "He came from the chaparral in the south."

Jennifer looked at Ronald and said,

> *"There are more things in heaven and earth, Horatio,*
> *Than are dreamt of in your philosophy."*

"Horatio?" said Ronald.

But Jennifer, with questions of her own for Rosamond, left Ronald in his peaceable confusion. "You say you serve as *protectress* for the naiads? Whatever for? Who wants to harm them?"

"No one at all for the life of my father, and for the lifetimes of my mother's mothers. But since he died, and his body was borne in the sacred barge to the

Western Sea, a king has arisen far to the south—the great El Ai (may his name ever perish). His empire grows by the desert hills of a thirsty land. The great El Ai is dissatisfied with the music of the chaparral and the drought-stricken brooks which sound in the place that he has chosen. He has lately heard of my sweet-voiced cousins and coveted them for his private pleasure. Ever since my father died he has come with his bands of thieves by horse, across the desert and into the gorge, to seize and carry away my cousins to bitter captivity far in the stinking pools of El Ai.

"I can do very little. And so it has been that Garth has given his permission for Colin and me to marry at last. For many years—the years of the Lava Beast—Colin could not be spared from his post in the western meadows, where he kept watch over the hapless marmots. The Beast yet lives, but his claws are blunted, and Garth has consented to our union so that Colin might help to protect the Amoenas."

"It's not all as practical as that," said Colin. "Garth too is a man who knows what it is to yearn and to love." He laid his arm upon Rosamond's shoulders and looked at her as if to scold.

"Garth?" said Jennifer. It was hard to envision a tender side to the stern old man she had met in the cave.

"Of course," said Colin. "Everyone knows of his former longing for the Lady Lira. When they were young and she was innocent, no two lovers loved as they. Whole days they spent—I have it in truth from Rosamond's father (may he rest and rise)—whole days at the foot of the falls at the head of the gorge, singing what the water sang, and joining their voice to the voice of the naiads. Whole days they rowed the river together in every season—the rush of spring when the meadows are flooded and dogwood blooms above the current, the green of summer when the grass is tall and thick with flies, the quiet of autumn when the flies are at rest and the stalks of grass are dry and rusted, the hush of winter when the walls are traced by fingers of snow on every ledge and the great falls hide in a shield of ice. Here at the tower she and Garth would end their journeys and scale to the very summit by daring and invisible ways. From the top they would laugh in the face of the sun and watch it set and rise again before they returned—no one knew how."

"But what happened?" said Jennifer. "Why aren't they together now?"

Colin started to answer but stopped, looking to see how Rosamond might choose to explain.

"It's a long story, and very short," Rosamond said. "On the morning of their wedding day in the western meadows, Lady Lira disappeared."

"Abducted?" said Ronald. "Kidnapped?"

"Everyone would like to think so," Rosamond said. "But she seems to have left by her own free will, and to have spent the rest of her wretched years in the service of the Lava Beast, preying for him on the hoary marmots roundabout, and praying to him—if half the stories about her be true—in her mansion within the obsidian cliffs.

"And Garth, brokenhearted, yielded his ax after many years to one William Arthur, his chosen heir, so that Lady Lira might be dispatched. Finally, he chose between his love and his land. The deed was done, and Lady Lira was delivered up to the jaws of the Lava Beast himself, after the ax had betrayed her into the crater lake of the North Queen."

"So that was the end of her?" said Jennifer.

"All of us certainly thought so," said Rosamond. "There was the marmot, of course, the one she called James, whom she had corrupted to her service. He ran away at the last moment—but now he has attached himself to the great El Ai (may his name ever perish)."

"A very big marmot?" Ronald asked.

"Yes," said Colin. "A whistle pig if you ever saw one."

"But lately," said Rosamond, resuming her story, "word has come of a curious statue set up in the barren courts of El Ai. It is the very likeness of Lady Lira, only now she is known and worshiped there as Lady *Lyra*. So even in death she seems to have gained new dignity. The great El Ai directs all his people to bow down before her. She is, he tells them, the only goddess, the great mother, mistress of earth."

Jennifer felt a twinge of dismay. "This Lady Lira—or Lyra," she corrected herself. "What does—or did—she look like?"

"I have not seen the statue," said Rosamond. "But in life her face was as beautiful as the faces of her sisters—the precious Stella, drowned with the stars at a tender age, and Lady Demaris, who yet lives among us. (She it is who brought up Colin from boyhood at their father's home in the meadows under the Center Queen.) Like her sisters, Lady Lira has the greenest of eyes. But her hair is black, a presage I suppose of her soul. Lady Demaris has hair that is the richness of cedar, and Stella's is a golden fire like the planets at dawn."

"*Is?*" said Jennifer.

"Is," said Rosamond. "She did not so much drown as commit herself to the stars and the waters high atop the North Queen. And she is seen in other waters as well. Wherever rivers flow free or lakes lie pure beneath the sky, Stella is there."

"Even," said Jennifer, "in a waterfall?"

"Oh, especially there," Rosamond said. She smiled. "You have seen her then?"

"I believe I have. And Lady Demaris at Chambers' cabin."

"And James," said Ronald. "And Garth, and William, and maybe even his ice ax, except now it's an oar—one of the two we have in our boat."

"By the Beast himself!" said Colin in wonder.

"And Lady Lira," said Jennifer in a miserable whisper. "I think I have seen her in my dreams." All of a sudden she began to cry. For days she had wanted to tell someone, and now she was telling three people at once. She cried till her cheeks were very wet and the front of her smock was smeared and stained. When at last she stopped sobbing she noticed that Ronald's arm was around her. He looked confused.

"Perhaps you have much to tell us," said Rosamond. "Let's clear the dishes and sit by the fire. It will be so much more comfortable, and give you a chance to recover yourself."

"I'm sorry," said Jennifer, getting up and feeling foolish for crying in front of everyone. She felt she had failed them in some way.

"No need, no need," Colin said brusquely. "You've said the right thing."

He stoked the fire and they settled into the cushions beside it, Rosamond leaning on Colin's shoulder and Jennifer propped up awkwardly against Ronald's knees. How long did it take, she wondered, for two people to learn to be one?

Rosamond nodded to Ronald first. "Give us your waking tale, Ronald, before Jennifer relates her dreams. One is as needful as the other."

Conscientiously, Ronald reported the story of their journey, with precise attention to time and distance and event, and rather less to how he felt about any of it. He faltered, however, when he came to the part about severing the rope on the bergschrund lip, and Colin groaned.

"Poor fellow," he said. "I met him once. Who knows? He might have learned to sing."

And when Ronald told about William's abduction, Colin hurled a stick in the fire. "That murderous marmot—may he be drowned and swallowed forever in the odious cesspool of El Ai."

"Can we get him back?" Jennifer pleaded. "William, I mean?"

"Garth will know," Rosamond said. "He will be here tomorrow."

"Garth or no, I will not marry until we do!" cried Colin. He jumped to his feet. "What shame it would be for me to lie in my Rosamond's arms and that man remain a captive in deep danger and disrespect. By the North Queen and all that is sacred, I swear it now."

Rosamond looked at him quietly for a long time. Jennifer wondered if she were disappointed at the sudden prospect of postponing their wedding day. "It is well," she pronounced with restraint. "You have said, Colin. It shall be so. Only, let us wait for Garth." She nodded to Ronald to continue his tale.

Ronald went on hesitantly, explaining the help the ouzel had given them coming down the river.

"So that's where he's been these few days," said Rosamond. "I had wondered at his absence. Truly, you had a reliable guide."

When Ronald explained their descent of the falls they expressed no surprise, though Colin admitted to feeling envious.

"Once in a lifetime a mortal may descend that fall," said Rosamond. "My father, Lord Amoenas, came down that way on the day he met my young sweet mother there at the bottom. It is a sign of a great commission—an honor and a great delight. You must cherish that day—it will nourish you in the steep dry years that lie ahead."

And then Ronald was finished, and Rosamond looked sorrowfully at Jennifer. For a moment, Jennifer kept silence. But then she told, reluctantly at first, her dream in the tent of the maze and the rose and Lady Lira, and of the actual rose she had plucked from the ax (which was Stella's, said Rosamond), and the dream of the dryad beside the cedar and of James the marmot gnawing at William, and of seeing Lady Demaris again, and finally—this took the most courage to tell—of her dream in the gorge of ascending the night sky high above the Three Queens and her sleeping self.

"So she lives," said Rosamond thoughtfully—"at least in the voice of her sometime marmot, speaking into your ear by night. It is strange, but one part of me is sorry for her yet. The three of them were such splendid sisters—and she suffered so in her cruelty. And now to have her depraved shadow seducing you in your dreams, Jennifer. It is altogether sad, both for you and for her memory.

"But rest assured, Jennifer, she is not your goddess within. With the naiads know your author without, and he will dwell richly within you. Lady Lira forsook and denied both him and his gifts, and her marmot would fain have had you believe we are self-created, each queens in our own realms, but the truth is something much humbler, and better. To serve and to worship in our small places is to be gifted with all creation, and to know the gift of our true selves."

"Amen to that," said Colin. "Except—I cannot confess such tender feelings for our dear departed Lady Lira. I have a mind, in fact, should I find her statue, to hack it to bits with a good stout ax and smoke them in the nearest fire. The old witch! You are too soft, Rosamond. She got exactly what she deserved on the North Queen, and I wish she had gotten it a good bit sooner than she did. Old James has a score to pay. I hope we get there before poor William is sacrificed to his live will and her dead pleasure. That's what I think. Sorry indeed!"

Rosamond sighed and exchanged a glance with Jennifer as if to say, with a certain melancholy, *Men!* But she chose not to reply.

By now the evening had grown late and the fire had begun to die. Ronald proposed that he and Colin sleep out by the cove to guard the boat from any harm—and leave the cottage to the women. Colin thought this a most sensible plan, and set about gathering wool blankets to offset the wet chill that lingered in the aftermath of the thunderstorm. Jennifer had half a mind to accompany them—it seemed rather odd to sleep indoors—but the thought of remaining with Rosamond was so comforting that she stayed with pleasure. So it was that they kissed their men goodnight at the door and watched them pace off into the moonlight to do their duty.

The two of them stood there in pleasant silence, looking out through the open doorway down the glistening lawns to the river. The air was cold on Jennifer's cheeks. She watched the glint and gleam of the water, the ghostly polish of canyon walls, and thought that she heard the distant sound of silvery singing. She found she was clasping Rosamond's hand in the innocent way she used to stand with her mother or a childhood friend. "I like this place," she said to her softly, "and willingly could waste my time in it."

"Let's," said Rosamond, and handed her back into the cottage.

She slept that night on a soft grass pallet in a separate room, dim and dry, closing her eyes amid the echo of naiad song that came in through an open window. But it seemed she had scarcely fallen asleep when she dreamed again of the garden maze, the turnings of path among tall thorny hedges. She came as before to the center of the garden, the enclosure of hedge about rose and fountain and beautiful woman whom she now knew to be Lady Lira, in death as in life. The woman stood tall in her crimson gown and regarded Jennifer knowingly.

"Pluck and find," she said again, pointing to the rose in the hedge. "Pluck and find the goddess within."

"No," said Jennifer. She felt surprise at her resoluteness.

Without even seeming to hear her, the woman plucked the rose herself, this time with a strangely mechanical motion. Immediately the red rose wilted in her hand, turning brown, then black, in a shrunken corpse of its fragrant self. The spring at her feet abruptly dried up. Most surprising of all, the woman herself began to age before Jennifer's eyes. Her clear fair brow contracted in wrinkles, her nose grew knotted with hairs and warts, and her emerald eyes became dark and deep-sunken. Her back stooped, her hands shook with the tremor of palsy, and her crimson gown hung tattered and gray.

"Pluck and find," the old woman rasped. "Pluck and find the goddess within."

Then, in her dream, a voice from behind Jennifer said, "Come out, dear sister. Oh, please, come out. You may still come out from the belly of the Beast. There is yet time, and you are yet loved."

Jennifer turned to see standing behind her the woman she'd seen in the waterfall, the woman that Rosamond had called Stella. She stood young and fresh and golden-haired in a robe of white. What struck Jennifer was the pureness of pleading in her face, the longing that no one should be lost. Here, she thought, was sisterly affection as she had never guessed could exist.

The hag that once had been Lady Lira repeated her hollow invitation. "Pluck and find. Pluck and find the goddess within."

"Oh sister!" cried Stella, and rushed past Jennifer to grasp Lady Lira by both hands. "Don't you see? I am here. You are given a chance to know the mercy from without."

Lady Lira paused a moment, as if dimly aware of a presence at the margin of self. "Pluck and find," she rattled out.

"Oh sister," Stella repeated softly. She went down on her knees, still holding the hands of the hag, and began to weep. "My poor lost Lira."

What Lady Lira might have done, Jennifer was prevented from knowing. For in that moment a clatter awoke her; outside her window she heard the hooves of many horses. And before she could separate dream from waking, the door to her room flew open with a crash.

Chapter 16
The Dark Divide

✳

WHEN RONALD AWOKE, THE MORNING WAS NO LONGER YOUNG. There on the sand in the shade of the tower, lulled by the steady surge of the river, he had slept deliciously and long. Colin's blankets lay broken like an empty cocoon. Ronald found his glasses in a boot beside him and put them on to look for Colin and find his world. The boat lay undisturbed nearby. The alder trees clumped next to the beach held out their leaves, sere and serene. Swallows swung across the cove, flash upon swirl, and arced high to their nests on the face of the tower above.

Ronald remembered what Colin had said about Garth and the young sweet Lady Lira climbing the tower to its top by daring and invisible ways. Invisible indeed. Now in the shadow of morning light the tower looked more than impossible to scale. Polished smooth by millennia of glacial ice, it raised its needled head at least a thousand feet above the river, maybe more. Geologically, the spire was an anomaly. Only the very toughest granite could hope to withstand the midstream force near the terminus of a valley glacier. Somehow the rock had remained. In the course of his fieldwork Ronald had climbed a few rock faces, but he could not imagine anyone wanting to venture out onto this one.

He was still reposing in his blankets, pondering the face of the tower with a strange mixture of scientific curiosity and metaphysical satisfaction, when he heard a howling in the distance, and soon saw Colin descending the trail to the cove at a run. It was Colin himself who howled as he went, and when he reached the sand he beat his breast and stumbled to Ronald in a frenzy. He stood shaking and panting for some moments, unable to speak, then closed his eyes.

"What's the matter?" said Ronald, standing up in his blankets. "Tell me. Please."

"They're gone," he said with a rasping sob. "Gone, gone."

"Who's gone?"

"My only love, your only love—my Rosamond, your Jennifer—they're gone, they're gone!"

"What? Dead?" He felt a sickening surge of panic, and grabbed both of Colin's shoulders.

"Not if we can help it, lad." Colin shrugged off Ronald's hands and spat on the ground in disgust. "Sleep on the beach to protect the boat—of all the misbegotten ideas! Taken in the night to El Ai—and probably the whole pack of naiads with them."

"You mean—"

"He means you have a long pursuit ahead of you."

Ronald turned—and there was Garth, white-haired and white-bearded, standing beside them, his pace of coming quite unperceived. It seemed oddly fitting for him to appear at yet another time of crisis. Still, Ronald was quietly amazed.

"Journeys have a way of begetting journeys," Garth said. "You must accept each one that comes. And you as well, Colin. Young Ronald was not at all wrong to sleep in the sand beside the boat, and you must not regret keeping him company. The contents of this bark are precious, and your faithfulness, Ronald, shall be rewarded."

With that, Garth stepped to the rowboat and reached inside with both arms. What he brought out, one in each hand, were not oars but axes—the axes that the oars had been on the Center Queen. He held the shorter out to Ronald. "Take this ax, the ax of the rose, of the pure drowned stars. Let it work its grace on those it may touch. Let it know the hands of a woman."

Ronald received the ax with care, and nodded in bewilderment.

Colin reached for the longer ax, the one that was William's, but Garth withheld it. "This ax I will keep for myself, and I myself will keep here until you return, to use it as I am used by it. I thought I would not hold it again, but with this ice ax now in hand I feel a rousing motion within me. As I see you here, ready for your journey, my old age knows the strength of its youth. Though much is taken, much abides. Go then, both of you, and return if you can to bear the body and to wed. You have my blessing and my hopes."

As Garth completed his benediction the sun emerged from behind the tower and flashed upon the silver head of the short wooden ax in Ronald's hands. He felt rather dazed. To wake and to lose and to leave in a moment was much at once. If only he could return to the glacier and simply finish his movement survey. To make the world into numbers in a data book—how much simpler that was than oars and axes capriciously interchanging themselves.

Instead of expressing this longing for a familiar world, Ronald allowed himself to be taken back up the path to the cottage. Halfway there, as they circled the tower, the path was joined by a trail that led down and across the natural bridge to the shore of the river closest to the Three Queens. This trail, Ronald imagined, must lead to the tall thin waterfall where he had stumbled into Colin, and thence up many a narrow ledge to the valley rim and the outermost skirts of the South Queen. When they reached the meadow in front of the cottage, Ronald saw that their path dipped down to yet another natural bridge that joined the tower to the opposite shore. Across this bridge, quite long and quite slender, a trail zigzagged up a ravine and disappeared at the southern rim. He didn't need Colin or Garth to tell him that this was the way they would be going.

The meadow itself was plowed by the hooves of many horses, clods of earth strewn everywhere atop trampled grass. The spring was muddied and manured, and the door of the cottage was wrenched askew, hanging halfway off its hinges. They walked inside, and the room that had brought such order and comfort the evening before now lay in shambles—the table collapsed, the cushions shredded, the ashes spread about the floor.

"And look here," said Colin, shaking his fist. He showed them into the bedrooms in back. In each of them the empty beds were deliberately cracked asunder, broken in two from head to foot. Suddenly Ronald was roused to a fury he had kept himself from feeling till now. He thought of Jennifer pertly recording his data in the survey book, and then of the marmot gnawing the pages, and all at once saw the violation—not of his numbers but of her fingers, the work of her hands.

"Neither heights nor depths," vowed Colin firmly, "neither river nor plain, neither thirst nor flood shall separate me from the love of Rosamond. What say you, Ronald?"

"Much the same," Ronald mumbled, "in regards to Jennifer, of course."

Colin looked askance at Ronald.

"He is saying what he can, Colin," Garth interposed, "and means as well and as deeply as you. Now, couple your words with deeds, and go."

Colin nodded, and they re-entered the common room. From the wreckage of the kitchen he gathered provisions for their pockets and slung flasks of water across their chests. "No packs," he said. "We're going light. Can you run, lad?"

Before Ronald could answer, Colin was out the door and gone. Ronald looked at Garth uncertainly and thought it best not even to say goodbye.

Then he was off, sprinting down the trail to the bridge, and onto it, just as Colin crossed to the other side. If he hadn't been trying to catch up to Colin he would have slowed to a careful walk—the stone arch was slender indeed, wide enough for a mountain horse quite sure of its footing but not any wider. As he raced across he dizzied himself with the perpendicular surge of the river, flaming with salmon some ten or twenty feet below.

Then he was over, and the trail plunged into a cedar grove and began to ascend a tiny stream. He couldn't see Colin. The way steepened into the ravine that he had seen from the cottage, and the cedar gave way to hanging thickets of slide alder through which the trail began to switchback in quick short turns, crisscrossing the stream at every traverse. The path was so narrow, so barely cut into the tangle of trunks, that he would not have thought horses could come this way had there not been the hoofprints to prove it. He ran up and up the green-gold tunnel, and still no Colin. His thighs ached and his lungs hurt and the ax grew heavy in his hands, and finally Ronald could run no more. The air was warm and close inside the ravine, and his shirt and knickers were drenched with sweat.

An hour later, or maybe two, after running and resting several times, Ronald found Colin impatiently waiting at the rim of the gorge on a mossy ledge. "Sorry," said Ronald, and planted his ax in pathetic exhaustion.

"That's what rowing a boat does for you," Colin huffed. "But rest your mind. That's the steepest it gets."

Ronald stood panting and looked back down at the river below them. He saw the ribbon of fall, just upstream on the other side, and the trace of a trail on the cliffs beside it. Behind the top of the waterfall was the forested skirt of the South Queen, silvered in its autumn ice, and behind the South, the familiar summits of Center and North, arranged in a column so as to obscure the saddle that held Chambers Lake. About the Queens the forest spread in every direction, broken only by golden larches and amber meadows and the creamy gash of the gorge below.

And within the gorge, directly before them, was the summit of the Tower of Otium, exactly even with their feet. It was flattened off at the very top, with a crack that separated two small pedestals, each no bigger than what a single person could stand on. With a very long rope one might construct a Tyrolean traverse from summit to rim. It seemed quite odd, Ronald thought, to be looking at a spot so relatively close at hand that he might never hope to visit.

Before Ronald had rested quite enough or drunk more than a sip from the flask at his chest, Colin sped off once again. From here, one trail branched left and followed the top of the canyon upstream. Ronald supposed that William had been brought that way. Their own trail continued up and away from the rim through open slopes of western hemlock, bearded with lichen and stolid in self-sacred shade. As Ronald gathered his nerve to continue, he thought of the ouzel he had followed through just such a forest to find the boat when it had escaped. He thought of the ouzel and unashamedly wished him back, and also wished for the finding now of more than a mere boat.

Newly resolved, he trotted on. The trail rose in gentler, longer switchbacks now, and Colin stayed one turn ahead, passing through the trees above him the opposite way as if he were going somewhere different, on another errand than the one that he and Ronald shared. He stayed one turn ahead, but no farther. This time Ronald kept Colin in sight, and this in itself kept him going in spite of a terrible stitch in his side. He balanced the shaft of the ax in his hand, moving it back and forth like a piston, and heard in his pain the lonely song of the varied thrush urging him on.

After more switchbacks than anyone would care to count, the hemlock thinned to Douglas fir and sugar pine along rocky ravines that hid a few scant patches of snow left over from winter. The trail wandered through dust and talus, humble phlox and blazing larch, and finally crested a real divide at a small gray tarn in a shingled depression. Colin was looking blankly at the water when Ronald arrived, each panting as hard as the other. The sun was dissolved in high cirrus scud, and far past its prime.

"Well run, lad." Colin put a trembling arm about his shoulders and turned him around. "You see where we've come." Ronald looked down a nearly endless forest slope to a distant suggestion of the gorge and the hazy shape of the Three Queens. He could scarcely believe how far they had run.

"And you see where we go." He guided Ronald around the tarn and stood with him where the ridge fell away at the opposite end. The trail plunged down through rocky clefts to a barren desert far below. No ancient hemlock interposed their verdure here. Close at hand were whitebark pine and juniper, then ponderosa and golden glimpses of aspen and cottonwood. And at the base of the ridge, stubborn groves of live oak lifted their arms amid skirts of gray-green chaparral. Beyond this, the desert opened south and east, dun beneath a strange dun haze. At its far extremity hills arose, barely distinguishable from the air. And at the foot of these hills lay a small dim spot, hazier than any other place to be seen.

"Behold El Ai," Colin said simply.

"Why all the smoke?" Ronald asked. "What's there to burn?"

"Not much," said Colin. "But the great El Ai requires every inhabitant of his great city to constantly burn an offering to him. Nothing live is sacrificed—or so at least I have heard—save the chaparral (which is live enough) and the few growing trees that are at hand. But farther and farther from hand they get. The plain before you was not always the completely barren desert you see—just as the river that drained its edge beside those hills did not formerly run dry. Each outlying citizen is also required to build a large reflecting pool beside his home—some, I have heard, are acres long. These are to mirror and multiply the glory of the great El Ai whenever he chances to ride past, just as the smoke is to fill the air with the precious incense of his presence."

"You have been there, then?"

"Never. But El Ai was the home of my mother, before she fled across the desert and found comfort in the shade of an oak at the foot of this ridge, the Dark Divide. In gratitude she gave herself to him, and I was born of mortal and dryad months later in the promised land of the Three Queens. My mother (may she rest and rise) told me all. I have never been to El Ai. I have always feared it would come to me, and now it has."

He sat down wearily, pulled a few broken biscuits from his pockets, and shared them with Ronald. As they ate, Ronald wondered what it would be like to have an oak tree for a father. He thought of his own, stern and inflexible, rooted in the wooden pulpit that he seemed to inhabit in Ronald's memory, world without end. In a way he too was descended from oak.

Colin pointed to the tarn at their feet, printed with the hooves of horses. "They might have been here at dawn," he said. "A place to rest and water the horses and tighten the saddles before plunging down the dry side and into the desert." He sank and sighed and looked back toward El Ai with lackluster eyes. Now Colin was the one that seemed spent.

"So what are we waiting for?" said Ronald. He stood up and refilled his flask in the tarn. And paused. For a moment he saw a face in the water that wasn't his own. It was the face of an old thin woman, weeping and moaning for some great loss. But the moaning was the wind, and the wind erased the face in the water. Ronald wondered if he had seen a naiad, and if he had, if it were one that had just been brought here or one that was native to this pool on the Dark Divide.

He wasn't even sure enough of what he had seen to report it to Colin. As they hurried down the trail at a run, jolting not panting around each switchback, Ronald kept the face in his mind, superimposed in a grotesque way upon the image of Jennifer. Though he was thus preoccupied, he took care not to turn his ankle, nor to slip on the carpets of needles that occasionally covered slabs of smooth black rock in the trail. Sometimes he went out of his way to kick aside a pine cone or two—especially those from the sugar pine that lay big as marmots across the path.

For this time Ronald led the way, gathering the strength that Colin seemed to be losing as the day drew on. They descended through groves of yellowing aspen in tall white meadows, feeling the tang of evening air. They passed cottonwoods beside trickling streams, and lost themselves lower down in head-high tangles of manzanita, just as they'd squirmed through thick slide alder coming up the ravine from the gorge. The ground became red and dry and hard. As the sun began to set, the earth agreed with its garish light, as fierce to the eye as the blood-soaked bark of the manzanita.

Just at dusk, they stopped descending and entered a grove of large live oak at the very edge of the desert plain. The day of running had taken its toll, and they sat in the shade of a gnarled giant whose limbs spread out and down all around them, offering rest. Ronald felt a sense of expanse and shelter, as if they had found an empty pavilion. It was peaceful and flat here. The ground was hard but they sat among stalks of white wild oats spread out among the trees like snow. Here and there a bright-limbed sycamore rose among the somber oaks.

Ronald had blisters on both feet, and was going to tell Colin when each of them heard something—voices, they thought—at the desert end of the twilight grove.

"Did we catch them this soon?" Ronald whispered. He nervously gripped the head of his ax.

"Hardly possible," Colin answered. "But stay here—I'll find out."

Colin crept off before Ronald could object. As he waited, night truly came. There was chirring of crickets, the clicking of a bat, and skitterings in the wild oats. When Colin returned, one star had come out and the moon had just begun to rise. The light of a campfire was visible far off through the trees.

"They're from El Ai, but they're coming, not going," Colin whispered. He sat hard by Ronald against the trunk of the spreading oak.

Laughter echoed from the fire, and Ronald wished that he could share it.

"A woodcutting expedition," said Colin—"more fuel for the sacred flames. They've completely denuded their own hills, so now they come this far. And there is another reason as well. According to their superstitions, El Ai will never fall until the wood of the Dark Divide comes marching against it. The great El Ai professes to scoff at this prophecy, but he isn't taking any chances. That's why he sends the woodcutters.

"We've got four of them on our hands—with six horses. And a very large wagon, I think. They haven't chopped down anything yet—they are just arrived. But they will turn in soon to rest themselves for their work tomorrow. And that, my friend, is when we borrow hooves for our feet and axes aplenty for our hands."

Ronald stiffened. "You don't mean—"

Colin shook his head. "No, of course not. I wouldn't murder the great El Ai himself in his sleep. We'll leave them here to enjoy the oaks intact at their leisure. By the time they wake we'll have crossed the desert and be waiting at the gates of the city. It will be quite simple."

Colin seemed to have regained his morning's energy and eagerness. Ronald too, aching and footsore, smiled at the prospect of cantering over the desert by moonlight. He lifted his ice ax, curiously out of place in this spot, and tapped it against the oak with approval.

"It is a good plan, my son," came a solemn voice. "Only this—*we* shall go with you."

Ronald jumped up. He could not tell who it was that had spoken. Then he saw Colin slowly rise and embrace the trunk of the tree itself.

Chapter 17
The Hands of a Woman

※

IN THAT SAME TWILIGHT, JENNIFER REACHED THE GATES of El Ai in loathing and relief. She had sat the same horse since the middle of the previous night, a sweating roan that shied on the switchbacks and lurched on the slabs, and that crossed the desert at a dismal trot which jolted her up and down in the saddle until her bones cried out for mercy. The prospect of journey's end was pleasing of necessity, but the farther they rode from the Tower of Otium, the more alien the land became. As gorge and hemlock gave way to desert and sage, her heart sank. This world was not her home.

At least she had a horse to herself. Each of the naiads was forcibly mounted between the arms of a swarthy horseman. They had struggled at first, singing in pain and trying to slip off the bows of the saddles, but when day had come they had wilted in the manzanita, and now in the desert they were all but dead, draped across the horses' necks like broken lilies.

Rosamond had the worst of it. The largest and burliest of all, the great El Ai, who had come himself on this expedition, had chosen her to share his saddle. He was rather big-bellied, with a pink scarf wrapping his bald head and a red silk shirt half-opened on his chest. To Jennifer he looked all too much like the disagreeable Escee. As he rode with Rosamond he constantly bent his cheek to hers, calling her his "pretty piece of Otium." He tried to share his cakes with her when they stopped to breakfast beside the tarn on the Dark Divide. And the sort of attentions he wished to give her now they were arrived at El Ai were all too clear. He had captured not only a choir for his court but an unwilling concubine for his bed.

But Jennifer had no idea what they wanted of her.

The men that opened the massive gate in the sandstone wall looked much like the ones on horseback beside her—not so much swarthy as carefully tanned, and for all their cruelty rather spiritless. For miles outside the city gates they had encountered strange rambling houses in the desert, each with its own reflecting pool and roaring bonfire at the door. The inhabitants stood next to their pools as the cavalcade passed, not even looking up at the horses but merely staring down at the water and repeating the words, loud enough so that Jennifer could occasionally hear them in unison, "I love El Ai, I love El Ai." There was no real fervor in the way they said it, but no real sense that they had any other sentiment to express, either. The men at the gate said the same thing. It was not only mantra, not only watchword, but apparently the sole means of communication. Jennifer's captors had talked and cursed and laughed and argued all the way over the Dark Divide, brandishing swords and battle axes in high spirits, but once they had got within sight of the city they had fallen silent, letting their weapons hang in their scabbards and only exchanging the reassurance that they, too, loved El Ai.

Outside of the city were no flowing streams and no standing trees. A long low bridge before the gate crossed a riverbed that was dusty and dry, and for miles about there was scarce a bush. The setting sun did not bring the tang of autumn cold but merely an anemic chill, bland and barely noticeable. It no longer seemed like autumn at all, nor summer neither. In fact, in El Ai it did not seem to be any season in particular. Every season, Jennifer guessed, was merely and purely the season of smoke. Her eyes smarted in the pall from the fires.

The horses entered the city proper at a tired walk—only it was not a proper city at all. The homes outside the city walls were richly furnished in spite of their irregular design, but the homes on the inside were mere hovels, crumbling huts of weathered sandstone looped and windowed in ragged decay. Equally ragged families sat beside cooking fires in the open doorways. Their skin held a native darkness deeper than the cultivated tan of the men in the cavalcade. None looked up as the party passed; none vowed their attachment to this place or to its august person, either. Jennifer wondered if the great El Ai, riding just ahead of her, was in any way offended by this lack of customary attention. But he was occupied just then in trying to nuzzle Rosamond, and did not particularly seem to care if anyone else loved him or not.

They wound through the darkening streets, past many more hovels and cooking fires, until they reached a sandstone palace raised in the very heart of the city. The front of it was all towers and arches silvered in the rising moon, the sort of place that Jennifer might ordinarily take interest in for the splendor of its architecture. As it was, she felt much too angry and much too tired to appreciate its finer features. They entered a large gate into a courtyard, where troops of servants bearing torches relieved the horsemen of their mounts. The naiads were passed to waiting hands and carried up a gleaming stairway like so many empty sacks of horsefeed.

"James!" thundered the great El Ai, swinging himself and his prize from the saddle.

"What?" said a voice. Jennifer could not see who had answered, but noted the voice was from somewhere very close to the ground.

"James!"

"What?"

"Open your flesh-clogged ears and listen! Lodge this brace of maids for the night. I would have them now but I must sleep. I trust none other to keep them close. Bring them to me when morning comes—that one first." He pointed at Rosamond.

"But the sacrifice, great one," said the voice. Jennifer had got down off her horse and now saw that the voice came from something sitting up like a dog. And not like a dog, either, but like a marmot—a very fat one.

"What about the sacrifice, beast?" said El Ai impatiently.

"It is set for dawn, at the waning of the full moon. Shall they attend you there?"

"Oh, very well," grumbled El Ai. He turned his back on the marmot and made a deep bow to Rosamond and Jennifer. "Tomorrow, my favored ones. Rest before pleasure." He made the pretense of a smile, and then with the help of several servants heaved his bulk up another stairway, opposite the one up which the naiads had been taken away.

"In the temple then," the marmot called after him. "We shall await you."

Soon Rosamond and Jennifer were left alone in the courtyard under the smoke-smeared stars with James the marmot. He turned his baleful eyes upon them, and Jennifer recalled the times she had met him before—in camp, on glacier, by riverside. A dozen epithets rose in her mind—*pig! brute! rodent! murderer!*—but they stymied each other and she kept dull silence. When he nodded his head and dropped to all fours they followed him mechanically.

He took them through a small door between the stairways and down a flight of sandstone steps to a dusty apartment lined with straw. There was no furniture, no window. A single candle burned in a niche. The marmot stood up and blew it out, then left the room and shut and locked the heavy door. They heard him shuffle back up the steps.

"Pig!" shouted Jennifer. "Brute! Rodent! Murderer!" She sat down next to Rosamond.

"He's deaf," said Rosamond in the dark. "Besides, he would take those titles as a compliment."

"I mean much worse than I say," said Jennifer.

"Of course," said Rosamond. She sighed.

And then Jennifer sighed too. "He may be deaf, but I'm the one who has been blind. I feel like—" She hesitated. "I feel like I've been in the dark this whole time. All the way across the divide and across the desert, I couldn't figure why I had a horse to myself. You I can see—but he wants me too. The great El Ai is getting hard up."

"Yes," said Rosamond. "The business is altogether disgusting, I agree. But—" She paused. "But in one small sense, you insult Ronald by what you say. To give yourself to a husband, Jennifer, you must believe you have something to give."

Jennifer was surprised to be handed this reproach, and hardly knew how to respond. "He was all over you!" she exclaimed. "How could you stand it?"

"It *was* trying," Rosamond said. Jennifer felt her shudder in the straw beside her. "His breath was rather like rotting carcasses of salmon that begin to wash up on the banks this time of year. But my dear lost naiads. I think of their poor desiccated souls almost more than I think of you or of myself, Jennifer. I cannot be sure they have survived the journey."

"Do you think they will come? Ronald and Colin? And Garth, perhaps?"

"They will try," said Rosamond firmly. "We must hope. And sleep."

There being no other or better choice, after many further commiserations they lay down together, nestling close in the stale straw. Jennifer did not sleep at first, though her limbs were sore and tired with travel. Her thoughts made pilgrimage to Ronald, wheresoever he might be. She wondered that he loved her at all, and if he loved her enough to risk himself in pursuit of her here. Looking on darkness with open eyes, she imagined his face

a jewel hung in ghastly night

and even then no quiet found.

Her sleep was restless. The marmot stood on one side of the river, and Garth on the other, arms upraised in execration or benediction, she wasn't sure which. The great El Ai rode back and forth across the bridges of Otium, and a voice repeated a lilting chant: "No such roses see I in her lips." An ice ax swirled above the tower unhanded by anyone, and Stella kneeled by the cottage fountain with her hands outstretched, proffering a burning coal. "No," rasped a voice. "Pluck and find. I am a woman of unclean lips. No, no."

Which was precisely what Jennifer found herself saying when the door to their cell burst open: "No, no!"

James stood implacably over them between two men with burning torches. "Yes," said James. "I say yes, and you must come. Think of it as your ceremony of dedication to the great El Ai. The time has come."

They rose reluctantly, stiff and sore, and followed the marmot back up the steps to the courtyard. The air was cool and pale and smoky in first light. He took them up the stairway that the naiads had been carried up the night before. Then he led them through a columned hall that opened into a great domed room with a high ceiling. Torches flared on pillared walls, reflected by a pool of water that took up most of the floor.

The marmot bowed upon entering and bade them do the same. Rosamond resolutely refused, and Jennifer followed suit. He bared his teeth in deep displeasure.

"Pig!" Jennifer said aloud. "Brute! Rodent! Murderer!" It felt good to say these things again.

He leapt at her, his teeth still bared.

"Down, cur!" said a voice behind them. It was the great El Ai, dressed in a pink silk morning gown and satin slippers with curled toes. He was accompanied by a troop of guards. "Who mars these maids, mars my pleasure."

"They would not bow to the Lady Lyra," James replied.

The great El Ai waved off this complaint. "They will bow to me, that is enough."

Jennifer, meanwhile, now that they had stepped into the high-domed room, saw what James was talking about. This was a temple, a sanctuary. The pool was filled with their languishing naiads, floating about like so many fallen aspen leaves. Arranged on each long side of the pool were solemn women in white robes.

"Ah," said El Ai, striding up to the edge of the water. "How are my pretty priestesses?"

The white-robed women did not reply but kept their eyes on a pedestal at the far end. Jennifer followed their gaze and gasped. For on this pedestal stood the woman of Jennifer's dreams. She was crimson-gowned, red-lipped, with raven-dark hair falling across her bare white shoulders. At her feet was a raised altar, and lying upon it was the bloodied and barefoot body of William.

El Ai instructed his guard to stay at the door, and following James, he took both women by the arm and guided them around the pool past the strangely immobile priestesses. As they drew closer to Lady Lyra, Jennifer realized that the woman was indeed a statue, just as Rosamond had said—beautifully painted, arms and chin and eye like life, but only a statue nonetheless. The goddess within was after all the goddess without, and merely made of stone at that. William, though still, was quietly breathing, apparently whole and undisturbed since she had seen him days ago in the hollow cedar by the river. When she got quite close she saw, however, that his heels had been hideously chewed.

The four of them stopped in front of the altar. El Ai advanced himself a little and ostentatiously fell to his knees. Jennifer saw that this crushed the toes of his satin slippers. She looked down at the top of his skull and marveled at his utter baldness; his head reflected the light of the torches that sputtered quietly on the walls. She thought to herself that at this moment she should have been filled with fear of him, or with pity for William, but no—she was thinking on crushed slippers and bald crowns.

The great El Ai spread out his arms before the statue and made his petition:

> *"Thou, Nature, art my goddess; to thy law*
> *My services are bound. Accept the blood*
> *Of this thy sacrifice and hear the praise*
> *Of these from Otium we bring to thee."*

He arose then, and judging by what he had just said, Jennifer wondered if she and Rosamond would now be required to speak. And how could they, now that he had made it clear that William was to be murdered at last before their eyes? Instead of turning to them, however, El Ai walked to the lip of the pool and summoned the naiads.

"It is now your time," he said to them. "I trust that you are refreshed from your journey. Sing to us one of the songs of Amoenas. Do it for my sake, and for the sake of your supreme goddess, the Lady Lyra."

Reluctantly, the naiads grouped themselves in the water, their sorrowful faces emerging as one. The dawn was breaking through windows in the entrance hall, and lent a pallor to their cheeks. They would not face the great El Ai or the Lady Lyra, but resolutely turned their eyes to the north and west toward the distant land of the Three Queens. A wordless harmony sprang up among them, mournful in a minor key. Then words came, song came:

> "By the waters of El Ai we sat down and wept
> When we remembered shining Amoenas.
> On dry sands we lay down our lyres,
> For there our captors required our praise.

> "How shall we sing the song of love in a strange land?
> If we forget thee, Tower of Otium,
> Let our hands know pain and withering.
> Let our tongues cleave dark to our mouths
> If we do not set Otium above highest joy.

> "Remember, O sisters, the men of El Ai,
> And how they swept upon us by night,
> Who sought in their souls to destroy the Tower,
> Who said in their hearts, 'Raze it, raze it!'

> "O daughter of the Beast, you devastator!
> Happy shall he be who requites you
> With that which you have done to us!
> Happy he who takes and dashes
> Your little one against the ax!"

The song ceased with cruel abruptness, and the naiads melted back into the water. El Ai was rigid with rage, and even James had heard well enough to know the last epithet was meant for him. He snarled at the pool, puffing out the full bulk of his hoary chest.

Then he turned again to El Ai. "The dawn has come and it is time."

From under the altar he pulled out a dagger with both paws. The hilt was long and the blade was longer. Solemnly he stood up and passed the knife to El Ai. The man stepped up to William's body on the altar, and the priestesses commenced a chant:

"I love El Ai, I love El Ai
And honor and obey his goddess,
The Lady Lyra, within us all."

El Ai raised the dagger over William's chest. His hand quivered, perhaps from his rage at the song of the naiads, perhaps from some remaining drop of the bittersweet milk of human kindness. Jennifer wanted to scream, to charge, to throw herself biting and kicking at the shoulders of the big bald man, but she stood unable to do anything at all, no less fixed than the statue itself.

"Let it fall!" urged James. "Do it, sire, and in the heat! It is blood well spent."

But woe to him who severs the heart, thought Jennifer, remembering what Garth had said.

"My lord!" came a voice. There were rapid footsteps in the hallway.

El Ai turned in an irritated daze. The ranked guards at the door of the temple opened up and allowed a ragged messenger to step up to the brink of the bath.

"The watch reports an advance against us. Fires quenched, pools dried up, the walls of the city soon to be threatened."

"That shall never be," said El Ai. But he let the dagger drop to the floor as if it should, and looked about vacantly. "The prophecy is that El Ai shall never fall until the wood of the Dark Divide shall come against us. And how should it ever? The Dark Divide is a desert away. And trees do not walk. And should they decide to, I send my woodsmen to prevent them with the edge of the ax. Say again, messenger. Bring honest news, or by the Beast I will sheathe this dagger in your heart." He picked up the weapon and held it like an obscene gesture over the water.

"The watch does not lie, my lord. And I among them—from the top of the gate I have seen them coming massed against us, rooting and writhing as no men move, bringing with them the shade of death. They are oak trees, my lord. Live oaks from the Dark Divide."

The great El Ai grew suddenly pale. He turned toward the altar, then started toward the pool again. "Remain here with the captives, James. You, my guards, come with me. Raise your fellows. We shall see what tales these be. Even now our ax is laid to the root of the trees. Every one shall be cut down and cast in the fire. Oaks indeed! Tumbleweeds, and a drunken watch. Come, away. I shall be back."

He strode out of the temple then, and his guards with him. Rosamond grasped Jennifer's hand and they stood very still in the menacing presence of the marmot. The sanctuary was quiet except for the murmuring of the priestesses that went on and on:

"I love El Ai, I love El Ai
And honor and obey his goddess,
The Lady Lyra, within us all.

"I love El Ai, I love El Ai
And honor and obey his goddess,
The Lady Lyra, within us all.

"I love El Ai, I love El Ai
And—"

"Do you, now?" came a voice. "Oh, do you really? If I've heard that once, I've heard it a thousand times here. You cannot tell me you truly love that mountain of flesh, nor this place neither, by what I've seen of it thus far. Don't think for a minute you're—Rosamond!"

It was Colin, of course, and Ronald by his side, standing now in the entrance of the temple after riding all night across the desert. And now they fairly flew past the priestesses, who did in fact desist in their praises. Colin carried a woodman's ax, and Ronald an ice ax that Jennifer thought looked strangely familiar. The silver head of the ax burned bright like the coal in her dream that Stella held in her outstretched hands. And this gave her an idea.

Before Ronald and Colin could reach the altar, the marmot sprang for Colin's throat. Colin dodged, and James plowed snarling into the wall. Colin turned, ax ready, and the marmot recoiled himself by a column. There Colin kept him at bay—the marmot ready to spring again, and Colin ready to chop him out of the air if he did.

Which left Ronald and the ice ax free and clear. He approached the two women in slow amazement and did not even say hello—which was typical of him, Jennifer thought. He paused with them beside the altar, and then as if put in mind of a promise, a vow made, he stepped around to the base of the statue and regarded it with a curious intensity, hefting the ice ax in his hands. The statue looked on coldly and firmly, the pale forehead, the hard green eye, the bitter lip possessing still an inert power.

"Lady Lira," Ronald said, "or Lady Lyra—whatever your name is—this time you're gone for good." He lifted the ax high and it trembled, just as the dagger had trembled over William's heart.

"Ronald," Jennifer softly implored, "let me." She had followed him around the altar. "It was I she ensnared. It was I who plucked the rose and the ax. I have the strength of a woman's hands. Let her suffer at mine, not yours."

Something in what Jennifer said awoke an echo in Ronald's mind. *Take this ax, the ax of the rose. . . . Let it know the hands of a woman.* He lowered the ax and offered it with both hands to her, a sacred gift.

"Now," said Jennifer, "step back." She gazed at the statue unsteadily and held the ice ax at her side. The painted eyes were proud and compelling. Even now they tried to enlist her loyalty. But Jennifer merely shook her head. Behind the glittering eyes she saw the vacant stare of the withered crone.

Then she knew what to say.

"Come out, sweet Lira," Jennifer called. "You may still come out from the belly of the Beast." She scarcely understood what they were, these words that came, but she knew they were the right ones to utter. "Be no longer the goddess within, and know the mercy from without. Know that you are loved, and live."

As she spoke these words, Jennifer reached the head of the ax as high as she could till the sharpest point of the burning pick was just touching the lips of the statue. At first nothing happened. "Come out, sweet Lira," Jennifer pleaded. "Come out, sweet Lira, be married today."

With those words a tear formed in the hard green eye of the statue and trickled down its painted cheek. Then one from the other eye. And another tear, and many more. The eyes blinked, warm and lovely.

"Come out, sweet Lira," Jennifer called.

Jennifer had the uncanny feeling that it was not she who was speaking, but someone else—someone like Lady Demaris, or the spirit of Stella in her dream. She marveled. Why had the words of Stella failed in her dream but now taken their effect? Was it the physical presence of Stella's ax, the touch of silver on lifeless rouge? Or was it that she, Jennifer, as Lady Lira's prey and victim, could be the sacrifice that saved?

"Come out, sweet Lira," she called again.

The red lips opened against the ax, like the flowering of a cold budded rose. "Oh," they sighed. "I am a woman of unclean lips."

From next to the wall the marmot snarled, and Colin threatened him with his ax.

"By this ice ax," Jennifer said, "and by the spirit of the one who made it, who planted the ash and buried the silver and shaped the hands by which it is formed, those lips are cleansed."

"Oh," said the statue. "Oh," and shuddered, releasing itself from the bondage of stone. And then the statue truly and fully came alive, stepping off the pedestal and into the arms of Jennifer, flesh upon flesh, and they wept together. And Rosamond joined them, and they wept all three.

Ronald stood by awkwardly, and Colin glanced back as best he could to try to make out what was happening. But he didn't want the marmot to escape or to spring, either one. Finally, Lira, still weeping and clinging close to Jennifer and Rosamond, made her way to Colin's side to address her marmot. Even off her pedestal she stood a full head higher than Colin.

"My marmot," she said simply. "James."

"What?"

"My poor corrupted marmot whom I have known from youth, when you faithfully joined me in the meadows, my constant companion in wickedness, even to my morning of death, I wake now to find you here, faithful still to my erring spirit. Be you faithful still, and join your mistress in life at last. Suffer this daughter of goodness to touch your lips with the ax of my sister, even as she has touched mine. Let it be so, James. There is mercy at last, and you may share it."

The marmot snarled sullenly, and grew very still. Jennifer slowly held out the ax, guiding the edge of the silver adze toward his curled lips. For a moment he sat quietly, as if to receive some transformation. But at the last instant, before the ice ax reached his lips, he sprang with a snarl at Jennifer. Before he got there Colin's ax sang through the light and sliced the marmot's head from its body in mid-air. Jennifer had hardly had a chance to recoil before the marmot lay at her feet, bestrewn and beheaded. As they watched in silence, the blood ran over the floor before them and poured into the flashing pool.

"I am sorry," said Colin, addressing himself to Lady Lira.

"It is as he has chosen," she replied. "And, I fear, as I have long ago chosen for him.

> *Happy he who takes and dashes*
> *My little one against the ax!*

The blessing is yours to keep, Colin. The mystery of wrath within grace, and grace within wrath. He kills only to make alive. We trust he shall. You have my love.

"And you, William," said Lady Lira, turning now to the body on the altar. "You too are now as I have wished, and how can I begin to say I am sorry for it? Ah, do you smile? Do you smile at me in your wounded sleep? Look! Look there! It warms my new-thawed heart that you do so."

She bent over William's face and wept, drying it with her raven hair. The others gathered around the body and saw that William indeed wore a peaceful smile of gentle contentment.

When Lady Lira had finished weeping, she cradled William in both her arms and picked him up from off the altar. Then she turned and addressed the priestesses. "You who stand there night and day to say you honor and obey me, obey me now. Each of you reach into the pool and bear up a naiad in your arms and carry her after me out of this temple, even as I carry with me this worthy man."

The priestesses, who had watched their goddess come to life without so much as batting an eye, now suddenly bestirred themselves to lend their helping hands to the naiads. Soon each of them stood with a willowy water nymph in her arms, ready to follow at command.

"Which way?" said Lady Lira to Colin.

"Our horses are by the door in the wall just west of the northern gate," Colin replied.

She nodded and led the way out of the temple and down the hall, striding smartly with William lying across her arms like a precious burden. Colin and Rosamond, Ronald and Jennifer, followed them out, arms entwined, no less precious to each other, and behind them dozens of white-robed women, arms dripping with versions of their better selves. They left in their wake a pedestal without a goddess, an altar without a sacrifice, the headless carcass of a hoary marmot, and a pool that flashed blood-red in the dying torches pale against the light of morning.

Chapter 18
Six Saddled Horses

✳

THEY FOUND THE STAIRWAY AND COURTYARD DESERTED, and passed through the gate of the palace into the streets of El Ai. Jennifer could hear shrieks of rage and hollow trampings far off, from the walls of the city and beyond, but El Ai itself was as sullen and quiet as it had been the evening before. The same authentically dark people crouched in their doorways beside their fires, turning their eyes on the strange troop of passersby as if an erstwhile goddess bearing a body, two young couples arm in arm, and a company of white-robed acolytes dripping with naiads were not at all a remarkable sight.

With Colin's instruction, Lady Lira led them to a door in the wall at the end of a dim and crooked alley. Men on the ramparts next to the northern gate nearby were shouting and pointing, but not at the escaping party. Once through the door, on the cityside bank of the riverbed, Jennifer saw what excited the lookouts. Across the river, spread about the suburban plain, great live oaks were afoot in the land. They advanced improbably on their roots, crushing houses, sucking up pools, beating out fires with limbs that reached like powerful brooms. The inhabitants fled in terror before them, though one band led by the great El Ai was attacking the trees with spears and arrows that stuck in the trunks and dangled there to little effect. One tree alone remained quietly rooted, shading a spot just over the riverbed. Jennifer did not recall it being there the evening before. Hitched to its trunk were six saddled horses.

At a word from Colin, Lady Lira led them down the crumbling bank, across the sandy wash of the river, and back up to the tree and the horses. She laid her burden at its roots and put her face to the bark of the trunk, speaking low. Then she paused as if listening for the oak tree to speak in return. Satisfied, she turned and straightened, addressing herself to the priestesses who stood obediently behind them.

"Thus far, my daughters, you have served me with constant if misdirected love. I now release you from that service. Lay down your burdens next to mine at the foot of this great fatherly oak, and go thy ways, never to praise Lady Lyra again except to remember the morning she was resurrected. If you wish to partake in her redemption, to devote yourself to the rushing water across the desert, I invite you now to share in our journey. This oak tree and his brethren will bear thee, along with the naiads you have borne. If you cannot bring yourself to this journey, the way is clear to return to the city across the river and through the door. Only, the time is short, and once inside, I bid you stay away from the walls. The choice is yours; I no longer can make it for you."

The white-robed priestesses looked perplexed. All about the city walls the marauding oak trees tramped closer and closer, and streams of people were clogging the bridge and crowding into the northern gate. All of a sudden, as if by a signal prearranged, the priestesses turned and fled as one, scrambling down the bank in a flurry and sprinting across the riverbed to the door in the wall, their white robes billowing out behind them. At first, Jennifer thought they had all left. But when she looked at her companions again she saw that four of the priestesses—the youngest and strongest—remained among them. One of them shyly returned her gaze.

"You have chosen well," said Lady Lira, and gave to each of them her hand. The four young women kneeled and touched their foreheads to the ground, but Lady Lira lifted them up. "You are not my priestesses; I am not your goddess. Together we are but broken sisters. We must learn to love each other well. More I will tell you. This much now."

Colin meanwhile had untied the horses. The army of oaks had completed their work of devastation outside the city and were now drawn up to left and to right on the bank of the river, encircling the walls as far as Jennifer could see. The gates were shut, the ramparts empty, the people all pent up inside. The rustling limbs of the long row of trees cast pleasant shade in the morning light that was already hot on the desert plain. Jennifer could half imagine a shallow river stealing beneath them, the calling of herons and croaking of frogs, and leisurely walks enjoyed by the few who might belong to such a place.

As this prospect crossed her mind a strange thing began to happen. At first she heard just a quiet patter, like the falling of leaves, or dewdrip on a foggy morning. Then it increased to a gentle rain, trickling down from twigs and branches as off the edges of great umbrellas. What began as a drizzle progressed to a torrent. Not only the crowns but also the roots of hundreds of trees began to gush great streams of water, sucked out of the many harbored pools of the suburbs and now disgorged in a thousand cascades down the bone-dry bank of the river and into the long-neglected channel. The water merely collected at first, or sank in the soil, but soon a river began to rise, spreading silty and deep from bank to bank and moving in a mighty current between the city and the desert.

Jennifer squeezed Ronald's arm. She whispered,

"*Dark brown is the river,*
 Golden is the sand.
 It flows along forever,
 With trees on either hand."

"On one hand, anyway," Ronald said.

Jennifer smiled. The Amoenas had trees on both hands, but it was green. She wondered when life would ever imitate poetry with complete precision.

At last the trees had given all the water they had. The river was filled to the very brim, and the sandstone bridge that linked the desert to the gate began to melt away in the current, falling apart in chunks and shards like a sandcastle in the rising tide until nothing at all was left of it. Jennifer was overjoyed to see it go. Now they could depart in peace, untroubled by fear of pursuit.

But the oaks had one more task to complete before they left. Suddenly, the tree they were under gave itself voice and shouted, "Now!" It clashed its limbs together like drums, like the mighty clapping of giant hands. The other trees took up the shout all up and down the desert river, beating their long stout limbs together in thunderous arboreal applause. "Now! Now! Now! Now!" Jennifer covered her ears in the din, and her insides shook, and the ground trembled. And all at once the tall deserted walls of the city tumbled outward and buried themselves in the depths of the river. The splash that went up over the desert soaked Jennifer and Ronald and all, and the trees stood clapping and glistening wet, shouting for joy.

The devastation was complete. The outlying houses and fires and pools were long gone, and now the wall of the city itself, leaving only a sandstone palace square in the midst of terrible squalor. Crowded in amongst the hovels were the suburban refugees, looking rather ill at ease among the darker citizens. Jennifer wondered if those who said they loved El Ai and those who hated it in their hearts would now come to some agreement about the place as a *place*, a watered nook beneath desert hills, a quiet land of little rain that might yet blossom as the desert rose it was meant to be. For Jennifer, it could never afford the pleasure of Otium, but she sensed it was no wasteland either.

Even as she caught sight of the great El Ai and his band of guards, staring blankly back at them from what used to be the northern gate, she hoped in her heart that he would somehow learn to dwell contentedly in the land in which he found himself. She could hardly help feeling pity for him. He looked dazed and foolish—and frightened too, when he saw Lady Lira standing among them. The supposed goddess held up her hand to wish him peace, but instead of responding he turned with his men and fled towards his palace, trampling and shoving their way through the masses.

"I hope we see no more of *him*," said Jennifer to Ronald. "You have no idea how disgusting he was to Rosamond—to me, even."

Ronald only smiled shyly, and brushed some oak leaves from her hair.

Lady Lira stooped and lifted William in her arms again. Colin mounted one horse, Ronald another, and Rosamond and Jennifer climbed up behind them. This conveniently left a horse apiece for the white-robed women, who were looking askance at the trees around them as possible modes of transport. When the horses and people had moved aside, the fatherly dryad let down his limbs and caught up the naiads into his crown, nesting them with the mistletoe. Then they all set off at an easy pace, Lady Lira and William in the lead.

The sun was high, but Jennifer felt the welcome shade of the oak tree marching along behind them, and then the shade of many oaks, the delicious cool of a moveable forest traveling with them across the desert. Birds called and swooped in the branches, and from their perch the naiads sang a song of blessing:

> "We lift our eyes to the Dark Divide:
> Return is sweet to the place of help.
> Swift are the roots of them that bear us
> To green bright waters."

Though Jennifer had hardly slept, the shade of the oaks and the song of the naiads so soothed her soul that the journey that day across the desert filled her with a strange and pleasing exhilaration. Ronald, she thought, must have been no less exhausted, but as she held him tight in the saddle she had no sense that he was tired. They exchanged many words in the long day's ride, but none unkind.

When evening came they caught sight of a campfire in a barren place at the very foot of the Dark Divide. "I have an idea whose that is," Colin said. As they approached they saw four figures run from the fire and dive under a nearby wagon.

"Woodcutters," Ronald told Jennifer. "We borrowed their horses. Perhaps now we can borrow something to eat."

They stopped their horses next to the fire. Lady Lira laid William down, and the forest of oaks dispersed themselves to their time-honored places and took root. The fatherly oak remained near the fire, though far enough from it to keep the naiads from discomfort. Over the flames hung an iron kettle on a makeshift tripod. Ronald and Jennifer dismounted, and she tested the broth. "Delicious," she murmured. "Almost as good as Chambers'."

"Not likely," Ronald said.

Colin, meanwhile, marched to the wagon with ax in hand and flushed the woodcutters into the open. "We thank you for your horses," he said, "and crave the use of them one day longer. In the meantime, we ask part of your supper, and blankets for the night." He held the ax in a menacing fashion as he spoke, so that the woodcutters, shivering with fear in the firelight, had very little choice in the matter.

"You speak much too haughtily, Colin." It was Lady Lira, who had come up beside him. At sight of her the woodcutters fell to the ground in absolute terror, pointing to their necks as if asking Colin to dispatch them then and there with his ax.

"They are from El Ai," Colin explained. "They came to destroy the grove of my father. I owe no more courtesy than I give." He sounded resentful, but also embarrassed.

"They are from El Ai," Lady Lira repeated. "And no less are you, O son of the south, your mother a priestess refugee from the very temple in which these women thought to serve me day and night. Methinks these men would make fit consorts for my women. As those may learn to worship aright, these may learn to care for what they cut before. Forgive them, Colin. They served El Ai with blind hearts, and knew not what they did. Mercy triumphs over judgment. If for me, how much more for the least of these."

The four men slowly lifted their heads, and Colin slowly lowered his ax. The former priestesses quietly gathered on either side of Lady Lira, and one by one and pair by pair she raised the woodsmen from the ground and put their hands in the hands of the women. It was done in a moment of holy silence. Jennifer thought she had never seen such a good and pleasant unity.

But then she saw that one of the women, the one who had gazed at her before, looked back at Jennifer and shrugged. *Not much choice here*, Jennifer thought.

Nevertheless those newly joined came back to the fire, and blankets were spread, and stew was served, and tales were told, and songs were sung, and the women danced, and along about midnight one of the woodcutters told a little story about their grandfather (for as it turned out, they were four young brothers).

"He had a lemon grove by the river, back when the river used to run," said the youngest one, the one who was paired with the priestess who shrugged. "His name was Sam, and his friends would ask him, 'How'd you learn to grow lemons, Sam?' And he would say, 'I look at what my neighbor does, and I just do the opposite.'"

Everyone laughed except the priestess, who looked again at Jennifer and rolled her eyes.

"What did you say his name was?" Colin cut in.

"Sam," said the woodcutter. "Sam of the South."

Colin grew agitated. "Did he have a daughter named Samantha?"

"Why, yes," said the woodcutter. "Yes, he did. Samantha is our long-lost aunt, sister to our departed father. He often told us she had been killed by the spirits of evil trees in the wild, and that is why he raised us to be woodcutters. Whenever our father spoke of his sister he would weep."

Now it was Colin who was weeping. "She was my mother," he said brokenly.

The woodcutters stood up as one, and the youngest said, "Our cousin, then." And then the brothers and Colin embraced each other and wept upon each other's necks, and Jennifer saw that the priestess who had rolled her eyes had now taken to dabbing them with the hem of her robe.

This reunion was still in progress, and the tears had long since turned to laughter, when one live limb of the fatherly oak took Colin aside. Colin seemed to confer with the knots of the trunk, and returned to the fire with a serious look. "My friends and cousins," he called to them.

Their laughter died.

"My father tells me he feels in his roots the fast approach of many horses. The great El Ai has found a way across his river, and is come in wrath to reclaim his captives. We must on tonight, over the Dark Divide in the stars, and make our stand at Otium. Our friends the oaks must keep their roots—we cannot ask them to do again what they can perform but once in a century. Only, my father shall accompany us to carry the naiads and guard the rear of our company. Rest is sweet, but the valley of the Amoenas is sweeter." As he finished his urging he poured a bucket of water on the fire, and it hissed and steamed in the light of the moon.

Jennifer was dreadfully vexed at the prospect of another night ride. She had been dreamily leaning her head on Ronald's shoulder, nearly ready to stretch out on the ground and sleep. All of her bones and muscles ached. But she got to her feet like everyone else and helped to find the horses that were scattered about in the wild oats. When the horses were gathered, she got up behind Ronald on the chestnut mare they had ridden that day across the desert. Colin and Rosamond mounted too, and the four new couples a horse to each. Lady Lira regathered William in her arms, and the oak tree took up the sleeping naiads. The strength of the oak tree Jennifer could understand, but the stamina of Lady Lira all that day and now tonight was far beyond her comprehension.

Then they were off, swift and silent, climbing through the dark tangle of manzanita up the reaches of the divide. In an hour they came to a rocky knoll from which they could look out over the desert. Colin saw a flash and churn approaching their camp in the moonlight, a column of horse, and pointed it out to all the rest. Jennifer breathed quiet thanks they were not on that

> *darkling plain*
> *Swept with confused alarms of struggle and flight.*

It was bad enough being just one hour ahead in the hills.

Lady Lira led them on with tireless strides, easily keeping ahead of the horses, which panted and sweated beneath double burdens. Cottonwoods gleamed in quiet ravines, and higher up, moon-pale aspen, quivering in the deep night breeze. The way became rocky, and pines appeared, and sometimes giant sugar cones came whooshing down around their ears like stones from space. When they got to the tarn at the top of the ridge, a faint rim of dawn shone over the desert. The horses were staggering with fatigue, and the couples dismounted to drink and to rest. The oak tree stood incongruously a few strides back on the brink of the pass, his twisted arms magnificently spread against the folds and dikes of shattered rock. Colin went to speak with him, and reported back that his father complained of the thin air.

"But it's down from here," he assured everyone, "and we've got to be farther ahead of them now than we were before." He no sooner spoke than they heard the sound of clattering stones from just over the pass behind them. Colin shot back up to the oak and uttered a groan.

The others did not even ask. They leapt to the backs of their tired horses and plunged down the northern side of the ridge, Lady Lira in the lead and Colin and Rosamond riding last by the lumbering oak. The moonlight was barely sufficient to show them the way through rocky defiles, and once they gained the hemlock forest it was dark indeed beneath the trees. Had the trail not been soft and wide they would surely have ridden themselves to disaster. Lady Lira called a warning for every switchback, and they wheeled each one at improbable speeds. Jennifer gripped with her tired knees as best she could but at every turn she felt herself nearly flung headlong into outer shapes of trunks and darkness.

Down, down, down they swirled, weaving back and forth through the forest till first light reached this side of the mountain and ferns and lichen began to show themselves in a blur. At last they reached the rim of the gorge, and Lady Lira came to a halt. "We can't stop!" said Colin, cantering up.

And then they all saw why she had.

The sun was on the point of rising just over the head of the canyon, there at the brink of the great falls. In its gathering light they could see across to the small split summit of the Tower of Otium, hovering in empty air above the center of the gorge. And standing on the downriver half of the summit, looking intently across the chasm into the eyes of Lady Lira, was the lone robed figure of Garth himself, no less statuesque than she had been on her pedestal in the desert temple. He held William's ice ax in his hand, lifting it high in solemn greeting. Jennifer could not make out his face from this distance, but she studied the profile of Lady Lira's and thought she saw there mingled parts of shame and longing. What Lady Lira might have said or wanted to say, Jennifer was ever afterwards curious to know. As it was, Lady Lira merely stood in her long red gown, soiled with travel, holding out William in her arms as if to offer restitution. Then Garth nodded, and Lady Lira nodded back, as if they had reached some final agreement or exchanged a mutual permission. The first rays of light broke over the canyon and caught the head of the upraised ax in a flash of fire that soon enveloped Garth's face and beard.

"Now!" he shouted, just as the army of oaks had shouted beside the river of El Ai. His voice rang and echoed across the gorge, even as they began to hear the pounding of horses above and behind them. With both his hands and all his might Garth pulled the ax back over his shoulder and brought it arcing over his head in a smashing blow to the pedestal of the second summit. A few small rocks split off from the tower and clattered away to the canyon depths. But Jennifer sensed that something greater than this had happened. Far away, from the head of the river, there came a sound as if the earth itself had groaned. A muffled surge, a sinking, a roar—and the ledge beneath them trembled slightly.

"This is the dolorous stroke," Lady Lira turned and told them. "Come, we must go."

A yell went up from the mountain above them, and they saw El Ai in the morning light, cutting straight downhill across the switchbacks with dozens of horsemen on either side. They did not wait for their pursuers to arrive. Lady Lira plunged into the alder ravine, and the horses after, the oak tree crashing behind them as best he could. "I am sorry, my cousins, you must pardon me," he kept saying to the alder thickets. "I must bruise your trunks for a greater cause. Let us pass, and cross yourselves against the hooves of those who follow."

Jennifer felt branches swat her right and left as their horse careened down the quick-turning trail. It was rather like falling down a spiral staircase and being beaten with whips and cords the entire way. But she did not mind—she was mostly afraid of falling off, which somehow seemed more terrifying in the light than it had in the darkness.

As they descended, the sunrise moved with them down the ravine, as if it were they who were bringing the dawn to the floor of the canyon. They could hear the curses of El Ai behind them, he and his horsemen hacking and slashing with swords and axes through the alder. The chestnut mare that Jennifer and Ronald were riding was starting to limp, as if it had lamed itself with exertion. They urged it on, but soon found themselves next to the dryad behind the others, and hearing more and more clearly the imprecations that El Ai poured out upon Lady Lira, and the Lava Beast, and the White Fawn of Otium—as if he had no steady view as to what he swore by or swore against.

At last the trail began to level in cedar trees beside the brook, and the oak tree was saying, "Pardon me, my brothers, a thousand pardons," as he snapped off the cedar limbs in his way. Ronald and Jennifer emerged from the grove on the brink of the river and saw the others already crossing the thin stone bridge, the deep current swirling below. Their limping horse took one look at the narrow span and put each hoof to a full lame halt.

"Move it!" cried Ronald. "We're almost there!" But the horse stayed put. They could hear El Ai come galloping up and slash at the oak tree right behind them. "Please!" said Jennifer, wondering what one said to a horse in a time like this. (*Giddy up* sounded too prosaic.) She made as if to threaten with her ax. But the horse wouldn't move.

Ronald leapt to the ground and pulled Jennifer with him. They ran at full speed onto the bridge and sprinted as hard as they possibly could to the other side. Lady Lira was there to greet them. She had laid William down on the bank, and told them to follow the others up to the cottage.

"You're staying?" said Ronald. "Shouldn't we all?"

"You must go with the others," Lady Lira commanded. "It is expedient that one should be sacrificed for many. This is my time."

Jennifer looked at William on the ground. Lady Lira said to her, "He too is in my charge. You must go, and go quickly."

She no sooner had spoken than El Ai and his band of horsemen came swarming around the oak to the bridge. They had mauled the trunk and hacked away some smaller limbs, and the wail of naiads rent the air. Lady Lira advanced to meet them, resolute, entirely alone. Ronald and Jennifer hesitated behind her, panting, and Lady Lira turned her head.

"Go!" she said.

And they turned and fled.

Soon they reached the others at the cottage, high above the narrow bridge. Their boat had been placed there, right on the doorstep beside the spring, and gathered around it were squirrels and raccoons and weasels and deer—even a mother bear and her cubs—as if all of them had come to flee El Ai as well. As curious as this assembly was, Ronald and Jennifer did not think to ask about it. They stood there wheezing, hands on their knees, right next to Colin and Rosamond and side by side with a pair of deer—antlered buck and glossy doe—and looked back at the bridge below them. It was still in shade, though the sun now shone on the cottage and the entire tower.

What Jennifer saw was Lady Lira standing face to face with the great El Ai, who had dismounted at the center of the bridge. They couldn't have been six feet apart. Lady Lira, tall and severe, was saying something with great firmness. She had no weapon, but El Ai was threatening her with a long cruel knife. From a distance it looked like the one he had wielded next to the altar. Half his men were lined up behind him on foot; the other half were still tormenting the oak on shore. Jennifer knew it had been their delay that had kept the tree from crossing the river. The thought made her stomach weak.

Colin was stamping and tearing at his hair. "Why did I let her persuade me up here? By the Fawn himself—for a son to stand by and to watch his father dishonored like this. O woe, woe, woe and shame upon my head!"

He wrenched himself free from Rosamond's arms and ran partway down the path—and stopped. The sun had reached the crown of the oak, and the dismounted guardsmen were bent on toppling the whole tree into the river. On the bridge, El Ai had edged closer to Lady Lira, probing the narrowing space between them with his knife. But Colin was no longer looking at the pair on the bridge or at his father. He was looking upstream, as the rest of them at the cottage were too.

From behind the nearest bend in the canyon they heard a roar like nothing their ears had heard before. Thunder could only dimly suggest it. The roar filled the canyon from wall to wall, onrushing, growing louder and louder like the deep increase of a kettledrum. Ronald gripped Jennifer's arm and shouted in her ear, "The glacier!" To himself he whispered, "*Jokulhlaup.*"

And then it was upon them—a wall of water and ice and stones and snags some thirty feet high, bearing down on the Tower of Otium like the alpine tidal wave it was. Colin just had time to sprint back to the cottage before it broke on the thin stone bridge in the first rays of the risen sun. The great El Ai was still flourishing his dagger, and Lady Lira standing fearlessly over him, and then they were gone, obliterated by the shock and thunder of the surge. The water smashed to the very doorstep where Jennifer and the others stood, and then rolled by in a giant flood, rich with earth and jagged icebergs, clashing rocks and whole red cedars torn by their roots. One old giant, curiously hollow and blackened at the base, came abruptly to rest in the deluged meadow before the cottage. Jennifer winced at its mangled side, its shattered limbs, and heard the dryad of her dream: *The river gives its life for me, and I shall give my life for the river. Gladly I shall lay it down.*

Where the bridge had been there was nothing to see. El Ai and his horses and men were crushed and drowned and washed away. But the oak tree, the naiads,

Lady Lira, and the body of William were no less buried and gone as well. A strange calm came upon the assembly in front of the cottage as the noise of the *jokulhlaup* pounded away from them down the canyon. They stood looking out over muddy water, the floor of the gorge made formless and void. Colin was weeping. Jennifer clung to the neck of the doe and to Ronald's side, and found that her cheeks were streaming with tears.

Chapter 19
Autumn Kiss

✳

FOR THE REST OF THAT DAY they rather gloomily set about fixing up the cottage. It was situated just high enough above the river to have been untouched by the glacier burst, but was still in a sadly vandalized state from the depredations of El Ai. The four woodcutters were fortunately just as good at joining together beds and tables as they were at chopping apart live oaks. The women helped Rosamond put her kitchen to rights again, and by evening the cottage was much as it had been before El Ai and his mounted guard had brought it to ruin.

Jennifer had half expected Garth to descend from the top of the tower and add to their remnant some grim form of encouragement. But all day long they saw neither ax nor beard of him. Even Rosamond, thinking on her hopes of a wedding, was put out that Garth did not show himself. "After all," she said, "he got up; he can get down." So while she and Colin readied some supper, Ronald and Jennifer stepped outside to look about the tower and the island.

The renewed order within the cottage was foiled by the chaos without. The waters had receded, and the terraces that led down through the shadows were choked with boulders and debris. Torn trees and snags jutted this way and that out of layers of mud like leaning corpses. The thin stone bridge to the south was gone, and in the turbid river below them a giant logjam butted up against the head of the island. As far upstream as they could see, the verdant shores of the pleasant Amoenas had been massacred as if by winter avalanche.

"What a sorry mess," breathed Ronald. He thought to himself that the can-yon might as well be dammed and inundated, if only to cover the wounds from sight.

"But look here," said Jennifer. "This *is* curious." She pointed to the washed-up cedar beside them, prostrate for its giant length, its roots appealing in withered agony to the sky. The bubbling spring flowed sweet and clear from the foot of the tower into the charred, wooden hollow, and already growing from the bark were tiny seedlings, green and tender against the sky. The log was nurse to numberless beginnings of its former glory, giving itself in death to life. There was promise here, and Jennifer felt strangely heartened.

They took the familiar path around the tower, or what they could see of it through the debris, and found that the bridge to the north had held. Given its mass, Ronald was not at all surprised. As they stood regarding it, however, they were startled to see in the westering rays of the autumn sun the bald dome of a white-bearded man who was striding toward them across the arch. He was robed and fat. As he climbed to meet them they both said, "Chambers!"

"Yes," he called back. "The very same, unchanged, untransmutable in identity and unimpeachable in name. One week older and a daylong worn in the soles of my boots. By the Beast, what a weary distance!" He sat on a stone and mopped his ample forehead with a handkerchief.

"Came to check on the boat, of course—on little *Amoenas*—and on you all, while I was at it. Saw the morning fracas in the pond and couldn't be sure there'd be anything left but food for salmon and slivers to sell for holy mementos to credulous maids at midnight dances in the meadows."

"Your boat's up at the cottage, Sir Chambers. High and dry," Ronald said.

"You'll find supper there too," said Jennifer.

"Pleased to hear it, very pleased," he nodded to each of them. "I think I'll just proceed that way, if you'll excuse me. Journey's end is a good place to start, if that's where you're headed." He got up to go and added by way of afterthought, "You wouldn't have happened to see anything of Lady Demaris now, would you have?"

Jennifer shook her head. "Not for days. She seemed in a hurry. A very busy person, I think."

Chambers nodded. "That she is, yes indeed. An undeniably busy woman." He clucked his tongue and strode away to his boat and his supper without so much as saying goodbye—not that he'd really said hello.

Ronald and Jennifer smiled at each other, then joined hands and made their way down the trail to the cove. They noticed at once that the sandy beach, unlike the rest of the island, was as clean as ever. "Curiouser and curiouser," Jennifer said. Then it was Ronald's turn to point. The alder trees by the shore were gone, and in their place was a large live oak, not native to this northern place but flourishing here at the placid waterside nevertheless. The forest downcanyon was mowed with precision to an equal height on either side of the riverbank. But here was the oak, strangely misplaced and undeniably alive.

"Do you think?" said Jennifer, dropping his hand. Its spread of branches, long and thick, looked rather familiar. She approached and saw that every limb was scarred but intact. "It is!" she cried, and touched its bark in renewal of acquaintance, tracing her fingers all the way around the bole. And then she gasped.

Behind the oak, under lasting arms, lay the peaceful form of a man on his back. "William," she whispered. He was resting there in the dying day as if not yet awakened from an overlong nap. They knelt beside him, and Jennifer felt his measured breath against her cheek. His face was flush with newness of health, his clothes dry, his heels intact. The bandage was gone from around his temples, and no wound showed. "Touch his side," Jennifer whispered. Ronald gingerly undid the parka and felt the flesh. It was healed and whole. He held his hand on the place and marveled.

The sun mellowed and ripened in lowland ridges of Douglas fir. The cove was alight, and out of the water sped quicksilver sounds of many voices. "The naiads!" said Jennifer. Their lovely faces encircled the sandbar that separated the cove from the river, and they filled the sky with a shout of gladness:

> *"Sing for love that never dies, for he*
> *Has triumphed, he has triumphed gloriously."*

The noise echoed off the tower and across the canyon like the aftershock of the flood itself, and Jennifer felt an exultation. She and Ronald remained on their knees beside the gloriously breathing body and listened to the song of the naiads.

When the last notes faded, and the naiads disappeared with the dusk, they both became aware at once that Garth was standing solemnly over them, ax in hand.

"Welcome, children, and take heart," he said. There was an ancient weariness in his voice. "Let us bear the body back to the cottage. Tomorrow the wedding, and then a journey yet for to go. You must row your friend down the rest of the stream to the Western Sea, and then your task shall be complete."

To Jennifer he looked sad as he spoke. It occurred to her that not everyone had been saved in the flood. She thought of the one for whom he might yearn—for

Lady Lira—and felt his sorrow. As for Ronald, he was simply curious how Garth had contrived both to climb and descend the smooth face of the rock, and how the blow of a single ax might communicate its local power to the heft and thrust of a distant glacier. But he didn't ask.

✻

The wedding took place at noon the next day on the sand of the cove, under the crown of the great live oak. Colin and Rosamond stood in the shade in their best white clothes with Ronald and Jennifer flanking them in knickers and smock. The four other couples had asked that morning if they might be married as well, but Garth had told them that Lady Lira had already joined them in word and deed when she had paired them hand in hand. ("They won't last long *here*," Colin whispered behind them. "The sort from El Ai—they can't stand the rain." To which Rosamond told him to be quiet, and to try to show more courtesy on his wedding day.) Ronald and Jennifer, after much conferring on their part, had asked Garth the same hopeful question. Or rather, Ronald asked in half-articulate syllables while Jennifer stood blushing by. But Garth told them their mother and father must come to give witness and consent, and bade them wait. And so they did.

Garth conducted the ceremony with weighty words that he read from a parchment, exhorting the newmade husband and wife to love and obedience, submission and authority. Jennifer watched to see which words were directed to which particular spouses, but it never was clear at any one moment to whom exactly Garth was speaking, and so she supposed that she and Ronald, like all those before them, would have to sort this out for themselves. Chambers stood beaming among the four couples from El Ai, his cheer a counter to Garth's grave countenance. Behind him the boat lay victualed and waiting, with newcut oars that the woodsmen had fashioned from the cedar log in front of the cottage. And next to the boat lay William on the sand, booted and ready, as amenable as he had been at any moment of the last many days.

Garth pronounced a benediction, the oak tree clapped its limbs in joy, and Colin and Rosamond sweetly embraced in a shower of leaves. The new-married pair then said their farewells to Ronald and to Jennifer. The two women clasped and cried; Ronald offered his hand to Colin, who brushed it aside and embraced him with a mighty hug. Then the woodsmen and priestesses led Colin and Rosamond back up the path to the other side of the Tower of Otium, there to hymn the blessing of a wedding song at the threshold of the bridal cottage. As the procession climbed from the cove, the naiads re-emerged and sang, haunting the air yet one more time with the pure calm music of their voices:

"This grassy terrace under the stone
Is all you need in October sun.
The trail leads upward into the snowbreeze,
Autumn kiss in the green-pooled canyons."

A cool fall wind swept down the gorge as if in answer to invocation. The column of couples rounded the tower out of sight, and the sweet song faded and ceased.

Sooner than they thought possible, Ronald and Jennifer stood with Garth and Chambers beside them, ready to place the sleeping William back in the boat. It was as if they had never left the crystal chamber deep in the ice of the Mirror Glacier. The river glided pleasantly away from the cove, calling them of its own sweet will to renew their journey to the sea.

Patiently, Garth raised his arms and pronounced once more a benediction:

"The tongues of sand and tide go with thee,
The arms of the floating maiden support thee,
The song of the ouzel lead thee aright,
And may—"

Just here he was cut off by the very song of the ouzel he had named. It came winging upriver, out of the forested valleys below, calling *bzeet! bzeet!* as it skimmed the water. Then it landed on the prow of the boat and made its customary bows. Ronald looked at Jennifer. She wanted to smile, but Garth looked too solemn.

"And may thy voice find praise with these."

Garth took both axes out of the boat—the long one that was William's, the short one that was Stella's once—and turned to plunge them into the water. Jennifer supposed he was about to change them to oars again, even though new ones had been provided. But before the axes touched the river he stopped and straightened in surprise. Garth looked downstream. The others looked with him.

"Well, I'll be blessed," said Chambers quietly.

Coming toward them, against the breeze and against the current, was the silhouette of a small wooden barge. Small it was, but large enough for three tall figures, crowned and veiled, to stand side by side in the flat-squared prow. They were female and feminine, greenclad in loose long gowns that trailed in the breeze as the barge came on at the slow speed of dignity. Ronald and Jennifer held each other's hands tightly. Each of them sensed that something more than the waterfall and its strange miracle was here. Nothing would become their journey down the gorge so much as this the leaving of it. Chambers mumbled beatifically. Garth just stared, his beard working in consternation.

The barge came skimming over the shallows at the foot of the cove, there where the naiads had sung by the sandbar, then crossed the calm and nudged the beach beside the oak. The three gowned women held absolute silence. Beneath crowns and veils their hair was all that told them apart—golden, auburn, raven black. The first stepped softly to the sand and took the shorter ice ax from Garth. She lifted her veil and Jennifer knew her for the merciful woman in the waterfall and in her dream—Stella of the alpine stars, utterly lovely and severe. The woman turned to Ronald and to Jennifer and pierced them through with a gaze that was so achingly good they could not bear it—but they wanted nothing more in the world than to be able to bear it longer. She thrust the shaft of the ax in the sand and left it upright just beneath their two joined hands.

Then she spoke:

> *"Nurture what is taken, restore what is thine.*
> *Friendship of opposition is ended;*
> *Contraries yield.*
> *You came in trouble, depart in peace."*

With measured step the second woman came ashore and took the longer ax from Garth. She stooped beside William and lifted her veil, and Jennifer saw it was Lady Demaris, lovely as well but suffused with kindness, a face of mercy less austere. With the head of the ax she very gently touched his lips, then laid it crosswise on his chest.

And she too spoke:

> *"When you wake*

You shall know that stars fade,
That night does not last,
That the sorrows of planets
Are the joys of morning,
That birds repair and blossoms
Kindle after darkness:
Nature's first lesson,
First hint, of grace."

Lady Demaris kissed his forehead and called him by name. "William, you have slept to know we accomplish more in our mortal wounding than in our heroic designs. Yours has been the better fortitude. Wake at last from things dying to things newborn."

As she rose from beside him, a smile broke upon William's lips. He stirred faintly, his eyes still closed.

"My sisters," said Garth, his voice quavering. "You have spared us much trouble. Let us help you place the body on board so that you may bear him to final healing."

He stooped to lift William in his arms, but the two women checked him. Instead of reaching down to William they ranged themselves on either side of Garth and took him by the elbows. Softly and firmly they guided him up onto the barge and presented him there to the third woman, the tallest and strongest. He gazed at the figure solemnly, and then Stella and Lady Demaris removed the veil of Lady Lira, whose face was so contrite with tears that none ashore could keep from shedding more besides. She fell to her knees and clasped his thighs in supplication, but Garth reached down and slowly raised her to full height. His shoulders shook as Jennifer watched him from behind. "No cause," she heard him murmur aloud. "No cause."

When he turned to look back, the barge had already left the shore. Chambers held up a hand of parting. "Goodbye," said Chambers brokenly. "Goodbye, my brother."

The barge crossed the cove to the bar, and Garth called out, "Let there be no sadness of farewell!" But his voice was shaking.

And then they receded down the current, the bearded old man, happy at last, and the three crowned sisters, queens indeed. Jennifer thought of the Fates in Ovid, three and terrible. But no, she decided—these were three as the gentle

Graces, the minglers of beauty and forgiveness. And thus they remained, green-eyed and haunting, in Jennifer's mind to the end of her days.

Sir Chambers' mind was apparently stayed on a single sister in particular. "One fine woman," he muttered distractedly. The barge was nearly out of sight. "Be a lucky man—" He cut himself off as if seized by a plan. While Ronald and Jennifer stood inert, he grabbed the two fresh cedar oars, tossed them in the boat, and shoved off into the cove.

"And where are *you* going?" called Ronald after him.

While the ouzel nodded from its perch on the bow, Chambers fitted the oars to the locks and sputtered the blades across the water in a frenzy of spectacular rowing. He reached the current just as the barge swept round a bend far down the river.

"*Festina lente!*" Chambers called back. "Hasten slowly, until you're late. And now I am. What I never was, that is." He threw up his oars in exasperation. "Chambers is willing. Who needs a pond when there is the sea?"

Ronald and Jennifer watched him diminish on the quickening current until the bend. And he was gone.

Chapter 20
A Suckling Babe

❋

JENNIFER AND RONALD WERE LEFT ON THE BEACH hand in hand. It was silent and they watched the river. They lingered in the breath of parting, alone again but part of all that they had met, and reassured by holy palm on holy palm in the touch of their flesh.

"I say!" said Jennifer suddenly. She felt the crowding of soft petals against their fingers.

Both of them looked and caught their breath. Planted anew and afresh between them, Stella's ax had bloomed again. A deep red rose had grown out of the burnished head and quietly enveloped their grasp.

It really is over then, Jennifer thought. *The healing is done.* They knelt to smell the reborn rose, to drink its scent, and Jennifer felt satisfied to leave it bending where it was.

"Hey!" called an anxious voice from behind them. "A little slack on this schrund here! Enough to get down this sunken bridge, if you think it will hold."

They turned to see William sitting up and holding his ice ax out before him as if to arrest an imminent fall. His eyes were open and peered without focus across the river.

"Slack! I said *slack!* What are you—" He gave a short cry and hurled himself chest first on the sand, digging in with ax and toes to make himself immoveable.

"William," said Ronald quietly. He leaned over and placed his hands on the knuckles clenched along the shaft of the ice ax. "I've got you. You can come out now."

William looked up and seemed to see him. Ronald slowly released his hold, and William his. He brushed his fingers across the sand and looked at the oak, the tower, the river. Then he stood up.

"I have had a dream," he said to Ronald. "I have had a most rare vision."

"And so you have," Jennifer suggested, wanting to be noticed as well.

"Yet I am doubtful where I have been, and ignorant what place this is." He carefully stood and looked about at the walls of the gorge, appealing to them in familiar wonder.

Jennifer stepped closer to William to make herself known, but before she could utter a word of greeting she heard a voice more constant and normal to her ears than any save one in the quiet of the grave.

"Jennifer!" it called from a distance. "How's my girl? Looking splendid, both of you, really—and William, what a pleasant and timely surprise."

They found themselves staring at the irrepressible Dr. Howe, who was striding across the sand of the cove as if coming to greet a host of visitors at his door.

"Dad!" she said uncertainly, meeting him with a modest hug. "How did—"

"A long day's push, I can certainly assure you. Down to Gwen's cabin for breakfast and across the base of Center and South to that goatwalk on the face of these cliffs. I can almost see why Escee preferred to fly. But poor Escee—a dreadful occurrence just yesterday morning. Inspecting the snout of the eastern lobe by helicopter at the very moment the glacier gave way—he must have just touched down by the stream gauge. Not that he didn't have the facts from me, and a proper warning. But a terrible thing—loss of human life and all that. And he such a good sponsor—a real believer in the scientific enterprise." At this he blinked his bushy brows, truly touched by at least one part of this tragedy.

"But the work must go on. Just as he'd have it. Nothing to do but hasten down here to inspect the dam-site. And—oh yes—at Gwen's this morning. She cooked us such a marvelous meal up at the lake last week—and told us you had all preceded her down to the cabin. Then she radioed later on that one of you had become indisposed, and we were so busy that all I could do was send our regrets. But this morning, when she reported that I'd find you here, I saw your instincts, stealing a march on the proper study of our cataclysmic aftermath. And what better place? The dam, of course, is out of the question, but think of the station for research that we could put here. That high broad bench on the other side of this granidiorite monolith is the perfect site for a Quonset hut.

"Ronald," he continued, putting a fatherly arm on his shoulders, "you don't know what a delight it was to see a glacier *really* move. Nothing like a *jokulhlaup* to demonstrate my little notion of entropy in glacial systems, the self-destruction of regulated bodies of ice in the long term. So difficult to observe in a lifetime, but here, we've seen it!—the resignation of a glacial regime to the ultimate laws of thermodynamics. We've got a whole autumn ahead of us here—the data can't wait until next summer."

"Here?" said Ronald.

"For science," said Dr. Howe. "As your advisor, let me suggest that for this semester, you quit your books. Throw classes to the winds. Let the gorge be your school, and nature your teacher." He winked and nodded suggestively.

Ronald looked at Jennifer, and she slyly shrugged. "Dr. Howe," he said, "I like this place—"

"Splendid, my boy. Absolutely splendid. And William—dear me, how one forgets. When I dropped by your cabin just this morning I found your lovely wife in possession of a suckling babe. Her water broke yesterday just at dawn. Somewhat premature, she said, but delivered with the help of three charming women whose names I have unhappily forgotten. And completely in health, nothing whatever to worry about. I offer you my congratulations."

With that he shook the father's hand with all due heartiness. But he might as well have been operating a pump handle for all the response he got from William, who stared past him to greater heights of incomprehension.

"Well, what is it? A boy or a girl?" Jennifer demanded.

"Bless me," said Professor Howe, scratching his head. "She told me, I'm sure, but as it is I don't remember. So much going on. This unfortunate business of Escee, and the *jokulhlaup*, of course—a whole new field of research. We'll have to close up the high camp soon—or winterize it—construct a cabin above the lake perhaps. Leave a crew there to keep an eye on our galloping glacier and move our base to this lovely island—and enough to do here to make use of our every minute."

"—and willingly could waste my time in it," Ronald added, firmly grasping Jennifer's hand. They stood in front of the ax and the rose so that Dr. Howe could not possibly see it.

"Eh? What's that?" the professor said. "In the meantime, of course, we'll drop by the Demaris Cabin to resolve the gender of this child. Easily done, and important to be certain about such things."

William nodded, and his blank confusion melted at last to a knowing smile that he privately exchanged with Ronald.

"Look at the forest trimline here!" sang Dr. Howe. He waved his arms like a great conductor summoning brass and drums to action. "Absolutely devastating. All to be charted—a catastrophic marvel of nature."

But William was already on his way, and Ronald and Jennifer grasped the elbows of the senior scientist to guide him after. They gained the path and crossed the bridge, and the rose bloomed on beneath the Tower of Otium.

BOOK III: WINTER

The Silver Spire

✳

[Y]ou are now sailed into the North of my lady's opinion,
where you will hang like an icicle on a Dutchman's beard. . . .
—Shakespeare, *Twelfth Night*

E

N ← → S

W

Silver Spire

Nor

Lava Field

Belknap Hut

← To the
Last Mountain

Three Queens
Wilderness

L. VETTE

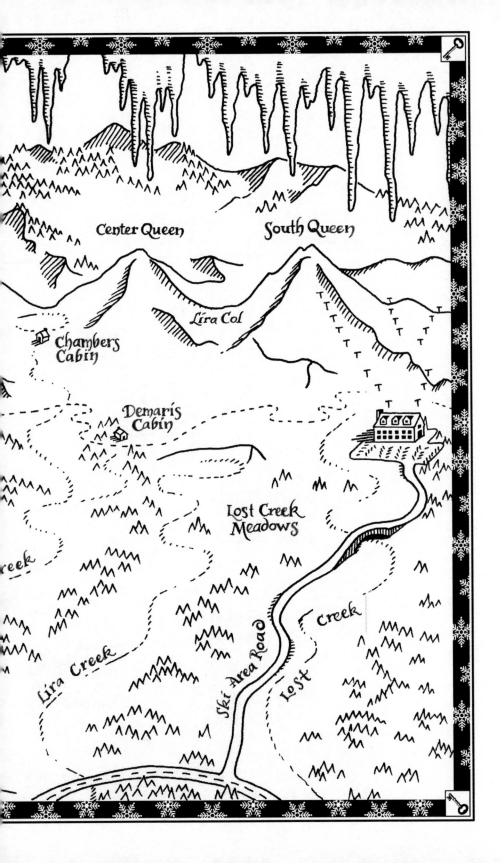

Chapter I
The Rusted Key

✳

When William broke onto the summit plateau, he finally stopped to remove the climbing skins from his skis. It was a golden-shafted afternoon, later than he liked. He had hoped to reach the top by noon, but the snow lay deep on the lower flanks of the Center Queen from a week of March storms, not to mention the entire season's accumulation. Even with mountaineering skis of extra width he had plunged to his knees while breaking trail; the going had been very slow. And on the lower skirts of the mountain, just at the top of the last moraine, he had set off an avalanche—a big one. It had swept his carefully switchbacked route in a shuffling hiss, planing the slope like a sharp knife across soft pine, all the shavings stacked at the bottom. Above the moraine, the glacier had offered smoother travel, the crevasses and seracs of summer choked and muffled with wind-beaten winter snow, but even here the surface had groaned in sudden settlings under his weight. It had left him uneasy, just like the snowpack.

Now as he stripped the mohair skins from under his skis, barehanded in spite of the wind, he wondered why he had bothered to come. The real reason, he suspected, was that the cabin had felt so empty—a week of storm, and no one home. With Gwen and Lara gone to the city, the walls had pressed like a vice upon his loneliness. In the bleak late winter, all by himself, it was perhaps inevitable that the sudden appearance of the rusted key had almost upended his mind.

The key. Had he brought it? With mittens off he checked his pockets, feeling a sudden thrill of panic until he remembered he had zipped it into the top of his pack. Relief, then. It would be no use to have come without it.

He had discovered the key yesterday while splitting off kindling from a twisted butt of mountain hemlock in the lean-to behind the back wall of the cabin. The drifts this time of year were high; by March he had to stair-step down into his workspace and use a lantern most times of day. That day, noon, was no exception. He had pared the sides of the butt with his ax and then taken aim for the core of the heartwood, hoping to cleave the piece in two in spite of its many knots and whorls. He half expected the ax to rebound, but the blade cut deep and the wood parted like double doors, more as if he had opened a lock than unseamed what nature had joined in a marriage of several hundred years.

That is when he saw the key, impressed on its side in one sheared face of the cloven heartwood, dark against the saffron luster. At first he had thought it a salamander, wintering in a woody crevice, or (even more illogically) a fossil of one. But as he pried it out he felt the cold and true of metal, and as he held it up to the lantern light he recognized the antique shape, and remembered its use. He sat in the woodchipped snow, dumbfounded.

The key he held was the key he had bitten in the center of an apple a full ten years before. It had come from Garth and led him to Grace and opened a silver register on the summit of the Center Queen. The last he had seen it, the key had flown in a glittering arc from his empty hand to the star-sky depths of a crater lake on yet another snowy summit. What was it doing here in the heart of a fallen hemlock? And what did it mean that he had found it once again? Or that it had found him?

Spindrift blew down into the lean-to and coated William like a crumbling sheet. He roused himself and carried the key back into the cabin and pondered it all through his lonely supper, the storm still veering at the windows, and pondered it in his empty bed, there in the loft where Gwen was gone. And then he slept.

In his dreaming—or in his waking, perhaps, for that is what it felt like—the woman he knew from that other time as Lady Demaris unlatched the door and came in out of the wind and dark. She threw back the hood of her cloak and unleashed her rich brown hair, snowdusted and fresh and lovely, looking around the embered cabin as if returning from long absence. She spied William asleep in the loft and climbed the ladder and touched the hand that held the key.

"For her to come, you must go," she simply said, and placed the key upon his lips. "Speak what the key says, go where it leads you. Set free the heart of the spire."

She looked much as his wife could, shedding concern from her deep green eyes. Which is why he had loved Gwen in the beginning, meeting her here in this backcountry cabin where he had first met Lady Demaris. Lately, though, Gwen's eyes had become more vacant, turned inward. It had happened in the years since Lara was born. In his dream, Lady Demaris stroked his brow and descended the ladder. She cast a last calm glance about, hooded herself, and slipped out into the storm.

William did not awaken then, but plunged into visions of avalanches and screaming winds and Gwen and Lara lost in the snow. And there appeared to him another visage, carved in the bole of an ancient tree, that he had not seen for a long time—Grace Foster's. The totem image of her face was rather perplexed, forehead knotted and rimed with ice. In his dream the storm had slowly toppled the old tree into a drift that completely engulfed it. As if he were the face on the tree he felt the cold against his teeth and awoke fearing Grace could not breathe. He touched his mouth. The key rested like ice on his lips.

So today, the first day of calm, he now stood poised on the rim of a high summit plain. *Go where it leads you,* Lady Demaris had said of the key. *Speak what it says.* William knew where the key had once led—to the iron box on the very top of the Center Queen. Not the box that was normally chained there, a modest container that held a ledger for signatures—but a massy, shield-shaped silver chest, embossed and engraved with a living scene of all the Three Queens Wilderness. This was the box that Grace had opened with the key, and that William had so far failed to discover on every subsequent ascent. It had been part of the old adventures, the other and greater wilderness that sometimes appeared within and beyond this present one. Yet it was not really *other* at all, William thought, but the true place that was there all the time. It was like the harmony he had once heard sung by the stars on the snowy rim of the North Queen. The music went on, and sustained the world, long after it seemed to stop:

> *But whilst this muddy vesture of decay*
> *Doth grossly close it in, we cannot hear it.*

Grace had written him this in a letter long after their quest had ended. It sounded right. The enduring music was something to hope for, just as he hoped that the massy shield would be there now, that because the key had come to him the mountains again would be transfigured. To speak what the key said, he was almost certain it was his turn to open the chest and read the poem—his part of the poem—in the ancient ledger. This time, after all the verse that Gwen had taught him in long evenings next to the stove, he hoped that he was competent to see the words for what they were.

Ah, Gwen. As he rolled up his skins and tucked them away in the top of his pack her name stung like the small needles of ice on the wind. He put his mittens and windproof overmitts on again and turned and looked at his willowy tracks, curving up the vast of the glacier. Farther down, the tracks were hidden behind the moraines, where anyway they were avalanched, but below and beyond in the thickly tufted alpine meadows he could see them winding out of the trees—not trees, but snow-blasted curtains of white—where their cabin waited in its own small clearing. The years there, the memories.

For all his present feelings of loss, it would have been an idyllic scene, an inspiring view, were it not for the quiet roar that drifted from the South Queen. The wind reduced the roar at times to a constant hum, like that of a persistent mosquito. But it never stopped, just as mosquitoes never sleep on hot summer nights. He looked down to the steep col between the two peaks, and across to the edge of the etched and fluted northeast face, the one long ago he had wished to climb. But as his eye traveled across the mountain to the edge of the gentle southwest slopes, he saw the silhouette of the ski lifts against the gold and blue horizon. And that was the problem.

Ten years ago she had warned him that the lifts were coming. Gwen was the backcountry ranger then, and knew very well what threats there were to the wilderness. First was the geothermal drilling—test sites by helicopter. They had fought it for years, in legislatures and newspapers and courtrooms, but finally in the midst of recession they lost the battle. The test drilling at Lost Creek Meadows had proved especially promising. A road followed where a trail had been, through the old growth of red cedar and western hemlock in Lost Creek Canyon, and selective cutting followed the road. At first it stopped at the grotesque forest of drilling rigs and aluminum barracks in the meadows, but conventional desire and wisdom pushed it just a mile farther to the very base of the South Queen, where the long and open southwest snowfields soon provided the most sought-after runs in the state. There was a brand-new lodge there now—he could see it in outline—and where once had been windy silences, crossed by the call of winter ravens, the slopes now echoed the latest hip-hop syncopating from outdoor speakers. There was even talk of bulldozing a groomed trail along the six-mile timberline path that led from the lodge to William's cabin—the Demaris Cabin—for the benefit of cross-country skiers. Or snowmobilers, if the wilderness boundary could once again be pushed back.

But William and Gwen and Lara had stayed—he now as the backcountry ranger, though money for this position was tight, given the new priority of roadside recreation. And in these times, the beleaguered Three Queens Wilderness, shrinking each day in maps on the walls of the capitol, was more front country than anything else, more buffer than substance, edge than entity.

> *Things fall apart;*
> *The center cannot hold.*
> *Mere anarchy is loosed upon the world.*

This is what Grace had written him, and this is precisely how William felt. His summer work had mainly become the hopeless policing of motorcycles and other off-road vehicles that illegally rutted the trails. His winter work, as a snow surveyor for the water district, was quieter except for the endless drone of the ski lifts. But this task too would soon become an anachronism. Newly automated survey posts were being installed on all sides of the Three Queens. They would be monitored not by skis but by satellite.

So things had been looking rather grim for Mr. and Mrs. William Arthur. And even apart from the effect of these inroads into their wilderness sanctuary, Gwen had changed since Lara's birth four years ago. At first she had been the defiant one, telling all objectors that the wilderness, that ceremony of innocence, was by far the best place to raise a child. But as William took over her backcountry duties, and she spent more and more hours at the cabin, and as Lara grew and desired friends (playmates and cousins that she had met on infrequent trips to the valley), Gwen's eyes turned to the city. The more the wilderness crumbled away, the more committed William became to staying put; and the more Lara increased in stature and awareness, the more distant and wistful Gwen became. Put off by his brooding, his silence, his implacable hold on the land, she had finally left to enroll Lara in a pre-school with real swing-sets. Skiing with daddy was not enough.

He was welcome to join them anytime. Perhaps, Gwen had offered, he could even get a job again in instructional technology or as a computer programmer. The forest service had real need of that sort now—the congressional mandate of multiple use required ever more ingenious ways of quantifying the values of the acreage entrusted to them by the public. Visitor days, soil stability, watershed volume, board feet, visual quality (or viewshed impact)—it all had to be entered and balanced in new programs each year. Balance, said William, for the forest service, was a spotted owl on one end of a teeter-totter and a DC-9 tractor on the other. (It occurred to him now that Lara also had teeter-totters at her pre-school.) The forest service only cared about the so-called needs of the growing population, and the population only cared about its needs, and the whole sick nation had nothing but the ideology of a cancer cell. Gwen would say yes, she understood, but wasn't he being just a little bit misanthropic, and why was it they were waiting so long for a second child, and maybe a third? Wilderness was nice, but it wasn't family.

William never knew what to reply at that point. To cope he invented a personal paralysis, a freezing of the heart, and in the end it coped his family right out the door. Not forever, but for now. *You are welcome to join us anytime,* Gwen had said. There was snow in her hair, their child on her back, and a shaky definiteness to her stride as she had skied away that morning.

His own strides over the summit plain were both shaky and definite as well. His skis skittered on windpack and thin ridges of *sastrugi*—miniature mountain ranges of snow blown into being by the wind. He more bumped and rattled than skied to the summit, a rocky nub thoroughly rimed and buried with ice. At the base he took off both his skis and stuck them heel-first in the snow. Then he unstrapped an old wooden ice ax, long-shafted and worn with use, from the loop on the back of his faded rucksack. This was the ax that Garth had given him years ago, the ax that touched off miracles.

It was just fifty feet to the top, but without creepers or crampons he had to chop out holds for his feet and sometimes bury the pick overhead to pull himself higher. He made it up in due time and stood tall in the westering sun, the yellowing light of late afternoon. The summit cast a lengthening shadow over the circular plateau, and he added the shape of his ice-axed figure to the very tip, a human point on the stroke of the sundial. Looking back, he could no longer see the drilling rigs or the lodge and lifts below the horizon, and could only hear a hum on the wind like that of flies that swarm the lower summits in summer. Overhead, a few thin cirrus clouds were ranking up from the southwest: in a day or less, another storm.

He must hurry, then. The box would be several feet under ice—but just where?

He sucked the frost on his beard to ponder, and held out the ax as if it were a divining rod. To his surprise, it dipped to the surface without his permission. Here then. In the center, of course.

So he chopped away, and the chips splashed up in his frosty beard and coated the chest of his dark green parka. It was not like splitting firewood, not that swift clean satisfaction, but more like cutting against the grain of a log that has fallen across the trail. The ax angles in first right, then left, and gradually the valley deepens. He was three feet down, his bent back starting to protest, when the adze sang against true metal. In the hole, a silvery gleam. He chopped and cleared and shoveled the chips away with his mittens until the box stood free and clear. Was it marred by his strokes? Not that he could tell. He sat on the edge of his newmade pit with his feet on either side of the register. It was not cast iron, exactly, and it did not have the stamped logo of the local alpine club on the lid. Instead it shone like the full promise of first light, a curious engraving all across its entire surface, fresh and distinct as if newly formed. Below this lid was a keyhole. It was, at last, the old box he had found with Grace.

Before reaching into the flap of his rucksack for the key, William crouched low to examine the engraved scene on the lid of the box. "Like the shield of Achilles," Grace had written him afterwards, once she had started the classics in college. Gwen had never welcomed her letters, and gradually William had ceased to reply. He had never gotten around to looking up this particular reference, and now the comment returned like an arrow.

He saw now in the silver picture the snowswept shapes of all three Queens— North, Center, and South—and the closer he looked the more he could see, even to the smallest detail. South of the peaks was Amoenas Gorge and the Tower of Otium, bounded by the Dark Divide which separated the green world from the southern deserts of El Ai. He had been there once, after a fashion, when Lara was born, but had lain unconscious the whole way, both there and back. Jennifer and Ronald, the research assistants from the glacier study project, had had to tell him all about it.

The South Queen stood sentinel above the gorge, and in the picture its flanks held neither ski lifts nor drilling rigs, just virgin snow. No parking lots paved paradise, and no plowed road led down Lost Creek. *As it should be*, William thought. *World without end. Amen.*

On the Center Queen he could see his ski tracks, even down to the cabin in the groves of trees. Wisps of smoke still curled from the silvery chimney, and by this he knew he could see the picture as Grace had seen it the day she had done her best to show him Lady Lira and her marmots pursuing them up the glacier below. The picture lived, even as the wilderness did. Before he had been blind to it; now he had the eyes to see.

The North Queen was rimmed with beauty, its crater corniced inward on the southwest side where Lady Lira had once been swept into the lake, cold blue in summer but frozen now and drifted with snow. On the near side, in a windswept pass, stood the drifted shape of Chambers' cabin, home to a rotund voluble man he had met with Grace—and never there, neither he nor his cabin, in all the years thereafter. On the far side of the North Queen, its forested flanks reached out and out and finally to the margin of a bleak and barren lava field. The trees stopped here as if at the ocean, and the lava, smoothed by winter white, rolled on and on and on to the north until it reached a silver spire, known on the maps by just that name. It was craggy and steep, a granite intrusion, almost as tall as the volcanic Queens.

William lingered on the scene, from the Silver Spire to the Dark Divide, with uncommon satisfaction. It was, in some ways, his reason for being, that in which he lived and moved. Almost reluctantly he took the key from the top of his pack and reached down, fumbling in his overmitts, to insert it into the obvious keyhole.

It would not go in. He shed one mitten and his fingers felt the terrible cold— the wind, the metal key on flesh. With a better grip he pushed the teeth of the key at the opening. But still no good. He got down close and saw the problem: the keyhole was filled with ice. His first impulse was to lick it clean, but fortunately he remembered stories of pump handles and foolish farmboys. He'd rather not freeze his tongue to the summit. He poked at the ice with his fingernails but made no dent. Next he tried the pick of his ax—just the tip—but this was too large. And the spike on the end of the shaft was too dull. He raised himself up out of his pit and noted new length in his shadow, lateness in the air, sharpness in the wind. The cirrus clouds were starting to thicken.

William began to lose patience. First he started tapping on the lock with his ax—gingerly, so as not to damage anything, and hoping to dislodge the ice. No luck. He stood and fumed. He wanted his wife, his wilderness back. What good was a key if the lock were frozen? Without really thinking, he planted his feet on either side of the pit he had dug and reared the ice ax over his head. It swung down hard, a swift arc against brittle sky, and the register rang like a silver bell.

The sound welled outward, ripples in a pool, and preternaturally held its note against the wind. William stood over the silver box, awed and a little ashamed, until the sound finally stopped. Then he crouched down to try the lid. But as he glanced at the picture again he noticed that three things had happened. Were happening, rather. All at once.

First, where forest met lava on the far side of the North Queen, he suddenly noticed a snug cabin on the edge of the trees. He must have overlooked it before. Smoke wandered up from the chimney, and through the window (the picture allowed him even this) he could see a pleasant young man with thick brown hair and woolen knickers, carefully seated by a fire. The young man held a knife in his hand and was carving a face in the butt of a log held upright between his knees. William looked at the face—and started. Its features were very much his own, right down to his anguished eyes and frosted beard. Then he saw that the whole cabin was filled with faces ingeniously carved in the same way. He marked Garth, and Stella, and Lady Demaris—and Lady Lira in versions both good and evil, as if there were actually two of her. And more faces he did not begin to recognize.

Then something very strange happened. All of a sudden the air by the cabin was filled with filthy winged creatures. They were large as eagles—no, much larger—but more like vultures in their repulsive form. There were four of them, and all four descended in a flock on the cabin, where they fouled the chimney, put out the fire with their dung, broke the windows with their beaks, and, finally, carried off the surprised woodcarver in their claws. The creatures flew like ungainly ancient lizards, like strangely feathered dinosaurs, and swung the carver across the sky high over the lava fields in the direction of the Silver Spire. William reached for the flying creatures as if to grab a wing from a wasp. But he could neither touch nor stop them.

Second (but really at the same time), the drifted door of Chambers' cabin, this side of the North Queen, budged open against the snow. Out stomped an ovaline, cloaked figure, silver-hooded and silver-bearded, with huge wooden snowshoes under his arm. He bent over to strap them on, and then proceeded down the gentle pass to the west, laboriously putting one enlarged foot in front of the other. His lips were moving as if he were talking to himself, and at one point he seemed to look William right in the eye with a rather over-obvious wink.

William waved in spite of himself. "Chambers," he whispered.

Third (and simultaneously), he saw a woman skiing down the near edge of the southwest slope of the South Queen, somewhat out of the regular run. Her face was obscured by a huge pair of goggles, and a garish ski cap partially hid the longish hair that streamed behind her. She was snowplowing in uncertain turns down a steepening grade. Rather a beginner, he could tell, and off route. She stopped by falling back on the seat of her pants, then stood up, dusted off her coat, and took off her goggles to clean them.

It was then he clearly saw her face—the same vexed eyes, the same pert nose, the same pouting lips he remembered. "Grace!" he called. Not the girl he had briefly known, but a young woman with cares and crosses. In the picture, she did not look up or answer.

Goggles off, Grace peered downslope as if checking the way. She looked right, then left. Then she shrugged. William was curious to see which direction she would choose. But he never got the chance, and neither did she. For suddenly the entire slope on which she was perched gave way like a white sheet yanked from a mattress.

"Look out!" called William.

But she did not hear. Grace was there, and then Grace was gone—lost in rumbling heaps of snow that clouded the air in the picture with a silvery plume, stripping the mountainside hundreds of feet across and down to the basin under Lira Col.

"Grace!" shouted William again. The ice ax shook in his hands.

After a while the silvery plume began to drift up and away, and the ruin of snow beneath was quiet. William looked away from the lid and into the wind and across the plain to the South Queen, now coming a whitish gold as evening neared. He could no longer hear the hum of the lifts. But a powdering of fine snow blew up over the rim, stinging his cheeks in an airborne cloud.

Chapter 2
A Home for Snow

❄

AT FIRST IT FELT LIKE A WATER SLIDE, or like slipping down a sand dune into a lake. But when Grace finally came to rest in the dark there was no swimming back to the surface. For that matter, she couldn't have said where the surface was. Her legs were twisted somewhere behind her, and her nose was thrust in the small cup of her gloved hands. They provided a breathing space, but she could not move them, no more than she could have resisted a thickening batch of concrete. The snow was that hard and heavy. And cold too—there was plenty of it down her neck.

St. Agnes' Eve, she told herself—*Ah, bitter chill it was!* And then, reverting to a childhood saying, *A mountain is a home for snow. But not for me*, she thought emphatically. *Not for me.*

Signs on the ski lift had warned of avalanche conditions outside of the marked runs. Grace thought she had come for a day of distraction, of falling down the slopes with the crowds. But as morning had worn into afternoon, she had begun to tire of standing in lines, of making small talk on the lift, of saying "Excuse me!" every time she wobbled into someone else's downhill path.

Late in the day she had gone into the lodge for a drink and watched a video in the bar called *Splendors of the Three Queens*. It was replete with masterfully intercut shots—most of them from a helicopter—of forests, snowfields, and summer wildflower displays. The female narrator had a confident and silky voice, inviting the public to see for itself what Mother Nature had to offer. Occasionally she would stop talking, and a string orchestra would take over. To Grace there was something not quite right about the images on the screen. She had known this place in another way, at another time, almost in another life. The video raised memories, only to subvert them. What she saw was a pale series of grotesque ghosts.

The final segment showed the rustic Demaris Cabin, cedar-shingled and walled with purply blocks of basalt. A fresh-pressed ranger waved from the door, then advanced to the camera to explain her careful guardianship of the multiple-use forest. "The land is for everyone," she insisted. "The forest service is here to help *you* enjoy your visit." She stood open-palmed with a rigid smile, and the picture faded to windblown treetops, orchestral credits, and a long shot of the Center Queen at sunset.

Grace left the lodge in deep disquiet, sensing a need not to go home but to leave the overrun part of this place, to see if the true locus of it were still there and would still have her. She snapped on her skis again and waited by the longest lift. It would close soon; the sun was dropping towards the valley and the wind was sharpening its bite. Her cheeks felt flushed with a tinge of wine but after sitting the lift to the top she was numb inside, shivering.

She disembarked and, with one eye on the lift attendant, edged across the top of the run to where it began to drop north to the headwaters of Lira Creek, smothered in snow below glacier and col. There were boundary markers here, day-glow flags on aluminum poles. She looked back towards the distant attendant standing at the top of the lift. When his back was turned, she slipped her skis into untracked snow and cautiously plowed over the horizon.

Once out of sight she stopped and looked. The basin below was wrapped in quiet. There were already several avalanche tracks on the far side, where noontime sun had set off some of the south-facing slopes that steepened under the Center Queen. The basin spilled down and over rows of clifftops to her left, past which she could see the descending lap of forest. She remembered a dwelling there in the lava cliffs, a mansion of sorts, and a spiky tunnel to the surface, and the sweet refuge of Lady Demaris and her cabin just beyond, a few miles along timberline.

It came to her then that this was what she had come to see—the old cabin— just a glimpse of the place where she had once felt safe. She saw the groves among which it might be, partway around the west side of the Center Queen, but from here the view was obstructed by a trailing shoulder of the mountain. If she paralleled the slope a bit she might soon see it.

So she tried this. But she found herself swerving more down than across, and by the time she could stop (or fall, that is) and look again she was much too low to see the area of the cabin at all. Worse, she found she had come down much too far to consider climbing back up to the top. Her skis were too slick to track uphill, and without them she would plunge too deep to make any progress. She tried edging up on the sides of her skis, but the slope was too steep and the snow too loose, and she only found herself edging in place.

This will never do, she thought. But what would? She called out several times, but she already knew that no one could hear her from far up over the lip, especially in the gathering wind. And she was becoming cold again, just standing there. So she decided on the inevitable: she would ski down the slopes to the basin and then try to chart a gently declining course that angled back across to the road in Lost Creek Meadows below the lodge. She didn't know much about avalanches, but something told her the less time she spent on the side of the basin the safer she would be.

So Grace had set out, snowplowing and falling by fits and starts, and was just beginning to think she would make it, scanning across the rest of her route, when the mountain gave way and rushed her into this cold solid dark.

She didn't know whether her skis were still attached to her feet—or her poles to her wrists, for that matter. She just knew that the snow was thick and heavy around her, and that the air in the pocket next to her face would very likely not last forever. She coughed involuntarily, perhaps to relieve the weight on her chest, and spittle ran from her lip to her forehead. It took her a moment to realize the significance of this. She was upside down. Her impulse was to right herself immediately, as a cat does in mid-air. But of course she could not. The indignity of it made her want to thrash in anger. But she could not do that either.

Of necessity her frustration wore coldly away, leaving behind it a dull fear. After a while she grew strangely placid and almost warm. There was time to consider. She thought of the phrase *her life passed before her eyes.* If only she didn't have so long—she rather envied the high-speed cinematic moment which was all some people had time for. But she used her uncertain time to advantage and composed a piece for tomorrow's newspaper in her mind:

> *Grace Foster, 27, died yesterday in an avalanche near the South Queen Meadows ski area. In spite of numerous warning signs she ventured alone out of the marked area onto steep and hazardous terrain. The ski lift attendant was quoted as saying, "Yes, she had a crazed look about her most of the day. And she couldn't ski worth beans."*

Foster is survived by an unfinished dissertation on Deconstructive Strategies in the Pastorella Episodes of the Sixth Book of The Faerie Queene. *Her graduate advisor speculated for the press that judging by the promise and progress of the dissertation, Foster's accident may well have been suicide. The coroner's office reported no evidence to corroborate this suspicion.*

Ms. Foster is also survived by a sophomoric husband, Lance Q. Lott, of Cravens Lane. The couple had been married for six years, but recently kept separate residences. Mr. Lott, a local hardware salesman, could not be reached for comment because of a college basketball playoff game being aired on cable television. The marriage produced no children.

She paused here in her composition, interrupted by a good cry that betrayed her attempts at gallows humor. Her throat convulsed (as her chest would have, had it room), and she swallowed in gasps between sobs. Afraid of using all her air, she finally managed to stifle herself. The brutal cold came on again. She fell into a shivering trance, and after a while no longer shivered, but just lay numb, not considering much of anything now, and rather incurious about her fate. *It happens like this,* she said to herself. *You fade away.*

And so she lay, and so she slept the sleep that approaches the sleep of death, until suddenly—she did not know precisely how much later—she became aware of something small and soft and furry whiskering against her nose. It brought with it air that was sharp and cold, and she took a deep breath that satisfied. It made her realize how stale her pocket of air had become until just then. She opened her eyes and saw the reflection of gray starlight in the confines of her breathing space—and four or five pair of tiny eyes peering half-closed into hers. Had she been something less than buried and frozen she might have started, but as it was she merely blinked at the pairs of eyes and said, "Hello," except it did not come out. It was as if her lips were frozen shut.

Then a bright light shone into her face. From her upside-down vantage point she could tell it was the moon, half-full in the sky. In its pale and perfect rays she now saw that the half-closed eyes belonged to a crowd of large mice. But not mice, really—these had longer snouts and wider paws. They were upside down with their backs on the moon. Then they were gone, and she felt cold and lonely in the moonlight. She tried hard to move her arms, but like her lips they would not obey her. Perhaps only her face was as yet uncovered.

So she lay there still, wondering how it was exactly her face had come to be exposed, and whether the rest of her ever would be, when suddenly, along one elbow and next to a hip, she felt a burrowing going on. Another one of the mouse-like creatures popped out beside her face, showering her mouth not only with snow but also with dirt.

Then she knew: not mice, but gophers. She remembered the maze of rounded ridges of earth in the meadows on her You-Can-Do-It Expedition. The red-bearded leader had confidently explained to them in his weary way that these were called gopher cores—the remains of earth-lined tunnels in the snow that pocket gophers had excavated during the winter. Once the snow melted away, the dirt linings collapsed into sinuous mounds on the grass. Grace remembered how soft and fresh the gopher cores had felt between her bare toes at the end of a long day of hiking. The recollection was almost otherworldly—she couldn't begin to feel even her toes now. If these gophers were really intent upon digging her out, she hoped it wouldn't take much longer.

As if wish were command, she felt the burrowings multiply on every side of her buried body. Before long she could shift her shoulder and nudge one elbow. Then her hips came loose, and she launched both arms beyond her head in a fountain of snow and began to drag herself out of her tomb, down and then up until she was sitting at eye level with the rumpled surface of the slope. There was dull pain in moving like this, somewhat as when you try to use an arm or leg that has fallen asleep. She was not so sure she could stand up.

So she sat and looked at the stars and moon going in and out behind patches of cloud, and thought the silvered basin beneath her a most beautiful place indeed. Grace was facing the nearly perfect symmetry of the Center Queen. She remembered racing to the summit with William, and going down inside of it, down to the warm-watered underground streams. She would have given anything to bathe in those warm waters now.

Curiously, the gophers gathered in her lap, a dozen of them, their work done, as if to receive her thanks. "I—I—I th-th-thank you all," she stuttered, and tried to touch them with her gloves. But they scuttled away, back into the tunnels of snow and earth from whence they came. Which left her rather lonely again, and not really out of danger. Where her skis and poles might be she had no idea, and in the open air it was colder than ever. In her condition, she couldn't possibly last the night.

She was musing her options, none good, when a small light appeared in the basin below. It was moving towards her unevenly, advancing and slowing the way a person strides uphill on skis. And as it came closer she saw that it was indeed attached to someone skiing up toward the avalanche track. When the light reached the toe of the track, fanned out in a rumpus below her, the figure paused as if wondering where to look.

"*U-u-up heeee*—!" Grace called, but her voice was tiny, out of breath. She rose partway, more on her arms than on her legs. "*Heeere!*" she called, this time louder.

The figure turned. The avalanche had carried Grace most of the way downslope, but the person still had to climb on skis through the snowy rubble to get to her. When he arrived (for it was a man, by the sound of his voice when he finally spoke), she could not see his face because of the brightness of his headlamp, the source of the light she had seen approaching.

"How did you know to look for me?" she managed to say, chattering it out between her teeth.

The man hesitated. "Grace?" he said.

Chapter 3
The Better to Carry You

❋

ALTHOUGH WILLIAM BRUSHED HER FREE OF SNOW and wrapped her in a thick wool blanket, Grace could not stop shivering.

"That's good," he said. "That's good that you are shivering." He dove back into his rucksack and passed her a hot bottle of tea. "Now drink this."

She could hardly hold it in her shaking hands, so he helped her bring the rim to her lips. As she drank, she felt a warmth begin inside and spread to her extremities. The shivering began to subside, and she gripped the bottle all on her own.

"You know, William," she said with a sigh, "it is such a surprise to see you again. Wonderful. Really." The night wind blew the tips of her hair, the parts that stuck out under her cap, and just for the moment she felt at peace. William looked as stolid and steady as she had remembered him. The beard was new, and it gave a seriousness to his face. His eyes held a little age, a little pain. Part of her wanted to ask about Gwen, but the rest of her realized she did not want to be asked about Lance in return, and so she refrained.

True to form, he skipped the small talk. "We've got to get you out of here and back to the cabin," he said. "It's five miles. Do you still have your skis?"

She shook her head slowly, and felt as if she had carelessly lost them. "They must have been torn away," she said. "The poles too."

He waved an arm. "They were downhill skis anyway. They wouldn't have gotten you far on the trail."

In his mind he was just as troubled by what he had recently found at his cabin as by the problem of how to get Grace back there with him. After seeing her overcome by the avalanche in the silver lid of the register, he had skied back down the Center Queen in record time, outrunning any possible slides he might have set off en route. His plan had been to pick up a sleeping bag and stove and head down the trail to Lira Basin in the wan hope of finding Grace, and finding her alive. What had so surprised him on entering the cabin as darkness fell was the strange sense that he had never lived there before. The furniture was much the same—an old wood stove, the wooden table and chairs by the door, and the cheap futon up in the loft. But the quilt that Gwen had patched was gone, and in its place lay a coarse wool blanket. And on closer inspection the futon was a mattress stuffed with stale straw. He looked about. The sleeping bags that should have hung from the rafters were absent. His camp stove was missing too—and his climbing gear, their books, their boots, the photographs they had hung on the walls.

At first, William thought that Gwen had paid a brief visit in his absence and taken a few things back to the city. But there was too much gone for that. And the cabin felt in perfect order, an old order—lived in, but not by him. He suddenly felt like a trespasser.

He couldn't dwell on it, he had told himself. There was Grace to think of. A kettle of tea simmered on the stove, and he quickly poured it into two thick bottles that stood close-by and wrapped them in the wool blanket. The headlamp he had in his pack. And he was gone.

Now that he thought of it, there had been two webbed snowshoes crossed over the door as he left, wide and wooden and not at all his. He wished he had strapped them to his pack. For he realized now that either he would have to return for those snowshoes or—as difficult as it would be—he would have to carry Grace on his back. He thought harder: it would take too long to return.

"The first thing we do," he said to her, "is get rid of those plastic weights on your feet." He pried off her ski boots and tossed them carelessly in the snow. From his pack he produced a thick soft pair of booties. "Try these," he said, and put them on for her. Her feet felt stiff in his hands.

"Feels great," she told him, "but how am I going to . . ." She trailed off in bemused silence as she watched William unload his entire rucksack in the snow. Then he unclasped a pocketknife and began to cut a gaping hole on each side, next to the bottom. "What are you—"

"The better to carry you in," said William.

"But you—" she began. Grace was thinking about her weight. She had added some pounds since leaving Lance and getting a start on the dissertation.

"I'll take that chance," William said, as if reading her mind. "Now drink off the rest of this bottle, because we're going to leave it, along with your boots and everything else." His headlamp had begun to dim. He stripped it from his stocking cap and tossed it aside. "This too."

Grace thought this odd, but noticed she could see his face more clearly now, and she liked that.

He threaded her legs through the newly cut holes in his rucksack and pulled the pack up high around her, tucking the blanket about her shoulders. She felt like a child being strapped into a high chair.

"All right," he said. "Let's walk, if you can, to the edge of the slide, and then we'll see . . ."

He put one arm around her shoulders and shuffled on his skis beside her through the debris of the avalanche. Her feet and legs felt wooden beneath her, like blocks and stilts. Once to the edge of the clean, pure moonlit snow, he stooped down in front of her and slipped his arms through the packstraps.

"Ready? Up." He shouldered her weight and rose unsteadily. At the same time the snowpack groaned and his skis pushed down a full foot deeper. It was a good thing he would soon have his own tracks to follow. Even downhill, he would never make it breaking trail. It had already been a long day; William was tired.

"How does it feel?" he asked her curtly.

Grace felt rather pleasantly crushed against his coat, her chin resting on the wool of his hat. "Fine," she said. "How is it for you?"

He didn't say. "Hang on," he told her. "Under my arms."

She just got a grip before the air began to rush in her face.

William angled downhill to the floor of the basin, plowing knee-deep beneath the surface so that Grace's booties skimmed the snow. Over the years he had become an accomplished skier in the backcountry, but even so, he didn't dare attempt a turn with Grace on his back. Once down he struggled for a bit, thigh deep, to regain his path on the flat. And once there he tested the surface and found to his immense relief that his tracks held. They had frozen hard in the hour since he'd left them.

There is not much to say about their five-mile journey except that if Grace had been less cold, and William less tired, they might have enjoyed it more than they did. As it was, he stoically put one ski in front of the other, sliding carefully between strides, and Grace watched the moon go across the sky, and then watched the trees go past as they entered the shadows of timberline. She could see her breath steam in the moonlight, and through it the endless parallel tracks curving gracefully up, down, around, and on, punctuated on either side by the ruffled pockets left by the baskets of William's poles.

After a while the rucksack was perhaps as uncomfortable for Grace to sit in as it was for William to carry. Her legs grew more numb than ever, but she didn't complain, she just hung on, and tried to imagine how much worse it must be for him. Eventually the moon set, but the night went on, longer and longer than even a winter night should last.

After little talk and fewer rests, and a good deal after Grace had given up looking for it, a cabin loomed in the starlight ahead, set among silvered groves and meadows. The snow was curled across the roof in a thick, layered cap that told the story of a winter. Smoke wisped out from the chimney, and orange light shone from the open door. Standing in it was a great-cloaked figure with arms outstretched.

"Ah!" he boomed. "*Semper lentus.* But I am sure you are here."

Semper lentus sed numquam certus, Grace recalled: "Always slow but never sure." The age-old motto of that age-old buffoon, Sir Chambers, whom they had met so long ago in the course of their first adventures. In spite of her exhaustion, she felt a wild hope in his renewed acquaintance.

William skied wearily the last rise to the doorstep. "You again," he said flatly. "I should have known." Instead of reaching to shake hands he simply turned and allowed Chambers to relieve him of his human burden. Then he sank down on his threshold and stared out into the night. He did not take off his skis until long after Chambers and Grace had gone inside. By then the sweat on his back had turned cold. He was shivering. And he found that he had started to weep.

Chapter 4
Doddering Uncles

✳

INSIDE THE CABIN, CHAMBERS HAD HUNG UP WOOL BLANKETS to screen a washtub to which he added successive kettles of steaming water. When all was ready Grace began to undress behind the partition. Her jacket, as she took it off, felt rather thick in one pocket. She reached inside and to her delight found there a small gopher, curled in a ball and trembling against her bare hand.

"Why, look!" she exclaimed, pulling it out and holding it in her open palm. It whiskered up at her hopefully and then tried to burrow down between her fingers with its shovel-like claws.

Chambers clumped over and Grace held it out between the blankets for him to see. "I found it in my pocket," she said. "These were the ones who dug me out."

"Bless me," said Chambers. "A pocket gopher. Right where he belongs, too." He laughed hard at what he had said, then offered to put the gopher outside, but Grace said no, she wanted to keep him (having decided it was a *he*). After all, this pocket gopher had saved her life.

So she tucked him back in her jacket pocket (with a more than motherly pat on the head), finished undressing, and slipped into the makeshift bath. The water was warm—it should have soothed her immeasurably. But at first it hurt. In her fingers and especially her toes the pain was deep. She was surprised to see how stiff and chalky white they were.

But eventually the strong ache subsided to a pleasant tingle; she watched the blood return to her extremities with a dazed kind of satisfaction. Real warmth came into her body, and drowsiness. She would have fallen asleep right there had the basin not been rather uncomfortable. It was round and wooden, not particularly made for sitting—more the shape of a bronze caldron in which one might boil herbs with a murdered king to bring him back to eternal youth. It was an old story she couldn't quite place in her present condition.

That night and far into the next morning, Grace slept the sleep of the dead, dreamless and sound. She awoke in the loft on the straw mattress and found the gopher under her pillow. Tentatively she touched her finger to its nose; he chewed on it with buck teeth. "We need to get some breakfast for you," Grace said, and looked at the shine of window in the loft. "Or maybe some lunch."

She found new clothes laid out for her beside the bed—or old ones rather—all wool. There were knickers and kneesocks and a huge knit sweater, under which she tucked her gopher. Her red nylon jacket and jumpsuit were nowhere to be seen. Which somehow was as it should be. As she clambered down the rungs of the ladder and saw William and Chambers already sitting at the table, she knew there would be a telling of tales and a making of plans.

She was not wrong. "Pancakes!" cried Chambers as she approached them. "We have too many pancakes! Please, help us!"

She touched William's arm shyly and took her seat. He was hunched over, head in both hands, staring a bit morosely at the remains of his last stack. At her touch he gave her a thin smile but turned back to Chambers as if to continue a conversation.

"You come here often, you say?"

"Periodically is more like it," said Chambers. "Intermittently. On occasion. Since she left. Someone has to look after the place. And it's a bit more comfortable here in winter than up where I live, as you might well imagine. Just me and the white-tailed ptarmigan, and birds that slow do not provide for scintillating conversation, which I need. And which I can make, even with myself, though I often get outwitted."

"By yourself?" said Grace.

"Oh yes, he's clever," Chambers nodded conspiratorially. He got up and heaped her a plate of pancakes from the wood-burning stove.

"Since *who* left?" William asked, though he thought he knew.

"Why, *she*," said Chambers, as if her name were too obvious or too sacred to mention. "Lady Demaris."

Grace remembered meeting her here. The brown smock, the green eyes, the sheer fertile motherliness. "Where did she go?" she asked.

"No one told you?" Chambers wondered. "Why, down the river with both her sisters—Stella, Lira—and with your uncle. It's been four years."

"Garth?" she asked. She hadn't seen him for that long—ever since graduate school had begun. But she had thought it her fault, not his.

"What do you mean, down the river?" William said.

"You should ask," Chambers shot back. "You were there, in body at least. After the toppling of El Ai, and the great flooding of the gorge, the three of them sailed down the Amoenas, and Garth with them. I followed them in my boat to the sea, and there I lost sight of their barge in the sunset, and there I slept on the shore. She came to me that night in my dream and told me to go back again to our Three Queens, and to watch over her cabin and mine until she returned for me."

Chambers' eyes were moist now, and Grace and William listened quietly.

"And when I awoke, the sand was warm and hollowed beside me. She had been there, and would be again."

Chambers got up and poured out the last of the batter into the pan. "So there you have it, a poor old bumbling fool for love. Ludicrous, isn't it? Sometimes I think my brother had it better. At least he knew why Lira wouldn't have him. And finally, you know, she came around. While I'm still waiting, after all these amicable years."

"Wait a minute," Grace said. "*Your* brother? You mean Garth?"

"The same," said Chambers. "I didn't want to shock you last time. This business of inheriting uncles can sometimes be hard on a girl."

"But how—"

"Yes, quite a surprise, I'm sure. You see, Garth and your father were brought up in the valley together by a strange accident. They were changelings, of sorts. Foster children. (And hence your name.) Garth found his way back. Your father never did. But you have, once in a while, like it or not. And a pleasure to see you again, Niece, by the way."

Grace rolled her eyes. Suddenly she felt indignant. "Next you're going to tell me," she said, "that Edmund Spenser is my great-grandfather, Lady Lira is my maiden aunt, and a new uncle is doddering behind each peak of the high country."

Chambers drew himself up in a way that reminded Grace his titled name was *Sir* Chambers. "As for Edmund Spenser, I've not heard of him," he began.

"He lived in England, a long time ago. I'm writing my dissertation about him."

"England?"

"Yes. A gloomy green island a long ways off that hardly seems to exist anymore."

"A pity," said Chambers. "Dissertated to death, I suppose."

"In a way, yes. More like self-deconstructed."

"A sad thing, to be sure," he nodded. "As for Lady Lira, however, I should hope she is your aunt indeed and no maiden by now." He flipped his pancakes and winked and nodded gratuitously, a full caricature of himself.

Grace found this hard to believe. She had never in her life met anyone who felt quite so evil as Lady Lira. Besides, hadn't she been done away with years ago in the summit lake of the North Queen? Hadn't Grace seen, and taken pity, with her own eyes? She knew Garth had loved her once, but still . . . she could not fathom it.

"I've heard it's true," William told her. "I'll tell you, later."

"As for further *doddering* uncles," Chambers continued, giving full weight to the adjective that Grace had supplied, "you have one more that I know of, if indeed he is still with us. That's Villard, our youngest brother, born to trouble as the sparks fly upward."

"What kind?" she asked.

"The normal kind. The sort that flare out in a great shower from a summer bonfire in a midnight meadow and erase themselves far short of the stars, where they so ardently aspire."

"I mean troubles," said Grace.

"Not much difference," Chambers said. "Still the aspiring kind. A man's reach should exceed his grasp, or what's a metaphor?"

"You really have been lonely up here, haven't you?" Grace said.

"It's been a long winter," Chambers admitted. "Not much to see in the pond, once it snows over. More pancakes, anyone?"

"But about Villard," William said, "and his sea of troubles."

"*Sea* is good, very good," Chambers said. "But it won't do with sparks, I think. It extinguishes them."

"He's quoting," said Grace, exasperated. "A poet."

"From where?"

"England again."

"Well, that explains it," Chambers said. "I think the mountains might have helped him. It must be hard to make oneself understood in a country that no longer exists. Pancakes?"

"But Villard," said Grace.

"Villard," said Chambers, "has everything to do with the ice ax that your friend William belongs to. I almost said *that belongs to him*, but that would be another thing, and far from the truth."

"I thought it was Garth's," William said.

"That's who Villard left it to when he disappeared. But it was Villard who first quested for it, enflamed by a vision to walk north on the Long Trail a year and a day to the land of Cold-Kiss, where the mountaintops are finally submerged beneath the burden of farflung glaciers, and the sun neither sets by night in the summer nor in the winter rises by day. Cold-Kiss—land of deep darkness, pure light, and ice as far as the eye can see. In his vision, on the southern border of that land, where the Long Trail ends and the Last Mountain rises its few feet above the all-encompassing glaciers, an old wooden ice ax stood in the summit, and on its shaft the letters burned: *TAKE ME UP.* This was his dream, and Villard bid us all goodbye one summer dawn to undertake it.

"The beauties and hardships of his journey are many to be told—the rivers, the beasts, the thundering glaciers—they are all written in the poem in the book atop the Center Queen. Suffice it to say he came to the final ripple of mountain and found the ice ax plunged in the summit just as it had been shown to him. The midnight sun of deep midsummer shone on the letters cut in the shaft. The head of the ice ax gleamed like fire. With ungloved hand he curled his fingers over the pick and slipped his thumb beneath the adze. And he found and felt, to his dismay, that the head of the ax not only gleamed like fire but also burned like fire. It was as a glowing coal in his grasp, as molten lava. Worse yet, he could not let go. The pain was searing."

Grace thought of how her frostnipped hands had burned in the washtub just before she had gone to bed.

"In his agony," Chambers continued, "Villard looked up and saw a beautiful maiden dressed all in white, standing before him on the summit. She had floating hair and flashing eyes that were dark as whorls and chips of obsidian.

"'Can you help me?' he cried, writhing this way and that. 'My hand is burning upon the ax, and I cannot let go!'

"'I can help you,' she said, 'on one condition—that you take me south to your home and people and there make me your wedded bride.'

"'Yes!' screamed Villard without hesitation. 'A thousand times! Only free my hand, before I perish!'

"'Then I shall help you,' she said. 'But you must remain true to your promise.'

"The woman stooped and took from the snow a pane of ice, clear as a window and thin as the first autumn freeze of a mountain tarn. She held it up between her hands and he saw her face refracted through the crystal pane. Even in his agony he thought her image more splendidly beautiful than ever. Then she shifted the pane in her hands and held it between the northern sun and the head of the ice ax. Instantly a refreshing coolness rinsed his hand. It was as if he had plunged it into a mountain stream. Villard began to let go, then hesitated.

"'If you want the ax,' the woman said, 'now you must take it, and take me with it.'

"He looked at her with an uneasy gratitude, relieved to be quit of mortal pain but astonished at the bargain he had made. Still, the more he looked, the more enchanting she grew in his eyes. He pulled on the ax, and it slipped easily out of the snow. At the same time the woman cast the ice aside, and it shattered on the glacier a few feet beneath them.

"'Many have tried,' she said to him, 'and many I have released from the burning, but none before you has taken the ax from its purchase here on the Last Mountain. I believe it has been granted to you because, unlike all the others, you intend to prove faithful. I am Media,' she said simply, 'and I am yours.'

"So in one adventure," Chambers continued, "Villard achieved both ax and wife—or sorceress, perhaps I should say, for as he soon found, her powers were extraordinary. Instead of beginning the weary trek back on the Long Trail, she simply caught him up in the air, each of them holding onto the ax, and they flew like the arctic wind over rivers and mountains without end. Three days and three nights they glided, cresting the ground that Villard had climbed and skied and toiled across for a year and a day. They did not set down until they reached the very tip of the Silver Spire, just across the fields of lava that lie beyond the North Queen.

"There Villard left her, for that is where she wanted the wedding to take place, and he took the ax and returned to the home of our reverend father, Oppie Belknap, in the forest beside the North Queen. He showed us the ax and told us of his great adventure, and Garth and I accompanied him here to the Demaris Cabin to invite Lord Linton and his daughters to the wedding on the Silver Spire. We planned even to descend to the Tower of Otium to invite the Lord Amoenas and his family as well.

"But we never got that far. The day we came to the Demaris Cabin was the day we learned that Stella, the youngest, had slipped away and given herself to the crater lake in the North Queen to live with the stars beneath its waters. She had done this the night that Villard had obtained the ax and promised himself perforce to Media, far away on the Last Mountain. Somehow, she knew. For as it came out, she and Villard had been secretly betrothed. The moment he chose against her, she vanished.

"Villard, as you might well imagine, was mortally ashamed and stricken. Apparently he had hoped to explain to Stella the inescapable nature of his bargain with the sorceress and to gain her eventual forgiveness. Now that Stella was gone, however, he only had thoughts for her. For weeks he kept a lonely vigil on the snowy rim of the North Queen, weeping his apologies to a woman who perhaps no longer could hear them. That winter he sat silent by the fire in our forest hut by the lava fields. We all still lived there with our father, now that Garth had found us again. But in late winter our father died, and we buried him under the first avalanche lilies of spring. When the snows were gone, Villard returned to Media's Tower, as we now called the Silver Spire—just visible to us across the lava. What he found and what he said there he never told us, but he brought back an infant son all wrapped in white that he said was his.

"So there we were, from things dying to things newborn in one short spring. The three of us tended the child as we could, but in deep midsummer, a year to the day after Villard had gained the burning ax, he quietly gave the ax to Garth and left the cabin late at night. That was twenty-seven years ago, and no one has seen him since.

"Soon after, Garth left to pursue his studies in the valley, and I took the child—Matheu, we called him—to my newbuilt cabin in the heather by the pond between the North and Center Queens. I needed to look in the water there. And I wanted to be closer—well—to certain people. At any rate, there I raised him until he came nearly of age and decided to take up residence in the family home in the hemlock forest by the lava fields—the Belknap Hut, we had come to call it, now that it had stood empty those many years. For Matheu had taken to woodcarving, and up where I live, far above timberline, there is not much wood to be found."

William, who had been listening intently, grew visibly anxious at these last details. He started to speak but Grace interrupted.

"I'm curious," she said. "Why did he give the ax to Garth? Why not to you?"

"Because Garth is the oldest," Chambers said. "I am one of the middle brothers. I've got my pond. Older and younger brothers do things; middle brothers see things."

"Oh," said Grace vacantly. She thought about herself, an only child. But the way things were emerging in her extended family, she didn't know if she could be too sure of that anymore.

"Since you see things in your pond," said Grace, "did you ever see your brother, or Media, in all these years?"

"Not a glimpse," Chambers replied. "Which is evidence, I think, of her powers. She's not a woman that wants to be seen except on precisely her own terms—through the ice, brightly, as it were. As for why I haven't seen Villard either, I can only ascribe that to her powers as well."

"But I have seen—something," William said abruptly.

They looked at him in great surprise.

"It was on the register atop the Center Queen—the silver shield. Do you remember it, Grace?"

"Of course!" she said. "And you could see it this time? I mean, see *in* it, the way I did, because of what the poem said were my *faerie eyne?* I'm proud of you, William. Really, I am."

He waved his hand as if he could physically brush aside the compliment. But he felt it deeply. Then, slowly at first, in halting stages, he told them about Gwen and Lara, and finding the key, and seeing Lady Demaris in a dream.

William told them about his long ski ascent of the Center Queen, his disappointment at not being able to use the key, and his loss of patience in beating on the lock with the ax.

When he got to that part, Chambers looked vexed, and was about to say something critical when Grace put a hand on his arm and said, "*Shhh*—you weren't there. We might have done something worse."

William gave her a grateful glance, and then described the three things he had seen in the picture. First, Grace in the avalanche.

"So that's how you knew," she whispered.

Then about Chambers leaving his cabin.

"I remember that wink," Chambers said. "I had a feeling I was being watched."

Finally he told of the young man, the wood sculptor, whom he now knew to be Matheu, and how he was carried away by the lizard-like birds that befouled the hut.

"Harpies!" said Chambers and Grace at once. William had no idea what they meant. He would ask later.

"And you say," continued Chambers, "they took him over the lava beds toward

Media's Tower?"

William nodded.

Chambers sat stunned and quiet. Finally he said, "Looks like we have an expedition ahead of us."

Grace looked at William. "Do you think," she said, "that's why we're here? Here in the other place, I mean—in the old place, the true place? Tell me, and be honest: were there any ski lifts in the picture?"

"None," he said flatly.

"And when you skied down the Center Queen to get me, did you see any ski lifts then?"

"No," he said. And this time he smiled.

Grace wanted to smile too, but she was starting to feel a little frightened.

She looked at Chambers. He appeared so comically aged and broken down and overweight that all at once she couldn't imagine setting out on such a perilous journey with him. "Chambers," she said, "do you really think you should go with us? You're bound by a promise to Lady Demaris to watch over this cabin, aren't you?"

"But it's my nephew we're talking about," Chambers blustered.

"And my cousin," Grace replied.

This seemed to catch him by surprise.

"William and I have gone off on this sort of thing before, and I suppose we can do it again." She meant to be stout, but her voice was cracking.

Chambers looked at them both rather meekly. "I suppose you are right," he said at last. "I am a foolish fond old man. I would just get in the way."

Grace felt a surge of pity. "No, Uncle," she said bravely. "You never have." She got out of her chair and gave him a hug, the first she had given anyone for a long time—at least since Lance had paid her a surprise visit on New Year's Eve. And bad as things had been between them, Lance was not unwelcome on that winter night. Now, as she hugged her rotund uncle, the gopher stirred beneath her sweater.

Chapter 5
The Winter Children

※

THAT AFTERNOON IT WAS CONCLUDED that Chambers would come only as far as the Belknap Hut, "to set it to rights," as he said. Grace and William would ski on across the lava to investigate the Silver Spire. They would climb it at least, to see what they could see from the summit, and hopefully find a clue of Matheu's whereabouts. No small part of this decision was Chambers' inordinate fear of heights, which he freely admitted. "I prefer my pond, frozen or unfrozen," he said. "Or a good mountain meadow. My climbing days are over—and I never did like them."

William listened patiently while strapping his ice ax to his pack—the same long-handled wooden ax that had once belonged to Garth, and to Villard, and to the summit of the Last Mountain. The ax, in fact, was just about the only thing he could find in the cabin that was his (and as Chambers had said, the ax was hardly William's at all). During the night the skis he had left outside the door had disappeared, and Chambers had outfitted him—and Grace too—with old heavy wooden ones, wide and long and graceful in a rough sort of way. With the skis came stout ash poles with leather-thonged baskets. Looking at this ancient gear, and the loads of food and blankets for their packs, William doubted they would make it to the hut in one day. Chambers insisted on using snowshoes, and that would slow them up even further.

To make matters worse, when they arose to set out at dawn the next morning, the cirrus clouds of the last two days had given way to gray skies that held the land in a promise of snow. "As if we had not had enough for the winter," William grumbled.

"Should we wait?" asked Grace. They were standing just outside the door, about to put on skis and packs. "Until it clears, I mean?"

William was put off by all forms of last-minute indecision. But Chambers spared him an unkind word.

"We could wait a week if we wait that long," he said. "And that goes for any month of the year." He shouldered his pack and the others did the same. And they set off in the cold dim light.

For Grace this start felt rather bleak. Her fingers and toes had grown quite numb in the short time they had loitered by the door. And now that they were traveling—William breaking trail in front, Grace shuffling her skis in his wake, and Chambers plodding slowly behind, snuffing out their tracks with his snowshoes—she could hardly keep her breath or balance. Of course she had carried a pack before, and had been on skis, but she had never tried to do both at once, and she found the combination not at all to her liking. Each huge ski—they were more like planks of wood on her feet—took considerable effort to shove forward, and they weren't even really going uphill. Then there was the constant matter of keeping the tips pointed in the right direction. For some reason she assumed that they would follow naturally in the broken channels that William left behind himself, like faithful dogs trotting in their master's footsteps. But the tips of her skis were more like dogs that turn aside to sniff in the brush. One second she would see them, sliding ahead in parallel progress, and the next moment one of them would have disappeared, completely submerged in the snowbank beside her, and she would have to stop, retreat, and then relocate her skis on the trail. Other times her tips strayed inward and crossed, like two puppies wanting to play. The first time this happened she fell face-first in the snow, and after many attempts to right herself she finally had to take off her pack, and then one of her skis, before she could stand up, and then she was so covered with snow, and so painfully conscious of having held up the others, that she wondered why she had bothered to come, and why she had had the hubris to suggest to Chambers that this was a trip for herself and William but not for him.

After a long mile or so she found she could keep her skis going in a straight line with a little reliance on her poles, planting them firmly with each step. But this soon tired her shoulders cruelly; her muscles there were already burning from the weight of her pack. She envied the gopher, tucked away in a pocket of her knickers, and recalled her ride on William's back. That was the way to go.

Before long, aching and gasping, she felt beads of sweat falling off her nose to her tongue, and she realized she was steaming with exertion. A stop then, to take off her parka and mittens and cap, and for a while afterward she felt relatively at ease in her movements, watching the snowy groves and parklands pass by in the gathering light. But then came a sudden drop, down the side of a steep ravine. William plowed straight to the bottom, contouring only slightly, and Grace followed after, hoping her rudimentary skills would somehow get her safely down. The broken trail bore her swiftly, faster than it had taken William, and she lurched right, into the slope, to slow herself in the untracked snow. Unfortunately her pack lurched with her, and kept lurching, and in a panic she swerved back left and found herself sailing headfirst, airborne, towards the base of the ravine. The drift received her impartially, as was its duty, and Grace found herself buried again, as if by another avalanche, her mouth this time stopped with snow.

It was Chambers who gently pulled her out. "You know," she said, "I really hate this."

Chambers and William said not much of anything, knowing there was nothing to say that a beginner would not twist to use against herself. In a little while, if things did not get any better, one of them would volunteer to carry some part of her load. But not yet.

They did suggest "an early midmorning break," however, and Chambers pulled out a bottle of something hot that made Grace feel a bit better about her prospects. By the time they all had drunk their fill, and Grace had relocated and reconfigured her skis and poles and backpack (and checked on the gopher asleep in her pocket), it had begun to snow.

The flakes were few and stray and lonesome at first, landing on Grace's lashes and nose and tumbling off the folds of her parka. Then they came in a thickening curtain, giving a sense of quiet inevitability to the forest and their progress through it. Perhaps it was the slow descent of the snow all around them, the stately measure of striding amidst such constant universal motion, that gave to Grace a new sense of rhythm. She was on a journey. It would sometimes be hard, and sometimes cold, but the journey was good. She was certain of it.

By noon they had dropped some way from timberline into thick woods, mountain hemlock molded with snow. William consulted a map and said they were not quite halfway to the Belknap Hut, and Chambers said that not quite halfway was quite good enough for lunch. Grace wondered where they would eat, for it is one thing to ski through falling snow and another to sit and shiver in it. She watched Chambers plod off, duckfooted on his snowshoes, to a large tree nearby. Its branches were indistinguishable in a solid sculptured skirting of snow that encased the tree like a thick white petticoat. Instead of stepping around the hemlock, Chambers plunged directly into it, first putting up the hood of his cloak to shield himself from the blocks of snow that tumbled down. And then he was gone, leaving only a black door in the tree behind him.

William followed, stomping down the snow at the entrance with his skis before taking them off and following Chambers inside. Grace came curiously after. By the time she got her skis off and peeked inside, William and Chambers had stomped a series of steps for her down into a small room, a private place, about the trunk of the hemlock tree. The branches bowed down and laden with snow formed perfect walls all around them, letting in a dim whiteness, a calm light, from the outside.

"Wonderful!" she pronounced.

They crowded close, sitting on packs and coats and blankets, and passing between them soup and bread and nuts and cheese and other good things that Chambers had brought. Grace had never felt quite so snug in her life. As she ate and drank and rested, two lines of a poem that never had meant much to her insisted on repeating themselves:

> *Thou hast light in dark; and shutst in little room,*
> *Immensity cloistered in thy dear womb.*

"Yes," she said aloud. "I suppose this is what it is really—a winter womb. And we are the winter children."

Chambers looked at her strangely. "A tree well, if you please," he said.

When all was finished, Grace lay back contentedly and idly studied the knots and rills on the bark of the tree in the soft light. When she looked with her head just to one side, she could almost believe she saw a face looking intently back at her. It seemed to be of a young woman, with wide knotty eyes, a broken-off stub of a branch for a nose, and an open whorl for a mouth that was perpetually agape in surprise. Dirty bits of goatsbeard lichen swept the forehead in a more than passable imitation of locks of hair. She was somewhere between plain and pretty (as Grace was herself, she felt), and someone to whom something was about to happen.

The harder Grace looked at the tree trunk the more the contours of the bark suited themselves to a sculpted portrait—chin, cheekbones, a suggestion beneath the lichen of ears. It was fascinating.

"What are you staring at?" William asked lazily.

Chambers cast a glance at the tree trunk and sat up carefully. "Herself," he said.

All of a sudden Grace knew it was true. The face she studied was the face she owned. And then, before the thrill of recognition could even begin to settle in, her wooden twin seemed to dissolve. The knots were knots, the bark was bark, the lichen merely wisps of lichen. Try as she might, she could not reconstruct them into her likeness.

"I don't see anything," William said.

Grace tore her eyes from the tree and looked at her companions. "Neither do I," she said hollowly. But her voice told otherwise.

The journey of the afternoon was a weary winding through the trees. The snow fell more thickly than ever, and had lost whatever spell it had cast to help them on their way in the morning. They slogged in silence, William thinking of Gwen and Lara, Grace of Lance and her dissertation about the utter meaninglessness of the apparently meaningful, and Chambers no doubt of his lifelong inadequacies, whatever they might be, that had so far kept him from winning the hand of Lady Demaris. And they all thought of the face in the tree, though Grace refused to talk about it.

By evening they were more than tired, legs leaden, shoulders aching, breath steaming in bitter rags of exhalation. They halted for a short break in an open meadow, and the snowfall stopped and the clouds parted and the early risen moon shone down on their dusted packs. The bottles of drink were no longer warm, and the clearing skies brought a deep chill into their bones. Grace realized she was thoroughly wet from the heat of exertion and melting of snow. She was shivering miserably.

William checked the map again in the twilight mixture of moonshine and alpenglow. The North Queen, now south of them, came unwrapped for the first time that day, its massive summit a pale gold against the clouds, glowing as if lit from within.

"Put the map away," said Chambers, wheezing in his snow-soaked cloak. His beard was clogged and dripping with ice. "I know the meadow well; it is but a mile at most from the hut. Even so, that is long for me. You and Grace go ahead now—I'll come after."

"We won't hear it," Grace protested. "We're staying together. Here, let me take some of your load."

Chambers stooped as if faintly humiliated by the offer. "Perhaps I shouldn't even have come. I did promise to watch over the Demaris Cabin, just as you said, and this is what I get for abandoning my post—a thorough soaking in the snow and making an exhausted fool of myself."

Grace and William did their best to disagree, and each took a bundle or blanket from Chambers' pack and strapped it atop their own. Then they skied on into the darkening forest, following the long, sinuous dimple of trail between the trees. Chambers lagged somewhat behind. All of them were too tired to move, but there was no other way to arrive—or to keep warm.

The moon rose higher, the darkness deepened in the shadows of the trees, and still they skied and plodded on. Grace was fairly sure that she had open blisters on each heel. And when the blisters had rubbed themselves into raw and pulsing certainty, she was perfectly sure that more than a mile had passed since the meadow. It filled her with a dull rage that the hut was not there where it was supposed to be. At every slight bend in the trail she looked for it beyond William's shoulder in the moonlit corridor ahead.

Of course, the only time she didn't look, for the mundane reason that in her fatigue she had crossed the tips of her skis again and collapsed face-first on top of them, was the time that William called back that the Belknap Hut lay just ahead. She extricated herself from the snow with this promise of rest and refuge, and then she saw it, across a ravine and up a rise, a stolid shape beneath trees and stars. Her anger at the hut melted.

She was just about to congratulate William for leading them here so durably when a cry of surprise rang out behind her. She tried to turn quickly around and naturally fell down again all in a heap, her skis and legs hopelessly tangled.

"Great gods! Let go of me, you slimy brute!"

It was Chambers that she heard shouting, but his voice, strangely, no longer came from behind but from somewhere far above, near the treetops, somewhere between snow and moon. A great stench passed over her face, and she caught a glimpse of huge flapping wings in the starlit sky.

She had no time to peer after them. A rushing of air, a braying screech, descended upon her where she lay prostrate in the snow. The foul stench intensified to a loathsomeness—she could not abide it. Suddenly, the light of the moon was shut out, and sharp claws gripped her shoulders and pack, lifting her partway into the air.

"William!" she screamed.

The tips of her skis were caught on something—a branch, perhaps—under the newly fallen snow, and the creature that held her flapped and pulled at her painfully, racking her in a terrible stretch. In a moment, she knew, her boots would be broken out of their bindings.

She screamed again, not a name or a call for help, but a full-lunged, inarticulate wail. Just as her feet were about to come loose she saw the silver head of an ax sail swiftly past. It sliced with a thud behind her head into whatever it was that so cruelly tugged her. A ratcheting cry pierced the night, and something foul dripped down her neck. The ax flashed by again and again, and then she saw it was William beside her, wielding the shaft with grimaces of pure disgust and astonishment. And all at once the sky released her. She fell to the snow like a discarded marionette and looked up into wings and beak and eyes that glowered in moonlight. They hovered as if ready to attack again. William stepped over her and gave one more swing with the ice ax, high and hard. Grace could not tell if the adze had struck, but she heard once more the screech, the bray, and nearly retched from the stench released all around them. Then the winged creature was gone, soaring away in a dark cacophony.

A long time after the cries had faded, William stood trembling in silence. Then he reached to help Grace off with her pack. "What's this?" he whispered. His hand recoiled.

Grace rolled out of her pack as if it were a shirt of fire. In the moonlight they both saw it—a severed claw. It was twice the size of a gnarled hand, still gripping the corded canvas.

Chapter 6
Works and Days

✳

The fireplace in the Belknap Hut was so bedunged that it took a full hour and much fresh fir to burn off the stench. By then, William had managed to board up the broken windows and Grace to shovel out most of the snow that had sifted in. They sank down next to the hearth and took off their dripping socks, warm at last.

"Poor Chambers," said Grace disconsolately. "I wonder where those—things—have taken him."

"No telling," said William.

"And where they would have taken *me*. Really, William, you outdid yourself with that ice ax." She looked at the ax propped on the mantle. The firelight played across its shaft and out onto many rows of carven faces, knee-high busts that circled the room in silent witness. She saw among them Garth and Lira and Lady Demaris, all quite solemn.

"It wasn't just me," he said. "The ax—I felt it leap in my hands." He looked at the ice ax wonderingly. "And we didn't do much for Chambers, did we? If only we hadn't skied so far ahead."

"Please," said Grace. "Don't blame yourself. You were doing what you could to get us to the hut. He was going very slowly at the end. You could only hang back so long."

"But it pays to wait," William said firmly.

Grace studied his troubled features and felt long-latent feelings of respect and affection stir within her, as surely as her pocket gopher stirred within the folds of her sweater. If she were not so very tired she could almost contemplate falling in love with this old friend and fellow adventurer, technically married though she was. But a strange queasiness in her stomach claimed precedence, something more than hunger pains. She had felt this way—in tinges at least—for almost a week. It was difficult to entertain romantic thoughts when she was not only exhausted but also close to throwing up. Not to mention still frightened. It had taken a good deal of prying to loosen the severed claw from her pack. She envisioned it creeping to the hut by night and scratching the door until it found its way inside.

"William, the winged creatures, the lizard-like things that you saw in the silver register—the ones that broke into the hut and carried away my cousin Matheu—did they look anything like . . . ?" She didn't have to finish her question.

"You can answer that with your nose," said William, nodding at the cleansed fireplace.

"So, Harpies again," she breathed, saying what she already knew. "So very odd."

"Can you tell me about these—Harpies?" he asked.

"Well," said Grace, "they are part of Greek myth—which is where I prefer they would stay. I had to translate Ovid for my Latin requirement last year, so I know it pretty well—at least his version. It goes like this."

She added another log to the fire and made herself more comfortable on the bare hearth. "The story begins with a prince of Thessaly named Jason, who tried to reclaim the throne of his father from his cousin Pelias, a usurper. Pelias said he could have it back on one condition—that he voyage north to the land of Colchis and bring back the Golden Fleece that had once belonged to another cousin of theirs, Phrixus. So Jason agreed and gathered a crew of Argonauts to go with him on this quest."

"Argonauts?" William said.

"That was the name of their ship, the *Argo*. Ergo, Argonauts."

"And the Harpies?" he asked again.

"I'm getting to them. En route to Colchis, Jason and the Argonauts stopped at an island on which they met a wretched prophet, Phineus, who had offended Zeus by sharing his knowledge of the future. To punish Phineus, Zeus afflicted him with these Harpies—described by Ovid as extremely frightful flying creatures, with hooked beaks and hooked claws, that leave behind themselves a stench. Real stinkers. What happened was, every time Phineus tried to get a bite to eat, these Harpies would show up and defecate all over his food. By the time Jason and his friends arrived, Phineus was skin and bones—he hadn't eaten in a good long while. But two of the Argonauts—sons of Boreas, the North

Wind—volunteered to defend him at his next meal. The Harpies made their usual disgusting visit, but afterwards the sons of Boreas caught up with them and would have cut them all to pieces had Iris not restrained their swords with a promise that Zeus would henceforth leave Phineus in peace."

"Iris?" asked William.

"The rainbow messenger of the gods."

"Nice," he said, as if this arrangement pleased him greatly. "And did Jason and company ever get the Golden Fleece?"

"Yes, they did," Grace assured him, "but not without the help of Medea." She stopped as if struck by an ax. "Good Lord!" she cried. "What's *she* doing here?"

William shot a look at the door as if someone were about to enter. Then he understood. "You mean, in the story?" he said. "Media's part of the story too?"

"Not Media, exactly. *Medea*, with the accent on a second *e*. But it's too close for comfort, isn't it? And she's more than just a part of the story—she's the very center of it." Grace stood up, perturbed at having overlooked this similarity in names. The pocket gopher came tumbling out of the folds of her sweater and onto the floor, where it scrabbled about with half-closed eyes until it nosed its way into a wet wool sock.

"Well," said William, "go on."

She did, over supper at Matheu's table, telling him about King Aetes, the bronze bulls, the dragon teeth, the terrible serpent that guarded the Fleece, and how the lovely Medea, daughter to the King of Colchis, helped Jason overcome all of these by her sorcery.

"The result of all this," she continued, "was that Jason promised to marry her, and took her back to Thessaly. There she helped him even further, by restoring his murdered father to life and by cleverly bringing the murderer, the false king Pelias, to his death."

"Back up," said William. "Something is repeating itself. You say Medea helped Jason obtain the Golden Fleece by sorcery. It seems our Media helped Villard obtain the ax by sorcery too—and likewise returned home with him to be his bride."

"Right," said Grace. She gave him a little encouraging nod. As a teaching assistant in graduate school she found herself doing this to students who were just beginning to catch on.

"So," he said, "did they actually marry, in the story?"

"They did, yes. And she had two sons by him. But then Jason, out of pure ambition, engaged himself to the daughter of the King of Corinth. Medea, as you might imagine, completely lost it. To revenge herself she not only murdered the princess of Corinth but also destroyed her own two children. Then she left. Took off on her flying chariot, I believe. And that's pretty much the end of the story."

"Her own sons? She murdered them too?"

"Oh, yes. Euripides, Ovid, Seneca—they all agree."

"So where does that leave us?" he pondered, sitting back from their lamplit table. "Are we dealing now with the same Medea, under a slightly different name? Is she somewhere near, perhaps still in her tower? Are these her Harpies, able to go anywhere and fouling everything they touch?"

"Tune in next week," Grace said with the gravity of a TV announcer. She thought of the confident narrator of the video of the Three Queens she had seen in the bar at the ski lodge.

"And the most immediate question, I suppose, is why she has sent her Harpies, if indeed they are hers and she has sent them, after you and Chambers and Matheu."

"Well," said Grace, "we're all related, for one thing. And all related to Villard, too. Do you suppose she's still hopping mad about being stood up? About Villard's engagement to Stella, I mean? It would fit the old story—though I don't much like what it suggests." She rose from the table and emptied the gopher out of the sock and cradled him protectively.

"But it's been so long," William objected. "Twenty-seven years. She could have come after them anytime. Why now?"

"Who knows," she shrugged. "But maybe things are different now with Garth and Stella and Lady Lira and Lady Demaris really gone." She looked at their images staring back into the fire. "It may be the rest of us are somehow less protected now. And when you think of it, William, not all of us are here all the time. Me, for example—and you."

"But I'm not part of your family," he said.

"Maybe you are, maybe you're not. Don't you ever wonder about Gwen sometimes? She's so much like Lady Demaris it's uncanny. I wonder now if they aren't sisters, separated across worlds, just like my father apparently belongs to this hut without even knowing it."

William didn't say anything. She sensed she had touched a possibility he wished to keep very private.

"I've another idea as well," she said.

"Me too," he mumbled.

"So what's yours?"

"It's that—" His voice faltered. "It's that I should never have struck the shield with the ice ax. As soon as I did it, I knew it was wrong. That silver engraving is sacred somehow—a true picture. The moment I attacked it, Matheu was carried away by the Harpies and you were buried by the avalanche. In using the good against the good, I feel I somehow threw this world out of balance and opened the door for some great evil." He solemnly put his head in his hands.

"Maybe so," Grace said comfortingly, "but perhaps those things were going to happen anyway. And if you hadn't seen us in the picture, you could never have rescued me and we would not be setting out to look for Matheu."

"Don't you see?" said William. "That's simply the property of the engraving—to help bring good out of evil. But it doesn't change what I have done."

"What you've done," she said, touching his arm, "is save my life twice over in two days. If you've made a mistake, it seems to me you're well on your way to correcting it."

He looked up at her gratefully. It was a look, in fact, that perhaps contained something more than gratitude.

"Anyway," she continued, "the idea I had was also about the ice ax."

"What's that?" he said.

"She might simply want it back."

"Whatever for?"

"It's a potent and mysterious tool, and after all, she is a sorceress. She might simply want the ax to complete her arsenal of power. As for what she had with Villard, it is the symbol of what he betrayed. And it may be her only instrument of gaining a likely suitor again. Years ago, Lady Lira wanted it, and wanted it badly. Remember? She thought she could use it to subjugate the land for the Lava Beast. Media may desire it to subjugate all things to herself in her own way."

"So we all could have gone for a ride tonight," William mused. "If you're correct."

Grace was standing by the fire now with the pocket gopher still cupped in her hands. As William spoke she let the gopher down on the hearth and watched him nuzzle the crevices between the stones as if looking for a convenient tunnel.

William rose from the table to watch. "What's that he's got his nose in now?"

Grace bent down. The gopher had his snout partway buried in a small opening cut into the heart of a rock. She picked him back up, and William stooped to examine the place.

"It's a keyhole," he said with strange excitement. He carefully dusted it off with his finger. "In sheer rock."

Grace looked. "Well," she said, "do you still have the key? No ice in this one. You wouldn't be needing the ax this time."

William averted his eyes when she said this, and Grace regretted her careless comment. "Sorry," she whispered. All the same, she wondered then if his striking the silver shield on the summit really was the very thing that had given Media her chance—had unleashed her waiting power.

William had drawn the key from his pocket and was working it into the hole in the hearthstone. Once held straight the key fit neatly, sinking all the way to the ring. He turned the shaft easily. Immediately, the entire stone in which it was buried levered upwards on a hinge, revealing a space just large enough for the few items that William carefully drew upward into the light. First was a bright sharp carving knife he unsheathed from a miniature scabbard. The wooden handle was dark and smoky, worn and smooth. He recognized the feel of it, then held it up against the ice ax and knew why. The wood of the shaft was identical with the wood of the handle.

"Brothers from the same tree, in the Land of Four Rivers," he said to Grace, and handed it to her. "Keep this."

"But doesn't it belong here?" Grace said.

"It belongs with your cousin Matheu," he replied. "Think of yourself as bringing it to him."

Next he held up a lock of hair, pure blonde.

"Stella's, I think," Grace whispered.

William nodded in tentative agreement, but in his mind he was thinking of Lara, his golden girl. He put the lock of hair in his pocket.

"What for?" Grace protested. To her it felt like graverobbing.

"If Villard is still alive," said William, "this might be a comfort to him." The possibility of meeting yet another uncle had not really occurred to Grace; she had assumed that Villard had disappeared for good. It was still strange to contemplate these new extensions of family. She was used to thinking of herself formerly as an only child, and now as a separated woman. She most often heard the word *family* on the lips of her avuncular chairman, who liked to welcome all the fresh assistant professors and graduate students as "part of the department family." A splendid fiction, as it turned out. For if you didn't make your tenure review or failed your exams you were out, divorced, disinherited. So much for family.

"Look at this," said William. In his hands now was a small book, bound with leather. By the wear and shine of the cover they could tell it was very old. William opened it in the firelight.

Oppie Belknap, Works and Days, the flyleaf read. The words were scrawled, the ink faded. He thumbed the pages. They quickly saw it was a notebook, full of jottings. Most of the entries were quite short and practical, thus:

> *Tear with lava, slice with obsidian, smooth with pumice.*
>
> *To hollow a cedar, let burn at core with coals, three days.*
>
> *Pole Spring dries in August, Upper Alder in September. For water in autumn, snout of Prouty Glacier is clearest.*

"As if he couldn't remember these things himself," Grace said.

"He knew them well enough," said William, flipping through. "But perhaps he foresaw a time when others wouldn't. We, for example."

He stopped near the end. "What's this?"

The last few pages held darker ink, clearer script. *Matheu Belknap*, it said. *A Note on My Recent Practice.*

"Read it aloud," William suggested, holding out the book to her.

"No, you," Grace said. "I had my turn ten years ago." She touched his arm encouragingly; inside, however, she was struggling with a new wave of nausea.

"All right," he said. "Here goes."

Grace sat down and held her arms across her stomach attentively, and William read:

> *"I have found this book with the aid of a key that came to me in the mouth of a white-tailed ptarmigan that followed me in the forest today. I have seen the keyhole ever since I came here ten years ago from my Uncle Chambers. I often fashioned roughcut picks of wood and stone to try the lock, but always failed. I find here some strands of hair—I know not whose—and will leave beside it my best knife, no longer having need of it, as I shall presently explain.*

"This book of my grandfather's contains much in the way of good and practical advice, some of which I have learned from my uncle, some of which I have painstakingly learned for myself, and the rest of which I have now committed to memory. I add to it my own discovery, which, if far less practical, is no less meaningful than the things written here before it.

"The discovery is this. For years now, ever since I was a boy, I have felt it my gift to carve faces from wood, to find their hidden forms in the grain and release them for all to see. I would walk far from my uncle's cabin by the tarn to find suitable material, and these ten years I have lived alone where wood is plentiful—here in the fir and hemlock forest next to the petrified sea of lava. With so many faces birthed by my blade I am not so lonely. My uncle has the mirror of his lake to keep him active company; I have this wooden cloud of witnesses.

"Like any carver, I suppose, I learned early on to rely upon the natural grain of the wood in hand to determine the shape and features of a face. Soon the cabin became full of the people I had carved in this way. Some I knew—family and neighbors in these mountains. Others were but reproductions of half-remembered glimpses of strangers. Still others bore resemblance to no one I had ever met—these faces often took shape so swiftly and surely beneath the knife that it seemed that underneath the bark they were already there. Their expressions often convinced me that actual people existed somewhere who might look at these carvings as if in a mirror.

"In time the hut became so populated I took to roaming through the forest and carving faces on snags and stumps and trunks of trees, leaving them to gaze where I made them. Of course I took advantage of whatever features offered themselves—cracks, splits, knots, bumps, whorls, splinters, stray bits of bark or lichen. I developed a sharp eye for these things.

"One day I walked until evening west and south on our part of the Long Trail, carving as I went. On this day a remarkable thing eventually took place. In the morning I hewed and carved at will, wresting the faces out of the wood. But on each one I spent a little less effort and time, merely connecting the natural features that already presented themselves. The farther I walked, the more my vision seemed to sharpen. By afternoon I was using my knife very little, just touching up what was already there. Then, at evening, I stopped beneath an old and craggy mountain hemlock. There on the trunk was the perfect face of a young woman who bore some slight resemblance to me. Her features were unerringly complete; there was absolutely nothing I could do with my knife to enhance her presence. I simply stood *and gazed until the sun went down, and all the while the woman seemed to gaze back.*

"Since then I have walked in the woods every day to look at faces and left my carving knife at home. At evening, by the fire, I sometimes use it just to let my hands feel the familiar motions. I have since carved the face of the lovely young woman I met in the hemlock, and trust that we shall someday meet. She now sits behind the others of my known family beyond the hearth. I say others of my family because of her strange likeness to them; I think her kin. Beside her is a strange figure, also a woman, that I also think I shall meet someday. But fear to. She is as threatening as the other is kind. I wish I did not carve her face, but I had to. She is one of the half-remembered strangers. No, not even half. She is but a dream of mine.

"Tomorrow I shall give the key back to the ptarmigan in the forest. My carving of Stella has already directed me to. Her lips have spoken, as they sometimes do. I think of her as my mother at times, knowing that my father loved her. I digress, however, from this surprise of my own few works and days. After carving a long time, it is better simply to see."

William quietly closed the book and put it back beneath the stone. This, at least, would remain here.

Grace was looking down at the floor, lips and stomach quivering. "Have you seen my gopher?" she said, wishing somehow to change the subject, the way people do when too affected by what is at hand.

William peered into the shadows. "There," he said, and pointed to signs of furtive movement behind the first row of faces.

She stepped over her Uncle Garth and found the gopher curled beneath the wooden chin of her own visage. Forewarned though she was by her cousin's story, she felt no less of a shock than when she had glimpsed herself in the hemlock tree. But this time she saw something motherly in her eyes, the comforting look of a Lady Demaris glancing down upon the creature in her care.

Next to Garth was an anxious face that derived from his. Villard perhaps. Grace moved it slightly to shed more light on her own. She caught her breath. Directly beside her wooden twin was the face of a woman she did not know, austerely beautiful but frightening, somehow, in the sureness of her gaze. Grace stepped back instinctively.

She stumbled, landing with a thump, and several of the faces around her fell over like dominoes. Then she heard a squeal of pain, almost human, and looked up sharply. The head of the woman had toppled directly onto hers, which had fallen in turn atop the gopher, pinning him to the wood floor.

She rose and carefully picked him up. "Poor baby," she said.

Chapter 7
The Lava Field

✳

THE NEXT DAY WAS GRACE'S WORST. After reprovisioning their packs they left the hut to its wooden faces and skied toward the edge of the lava field. The sun was out, and the sky was gloriously clear. In the warming air, huge clumps of snow were cascading off the trees and cratering the surface below. Just before they reached the lava, Grace took a direct hit. It was like stepping into a waterfall, or a swift and vertical avalanche, and it knocked her down flat on her pack. "Oh, please," she groaned, plastered and heaped with twigs and cones and needles and slush. "Not today." Her stomach was churning more than ever.

William pretended it wasn't funny, but not very successfully. "Let me help you," he said, and offered his hand a little too ostentatiously.

"As if you could," she grumbled at him. She had detected a less-than-distant attention in his eyes and manner during the evening in the hut. This morning it was unmistakable: William had a crush on her. In one sense it was about time. It wasn't as if she didn't have some feelings herself. But each of them was still married, in theory at least. He had told her more of his story by the fire, and she had divulged parts of hers. This business of being married could be inconvenient. Even more so was her growing suspicion about the reason for her nausea. That New Year's visit—if only she had not given in to Lance's whining. And the punishing irony of it all—to be pregnant with the child of a husband she hardly cared for anymore. She had a dissertation to write, not to mention a budding winter romance to attend to. But her stomach gave her relish for neither. The notion of skiing ten miles today across an open lava field gave her even less cause for celebration.

She struggled back up on her skis herself, then followed William out of the trees and up the slope of what seemed to be a huge white wave about to break across the forest. From the top they turned to look again at the small stone hut above the ravine. Snow-decked firs swept back and up to the open flanks of the North Queen, newly clothed in the morning sun with the dazzle of yesterday's fresh snow. A plume in the air by the crater rim showed the power of the winds on the summit. Where they stood it was still calm.

In the other direction, due north, an undulating plain of white spread out before them, far and wide. In the summer it would appear a dark and craggy chaos of lava, full of ragged bluffs and trenches twenty- to forty-feet high and deep. There was a path—the Long Trail—which crossed the lava in clever ways, but they would not be able to find it. William sighted carefully on the tip of a silvery needlepoint across the plain.

"Is that the tower? Media's Tower?"

He nodded faintly. To both of them, it looked far.

Their progress was not swift. What had looked like gentle undulations from their perch on the brink of the lava field were really a series of dips and banks and half-hidden grottos, somewhat gentled by the layering of winter snows but real obstacles nonetheless. There was no gaining the sort of rhythm they had found the day before in the forest. Often Grace would plunge down into a hollow much deeper than she had thought, then gingerly sidestep up a ramp that was likewise much steeper than it had appeared. Other times she would brace herself for a huge drop, only to find the surface remained perfectly flat. Ridges and corridors raised their hopes as reasonable avenues of travel, but eventually these ways dead-ended, sometimes abruptly, and then they would have to backtrack. The lava field was a maze without a correct passage—at least none that they could see. Indeed, seeing was the problem. The glare of white in the shadeless sun was what made it hard to discern the rise and fall of each approaching slope and declivity. They had little more to go on at times than the length and lay of their own shadows cast across the snowscape.

And so the two of them grew hotter, and their packs grew heavier, stuffed as they were with castoff parkas and sweaters and mittens, and Grace's nausea seemed to increase with every wayward slip and step. By midday they were still much closer to the North Queen behind them than to the Silver Spire ahead. They collapsed on a fragile crest for lunch, sunburned and deeply discouraged.

"Are you sure you're going the best way?" Grace said. Her voice was tinged with accusation.

William pointed to the spire in reply. "We're going the right direction," he said. "I know that much."

They looked at the Silver Spire together, regretting the distance it firmly kept but not at all anxious to get there either. It glinted in the noontime sun, packed and sheathed with snow and ice.

"You bring a rope, William?"

He touched the bottom of his pack and nodded. "Creepers too. And ice daggers, since you don't have an ax."

She imagined dangling somewhere on that icy face while fending off her morning sickness. "I suppose we'll do just fine then," she meekly said.

William turned his gaze to the west. "Look," he muttered. "Fog coming—the whole horizon."

Grace did not yet glance at this fog for the simple reason that something on the Silver Spire had caught her eye. She saw four black specks, no bigger than flies from this distance, arise from the top and circle the summit in the air. She tugged at William and pointed them out. "Harpies?" she whispered.

"Not rosy finches, that's for sure."

Even as they watched, the specks stopped circling the spire and turned towards them, swooping down the forested flanks at the base of the tower and out over the lava field.

"Down here," said William. He had already slid off the narrow crest on which they sat and squeezed himself down into a hollow. When Grace joined him, he was unstrapping the ice ax from the back of his pack. She felt the gopher stir in her pocket. If only they could tunnel under the snow too. Then she saw that William was doing just that, furrowing the bank with his adze to make the beginnings of a hideaway.

"You can help," he said. "Clear it away as I dig."

She got on her knees and scraped the snow away from behind him in armfuls. The work went fast. Soon they had made a cave for two and crouched inside atop their packs. Their skis and poles lay buried outside.

Grace was wet from scooping the snow and began to shiver in the shade. This was the truly annoying thing about the mountains, she remembered. One moment you are dying to shed everything, and the next you are needing all the clothes you have and more. She was just deciding to slip off of her pack for a moment to retrieve her parka when she heard the bray and screech of the Harpies, high above.

They both froze. The sound got louder, then fainter, then louder again. The

Harpies seemed to be slowly circling overhead, trying to locate their human prey. Grace quietly held on to her gopher, as if doing so would stave off harm. For a while the bray of the Harpies ceased. She dared to hope they had gone away. But just as she thought it was safe to move, the braying returned, this time with the loathsome smell.

And so it went through the afternoon, the Harpies approaching and then retreating in waves and tides of stench and sound. Grace did manage to get into her warm clothes, so when the fog finally came she was ready for it. The air outside became suddenly luminous, thick with light. They could still hear the Harpies; the Harpies, however, would not be able to see them.

William was first to step outside. "Total whiteout," he whispered happily, and started to unbury their skis.

Grace crept out and cautiously clambered up to their crest. In every direction—before and behind, left and right, up and down—her eyes met with an opaque radiance, not gray as fog can be in a forest but blinding white. Two things she was immediately sure of: first, it would be harder than ever to estimate the surprising contours of their path; second, it would be harder still to maintain a direction of travel steadily aimed at the Silver Spire. She was fairly sure that Chambers had not left them a compass. Yet they would have to go on. To wait for the fog to clear would be to invite another visit from the Harpies. She heard their cries but they were far off now. For the moment she did not fear them.

William brought up her skis and pack in a bustle of efficiency.

"What now?" she said. "Will we have any idea where we are going?"

He looked about and his face fell. They could not even tell the position of the sun, let alone the Silver Spire. "Just look for moss on the north side of the trees, I guess."

She laughed sourly, punching her skis through an overhang of snow on their crest. They watched clumps and snowclods slide into a hollow below.

"Actually," he said, "there may be something to that. You see this cornice you just knocked off? It points northeast. That's because most of the storms in the Three Queens blow out of the southwest. If we watch the cornices, and go just a little left of their lead, we'll be headed due north for Media's Tower."

In spite of herself, Grace was filled with admiration. "You must be pretty proud of yourself to have thought of that." The way she said it, she wasn't sure it had come out as a taunt or as a compliment.

So they set off into the thick fog, the ups and downs all the more unpredictable, the occasional cornice lending them guidance. By evening, however, the ups and downs had just about done them in. The radiance had turned cool and gray, and they both knew, in their dregs of exhaustion, it was not likely they would cross the lava by nightfall.

Grace was about to turn aside to relieve the queasiness in her stomach when she saw something moving beside her. Or some things, rather, for it looked as if a covey of snowballs were slowly rolling away from her feet. She had seen and heard shapes and voices for hours, of course. Her eye and ear did more to create than to perceive their world in the fog. For a while she had imagined that Lance was skiing behind her, mocking her each time she fell. "What are you doing here?" he would whisper. Lady Demaris had beckoned calmly from just ahead, and from time to time Garth had appeared alongside of her, his white hair blending into the mist. He spoke just once: "It's not that difficult, you know." He said this by way of reassurance, from some perspective above the fog and beyond her heavy skis and pack.

So she supposed that these white things at her feet were just as imaginary as the rest. She waded into them carelessly, the way you would step among chickens in a barnyard. But to her surprise, rather like chickens these snowballs scattered, clucking softly. She dropped to one knee. Surrounding her were a flock or family of plump white birds, perfectly blended with the snow except for short black claws, stubby black beaks, and glossy black eyes now trained upon her. When she reached out to touch them they shuttled backwards on fat feathered legs—legs that looked for all the world like absurdly formal pairs of spats. But the birds did not fly away.

William appeared over her shoulder. "Ptarmigan," he softly said. "We must be getting close to the edge."

"Charming," said Grace, and she meant it. She liked the way they milled about amicably, willing to share their company. When she really listened, they sounded more like doves than chickens. There was something soothing and comical about them.

Suddenly the ptarmigan formed themselves in a line and wobbled off into the fog. The cooings and cluckings began to fade.

"Chances are," William said, "they know the best way ashore. I say we follow them."

"Gladly," said Grace.

So follow the ptarmigan they did, marching on skis at the tail end of the feathered procession. Before long they realized they were no longer skiing up and down the many tiresome humps and hollows, but traversing a narrow corridor that trenched its way clean and true through the snowcovered jumble. Darkness fell and still they traveled, striding easily down their hallway and sometimes even riding slowly on long gentle inclines. Grace had the feeling of coasting on a horsedrawn sleigh.

Eventually it occurred to William what they were in. "This must be an old lava tube," he told Grace, "where the magma flowed underground. Caved in. A subway without a roof."

The fog brightened with the rising of the moon. They could see their breath as they followed the sound and shape of the ptarmigan, coursing onward as if in a dream. Grace's stomach had quieted, and though very tired she felt now she could go on indefinitely. There was a certain strong pleasure to it: they thought they had found a way that would last. So it came as something of a surprise when the walls of their corridor melted away and the ptarmigan utterly disappeared from sight and sound.

"Did they fly off?" Grace asked.

"Not likely," said William. "They hardly ever take to their wings."

He searched about in the barely lit gloom. "Here," he said. "They've all disappeared in this hole."

Grace stepped over to look. As she did so, her face struck a muffled branch that unloaded a pile of snow onto her shoulders. "I think we made it," she weakly said. "I just ran into a tree."

William took out a lantern and lit it. By its circle of light they examined the skirts of the snowclad tree—a grand fir, William said—and found a spot to tunnel into it just as they had done with Chambers at lunchtime the day before. They found the ptarmigan quietly nestled together inside.

"Sorry," said Grace, "but you've got company for the night."

William hung the lantern on a branch and they flattened a spot on which to rest. After supper, as they crawled inside the cold embrace of their waiting blankets, Grace looked about the tree with a weary sort of satisfaction. The ptarmigan cooed softly behind her, and the lantern threw its spotted light across limbs and lichen and snowsnug walls that returned a calm glow of their own.

William rose to extinguish the light. Just before he did so, her gaze meandered to the trunk of the tree. *I hope it's not me again*, she told herself. And it wasn't.

But there *was* a face. In the instant before the light went out, she caught a glimpse of a young man, lips pursed in thought. He was pensive, alert—and alarmingly, he looked very much like Grace herself, as if he were a fraternal twin. His wooden eyes seemed to look deep into her own, as if searching for something that even she could not yet see.

Chapter 8
Not So Bad

✳

GRACE AWOKE IN A SOFT GRAY LIGHT and missed the sounds of clucking and cooing that had lulled her to sleep. The ptarmigan were gone. William too had broken out of his blankets beside her and disappeared. She was left in a slow cool silence to contemplate her aching limbs and morning sickness. She had slept with her boots tucked next to her hips in hopes of keeping them supple and thawed. She felt for them now—the leather was cold but still unfrozen. As she pushed her battered feet inside, her eyes fell on the trunk of the tree, blistered and runneled with sap and ice. The face was gone, as surely as the ptarmigan. She wondered if it had merely been a sly trick of lantern light, a longing in her heart for a twin.

Outside the entrance to their tree the fog hung still and deep. Grace found William crouched in a pit, blowing on a stack of twigs. Presently they erupted in flame, and he added sticks from a ready pile. She slid down next to him and saw that he had built a platform of hefty branches on which to keep the fire from sinking into the snow.

"Ingenious," she said. "We'll have to keep you on as our Sherpa—at least for another day or two." She stretched out her frozen fingers and felt the warmth come into them. It spread down into her bones like summer stirring in her side.

"With the fog," said William, "I thought we could afford to." He looked up warily.

Grace followed his gaze. "You really think we should climb into the claws of those Harpies? I feel like they're just waiting for us up there."

"If the fog holds, we ought to make it safely enough. As for what we find when we get there—well, we still have the ax," he said.

"And the knife," she added, none too hopefully. "I suppose Matheu wouldn't mind if we used it—a little."

William heaped a pot full of snow and set it on the edge of the fire. Soon they would have hot tea.

"But which way is the tower?" asked Grace. "We've no ptarmigan to take us there, even if they wanted to go."

"We just go uphill," said William. "All ways lead to the tower from here. I think Chambers packed some skins for us. We should be all right."

Grace wondered why people used the words *all right* when what they meant was something just short of *all wrong*. Which was how she felt about climbing the spire.

A little tea, a little bread, improved her spirits, and as it turned out, Chambers had indeed packed the skins to give their skis purchase on the approach to the spire. Grace was not ten steps out of camp before she wished she had worn them the day before in the lava field. "They would have saved us so much slipping and sidestepping," she said to the gopher curled in her pocket. "Why didn't he tell me we had these?"

As William was several paces ahead and conveniently out of earshot, she found him easy to blame. Particularly as the slope got steeper. They switchbacked up through well-spaced trees and ghostly snags, William striding manfully, Grace stutter-stepping to keep up, her breath ragged, her gorge periodically rising. She remembered what it was like to climb a glacier on a rope behind him, trying to match her steps with his. But there was no rope between them now, and she felt he was always just about to disappear up into the fog and leave her permanently behind. She was tied to him by her own umbilical cord of fear.

After a time they left the trees and snags behind. The mists brightened and the slope became unbearably steep, even with the help of the skins. Grace felt herself digging in the tips of her poles and leaning hard on them for balance. Sometimes, one ski or the other would scratch and slip on a layer of ice beneath the surface.

Just when Grace was about to demand they break out the rope, William stopped and touched his pole to a wall of ice. With his skis he stomped a platform for Grace, then took them off and dug them deep, heels first, into the slope. She joined him there and felt the ice through the palm of her mitten. It was not clear and smooth as she had expected, but mottled and draperied in white, more like a freezer badly in need of being defrosted than the translucence of cubes in a tray. Still, it was slick and steep and cold. She wondered how they would ever get up it, even with creepers and ice tools.

She let William strap the creepers to her boots, feeling a little like a child. "Sorry," she said when he had finished, "but do you have anything in a size 6, double E?"

By way of answer he placed a pair of short sharp daggers in her hands. "Set them lightly," he simply said. "They don't need to go in as far as you think. The same goes for your front points."

She looked down. Two fangs of iron angled out beneath her toes on each foot. Already the cold of the creepers was burning through the soles of her boots. As William knotted the end of a very old, very frayed rope about her waist, a breeze kicked up and moaned across the icy face.

"All right," he said, shouldering his pack and hefting the ice ax in his hands. "Like this." He swung the ice ax high and deftly overhead. When the pick found purchase, sending a tinkling of ice on them both, he gingerly kicked the front points of one boot and then the other into the ice. Grace saw him suspended above her in the fog, risen as if by levitation. He seemed hardly attached to the ice at all.

"Not so bad, eh? Just hold your feet steady. Don't drop your heels too far or you'll slide out." He looked down at her sharply to make sure she understood.

Grace merely nodded.

"Wait till the rope's paid out. Then I'll find a stance and bring you up."

"What if you fall?"

"I won't," he said. "It only looks vertical."

Then with one hand swinging the ax, the other carefully pawing the ice, he stepped up into the fog and was gone. Grace watched the rope uncoil and rise behind him, a silent snake dance, she the charmer. She heard the muffled chink of the ax, the crunch of the creepers, followed by rattling shards of ice that stung her cheeks and bit down into the snow.

When all of the rope had followed after she felt it tugging at her waist. "That's me!" she cried.

There was a moment's pause. Then she heard his voice, small and distant. "Come on up!"

She poked at the face experimentally with her daggers and found they refused to penetrate far. Nevertheless she plunged them high over her head and kicked her front points into the ice. She stood there, trembling, inches off the snowy platform, and felt a strange new ache in her calves and forearms, not to mention the familiar one in her shoulders. The weight of her pack was pulling her backwards into space.

"Relax!" called William. She looked and saw that the rope was trembling from her waist.

She took another step, and another, and then plunged her daggers higher, this time finding easier entry. She began to loosen her grip on the handles, let her feet rest on the front points. William was right: it was not so bad. By the time she reached him she had found a rhythm of ascent that reminded her of skiing through the falling snow.

William was perched on a tiny ledge he had chopped out on top of a bulge. The pick of the ax was angled deep in the ice above him, and the rope was looped over the adze to arrest any slip she might make.

"Stand still," he said, showing her where to place her feet. "I'm off again."

True to his word he wrenched his ax out of the wall and disappeared once more in the fog, leaving her on the tiny ledge beside the neatly coiled rope. At least she was warm from all the exertion of getting here. She looked down and saw nothing at all to make her dizzy or to help her chart their upward progress. She felt the illusion of not having left the bottom of the spire, of not being able to fall. *The beauty of fog,* Grace reflected, *is what it doesn't let you see.*

Soon the rope was gone again, and Grace with it, scrambling up an easier pitch of lower angle and softer surface. At the end of it she found that William had sunk the ice ax in by its shaft, looping the rope just under the head to belay her up.

A steeper pitch followed, on which Grace required a certain amount of tension on the rope. Then several moderate ones, more like their first. Then an easy part, and a nasty bulge on which William showed her how to belay him, leaving his ice ax for that purpose and borrowing her pair of daggers. Eventually she lost count of the little ledges she had stood on, watching the rope sift out of sight and feeling the sting of ice flecks ricocheting off nose and lips. And still the fog lay wrapped around them.

In the afternoon, after a quickly nibbled lunch, the mists began to thin and brighten. William thought they might be starting to climb out the top of the cloud. "We'd best hurry," he said. "We don't want to be caught in the open. The ice is softening—have you noticed? I think we can both climb at once, without a belay. Just call if you need help."

Grace shrugged. It was still easy to believe she could not fall. She waited for him to lead out; when the rope was once again stretched between them, she followed after without pausing. And followed. And followed. Instead of their ritual of start and stop, Grace pursued him continuously, moving upwards with a poise by now measured and practiced.

The fog became even brighter, and began to shred apart in pieces. Just as she reached the relative safety of a ramp, a huge hole opened in the mists beneath her. She froze for a moment. There were snags and trees and a thin wandering line of tracks on the snowslope far below—so far below that it seemed a wholly separate world, divided and distinguished by a firmament of sheer ascent. Before she could fully adjust her perspective the mists beneath her closed again, and she felt a sharp tug on the rope that reminded her to continue climbing. The capricious clouds opened above her, and she caught a glimpse of William plodding duly up the end of the ramp like a tortured soul ascending the Mount of Purgatory. Above him she saw steeper ice, a fluted crest, and brilliant patches of blue sky. Then this picture too was erased.

She caught up to him at the top of the ramp, standing in a natural pulpit next to an almost window-like sheet of ice that was very nearly vertical. A detached column, thick as a sapling, stood guarding the ice sheet.

"We belay this," William said. He was looking upward. The fluted crest that Grace had seen was just above them, flitting in and out of the fog.

"Is that the top?"

"Close to it, anyway." He squeezed behind the pillar of ice, pressing against the window sheet, to create for himself a natural belay.

He looked up at the pitch again, a luxury they had seldom had. "I see bulges below the crest. Mind if I borrow one of your daggers? From the top I can pretty much pull you up."

For a moment Grace resented the thought of being hauled up like a sack of supplies. But it occurred to her that William was just being practical. She gave him the dagger, and he headed up.

As William climbed, and she watched the rope curl round the pillar, a wonderful thing began to happen: the fog simply melted away. She found herself in glorious sunshine of late afternoon, the light pouring over a solid layer of clouds at her feet, a golden mass that reached whole and entire to the distant summits of all Three Queens. Her struggles and suffering lay underneath; it was as if she had graduated to Paradise. The view was so sudden, so wideflung, that after a day and part of another in the fog it had the force of revelation. She knew she should feel afraid of the Harpies, but Grace had a feeling instead of wild surmise—of seeing, of knowing, an entire continent of the spirit.

It was an act of discipline to turn her eyes upward again to check on William's progress. He was just under the crest now, struggling a bit with the bulge he had seen from below. She gripped the rope about her waist in the way that he had quickly taught her, glad for the added strength of the pillar. She studied its smooth and shapely extent, and the gleaming surface of the tall sheet of ice behind it. In the full strength of the sunlight she could almost see her reflection. In fact, she could. There was her face, there were her eyes, gazing back at her from the ice. She saw a look of alert concern, of worry even, of tiredness after a long day. And also a hint of eagerness, of frightened curiosity. The hair was of the proper length, falling down just to her shoulders, and well brushed too, the way she liked it.

This gave her pause.

With her free hand, she felt her hair, knotted and tucked under her cap. "The person I see," she very slowly said to herself, "is not the person that I am." She waved at her erstwhile reflection. After hesitating, it waved back, wide-eyed, wondering.

"Watch me," called William.

No, thought Grace. Watch *me*. The person in the ice kept looking.

She heard a scraping overhead, a cry of surprise. Suddenly William was hurtling past her, a blur of wool and flesh and iron. *This too cannot be happening,* she quickly thought. The rope from her waist went cruelly taut about the pillar and slammed her against the window of ice. There was a crash, a splintering, as of crystal, and suddenly she was released inwards, falling into the other side of the looking glass. Grace landed abruptly.

When she opened her eyes, she was lying on the floor of a small stone chamber, clutching a severed rope at her waist. Bending over her with a quiet look of fear and concern was a young woman in a white robe whom Grace could only recognize as her perfect self.

Chapter 9
Millican

✳

THE STRANGE BUT FAMILIAR YOUNG WOMAN was first to break the silence. "All of my days," she whispered, "I have seen neither girl nor woman my own age. And now to see one so like me as to be myself. It is altogether too wonderful."

Grace did not say anything. She took in the sparsely furnished chamber, the face above her, the rope in her hand. She gripped it still as if William were dangling on the end. But the rope was cut. The fact numbed her.

"Are you well?" asked the woman. "Are you hurt in any way? How foolish of me to dwell on my own astonishment when you may be dwelling in pain."

Grace looked from her to the rope again, still speechless, then turned her gaze to the window of ice. What she saw made her start to her feet, skating across the stone floor with her iron creepers. "It's not broken!" she cried aloud. "I broke through—just now I did, you must have seen me—but it's still there!"

"Of course it is," the woman said sadly. "No one has ever broken this window before, and you could not expect it to stay broken for very long. I am surprised you got in at all. Though now that you're here," she quickly added, "I am very glad you've come."

Grace crossed to the window and pounded on it with the heel of her mitten. It didn't even shake. The ice might as well have been granite, just like the walls of the room.

"I'm afraid it's no use," the young woman told her. "You're inside now. But I do want to help. You look so—troubled."

"I have a friend," Grace shrugged. "Or had one, anyway. We were climbing the side of the spire. He fell." She held up the end of the rope, and her eyes welled with tears at the sudden strangeness of separation.

"You have a friend," the woman said, and shyly touched Grace's hand. "Millican is my name as I know it. Since we are so much alike, and since you come by such miracle, I shall be closer than a sister. I am sure of it. When I saw you through the pane of ice, my heart stirred like a child within me."

Grace looked at Millican through her tears and saw a tremor in her kindness, a habit of fear inbred by hard use. Yet she also saw a fierce determination to love. She gave in to the sorrow she felt, the comfort she saw, and grasped both of Millican's hands. And wept. And wept.

Finally she said, "My name is Grace. I can't say why but I'm glad you're here—that we are here."

Millican nodded graciously and led her to a stone-carved bench where they sat together. Grace bent over to unstrap her creepers, and Millican was soon down on her knees to help.

"There, thank you," Grace said. "But tell me, please, who you are—and what you do here? I'm feeling so—confused, I guess."

She was also feeling sick again, and rather tired, now that the shock of William's fall and her strange entrance into the room had just begun to wear off. But she was not cold, though everything in the chamber was stone. What color of stone she could not say, for everything in the room was suffused with a golden light that came from the window of ice. Then, even as she watched, the ice began to swirl green and violet and deepest blue, shifting like a kaleidoscope in sequent patterns. The colors played across the room like reflections of sunlight from a pond upon branches of trees overhead. It made her a little ill to watch, but it also drew her fascination.

She had been gazing at the window for several minutes when she realized Millican was speaking to her, replying to a question she might have asked.

"Oh, it's got you, hasn't it? It often catches me, too. But now I have something—someone—more warm and real to look upon. Try to turn away, Grace. Hold my hands and look at me. You asked for my story. I want to share it."

This simple duty was surprisingly difficult. Grace turned from the colored window, but she kept on wanting to look back. A pattern, a color, might go by that she would miss. She felt greedy to see them all.

But Millican's eyes held a sweet imploring all their own, and gradually Grace found solace there, and was able to anchor her dazed attention in what Millican called the warm and real. Added to this was a cup of something cool but sweet that Millican gently placed in her hands. Though colors flashed in the window of ice like a neon version of the northern lights, Grace was ready to hear her story.

"I have lived here in the Tower of Light all my days," she began. "Not alone, but with my mother, who by her powers hollowed our home from solid rock."

"Your mother?"

"Yes. Archimaga, Duessa, Media—she goes by many names, just as all of our windows of ice go by many colors. As for what I do here, I have long begun to wonder myself. As my mother is a sorceress, there are no household tasks to speak of. Meals appear from her magic caldron, drink is provided at any time at my silent request—just as I have asked one for you. The tower stays warm of itself—or just this side of cool, anyway—without aid of any fire. And no dust falls—there is nothing to clean—since we are sealed completely off from the outside. I know these things—about dusting and burning and preparation of food and drink—because my mother speaks of them often. In order, I suppose, to instill within me gratitude for her provision.

"But as you see, I am so well provided for that I often wonder what difference there is between my live flesh and this stone bench we rest upon. I have chosen this room in the tower because the window looks south. When the sun is strong the colors in the window clear and sometimes I can see through to a different world, the one I think you have come from. I long for it sometimes. Before you entered I saw across a floor of cloud to the breasts of three distant mountains—I think of them as part of a place of true belonging. Other days, when the cloud is gone, I see far down to the bottom of the tower, where rows of men—I think they are men—wave their hands and hair in a dance. But for much of the year they are white and still."

Grace looked perplexed, then almost laughed aloud. "They are trees," she said. "Their tops and branches blow in the wind. In winter they are covered with snow. Just this morning I slept in one."

"How very wonderful," Millican said. "But tell me, what are trees? And wind? Clouds and mountains I know from my mother. Not that she meant for me to know—but in spite of her care, she sometimes slips."

"A tree," said Grace, embarking on earnest explanation—"a tree is a living thing."

"As we are?" Millican asked.

"Almost," said Grace. "But it always stays in the same place."

"Like me, then," Millican said.

"Yes, but it reaches high up into the sky, with many arms, and they sway there in the moving air. That is the wind. That is their compensation for remaining in the same place."

"This wind," said Millican, "what does it feel like?"

Grace thought a minute, then gently blew into her ear. "It is like that," she said. "But wilder, and stronger. It is the sky breathing."

Millican's eyes shone with pleasure. "To be in the wind," she whispered fervently. "That must be life itself." Her eyes drifted to the flashing shapes and colors in the window, not held by them but held by a longing to see and feel far beyond them.

"Do you love your mother?" Grace asked suddenly.

Millican looked back from the window and pursed her lips in a long silence. "I have as yet obeyed my mother, and lived uncomplaining in her presence. But *love* her? That is a word I hardly know, like *trees* and *wind*. Certainly my heart is not moved in her presence the way it has already stirred in yours."

"And your father?"

"I have none that I know of. There is nothing I ask my mother more often. But the more I ask, the colder she becomes, and bids me rest my thoughts in the windows and think myself fathered by them. And in a way I have done so. I saw no men that were not trees until four nights past. The ice had cleared in a dazzling moon. I was looking into the silver light when one of my mother's Birds of Paradise—"

"Birds of Paradise?"

"That is what she has taught me to call them, though once I heard her name them Harpies. One of them suddenly flew across the face of the moon on his way to the tower. A young man, I am sure of it, hung nearly dead in its talons. I pestered my mother with questions about him the next day. She answered me nothing, suggested even that I had imagined what I saw. But I know I did not. In the light of the moon I caught a glimpse of the young man's face. Like yours, Grace, it seemed almost my own. In the outside, is every countenance thus alike? Or is it that we are brother, sister, or cousin perhaps? I know these terms not from my mother's lips but from certain books I have taught myself to read in her study in times when she has left with her Birds of Paradise. In all other parts of the tower books are forbidden; only the windows are to be looked upon. But what think you, Grace? Do you know the young man I saw in the window? Do you know who you yourself might be?"

This last question caught Grace by surprise. She felt for the gopher deep in her pocket as if for her identity and without thinking brought him out for Millican to see. Even as she did so the ground of her stomach crumbled again in queasiness.

Millican stroked the creature timidly, then looked up. "Is this some part of you as well?"

Grace nodded yes, then no, then shrugged her shoulders and doubled over with nausea.

"Grace, are you ill?"

"I suppose I must be," she quietly admitted.

"Is it food, or drink, or rest that you need?"

"No, it's just my—pocket gopher." She nodded at him in her palm.

"By all means, put him back then," Millican insisted. She folded Grace's fingers around it and pushed her hand back towards her pocket.

"Thank you," said Grace. In spite of her illness, she wanted to say the things she knew. "Millican, whether we be sisters I doubt. Cousins perhaps. But as for the young man you saw, I now think him your twin brother. His name is Matheu; I believe he is in grave danger. That, in fact, is why I have come." It sounded all so dramatic to speak this way. She wished she were not on the verge of throwing up.

Millican stood up, agitated. "I do not know how to feel—happy for a brother or sorry for his danger; glad for your presence, Grace, or in mourning for your friend. And—oh, you are ill again, I can tell. How foolish of me to keep you talking when what you need is to lie down. Here, please, hold my arm."

She took Grace to a stone bed in a shadowy corner and sat her down on the edge of it. The window at the end of the room flashed no new colors. It had settled into a dull gold, purpling with the evening light. In the silence of this glow, Millican slipped off Grace's cap and, sitting beside her, began to brush her matted hair, working out the knots and tangles one by one. In a matter of minutes, Grace's hair fell just as neatly to her shoulders as Millican's own.

Then Millican rose to her feet again. "Sweet cousin," she said, "rest here for the night. I cannot sleep while this weight of news lies heavy upon me. Take my bed, and I shall betake myself to search the tower for my brother. Matheu, you say. A Matheu to go with Millican. Pray the gods he may be alive."

"Yes, let's," Grace said weakly.

Millican kissed her on the forehead and quickly moved to a stone door. Here she paused. "I had almost forgot," she quietly said. "My mother will soon be here to bid me goodnight. It is out of affection, she says, but I think it is to keep me in place. How can it be that she will find you in my stead?"

Grace had already fallen back on what she saw were very clean sheets. She felt as tired as she did sick. But the thought of meeting Media—or Medea even— all by herself in this room brought her bolt upright again. "We must exchange clothes then," she nervously said.

Millican, in her long white robe, contemplated the idea. "Of course," she whispered, sweeping back to the bedside. "We look so much alike that in the dim light of evening not even our mothers could tell us apart."

And so it was done, over Grace's half-hearted protests that her wool things had been sweated and slept in for four days running and were likely to be terribly foul. She was getting the much better end of the bargain, slipping on Millican's cool white garment that would do quite well for a nightgown. When they were finished with the exchange, Grace had the oddest sensation of looking at herself in a full-length mirror. For there stood Millican in boots and knickers and sweater and cap, for all the world the very person who had crashed through the window that afternoon. And evidently for Millican the feeling was very much the same.

"You are none other than myself," she said. "The gown fits?"

"Perfectly," said Grace. "And my clothes?"

"A match," said Millican, stretching her arms and taking a few experimental strides. "This must be how it feels to walk about on the outside. I shall pretend I am beyond the window."

She picked up the ice dagger, loose on the floor beside the cast-off creepers. "Shall I need this?"

Grace thought a minute, leaning back on Millican's pillow. "No, put it in my pack, with the creepers. Or, just bring it all over here."

She did so without too much trouble. Grace pawed through the pack, stifling a wave of queasiness, and pulled from the bottom the finely curved knife she had taken from beneath the hearth in the Belknap Hut. She unsheathed it and held it up in the deepening twilight. The edge was sharp.

"This was your brother's," Grace whispered. "I hoped to bring it to him myself. Perhaps you can. And perhaps it can help to release him."

Millican received it with reverence and slipped it into its ornate sheath. Then she tucked it into her pocket, only to find an impediment. "Your gopher!" she said, fishing it out for her.

Grace smiled and laid him under the covers. Millican turned to stow the pack out of sight in an alcove across the room. While she did so, Grace slid the ice dagger under her pillow. Somehow, she did not want Millican to see.

"Now, quickly, for soon she comes," Millican said. "When my mother arrives, with a circle of ice shining in the palm of her hand, she will first ask what you have seen in the window today. You must answer, 'I have seen the most beautiful colors, Mother, in the finest patterns.' 'You are at peace, then, my daughter?' she will say. And you must answer, 'Yes, Mother, I am at peace.' 'It is well,' she will say. 'Goodnight, my daughter.' 'It is well,' you must reply. 'Goodnight, Mother.' Then she will tuck the covers about your shoulders and kiss you on the forehead and leave. All you must do is lie silent, and she will not return until morning. Can you remember and perform all of this?"

Grace nodded.

"Your safety and mine depend upon it. Never before have I ventured into the tower at night while my mother is present. Good night, my cousin. We shall speak much more hereafter, as our leisure and health permit."

She tucked her in, just as she said her mother would. "Is it well with you?" she whispered.

"It is well," Grace found herself saying. She closed her eyes and received a sisterly kiss on the lips. Then she heard the door open and shut, and Millican was gone.

Chapter 10
They're Waiting for Us

❋

WHEN WILLIAM CAME TO CONSCIOUSNESS he was dangling on the icy face, his feet drifting inches above a wide and snowy ledge. He could not say how long he had hung there. The rope stretched taut from his waist up over a lip of ice and out of sight; the ax and dagger were stuck fast in the ledge beneath him. His mittens were gone, and dried blood covered his hands. And his nose and chin felt thoroughly battered. He lifted his fingers to his face and thought he touched a wreckage of flesh. But he could move his arm without too much pain. He tried the other—sore, but workable. His legs, however, were a different story. Try as he might, he could not lift them. Yet they did not hurt; it was as if they had fallen asleep. And judging by the tightness of the rope about his waist, perhaps they had.

His memory of falling was slight. He had been about to place the pick of the ax over a bulge when the ice dagger had popped free. It would have been the last move of any real difficulty before reaching the summit crest. He remembered thinking he had made it, and for all the uncertainty of what awaited them on the top had begun to feel the pride of a successful ascent. But suddenly the top of the bulge disappeared as he slipped off. There was nothing for his ax to bite. He had felt cruelly cheated. And his long fall, so dramatic to watch no doubt, had only felt like a slightly elongated moment of surprise. He did not recall losing his mittens or hitting his face, or even reaching the end of the rope.

Now, checking himself for injury and swaying slightly against the ice, he wondered if Grace were still holding him on belay. With the help of the pillar she probably was. Otherwise, how could he still be hanging here on the mountainside?

He leaned back as far as he could without the help of his useless legs and peered upwards. He could not see past the lip of ice that was forty feet up. "Grace!" he called. His voice came out like the broken bleating of a sheep. He cleared his throat and tried again. "*Grace!*" That was better.

Still, his words fell dead in the air, trapped he was sure in the space beneath the overhang. For the first time he noticed that the sun was out, shining across a field of cloud in evening strength, not far above the horizon. His bloodcaked hands glowed an eerie orange, as if on fire, but even in their deep hurt he could feel they were getting desperately cold.

Out of habit, William did what he usually did when unable to make contact with his belayer: he tugged gently on the rope. To his wounded fingers this did not feel gentle, and he grimaced in pain. He received no answering tug on his waist, however slight, and after weighing his options decided to risk a harder pull. He knew it would hurt; it took a good while to place his fingers high on the rope and prepare himself for another jolt. He downcounted, took a deep breath, and jerked hard. Suddenly he was sitting in the snow by his ax with coils of rope looping down upon him like rain. The end fell across his knees. It was sliced and frayed.

What this meant began to seep dully into him like the cold. Possibly Grace had tied the rope about the pillar and cut herself free. More likely, the rope had been severed in the shock of his fall, Grace had tumbled from her perch, and by merest chance the end of his rope had wrapped itself around some projection and withstood his fall, though not his subsequent tugging and pulling. The more he considered this possibility the truer it became in his mind. Unrestrained by a rope from above, Grace would have fallen far past the ledge that held him, perhaps all the way to the bottom of the spire. He dragged himself to the edge and looked down. The ice wall plunged to the placid layer of cloud and vanished. There was no telling what might have fallen through. He stared at the clouds and felt disconsolate and ashamed.

What he did find here were his mittens, perched half-torn on the edge. They were frozen stiff. He made himself put them on, even though the hard wool ate at his hands. His eyes watered. Without realizing it, however, he had raised himself up on his knees. He decided to try standing, and clutched at the shaft of his ax for support. To his great relief he was able to wobble to his feet. Both legs were unbroken. He knew a man who had shattered his shins on the top of a peak in the Karakoram. It had taken a week to crawl to safety in a terrible blizzard. William smiled bitterly. At least he could walk.

But where, exactly?

He gripped the head of his ice ax in an agony only scarcely less than what Villard must have felt in his hand on the Last Mountain. The ice dagger he merely dropped handle first into his pocket. To stow it in his pack would take the suffering of unimaginable dexterity, as would loosening the knot at his waist. He took a few halting steps to what looked like the dead end of the ledge on the east. But once there he found it merely turned a corner and began to ramp gently upwards.

So he shuffled onward, trailing the damaged rope behind, not knowing quite what to hope for. His creepers had been knocked rather loose on his feet, but they would have to do—there was no question of trying to restrap them. As the ramp continued to curve upward, onto the eastern side of the spire, he soon reached a line of shade that separated him from the sun. He was cold already, but entering this shadow was like stepping onto the moon's dark side. He had long noticed that high places, underneath their sublimity, can have an alien feeling about them. They are places where people do not belong. This feeling increases as night approaches; he had never felt so alien on a mountain as now.

In spite of this feeling, this aching hollowness inside that made a cruel complement to his lacerated and aching flesh, William kept plodding upwards. Several times it seemed the ledge was about to give out—but it always continued around each corner. Often it narrowed, and he set the ax in the wall for balance. But it never narrowed too far. Presently the corners and bends came sharper and sooner than before, and William realized he was getting close to the top of the spire. Then, anticlimactically, the ledge simply ended on a flat terrace. He was back in the sun, and the sky was golden all about him. The top of the tower was the shape and size of a small pond. On the far side was a gentle mound with what looked like a door in the side of it. Or a window, rather, glazed with ice.

As a matter of habit, a way of arriving, he walked to the center of the tiny plain and plunged in his ice ax. Never had he felt less like a conqueror. *Now what?* he thought to himself. The sun had touched the bank of clouds and would soon be gone. Leaving his ax upright in the summit, he advanced to inspect the window of ice. It was rather similar, though much larger, to the sheet by the pillar at their last, fatal belay. He pressed against it with his shoulder, then rubbed the ice with the sleeve of his forearm. Quite solid it was, and opaque. And yet he had the uncanny feeling it was an entrance of some sort. Those Harpies required some ingress—surely they did not bivouac on the bare summit. Unless they came from somewhere beyond . . . He scanned the firelit northern horizon, tossed with peaks above the cloud. Beyond the spire the mountains multiplied in a maze. So many to climb—if one wanted to.

Thinking of the Harpies again made him feel naked without his ax. Hands aching, he turned back to where he had left it. To his great surprise, there was no ax. In its place was a tree, a green-leafed sapling, and all about it the snow had receded from a small circle of rich green turf. Aside from this miracle of transformation, it was the sheer shock of verdancy that at first astonished his senses. If all you have seen for months on end are the whites and silvers of winter snows, even a single blade of grass is enough to make you die of wonder. He remembered the feeling of descending to meadows at timberline after days or weeks on a glacier. The flowers would awaken his mind from stoic slumber; on the mountain his body was a machine, in the meadows it was living flesh. Now, somehow, spring had invaded the pinnacle of winter's achievement, planting herself in a high barren garden.

He took a step closer and saw that someone was sitting against the far side of the little tree. It was a small person—a child, perhaps—and from what he could tell, not at all dressed for the cold. He caught a glimpse of soft blonde hair and white summer dress, and a short pink arm extended in a gesture of play. Warily he circled about for a better view, treading closer to the edge of the green. When he saw her face he came to a standstill.

"Lara!" he cried. For before him sat the innocence of his own daughter. He collapsed to his knees on the ice and snow at the very edge of the green turf, just out of her reach. But she did not reach for him. Lara sat barefoot and cross-legged against the tree, waving each arm in turn as if imitating a grown-up who has something important to say. She seemed to be talking in just the manner she often did while playing with invisible friends. William had sometimes found her thus in a little grove behind the cabin, speaking in a reverie. It had never been easy to interrupt her.

"Lara," he called out more softly, hoping to ease into her game. But her eyes, though turned in his direction, looked inward without seeing him. He spread out his arms to welcome her, then let them collapse in a mild sort of exasperation so familiar to him from the last four years. For some reason he kept himself back from the grass. It seemed to him holy ground.

"No, no," she lectured someone, wagging her finger. "Papa has to stay. You have to go without him. If you're good, maybe you can visit Papa."

William shuddered. "Yes!" he shouted. "Or no—no! It doesn't matter! Come always—good or bad. Can't you see, Lara? I'm the bad one." He held up his ragged hands again, this time as if in prayer. Each finger was in cold hard agony.

"All right," she said. "Be that way. But no supper for you tonight." Her eyes grew expressively stern. "Not unless you wash your hands, anyway. You know better than to come to the table like that."

At this William began to weep.

"What? Locked yourself out again? Here, give me the key. I know you have been playing with it, even after I told you not to. Someday you must learn how to use it. But hurry, it is getting dark. Let me have it. I'll let us both in." The girl held out her hand toward William impatiently. Still, however, she was not really looking at him, nor at any exterior object.

William did not know what to think. Never in the past two weeks had he so felt his separation from his daughter. Yet there she was, beseeching him for a key.

A key.

He gripped the end of his right mitten between his teeth and tore it away from his wounded hand. The scabs came with the wool, and he screamed. Lara gave no sign of hearing. Fresh blood dripping from frozen fingers, he forced them down into his pocket. Yes, it was there. He made himself grip the shaft, the ornate ring on the end. Twice it slipped out of his grasp, as if it were a live thing seeking a deeper hold in his pocket. But in the end he brought it out, bright with blood, burning in the sunset, and handed it to his waiting daughter. In the moment before he released his hold, a thrill of warmth passed through his entire body.

She held the bleeding key in her palm and gave a wary smile of approval. "It's about time," she said peremptorily. "They're waiting for us."

In that moment the sun sank beneath the clouds, and Lara vanished. Not into darkness, for the spire still burned in an alpenglow. But completely vanished— she and the grass and the leafy sapling. William found himself on his knees, one hand outstretched in the direction of his lonely ice ax, planted where an ice ax should be—in the ice. He looked at that hand, still bare without its mitten, and saw that the flesh was as pink and as whole as his daughter's arm. There was no trace of blood or wound or scar. He flexed his fingers and found no pain, not even a memory of it in the bones. Quickly he bit off his other mitten and found his left hand likewise healed. With both hands he touched his face. It felt whole, neither torn nor bruised.

Without even bothering to put on his mittens he gripped the silver head of the ax and felt it newly warm to his touch, like the live clasp of a human hand. He lifted it easily from its purchase and walked sedately back to the door in the brow of the summit. Somehow he was not surprised to find the ice completely gone.

Chapter 11
Let a Man Sleep

✳

WILLIAM HAD NOT GONE MANY STEPS BEFORE HE REALIZED his creepers were skating and striking sparks on a stone floor. He sat down and unstrapped them, marveling at the strength and suppleness in his fingers. In the half-light he untied the rope from his waist and gathered it in, coiling it in a proper skein. Then he stowed the rope and the creepers inside his pack and took out the lantern. When he lit the candle, speckles of warmth fell upon a widening passage, curving downwards. He remembered the time that he and Grace had spiraled into the bowels of the Center Queen, and wondered if he were about to embark on another long and dark descent. Shouldering his pack and readying himself with lantern in one hand, ax in the other, he took a last look back at the doorway, expecting to get a final glimpse of the twilight open air. But the lantern light reflected off a sheet of ice. Once again the door was closed.

Somehow it hardly mattered. He resolutely set his face for the inner journey and began to stride along the passage. His path ramped downward, always to the left, with a gentle regularity. Soon, however, a familiar smell began to assault him—a stench, rather—the loathsome odor of the Harpies. He held the lantern higher before him and stepped more cautiously, keeping the ice ax balanced and ready in his grip. Soon his boots began to crackle tiny bones and send up plumes of loose white feathers. He stooped to examine them.

Ptarmigan.

So, he thought, *a gourmet diet for these monsters.* He would rather see these odd birds nested in a snowclad tree than massacred on a stone floor. On this scale, death seemed hardly natural—if indeed it ever were.

William rose and resumed his descent. As the stench thickened and the bones and feathers multiplied, he prepared to meet the slaughtering Harpies at every turn. Presently the passageway opened out in a wide cavern, spaciously roofed. He stood at the edge and moved his lantern right and left, unable to see its extent. Rather than walk into invisible danger, he decided to announce his presence.

"I've come!" he shouted, holding his ax and lantern aloft.

"Come, come, come," said the cavern, echoing back.

"You can't hide!" he announced.

"Died, died, died," said the cavern.

Not knowing what else to do, he began to step out into the chamber, turning his eyes this way and that to prevent any surprise encounter. His steps echoed hollowly, like the drip of water in an underground pool. Nothing else broke the silence. But the smell in itself was deafening. And still he walked over bones and feathers of ptarmigan.

When he reached the other side of the cavern, his lantern shone on a small door, made not of ice but of stone. There was no latch or handle or doorknob of any sort, just the smooth oval outline of rock set in rock. He wondered how he might open it. His first impulse was to knock, but he abandoned this as too polite for the circumstances. Better to use force, he thought. Accordingly, he was about to shove against one side with the back of his arm when he saw something heaped in the shadows nearby. It was to his left, just at the edge of the lantern light, slumped against the wall of the cavern.

He moved toward it cautiously, ax at ready. But he soon relaxed his hold on the shaft when he saw that the shape was not *it* but *they*, two old men bent fast asleep, arm in arm and heads together. William shone the light in their faces.

"Chambers," he whispered. For one was he—clothes torn, face scarred, smudged and befouled from head to foot, but assuredly Chambers nonetheless. His bald crown was partially covered by a mat of silvery red hair that hung down from his fellow sleeper. His was a face that William dimly recognized but did not know. Then it came to him.

"Old Villard," he breathed. "Your dearbought ax has returned to you at last."

Villard's clothes, if Villard it was, were so ragged and worn as hardly to be clothes at all. They seemed caked onto his flesh. His feet were bare, and his face was long and gaunt and sad. Even in sleep he projected a stark hopelessness. By the slack hollowness of his cheeks it appeared he had not eaten well in a long time.

"Ptarmigan doesn't agree with you?" William said softly.

The sleeper said nothing.

William leaned down and gripped the shoulders of the two brothers. "Chambers! Villard!" he said in their ears.

No reply.

He shook them gently, and shouted this time. *"Chambers! Villard! Wake up!"*

The cavern echoed, and both sleepers slumped back together, breathing in quiet unison.

William did not know what to make of this. For the moment he decided to let them rest and to return his attention to the door. But before he did so, to salve his conscience at leaving the men defenseless in this den of Harpies, he slipped the ice dagger out of his pocket and placed the hilt in Chambers' hand, wrapping his sleeping fingers around it.

"Keep it well," he whispered. "I hope you have no use for it before I return."

William picked up the lantern again and followed the rock wall to the door. He placed his arm and shoulder against it and once more was about to push when a beating of wings, a terrible cry, broke the silence. A bray, a screech, entered and answered, and the cavern was filled with cacophonous echoes. William trembled, even as the reek of the place redoubled around him. The Harpies were back.

In the lantern light he at first saw nothing. For a brief moment he told himself to get through the door and save his skin. But what of Villard and Chambers behind him? In retrospect, it would be nice to think that William made the deliberate choice of staying to defend his kind. But everything happened much too fast for him to be sure he really had chosen. For suddenly a pair of yellow glowering eyes came sweeping towards him out of the darkness. He just had time to set down his lantern and take firm hold with both hands on the shaft of his ax. Then he saw the blur of wings, the outstretched talons fast approaching.

Once, in the eastern reaches of the mountains, he had come upon an enormous goshawk perched on the limb of a ponderosa. To protect her young it had swooped and dived him repeatedly, sometimes even running its claws through his hair. He had taken up a stout branch, stood his ground, and hopelessly swatted at the bird each time it came. Finally he had sprinted for a thicket, only to be knocked down from behind before he reached it. Then the goshawk had let him be, prone on the ground with a trickle of blood on the back of his head. Now in the cavern he had the advantage of an ax, but little light, and nowhere to run. And he had an idea the Harpies would not be content to knock him down.

With the first swing of the ax he missed. The Harpy wheeled past with a shudder and William felt a tearing and burning along one forearm. It had managed to scratch him with its talons. He did not have time to inspect his wound, for no sooner did the first attacker veer away than a second bore in upon him, eyes glowering, claws outstretched. This time William aimed well. He swung the ax high over his head and felt a thud as the pick swiftly buried itself directly between the yellow eyes. For a moment he felt a great weight balanced on the ax above him; then a mass of scales and claws came raining upon him, knocking him down.

He scrambled up and retrieved his ax just in time. Another Harpy was homing in from directly above, barking like a ravenous dog. He slashed upwards with the ax in a desperate underhanded blow. As if self-guided, the adze broke the belly of the bird as a large knife opens a melon. Entrails came spilling out like a thundershower, and the Harpy met the floor with a shriek.

Two down, and in the midst of this sudden gory business William felt a flush of pride. This was when the third Harpy drove into him hard from behind, just as the goshawk had in the pine forest. The blow this time came square in his back. Only the blankets in his packsack saved him from injury. But his ax went skittering into the dark, and he slid face-first across the floor. When he came to a stop he found he was unable to breathe; the Harpy had knocked the wind out of him. He turned over, practically paralyzed, and saw the Harpy circle back out of the darkness. It came to rest just beside him, as if aware of his sudden incapacity and willing to destroy him now with an air of leisure. William was still gasping for breath as it brought its beak over his chest. Weakly he put up his arms and tried to roll out of the way. But he knew his efforts would be too feeble.

Suddenly the Harpy gave a great scream, not of triumph but of pain. It shuddered over him, then collapsed just at his side. He gained his breath and sat up. Standing behind the body of the beast was the shambling, portly figure of Chambers, a dripping dagger in his hand.

"You'd think they'd let a man sleep around here," he said. He offered his hand and raised William to his feet. "All this shrieking going on. It's enough to wake the dead."

William was about to embrace him in gratitude when Chambers was literally torn from his grasp. It was as if he were shaking hands with a person who was suddenly run down by a train. It occurred to him then that he had seen four Harpies in the lid of the silver register, and that he and Grace had likewise seen four emerge from the tower. In all likelihood, one more was left in the cavern, and had just snatched Chambers away. Quickly he searched about in the circle of light not only for Chambers but also for his wayward ax. He saw it glinting against the door and ran to get it. The ax was no sooner in his hand than he heard a cry from the outer darkness—a human cry of terrible pain. Then, to his horror, the cry changed to a tearing, slathering sound that came from a human throat. He grabbed the lantern and rushed to the sound. In the first reach of candlelight he saw the fourth and final Harpy, standing on a single claw and feeding on the bloody remains of Chambers' chest.

It was too much, too awful a sight for William to bear. Heedless of the consequences, he flung the lantern at the Harpy and hurled himself into the ensuing darkness, letting loose with a terrible yell and flailing the ax in all directions. He saw nothing, but beak and claws and wings and ice ax filled the vision of his body. Somehow he felt the position and presence of his adversary in a way that allowed him to land blow after telling blow. It was as if the ax itself shone in the darkness, cutting into the black rind of the enemy. Then once again, as quickly as it had begun, the fight was over. He found himself panting, ax in hand, in absolute silence.

For a long time he waited for another sound, the beating of wings or the labored suspiration of breath. But he heard only the drumming of his heart in his ears. He took a step in one direction and met the body of the Harpy, still as the stone on which it lay and overwhelming in its stink. Three steps the other way brought him to the form of Chambers. He bent down in the darkness to find his face and touch his neck. There was neither breath nor pulse; the flesh was already starting to cool. William's fingertips came away wet. He did not even consider exploring the open wounds he had seen on the chest.

He would like to have said something, kneeling there by the body of this most hearty man who so recently had saved his life. But words did not come, and he sensed they would only be mocked by their echoes. It was enough to be mute with grief.

As he knelt there, a sudden snore parted the air and gave him his bearings. *That must be Villard*, he thought, *still asleep*. Reluctantly he left the sanguine body of Chambers to molder in darkness and made his way to the younger brother against the wall. With his hands he touched the matted hair, the hollow cheeks.

"Still asleep, old man?" he said. "A brother gone, and you not know it?" He wondered why Chambers had awakened and Villard not. If they slept by some design or charm, might it be that Villard had lain longer and heavier under the spell, and that Chambers had been not yet fully weighted by it?

"If you would wake up now," he muttered, "I could use your help."

But there was no change in Villard's breathing. He might as well have been speaking to a metronome.

William sighed. "So long, then. Until I come back."

Once again he left the man and made his way to the stone door. This time he moved very slowly, feeling the wall at every step until his fingers pressed against the doorway's outline. He considered throwing his weight against it, or even attacking it with the ax. But sick of violence, he simply knocked.

In the last hours he had encountered many surprises. But now came perhaps the greatest. Sweetly and slowly, the stone door opened inwards, and standing behind it, holding a glow of light in her hand, was a comely young woman dressed to climb a mountain in winter.

"Grace," he whispered.

Chapter 12
The Rose and the Lily

✳

AFTER MILLICAN HAD LEFT, Grace felt the chamber gradually darken as night fell. She was almost too exhausted to sleep, the old queasiness fresh inside her. But it was a comfort to be lying down, even on a bed of stone. The pillow was real and soft enough, and the surface she rested on warm if firm; she had it far better than Jacob in his desert repose. But Jacob had only a brother to contend with; she had an ancient sorceress—in Ovid's terms, the *senex venefica*.

She hoped that Media would come soon, so she could act her part in the interview and try to find rest for the night. The waiting and expectation were hard. Grace had once had a role in *Macbeth*—as the wife of the good Macduff—and she remembered the hollow forgetfulness that used to swirl inside of her in the moments before she went onstage. The time for her entrance always came before she was ready.

So when a tall and dark-haired woman opened the door, a circle of ice shining in the palm of her hand, it was all too soon after all. The woman glided to the bedside, a long robe sweeping behind her. The garment flashed a fiery rainbow of many colors, much like the window of ice when it first had captured Grace's attention. The cold light from the woman's palm, upraised as if in a gesture of peace, was enough to illuminate all her features—thin lips, sharp nose, and large dark eyes to match her hair. If she were the same Medea of ancient times, she did not begin to show her years. But as Grace met the woman's gaze, it seemed to her that all the years had accumulated in her cunning. The eyes she saw were as careful and close as Millican's were clear and generous.

The woman sat on the foot of the bed and appraised her with a practiced look of conditional approval, just this side of suspicion. It was the sort of look Grace had often received from her own mother, and put her on familiar if uneasy ground. The best tactics, she knew from experience, were to speak with quiet but unassertive confidence and never to glance down.

Media looked at her silently for a long time, as if testing the younger woman's resolve. Grace remembered an interviewer for graduate school who had done the same, staring her down in a way that would be impolite in almost any other setting. Grace had stared blandly back, as if to say, *We can do this all day if you like, but wouldn't it be better to talk?* And so Grace stared back at her visitor now, for the added reason that she dare not depart from her script in which she had the second line and not the first.

At long last the woman spoke, shining her small circle of ice directly into Grace's face. "How sunburned you look tonight, my daughter—and yet how pale. What have you seen in your window today?"

Grace hesitated. She was sure she had heard this smooth and silky voice before, but could not remember where. The voice was one of modulated and even control. It both knew and could say everything.

"I have seen the most beautiful colors, Mother, in the finest patterns," she finally replied. "Sometimes the sunshine came in so strongly it burned my face; other times the colors and patterns turned my countenance white with amazement."

Media looked at her with barely veiled curiosity, as if waiting for further explanation.

"The rose and the lily," Grace went on—"they are nature's way with our complexions." She was getting farther out of her text each time she spoke, but couldn't seem to help herself.

"But you, my dear, have more of the rose and more of the lily than ever I saw." She paused for a moment. "And where have you learned these pretty names? I am sure you never heard them from me."

"Names?" said Grace. "Of the flowers, you mean? I—um—read them, I think. Yes, I remember. They were part of a poem:

> *Nor did I wonder at the lily's white,*
> *Nor praise the deep vermilion in the rose;*
> *They were but sweet, but figures of delight,*
> *Drawn after you, you pattern of all those.*
> *Yet seemed it winter still. . . ."*

She trailed off, keenly aware of Media's eyes.

"And where found you this poem, Daughter? I am sure it is not in my house."

"Where?" said Grace. "Why, it came to me—today in fact. The words were written on my window—part of the patterns that so amazed me."

Media looked at her dubiously, then seemed to relent. "You are at peace, then, my daughter?"

"Yes, Mother, I am at peace."

"And yet you look uncommonly ill for one so peaceful. Is there nothing that disturbs you, my daughter?"

"A slight queasiness in my stomach, Mother. That is all. The colors were so wild today. And I am so unused to reading—so untutored, as you know—that I found the effort quite nauseating."

"Yes," said Media. "That is the nature of reading, I have found. Best just to enjoy the windows—the colors in them—and to ignore any distracting words that may appear. But as for this discomfort you report in your stomach—I have a way to rid you of it."

As she spoke a brilliant gown suddenly lay folded across the sleeve of her own. It shimmered like fire, throwing off colors like the robe she wore, like the window of ice.

"Wear this instead of your plain white gown. You are of age to do so now. It will purge your queasiness inside, and root out the cause of it. This robe will make you free to pursue the tasks—arduous tasks—that will make you strong and independent."

"You mean," said Grace, only half-feigning astonishment, "there will come a day I will leave this tower?"

"The day may come, and soon," said Media. "I have raised you unstained by the world that you may the better conquer it. To wear this robe is to arrive at your true home and truer self, and to defeat all encroachments within. Only what grows inside of us can hold us back. Sometimes we must prune the rose to prevent the thorns. To construct a life, a tower, a song, is in the end to deconstruct. The great dance of Acidale is finally absence, a universal emptiness. The meadow there is ice and rock. There is only the Silver Spire, the Tower of Light. To leave will only be to return. Your true home elsewhere shall be here; your independent self shall be me."

"You, Mother?"

"We, if you like, my dear daughter. I give you the gift of the robe. I shall leave it with you. When I come in the morning I hope to see you wearing it."

Media placed the gown on the bed and stood up, bending upon her a knowing glance. Just what she knew Grace wasn't sure. Media's reference to the Mount of Acidale, the locus of Grace's dissertation on Edmund Spenser's *Faerie Queene*, had left her limp beneath the covers.

"It is well. Goodnight, my daughter."

"It is well," faltered Grace. "Goodnight, Mother." Her eyes closed in frightened relief before the door opened and shut.

Once again she lay in darkness, feeling the weight of the robe draped across her feet. Had it been left for Millican, or had Media known Grace for the imposter she was and left the gown specifically for her? She suspected the woman had seen through her verbal disguise. Yet if she had, why had she not exposed her outright as someone other than her daughter? Why the pretense? And why the gift of the dazzling robe?

Media had been so self-assured and knowing in the things she said. In spite of herself—or perhaps because of herself—Grace found these qualities terribly attractive. The final absence of Acidale—its universal emptiness—these were the very conclusions that she herself had been working towards. The Graces, the dancers, the singer on the mount—all finally disappear and thus betray their lack of presence. What so many had taken as Spenser's ultimate affirmation of beauty and order and harmony was really a wasteland in disguise, self-subverting and lacking in all but passive reflexivity. The episode, the entire poem, had been valorized with arbitrary significance by a long tradition of logocentric interpretation. Her task—her arduous task—was to expose the poem for the hollow vessel that it was, to free all future interpretive communities from the burden of inscribed meaning. She felt like Media, holding up a circle of ice to illuminate a darkened room. Sometimes, in meetings with her weary advisor, she had had glimpses of this mission. But never before had she felt so heroic about completing her dissertation.

It was an exhilaration qualified only by a returning queasiness in her stomach. With it came the sudden force of familiar words:

> *Let me not to the marriage of true minds*
> *Admit impediments.*

This marriage, she now saw, was the wedding of her intellect to that of the world of scholarship. And Shakespeare was right—nothing at all should get in the way of the cutting edge that was bound to result. The robe at her feet became in her mind her academic regalia, its fiery colors as superior to sober black as her work would be to tired traditional ideas.

It would be an easy thing, she realized now, to file for a simple divorce. For all she knew, Lance had already beaten her to it. That would be one impediment down. And as for the child—she must treat it as a simple mistake, and erase it as a wayward word can be emptied from a computer screen. Surely the robe, through some great magic worked upon her inner being, would do that much. She realized what a gift it was that lay in her choice, and praised the giver in her mind. She was beginning to like the mother more than she had thought she would from the daughter's report, and wondered now at Millican's suspicions. In fact, Millican was starting to strike her as someone afraid of her own freedom. She had a kind and generous presence, to be sure, but her goodness was something too naïve ever to be a powerful force. And what Media had in abundance was power. Grace realized she admired this and rightly desired it for herself. The robe, she saw, was means and symbol for taking charge of her own life.

And so, finding reason after reason to bolster her case, Grace wearied herself to sleep. In her agitated state of exhaustion her dreams were more than usually troubled. Out of a chaos of ptarmigan and woodcarved faces she found herself whirled into a dim bare room. In the corner sat a bent figure. When she approached, the figure looked up. It was Lance, her husband, though she hardly recognized him. For he was crying, his dull strong face contorted with a terrible anguish. Waking or sleeping, Grace had never seen a person quite so broken. She stopped directly in front of him, and though he was looking in her direction he did not seem at all aware of her obvious presence.

"Grace left me," he said flatly, his voice dead with disbelief. She had a sense of deep calling to deep, of one lost soul reaching out to another. For a moment it seemed he actually saw her, that she in her dream had broken into an actual room where Lance at that moment was sitting.

And then he was gone—or she was gone—and she saw instead a more composed version of her stony husband, standing at the counter of the hardware store at which he clerked. A strange woman in a strapless shimmering opal dress was leaning over the counter in front of him, asking him questions about a remodel of her kitchen. He was answering them with tact, patience, and good spirits that seldom if ever entered their conversations at home. The woman had her back to Grace, but she could tell by the way that Lance's eyes kept drifting down that the woman was reasonably well endowed, and displaying her wares like fruit on the counter. The conversation turned on certain pipes and fittings, and ended with her invitation to Lance to inspect the work-in-progress firsthand right after work. He readily agreed to come, and the woman turned to walk away. She looked then directly at Grace, and her face was the face of Media, all poise and craft. The sorceress came straight toward her, then opened her arms and caught Grace in a sudden embrace. The touch of her dress was the touch of fire.

Chapter 13
Media's Charm

✳

BEFORE THE YOUNG WOMAN COULD REPLY, William noticed that what he had thought was a candle in her upraised hand was merely a glowing piece of crystal—of ice, even. "Whatever is that?" he demanded.

She regarded the shining curiously, as if only now aware of it as something to remark upon. "Light for our steps," she simply said. "Stored up from summer, I suppose. It has to go somewhere, and the tower is very dark at night."

She kept her eyes steadily upon him, as if trying to remember who he was. Everything about her was Grace—clothes, features, hair, hands. And yet there was something not Grace in the way she spoke and looked at him—a vacancy, a wavering calmness. It occurred to him that she had been hurt, or drugged, or charmed.

"Grace," he said again, beseeching. "It's me, William. Are you all right?"

She nodded rather uncertainly.

Ax in one hand, he threw his arms around her neck and brought her body close to his. She meekly submitted, and her breasts were warm and full against him under the roughness of her sweater. He had longed for this.

When they drew apart, she held his arm. "You are bleeding," she said.

He saw that his forearm was deeply scored. She bound it with a handkerchief, her fingers nimble about the wound. He liked the feel of her touch on his flesh.

Then she looked directly in his eyes again. "William," she said, as if trying the name for the first time, "there is much I cannot now explain. Only this: I have found Matheu, hidden in an outer chamber. He is as like to me as my own brother. I have cut him free from the cords that held him with his knife, but nevertheless he remains bound to a stone chair by invisible strands. We must see if your ax can help. I know by it you have contested the loathed Birds of

Paradise—"

"Birds of Paradise?"

"Harpies," she said. "The shaft still drips with their stench. Perhaps it will prove as effectual in the tower proper as it has in this filthy den."

The cadence and diction of this speech struck William as the slightest bit too quaint and formal to be coming from Grace's lips. But he said nothing, and obediently stepped aside as she swung the stone door shut behind him.

She took his arm—the unwounded one—and hurried him down a broad and curving flight of steps. After a long and breathless descent they passed through an archway and into what appeared to be a vaulted chamber, larger perhaps than the cavern in which he had fought the Harpies. The handheld circle of ice did not begin to illuminate the reach and extent of the room about them, but the muted echoes of their steps suggested a vastness that loosened his imagination.

They were partway across this open floor when she suddenly took her hand from his arm and cupped it around the light in the other, as though in prayer. They both stopped. She carefully put her folded hands behind his back, as if to hide the glow that escaped between her fingers. William sensed he should not say a word, and he soon found why.

Slowly passing high above them he saw the glow of a light like theirs. It went laterally at a walking pace, as if held by someone traversing a gallery built into the wall of the tower. The light, he was sure, could not reach the darkness in which they stood. Even so, William felt a thrill of naked vulnerability.

Presently the light paused and gestured out into the room. He saw behind it an outstretched arm in a glittering sleeve, and above the arm, the suggestion of a woman's face, high-cheeked and thin-lipped. The eyes, strangely underlit, were dark sockets, a nothingness. The woman looked out over the room in steady silence. Then the face withdrew and the light vanished. He thought he heard the shutting of a door.

His companion quickly uncapped her light. "We must keep on," she whispered. "Make no sound."

He felt her hand on his arm again and found himself whisked across the floor, running on tiptoe. He was out of breath, trying hard not to pant, when they reached a door on the opposite wall. They opened it with a simple push and slipped inside. The door closed softly behind them.

"Who was that?" William whispered, venturing to breathe aloud. "Media?"

She nodded sagely.

William was pleased at their escape, not only for his own sake but for the alertness it showed in Grace. Here was no charmed sleeper, but a woman who knew her enemies. He regarded her again in boots, knickers, and ragged sweater. There was no telling what she had gone through since he had fallen. He liked a woman so tough and adaptable, so native to these surprising mountains. Gwen might turn tail and head for the city. But here was a wilderness woman.

They were standing now in a smaller room, high-ceilinged and windowed with a slab of ice that reflected the light in a deep black shimmer. Facing the window, its back to the door, was a high-backed chair made completely of stone. They slowly approached it from behind, and William felt an inexplicable sense of dread. At the same time a wave of weariness washed through him, a sense he should have taken his rest hours ago, that his body was pressing its mortal limits. For a moment he found himself hoping that the chair would be empty, that he might sit and simply sleep.

So when they passed to the front of the chair and light fell on the sleeping face of a young man, William was dimly disappointed. Scraps of rope lay on the floor where they had been cut away. The sleeper sat regally unencumbered in a long white robe, both arms resting on arms of stone and head tilted just slightly to one side. The young man's face was a handsome version of Grace's own.

The woman touched one weathered cheek, downy with beard. "Matheu," she whispered. But he no more awoke than Villard or Chambers had for William.

"You see," she said, turning away from the sleeping figure, "he is not now with us. At twilight his eyes were open, gazing upon the colors of the window. But even then he made no answer. Waking or sleeping, I fear he is bound by Media's charm."

William heard her only faintly, as if from very far away. His legs were heavy, his head too great a weight for his shoulders. There was a faraway clatter as if his ax had dropped to the floor, and then he felt across his face the cool stone that could have been a lover's caress.

Chapter 14
The Sparkling Robe

✳

WHEN GRACE AWOKE, the room and bed were streaming with light. The window was charged with swirl and color, radiant reds and crushes of blue and violet. Her eyes were drawn and held by the ice and remained there in a dull but restless exhilaration. She did not particularly want to look at the shapeshifting hues in the window, but it was too hard to do anything else. As she gazed, newly awake, her memories of William and Chambers and Millican came slipping back in no clear order, an irrelevance, a faint intrusion, dismantled and dispersed by the colors that hurtled by in momentary fragments, one displaced and dissolved by the other. She had read of the Great Dance of the suns and planets and constellations, slow and stately and guided by angelic intelligence. This seemed a mockery of it, some indoor travesty of the world, a supremely nervous juggling act that held the senses only to demean and degrade them.

Grace was dimly aware of this loss even as she succumbed to it. And yet she felt helpless to detach herself. An ancient prayer began to sound in the back of her mind: *Our hearts are restless, until—until . . .* What was the rest of it? Her mind seemed suddenly blank. It didn't matter, really. Did it? *Our hearts are restless,* she tried again. *Until—until . . .*

How long she continued in this state of vague hypnosis she did not know. What broke it was the stirring of her pocket gopher under the covers, fur and claws and small wet nose all burrowing against her side. Somehow, while she slept, the gopher had gotten under her nightgown. Her first reaction was to strip the creature away from her as if it were an intrusive leech. She threw off the covers and caught it a blow, then got to her knees and shook the gopher out the bottom of her robe. He came down with a bump on the bare sheets and instead of curling into a ball lay rather limply on his side.

Got him, was all Grace thought to herself. It would teach him a lesson for presuming to be so intimate. Her eyes then fell on the sparkling robe that lay across the foot of the bed. In the shifting lights and colors of morning it shone more splendidly than before, burning like a rainbow of fire. In the confusion and distraction of waking she had forgotten her intent to put it on, forgotten in fact that it was there. Now it seized upon her desire as it had the evening before.

Tremulously she reached for the robe, an unimaginable coat of colors, and even without quite putting it on began to feel its cleansing power about her shoulders. First, however, she realized she would have to remove the white robe that she was wearing. She slipped it easily overhead, then paused on her knees, naked and vulnerable, ready for the veil of a new garment. At this moment the nausea invaded again. With weak hands she traced the outline of her womb, the tilt of her breasts, places of nurture and nourishment. The queasiness, she knew, would pass. Motherhood, however, would not. A child would require her milk, her sleep, her constant care. It would need a father; it would not need a dissertation deconstructing *The Faerie Queene*. All she had to do now was to put on the robe. The nausea would pass at once, and the dissertation would be her infant until it grew to astonish the world. In a single stroke, she could be mother and midwife and husband to her own maturing intellect. The urge to have a real child could easily be seen for what it actually was—a death wish of the primitive self. Children were the result of fear; her way was the sophisticated path of courage.

She had reached once again for the splendid gown when her eyes fell on the limp gopher, stretched out by her bare knees. Next to his mouth a spot of blood stained the sheet. She contemplated it dully, from the distance of a disengaged heart, then picked up the robe between her fingers. Her eyes, however, did not leave the stricken gopher. With her other hand she scooped it up carefully and counterpoised it with the robe, as if she were within herself a fragile human scale of justice.

And then, in spite of her resolve, she found herself beginning to ponder. For some reason it came to her in a slow rush of memory what she had felt when trapped in the womb of the avalanche. Were it not for the pocket gophers, her life would have been stilled there. They had labored to release her for no benefit to themselves, yet they in a way had given her a second birth, a salvation from cold death. In her hand lay the limp lesson of her ingratitude; in her womb lay the quick possibility of their gift, of her repetition of what the gophers had opened to her.

As quickly as they had been kindled, the glories of her dissertation began to fade. They were like the smile on Media's mouth,

> *the deadest thing*
> *Alive enough to have strength to die.*

She stroked the gopher with her thumb and held it against her cheek, her lips, and finally her breast. "Live, child," she softly said, and when it finally stirred in her hand she kissed its nose and placed it gently beneath the covers. Then she dropped the colored robe and quickly donned the white one again.

"Die, self," she whispered more fiercely. From under her pillow she took the dagger hidden there the night before. Then, catching up the brilliant gown, she leapt to the window with eyes averted from its pull and staked the garment to the ice with one wild swing of the dagger. It sank deep, and she left it there, skewering the robe to the window, as she sank back upon the bed, overcome by what she had done. For a moment the robe redoubled its opalescent brilliance—a flag, a banner, a tapestry—scintillating the magic of the window. Then suddenly it burst into flame, no longer something akin to fire but fire itself. Grace felt a hollowness in her throat as she watched it burn. She remembered the cruel coat of poison that Medea of old had given to Jason's Corinthian princess. *Colchis arsit nova nupta venenis*, as Ovid had put it: "the new wife burnt by the Colchian witchcraft." Grace realized in horror that the robe burning before her eyes would have destroyed far more than her unborn child. The price would have been the immolation of herself—and not just the false self she hoped lay nailed and burning against the window now, but the true self she might yet become.

So she watched the robe and her old self burn with a dazed sort of gratitude. She was so absorbed by her narrow escape that at first she did not notice the effect of the flames. Quite simply, the window was melting. All the exotic dance and color had drained from the ice; it was literally dripping now with the clear silver light of morning. And still the robe burned, unconsumed like a bush in the desert. The meltwater ran like a stream from window to floor, pooling on the stone by the bed and rolling on towards the door. Grace caught the gopher up in her hands and clutched him against her chest in amazement. Still, still the robe kept burning.

Suddenly she felt on her face the clear breath of open air. The top of the window had now melted completely away, and the sky beyond was bright in the ocean of itself. The rim of ice descended like a sash being lowered. Soon it reached the dagger and robe, and they matter-of-factly fell away, outward, into the abyss, just as William had lost his hold and plunged down the side of the spire. Grace felt a lightening of her heart as the robe and dagger disappeared. The fire was gone.

Yet still the window vanished away, dissolved now by the steady force of an entering breeze, no longer a breath of air but a strong west wind, warm and full and replete with desire of new life. Grace rose from the bed and stood in the window, letting the wind stream through her hair and billow her robe in swelling rounds. The last of the ice gave way at her feet, and she looked out across the shimmering white of the lava plain to the graceful and familiar rise of the Three Queens.

She held up the gopher in her hands as if in offering, as if in prayer. "We're going back," she whispered to him. "I begin to feel it."

Grace turned and saw the sheets from the bed arcing like sails across the room. She ran to catch them, tucked them back where they belonged. Then she found herself blown back to the stone door. Her bare feet trembled on the threshold.

"Shall we go?" she asked the pocket gopher.

He stirred in her hands, and she stroked his head.

"As you wish, then."

She set him gently on one shoulder and with the other pushed open the door. It swung out easily, but she was not able to shut it behind her. The wind from the window would not allow the door to close. But Grace hardly noticed—she was too busy taking in where she was. She found herself on a narrow veranda, a low-walled gallery, high on the edge of a vaulted dome of interior space. Light and color swirled in through magnificent circular windows of ice, as many above her as below. The whole was enspiraled by tiers of galleries like her own, circling the walls of the dome in succession. Some were connected by stone ramps, others by stairs; all passed row after row of doors, none open. But it wasn't the doors that set her agape so much as the vast interiority of space—a vastness that at first seemed to enlarge her spirit but finally brought profound confinement. It reminded her of cathedrals she had visited in that dying country of England— grand and impressive when you were in them, but what a feeling of freedom it was to escape again out into the open air. This time she had brought the open air with her, flinging itself through the door at her back. The wind made her feel fresh and determined, ready to work. In spite of what Millican had said about the lack of chores in the tower, there was spring cleaning to be done.

Grace stood poised on the inner edge of the low-walled gallery, wondering where and how to proceed. The righthand way ramped gradually downward, the left went level to an upward stair. Both were lined with a myriad of stone doors. "Down," she whispered to herself. She had climbed enough.

And so she drifted down the ramp, curving past door after door, and encircled the dome twice over before she descended a flight of stairs to the broad, bare plaza at the bottom. The circular floor was surrounded by even more doors at a great distance on every side. One, she felt sure, should be chosen. Which one, she had no idea—and she was not about to venture out into so open a space. On the galleries she had felt half-hidden; on the floor of the dome she suddenly felt vulnerable. So she hesitated there at the foot of the stairs, feeling even at this remove the warm breath of the west wind from her chamber door high overhead.

All at once a cry of pain erupted from behind a door directly before her across the plaza. "No!" it sounded, a man's voice in agony. "I will not! I will not!"

Grace started and ran for the door. Impossible as it seemed to her, she was quite certain the voice she had heard belonged to her fallen companion.

Chapter 15
Delicious Air

✳

WHEN WILLIAM FELL ASLEEP ON THE STONE FLOOR he was plunged into dreams of desire—and not for his long-lost Gwen but for Grace. She appeared to him in a diaphanous robe of flashing colors that barely concealed shapely thighs and ample breasts. He went to meet her with arms outstretched, and she paused to regard him with a curious look, one part pity and three parts scorn—a look so entirely self-possessed that she seemed to be gazing not at him but into a mirror.

"Grace," he whimpered, choosing not to mind her expression but hoping to enslave himself to what he glimpsed beneath the robe. "At last, at last."

He was just about to encircle her waist when suddenly her figure changed to a pillar of ice. His hands went slipping down cold smooth sides. All at once he was falling, whistling in thin cold air past the icy ramps and cliffs of the spire, this time with no rope, no ax, no hope of arrest. In the dream he plummeted to the base of the tower, writhing and shouting, and just as he cratered deep in the snow he woke into another dream in which Grace was approaching him as before, wearing her filmy, fiery robe. Once again he yearned for her, and reached, and fell. The dream repeated itself all night. Sometimes he actually felt the warmth of her flesh before it congealed in a frozen pillar, and once she even called his name.

That is when he finally awoke.

He lay exhausted on the cool stone floor. Light flamed through a translucent window of ice in a strangely exotic dance of color. The one called Matheu was still seated in a stone chair directly above him; his eyes were open but fixed with a glassy stare on the window. The one called Grace was standing beside him. She looked wan and tired in the wheeling light, as if she had watched over William and Matheu the whole night through. She held Matheu's carving knife in her hand, but listlessly, as it served no purpose.

William slowly got to his feet, half-intending to re-enact the better part of his dream and embrace her. But she looked rather homely in a gray wool sweater; he could almost smell the perspiration and grime woven into the knit. Besides, she was no longer looking at him. She had turned toward the stone door. It was opening.

He saw her cower before he saw who had entered the room. She shrank back towards him, hiding the knife. And through the door a startling figure broke upon them: an ageless woman—thin-lipped, high-cheeked—in the same gauzy, flashing gown that Grace had worn all night in his dreams. His first response was not to reach out his arms with desire but to stoop down and pick up his ax, which lay discarded on the floor.

"William," she said, calling his name as Grace had at the end of his dream. She stopped with her hands on the top of the chair. "How thoughtful of you to bring your ice ax."

"You are—Media?" he stammered.

The younger woman shrank still further away, but not before Media snatched the knife out of her hand.

"Mother!" she protested. "Please, no!"

William raised his ax in protest, stepping up to the side of the helpless. But his gesture of protection was not wholehearted. Since when had Grace called this woman mother? Without meaning to he looked to both for an explanation.

The older woman—or the ageless one—regarded him with the same mingled countenance of pity and scorn that the image of Grace had worn in his dream. "I see your confusion," she said to him with the air of a hostess. "You lack a proper introduction to everyone present in the room. But you are quite right—I am Media. This is my long-lost son, Matheu, enjoying the morning light in the window, as he has each day of his visit. And this is my daughter, Millican, masquerading as one of your own missing companions—for what reason I cannot be sure. But I have only just visited your friend Grace. I offered her far better clothes than these my daughter by some strange whim is wearing. When last I saw her, she was simply burning to try them on."

Media interrupted herself with a trill of laughter.

"But where is she now?" William demanded.

Without waiting for an answer he turned to Millican, looking at her with new eyes. "Is she telling the truth?"

"Yes," she nodded, the word barely audible. Her eyes began brimming with tears. "I did not mean to deceive you," she said. "I just wanted your help. I didn't know if you'd come with me if you thought I were someone other than Grace."

William looked back sullenly, caught between anger and understanding. "So where is Grace, then? Where is she now?"

Millican pointed cautiously upward. "In my room, I yet dare hope. I left her there. She was feeling ill, but in good spirits."

"And I have cured her of that illness, rest assured," Media added. "But there was, I regret, something caustic in the cure. Unless your Grace has the powers of a phoenix, I am afraid that as of this morning she has fallen into her own ashes. A terrible end, but I can't have people breaking in and corrupting my children now—can I, William?"

"Mother, you didn't!" Millican wailed.

"As you say, I didn't," Media responded. "I left the choice entirely in her own hands. I have some experience, however, in the way women choose."

Millican wept, and William raised his ax again, trembling with outrage.

"Careful with that," Media warned him. "You do not yet know the real reason of your coming. These many years I have been cheated of the ax you hold. And now, finally, I have drawn you here to re-deliver it into my hands. You may put it down, by the way. I know you cannot hurt a woman. Don't worry—I won't wrest it from you. The ax is given, never taken. That is its way. The choice shall be entirely yours."

"As it was for Grace?" he said suspiciously.

"Well, yes," she said with a smile. "I have some experience, as well, in the way men choose."

"What is my choice, then?" he asked, lowering the ax to his side.

"Simply this. You somewhat know my daughter, Millican. It is she you have adored in your dreams. Take her, keep her, be Lord of the Tower of Light, the Silver Spire. You may even have custody of her brother, who is sure to adapt his artistic talents to enhance the décor of your inner palace. Simply leave me the ice ax, and I will quietly depart for the north, for Cold-Kiss, the land of my birth, where I lived my life before my betrayal. That's all I ask, a poor moiety to all I give."

William set the ax resolutely spike-first on the floor before him, holding firmly to the pick and the adze with both hands. Millican looked at him almost hopefully. For just a moment he allowed himself to imagine a life together with her. If Grace were gone, wouldn't she be the next best thing? In the tower they could take their pleasure continually: here was world enough and time. He would never have to worry that she would long to move away to the city.

"It is settled, then." Media opened her hands for the ax. "I see that your heart knows its belonging."

William tightened his grip on the ax in disregard of his fantasy. In his mind's eye he suddenly saw a little girl sitting against the trunk of a sapling. *You know better than to come to the table like that.*

"No," he muttered.

"What's that?" said Media sharply. Her hand had almost closed on his.

"No," he repeated with strength and clarity.

It's about time, his daughter scolded. *They're waiting for us.*

Media's eyes grew narrow. Her robe flashed fiercely in the light from the window. She pointed to his hand on the ax and appealed to Hecate, the triple-crowned goddess of the night, in what must have been a fearful curse. Most of the words he did not know, but their terrible effect was clear. For instantly the head of the ax began to burn like a red-hot iron in his hands. Worse, he found he could not let go.

"I will let you speak again," said Media. "The choice still lies in your power. To rid yourself of this wholly unnecessary discomfort and to gain the hand of my beautiful daughter, simply surrender the ax to me."

William had never felt such agony. The flesh of his hands, though still clean and whole to the eye, was searing like meat over hot coals. His arms shook, his body trembled, as he writhed about from foot to foot.

Millican looked on helplessly, reduced to tears.

Media spoke with delicious leisure. "What say you now, William?"

"I have a wife already!" he pleaded.

"That's never stopped anyone before," said Media, as if affronted by the objection.

"And a daughter," he sobbed.

"Nor that," she added.

Media smiled coolly and nodded at his hands on the ax. The heat, if anything, seemed to intensify. "And now," she repeated, "what will you answer?"

William found himself panting and gasping, as if straining for a final breath. To rid himself of his suffering, he suddenly felt he would promise anything.

But not everything. It was Lara's voice, surging with the pain inside him.

But not everything. And this time it was Gwen speaking, her long-forgotten wisdom and warmth.

"No!" he shouted, howling like a dog at Media. "I will not! I will not!"

Her lip curled, and her hand shot out to catch her daughter by the hair. She pulled her head down close to her brother's and tilted it back to bare her throat. With her other hand she brought the blade of Matheu's knife close under the chins of brother and sister.

"You spurn her then," Media said with a measured ferocity. "Perhaps in addition to your own dire suffering you would like to witness my daughter's death throes—both hers and her brother's. Such a terrible waste of beauty and talent."

Even in his agony William stopped writhing, smitten with shock. Millican's throat was pale and trembling above her sweater; Matheu looked blandly out at the window, the sickening colors playing across his earnest face. This time William would have to relent, not for his own pain but simply to save the life of another. Of two others. There would be no wedding. He would find his way back to Lara and Gwen and simply explain.

The burning of the ax began to overtake him again. He was feeling faint. The words formed in his mind: *I will.* He opened his mouth, about to say them.

But before he could, the door opened behind Media. In stepped Grace, barefoot in a plain white robe that billowed in a breeze from behind her. William felt the wind from the door wash over him—fresh, strong, a warm coolness. Instantly the heat of the ax began to die away in his hands.

Media whirled as if she had been struck from behind; she held the knife no longer at the throats of her children but outstretched towards the open door, both hands fast on the hilt.

"What do you here, you foolish girl?" she snapped at Grace. "Where is your robe? What is this wind you dare bring with you?"

Grace said nothing, but merely held the door wide open, letting the wind pour all the more strongly into the room. William found to his amazement that his hands were cool and whole and steady. The ax had lost all trace of its burning. Media, though, was apparently feeling an opposite effect.

"My hands!" she cried. "You have ignited the knife, you little witch! I cannot let go. They burn! They burn!"

In that moment it looked to William as if she would rush with the knife at Grace. He let go the head of his ax and grasped it by the shaft to pursue her. But before he took a single step, a burst of wind suddenly seemed to root Media firmly in place, halfway between the chair and the door. She was shaking and writhing and wailing there, the knife dancing over her head. William stood uncertainly by the stone chair and its occupants. He looked to Grace and their eyes met, a partnership for working days.

"Not her," she said, pointing at Media. "Get the window. What we need is more air."

William nodded and promptly spun about on his heels. The sheet of ice was fully as tall as a stained glass window in a cathedral. Were it not for the unholy dance and swirl of synthesized light, William would have felt all the shame the iconoclasts should have in long-ago days of Reformation. As it was, he simply had a job to do; the ripeness of his ax was all.

He reached the window on a run and deliberately planted both feet as he swung the ax high over his head. It fell like a dread two-handed engine and splintered the ice in a mighty crash. Great jags and slabs of it smashed to the floor, and the wind pounced through like a hound of heaven, cleansing the room with strength and light, the true light of morning come. What was left of the window was torn away by the force of the air and hurled across the room in fragments that burst against the walls and floor. What had come in the door was a skipping breeze; the window had let in a full gale of warm, strong, delicious air.

What happened next was a great surprise to everyone except perhaps to Media herself. She wailed and wept just as before, her hands clasped to the burning knife, making such a scene that even William, so recently her victim in so similar a circumstance, began to cast about for ways he might alleviate her pain. Grace and Millican evidently had the same idea, for they all found themselves ringed around her writhing body, out of reach of the slashing knife but hands outstretched nevertheless to help in some instinctive way. But suddenly William realized there was much less of Media to help than there had been just moments before. As the warm full wind blew through their circle, melting the shattered ice on the floor, Media herself seemed to be diminishing in size and stature. At first he thought she had dropped to her knees, but then he saw she had only done so because there were no longer legs beneath her knees to support her. And then there were no longer knees, or thighs, and her splendid gown was gray and dank in the morning light, wilting and curling like leaves, like ashes, long dead.

She looked up at them piteously, still contorting about the knife. "For the love of my husband, shut the window!" she cried aloud.

"We can't, Mother," Millican said quietly. "It's open now. It's time for us all to go outside."

What Millican said had a strangely calming effect on William. He merely watched, not in triumph but in simple sadness, as Media gradually disappeared into the floor. Soon only her torso was left, and then not even her breasts or shoulders. Her arms disappeared from the fingers inward, the knife falling away to the floor, and then all they saw was her upturned face, looking at them with a grim and quiet resignation framed by her mane of dark thick hair.

"Remember me," the pale lips said. "Remember me, that I was great." Then the face dissolved like the last remnants of Ozymandias in the desert, and the hair vanished in a gust of wind.

They stared at each other, dumbfounded. Except for the wind, the room was silent. It was the sort of moment in which there was so much to say that nothing could be said at all. But it did not last because quite suddenly someone had the urge to speak.

"Where are we now?" came a pleasant voice.

They all looked at the stone chair. Matheu stood next to it, stretching his arms and gazing lazily out the window. Apparently he had only been addressing himself, as one who lived alone might do. He yawned and turned and suddenly caught full sight of the three of them. His eyes blinked and his forehead furrowed in a concentrated effort of memory.

"I recognize you all," he said. "Unfortunately, I have never known your names."

He approached their circle as if to introduce himself, and his eyes fell to the floor at their feet. "Oh, so you've located my knife, have you? A good knife, but I've found I can see better without it."

He still got no response from them. They might as well have been gnarled trees, shaggy with lichen and scoured by storm.

"A bit windy, isn't it? I like the wind myself," he said.

Chapter 16
Ptarmigan Feathers

✳

MILLICAN WAS THE FIRST IN THE RING to finally respond. She broke from the circle and flung herself upon her brother, clutching him in her wool-clad arms. She was weeping again.

He held her close, then stepped back to regard her with care. "You," he said, "are the face in the hemlock. Some kin of mine, I have always believed."

"I am your own dear sister," she sobbed—"your twin, Matheu. I am Millican."

His lip quivered. Then his entire face opened up with joy like a flower, and he pressed her to him, stroking her hair. "Millican," he slowly said, testing the sound of it. "Millican. Not only sister but my own self. So much more than I dared hope."

He looked up from this tender embrace to see Grace and William shyly watching a few steps away. "But who are these two persons?" he asked, turning Millican around in his arms. "Is this woman our sister as well? And is this our brother? She especially looks much like us, does she not?"

Grace stepped solemnly forward and took his hand. "I am not sister but cousin, Matheu. Grace is my name, and this is William, no kin of yours but keeper of your father's ax and our chief rescuer from this tower."

William awkwardly offered his hand, and Matheu shook it heartily.

"My many thanks," he said to him. "But I hardly know what to thank you for. I know I was taken some days ago—or years ago, for all I can remember—snatched from my cabin one winter evening by the cruel claws of foul monsters. They brought me to the summit of the Silver Spire, and thence to their wretched den, where I think they would have devoured me had not a woman of fierce countenance taken me from them and bathed my hurts in a bronze caldron. I emerged unscathed from the seething waters, my wounds made whole. I recognized the woman then—I had carved her face many times, always fearing what I made but unable to do otherwise. But in spite of my queries, she steadfastly refused to tell me who she was. Only, she dressed me in the plain white robe that I wear now and led me through the dark to this room, where she bid me rest in this stone chair.

"And rest I did, but in a peculiar sort of restlessness. At dawn I woke, after a fashion, to a dancing sea of colors in the window, fascinating to me, of course, but ultimately devastating, for they refused to take any definite shape, neither of themselves nor in the fashioning of my mind. The shapes and colors seemed wholly abstracted from any flower or stone or star. Trees have faces, but this window of ice had none. It seemed a power intent upon turning my vision to formless chaos. Years of looking at light and wood were whittled away. I could no longer see. I could no longer move. And I could not take my eyes from the window.

"Now that the window is gone, I find I am released from the chair, but how I know not. And who or where the woman might be who put me here I know not either."

Millican looked at him soberly. "She is our mother," she softly said, "and she is no more. In the moment that you woke, she vanished."

Matheu considered this in silence. "There is a kind of sadness to that," he finally said. "But I am not sure where it lies."

"Here," said Millican, pointing to her breast. "However evil she may have been, she still lies woven in our hearts."

Matheu nodded approvingly. "Well said, Sister," he murmured.

"But Matheu," said Millican suddenly, "do we have a father? Do you live with him, just as I have lived with our mother?"

"Alas, Millican, we had a father. He died of grief for the purest woman there ever was, the lovely Stella—both for her death and for his forced betrayal of her at the hands of another. I can carve for you his face, but I never knew him beyond my very earliest days."

Millican looked down at the floor. "I had such hopes," she said brokenly. "Such hopes for a father in spite of such a mother."

Here William spoke up, putting his hands on both their shoulders. "Take heart," he said. "It is my belief your father lives. He sleeps, but he lives. I think I saw him last night here in the tower."

"Where?" said everyone almost at once.

"In the Harpies' den."

"The same monsters that brought me here? Then he will have been torn to pieces," Matheu lamented.

"Not so," said William. "By the strength of the ax and help of Sir Chambers, the Harpies have lain dead and bleeding all this night. It is Chambers who lies dead near his side."

"Chambers!" said Matheu. "It cannot be. For sixteen years he was more than a father to me. "This—this is hard to bear."

Grace too was trembling inside at this strange news. "William, take us to him," she begged. "Perhaps there is something we can do?"

"And our father," said Millican. "Perhaps we or the wind can awaken him?"

All were agreed on at least this hope, so without delay Grace ushered them out of the door and into the central vaulted dome. Here, an entirely new scene awaited them. The entering wind had blown up into the highest reaches of the dome and begun to melt the circular windows that criss-crossed the giant chamber with shafts of light. Colors no longer danced in the air; instead, streams of water were wafting down from the melting ice. Pockets of blue and open air were starting to clear overhead, and with each new hole the strength and freshness of the wind invaded the dome with mounting energy. The four of them were not halfway across the vast stone floor, threading the music of waterfalls, when the rows of doors that lined the galleries all around began to open in bursts of sound, flapping in air like aspen leaves.

"I always dreamed it could be like this," Millican said, and held her arms up into the wind as if she could swim in its changeable currents. Indeed, the growing force of the wind was starting to blend the waterfalls (or *windowfalls*, as Grace later thought of them) into a general whirl of rain.

To keep dry, they took cover under a crumpled bedsheet that was lying in the center of the floor—Grace realized it must have blown down from Millican's room. Holding it tightly over their heads, they bunched together like friends under a small umbrella and sprinted for the opposite door, an open archway, next to the stair that Grace had descended. They had just reached it, and were sitting on the steps inside, panting for breath, when the windows began to come down in earnest, crashing to the floor like chandeliers let loose from the ceiling. It seemed to Grace like loads of snow slipping off boughs of the forest in thaw—except louder, and grander, and to greater effect. The slabs and shards of the great ice windows came whistling down and exploded on the stone like announcements of a world restored. Soon the galleries across the way were spilling ribbons and sheets of water down to the floor in a grand circular cascade, tier upon tier, and little by little the dome began to fill and flood against the steps on which they sat.

"Do all of the rooms have windows?" asked Grace.

"Every one," Millican nodded. "They must all be melting."

"And all the ice on the mountain with them," Grace said in quiet amazement.

Now a cascade from the galleries directly above them began to fall, hiding the dome in a curtain of water. The flood at their feet had risen to the second stair.

"Let's go," said Grace. She was feeling impatient to find Sir Chambers.

"No," said Millican, seized by a thought. "Wait here. Please, just for a moment."

Before they could stop her, she had plunged knee-deep off the stair and disappeared through the curtain of water.

"Wait," called Matheu. "Millican, it's not safe!"

He rose to follow but Grace held him. "She's the one who said to wait, Matheu—and she's lived here all her life. Sometimes it pays to listen to your sister."

Matheu looked at her in surprise, as if he were not sure how much he liked this kind of spirit in a cousin. "Yes," he said finally. "I suppose you're right." He sat back down on his step. "It's only that, having just found her, I don't want to lose her again."

"Nor do we all," Grace said more softly. She touched his arm and he smiled warily. "But we can't always be the ones who are carving, remember?

> *There's a divinity that shapes our ends,*
> *Rough-hew them how we will.*"

"And that's true too," said Matheu.

So they sat. And waited. The water had risen another step, and Grace, in spite of her borrowed wisdom, was growing very impatient again. Then, when she was about to say they should go to look for her after all, a bronze caldron came bobbing through the waterfall, and Millican behind it, wading now up to her thighs. She shivered as she climbed onto the stairs.

"That's the caldron that cured my wounds," Matheu said. He hauled it up on the stairs beside them. "You don't suppose it could—"

"Raise the dead?" Grace suggested. For suddenly she remembered the way in which Medea had brought the murdered father of Jason back to life.

Millican sponged herself with the bedsheet and held up a stained and crumpled parchment. "With the right ingredients, yes. I just had time to tear this page from a book of our mother's in her study."

"There is white magic as well as black," Grace said. She knew this from her own studies.

"Yes," said Millican. "And, in her earliest days, I believe that our mother may have been an accomplished mistress of the former."

"Which means—" said Matheu.

"Yes, which means that, in our innocence, such power may yet be ours to command. We must try, anyway. We must do what we can, and allow to be done whatever good is waiting to happen."

Without any more questions, William and Matheu shouldered the empty caldron between them and staggered up the winding stairs. Millican led them, lighting the way with a strange glow that appeared in her palm. Grace came just behind, lending a hand to balance the caldron when she could. The wind seemed to lift them upward; before they reached the top of the stairs a trickle and then a stream of water had begun to cascade from step to step.

After several rests, they came to the door of the Harpies' den. It was wide open, held by the wind, which had begun to scour the stink and stench from the place. A stream of water ran across the middle of the floor; in the light from Millican's palm the air at first seemed filled with snowflakes. William surrendered his side of the caldron to the floor and simply said, "Ptarmigan feathers."

They stood then, panting just inside the door, and peered about in the partial light. "Where is our father?" Matheu asked.

From next to the wall, in the shadow of the caldron, they heard a huge yawn. All four of them whirled about. The man in rags, the relentless sleeper, was stretching his arms and looking about from his seat on the floor.

"Getting drafty in here," he grumbled. "And time for breakfast, I would think."

Matheu and Millican were immediately at his side, helping him up.

He looked back and forth at each of them without a trace of recognition in his eyes. "Aren't you a pair," he said approvingly. "Faces to make your parents proud."

"Father," said Millican, "you are all the parents that we have. This is your son, and I am your daughter."

His beard wobbled, and he sank, limp, back down to the floor. Matheu and Millican caught him up again in their arms.

"Twins," he said, shaking his head. "I wish she'd told me."

As moved as she was by this reunion, Grace was impatient to locate Chambers. "Millican," she whispered, elbowing in. "Hold up your light so we can see."

Obligingly she raised her hand and illuminated the cavern about them. There appeared no trace of the Harpies—as if they, like their mistress, had melted away—but both William and Grace saw the body of Chambers at once. It was badly mauled. William hurried straight to it, but Grace could not bring herself to follow.

"Millican," she said again. "The ingredients for the caldron. What are they?"

Weeping over her wakened father, Millican thrust the parchment at Grace. "That is the charm," she said. "I will join you straightway."

In the glow of Millican's upraised palm, Grace made the parchment smooth in her hands. It was covered, she saw, with an antique script. *A Receipt*, it read in bold letters across the top, *to Bring Back Life That Hath Wrongfully Been Taken Away.* What followed was a brief rhyme:

> *At sunset of the equinox*
> *With true-skilled knife and starry locks*
> *Join the flower of Rosamond;*
> *Restore to life what Death hath stunned.*
>
> *Find the flower atop the Spire*
> *When the wind and sun conspire.*
> *Send alone a maid with child;*
> *Save a life to save the wild.*

She put down the parchment breathlessly, and all at once felt the old ache of nausea, and the warm poke of her pocket gopher on her neck.

"William!" she shouted across the cavern.

He was bending over Chambers' body.

"William! When is the equinox?" Had they already passed it? She had lost track of the days.

"The what?" he called back.

"The equinox! The spring equinox!"

He walked back to her absent-mindedly, calculating on his fingers. "Friday I found the key. That was the fifteenth."

"The Ides of March," Grace said.

"Let's see. Saturday to the Center Queen, Sunday at home, Monday to the Belknap Hut, Tuesday across the lava, Wednesday up the spire. So here we are, Thursday, the twenty-first. Today is the equinox of spring."

"Good," said Grace, a thrill going through her. "Just one more question: how do I get from here to the summit?"

Chapter 17
So Many Graces Gathered

✳

IN THE SOFT LIGHT SHINING FROM MILLICAN'S HAND, Grace ran across the Harpies' den to the far entrance that William had pointed out to her. Once inside the curving tunnel, she found that the light was gone. Grace felt her way along the wall as quickly as she could in the dark, her bare feet splashing in cool water that ran along the floor of the passage. This went on for a long while—so long, in fact, that Grace began to wonder if William had pointed out the wrong passage. But the wind at her heels and the wind in her face—coming, it seemed, from both directions—kept urging her, onward and upward, and she did not turn back.

In time a hint of light appeared, and the floor of the passage turned warm and dry under her feet. She rounded a corner and saw before her the mouth of the cavern, framing a swath of sweet blue sky. Almost shyly she crept to the threshold and peered out.

What she saw was the summit indeed, but not the summit she expected to see on the Silver Spire. For the circle of space was not silver with ice but green with grass, a springtime meadow, a raised altar to the goddess Flora. More surprising yet, she was not alone.

Near the entrance a blonde young man, bare to the waist, sat neatly cross-legged in knickers. His back was to her, and in his hands was an instrument like a wooden recorder—something old and plain to pipe on. He was just raising it to his lips. Beyond him, on the very center of the summit, three tall figures were poised in a ring, and another stood modestly in the center. All of them were women, she saw, dressed in gowns that reached to the grass: one blue, one green, one red in the ring, and the one in the middle all of white.

Before she could really glimpse their faces, the man began to play his pipe.

The sound of it was like birds returning north for the summer, heightened into a human melody. The ring of women began to dance—blue gown, green gown, red gown swirling about the central figure in white. And now Grace saw the faces of the dancers.

"It can't be," she whispered to herself. And yet it was. All three sisters—queens, really—were circling before her arm-in-arm. Stella romped in the blue robe of hope and sky, blonde hair streaming behind her in the wind. Lady Demaris flew beside her in forest green, laughing and tossing her unbraided chestnut hair. Then Lady Lira, raven-haired and gentle at last, wearing the crimson of her redemption from death and darkness in El Ai. None of the three so much as even glanced at Grace. They were all turned inward on the cynosure of the woman in white, a strawberry blonde who stood in simple, mannerly acceptance of their attention. Grace was not sure, but under her robe the woman seemed to be with child. She was beautiful in the fullness of her figure and face. Try as she might, Grace could not recall ever seeing this woman before, unless perhaps among the forest of wooden faces in the firelight at the Belknap Hut.

The piping and dancing went on and on, and as Grace watched, it occurred to her that none of the persons taking part had place or self apart from the others. The identity of the young piper lay in the dancers he piped for, and theirs in the beauty they admired, and hers in them all, and all in the bird-like notes in the air, which themselves took part in the grass and wind and farflung sky to the ends of the earth and the limits of heaven—and perhaps even in heaven itself. The point was to perfect oneself only in one's membership in the harmony, the local dance of birth and death in which we find ourselves for a season, the echo of a greater dance which is and was and ever shall be. This, it suddenly came to her, was the significance of her having seen her likeness in others—in Matheu and in Millican—and even in the faces of trees. She was twin, cousin, daughter and mother to the world, and must step with it or step out of it altogether—and so step out of her one true self.

So enthralled was she by this realization that she literally stepped out of the cave, hoping to be allowed in the dance. But the moment her foot touched the grass, all four women completely vanished into the wind. In the twinkling of an eye they were gone.

The young man jumped to his feet and whirled about, dashing his pipe to the ground in frustration. "What do you here?" he demanded.

Grace now recognized him at once. "Colin," she said. He was the one who years before had helped Lady Demaris watch over the marmots.

"Yes, Colin," he repeated. "Who knows not Colin Clout?"

"I'm Grace," she said cautiously. "I met you at the Demaris Cabin, long ago." He nodded vaguely.

"I'm so sorry to interrupt. I didn't mean to." She paused to consider. "I hope they'll be back."

"No time soon that we can predict," Colin scowled, putting both hands on his hips.

"But they haven't really stopped, have they? They are still dancing somewhere, I hope?" In her heart she was sure of it. The pause in the dance was not vacancy but separation, not absence but the limitation of human sense. She did not feel empty; she felt the sweetness and ache of longing for something that was sure to return, that had continued and would continue until someday she was fully part of it.

"No," said Colin wistfully, "they have not stopped."

"But Colin, tell me," Grace addressed him. "You I know, and the three sisters I recognize. But who was the woman in the center?"

"That," said Colin matter-of-factly, "is my fair Rosamond. No goddess like the other three, but graced by them to be another Grace."

"Like me?"

Colin went on as if he had not heard her:

> *"Another Grace she well deserves to be,*
> *In whom so many Graces gathered are."*

"Why," said Grace, "this is getting terribly familiar, and so like a riddle of myself."

"You must solve your riddle to the music of the wind," Colin said.

"Then play again, won't you?" asked Grace.

But looking on the grass where Rosamond had been, she saw something white on the ground. She rushed past Colin and stooping down found a small white rose, plucked but not wilted. She picked it up and pressed it to her nose in the wind. It smelt fresh and clean like the air around her.

"Colin, look!" She turned around to show him what his love had left.

But he was gone, vanished she supposed in the cave for petulant reasons of his own. She returned to the entrance and peered in. "Hello?" she called. "Colin?

Hello!"

Soon she heard footsteps down the passage. "Coming! We're coming!" came voice and echo.

Out stepped William, the bloody hulk of Chambers' body across his shoulders. After him came Millican, supporting her father, and Matheu staggering under the caldron.

"So here you are," William said, laying Chambers out on the turf. "What was all that hurry about?"

Villard sank down on the grass, shielding his vacant eyes from the sun. Matheu set the caldron beside him.

Grace spoke to William as if he had not spoken first. "You didn't pass anyone on your way up?"

"More ptarmigan feathers," William reported. "But not a soul."

Chapter 18
As I Say, When I Say

✳

THE SIX OF THEM NOW STOOD AND SAT AND LAY ON THE SUMMIT, dead and alive, in the warm wind of afternoon. Grace had her first close look at Chambers, bloody and torn, and turned away, sick at heart.

But Millican stood with her arms in the air. "It is so very beautiful, Grace. I am here at last, on the great outside. And here on the summit, the roof of my world, it is even so as I have read:

> *When she shall die the Spire shall spring*
> *In grass and flower and Graces' ring.*

Who the Graces may be I do not know except for you. And here is the grass. And where is the flower?"

Grace held the white rose up in her hand and with the other returned the parchment recipe, quoting again the first quatrain:

> *"At sunset of the equinox*
> *With true-skilled knife and starry locks*
> *Join the flower of Rosamond;*
> *Restore to life what Death hath stunned.*

Here is the flower of Rosamond, Cousin. In Matheu's hand find the true-skilled knife. In William's pocket rest starry locks, the golden hair of your ancient father's one true love, the sky-drowned Stella. Take all three for sunset of the equinox this very night."

Millican received the rose. Then Matheu gave her the carving knife, encased in its sheath, and William dug deep in his pocket until he found the lock of hair. He first showed the lock to Villard, who was still turning his eyes from the sun. It seemed to revive him, to open his gaze, to help him bear the beams of light.

"At sunset then," Millican said. "For this we brought the caldron here. Let us rest meantime, and then fill the caldron from the spring." She pointed to a fountain of water bubbling from the center of the summit. Moments ago, Rosamond and the three sisters had stood and danced in the same spot.

"That wasn't here when I arrived," Grace insisted.

"Perhaps it came because of you," said Millican. "So much else good you have brought with you—this would be the least of your graces. But come, drink."

They all five walked to the fountain and kneeled and drank, realizing only then how thirsty they were. The water had more clear sustenance to it than any water Grace could remember. It seemed full of life and light, more like bread or wine than water.

Old Villard rubbed the spring water into his face and beard and hair, clearing out the stench and matting of long years of sleep with the Harpies. His eyes gained a youthful brightness, and his haggard features cleansed themselves to a hale and wholesome heartiness. "Who knows how long I have been in there?" He turned to Matheu and Millican. "How old are both of you now?"

William, meanwhile, retrieved the bloody body of Chambers from where it lay by the cavern mouth and gently washed its wounds in the fountain. When he had finished, the old man was no less dead, but certainly more like himself and bearable to look upon.

When all of them had drunk and washed, they sat simply chatting in a rustic row, speaking more of the wind and the sun and the feel of the grass than of any of the momentous events and histories they had to share with one another. It was odd, Grace thought afterwards, that they did not spend the time catching each other up on themselves. But at the moment their own stories seemed strangely inconsequential. There was a feeling of quietly waiting for sunset, of drinking in the farflung view that was all around them, of sharing the fountain of the world.

To the west, in the home of the warm full wind, they saw the sparkle of the sea over ridges of fir and cedar and hemlock, darkened now in the shedding of snow. Northward, a pleasing chaos of rivers and mountains stretched to a snowbound horizon. One could lose oneself in the deep canyons and waterfalls and hanging glaciers. The peaks were jagged, sharp with arêtes and needled pinnacles. To the east lay a land of dry buttes and open sagebrush, ponderosa and pinyon pine. The view was brown and dry and clear, an exhilaration of unfenced roaming.

But the direction they looked most often was south, across the sweep of the lava fields now flecked with red where the windworn snow had melted from the pressure ridges. Beyond the red-tipped fields of lava the forest spilled from the threefold laps of the generous Queens, which rose in a fecundity that seemed quite at odds with the barrenness of the Silver Spire. But now the spire dropped away on every side in walls and corners not of ice but of sculpted granite, bright and wet in the westering sun. The tower was not alien ground, the dark side of a troubled moon, but now simply a place to be at rest. And come sunset, they hoped it too would give new life.

At long last, the mound that held the cavern entrance began to cast a shadow across the rest of the summit. William and Matheu filled the caldron in the fountain, and Millican touched her hand to the bottom underneath. Directly the water began to steam, and then to boil.

"Now," she said:

> *"William, with thy ice ax stir;*
> *Save him as you murdered her."*

He winced at the mention of murder, but she reassured him. "Even the best and most necessary deaths are wrong. But peace, William—I of all people bear you no malice."

So he put his ice ax headfirst into the caldron, and holding onto the shaft near the spike, began to stir the boiling water.

"And now," she said, distributing the three ingredients to the others, "do as I say, when I say."

She stood back and raised both hands:

> *"Brother, plunge thy true knife in,*
> *Heal the wounds of kith and kin."*

Matheu carefully unsheathed his knife and dropped it into the center of the caldron.

Then Millican turned to old Villard:

"Father, add those locks of hair
Cropped from stars and sky and air."

Villard stepped up to the caldron and somewhat reluctantly parted with Stella's bright blonde hair. "For Chambers I'll do it," he grumbled half under his breath. "No one else, I think."

Then Millican turned to Grace.

"Cousin, drop the gentle rose;
Be the end of Harpies' woes."

Grace held the rose out over the caldron and let it slip down into the seething. She stepped back, and William continued stirring the potion with the head of the long-handled ax.

At a nod from Millican, Matheu picked up Chambers' body. A gust of wind blew full and strong, and the sun just touched the horizon.

"Uncle, now you enter in;
Rise to be what you have been."

William stood back, and Matheu laid Chambers gently in the bubbling water. His bulk and girth were completely submerged. Everyone stood very still, and the sun sank slowly into the glimmer of the Western Sea. The burning globe was half submerged, then three-quarters, then only holding a candle flame above the horizon. Then it was gone, and the summit was bathed in the dusk of a final alpenglow. For a moment Grace feared nothing would happen, that they had only succeeded in boiling Chambers into a terrible parody of one of his favorite soups or stews.

But then a shining head of gold-bronze hair thrust wet and streaming out of the caldron. "I say," it bellowed, "what am I doing here in the soup? I won't vouch for the flavor of this one. *Numquam certus*, I always say. And now in perfect particular." He rose up and stepped completely out of the water.

"Oh, but Sir Chambers," Grace said, rushing up to him eagerly. "You *are* in perfect particular."

What huggings and weepings and general rejoicings took place then can only dimly be imagined. Suffice it to say that with Millican's mysterious help, Chambers actually did contrive to prepare for them all a fresh caldron of lentil soup, and as night gathered and the stars shone thickly about, they served themselves again and again without scorching their fingers, even though the soup was hot and their hands were the only ladles they had.

Thoroughly warmed, and sheltered somehow against the wind (Grace thought this might be Millican's doing), they sat and tried to tell their stories. But they kept getting sidetracked—Chambers especially—into the most uproarious jokes. Soon everything—their deaths and trials and long captivities all included—had somehow become the stuff of infinite laughter. They threw back their heads and howled and bellowed at the stars until the tears came down their faces. Then someone would try to speak in earnest, and they would all fall to laughing too hard for words again.

And the stars. Once the hilarity had passed, they simply sat and looked at the heavens. It seemed to Grace they were sitting not so much under the stars as in and among them, twinkling lives given their brief moment in the circling ring of the Great Dance. More than ever she felt a longing to be and continue her part in it. Chambers and Villard were pointing out the new spring constellations— The Marmot, The Ouzel, The Gopher, The Fawn—and Millican was drinking them in, feeling for the first time their clear sweet influence. William held his ice ax before him, meditating, and the head of it shone like an earthbound star, clasped inside the jewel of his hand. And Matheu lay quietly on his back. "I see," he murmured, "a thousand faces."

At some late hour they fell asleep, pillowed one upon the other, warm as the family they had now regained and become. Afterwards William called it his most unlikely and yet most comfortable bivouac of his climbing career. The night deepened, the stars wheeled by, in perfect peace.

Before dawn, however, when only the grayest of light touched their faces, Villard shook them all awake. He looked pinched and nervous. "She came to me in my dream," he shuddered. "A most fearsome spirit, wandering the wastes of the north, of Cold-Kiss." He could not cease trembling as he spoke.

The others rubbed the sleep from their eyes, trying to give him their waking attention. Grace felt her stomach lurch as she sat up.

"She appeared to me with a long sad shriek," Villard continued. "I cannot tell you everything that passed between us. Not everything. But I can say this. At last she has forgiven me my betrayal of her promised hand."

Hearing this, Chambers started to his feet in indignation.

"No. Sit down, Brother," Villard told him. "It *was* a betrayal. I did not keep my word. Worse perhaps, I kept my promise initially and then forsook it. I do not blame her for her anger. That is the second part of what I can say: she has confessed her bitterness, and I in turn have forgiven her my years of sleep, and have promised to care for Matheu and Millican—or more likely, to be cared for by them. For your sakes, children, I cannot regret my errors. But all, I say, is forgiven now."

"I add to yours my pardon," said Millican.

"And mine," said Matheu.

"I'll think about it," Chambers said. His fists were clenched. "The gall of that woman. The last thing she said before sending me off to sleep in that den was that she was dreadfully weary of my prying about in that tarn of mine. As if it were any of her business what I choose to see in my pond."

Villard smiled weakly and clapped his brother on the shoulder. "And one more thing she bid me speak, and this I daresay you will like: the ice ax, once again, will fly, and bear all of us home together."

All of the others released a sigh—especially William, who had checked for the circling ramp of ice in the afternoon and found that it had melted away. Secretly, they had each been wondering how they would descend the tower. And this was a far more wonderful way than any of them had dared to imagine.

Grace touched Millican's cheek and pointed to the morning star in the paling sky, hung astride the silhouette of the North Queen. To her the distant planet of love was blossoming like a white rose.

Chapter 19
Farewell, My Home

✳

THEY GATHERED ON THE SOUTHERN BRINK, where the spire plunged down to a ghostliness beneath their feet. The stars still shone around and among them; only the edge of the eastern sky was beginning to brighten over the desert.

"Farewell, my home," Millican whispered. "I shall not miss you much, I think."

William passed the ice ax to Villard, who gripped the head of it cautiously with his left hand. It was as if he were still wary, after all these years, of being burned. Villard extended the shaft sideways so that Chambers could grasp it near the spike. Then each of the brothers held out his free hand; Millican took hold of her father's, and Grace of Chambers'. Then Matheu joined hands with his sister, and William with Grace, so that all of them formed a handclasped line with the ice ax as the central link.

Grace half expected a moment of terror in setting out, something akin to the way one feels in leaping from a precipice high over a mountain pool, or in backing off a cliff on rappel, as she once had done on a You-Can-Do-It Expedition. But it was not that way. The western wind, which had blown all night, simply lifted them off their feet and sent them sailing high over the dim down land. They swooped to the east, and then as if correcting itself the ice ax turned across the wind directly for the shimmering bulk of the North Queen. Grace felt her feet stretch out behind as she held tight to Chambers' and to William's hands. It was as if she were floating in water. Her white robe billowed softly about, and she felt the gopher nuzzling beneath her streaming hair, just over the top of her shoulder. When she turned her head to look back, the Silver Spire was already well behind and beneath her, its turfy top coming to light. She could just make out the empty caldron gleaming beside the crystal fountain.

For long years after, Grace remembered the feel of flying among the stars. It was a feeling of unfettered freedom, though all of them were bound hand in hand. To let go would be slavery to the punishing gravity of self; to hold on was lightness and liberty, the joy of one consisting in all. As the dawn light spread, the lava fields took shape beneath them, swelling and falling in all directions. The savage ocean was gray, then gold, and then, as sunrise broke the horizon, a flush of rose, as if lifeblood had been spilled again across the land. The Three Queens found their morning splendor, and as Grace looked across her row of companions she saw the beauty of each one—faces shining, hair swept back. William had lost his careworn countenance; his eyes seemed to be straining for the cabin he knew in the western lap of the Center Queen. Chambers and Villard looked positively youthful again, immortal perhaps, their beards reddish and golden in rays of sun. And Millican held Matheu's hand as if the world were all before them, which it was, to be seen and learned.

Still they flew on. The sun climbed into the fullness of morning, and the lava field turned blinding white. Ahead of them lay the welcome dark skirts of the forest, and as it approached, they all became conscious that the ax was dropping them gently downwards. The furrows and crests of the plain beneath them became more clearly visible, the rockier parts now free in the wind. Grace was recalling their torturous journey on heavy skis when William squeezed her hand and nodded.

"Look down," he said.

At first she saw nothing. Whatever it was, she wished that he would point it out with his free hand.

"There," he said. "Ptarmigan."

And then she saw them, all in a row, six white snowballs scooting across a lava crest. *A parade,* she thought, *of earthly belonging.*

And then the lava field was gone, and they were sailing through the crooked tops of mountain hemlock and hearing the sound of boughs and branches tossing and sighing in the wind. "So these are true trees, Brother," Grace overheard Millican say. "I think them very much alive. You will show them to me, every one?"

Very soon the Belknap Hut hove into sight, just across a familiar ravine now filled with the rush and roar of snowmelt. Atop the hut, smoke was curling out of the chimney. *Whoever could be here?* thought Grace. She did not have long to wonder, however, for the ice ax brought them quickly down in a mad tumble on a very wet snowbank just outside the door of the hut. They came somersaulting to a stop, all laughing again like wild children just as they had the night before. Grace was first to skip to the porch, for her boots were still on Millican's feet, and the snow was cold against her own. As she stood there waiting for the others, the door opened and out came a woman in a long blue gown, blonde hair streaming past her shoulders. Her face wore the soothfast fairness of hope.

All laughing stopped. Villard approached in a crazy stagger, punching holes in the snow to his knees. Then he faltered and collapsed on the step. "Stella," he choked. "You have come."

She nodded, descended, arms open.

"You have come," he repeated brokenly—"to live with me and be my love."

She held his face and spoke softly to him, so that Grace alone overheard:

"And we will all the pleasures prove
That valleys, groves, hills, and fields,
Woods, or steepy mountain yields."

She raised him up and embraced him sweetly until the others came shuffling near.

Then Villard stepped back and put one arm about Matheu and the other about Millican. "This—this is my son, my daughter. You will be mother to them as well?"

"Most sincerely," Stella replied. "With all my heart."

She kissed them both and then lifted her eyes to include Grace and William and Chambers as well. "You are welcome each one. Three to be mine, three to be guests, and all to breakfast."

The morning feast that she had prepared for them beggared description. There was hot-buttered toast and thick rich oatmeal with raisins and spices, and omelets made of ptarmigan eggs (freely given, Stella assured them) that were dripping inside with melted cheese and wild onions. They washed it down with endless mugs of mulled cider and steaming chocolate, and when they had finished, which was long after they had begun, even Chambers declared himself satisfied. "Amazing," he said, "how a little travel vastly increases one's appetite."

He was just settling back from the table, prepared to enjoy a leisurely process of digestion, when Stella turned to him and said, "Not too comfortable, Sir Chambers. Your morning flight is not yet over. You too have a guest awaiting you—at your own cabin."

At this, he shot up out of his chair like a pyroclastic volcanic eruption. "You don't mean—? She wouldn't have finally—? Not—?" For once in his extravagantly articulate life, he could not finish a single sentence.

Stella sat back and looked at him slyly, relaxing the accustomed rigor of her gaze. "Go and see, dear brother. I tell you no more."

Chambers grabbed William by the arm and pulled him forcefully out of his chair. "Get your ax, man. Why do you insist on being so dilatory? You heard the lady. Company waiting. Perfectly rude to delay any further."

William smiled, and Grace, who was talking with Millican in front of the fire, could not help laughing at all that she had overheard.

"I see I must go now, Cousin," she said. "Let us ever be friends."

"Yes," said Millican, eyes glistening. "I have found more of myself in you than ever I thought possible."

The two young women wept and embraced, and then at the last minute decided to re-exchange their clothing, so that Grace would have proper attire for whatever her mountain journey might bring. From outside the door they heard Chambers grumbling. "No sense of respectful punctuality left in this addled world. As if we had all day to try on clothes."

But soon enough Grace re-emerged in her old wool garb, her gopher safe in the pocket of her knickers. On the porch she bid adieu to everyone, and William with her, while Chambers waved impatiently from the wet snowbank where they had landed. "We're getting late for lunch, I think," he called to the others. "Absolutely and expressly time to go."

At last Grace and William descended to him, the rush of wind and trees in their ears. The forest was still tossing about them. This time they all three put a hand to the ice ax, Grace in the middle of the shaft and William and Chambers on either side. For a moment they were simply standing on the snow, all feeling the slightest bit foolish to be holding onto the ax together. And then suddenly they were whirling aloft, looking down at the waving foursome on the porch of the Belknap Hut and sailing over the restless treetops. There was not even time to shout goodbye.

It did not take long to see the ax was taking them directly up the broad slopes of the North Queen. Soon they were rushing past timberline and crossing clownish humps of moraine. Without touching the mountain they were climbing it to the very top, skimming over the snowdraped glaciers where only the largest crevasses were open, yawning against the whelming drifts. But they needed no rope, no bridges, to cross them. The ice ax flew unerringly to the rim of the crater, where it dusted their toes in the cornice lip and flung them speeding across the hollow at the center, the blue clear lake still overlain and winterbound. Then over the opposite rim they raced, hurtling down a broad couloir that narrowed like an hourglass (Grace was almost sure that she and William had once climbed through it) and then opened onto the lap of a glacier that spread below them to a saddle that separated the North from the Center Queen. There near the shore of a tarn still frozen they saw the shape of Chambers' cabin, as distinct against the windswept flat as Grace remembered the caldron to have last appeared on the dawning summit of the Silver Spire.

"Look!" shouted Chambers. "Smoke in the chimney! As absolutely certain as the celerity of this splendid ax. *Semper rapidus, semper certus,* as I've always insisted. She's got the home fires burning."

And so they were. The ax no sooner brought them to a skittering stop on a windworn drift at Chambers' step than out the door came Lady Demaris, all in green, urging them to come in quickly out of the cold.

"And me too? That is, I as well? As much as to say, myself included?" Chambers stammered. He stood knee-deep in the drifted snow and began to shake, looking up at the woman of his deepest dreams as if she would surely disappear as she had so many times before. Grace thought he had never looked so pathetic or so beautiful—the picture of a perfect longing.

"Yes, you too, my dear Sir Chambers," said Lady Demaris merrily, letting the wind blow once again through the rich sheaf of her chestnut hair. "For pity's sake. You'll freeze in the wind otherwise, you old goat. By the way you have gone flying about, anyone would think it were spring."

She allowed herself to be gently kissed—as gently, that is, as Chambers could manage—and soon for the second time that day the travelers were inside a warm cabin enjoying a magnificent meal. This time it was stew and beans and fresh-baked bread, and a root-stuffed pie that was so much better than it sounded that Chambers and William had three or four slices apiece. Grace was hungry not so much for the feast before her as for the delicious sense of returning to a place from her past. Chambers' hearth was warm and familiar and laden with memories, not least of which was the love she had first felt for Lance. There by the fire he had lain near death, so beautiful in his golden youth, a victim of Lira's poison berries. She gazed once more on the polished, egg-shaped chimney stones and felt a smile that seemed to start inside her womb. In a quiet, inner way it was possible to re-imagine a true affection for her husband. And while she was here in Chambers' cabin, there were so many things she wanted to ask of Lady Demaris—not to find out anything in particular, such as where she had been (and where Garth and Lira still might be), but just to enjoy her motherly attention and presence.

When the last crumb was eaten, however, it was Lady Demaris who turned her questions upon them. "William," she said, "do you fear to leave this place?"

"This cabin?" he said.

"The whole place. The place we live and hope to care for. Do you think it cannot live without you?"

He said nothing, caught by surprise.

"Know this. The winds that brought new life to the Silver Spire brought death to what you so fiercely hated near at hand on the South Queen. Avalanches— greater than those that buried Grace—have closed over the western slopes. Those who come there will not return. They will seek another, safer place to extend the empire of Media. This happened when you were far away. You did not do it, though it happened in part to be done by you."

He looked at her blankly still, key-cold and deathly silent. *Speak what the key says,* she had said. It occurred to him then that the key said nothing at all. Or perhaps it had. *After carving a long time, it is better simply to see.*

Lady Demaris addressed him again. "Your family awaits you at my cabin down the hill. Sometimes you shall live with them there, and other times—more times than you like—you shall go with them to the valley below. But remember, William. Take love with thee:

> *then wilt thou not be loth*
> *To leave this Paradise, but shalt possess*
> *A paradise within thee, happier far."*

Without waiting to see whether William had fully understood, Lady Demaris turned to Grace. "You, Daughter, have learned more already than I can tell you. Your husband awaits you at trail's end. Rather, he will have come when you arrive. The tracks that Gwen has left this morning will guide you out by evening light and keep you atop the softening snow. Let the love of your dear cousins—your other and deeper and truer selves—direct your heart and keep your thoughts."

She smiled and kissed Grace on the forehead.

"Now, listen, both of you. Sir Chambers was right. You must not wait. The sun hastens toward the west. The skis that you left at the foot of the spire are even now outside the door. You will take no packs. And the ice ax, William, must stay with us."

This staggered him. "Forever?" he said in a quiet voice.

"For now," she said. "You must use it as you are used by it. And perhaps the ax will make good use of your hands again. For now, however, what lies ahead of you lies below you:

> *There is an art of conducting oneself in the lower regions*
> *By the memory of what one saw higher up."*

She solemnly ushered them both to the door, where they found their wooden skis and poles leaning against the side of the cabin, just as Lady Demaris had said. This time it was Chambers who delayed their parting, pawing at them tearfully again and again like a sorrowful bear. Then their skis were on, and mittens and caps retrieved and donned from forgotten corners of the cabin. When all was ready, William gave the ax to Chambers and asked him to keep good care of it.

"I will guard it as my life," said Chambers.

"But consider," said William. "You've lost that once already."

And then they were off, skiing side by side down the gentle slope away from the cabin, heading into the afternoon sun. When they reached the shore of the frozen tarn, Grace and William turned to wave.

And the cabin was gone.

Chapter 20
Into the Earth

✳

THE RUN DOWNHILL WAS PLEASANT AND SURE. Grace liked the feel of skis again under her feet, and of slipping down the hills and ravines, sometimes following William's tracks and sometimes making her own. The way was not so steep that she had to worry about her balance, but not so gentle that she had to make the effort of striding. She merely had to stand and glide—as self-possessed as an owl in moonlight sailing across an open field.

And so they descended, slowly and simply against the delicious breath of the wind, making effortless contours through untracked snow. They came at last to the stubby snags of timberline, gale-scoured and ice-sculpted, and then into the rich-smelling hemlock groves that dotted the parklands lower down. Soon they heard sounds of running water, though as of yet there was none to be seen, and sounds too of jays and finches and nutcrackers that flitted and sang in the blowing trees. It was an alpine world come alive again, and they were in it, and that was enough. Poised between the encouragements of Lady Demaris and the joys and trials of family, each of them felt the truancy of wilderness, the satisfaction of everyday friendship here and now. It was not the sort of moment that Grace would later describe as one she most wanted to live over again, but it was a moment in which they were nevertheless most alive, feeling the normalcy of their pulses as surely as their skis felt snow beneath wooden grain.

Grace wanted to stop and say something fitting to William before they reached the Demaris Cabin, but she was not tired or thirsty or hot or cold and could think of no excuse to stop. She wanted to define somehow their common bond, to wish him as well with his waiting spouse as she sensed he wished her well with hers. But some things, some relationships, were perhaps best left uncharted and unspoken.

She had just given up on the idea when William suddenly paused before her. He was on the edge of a knotted clump of whitebark pine, peering down across a clearing. Grace stopped at his elbow and looked. It was nearly evening now. On the other side of the open space, across a ravine, a familiar cabin held its ground, smoke rising like mist from the chimney.

He looked at her. "I guess this is it," he said in a husky sort of understatement. "Thanks for everything." Leaning across from his planted skis, he tried to give her a generous hug, but he couldn't quite reach her without falling over. "I feel like I should—" he began. "It's just that I—I wanted to . . ." He trailed off, wordless.

"William," she said, "you really don't have to explain."

She held out her mittened hand. "Friends?" she said.

"Friends," he affirmed, and shook her mitten heartily. "More and less than ever, I think."

She remained in the shadow of the trees while William skied the last stretch to the waiting cabin. Before he had climbed up out of the ravine a little girl—a little blonde girl—burst out the door, hands on her hips. "It's about time," she said. "Dinner is waiting. You have to wash your hands, you know."

Before William reached his daughter, Grace had already slipped away behind the trees. She found the suggestion of a trail below the cabin, a faint hollow of indentation, and followed it south for several yards, struggling in the soft snow until she came to Gwen's fresh tracks. They were smooth and hard, easy to keep. As the sun dropped into clouds in the west, she traversed the mountainside up and down from hill to hollow with skillful steps. From vantage points between the trees she considered the cloud front on the horizon. The thaw was anomalous, she knew. It would be replaced by spring storms not all that different from those of winter. But it was the promise and hope that counted.

Under each ravine that she crossed she heard the sound of rushing water, sometimes muffled under the snow and sometimes clear and distinct beneath her skis. Finally, at dusk, just a mile from the trailhead, she came to a crossing where the melt had broken the cover of snow. Upstream and downstream she saw no bridge. So she took off her skis, unlaced her boots, and prepared to make an icy wade.

At the water's edge, among the roots of a grand fir, her toes suddenly touched bare soil. She crouched and poked in the freshness of the dirt with her finger. Something in the soil was green, sprouting: the first shy tip of an avalanche lily.

It was then that she felt the familiar stirring at her side. Carefully she reached down into her pocket and scooped the gopher into her hand. In the failing light she held him up close to her eyes. For just a moment her nose touched his. Then she released the pocket gopher into the glistening roots of the tree and saw it go, born again into the earth.

BOOK IV: SPRING

The White Fawn of Otium

✳

Sweet lovers love the spring.
—Shakespeare, *As You Like It*

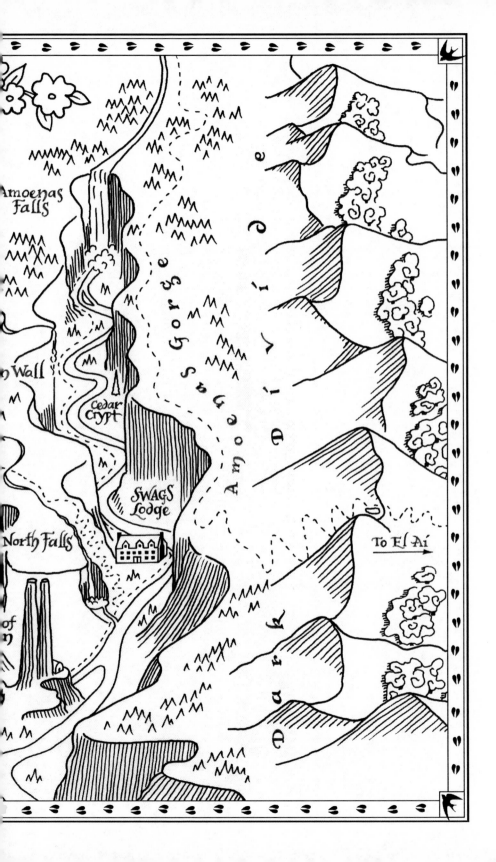

Chapter I
The Cedar Crypt

✳

Now EIGHTY FEET UP, Lara could no longer be sure that her client's knot was correctly tied. From where she was seated on mossy granite, the rope led from her right hand around her waist and down between her dangling feet through a partly open chimney of rock to a man in a skintight spandex suit who stood uneasily in the meadow. He had once been athletic, she could tell, but now was slightly overweight, and in any case looked rather ridiculous in pink. She had never caught on to lycra herself, and preferred the faded, baggy wool knickers that Roper had given her for her birthday. Though they did itch, especially on a damp ledge.

Right now she wished that Roper were still on the grass below so that he could check on Pink-Man's knot. Not Pink-Man, she corrected herself, but a Mr. Lott. Lance, he had told her to call him. But Roper was already off the ground with another client, Lance Lott's rather anemic son—a college boy— somewhere around the corner of the buttress. She had just heard Roper call down that he was off belay, just as she was, anchored to the rock and waiting for his client to climb. They were probably doing Harm's Way, a beginner's route on this part of the south wall of Amoenas Gorge. In early May, the sun was getting high enough to warm and dry this side of the gorge for another season. But there were still seepages, mossy wet spots, and she was sitting on one of them. Higher up there was still snow on the topmost ledges. Roper would be in morning sunlight where he was, but on her side of the stone prow, Lara sat in dank shade that extended upwards a full two thousand feet to the rim—part of why this climb was called the Cedar Crypt.

They wouldn't be climbing anywhere near that far today—not to the rim. And if Lance Lott were improperly tied to the rope, they wouldn't be climbing anywhere at all. She had checked it for him—a double bowline with a follow-through safety—before she had left the ground, but as soon as she had anchored herself on the mossy ledge he had untied and disappeared behind a giant western red cedar—the only one remaining on this side of the gorge. It was like that with clients who talked the most and the loudest about their prowess. Get them to the base of a cliff and their bowels started bubbling like a witch's brew. He had re-emerged with trembling hands and re-attached the rope to his harness with a look of amnesia on his face.

"How's that knot?" she called down. He had moved so that he was now obscured by the branches of the red cedar that grew up alongside the face.

"Good—I think," he shouted back. "The rabbit comes out of the hole, around the tree, and then—back in the hole? Or does he break out of jail and shoot the sheriff? I forget which."

Lara groaned. "Listen," she said. "Maybe I better rappel down just to check."

"Just kidding!" Lance Lott shouted. "Really, I got it. Trust me on this."

"You're sure?"

"Listen, honey, I went on a You-Can-Do-It Expedition with that red-bearded boss of yours before you were even born."

Lara didn't say anything. At the moment she felt that if indeed the knot were mis-tied and the man fell off the end of the rope the world would be a richer place.

"On belay?" she heard. This was the official signal. He was checking to see if she were securely anchored and ready to bring him up on the rope.

"Belay on," she answered.

"Climbing!"

"Climb on." This last was her signature on the contract. She pulled the rope in quickly at first to get rid of a few feet of slack. Then she felt him on the end of the line, something like a big fish. Her task was not to reel him in as dead weight but to keep him loose and let him climb on his own power. If he slipped, the running rope would cinch itself about her waist. He would fall a few feet—the rope did stretch—but essentially he would dangle at his point of departure until he cared to try again. Most of the guides for the School of Western Alpinism Guide Service preferred to use a mechanical belaying device, but Lara liked the old-fashioned hip belay, just as she liked her woolen knickers—she hadn't dropped anyone yet. In the same way, the other SWAGS guides used the more modern figure-eight follow-through to tie in their clients, but Lara stuck with the double bowline. To her it was a matter not only of elegance but also of tradition. These were the ways her father had taught her, back when she was the youngest climber, boy or girl, to touch the rock in Amoenas Gorge.

"Do I take this out?" Lance Lott had scrambled twenty-five feet to the first anchor point at the bottom of the chimney. Here she had slotted a steel wedge—a nut or chock—in a tapering crack. The nut was slung on a perlon loop she had clipped to the rope with a carabiner. This whole arrangement was to keep her from sailing to the ground as she had climbed. If she had slipped five feet above this piece of protection, she would have fallen ten feet, theoretically held by Lance Lott's belay from below. (She always had her clients use the foolproof belay devices.) On her ascent she had strung a series of similar anchors ten to twenty feet apart, selecting them from a whole collection carefully arranged on a sling over her head and shoulder. That was half the skill of leading. The lowly duty of the climber who followed was to take this protection out—or to clean the pitch, as the process was called.

"Yes!" she called down in response. She had instructed him beforehand, but like most clients, Lance had forgotten under the duress of the climb. "Unclip the rope from the carabiner and lift the chock out of the crack. Don't yank on it."

"Don't what?" he said. She could see him now between her feet, pulling on the sling as if it were the starter cord on a lawnmower.

"I can't get it," he complained. "Why did you jam it in so far?"

She pondered this accusation in silence, then gave the rope a little tug. "Just leave it," she said. "I'll get it later." It was her favorite size and shape of chock—a number 8 stopper—about as large as her two thumbs side by side. She didn't like the idea of leading the next two pitches without it. With her free hand she flipped her blonde hair out of her eyes and settled in for a damp wait. The next move after the stopper was the hardest. Lance Lott would no doubt get stuck.

For a long time there was no more than tentative motion down below. She contented herself with studying a chartreuse splash of lichen beside her, giving the rope an occasional flick to test the presence of the climber. Swallows arced along the rock, swinging away, slashing sky, threading the outstretched limbs of the cedar. The tree was shaggy, huge, old. They would only overlook it when they reached the Cedar Sidewalk, a comfortable ledge that linked the top of their climb with Harm's Way. The plan was to join Roper and young Lott and rappel down to the ground together with both ropes.

But even from here she could see through the branches of the cedar to the meadow dipping down to the river, green and swollen with spring melt, and beyond the river through flowering dogwood and alder groves to the far side of Amoenas Gorge. Framed in the cedar boughs were the first four pitches of the Fawn Wall, a rosy slab that glinted with spots of almost silver glacier polish. She and Roper had put up the first three pitches last week; as yet, the fourth existed only in their imagination. The climbing had proved more difficult and yet more pleasing than anything she had ever attempted in the gorge—harder even, so far, than the east face of the dread Tower of Otium, another of their current projects. The wall had first offered them a long, meandering, finger-breadth crack, and then delicate moves up and across a sweeping face on tiny nubbins. Only sunset, after a late start, had brought them down. There was no telling how many pitches—and days—it would take to reach the top. For there, under the glacier-clad summit of the South Queen, the valley wall rose to its highest—a full three thousand vertical feet from river to rim. From where they had abandoned the climb, they had seen overhead the dark suggestion of overhangs and the wisp of a seasonal waterfall draining the snows of the high country. The wall was so high that the fall was scattered apart by the winds before it could reach the valley floor. Where they had been climbing they only felt an occasional drop, slinging down across the face like a spring swallow. Other than that the route had proved warm and dry, and it looked even more so now, beckoning her in the full morning sunlight, a preferable place to this shade and damp. She would so much rather be there with Roper than here with yet another in a series of boorish paying customers. Climbing could be so deeply beautiful at times that working as a guide could feel like a form of prostitution—sometimes almost literally so. Especially the male clients seemed to be buying merely her companionship, the chance to be linked to a fair-haired girl, if only by a rope.

"How do you get up into the chimney from here?" Lance whined. "I thought these shoes were supposed to stick on anything. I paid enough for them."

She looked down at his upturned face, rimmed with woven gray-brown curls. "The secret," she said, "is to think pure thoughts."

"Not a chance, honey. Not while I'm looking up at those pretty little eyes of yours." He laughed long and loud, something like a donkey.

"In that case," Lara advised, "take your left foot, the one you've got on that little nub."

"Okay," he said.

"Reach it up high."

"Okay," he said. "I'm doing it."

"And stick it in your ear."

For a moment it looked as if he actually would. His foot scrabbled upward, found purchase, and his hands made an ungainly lunge. "Falling!" he screamed.

Reflexively she braced herself and tucked the rope across her waist. It tightened briefly about her hips, then went strangely slack. She heard sounds of a tumble, a soft thud on the grass below. Lance Lott lay flat on his back beneath the cedar, entirely ropeless.

Silently she swore to herself, not so much concerned for him as for her professional future with SWAGS. This was only her second year. For something like this, old Savidge would sack her. If the client were hurt it would go even worse. All that pink lycra lay perfectly still.

"Lance!" she called down. "Mr. Lott! Can you hear me?"

There was no response.

"Don't go away!" she yelled incongruously. "I'll be right down." Accordingly she stood up and loosely coiled the excess rope in her hand. She untied herself from the end and clipped the loose rope through her anchor—an ingenious web of cords and slings emanating from three separate chocks. Then she tossed the coil to the ground.

"Rope!" she called. The end of it swatted Lance across the face, but he did not flinch. A bad omen. She evened out the ends of the line until they were both touching the ground. There was just enough. She crimped the doubled rope into a bight, snaked it through her descending ring, and clipped the ring onto her harness. Only now, still standing on the mossy ledge, did she unclip herself from the anchor. Then she leaned back away from the cliff, let the rope slide through her fist, and nimbly began her rappel, walking her feet down the rock.

Halfway down she turned to look at Lance again, hoping to better gauge his condition. Her first thought upon glancing below was that someone was bending over him, that Roper perhaps had heard the cry and descended to investigate. But it wasn't Roper. It was not, she almost immediately saw, any man or woman at all. It was a fawn, a white fawn, nuzzling Lance Lott in the face.

This struck her as so entirely strange—first, that a young deer would approach so boldly, and second, that it would be so purely white—that Lara hung speechless on the rope. And why should she shoo it away, when it seemed to be touching the stricken man so tenderly? Before she could think of anything at all to say, the fawn lifted its head and turned to look at her steadily with liquid eyes. Whether those eyes held sorrow, or reproach, or curiosity, Lara could not begin to tell. She was sure, however, they were not indifferent.

It was Lara who broke off gazing first. It was her duty after all to reach the victim as rapidly as possible, fawn or no fawn. Facing the cliff she rappelled again as quickly as she could, dropping out of the bottom of the chimney and past her stopper—now hopelessly wedged deep in the crack in which she had placed it. She almost paused to work it out. Certainly it meant more to her than Lance Lott, and this very knowledge chilled her. Below the stopper she checked the rock for signs of blood. They were there in plenty, in smears and splotches, hop-scotching the pearl-gray granite to the ground. She stepped around them carefully. Why, oh why, had she not insisted he wear a helmet?

Once on the grass she unclipped her descending ring and whirled about. The fawn was nowhere to be seen. In the last ten seconds it had vanished.

And Lance was sitting calmly upright.

"You were wrong," he said. "My ear didn't hold."

She knelt by his side, carefully checking all parts of his body that she could see for bleeding wounds. "Lie down," she said. "Don't try to sit up just yet."

"If you insist," he said blithely. "I'll lie down for you any day."

Both hands working in symmetry, she examined him from head to toe. She could find no cuts, no bruises, no broken bones. In fact, he did not report the least bit of soreness. "You sure you're okay?" she asked him incredulously.

"Fine," he said. "Just a thirty-foot drop. I had all this soft grass to land on. But hey, if you want to check me over again, I think I could get into that." He leered at her and laughed like a donkey again.

She turned away in confused disgust, scanning the few feet of rock above them. The bloodstains had completely vanished. She rose to look more carefully. In their place were vibrant whorls of fire-orange lichen. Could it be she had only imagined the spots of blood? The fawn, for that matter?

"Or maybe you could teach me that knot again," Lance Lott suggested. "Demonstrate. Show me where that cute little bunny goes back in the hole."

Chapter 2
Harm's Way

❉

To the redounding credit of Lance Lott, he insisted on giving the Cedar Crypt another go. His bowline securely tied this time, he made it into the rock chimney with only a little winching on the rope from above, and managed to complete the pitch and two more by midday. The ledge at the top was in full sun, and so broad that they could walk it unroped. Lara led him east around the prow of the buttress and into an alcove directly above Harm's Way. They were no sooner settled there, unlacing their tight rock shoes, than a strong hand locked its grip on the edge of the terrace. It was followed by a shaggy blonde head.

"Lunchtime, mates," it said. Another hand appeared on the ledge and plucked a scrap of wet moss, holding it up. "And the house dressing today, love?"

Lara stifled a laugh and fished a stuff sack out of her pack. "Not again," she sighed, peeking inside and hitting her head in mock anguish. "We left the blue cheese at the lodge. All we have is thousand island, ranch, and vinegar." It was a little routine, a formalized greeting, they liked to practice in front of their clients.

The shaggy blonde head shook wonderingly side-to-side. "Guess we'll be going then. Have to try the next eatery up the street." The face started to disappear.

Lara could tell that Lance Lott might have laughed if he did not feel so envious of the fun they were having. She realized how relieved she was to be rescued by familiar company.

"Roper," she said, "get your British butt back up here. Table for four, and we'll make it up to you with licorice. Maureen packed a whole red rope, enough to rappel down on."

"Now that's more like it," he said, re-emerging. Roper mantled the ledge in a bound, chocks and carabiners jangling, and in a series of sure swift strokes had soon woven a web of anchors in a pair of cracks at the back of the alcove. Attaching himself, he leaned out over the edge and called that he was off belay. Then nonchalantly he settled into the space of rock that separated Lance from Lara, pulling the slack through a slotted ring attached to his waist.

"Belay's on!" he shouted.

There was a faint reply from below, and Roper shouted back again, granting his permission to climb.

"So, any adventures this morning, comrades?" He looked back and forth, inviting an answer from either side.

There was only a short pause.

"A cruise," said Lance. He turned to Lara. "How hard did you say that was? I was hoping for more of a challenge."

"That one move is 5.7," Lara replied. "The rest of it is 5.5."

"What move was that?" said Lance. "I guess I hardly noticed it."

Suddenly the rope went tight through Roper's ring. He clenched the line between his fingers.

"So how's my boy?" Lance asked. "Slowing you down a little bit, is he?"

Roper gave him a pained look, not easily explicated. "A little slow, but terribly interested to learn. I've never seen anyone practice his knots so thoroughly."

Lance was stuck for a reply, and Roper started pulling the slack through his belay device again. Before very long, after several more stops and starts, a nervous, sweating, pale face of a young man with a shock of brown hair in his eyes appeared like a puppet on the rim of the ledge. He looked abashed by the unexpected size of his audience.

"Off belay?" he said weakly.

"Not till you get up here, out of Harm's Way, you're not," Roper said, and motioned him up over the lip.

The young man staggered to his father's side and looked over at Lara shyly. "I hope we haven't kept you," he said. "Waiting, I mean."

"Not at all," Lara replied. She was surprised to feel the words come forth so earnestly.

"The lady's being polite, Purse," Lance Lott interjected. "The fact is, your old man is starving. If you had taken any longer I would have cut the rope with my own hands."

The young man visibly blanched. Whether out of fear or embarrassment—or both—Lara could not tell.

"Where's that licorice?" Roper yawned, brushing a pile of rope aside.

"Purse?" said Lara, as if to herself.

Taking this as an invitation, he hesitantly stepped around the rope to her side. "I forgot to ask you in the boat this morning if that is your real name."

"Percival, actually," he said. "You can call me either one."

"Do you have a preference?"

She could see him thinking it over, as if it were difficult to decide. "Purse is easier," he shrugged.

"Your first climb?"

"My very first." There was in his voice a slight tinge of pride and wonder.

"Congratulations then," said Lara, and she stood up and quite solemnly shook his hand. Their eyes met as their hands touched, and for the second time that day Lara felt caught by a gaze that expressed much but said little. The rest of him was certainly unprepossessing. In his stiff new khaki pants he was all shyness and awkward boyhood compared to Roper's animal sureness of body and manner. And he was not someone who spent time out of doors—the morning of climbing into the south had given his nose a blazing sunburn.

Purse dropped her hand and looked down at his harness like a startled thing. "Should I untie from the rope?" he asked no one in particular.

His father and Roper had joined forces to unearth licorice and lunch, and paid him no mind.

"Yes, certainly," Lara told him. "We're safe here."

He grappled with it uncertainly, then gave her a rather miserable look. "It's gotten pretty tight," he said. "I guess I fell on it quite a bit."

"Let me see," Lara said. She stooped to feel the knot at his waist. This was a routine gesture for her—people were forever needing help with their knots. But this time it felt strangely intimate. She pushed and pulled on the bights of rope, all the while conscious of his shifting weight—without meaning to she was rocking him back and forth on his feet. "There," she said, the knot dissolving onto the terrace. "You're free now."

"Thank you," said Purse, shyly looking at her again. "I thank you."

Not *thanks a lot*, or *thanks*, but *I thank you*. As if it had been the most natural thing for him to say. Lara marveled.

Purse retreated and took a seat next to his father, and Lara sat down again beside Roper, a small distance from their clients. "So," muttered Roper, smacking his licorice, "have you met your bloody Prince Charming? Think if you kiss him he'll stop looking so much like a frog?"

Lara colored. For the last three weeks, ever since the beginning of the season, Roper had been, except for Maureen, the one she spent her time with, whether on working days like this or on the occasional afternoon off. The Fawn Wall loomed directly across from them now, in pale rose and silver splendor, a reminder of their joint ambition. Lara and Roper were possibly the best climbers that old Savidge had ever employed.

"You'd better know your *litt-ur-a-toor*. The bloke's a bloody English major at an actual university. Not like you—a term at the city college if and when you feel like it."

"What's going on?" she whispered fiercely. "I untie someone's knot while you're rooting around in the lunch sack, and suddenly I'm open season?"

She looked deliberately past him to Purse. "Getting enough over there?"

"Plenty," said Lance. "Such as it is. Where's the beer?" He belched and laughed.

Purse passed Lara some sausage and crackers, and Roper gave them some lemonade. Finally they shared some gorge bars that Maureen had baked at the lodge.

"What's in these?" Lance marveled.

"Marmot dung," Roper said. "A closely guarded recipe."

Purse chewed his for a while before pronouncing, "I think them very good."

Lara would tell Maureen this. Not only what Purse said, but how he said it. From where they sat on the Cedar Sidewalk, three hundred feet above the narrow valley floor, they could look west to the little lodge on the far shore of the shining Amoenas. It was perhaps two or three miles downstream, an oversized log cabin with a small dock on the water. Behind the lodge a zigzag trail steeply climbed a broken cliff, and next to the trail a stunning fall dropped from the rim, at this distance a static but brilliant ribbon of white. Spray from a plunge pool shot out from a grove of trees. She could just hear the crash of water. The sound was overwhelmed, however, by the motor of a powerful jetboat, now leaving the dock by the lodge. It swung upstream, roostering into the green swift current like a live and angry animal, wounded in some secret way. The whine got louder as the boat made its way upriver.

"Will it wait for us?" Purse asked anxiously.

"It's going all the way up to Amoenas Falls, mate, at the head of the gorge," Roper said wearily. "We'll catch it on the way back. Plenty of time to abseil down. Unless you want to fly," he added.

Lara gave Roper a twist in the ribs with a carabiner but said nothing. All of them lazily followed the progress of the boat, charting its passage through willow and alder and spring-green thickets of dogwood. In many places the valley was simply open meadow or fields of fern, home to well-fed mule deer and cinnamon-colored black bear, though Lara could see none at present. And on either side, on and on, the rock walls rose steep and smooth, rebounding the whine of the jetboat. There were prows and columns and shields and arches, impossibly upheld overhangs and deep recesses thick with moss. To the practiced eye, and Lara had one, this terrain was crisscrossed by invisible paths, some well known and others yet-to-be discovered. One reason she and Roper had brought their clients here today was to get this view from the Cedar Sidewalk of the upper portions of the Fawn Wall.

"Have you been looking at the overhangs," she whispered to Roper—"about two-thirds of the way up? Think they'll go?"

He pulled a small pair of field glasses from the top flap of his rucksack. Looking through them he studied this crux, then handed the glasses to Lara without comment.

She saw for herself. The overhanging section of wall, a huge roof, was broken only by a slippery groove, black with lichen and water stains. Above this groove blew the stray wisps of the intermittent waterfall. By late afternoon, at the daily height of the snowmelt, the waterfall would reach farther down. "So we might have to wait until autumn," she said, lowering the binoculars. "When the runoff slows down." Above the groove the fall of water wavered in dissipating sheets, catching the sun in airy rainbows.

"Grand prize for that bit of deduction, love," Roper said. "But there's plenty to work out until then. About seven hundred meters' worth."

A flight of swallows came skimming by, hurtling like stones that for some reason were falling sideways. Lance, who had been gesturing across the meadows, rhapsodically explaining something to his son, reached over for more red licorice. "What are you looking at there?" he said, noticing the field glasses. "Bird-watching?" He said this with a slight sneer.

"I should like that," Purse said.

"Here," said Lara, passing the glasses down to him. "Tell me what you can see."

Purse took the glasses solemnly and looped the strap about his neck. He trained the lenses on the top of the cedar just left of them.

"You don't need the binocs for that," his father said contemptuously. "If there are any red-breasted tit warblers in that tree, you can just use the naked eye. Try that meadow across the river, the one I was telling you about. See what we have to dispose of before we file that godalmighty environmental impact statement."

"For what?" said Lara, instantly alarmed.

"Nothing much. Golf course, tennis courts, swimming pool. And a real hotel—something more than that tiny log shack of yours. A modest destination resort. Maybe two golf courses. Plenty of room, after all."

"But this is wilderness," Lara said indignantly. "And protected as such. The lodge, the jetboat, and the research station down at the Tower of Otium are the only legal exceptions."

"So far they are," Lance replied. He stretched his arms over his head, apparently bored by her objections. "But you need to understand. People want to do more than just climb rocks or hike trails or ride to the falls in the little boat. We have to give them something to keep them occupied. Maybe an ice rink. And a mall too—a small one, of course."

Lara was so amazed by this spandex insolence that she could think of nothing to say.

"I know what you're thinking," Lance said. "But trust me, the whole project will be developed with the utmost sensitivity to the natural surroundings. In some ways it will look even better. We'll clear out the dead snags and plant ten trees for every one we have to remove. And after we're through, those meadows won't be nearly as wet and marshy as they get in the spring. Fewer mosquitoes, better hiking—an improved natural paradise."

Lara felt tears coming.

"And what would you say to a soak in a hot tub after a long day on the rock? Think of the benefits for yourself."

"Now you're talking, mate," said Roper. "Compared to the Lake District, this place always did seem to me a bit under-civilized."

Lara looked at him hard. He was serious. She rose abruptly and walked to the far side of the alcove. Her father's blood ran much too deep in her veins to brook any further compromise of the Three Queens Wilderness. In her opinion, the jet boat was more than obscenity enough. Meanwhile, Roper and Lance huddled together, exchanging visions of the future, and Purse looked steadily through the glasses at the precariously pristine meadow. She suddenly wondered what he thought.

"Lara," said Purse. It was the first time he had used her name, and his voice was strangely animated. "I see something. In the meadow. Directly under that big wall, right where the waterfall would hit if it could come down all the way."

"Well," said Lara. "What is it?"

"I've never seen one quite like this—not here. At Oxford, I think, Magdalen College, fenced in. But not here."

"What do you mean?" she said, trembling.

"It's a deer," he said. "A small one. And it's pure white."

Chapter 3
The Climbing Art

✳

"But I thought you liked Roper. Or were starting to, anyway," Maureen said. She was seated on her cot in the moonlight in the upstairs room she shared with Lara. Supper was done for the dozen or so visitors to Amoenas Lodge, and the dishes were at last washed. Maureen was brushing her thick dark hair in long, slow repetitive strokes. It was a way of distancing herself from the world downstairs, of falling into a happier calm.

Lara was more agitated. She stood looking out their window, rocking back and forth on her heels and squeezing a rubber ball in one hand for finger strength. A day with clients never left her feeling she'd gotten enough of a workout, and her purpose this spring had been to keep herself ever and always fit and ready for the Fawn Wall. Tonight, however, her restlessness was more than this. A waxing moon of early evening flooded the meadow behind the lodge, and just beyond it she saw and heard the long fall gleaming in the silvery dark and beating and puffing among the muffled shapes of cedar. She could not tell the spring gust of the waterfall from the fluid pulsing of her heart.

"It's hard to explain," Lara said uncertainly. "Roper's fine to be around—and very funny. And great to climb with. But sometimes it seems . . ."

"Seems what?" Maureen asked, her voice as smooth as her well-brushed hair.

"Sometimes it seems there's no more to him. That everything is on the surface—and none of it's bad, but that's all you get. I mean, have you ever seen him read anything but the climber's guide to Amoenas Gorge? Or talk about anything more than new routes?"

"Not to be rude," Maureen put in, "but you could be describing yourself for the last few weeks."

"Yes, I know. It's so easy for me to slip into that. And, well, maybe he does it just to please me—to give us something to talk about. I like to climb as much or more than he does. I think I will all of my life."

She paused, still staring out at the falls. "Sometimes, when I look up at the Fawn Wall as we were today, I think it will be the ultimate climb that will make everything else all right."

"Which is a lot to expect from a slab of rock, dearie," sighed Maureen.

"And I know that," Lara insisted, turning away from the moonlit window. "At least sometimes I do. But I don't think Roper is capable of either knowing or not knowing it, if you see what I mean. For him it's just a dreary habit he's fallen into, not a pursuit of the soul that one can affirm or deny."

"Eloquent," Maureen nodded, putting down her brush at last. "You must be reading more than the climber's guide after all."

"Not lately I haven't," said Lara. "But when you grow up half your life in a backcountry ranger cabin, you tend to get read to a lot. Thank my mother."

"As well we should," Maureen agreed pleasantly.

Lara nodded. She let her ball slip to the floor, where it bounced through a patch of moonlight and into darkness. Her parents lived a dawn-to-dark hike away, in the meadows under the Center Queen, still carrying out their duties for the forest service. They lived such a plodding life, it seemed to her, making their rounds through woods and meadows and over the occasional glacier. She had chosen the daring of big-wall climbing almost in protest. It was her father, William, who warned her most often of the dangers and the disappointments; her mother, Gwen, who let her go her own way. For some reason, at this point in her young life, she had felt the need to keep her distance. When her parents happened to drop by, a certain awkwardness came with them. Deep down she knew that she loved them. But she also wanted to do without them. When Lance Lott had listed his plans for the meadow under the Fawn Wall, part of Lara had winced to hear herself reply in the way her parents had scripted her.

"But what happened today," said Maureen, earnestly taking Lara's hand and drawing her down on the cot beside her, "that would change your mind about Roper?"

Before Lara could frame a reply, there was a sharp rap on the door. "Yes?" she said. It swung open quickly. Lantern in hand, their aging employer, Park Savidge, stood over them. In the light of his kerosene lamp his balding head looked pale and shriveled, his beard more silver than red.

"Just wanted to brief you girls about tomorrow," he said abruptly. "Lott and I will be touring the upper gorge in the boat. We'll be needing an early breakfast."

"Climbing something?" Lara asked innocently. "I think you'll find him an excellent client."

"No," said Savidge, "an inspection tour. He wants to get the lay of the land. We—he's got some ideas to help make the School of Western Alpinism a more effective operation."

"Lunch?" asked Maureen.

"Pack one. The best you have. And a little wine, if you've got it."

"Naturally," Maureen said.

"Anyone you'd like me to climb with?" Lara said.

"No," said Savidge. "Everyone who went out today wants to take tomorrow off. Except that pair from back East—but they don't need a guide."

"So Roper and I can spend the day on the Fawn Wall if we like?" It was almost too good to be true.

"If he was available you could. But he's coming with Lott and me."

Lara's face must have fallen, for Savidge added, "Don't blame me. He was the one who asked to come. Who am I to get in the way of a young man who seems to have the real future of SWAGS at heart? If you want to climb, take one of the younger guides—some of them need the experience. Why we haven't been hit by a lawsuit yet I do not know. Some of these kids spend so much time soloing without a rope they've probably forgotten their knots—or how to teach them, at any rate. It's enough to make an old man want to retire and play golf."

Without waiting for a reply, he left, shutting the door and leaving them in darkness again which gradually silvered itself with the moonlight.

"Is that what happened?" Maureen asked. "About Roper, I mean? Has he found an interest other than climbing after all?"

"Yes," said Lara. "I saw some of it today. That Lance Lott fellow—you've seen what he's like—was sketching his plans for hotels, tennis courts, I don't know what all, and Roper simply fell down and worshiped at his feet. The whole boat ride back they were thick as thieves, plotting away. All this time I thought he loved the gorge like I did. But for him, I guess, it might as well be a gymnasium. And if there's money and comfort in improving the gym, he wants to be in on it. Next they'll be planning a temperature-controlled plexiglass dome over the entire gorge for year-round activity, just in time for the Climbing Olympics. They'll build grandstands on the fairways, and then spray-paint lanes on the Fawn Wall for the lycra types to go sprinting up in record times. The losers will throw themselves off the rim to demonstrate the utter agony of defeat for the television audiences. There will be safety nets, of course, not to mention instant replays."

"Lara," said Maureen gently. She was squeezing her hand. "It may not be as bad as all that. But I'll agree with you that Savidge has been a lot more interested in the jetboat service this spring than in guiding climbs. And this Lance Lott and his family have certainly gotten the royal treatment. I like his wife, though. Have you met her?"

"The one in the wheelchair?"

Maureen nodded.

"I haven't really talked with her. Just their son."

"Oh, I know. She spoke of him often today."

"So you were chatting her up, were you?"

"She wheeled herself right into the kitchen and insisted on helping me with supper. First time anyone's done that. And she was helpful. Peeled and mashed a whole pot of potatoes."

"What did she tell you about herself?"

"Very little, actually. Simply that her name is Grace, that she met her husband on a You-Can-Do-It Expedition in the Three Queens a long time back, when they were in high school, and that Savidge was actually their leader."

"Hah!" said Lara. "That would drive anyone together for comfort."

"But she didn't say that much about herself, actually. Except—oh—I did find out that she is a writer—of children's books. At least that's what the titles I finally got out of her seem to suggest."

"What are they?"

"Hmm. There's a question. *The Lady and the Lava Beast*, that was one. And something longer—*The Marmot, the Witch, and the Rowboat?* Also, *The Flying* Ax, or *The Magic Ice Ax*—something like that."

"*Puff, the Magic Ice Ax?*" asked Lara.

"No," said Maureen.

"Just checking," said Lara.

"But she mostly talked about Percival."

"You mean Purse?"

"Well, *she* never called him that, though I imagine his father does. She and her husband do seem to have a different perspective on things, their son included."

"Their son most of all, I'll bet," Lara mused, letting go her friend's hand and recrossing the room to the window.

"She seems very proud of him," Maureen continued. "At Oxford and all, studying English literature. But she seems protective of him too."

"Who wouldn't be? I mean, with a father like he's got." She wondered what this gentle woman saw in her husband, but decided not to ask it aloud.

"The funny thing," Maureen went on, "is that she mostly asked about you, Lara."

"About me?" she tried to say casually, looking out onto the meadow.

"Yes. Apparently she knows your parents—your father, at least. And for that matter she said she had met my parents as well."

"At the research station at Otium—on the boat ride up?"

"No," said Maureen. "That is the curious part. It was long ago, on the same trip on which she met her husband."

"Just think," said Lara. "If those bratty kids on that You-Can-Do-It Expedition had been roped together a little bit differently, Lance Lott might be your father. Not Lance and Grace, but Lance and Jennifer, sitting up in a cedar tree."

"There is providence in the fall of a sparrow," Maureen replied.

"And in the fall of a client too, you suppose?" Lara said. She turned away from the glowing window. "Maureen, you're not going to believe this, but our Mr. Lott took a thirty-footer right onto the deck today."

"You let him lead?" Maureen asked incredulously.

"I let him fertilize the old growth," Lara replied, "and I was too far away to recheck his knot. He peeled right off the end of his rope."

"But he's okay?"

"Perfectly—if that's what you want to call his normal state. And he's too embarrassed to tell the others, so I think I'm safe. But *please* don't tell anyone, especially that helpful wife of his."

"That will be hard. She might see the humor in it."

"Well, I don't. What did she want to know about me, anyway?"

"Nothing in particular," Maureen said slowly. "Just whether you were—happy, I guess."

"Well, that's very odd," Lara said indignantly. "Who does she think she is? My fairy godmother? So, what did you tell her?"

"About Roper, a little. And all your talk about the Fawn Wall. She seemed very interested."

"In what way?"

"She said she was not at all surprised that the Fawn Wall attracted you. She said it was right. She said she wished—"

"She said she wished what?"

Maureen lowered her voice. "That you would take Percival on it."

Lara was so shocked at first she could not make a sound. Then she let out peals of laughter. "Percival!" she gasped. "Sir Percival, the climbing wonder? Maureen, he must have taken nine falls on Harm's Way with Roper this morning. And that's 5.4—the easiest multi-pitch climb in the gorge. Do you know what the Fawn is? It's 5.11, and that's just the first three pitches. Higher up it's overhung. Radically. We don't even know if it goes, and what we've put up so far has some of the hardest moves that anyone has ever done in Amoenas Gorge. Where does this lady get her reality?"

"Well," said Maureen, with the air of someone standing up for a new friend, "when you came back this afternoon I could tell she was disappointed to learn that you had climbed with her husband and not her son. I guess I am curious if you like him at all. He's so quiet and serious—and cute, in a way. Not like most of the boys who come up here." There was a moonlit pause. "And certainly not like Roper," she added.

"Sounds like *you're* the one who likes him," said Lara. "I'm sure you can get the mother's blessing. And I'd be glad to loan you my rope to tie the knot on the Fawn Wall."

From the quiet look on Maureen's face, Lara could tell she had overreacted. "From a distance, I like him," Maureen said—"a Platonic distance, I believe. But maybe you could tell me what he is like closer up?"

Lara felt a stab of jealousy, then realized her friend was telling the whole truth. She knew she owed her nothing less in return. "He's—he's—oh, Maureen, I admit it. I don't get it at all, but to you I'll say it. He seems to have charmed me a little. I don't know how. I think it must be pity, really. He's so pathetically misused by his father. And to have such a matchmaking mother, too—it must be hard."

"She's not that way," said Maureen. "Not really."

"Whatever," said Lara. "But would you believe it? After supper he gave me this." She fished a paper out of her pocket. "It's a little poem. He must have written it after we got back to the lodge."

"Private?" said Maureen.

"I guess not," Lara sighed. "Nothing else about my life seems to be." With something of both relief and reluctance she held the paper up to the moonlight in the window and slowly read the poem aloud:

"If by thy hands my knot may be undone,
How much the more my heartstrings by thine eyes?
The one released where nimble fingers run,
The other by thy fixéd gaze thy prize.
No fall have I to fall into thy grace,
Securely knotted to thy better part;
To fall were not to fall when thy sweet face
More sweetly urges on the climbing art.
Nor do I blame my artless lack of skill
To look upon thy face or feel the touch
Of thy deft fingers, though I do but ill
In learning to ascend this face, for such
*   Is thy dear pity in thy hands and eyes*
*   That sinking in them I shall learn to rise."*

Maureen kept an appreciative silence, even after Lara had finished.

"Well," said Lara, lowering the poem, "think his mother wrote it for him?"

"What do you think?" Maureen asked.

"From what you've said, I wouldn't put it past her. But we only returned an hour or two before supper. That's not long enough for her to have known."

"Known what?"

"That I untied his knot today—which is where the poem starts. And I doubt he would have told her about it. Because, in a way, that's how we met. I didn't pay much attention to him on the boat in the morning."

"So what you've got—"

"Is a genuine love sonnet, written by a genuine student of the Queen's English."

"And how does that make you feel, Lara?"

Lara turned to the window again as if looking outside to find an answer. The moon was gaining height in the sky, and the meadow below was shining and still. The entire lodge seemed asleep. She was aware of the sifting sound of the waterfall, glowing above them as if it were the moveable means by which the moonlight spilled its magic down onto the valley floor and into the current of the Amoenas. She felt terribly unsure of herself, but she also felt a perfect peace in her surroundings.

Ne'er saw I, never felt, a calm so deep!
The river glideth at his own sweet will. . . .

She knew a bit of poetry herself, she reflected—as if knowledge of it were part of a contest.

She was just about to turn around and tell Maureen that she didn't know just what she felt, when something caught her eye in the meadow. A figure in a wheelchair was with great effort moving herself through the tall grass, stubborn arms straining against the entangled hubs. Purse's mother, she had no doubt. But why would she be out so late, in a place so unfit for her means of motion? Halfway across the meadow the woman stopped, looking up at the moon and at the waterfall, her silvered hair half-fallen across her face. She seemed to have gotten as far as she wanted. She seemed, in fact, to be waiting for something.

Lara was only half-surprised when out of a shadowy thicket of alder a small white fawn advanced to meet the woman in the wheelchair. Without a trace of skittishness it laid its head upon her lap and allowed her to stroke its neck. The woman seemed to be speaking to the fawn. A strange communion was taking place.

For some reason, Lara couldn't stand it. With both hands she raised the sash, letting in the cool night air. The lattice squeaked, and the fawn and the woman looked up with liquid eyes. For a moment Lara held their gaze. Then, in a flash, the fawn turned and skittered across the grass to the trees.

Maureen was now at Lara's side, looking out. "Whatever are you—" she started say, and then caught sight of Grace in the meadow. "Why, Mrs. Lott," she said in surprise. "Can we help you in any way?"

Chapter 4
Some Bloody Assignment

❋

THE GRAY LIGHT OF MORNING brought with it the sound of rain on the roof of the lodge. The air outside the open window was cool and damp, misty with the smell of cedar from under the falls. Lara crawled out of her sleeping bag and quickly dressed. Just why she felt in such a hurry, she wasn't sure—certainly there would be no climbing on wet rock. Maureen's cot had long been empty; she had as usual risen early to prepare breakfast down in the kitchen. Lara sometimes resolved to help her but never did. Maureen did not seem to mind, but the appreciation she had expressed for Purse's mother had pricked Lara's conscience—a little.

A few of the guides were loitering in the upstairs hallway when she stepped out, Roper among them. He became curiously alert when Lara emerged, pausing in mid-anecdote, something that was just about to raise a laugh.

"Hello, love," he said with a tentative playfulness. His blonde hair was matted and splayed in all directions.

"Going upriver, are we?" said Lara.

"If the rain stops," he replied. "You going too, then?"

"No," said Lara. "I didn't mean it that way. Thought I'd do a little climbing—if the rain stops." She broke off with a timed abruptness and headed past him down the hall.

"It's not what you think," he called after her. There was an edge of frustration in his voice. "We'll climb the bloody wall, Lara. You know that. Not today, that's all."

But she was already down the stairs.

The landing led directly into the common room. Half a dozen clients and climbers were lounging about the remains of breakfast at the long table. Others were drifting about the stone hearth where someone had built a fire. The shifting light on the rough-hewn walls created a cozy ambience—too cozy, as far as Lara was concerned. It was the sort of place that was nice enough for dawn and dusk, but to spend all day here would tax almost anyone's patience. The clients would get irritable, and poor Maureen always took the brunt of it. In wet weather, Lara either stayed in her room or walked outside in the rain. Through the large window that faced the river she could see it falling steadily, hiding the far south wall of the gorge behind shifting gray and gauzy curtains.

She sat down quietly at the table and noticed for the first time that Park Savidge and Lance Lott were sulking in the rocking chairs in a recess behind the chimney, glancing restlessly out the window. Lott was rocking back and forth maniacally, like a spoiled child; Savidge held himself perfectly still in a meditative sullenness. There was for Lara at least some pleasure in watching it rain on the unjust. She was wondering, however, where Purse might be—and his crippled mother. What could she possibly say to him after reading his sonnet—and to her after watching the strange encounter with the fawn?

Maureen appeared from out of the kitchen. She gave Lara's shoulder a little squeeze before sweeping up the dishes from a pair of climbers at the end of the table. They were from the East Coast, the sort who came with brand-new gear and a pristine guidebook, eager to check off classic routes and disgruntled until they did so. They asked something of Maureen, who referred them to Lara with a nod before leaving the room as swiftly as she had entered it.

"Hey," said one of the climbers, not bothering to introduce himself. He had dark stubble on his chin. "Ever been up on the Fawn Wall? There's nothing about it in the guidebook." His voice was hurried and flat and nasal. It scared her a little. Lara imagined him and his partner pulling through the overhangs two-thirds of the way up with mechanical efficiency.

"What if I have?" she said a touch defiantly.

"Just asking," he pushed.

She sighed. Savidge seemed to have overheard and was glaring at her from across the room. The SWAGS way was not to offend the customers. "No one's been to the top," she conceded. "The first few pitches go 5.11."

"What about the roof?" asked the other man. His face was thin, pale, and very determined.

"Nobody knows. And it won't be in shape until September. The runoff keeps it wet until then." She hated herself for saying so much.

Both looked vaguely disappointed—vaguely because she could tell they were not sure they believed her.

"What about the Tower of Otium?" said the first man. She wondered perhaps if he were a lawyer. Or maybe everyone from the East Coast approached table talk as an art of aggression.

"Well, what about it? Three miles down-valley, at the magnificent entry point to Amoenas Gorge. You probably saw it on your way up, passing under one of formerly two natural stone bridges that connected the island tower to the banks of the river. The other bridge was swept away in the *jokulhaup* flood of just twenty-four years ago." She could get into this Chamber-of-Commerce happy talk.

"The guidebook says the south face goes 5.9."

"Indeed it does."

"And the west face and the north face each go 5.10."

"Exactly so."

"What about the east face?"

Lara felt her face flush with displeasure. The east face of Otium was another one of her goals for the season. Two thousand feet of polished granite that swept to a needlepoint in the sky, and no one yet had found the key. The guides called it the Wall of Early Morning Fright. Because of its position facing up-valley, the rock had been ground more slick and smooth and seamless by the glaciers of the Pleistocene than any other cliff in the gorge. The surface was more like glass than granite, especially the first four hundred feet. Lara and Roper had pushed a route almost to the top of this smoothest section last September, and had done their best to keep it a secret.

"I wouldn't know anything about it," she said. "But the west face is certainly a classic."

The two men exchanged a glance and then nodded to Lara as if they were dismissing her from the witness stand.

She got up and entered the kitchen, looking for breakfast. Maureen was washing dishes, and Grace Lott was drying them for her. "Hey," said Lara, dipping into a bucket of granola, "thanks for the interview, Maureen. A delightful pair. Charming to speak with."

Maureen smiled quietly. Lara saw that Purse's mother was looking at her with keen interest. She dried a hand on the towel in her lap and reached it forthrightly to Lara. "Hello," she said. "We haven't really met yet. I'm—"

"I know," said Lara, interrupting. She felt confused by her own rudeness. Seen in dim daylight, Grace's hair was still partly silvered, not so much from age, thought Lara, as from pain and patience. Though she sat in a wheelchair she had the presence of someone standing nobly erect—not proud, but self-possessed.

"Yes," said Grace. "We know." There was no challenge here. Just a clarity.

Maureen excused herself to gather more dishes in the common room. Lara had an idea she would not return right away. So she ate the granola she held in her hand and then began to wash the dishes. Grace dried them quietly.

Finally, Lara decided not to delay. "About that fawn," she said. "I saw you, you know."

Grace nodded.

"And Purse and I—I mean Percival, your son—we saw it with the field glasses yesterday, beneath the wall. The Fawn Wall."

"Yes, he told me."

"And—I might as well tell you this—I saw it myself yesterday morning, at the bottom of a climb. It was very close to—your husband."

"Yes," she said again, "he told me."

"Your husband told you?" Lara asked incredulously.

"No," said Grace, and here she surprised Lara by breaking into a beautiful laugh, the kind of laugh that suggested she had once been young, and climbed many mountains.

"Then *who* told you?"

"The fawn," she said simply. "The white fawn. The White Fawn of Otium."

Lara let her hands drop, dripping dishwater down her thighs.

"Don't act so surprised," said Grace. "Deep down, you're really not."

What did surprise Lara, when she thought about it, was how true this felt. Each time she had seen the fawn there had been a strange inevitability in the way it had come, as if it were destined to cross her path at just those moments.

"Maybe I'm not surprised," she said slowly. "But that doesn't mean I know who he is, or why I've seen him, or what he tells you."

"Of course not," Grace reassured her. "That takes a lifetime. Maybe more. And first you need to climb the wall."

"And why is that?" Lara demanded. "That's something *I* want to do. Why should it be a concern of yours? Why turn it into some bloody assignment?" She was surprised to hear herself talk like Roper.

"The things we most want to do," said Grace, speaking very earnestly, "the things that are suggested to us by our deepest selves—who is to say they are not really our life assignments, and who is to know who the assigner really is?"

"Your white fawn?" Lara shot back scornfully.

"Yours as much as mine," said Grace. "Perhaps more than mine."

"And what does Purse have to do with it?" Lara asked, feeling bolder. "Why are you pushing him on me?"

For once, Grace looked perplexed. "Tell me the truth," she said in a low motherly voice. "How did he do yesterday?"

"He's a charming boy," Lara replied. "I don't mind saying I'm half in love with your son, Mrs. Lott, but—"

"Grace," she said. "Call me Grace."

"Okay. I'm glad to have met your son, Grace. But he's no climber."

Grace smiled sadly, as if her suspicions were confirmed. "But you will keep him tied in, won't you?"

"That wasn't my fault!" Lara protested. "Your husband—he untied when he wasn't supposed to. Anyway, he's all right now. I don't think he even knows what happened."

"He seldom does," Grace said gravely. "No, Lara, I'm not blaming you for anything. I just want you to give my son another chance. Be patient with him. See if he can learn to climb."

"You still haven't told me why," said Lara.

"Just think of it," Grace said wistfully, "as a little assignment. Not mine, but yours."

At that moment, Maureen came through the door again, her fingers blossoming with cups. "I've just been talking with Purse," she said. "I was telling him about Otium, and the research hut where my parents live, and he said he would love to walk there today."

"In the rain?" said Lara.

"Isn't that what *you* do on days like this?" Maureen said slyly. "But I told him I couldn't go, on account of having to make lunch for everyone. Perhaps you could go, Lara?"

Lara felt both of the women looking at her. "But I don't know your parents all that well, Maureen. I would feel so awkward just popping in on them. And it's too wet to walk all that way without stopping in to dry off for a good bit. I'm afraid I'm—"

"I'm afraid you're just afraid," said Maureen, laughing at her.

"Listen," said Grace. "My husband and I would be glad to take care of preparing lunch."

"Your husband?" said Lara.

"Yes," she said emphatically. "Maureen, you and Lara just take your time on your hike with Purse and enjoy a visit with your parents. Give them a good hello from us. Ask if they remember the time that Lance and I ran away from the group and gave old Savidge such conniptions."

"But, Mrs. Lott—" Maureen protested.

"Please," she insisted. "It's Grace."

Chapter 5
Sublime Exactly or Picturesque?

❋

By THE TIME MAUREEN AND LARA HAD PACKED A RUCKSACK the rain had faded to a drizzle, and when Purse finally joined them on the porch of the lodge the clouds were beginning to part.

"Good morning," he said to Lara shyly, and she felt herself smile.

He touched the sleeve of a blue cagoule that he was wearing. "Do I keep this on, do you think?" The question was utterly childlike; he could have been speaking to his mother.

"Well," said Lara indulgently. "Is it raining?"

Purse walked down the steps to the meadow and put out his hand. "No, I guess not." He looked down at his legs. "But the grass is wet. I think I'll leave my chaps on for just a bit."

"Good idea," Lara told him, but not in scorn. In spite of herself, she was utterly charmed by his innocence.

Maureen led the way downstream on a muddy path through tall green grass and fern, their wet rain gear swishing loudly between their legs. The swallows were flying, invisible birds were singing under cover, and Purse was whistling quietly—some classical piece that Lara did not recognize. They hadn't gone far, however, before song and tune were obliterated by the manic roar of the jetboat engines pulling away from the lodge behind them. Savidge and Roper and Purse's father were no doubt headed upstream on their tour of inspection. When the sound faded the fields and groves were strangely quiet as if recovering from shock. Purse had stopped whistling.

But the gorge was soon a fine and private place again. Everywhere was the steaming fragrance of damp and leaf, the astonishment of things that grew. The three of them pushed through dense wet patches of bluebells and forget-menots, through deep purple of lupine and larkspur, the crimson and yellow of columbine. They passed meditatively in and out of the cool shade of thickset alders, and mingled their faces with constellations of wet, white dogwood blossoms, each blossom catching the occasional sunbeam and gathering it into a greenness. The granite cliffs, beginning to appear on either hand, gleamed like newly polished mirrors, and the river murmured at their feet.

"I've always liked the dogwood," Purse remarked. He was walking behind Maureen and ahead of Lara.

"Oh, why's that?" Maureen and Lara said at once.

"The whiteness of the petals, I suppose. And the color of green inside of them at the very center. A hopeful color—the sort of green that says sunshine and high water and longer days."

"How true," said Maureen.

"And the white on the green," Purse continued, "is like the whole world that matters, like the Three Queens rising out of the old growth forest."

"So you've been here before?" said Lara, inwardly marveling at this description.

"Not much in the gorge," he said. "But before my mother's accident, we used to hike in the high country from time to time. And sometimes partway up the peaks."

"Your father too?"

"No," he said quietly. "Not my father."

"Ever go to the Demaris Cabin?"

"The one below the Center Queen?"

He looked back, and Lara nodded.

"Yes, I know where it is. We went by on the trail several times. But we never stopped. Mother said the rangers who lived there didn't want us to bother them."

Maureen paused ahead of them and shot a meaningful glance at Lara. Purse intercepted it, just as she had no doubt intended. "What?" he asked. "What did I say?"

"Those rangers," Lara said slowly, "are my parents. That's the cabin where I grew up."

"Really?" said Purse.

"Really and truly."

Maureen at this point scrambled over a huge snag that had recently fallen across the trail. Purse and Lara were left for the moment by themselves.

"And Purse," said Lara, catching his hand, "you should have stopped." Her heart was beating in her fingertips. She hardly knew what she was doing. "That way I wouldn't have had to wait so long."

Once again their eyes met, his not quite so frightened as they had been on the ledge the day before. He brought her hand to his lips and kissed it.

"Now that's quaint," she whispered. "Just like your poem. And as beautiful as your poem, too."

He said nothing, just trembled a bit while still looking into her eyes.

"You guys coming over?" Maureen called from across the log. "There's a way around if you want."

Lara released Purse's hand and looked at the downed snag without really seeing it. "Let's walk around," she said. They pushed their way through thick bracken, and by the time they rejoined Maureen their faces were drenched, sparkling like the rain-heavy fronds.

Maureen looked from one to the other, and seemed to guess something of what had just occurred. In spite of this, or perhaps because of this, she restarted the conversation as they continued down the trail. "If you don't mind my asking, Purse, what exactly was your mother's accident?"

"Oh . . . that," he said darkly. Lara felt him pull away into himself.

"You do mind, then. I'm sorry."

"No," he said. "It's simple to tell. It happened in the car, five years ago. I'd just turned fourteen. We were driving up the Lost Creek Road to the trailhead under the South Queen. A log truck coming the opposite way cut a blind corner. It had a full load—a single section of old-growth hemlock about the size of the one you just climbed over. Somehow I was all right, thrown from the car all the way into the creek. But Mother, her legs were mangled—almost beyond recognition."

"How awful," said Maureen.

"So this is the first time she's been back—to the Three Queens Wilderness, that is. And she didn't want to come, actually. She thinks these jetboats an intrusion—like motorcycles in the Sistine Chapel, I've heard her say. Savidge tried to take her picture several times on the way in, presumably to show everyone how jetboats help the handicapped enjoy the beauties of the wild, but she wouldn't let him. Finally he got a photograph while she wasn't looking. I saw and told her. Then while *he* wasn't looking she tipped his camera into the water."

Lara burst out in delighted laughter. There really was something to like in this woman.

"Then why did she come?" said Maureen.

"For my father's sake," he said. "Or because of him, anyway. My father used to be a hardware clerk, but now he is a developer. He met Savidge in a pub—excuse me, a bar—last winter and they've been making plans for the gorge ever since. Mother doesn't begin to approve of any of them, but I believe she thought if she came along she could at least control the damage. And she wanted me to learn to climb, something I've never been very good at, especially since we ran into that log truck."

"But you're learning," said Lara gently.

"Yes," he said. "With a little help." For a moment they joined hands again behind Maureen.

But not for long. From behind them came the hurried sound of steps in the path—the pushing of ferns and the splashing of puddles. Purse and Lara instinctively let go their hands and stepped to either side of the path. From around a corner, stooping under a branch of dogwood but snapping it off with their towering packs, came the two swift climbers from the East.

"Hello," said Lara, with more kindness than she had bestowed on them in the lodge. "Heading out?" It was a long trail down the river, a twelve-mile walk without the jetboat.

They hardly looked at her and grunted. Without stopping they passed between the young lovers and then shouldered past Maureen.

She turned and said, "There's two climber boys in a hurry. What do you suppose they're up to?"

"Beats me," said Lara. "Maybe they're late for a wilderness etiquette seminar?" As she spoke, however, she had a feeling they were not hiking out to the trailhead. These kind of climbers were the boat-riding type. Most likely they had got wind of her innocent stroll to Otium and become alarmed, thinking she was stealing a march on the Wall of Early Morning Fright. This afternoon, as the rock dried, they would no doubt fix ropes on the first few pitches, then set up camp to be ready for a full attempt first thing in the morning. Hah! Where was Roper when she needed him? Out playing real estate in the boat.

As she mused, the three of them walked on quietly, feeling again a strange kind of violation with the sudden appearance of the climbers from the East—just as they had with the noise of the jetboat. The passing of the rain, the coming of the sun, had lost its edge of morning freshness. Their spirits were lifted again, however, when the trail rounded a bend in the canyon and gave onto a splendid clearing from which they saw the Tower of Otium rising from the river itself not half a mile downstream. It was nearly a full two thousand feet from its broad base to its narrow summit, a pearl-gray pinnacle that matched the height of the canyon rim on either side. The face of the rock, rinsed with rain, was steaming in the noontime sun. Underneath it, terraces of wood and lawn reached to the water in lovely tiers. On the topmost terrace, close to the bottom of the Wall of Early Morning Fright, sat the research station that was Maureen's home. It was rather ugly, actually, something Lara knew her friend was fairly sensitive about. The station was simply the squat half-tube of a Quonset hut, brought in by helicopter just before Maureen was born. It was now rusty and dilapidated.

"Very fine," Purse said admiringly, taking in the entire scene. Without meaning to they had all stopped.

"But it's not the nicest house," said Maureen apologetically. "Not like the Demaris Cabin."

"Maureen!" pleaded Lara. "It's not your fault."

Purse didn't seem to hear them. "I can't decide if the overall effect is sublime exactly or picturesque."

"What's the difference?" Lara said. If someone else had posed the problem she wouldn't have cared.

"The sublime has something terrible in it. Terrible as in terrifying. It's a grandeur that frightens, and that's part of its proper effect. A storm at sea, a calving glacier, a river in flood. It's beautiful, but it can hurt you."

"The Tower of Otium never hurt me," Maureen said.

"Me neither," Lara added. "Not much, anyway." In the interest of truth, she was remembering a fall she had taken.

"That's as its name suggests," Purse replied. "*Otium*—that's Latin for the distinctly pastoral quality of pleasurable peacefulness. It's what Shakespeare meant when he said there was no clock in the forest. Which is more the feeling of the beautiful or the picturesque—a place where one willingly wastes one's time without it being a waste at all, because it doesn't need to be saved for anything. The picturesque landscape is arresting but not challenging—though it incorporates roughness and irregularity, it doesn't threaten, and it doesn't inspire heroic response."

"You call climbing heroic?" said Lara. For some reason they all started to walk again.

Purse thought about it. "There's risk," he said. "The climber responds to some sort of challenge she feels from the landscape. It's not the same as sauntering down this path, is it?"

"I suppose not," Lara agreed.

"But what if you don't want to climb it?" said Maureen. "I never have. I'd rather sit here in the meadow and look at the tower reflected in the river when it quiets down on an autumn day. To me it is simply beautiful."

"No," said Purse. "To you it is picturesque—something between the placid safety of the beautiful and sheer terror of the sublime. You have the same impulse as did travelers in England some two hundred years ago. When they saw a scene they liked in the mountains, they would pull out an actual framed mirror, hold it up, and admire the landscape backwards, safely bordered and contained. For Lara, no mirrors. She's got to put her hands to the rock."

Lara felt strangely pleased, as if he had paid her a compliment. Even so, she protested. "But it's not just heroes who touch the rock. So do artists. So do dancers. It's not all danger and daring, Purse. Hardly any of it is. You'll see."

"On that?" he said, looking at the tower fearfully.

"No," she replied. "I'm afraid we don't have the time—'to waste,' as you say— or the gear on hand. But there are other walls and other days. There's much more being than doing up there. Finally, the sublime and the beautiful run together and dissolve when you're inside of them. You don't arrive at anything so standoffish as the picturesque. You are simply left with the place itself, and your hold on it—or its hold on you."

She paused on the path to see how he took this, a little impressed by her own surge of eloquence. "Do you like it in England, when you're in school?" she asked quietly.

"No," he said. "But I feel safe there. I imagine you'd find it—claustrophobic."

"Maybe," she said, taking his hand and drifting down the trail once more behind Maureen. "I think it would depend on who I was with. The grandest mountains can be confining with narrow companions, I've come to think."

"Like me?" he said nervously.

"No, silly." And suddenly, without planning to, she stopped and kissed him full on the lips. And she lingered on it. There was no clock in this kiss at all— and much pleasurable peacefulness. By the time they thought to pause, Maureen was many steps ahead and had the sense to keep going.

"So," said Lara softly. "Was that sublime exactly or picturesque?"

"To me," said Purse, "it was simply beautiful."

So they kissed once more, and when the two of them started hiking again he surprised her with a little song:

> *Little climber, little one,*
> *Made my bowline come undone.*
> *Do you love me,*
> *Do you, climber girl?*

The result was this: Maureen had been visiting with her parents a full half hour before there came a shy knock on the door of the shabby Quonset hut at the foot of the Tower of Otium.

Chapter 6
Can You Stay?

✳

"Why, Lara," said Maureen's mother. "Come in, please. You and your friend. Maureen's been telling us all about you."

Lara looked at Maureen seated beside a table that was snowed over with graphs and reports. From the look on her face she could not tell what *all about you* really meant. And in some ways she did not care. Love was love, however sudden and unlikely, and she saw no good reason to hide it. She gave Maureen's mother a familiar squeeze, shook hands with her more reserved father, and introduced them both to Purse.

"It's Jennifer, please," the woman said, noticing Purse's hesitation. She took one of his hands in both of hers, holding it like a precious gift.

"And Ronald," said the man. Though not old, he was almost bald. He pushed aside the mountain of papers on the table and invited them both to sit down. They were in a makeshift kitchen, lit by windows on either side of the wooden door. Behind them the hut arched back into a darkness, stacks of notebooks and oddly shaped research equipment reaching into a cluttered void. The living quarters, Lara knew from previous visits, were somewhere at the end of this tunnel.

Before long, Maureen's parents were serving them a late lunch, and talk drifted comfortably around the table. Purse was politely asking Ronald about their research.

"This station," Ronald patiently told him, "was installed twenty-four years ago, just after a catastrophic flood released from under the eastern lobe of the Mirror Glacier, the source for the Amoenas River. Here in the gorge, only the trees on highest ground withstood the floodwaters. At the time there were plans for a dam on this site, joining the Tower of Otium to the walls of the gorge on either side. But the violence of the flood made the notion of a dam impracticable. The glacier is not likely to burst again for many years, but no one wants to put money into constructing a dam only to see it wash away. That, and a few people want the gorge to remain as it is."

"Just a few," his wife put in wistfully.

"But what do you do here?" Purse asked.

"We're here to monitor the water volume day by day, to make geologic observations of various sorts, and also to do a more general reconstructive study of vegetation in the gorge—to see how it repairs itself in the immediate wake of the *jokulhlaup*."

"The what?" said Purse.

"The glacier burst. The flood," whispered Lara.

"So far," said Ronald, "the flora has come back rather well."

"And so have the developers," Jennifer sighed.

"You mean they want to construct the dam after all?" Purse said.

"No," said Jennifer. "But people are willing to make much smaller investments as the memory of the *jokulhlaup* fades. Now that the gorge is looking rather scenic again, the jetboats have come, as you know, and the climbing lodge too, thanks to our neighbor Park Savidge and certain of his friends in high places. And yes, it's employment for our daughter, and a good job for a talented girl like Lara, to be sure, but the gorge is not the serene place it used to be. And if rumors be true, we haven't seen the end of it. If we're not careful, the valley floor will be one big putting green."

"Jennifer," her husband said, patting her arm. "Don't exaggerate. It's not quite fair to push our opinion on new acquaintance."

"That's fine," said Purse, reassuring them. "I liked it better before the lodge myself."

"And to think where he put it!" Jennifer exclaimed, in no way deterred from her disgust. "The jetboat is docked in the very place where—where—"

"Where what, Mother?" Maureen asked quietly, trying to calm her.

"Where the naiads sang," she whispered fiercely. It was as if she had lost her voice. Ronald patted her arm again but suddenly she began to weep. She looked vaguely about, as if everyone were invisible to her, and abruptly rose and left the table, retreating into the hollow cave of scientific paraphernalia. In short order, Maureen and her father excused themselves and went sailing in pursuit of her.

"What's a naiad?" Lara asked Purse.

"They're demigods," he quietly said. "River spirits. Beautiful and female. The Olympians never saw one they didn't want to chase. Sort of like you, I imagine."

"Which makes you an Olympian?"

He flushed slightly, then said, "But is Maureen's mother all right, I wonder? In the head, I mean?"

"Really, I don't know," said Lara. "They're awfully isolated here. I don't think they go down in the winter, as we used to do when I got older."

"So one comes to imagine things."

"Perhaps. But Maureen's mother is a canny woman. She knows every bird, flower, and fern in the gorge on a first-name basis. When you are at home in a place as much as she is at home here, you might care more deeply than others can care. And you might see things that others can't."

She paused, not knowing if she really wanted to travel this path.

"Go on," said Purse. "What is it you were about to say?"

She felt as if he had read her mind. "Well, take that white fawn, for example. The one we saw in the field glasses. You might have such deer penned up at Oxford, but here in the wild, no one would believe such a thing."

Purse nodded.

"And Purse," she went on. "Speaking of mothers, I saw the fawn with yours last night. She was petting it outside the lodge. No, *petting* is the wrong word. I almost felt—"

"Like what?" he said.

"I almost felt as if they were speaking to one another."

His eyes flicked nervously. For a moment he was silent. "They were," he said slowly. "They have been, for five years, ever since our accident."

"What do you mean?"

"I mean that the first thing my mother saw when she returned to consciousness on that gravel road, before even the truck driver could climb down out of his cab, was a white fawn. It made no sound, just looked at her calmly. She told me that when she saw that fawn she knew somehow that she and I would be all right. She felt at peace. The truck driver never saw it. And I never saw it after he fished me out of the creek. All the way to the hospital, bleeding in the cab of that truck, she kept asking us about the fawn."

"So yesterday—"

"Was the first time I ever saw it for myself. It came to her bedside week by week as she convalesced, and later came to her in our garden. I had to take her word for it, and believe me, I was worried about her mental health. I thought perhaps all those children's fantasies she likes to write had taken over her mind for good. Eventually, the fawn spoke to her. She would never tell me what it said, but I have an idea she brought me here on his advice."

"*His?*"

"Oh yes, it's a young male. Just the thing a woman married to a father like mine might dream up, I realize."

"So you thought—"

"I didn't know what I thought. I wasn't going to argue with her. But now that I've seen it, that *you've* seen it—"

"Look!" said Lara, interrupting him. She was pointing out the window to the left of the door.

Maureen returned from the back of the hut at just this moment and found them peering outside.

"It's our climber boys," Lara told her. "They've pitched a camp down by the water and have come up here to look at the tower. *Veni, vidi,* but no *vici*—not unless they're *really* good."

"A little jealous, are we?" said Maureen.

"Me?" said Lara. She opened the door and led them out. The two climbers from the East were uncoiling a rope in the shade at the base of the tower not far away, on the other side of a little spring. The rock above them rose not quite sheer but very smooth, polished by its many encounters with ancient ice. Below them the island dropped in tiers to a canary-yellow tent by the river, and beyond the tent the Amoenas Gorge unfolded its quiet splendor of meadow enclosed by granite walls.

"Is your mother feeling better?" Purse asked.

"I'm not sure," Maureen said. "She's been this way ever since Savidge got special permission for the lodge and jetboats. She takes it very personally."

Purse mused upon the scene upriver. "As well she might," he said with a surprising firmness.

Lara was conscious only of the climbers beneath the Wall of Early Morning Fright. They had spotted the line that she and Roper had pioneered the summer before, a hairline crack just big enough for the fingertips that traversed at an angle up and right, away from the hut. Roper had set a pair of bolts where the crack petered out. This was the end of the first pitch. Beyond that point, the route followed almost imaginary rough spots on slick polish, wandering more or less straight up. An occasional bolt protected two more pitches, above which Lara had taken a forty-foot sliding fall in search of a way. Bruised and shaken, she had rappelled back down to the ground, and Roper with her. From below they could see that a pendulum swing from their highest anchor might have gained them a small flared crack to the left, directly above the start of the climb. But it would have to be a very long swing, one perhaps that was not even possible.

One of the men was now inching onto the delicate fingertip traverse, his partner paying out rope behind him. The movements of the leader were very far from elegant but nevertheless strong and sure. He was quivering with determination. Twenty feet out he rested on the strength of one wedged finger and slotted a tiny wired stopper into the crack, clipping the rope that trailed beneath him into this provisional anchor.

Purse and Maureen were now watching alongside of Lara. "Wish you were up there?" Maureen said.

Lara frowned.

"You'd never get me on something like that," Purse whispered.

Lara looked at him quizzically, almost contemptuously. "And why not?" She tried to speak gently, in the language of love, though for the moment she seemed to have lost the feeling.

"Looks much too hard for me, thank you," Purse said firmly. "I came here to learn a little climbing, remember? Not to die."

The climber put in a second piece of protection now, another small stopper, farther up the crack. He was just about to clip his rope into it with a carabiner when his feet gave way. His entire body came smearing down the steep face, hands clawing for purchase. When he was perhaps ten feet above the ground his first stopper began to hold him, swinging him in a comic arc directly into his belayer. The two of them collapsed in the spring with a splash, then jumped up, cursing each other.

Purse had turned rather white. "See what I mean?" he said uncertainly.

Lara didn't hear him. In spite of herself she had burst out laughing. The climbers stopped cursing each other and looked darkly over their shoulders. "Are you boys all right?" she asked, her voice dripping with insincerity.

"Lara!" Maureen whispered firmly. "Don't. You shouldn't. They really might be hurt, after all."

But the two climbers appeared undamaged. With some reluctance, the leader was giving his slings, chocks, and carabiners to the belayer. The other man would give it a try.

Lara shrugged.

"Do you think," said Purse, "it might be time to head back?"

"But would you like to stay?" Maureen asked.

"Oh, yes. But I thought you needed to get things ready for the evening meal at the lodge."

Maureen smiled. "Normally, yes. But your mother is a surprising woman. At the last minute she volunteered to take care of supper as well. *And* breakfast. So we can all stay for the night if you wish. The clouds are gone, and it looks as if we can sleep outside."

"But your mother?" asked Purse.

"It will be the best thing for my mother," Maureen said. "Lara, how about you? Can you stay?"

A bit sheepish about having taunted the climbers, and also anxious to track their progress, Lara agreed. She sought out Purse's hand with her own to let him know he didn't have to prove himself on the Tower of Otium. A shy smile crossed his face. She could feel his relief.

Just then Maureen's parents stepped from the door, her father looking care-worn but her mother beaming and newly spirited, as if nothing had happened to disturb her. She caught sight of the two climbers. "More visitors?" she pleasantly asked.

"No, Mother. But we're all three staying for the night, if that's fine with you. I can help with supper—we all can—and we'll sleep outside. It's warm enough now."

Her parents looked at one another.

"We can build a fire on the lower terrace. We could all eat there, just like we used to, Mother, when I was little and you told me we were camping out."

"That will be splendid," Jennifer said. A full soft smile on her face suggested that she really meant it. The swallows went slashing and arcing across the face of the tower, now dark in the shadow of afternoon. The air was full of gift, of rest. There were dogwoods over the door of the hut, and their topmost blossoms still held sunshine. All this to revel in, and then a call from up on the face.

"Off belay!"

Lara dropped Purse's hand. The new leader, clipping into a pair of bolts, had polished off the first pitch in record time.

Chapter 7
The Pendulum

✳

WHEN THE SHADOW OF THE TOWER OF OTIUM HAD LENGTHENED into the fragrance of night, Lara was lying awake in a sleeping bag next to the embers of a fire. Purse and Maureen were breathing softly on either side of her, heads upturned as if to receive the gentle influence of the stars. It was pleasant to lie away from the lodge, to feel the breeze course down the canyon and toss their hair with the scent of glaciers far upstream. Their talk had eddied with the far-off murmur of the river and finally died with the life of the fire. Purse and Maureen had almost certainly been asleep for some time.

But no sleep came for Lara. The pair of climbers from the East had reached the top of the third pitch by late afternoon and rappelled down, leaving their ropes fixed in place. Lara had seen them point back up at the flared crack they would have to pendulum to in the morning. They had not only guessed the route, but had shown they had the skill to climb it. Which left Lara as deeply depressed as a winter toad.

It made her wonder what this surge of romantic feeling for the pale and scholarly Purse amounted to after all. Just that morning all she had been able to feel was the strange soft texture of his lips, his quivering arms as they had held her on the path. Now, all she wanted was rock beneath her fingertips and someone to share a rope with her. And that someone, despite his mother's fondest hopes, could most assuredly never be Purse, who could untangle the picturesque from the sublime more easily than he could untie his own bowline. If anything, he seemed more responsive to the calm inner waters of Maureen. Lara had noticed how easily the two of them had quietly talked each other to sleep while she had brooded about the tower.

The moon, a little less than full, had risen from the upper gorge and illuminated the folds of her bag and the soft turf all around her. She raised herself and saw the tower struck with silver. The bolts on the face were twinkling there like little stars, linked by a thin dark line of rope. She could even see, as if it were daylight, the small flared crack that began its journey high above the Quonset hut. The slight voice of the wind, the tiny speech of the bubbling spring, the far-off murmur of the river—all said one thing and the same. There was no reason to wait until dawn.

No reason, that is, but the lack of a partner. She lay back down in dark frustration, grinding her teeth in just the way her mother had always begged her not to. And then, above the sound of the wind and spring and river, she heard footsteps. Not the furtive scampering of a squirrel or the almost noiseless approach of a bear, but a human tread, soft and deliberate. Her first thought was that the pair of climbers from the East had returned to finish their work by moonlight. The opportunity must have been as apparent to them as it was to her. But instead of approaching the base of the tower the footsteps neared the fire below the Quonset hut. Lara lay very still. Someone was standing quite near. A stick stirred the embers into flame, and she heard a whispered voice: "Lara."

She sat up. In the light of the new-sprung fire, she saw the face of the one she realized she had been secretly hoping for. "Roper!" she whispered. "What are you doing here?"

He was standing at apparent ease with a full pack bearing down on his broad shoulders. Though the night was cool enough, his face shone with perspiration, evidence of a long hike. He didn't answer her question at all, but just grinned.

"What do you have in that pack of yours?" It looked like a crushing load. "A rope, maybe?"

"Two," he said. "And your shoes, and harness."

"Roper," she said, "those guys from the East, they followed—"

"I know," he said. "Get up. Let's go. I think it's just light enough."

Without further word she swung out of her sleeping bag and put on her boots and sweater, taking care not to disturb Maureen and Purse. As she got up to leave they each rolled over into her space, nestling against each other in sleep. Quietly she touched Roper's hand and saw the merriment in his eyes. Putting his finger to his lips, he turned away and walked toward the base of the rock. Lara followed. The heavily laden figure before her moved as nimbly as a deer.

He set down his pack not at the start of the angling crack but at the place where the rope touched down directly beneath the first belay. Lara caught up to him as he started to unpack their gear. For a moment she stood silently, looking at the chain of rope that ascended the face in the moonlight.

"No," she said, "I don't want to use their lines."

"But they're fixed and ready," Roper said. "Think of the quick start it will give us."

"No," she repeated.

"We've already climbed these pitches, Lara. We want to be fresh for the hard stuff—or whatever's ahead."

"I know," she said. "I know, I know. But I just think we should do the whole thing, bottom to top. On our own."

He thought about it, buckling on the straps of his harness. There was something in him, Lara guessed, that was leery of offending her. This whole idea of showing up in the middle of the night for a first ascent was probably penance for joyriding with Savidge and Lott in the boat all day. And if it was, she would make him pay on her terms.

"All right," he said. "We'll be bloody purists. Only—"

"Only what?"

"Nothing," he said.

"What?" she persisted.

But he wouldn't speak. He gathered up the gear in his arms and carried it to the base of the crack, some distance to their left. The spring issued from under the wall just here, filling a shallow rippled pool with broken stars. They each took a long drink before filling up their water bottles that they would store in the big pack with a bit of food and some extra clothes. After each pitch they would haul the pack up after themselves.

Lara went through the familiar motions of donning her skintight climbing shoes, soled and skirted with soft rubber. They stuck cold on her bare feet, and squeezed her toes with a welcome pain. Climbing was an art wherein, no less than in ballet, one must suffer to be beautiful. Next she threaded her legs through the loops of a wide-belted harness, cinched up the straps, and clipped five dense clusters of carabiners to her waist. Over one shoulder and across her chest she slung a grouped assortment of chocks—hexes, stoppers, and mechanically retractable cams that would find use in the flared crack they hoped to reach. And across this rack of chocks she draped a bandolier of nylon slings, multicolored in daylight but all pale in moon-glow. Now she was equipped and ready. She tied back her hair in a swift motion and dipped her fingers into a bag of gymnast's chalk that hung on her harness. In the silvered dark she could just see the first thin holds for her fingertips.

"Care to tie into the rope?" Roper held up the end out of a loose pile at his feet.

She felt herself blush. Of all the things to overlook. Quickly she took the rope from his hand and tied it in a double bowline into her harness. "Did I tell you about Lance Lott?" she said.

"Lance Lott, that intrepid pioneer of the sheer cliffs of Amoenas Gorge? What about him?"

"I'll tell you later. You'd laugh too much if I told you now, and wake up the others. On belay?"

"That depends," he said.

"On what?"

"On whether you leave the bloody ground. Love."

She stroked his hair, streaking it with chalk. "Just don't drop me, okay?" There was a special pleading in her voice.

The edge of rock inside the crack bit into her fingertips, and she levered her feet high up against the face. Keeping her arms as straight as possible, she rested in a crouch for a moment, then reached for the next faint holds, locked on, and let her feet follow again. She climbed more by faith than sight, trusting the texture of the rock to guide her on from stance to stance. The summer before, she had actually climbed with a blind man for most of a week. After watching him for several days she had realized that he saw the rock through his hands and feet more clearly than she often did with her own eyes. In the moonlight, then, all things were possible.

Like the climber in the afternoon she slotted a stopper in the crack, then another higher up. She took care clipping into the second one, keeping the pressure of her feet against the sloping glacier polish. With each move she found herself edging up carefully on the sides of her shoes, needing only the slightest rugosity in the rock to keep her aloft. For her it was a rhythm, a dance, a condition of being entirely awake and yet part of a trance of concentration. Some climbers liked to chat away as they advanced, but Lara and Roper always kept a pact of silence while one or the other was leading a pitch. The banter was kept for when they passed at each belay. Lara was so engrossed in her work that the pair of bolts at the end of the pitch emerged beneath her hands by surprise. She clipped into the sling that joined them and leaned back against the anchor, straddling the rope the other climbers had left dangling from here to the ground.

"Off belay!" she called softly. Soon she was working her own rope about her waist, hauling it in as Roper traversed the crack behind her. His progress was only interrupted at each shining piece of protection, which he deftly removed with a single movement of his hand before clipping it onto his own harness. This, she remembered, was real climbing. She thought of Purse with a certain pity and condescension. If he couldn't know this, he could never know her.

Roper reached her and clipped in. He was trailing a second rope that was tied to their pack on the ground. With practiced hands he rigged a pulley and brought it up. The pack slipped easily up the rock, scraping softly. For an unknown climb of this magnitude, they were going light. When the pack had joined them, Roper hung it on the anchor and turned his eyes to the pitch above.

"So what happened to Lott?" he asked.

"Lance Lott?"

"Who else? Your teacher's pet?"

Lara groaned. "Please," she said.

"Lance, then. Our hero in pink."

"Promise you won't tell anyone?"

"I swear," he said. "By the bloody gods."

"Well, yesterday he fell thirty feet, right off the end of the rope."

"No."

"Yes. He untied after I'd led the first pitch, and he tied back in with only half a bowline, I guess—I couldn't see it. He got to the crux and cratered—on the grass."

"Like this?" asked Roper. He reached over and untied the fixed line left by the climbers from the East. With a small flourish he let the end slip through his fingers. It made a sound like rain on the ground below.

"Roper!" she hissed. "How could you?"

"Did I drop something?"

She burst out laughing. It was too hard to be angry.

"Don't wake the others," he warned her. "I'd never have done it if I knew you planned to give us away."

"I don't plan much of anything these days," she said. "Not even this." And she leaned over and gave him a kiss. When they parted, his eyes were bright. She snapped the rope that led to his waist.

"Now get your British derriere out of here." She handed him the remnants of her rack and slings, and carefully transferred the carabiners from her harness to his. "You're on."

He left so quickly she could hardly pay the rope out fast enough. Stepping right and then left of the second fixed rope, he wandered up the gleaming face as if holdlessly levitating himself. She knew there was great effort involved, fingernails dug firmly into tiny nubbins and calves and toes that ached with strain. But any observer would have thought Roper was out for a vertical stroll. He stopped only occasionally to clip one of the two ropes trailing behind him into a bolt, and once into a sling placed around a flake. At intervals, Lara could attend to the view—the dim shape of the hut below, the embers of the fire beneath it, and over the tangle of turf and dogwood the broad expanse of the shining Amoenas, coursing at its own sweet will. The walls and prows that rose upstream in silver shadow were all ones she knew well—Queen's Throne, Marmot Buttress, Harmony Ridge, the Footstool. (On the Footstool there was a climb they had named for Savidge—The Quitter—right between SWAGS Away and Lost in the Wild.) Her life was here, her past, her purpose. Far beyond the bend in the canyon she could see the upper reaches of the Fawn Wall, its stripe of fresh waterfall fraying in the moonlight.

When Roper reached the top of the pitch she let him haul the pack up first in case it became entangled in the fixed line. That done, upon his signal she clung to the rock once more and stripped the anchor, leaving only the bolts in place. It was a relief to move again. She was stiff and slow on the first few moves, then found her rhythm. With no crack to guide her it was even more a game of Braille. But her hands and feet were alive to the task, touching the rock in just the right places in small moments of fleeting balance. To be saved one thousand times in the night, that was the meaning of the climb. The only annoyance was the hanging rope that their rivals had left. Sometimes it obscured the best holds—she had to be careful not to step on it lest she slip.

At length she reached the hanging pack and Roper beside it. Silently she clove-hitched herself to the anchor, another spaced pair of bolts, and then reached over to pat the offending rope. She untied it with a wicked smile and let it drop. "We're cruising," she said—and kissed him again, a little more passionately.

"This gets better each time," said Roper. "What happens when we get to the top?"

"Don't get greedy," Lara replied. But she kissed him again anyway. It was the whole tower, the length of the gorge, the entire wilderness bathed in the moonlight that she kissed. It was only Roper by unconscious synecdoche. Part of her wondered if he would feel enlarged or diminished by this thought. Most likely, he wouldn't understand it at all. Purse would—that's what she liked about Purse. But Purse wasn't strong enough to be part of what mattered. He could only entertain notions about it. Then again, Roper had his own disconnections.

"So how was the boat ride?" Lara said, pulling away as they hung side by side in the dark.

Roper stiffened. She could feel it. "Long. Dull. Not like this."

"Did they decide anything?"

"Some things," he said noncommittally. He began to hand her the rack and slings.

"Are you in on it?"

"Listen," he said. A carabiner slipped from his hand and went battering down the cliff to the ground, now two hundred fifty feet below. He cursed in frustration. "Lara, where I come from—in the Lake District—the mountains and people have gotten along together nicely for hundreds of years. No one complains. It's just some of you here that have this bloody hang-up on—virginity." He smiled slyly.

"On belay?" she said curtly.

"It's going to come, Lara," he said. "It's just a question of how it will come. They're going to do it Bavarian. I think it will look bloody pleasant, myself."

"Climbing," she said. In five moves he was far behind.

This pitch was more of a struggle. The bolts were spaced farther apart, and the route was much more devious, winding through the glacial polish in sudden traverses and off-balance diagonal lunges. Her fingers became iron hooks as she pulled herself from hold to hold, and her toes cramped on the tiny nubbins. All this face and friction climbing with hanging belays—it was time they rested on a ledge. But the end of this pitch, as she reached it gasping, was just another pair of bolts, winking like contemptuous eyes on the otherwise featureless wall. This was their high point from the previous autumn, unless she counted the twenty more feet she had scrabbled out before falling while trying to drill another bolt into the rock. Odd, to think that her body had once hurtled past this point in space. She looked upward. From here it steepened considerably. Between her and the stars was at least another thousand feet of smooth stone.

She pulled up the pack and then put Roper on belay. He climbed quickly, zigzagging up beneath her without any apparent struggle. This irked her. At least he could have the decency to pause and make it look difficult. But no, he had to show her up. He was halfway when she decided to unclip the last of the hanging fixed ropes. She let it slip and the tail slapped him in the face.

Cockney curses ascended the rock. "What are you doing?" he called angrily.

"Sorry," she said. But she knew she wasn't.

When he rejoined her, the gibbous moon had almost merged with the top of the rock. Past the upper gorge the horizon was tinted with only the faintest glimmer of dawn. They were in for their darkest hour.

"I thought you were out of the way," she said. "I don't know what got into me. Are you all right?"

She saw with alarm a stripe on his cheek where the rope end had cut it. "Can I bandage that? Did we bring the kit?"

He shook his head. "Too much weight," he said, but he pawed through the pack anyway, pulling out a hammer and drill and hanging them on the side of his harness.

"Here's where you lower me for the pendulum. About seventy feet to start with. More if I ask it. If that crack goes all the way up we won't be needing to place any bolts. But I want to be ready, especially to back up the next belay."

He wasn't about to let her kiss him. She could tell that. But she was sorry already for what she had done, in part because she realized now that the tension from a third rope could help her follow his pendulum much more safely than without it. Borrowing his belay plate, she gave him all the gear he would need and lowered him back down the route. At seventy feet he hung like a plumb bob, distant and lonely, an appendage to her vantage point four hundred feet in the air.

"Okay," he said. "Lock me off."

She tied the slack into the anchor and let go. All she had to do now was try to stay out of the way.

Hands held out to keep himself away from the face, Roper took a few tentative steps to his left. He didn't get far before the rope began to swing him back again, and he didn't fight it—he began running the other way, back to his right, arcing across the moonlit face. When this momentum began to fade he changed directions once again, sprinting faster and farther back to the left, the direction he really wanted to go. Lara watched him seesaw back and forth, a little farther each time, all the while dancing herself to keep out of the way of the rope swerving under her feet. Finally, when he had run his arc as far to the left as the radius of rope would reach, instead of turning to reverse direction he lunged in a dive across the face, arms outstretched. For a moment he had hold of something. She heard sounds of scraping as he tried to pull himself into the crack. But apparently the rope was too tight. Suddenly he came swinging back, upside down, cursing his way across the cliff.

Eventually he righted himself and came to a halt. "About five more feet. That's all you can give me. I'm almost to the bottom of the crack as it is."

She untied the slack and let a little rope through the plate.

"Okay," he called. Immediately he began trotting the course of a new arc, wider this time. At the apogee of his pendulum he lunged as before. Lara heard more scraping noises, and this time he didn't return across the cliff.

But now, she knew, came the truly nerve-wracking part. Somewhat below her now, he would have to climb the crack to a point above her before putting in protection. Otherwise the drag on the rope would be too great. A fall, however, would cost him a swing too great to imagine. Quickly she untied the slack and put him back on a moving belay. She heard him fighting up the crack. It was shallow and slippery, she had no doubt. But if he could make just thirty feet he could jam in a couple of cams and they would be on their merry way.

She watched his muffled shape in the moonlight gradually rise far to her left. Now he was even with her, now just slightly beyond. He paused and she heard the crisp snapping of carabiners. He had gotten a piece in. From where he was he waved to her, then continued his upward progress. She slowly paid out the rope—a foot here, three feet there, with many pauses—until there were only inches left. There came a longer pause than usual, then his voice.

"Lara! I'm off belay. I'm on a bloody ledge! And it's a good crack—just a few sharp edges is all."

For a moment she saw him against a corner of the moon. Then it passed beyond the tower, and they were in darkness. The dawn was still a mere fore-shadowing.

No matter. If the blind could climb, so could she. From long practice she knew what to do. First she unclipped the pack and at his signal let it slip into the darkness. She heard it scrape the rock as it swung; that was her, in effigy. When it came her turn to unclip she would likewise swing, not in the incremental fashion in which Roper had controlled his progress, but wildly and suddenly through the dark. If she kept her balance and wits about her, brushing by the glassy smooth face like a cat, she would eventually come to rest at the base of the crack, or perhaps a few feet farther down. On Roper's belay she could then climb directly up the rock to join him. With a rope from above it would not really matter how hard the crack or dark the night might become.

"Got me?" she called.

"You're on!" he shouted.

She hesitated. For a moment she heard or perhaps imagined a plaintive voice rise from below. "Lara!" it called. "Come down! Come down!" *Purse*, she thought. That made up her mind.

She unclipped the carabiner and let go.

Immediately the invisible rock was whirling past, skimming under her fingertips. Her stomach felt its weightlessness as she sank and flew, swiftly tilting into the void. *Too fast*, she thought. Soon she should be bottoming out and swinging upwards. Now. Now. But not yet. She felt the rope catch on something far above her and then grow slack. She was swinging, sailing, into the dark. Not up. No longer across.

Just down.

Chapter 8
His Moonlit Dream

✳

IN HIS MOONLIT DREAM, Purse was swimming up a cool, dark river. The power of his arms was stronger than the current, and he surged upstream at will like a salmon. Great cedars rose on either bank, and walls of granite silvered the sky. He seemed to be in Amoenas Gorge.

His arms pulled hard against the water because a ship—a black ship with a black sail—was close behind him. Many long oars were stroking the river in unison, and the evil-looking prow of the boat was gaining on him. The prow was carved with a dragonish figure that glared and snarled in steadfast silence.

He was nearly out of strength and breath when he rounded a bend and saw the gorge was at an end; the walls of granite had come together. From high above, over the rim plunged a waterfall. The entire river dropped from the stars to a foaming pool. The fall and the pool were white as the moon, illuminated as if from within. There was no roar: the water fell soundlessly.

He swam into the foam of the plunge pool and felt a sweet invigoration. The ship came close behind, but began to swirl in the many eddies and crosscurrents. Figures on deck began jumping and waving. They had lost the pursuit. Showers of arrows slit the water all around him, but he swam on safely, across the pool to the very base of the waterfall, a shining veil. Here he paused, treading the water and lifting his head to look through the spray to the top of the fall. He seemed to be waiting for someone.

It was Lara.

Impossibly high against the moon, only a very tiny figure, she slipped across the brink of the fall and began to float quickly downward, involved in the collapsing veil. He felt for her a desire and an anxiety. As she flew down the face of the fall, hair flowing silver in spray, Purse swam directly into the cataract and held out his arms. In a moment she fell into them, crushing them both beneath the water. They swirled beneath a canopy of spreading foam, cool and slick against each other. Then suddenly they surfaced in darkness behind the fall and touched wet rock. Lara was nuzzling him under the chin. He suddenly felt very cold, and heard her shout as if in a whisper, "Belay off!"

With a shiver he awoke. He was half out of his sleeping bag, his arms entwined about the sleeping form of Maureen. The back of her head, her smooth hair, was lodged beneath his Adam's apple. He drew back. Lara's bag lay underneath them, completely empty. Careful not to disturb Maureen, he sat up and drew on his jacket. The fire at their feet was dead, just silvery ashes under the light of the gibbous moon about to sink behind the tower.

He turned and looked at the smooth rock face, remembering the climbers of the afternoon and Lara's coldness to his fears. In the shadow of the moon it appeared to him more frightening than ever—the pure and merciless sublime. What was there about it which drew her on? That part of her scared him— more perhaps than the tower itself. And where was she? Where had she been drawn in the night?

Perhaps Lara had returned to the lodge. He had noticed of course the camaraderie she shared with Roper. Perhaps they had planned a climb for tomorrow. The possibility bothered him. Not only was Roper his obvious rival, but Roper was also quite obviously his inferior in both intellect and sensibility. Two days before, on Harm's Way, Roper had mocked his every question about the geology of the gorge, his allusion to certain passages in Tennyson about the valley of Cauteretz in the Pyrenees, and his apt quotation from Shakespeare about

daffodils,
That come before the swallow dares, and take
The winds of March with beauty.

Roper had said that it was May, and that daffodils did not grow in the gorge. The fellow could climb, there was no gainsaying that, but there was something unutterably coarse about him. Purse was more than willing to grant his superior athleticism, but he sensed a stubborn unwillingness on Roper's part to grant in turn his scholarly prowess of poetry. He had just as much right to Lara's attention as Roper did, but on different grounds. Roper was simply too dim, or too jealous, to acknowledge this. And when push came to shove, Purse feared that

Lara, though intrigued by his weakness, would choose the climber over the poet. Indeed, it appeared she already had.

Without quite knowing where he was going, Purse slipped on his boots and rose to leave. Maureen now lay at his feet alone. A calm and beautiful girl, to be sure. Had he wanted to, he could have lain till dawn beside her, holding her quietly in his arms. When she awoke it was possible that she would not make any objection, that a new and sweeter belonging could begin. But he wanted Lara. Not the limpid pool in the river, but the swift fall, taking the winds of March with beauty.

He looked up. Something at the base of the tower, white in the shadow, caught his eye. Whatever it was stood perfectly still, watching him. As if swimming the river in his dream, he advanced toward it. He was conscious, too, of voices and footsteps far behind him. He recognized the tone and tread of the pair of climbers from the East, no doubt getting an alpine start. But in his mind they were chasing him—the ship, the oars, the dragonish snarl. He broke into a clumsy run.

He had not quite reached the spring at the base of the rock when the waiting figure resolved itself into the fawn. It stood weakly poised on four thin legs, gazing at him. Then it dipped its muzzle into the pool and quietly drank. Purse slowed to a walk. The whiteness of the fawn and the glint of stars in the broken water around its lips were the only light under the tower. He approached from the far side of the pool, and the fawn cautiously raised its head, eyeing him once again. Purse stopped at the edge of the water. Slowly he reached his hand across. The fawn seemed to wait for his touch.

Just as the tips of his fingers felt the warmth of its breath, the water dripping from its nose, Purse heard a cry far above him: "Got me?" It was Lara. He was sure of it. In that moment the fawn bolted. Purse was left with his hand outstretched across the spring, but now looking upward.

"Lara!" he shouted. "Come down!" He had no idea what he was saying, but he said it with all his heart. "Come down!"

He heard a long soft scraping high above him, and a small scream. It was too dark. He couldn't see. The scraping and bumping descended upon him, a sparrow's plunge, the dare of a swallow. He stumbled in terror into the pool. Something came wooshing downwards—he held out his arms if only to protect himself. Almost soundlessly, as if in a dream, into them came the entire weight of his fallen desires, crushing him into the veil of water.

Chapter 9
Moraine

❋

"You are here," said a voice. "Just as he said, you are both here."

Lara looked up. She was reclining against a rock wall next to a spring; not far away a shaggy cedar let in shafts of morning light. The tree was immensely old and tall, and full of songbirds. Purse was sitting close beside her, raising his head and rubbing his eyes.

"It is the fawn who has awakened you, I think. I saw him from the door of the cottage. From such a deep sleep perhaps only the fawn could have brought you awake."

Lara turned now to the voice. Standing beside her was a young woman, simply featured, who stood barefoot in a long green smock. Her hair was a pleasing color of brown, and fell far past her shoulders.

"Maureen?" said Lara, not at all sure that it was.

"Almost, dear sister," said the woman. "Moraine is my name, born at the foot of the ancient glacier, sole daughter of my lost parents and until now the only remnant of Otium."

"Remnant?" said Purse. "How is that?"

"I will tell you," Moraine replied. "But first I must know you, and whence you came."

Lara and Purse looked at each other, and then at themselves. Their feet were bare, just like Moraine's, and Lara wore neither rope nor harness. Lara felt at a total loss. "I—I thought I was climbing. On the tower," she said.

She stood up to scan the rock. There was the flared crack, high above, but Roper was nowhere to be seen. Slowly she retraced their route—the delicate traverse from the spring, the friction ascent, the pendulum. Something was missing. *Some things.* There were no bolts. She looked to her right, underneath the first three belays. There were no ropes piled on the ground—the ones they had let fall in the night.

She turned again to face Moraine. "I must have fallen," she said lamely.

"You did," said Purse. "I caught you. Here." He pointed to the water.

Lara looked away from him, dark lines of thought on her face. The pendulum. Something had cut loose on her swing.

"You couldn't have," she said flatly. "I was four hundred feet up."

Now it was Purse's turn to look perplexed. Moraine stood by as if to oversee the discussion.

"Then, are you hurt?" he asked.

"Are you?" said Lara.

They stretched their limbs and took trial steps about the spring.

"Not even sore," he said.

"Me neither."

They stood shyly together and joined hands. "And where's Maureen?" Purse asked the woman. The panic on his face had increased.

"Moraine," she corrected him. "I do not know any Maureen."

"But she grew up here!" Lara protested. "Right in that—" She was going to say *Quonset hut*, but as she pointed to it, that is not at all what she saw. A little way off stood a handsome cottage of granite and timber. The door and shutters were curiously shaped and carved.

"How rude of me to keep you waiting," said Moraine. "I should invite you in for breakfast. But I really must know your names."

"I'm Per—"

"No, let me guess," Moraine interrupted. "Percival. And you must be Lara." She looked rather pleased with herself.

"But how did you know?" Purse demanded.

"I received word of your coming," said Moraine. "A great-uncle of yours, I believe."

"But I don't have any great-uncles."

"Oh, this one has been absent a long time. Since before you were born, he said." She let the words settle in. "But please, do come join me for breakfast. It's been ever so lonely here, since they took my parents away. If it were not for Garth and Lira and the fawn, I don't know what I would have done. And now that you are here to help me, I really do feel my spirits lighten. Really, I do."

She held out a hand to each of them, and brought them with quiet ceremony along the base of the rock to her cottage, where they crossed an intricate threshold of stone. Inside, a sunlit kitchen opened onto a round cedar table some ways from a fireplace. The morning here was as cool and fresh and pleasant as it was without. It was as if they were not indoors at all. A fire would have ruined the feeling. Lara looked about at the low-beamed ceiling, the many old books along each wall, the ferns that seemed to crowd through the open windows. She glanced at Purse and saw on his face a look of deep satisfaction, as if he had found his ideal dwelling. "Green to the very door," he whispered.

Before long they were all seated about the table, finishing a delicious breakfast of eggs and salmon and baked brown bread. The food gave to Lara and Purse a faint sense of normalcy. And yet, from the moment they had entered the cottage, what they had felt was a deeper sense of ease and belonging than drab normalcy ever offered. The pleasure was so unexpected and exquisite that both of them wanted to stave off explanation for fear the feeling would diminish.

But they were also undeniably curious.

"You say a fawn awakened us," Lara said. "Was it a white fawn, by any chance?"

"Not *a* white fawn. *The* white fawn. The White Fawn of Otium."

"So you have seen him before?" Purse said.

"Hardly at all," Moraine admitted. "He comes only in times of danger."

"Such as now?" asked Purse.

Moraine nodded. "And I think that he has brought you here to be of help."

"I can almost believe it *was* the fawn who saved us," said Lara. "I have seen him heal the fallen once before."

Purse looked at her sharply.

"It was your father," she faltered. "I'm sorry. I was too embarrassed to tell you. Because it was my fault, really. He fell off the end of his rope because I couldn't check the knot. I thought that he had crushed his head or broken his neck. But the fawn touched him, and he was well. At the moment I was angry with him. Yet the fawn nuzzled him, breathed upon him. It's a terrible thing for me to say, but your father seemed so—undeserving. And he doesn't even know it happened. He regained his life only to keep being so awful to everyone, and to carry out his plans for the gorge."

Purse put an arm around her and looked down. He didn't seem to know what to say.

"No," said Moraine, "none of us are deserving, Lara. But the white fawn keeps coming from time to time. He visits and succors whom he will. I do not know his purposes. But it is written on the top of the tower that they are good."

"And yet, Purse's mother—Grace," said Lara. "Her useless legs. Couldn't the fawn have prevented that?"

"I do not know," Moraine said quietly. "I often wish the fawn had come before they took my parents away." She looked at Purse. "It is something to ask Garth."

"Garth?" he said.

"Your uncle."

"I told you I don't—"

Lara put her hands on his knee. "Purse," she said, "Moraine has troubles of her own. Perhaps we should hear her story first—then hear more of ours."

Purse nodded, acquiescing.

"In truth," said Moraine, "my story and yours are joined, and to tell one is to tell the other. To start with my parents is to get to the uncle you now deny."

"Go on, then," Lara said. "Take your time."

Moraine paused to pour them all tea, and then began in a formal manner. "This cottage," she said, "was built many years ago by the Lord Amoenas, my grandfather, the first of mortals to come to the gorge. He met and married the most beautiful of the naiads whom he found at the foot of the great falls, and made this cottage beside the spring at the base of the Tower of Otium because this spring was a favorite of hers. From it, she said, came all the songs that the naiads sang. The Lord Amoenas and his bride had a single daughter, Rosamond—but my grandmother died soon after her water broke, and melted back into the river. The Lord Amoenas delivered his daughter in his grief and raised her until she came of age. And then he too passed away, and went to be with the dust of his fathers.

"Rosamond—that is my mother—all alone kept house here until she married Colin the herdsman, who served under Lady Demaris in the meadows below the Center Queen. In those days he helped to protect the marmots from the Lava Beast. When Colin came to the gorge, however, he was sent by Garth to defend the naiads from the depredations of El Ai, the desert prince far to the south who had begun to make ruinous raids upon the gorge. The great El Ai was swept away in the glacier burst that crushed the south bridge to the island, and afterward Garth was taken down the river in a silken barge with the three sisters—the Ladies Lira, Demaris, and Stella."

"These names," said Purse. "They are sounding familiar. I think some of them are in my mother's books."

Moraine simply nodded, as if the names should be familiar to everyone. "The four of them sailed far away for many years—some say to the world's end in the Western Sea. Four years later it was rumored that Demaris and Stella had returned—to marry at last the two brothers Chambers and Villard on either side of the North Queen. But the third brother, Garth, and his beloved Lady Lira were never heard of again. Never, that is, until some few days ago.

"I lived here with my parents in peace for all of my twenty-two years, and the tale of my curious woes is a recent one. Four days ago, after hiking to the northern fall some three miles upstream from here, I was returning across the stone bridge when I saw a low black ship beached in the cove on the downstream side of the tower. It had many long oars, and a furled black sail, and an evil figurehead—like a dragon. On the sand in the cove were bands of men, some in black, others in outlandish pink. They were tending fires built up against the rock. Later I saw the smoke had left great black streaks on the granite.

"Then I heard my mother and father cry out from the cottage. Another band was wresting both of them out the door. I saw the men set fire to the back of the cottage and carry my parents around the tower toward the ship. I did not know what to do. I tried to scream but fortunately I only fainted, and because I lay prone on the bridge I was never discovered. I was awakened by a heavy rain. The fires were gone and the cottage was no longer burning. And the men, and the ship, and my parents—had vanished."

"How perfectly awful," Lara said, and Purse nodded. "Do you even know which way they went—upstream or down?"

"I do not," said Moraine. "And that is the worst of it. However, when I got to the cottage the fawn was waiting at the doorstep. I had never seen him before. He let me put my arms around him and breathed a certain warmth back into my heart. Then he was gone, and I cried myself to sleep in the cottage. And in the morning, when I came into this common room, Garth and Lira were seated here at the cedar table. I knew them from my parents' stories. Garth was tall, and very old, with cascading hair and beard that shone so white it was almost silver. And Lady Lira had green eyes, like all of her sisters, and raven-black hair. She had once been cruel, but I found her wholly kind. They each enfolded me in their arms, and spoke words of comfort—I can't begin to remember them all.

"Finally, Garth said, 'This is not work for the ax, but for the cup, and the blood of the fawn.'

"'The blood of the fawn?' I said to him. I did not like to think of the fawn as wounded and bleeding.

"'Even he,' Garth said. 'But you must wait. You must wait for the cup. For it is not you that shall seek it but another. You shall find him sitting beside the spring, under the tower, three days hence—and a young woman with him like yourself. You shall call him Percival, and the woman Lara, and they shall be your help in the name of the fawn. Percival is my niece's son, but knows not me. You must give him this.'"

"Give him what?" Purse interrupted.

"This," said Moraine, and pulled from her lap a piece of parchment. She handed it to him, and he smoothed it out upon the table. There was writing on it, in antique script. The first capital letter, a *T*, was made to look like a large wooden ice ax. At least that's what Purse said later on. To Lara it looked more like an old-growth cedar. In any case the letter was enlarged and illuminated beyond its normal capacity.

"It's a poem," said Lara.

Purse gave her a look that said he knew. "A Spenserian stanza, to be exact. Usually part of a longer narrative."

"Well," she said, admiring but nonplussed, "read it, why don't you?"

So he did:

> *"The fawne, the cvp, the vallie all do yearne*
> *To be vnited in the shedding grace*
> *That from the cvp shall spill vpon the ferne,*
> *The flower, the cedar of this stonie place.*
> *Who finds the cvp mvst certes soon abase*
> *His pride of knowledge or her pride of skill;*
> *What thinks he sees or thinks that she can face*
> *Be nothing to the svm of good or ill.*
> *Go, seek the cvp behind the fall. The fawne they kill."*

They were all quiet. Lara didn't like the last part about someone killing the fawn. "Who's *they?*" she asked. "Who's after the fawn?"

"The people in the ship, I suppose," said Moraine. "Garth would only tell me they were from the East."

"Like the climbers," said Lara.

Moraine shrugged. "I did not see them touch the rock—except for their fires."

"Let me get this straight," said Purse, still staring at the parchment on the table. "We're being sent by this mythical uncle of mine to find a cup behind a waterfall?" He tried to sound contemptuous. "What's next, the Holy Grail?"

Moraine looked pensive.

"What I'm asking," he said, "is how is this supposed to help your parents?"

"I do not know," Moraine said. She seemed to weigh a further comment.

"And—" he prompted, catching her pause.

"And according to the poem," she said, "neither do you."

"What do you mean?" he said uncomfortably.

"Our knowledge is limited," she said. "It is better to obey than to know. It is better to be lowly wise."

"Milton," he said, looking about as if someone were hiding in the corner. "I bet you have him on your shelves."

"I know no Milton," Moraine said. "I only know what is said to be written on the summit of the tower."

"Well, I'm not up to this," Purse said miserably. "I'm going back to the lodge." Even as he spoke, however, he realized the lodge was no longer there.

"Purse," said Lara. Her voice was measured. "I think you have to be up for this—that *we* have to be up for this. I think this is why we are here."

He sat for a moment in convoluted silence. "I see," he finally said. There was a flatness in his voice. "So where are we going, exactly? Where is 'the fall'?" But he already knew. He had been behind the fall in his dream.

"There are several," said Moraine. "But the greatest is at the head of the gorge, where the river drops from the high country. It is ten miles. Perhaps eleven."

"Barefoot?" he said weakly.

"You will find the grass very soft, Percival. I never use shoes myself. They are a form of separation. You will feel more, and gain the real strength of the ground."

Purse gave Moraine a scornful look that Lara suddenly recognized as inherited from his unkind father. It made her squirm with embarrassment.

"Moraine," she said, "we are glad to go. Will you come with us to find the cup?"

"I am to stay here," she said. "To welcome my parents when they return. So said Garth and the Lady Lira."

"And where are they?" Purse asked.

"I do not know," Moraine said. "The two of them crossed the bridge and vanished. That was three mornings ago."

"They literally vanished?"

"In a manner of speaking. Perhaps they just kept walking. Perhaps you will meet them someday soon."

"That would be nice, I think," said Lara.

Purse was silent on the matter. He suddenly asked, "This cup—what is it? What is it good for?"

"I can only tell you what every creature in the Three Queens knows by heart:

Never false and ever true,
Ancient eld and ever new,
Ever full and ever spilled,
The cup is as the fawn hath willed.

That I was taught since I could speak. It is written atop the Tower of Otium."

"A rather inaccessible book, that," Purse said wryly. "Do you have a copy in the cottage?"

"No," said Moraine, "but you will find it written throughout the gorge, if only you look hard enough. Even the stones and stars can speak, if you but let them."

Purse had no answer for this but a sigh.

Together they cleared the cedar table. The morning was late, nearly dissolved. "Shall we pack a lunch—and a dinner or so?" Lara asked brightly.

Moraine led them to a pair of rucksacks beside the door, the olive canvas ripe to bursting with provision. "I packed these for you last night," she said. "That way, when you came in the morning, I thought there would be no delay. You will find food enough for several days, and water aplenty in the river."

After some discussion of which pack might be heavier, and who might best be suited to carry it, Purse and Lara put on the rucksacks, tightened the straps about their shoulders, and stood in the doorway to say farewell. The sun now shone directly down upon the doorstep, much as it had upon their arrival the day before. The dogwood blossoms were all alight, cool and clean in the noon of springtime.

"Goodbye, Moraine," Lara said simply. She reached out for both her hands. "I feel I have known you for more than a morning. I hope we'll be back before many days."

"The fawn go with you," Moraine said. "With both of you."

But Purse had already turned to leave.

Chapter 10
In a Watery Way

✳

"YOU WERE RUDE," SAID LARA. They had crossed the natural stone bridge that joined the island of Otium to the north bank of the Amoenas, and their bare feet were settling into the damp and duff of the meadowy trail.

"I was scared," said Purse. "I still am. I would rather have stayed in the cottage."

"With Moraine?"

"I suppose. But with all those books, too."

This struck her as a bit odd. "You really like to read, don't you."

"Don't you?"

"Yes, but did you hear Moraine? The gorge is a book—the trees, the river. This trail we're walking—it is a story. Sometimes I think you like the books that come on a shelf because you can close them whenever you want and put them back. They're safer for you."

He thought about it. "I don't think I'd put it that way. But you can, if you want to. As I said, I'm frightened. Unlike my father, I can admit it."

"But like your father, you know how to belittle people. You should have just said you were scared and not taken it out on Moraine."

He walked in silence a long time. When he spoke, his voice was slow and deliberate. "It's not just me I'm scared for, Lara—it's the whole world. It seems to be set up all wrong for everyone. I'd like to think this white fawn can set it to rights, but so far he hasn't done an impressive job."

"Perhaps we should do ours," said Lara.

"There you go," he said with renewed petulance. "Being so brave all the time. Do you really think that climbing these cliffs of yours makes anything happen? Does it solve anything? Prove anything? Leave you with anything beside your so-called 'pride of skill'? Because the poem was about that too, you know—not just my wormy pride of knowledge. It was talking about your Tamburlaine as much as it was my Faustus."

Now it was Lara's turn to ponder. "No," she said carefully, "climbing makes nothing happen. It's like poetry in that way." She surprised herself with the calmness of this reflection.

"But Purse," she added, "I'm not always brave—not about everything. When I fell last night, I'm glad you caught me—if that's what you did. And we can both be glad for the fawn, I think. And now for Moraine, and for Garth, and the cup. The world may be all wrong, but I'm beginning to think it is also full of strangely interconnected goodness, as tenuous and invisible as the way up the wall from valley to rim. I'm brave enough to see some of that already. Can you see it too?"

"Almost," said Purse. "Not yet. But I'm walking, am I not?" He reached ahead and took her hand and made her stop, and she kissed him sweetly. They were at the bend in the canyon with the last view of Otium, the place they had embraced before.

"Sublime," said Purse drolly, looking at Lara and then at the tower. "A fearful wonder."

"It is," said Lara earnestly. "But I wonder where everyone is, don't you?"

They were still wondering an hour later when they reached the meadow underneath the northern fall. There was a trail junction here, one path leading up steep ledges beside the fall to the rim of the gorge, and the main path continuing through alder and dogwood up the river. But there was no lodge, and no dock—not even a hint of their ruin. Purse and Lara sat down in the tall grass for a late lunch of bread and cheese.

"It's funny," said Lara.

"Not at all."

"It's strange, I mean. The gorge looks just as it did before—the river, the meadow, the dogwood. Even that patch of Queen Anne's lace, right down there by the water. And the remnant cedars under the fall. It's not like we've traveled in time. I'm sure Maureen's father would tell us the valley we're in is recovering from the glacier burst that wiped out the lower cedars, just like the valley we knew. Yet the lodge isn't here, and apparently never *was* here."

"And yet the valley itself—" Purse paused, intent upon the crimson strokes of a clump of paintbrush at his feet.

"—seems more here than it ever was," Lara continued. "More, more—"

"More revealed," said Purse firmly, looking about at the blue sky, the quiet walls, the swallows swinging across the rock and the ouzels skimming along the river. "Better disclosed. Not just sublime, but

a sense sublime
Of something far more deeply interfused."

"Meaning?"

"Meaning it has been transfigured in some way." He held up the bread in his hand as if by way of illustration. "Or that we have. Somehow, Lara, we have gotten into the real world, the world our world wants to be, the world our world really is if only we could die of wonder."

"Does that scare you?" she suddenly asked.

A slow smile spread like a discovery across his face. "It gives me," he said, "great pleasure."

He leaned forward to pass her the cheese, and their hands touched—and lips might have followed had not they heard at that very moment the sound of music, voices singing from under the bank where the dock had been. Lara and Purse looked at each other and dropped their bread and cheese in the grass. Had they arisen and walked to the water's edge they could have peeked over the bank and seen the voices that lay out of sight. But they stayed where they were, without moving. "The naiads," Lara whispered. "Remember what Maureen's mother said?"

Afterward they could not agree on exactly what the singing was like. Purse thought there were words being sung, though he could not say what they were, but Lara heard only wordless notes, sweet and wild, yet ordered in a harmony of birds at dawn, or of a wind chime in the afternoon when you are all by yourself in a lonely place of rest and peace. The music drifted on in that way, as if it had never really started and had no particular reason to cease. Just hiking along, they might have mistaken the ongoing sound for the gentle rippling of the river.

But though the music seemed to seek no end, it suddenly stopped. They soon saw why. Coming downstream, around the bend in the river where the creek from the base of the northern fall went tumbling into the broader current, a jet-black ship slipped suddenly into full view. Purse and Lara flattened themselves in the tall grass. It was not a large ship, more like a galley with many long oars now resting in air and a short mast rising from a single deck. The bow reached forward in the figurehead of a menacing dragon. To see just the dragon alone was enough to make Lara tremble. It sent a fear as black as the ship through her bones.

"Look there," Purse whispered. "On the deck."

There were many figures gathered there, all dressed as black as the ship itself. All save one, that is—a man in pink who stood in the prow behind the dragon. She started even more when she saw him.

"Purse," she said, "he looks like—"

"My father," Purse said miserably.

"And those two up in the rigging, they look—"

"Yes. Our friends the climbers from the East."

"And—by the tiller!"

Purse saw, but chose not to rub it in. What appeared to be Roper and Savidge stood side by side in the stern of the ship, guiding it swiftly down the current. There were others on the deck as well, and Lara dimly recognized some of them as former visitors to the lodge. But the boat slipped by too rapidly for her to begin to see them all. That, or perhaps she was too shocked by what she had already seen to take in more.

As quickly as the ship had come it coursed away, floating behind a curtain of alder and down the stream. Purse and Lara slowly raised themselves from the grass.

"Did we really see—who we thought we saw?" Lara said. Her voice was quavering.

"Maybe we did," Purse said. "Maybe they're really just—marauders." He tried to laugh, the word sounded so comical. "Here in the real world, that is."

Lara felt an ache in her throat. "I don't like this," she choked. "I don't like seeing all those people on that ship. I don't think it was really them."

Purse was silent for a moment, taken by a sudden thought. "Well," he said, "maybe it wasn't—them, that is. Remember Moraine? She wasn't Maureen, she was just her stand-in apparently—her real-life counterpart."

"Then what does that make us?" wailed Lara—"in this so-called real life of yours. Ghosts and goblins of ourselves? And who is your mother going to show up as?"

Purse stole an arm of comfort around her shoulders. "As something better than she was, I hope. As someone without a wheelchair. We've left our books and ropes behind—perhaps she can leave her crutches as well."

Lara shut her eyes tight and thought about this, dimly heartened that Purse had become the one with hope. Then she heaved a great sigh, wiping away a gathering tear. "Well," she said, "shall we get on to the head of the gorge? It's been a rather exciting lunch, I think. Better than most I've had at the lodge."

They got up, restuffing their rucksacks. "I wonder, though, where Moraine's parents are, don't you?" Lara asked. "You don't suppose they could still be below deck?"

Purse didn't know. And, in fact, Lara did not stay for his answer. Out of thirst and curiosity, she went down to the bank where the dock had been and climbed down to the riverside. She scooped the water to her mouth and in the stillness of an eddy watched her reflection. Except somehow there were two of them, peering back from under the surface. And one looked, in a watery way, for all the world like Maureen's mother, Jennifer.

Chapter 11
A Different Kind of Courage

✳

By the time that Purse and Lara were walking beneath the Fawn Wall, the sun was well on its homeward way to Otium. It was that timeless time of day that is somewhere between late afternoon and early evening. The trail passed close to the riverside here, and a sloping meadow separated them from the cliff. A single cedar grew there at the base of the rock, just as another remained on the opposite side of the gorge where Purse's father had fallen a scant two days before. Lara gazed up at the wall as they went, recalling the wish of Purse's mother that he be the one to climb it with her. She still wondered how this might be possible. With five miles yet to go to the great falls of the Amoenas, Purse was lagging behind her pace, demanding a rest.

"Please," he bleated pathetically.

She turned and watched him emerge from shadow into the latening light of the meadow. When he had caught up she saw he was limping.

"What's the matter?"

Purse grimaced. "Apparently, there are thorns in this perfect world of ours. There's one in my foot, anyway." He plopped down in the grass by the trail and held up the afflicted foot for her inspection. "If we were meant to walk without shoes—"

"We would have been born with feet," said Lara, gently rubbing the dirt from his sole. She found a large splinter of wood in his heel but was unable to nudge it out.

"Let's soak it in the river," she said. She helped him just a little further down the path to where it dipped to the water's edge. But they stopped short, and Lara lost all thought of extracting the splinter.

For here the bank had been caved in, and the meadow churned to a berth of mud. It was as if a leviathan had hauled itself up onto shore and turned the grass into a wallow.

"The ship," said Purse. "The dragon ship was here today."

Lara began to skirt the mire. There were footsteps all about in the beaten grass. At a point farthest from the river, the steps converged in a broken path that led toward the Fawn Wall. Fern and flower were flattened in a trampled swath.

"Look here," she said as Purse caught up to her. "Shall we follow?"

He nodded grimly, still mindful of his heel but not about to complain. Not now.

They picked their way out of the light and back into the shadow of evening. The wall above them loomed like a grim visage, beetle-browed where the overhangs jutted out high above. At the very top was the ghost of a waterfall, still reflecting the alpine sun, a goodness that was almost gone.

A little way from the river, Purse paused. He bent down and brushed his hand along the ground, then ran his fingers across his arm. Lara looked over his shoulder.

"Blood," he said quietly, pointing to the darkened grass.

"But it has to be hours old," said Lara.

"I know," said Purse. *"Ancient eld and ever new."*

"You mean—"

"I hope not. Just a guess."

But he was right. They followed the trampled trail through the grass, dotted now with pools and patches of fresh blood, until they came to the giant cedar at the base of the Fawn Wall. It was shaggy, and old, and fire-scarred. The first branches only began far overhead, and they swept across the face of the cliff like lasting arms. On the downhill side of the tree was nothing gruesome. But nestled between the trunk and the stone on the uphill side was the peak and period of their fears.

Here lay the white fawn, spindled with a dozen arrows, glassy eyed in its own gore. Worse, perhaps, on either side against the tree were propped the bodies of a man and a woman, each with a dagger stuck in the heart. The man's red beard and the woman's blonde hair were fouled with blood. Their clothes seemed to have once been white.

"Colin and Rosamond," Lara whispered. "Poor Moraine. However can we possibly tell her?"

"And the fawn," said Purse, reaching down to touch its neck. "They killed him. They really did." He looked about stupidly.

Without knowing why, Lara threw her arms around the neck of the fawn and began to weep. The blood from its wounds was warm and wet, but the body was cold. Then, with both hands Lara began to tear away the arrows from the flesh of the fawn, as if she could reverse the flow of his life's blood by removing what had pierced it out.

Purse, likewise, carefully removed the daggers from Moraine's parents as if their deaths could be undone. When they had finished, they threw the weapons far away into the meadow and wiped their hands clean on the grass. Lara leaned against the wall and moaned softly, digging her nails into the rock as if somehow it could sustain her. *The ultimate climb,* she thought to herself bitterly, *that would make everything else all right.* Purse slipped in the blood of the fawn and found himself clinging to the tree.

For a long time they did not speak. The shadow of evening slipped completely across the valley. The belching of frogs and the scratching of crickets began to echo from wall to wall. A cold wind began to blow from the head of the gorge, and the branches of the cedar groaned. It could have been the world's last night.

"I think," said Lara, finally turning from the wall, "we must still go on to seek the cup. Or one of us, anyway. It wouldn't seem right to desert the fawn and these poor people, even if they are quite dead."

Purse looked up from the tree and nodded. "I'll stay," he said. "You know the way better than I. Besides, my splinter."

"Your splinter," said Lara, with the pained look of one who had completely forgotten. "Let me see it."

He sat down against the tree and she lifted his foot. It was smeared with blood. She wiped his heel clean with her sleeve and squinted at it in the dusk, scraping and pinching the skin with her fingers.

"There's no splinter here," she said. "Not anymore."

"There's got to be," Purse said. "It was in deep."

"You sound like you miss it."

"No. But—"

"What?"

He realized he was thinking about the dream he had had of swimming upstream to the waterfall with the black ship close behind. He remembered the arrows, the crush of water, the hollow darkness behind the falls. "Lara," he said desperately, "how am I supposed to get on the other side of a waterfall?"

"But you just said you were staying. Did you change your mind?"

"No. I mean, I don't know. I mean—Lara, it's just that I had a dream last night that I swam there, right through or under the great falls. On the way I caught you coming down. Except that part already seems to have happened. But because of the dream I have this strange and terrible feeling that I am the one that has to go. Even though I don't want to, and even though you're the brave one."

This gave Lara pause. She was not so sure she liked the idea of spending a lonely night with the dead. For her it would be easier to hike up-canyon in the dark and face the danger of the falls. But what was she thinking? Why did it have to be right now?

"You know," she said, "maybe we're rushing this whole thing. Why don't we just camp here—" She looked at the bodies. "Or nearby, and make up our minds in the morning. It's not like we have a deadline to meet or anything."

"*Deadline?*" Purse winced. "It looks as though we've missed that already, Lara." He stared again at the bleeding fawn, the corpses pale in the dusk. Quite deliberately he closed the eyes of Colin and of Rosamond. "I can't believe my father would do this. Or even someone *like* my father." He shook his head.

"What do you say?" Lara pressed. "Do we camp?" She shivered in the gathering dark.

Purse did not seem ready to answer. They both looked down at the river, perplexed. Whatever light was left in the valley seemed to have been collected in the moving surface of the water. It glimmered and glowed, a shining path, a lifeblood that could never be let out forever, but always came, and kept on coming. Beyond it was the craggy buttress of Cedar Crypt and Harm's Way. Their climbing there felt years in the past.

"Right now," said Lara, "I wouldn't mind seeing that awful jetboat." She thought of supper in the lodge, and her little room, snug with Maureen. She was trying to remember what warm clothes or blankets there were in the bottom of their rucksacks.

"What's that?" said Purse, sitting up. "Down on the water."

She followed his arm. Just downriver, a dark shape was laboring against the current, many arms extended in unison into the water. Her heart sank.

"The ship," she said. "As if they had not done enough."

"Yes," said Purse. "Why would they be coming back? Unless they have taken—"

"Moraine too?"

They looked at each other and both rose to their feet at once. Staying low, they crept back down the trampled meadow and hid themselves in a clump of alders just at the riverside. Lara felt herself breathing hard. Through the leaves, the first stars had gained the sky.

"There," said Purse. Into their restricted view, latticed by the trunks of the alder, the black ship slowly came. All of the oars were moving hard against the current from portholes under the deck, and someone—it sounded like Savidge—was calling out the strokes in time. A lantern burned in the mouth of the dragon, another in the stern. By the light of the last they could just make out the fiercely intent face of Roper, alone at the tiller. The rest of the deck was too dark to see. As the ship passed by the alders, however, they heard voices from the base of the mast.

"Where?" said one. "Tell us where."

"And for what?" said another, equally demanding.

Lara recognized the voices. It was those grand inquisitors, the two climbers from the East.

There was a sound of sobbing. "I already told you. The waterfall. They left to go to the great falls."

Purse gripped her arm. They both knew it was Moraine.

"But where is the hiding place, precisely? And what is it you sent them for?"

There was more sobbing from Moraine.

"Tell us," said the other, "or it will go hard with your family—and even worse for your two friends."

The sobbing continued, and the ship moved away in the night. Purse and Lara strained their ears, but could hear no more. Slowly they disentangled themselves from the alder screen and stood in the cold mud by the river.

"The beasts!" hissed Purse. "The absolute animals! I'd like to swim out to that ship right now and—"

"Get yourself butchered?" asked Lara.

He clenched and unclenched his fists in the air. The sky about them was fast filling up with stars, blown into being by the wind.

"We're not camping," Purse said decidedly. "We're going upstream to get that cup before they do, and we're going to rescue—"

She cut him off. "Purse, I have this funny feeling. If they do decide to harm

Moraine, I think they will bring her right here to the cedar at the base of the wall. It would be their way—the cruelest possible end for her. And if that happens, one of us should be here to try to prevent it. We might outrun the ship to the falls, but we'd never beat it back downstream."

"So you want me to stay?"

"For me it is harder. It will take a different kind of courage. I would like to run ahead to the falls—of course I have been there, I know the trail. But tonight, on account of your dream, I think it is you that knows the way. That's how it feels to me, Purse." She touched his hand, shivering.

He started to answer, but something in him ceased to argue. The light from the stern of the dragon ship was pulling farther into the distance with every word and wasted breath.

"All right," he said, and felt his rucksack fall from his shoulders. "I'm off belay."

Chapter 12
The Plunge Pool

✳

BY THE TIME PURSE WAS SHORT OF BREATH, he had drawn abreast of the slow but steadily moving ship. Fortunately, the trail was screened from the river here by a thicket of willow. He could feel the path much better than he could see it; running in the dark was a matter of trusting his feet to guide him. But he was no runner. At Oxford, he had loved to walk on the bank of the Isis while classmates came sculling by in their shells on the water. He had not had to keep up with them. And now it appeared, as his breath grew sharp and his arms grew tight, that keeping up with the black ship would be the best that he could do. He wanted, of course, to outrun the ship to the falls. But there were a dozen or so of them, all pulling on the oars, and all he had were his bare feet and his weak lungs—and perhaps four miles to go. It was hardly fair.

He was thinking such thoughts, over and over with the ragged rhythm of his legs, when he suddenly noticed that the lantern lights in the bow and the stern of the dragon ship were no longer blinking through the trees but shining steadily on his right. The willow thicket had dissolved, and nothing now separated him from the river. He heard a shout, and saw the face of his own father, a fellow traveler, leaning toward him across the neck of the twisted dragon. The eyes were wide with surprise, and fear, and then suddenly narrowed in deep hatred. But in that instant Purse knew for the first time that the fear was deeper, that the distance he had long endured was ultimately founded on fright.

Overcome, he slackened his pace even further, not knowing where he could hide. His father slipped upstream, and the stern of the ship drew even with him. There was Roper, not with his hand on the tiller but holding a bent bow to his cheek, arrow notched. Purse bolted just as the string twanged, and something went zipping behind him into the darkness. He felt himself sprinting as never before. His father's face came up on his right again, then disappeared behind a timely row of alder. He heard another twang behind him, followed by a hollow *thunk* in the trunk of a sapling next to his head. His legs pumped even faster. His feet found the trail without even trying.

Some minutes later—he had no idea how many—the trail met the bank again, and he slowed just enough to cast a look back down the river. To his great relief there was no ship in sight. For the moment he had outdistanced it. And though his adrenalin had peaked, he did not stop running. This time it did not cost the same effort as when he had started. His body felt made to run, riding on a second wind that carried him up and up the trail into the barely starlit dark. It occurred to him that a strong man really could run his course with joy.

He heard no sound save the beating of his feet, the surge of his breath, the wind in the grass, the glide of the river against the bank. An owl occasionally swooped beside him, or hooted in the branch of a tree, and unseen creatures scurried through the brush sometimes when he rounded a sudden bend in the trail. The walls of the gorge rose black and tall on either side, and stars were now strewn thick in the sky. Hemmed in by either rim, they seemed themselves a pathway to follow overhead.

But his second wind did not last forever. His thighs grew heavy, his feet sore; he felt himself wearing out once again. He had no idea how close he might be to the end of the trail, and not much clue about what he would do when he got there. *You're hopeless! Your father hates you! Your mother can't help you! Her fawn is dead!*

He was just beginning to hear again this old voice of discouragement when another voice, an older voice, made itself known as the trail rounded a turn in the gorge. Through the air came the spray and sound of acres of water sifting the sky, then reverberating on rocks and river like a pounding drum, echo on echo. Purse ran ahead up a rocky switchback crossing over the toe of a buttress. Stones in the trail cut his feet, but he hardly knew it. At a narrow crest he came to a halt. There, a scant half-mile ahead, the Amoenas River poured from the lip of the gibbous moon, which was just peeking over the head of the gorge. The falling water sent wreaths and plumes across the stars, and the ferns at his feet were waving and wet, even at this modest distance. The foot of the falls was hidden away in moonshadow.

From his vantage point, he looked downriver. Perhaps only a quarter-mile behind him, the lights of the dragon ship glowed on the river like fallen stars. It was still coming on. He could pause no longer.

In the moment he had looked and lingered, the moon completely crested the rim and brought its light upon the rest of his journey ahead. The trail switchbacked down to the river, and now that he could see the many rocks in the path, he found that he was not really running, but picking his way to avoid hurt. By the time he reached the river again he feared he had lost precious time. He looked back. As far as he could see in the spray, the black ship had not yet rounded the buttress behind him.

He felt luck, but also hurry. *Go on!* he told himself. *Go on!* The trail ahead was rocky still, and now slippery as well. For here the boom and mist of the falls rained all around him. In the moonlight it was a swirling fog. He fought his way over the stones, bruising his heels, stubbing his toes, getting wetter and wetter with every step. Finally the path gave out altogether on the margin of a vast pool at the foot of the falls. The spray flew hard and horizontally into his face. He was quite soaked, and thoroughly chilled. As in his dream, the water before him roiled like an ocean in storm. Waves and eddies of foam piled up in all directions. He could just make out the crash and plunge of the actual waterfall in the distance. The weight and sound of it were prodigious, the stuff of fear and not of wonder. To admire this fall one needed to be considerably farther off. He saw at once there would be no walking around the pool and somehow slipping behind the curtain unscathed—the cliffs hemmed in on every side. If he were to encounter the falls he would have to swim through the chaos of the plunge pool. Once across—if indeed he could get across—he had no doubt the falls would smash him to little pieces. He would end like Orpheus,

> *When by the rout that made the hideous roar*
> *His gory visage down the stream was sent.*

He hesitated, shivering in uncertainty. He turned, even, to go back. But what he saw, laboring up the river behind him into the hard-driving spray, frightened him even more. It was the black ship, wavering now in new complexities of current, but no less determined to overtake him. Purse did not so much make up his mind as feel himself act. He stepped into the swirling pool and dove headlong into the foam. The water was cold, but no colder than the wind and spray, and the bubbling water even brought a certain strange exhilaration.

With strength of fear he struck out swimming, arms pulling one after the other in great strokes. He was almost halfway to the fall when suddenly he felt himself sucked to the left, swiftly whirling round and round toward the cliffy shore. It took him a moment to realize he had been drawn into a giant eddy. He was carried nearly into the rock and then suddenly pulled round again, back once more toward the outlet of the plunge pool where he had started. And there, to his horror, the black ship was just nosing into the waters. The current bore him directly under the mouth of the dragon. He felt himself just about to slip under the prow of the ship when the eddy shot him out again, toward the falls.

This time he knew he had to escape the leftward thrust that was coming. Instead of swimming straight for the falls he threw all his effort into pulling for the right-hand shore, hoping to counteract the swirl. The ship was wavering just behind him, drifting in the giant eddy and wary perhaps of the great falls. He was stroking hard, hardly daring to look up, and trying to think like a water ouzel, a beaver, a salmon. There were muffled shouts. Something sharp grazed his lips, and he felt them ache with a bleeding pain, as if he could speak no tongue but the always silent language of suffering. But he kept swimming— hard, harder, harder even than he had run—and finally he saw he was out of the eddy and almost to the great falls, which existed more in overwhelming sound than substance.

In the hesitation of half a moment he looked up at the sailing moon, rain-bowed against the spray, as if to ask it what to do. Then he lifted his head and looked across at the black ship, twirling end past end at the far side of the boiling pool. It occurred to him he might yet be able to swim downstream, out of its reach. Perhaps he could even slip by without his father's noticing. The falls beside him thundered like an angry god, bent on human sacrifice. He saw no good reason to offer himself.

In that moment, buffeted by the churn of water, tortured by doubt, he suddenly saw in the veil of the fall—or thought he saw, shimmering in the confusion of moonlight—something that completely surprised him. It was the stately figure of a woman in white. She was looking right at him, not proudly but with a composed mercy. She seemed even to extend her hand out of the pounding curtain of water. Without knowing that he had decided, Purse swam the few last yards to the fall and reached for the outstretched fingers of the woman. His hand closed on empty spray. There was nothing there.

But it was too late to swim away. He felt pulverized as if by a thousand granite boulders. The world became an immense and sudden rush of white that plunged him deep, deep, deep, beyond the reach of the farthest star.

Chapter 13
Keeping Watch

✳

FOR LARA THE NIGHT WAS VERY LONG. As soon as Purse had slipped away, she wanted to run and overtake him. But something held her rooted to the riverbank, watching again and again in her mind his angular and awkward gait as he had labored into the darkness. No, she finally told herself, it was his errand. Hers was harder—that ancient and most human duty of keeping watch over the dead.

In no particular hurry she carried both their rucksacks back up to the cedar tree at the foot of the wall. She forced herself to see that the bodies were still there. Between trunk and rock they rested in dim outline. She could almost think of them as merely asleep. But she would not choose them for bedfellows—just the thought of it made her shudder. She turned away and walked up-canyon along the wall until she found a sandy shelf. This would do; it was still within hailing distance of the dead. Here she sorted through both rucksacks, finding a pair of thin wool blankets. They would have to be enough for the night. There was still a breeze, and May was cool in the depths of the gorge. Once nestled inside the blankets she chewed part of a loaf of bread that Moraine had packed. But she scarcely felt hungry—she ate the bread more for something to do than for any nourishment.

Lara felt sure she would not fall asleep for a long time, if at all. The river made a quiet shimmering under the meadow, and minute by minute the stars thickened overhead. In an hour or so the moon rose from the head of the gorge. She lifted her head to look at it and felt drops of water in her face. But she saw no clouds. A faint shining far above her on the cliff reminded her of where she was, directly beneath the evanescent waterfall that shot from the rim. She fixed her eyes on the fading fall and wondered if she would ever feel it by her side, high on the rock. In the moonlight she examined the face just above her. It was split by a long fingerbreadth crack, the same that she and Roper had climbed the week before. The crack began at her sandy ledge. In the moonless dark she had not realized she had chosen the start of the climb as her place of rest. She wondered what she would do if Roper once again awakened her for a moonlight ascent. But he wouldn't have to awaken her. Both of her feet were very cold now—she sat up and wrapped them inside one of the rucksacks.

From her sitting position she could see the fawn and the unhappy couple silvered and silent, taking their deserved repose. And perhaps this was the blessing of death, a cessation of suffering, peace after trouble. In the moonlight it seemed almost enough. She thought of her mother, her silence in the face of such things. What could she say? And her father too. What did he want out of death? She tried to imagine how she would feel if the two bodies next to the tree were those of her parents, not the parents of someone she had just met. But Moraine felt more like someone she had really known all her life. And what did it mean to know somebody, or really to love them? She thought that she had loved Roper, but she had not loved the Roper she had seen on the ship. And she thought now that she loved Purse. But he was gone, and she was left with the bloody remains of someone's parents, and a dead fawn. And how could she love a dead fawn?

She got out of her blankets and disentangled her feet from the rucksack and walked back to the cedar tree. The wind made the cedar sway, and an owl called from high in the branches, asking her who she thought she was. She laid her hand on the neck of the fawn and felt there the white fur, the freshness of blood. A warmth spread inside of her, but nowhere else. The fawn and the people were still dead. She went back to her sandy shelf and got back into her blankets. She was warm now, and her thoughts were strangely put to rest. Without meaning to, she fell asleep.

In her sleep she dreamed she was resting on the sandy ledge at the foot of the wall, just as she in fact was. Roper came hiking up and across the silvered meadow and touched her shoulder. In her dream, his fingers were wet. She saw that he was pale and dripping, as if he had come to her from the river.

"Lara, the wall," he simply said. "The Fawn Wall." He began to unpack a sodden rucksack full of moldy, muddy ropes.

"But the fawn is here," Lara answered. "We don't need to climb the wall to find him."

"He's dead, Lara. He's bloody dead. I killed him myself so he would no longer be in our way. Now he can't stop us."

"But he never would have," Lara said.

"He didn't want *anyone* on his wall," Roper insisted. "He thought he could keep it for himself. *Virgin territory.*" He drew out these last two words derisively.

"Listen," he hissed, stooping down close to her face. Water kept dripping from the wide mat of his uncombed hair. "Didn't you know that bloody deer was hiding something on top? Something you can find only by climbing there? Something that will make you set for life? It's a cup, they say. And it has strange powers."

He lowered his voice and stooped even closer. "Drink from it, and you'll never fall from a climb again."

He drew back as if to gauge the impression he had made. "Think about it. The first ascents we could do, Lara—you and me—the biggest of the big walls all over the world. Patagonia, Baffin Island, the Karakoram. They would all be ours, every route—free, on sight, unroped. We would become the all-time bloody finest climbers in history. Think of all those suckers who will break their backs just trying to follow the first pitch of our forty-pitch routes. Not a soul will be able to compete. They'll all literally die trying, and we'll write their bloody obituaries to fill up half the space in all the climbing rags. In the other half we'll make them all drool over our exploits—those that are still alive, that is.

"Look!" he said, and pointed to a pair of figures dragging themselves out of the river in moonlight. They came trudging toward the base of the wall, and as they approached, Lara saw that they were the climbers from the East. Only now they were as bedraggled and pale as Roper was, shedding water the way the fawn kept shedding blood. They set their packs down almost on top of Lara. It was as if she were not there.

"So," said Roper, "are we going to let them get a head start on us? If they get to the cup first, they'll drain it to the dregs and toss it from the rim. You can be bloody sure of that."

The two climbers uncoiled a pair of ropes all hung with slime, and draped their shoulders with eels and spotted salamanders. One of the men started climbing up the wall with a strange mechanical regularity, stopping to crush a salamander into the crack at infrequent intervals. The rope behind him apparently threaded itself through the jaws of each unfortunate creature in turn. At the top of the pitch he looped an eel about a flake and began to belay his silent partner. The rock glimmered wet in their wake.

"Lara, what are we waiting for?" Roper demanded.

"The fawn," she heard herself say in reply. "We're waiting for the fawn."

His face turned into a white moist sneer. "A long wait that will be!" He stood over her, shaking as if in a terrible rage. Then it seemed, though the shaking continued, that he turned merely nervous with fear. Or perhaps he was just shivering with cold. She reached for his palsied hand. It was ice.

"If you touch the fawn, he will make you warm," Lara said.

"I have touched the fawn and killed it," he said, not passionate now but without almost any affect. "I only wanted to climb the wall and dance on his grave, but you won't come."

She held on to his cold white hand.

"Lara, the wall. The Fawn Wall."

And the hand melted into water.

When Lara awoke, the stars had begun to pale in the sky. She was holding on with one hand to the base of the small crack in the wall. Inside the crack, the rock was damp. Cautiously she withdrew her fingers and carried with them a tiny frog. It was gray and wet, no bigger than the top of her thumb. One moment it was there in the faintness of dawn, connected in surprise to her flesh. A moment later it leapt into the shadows of the dew-drenched meadow and hid beneath a clump of paintbrush. When it began to croak from its new niche in the world, Lara was amazed that so great a sound could trumpet from so small a creature.

Chapter 14
Behind the Falls

✳

AT FIRST PURSE THOUGHT HE WAS DREAMING. His face was lying against cold rock, and his legs were drifting in water that pulled in and out like a changing tide. It was a free yet safe feeling that brought to mind his very first swimming lesson. He had clung to the side of the pool and let his feet float away as if they belonged to someone else; the water would take care of them. Purse opened his eyes and found he could breathe. Of course, he had been breathing long before that, but now that he could see dim light he was somehow sure there was air to be had. But his lips hurt as the breath passed between them. They seemed terribly chapped, wounded even.

As his eyes adjusted to the light he saw he was in a cave of some sort. After a time it occurred to him to pull his legs out of the water. This took little effort. He paused for a moment on his knees, his sodden trousers dripping on the rocky shore. Then he tried to stand. His legs felt spent, but his feet were the worst of it—sliced and bruised from heel to toe. It would almost be easier to crawl. He sat against the side of the cave and tore off the sleeves of his shirt, wrapping and binding both feet to make something between a shoe and a bandage for each one. Then he carefully stood up again. That was better.

All this time he realized he had been listening for something he did not hear—or hearing something he did not expect. This was an almost perfect quiet. The thunder of the falls was gone, erased from the air. But he could not be very far from them, here, in the silence. He looked back in the dim light at the black water from which he had come. There was only a small space of it, a lapping well, surrounded by rock. So that was it—a subterranean piece of the plunge pool, rising into the calm of a cavern. What were the chances of coming to the surface in just this place?

Grateful, he began to walk. The passage was not a large one—just taller than he, and wide enough for two abreast—but it soon became very dry, once he had left the reach and splash of the shifting pool. The light in the cave was indistinct, as if coming from somewhere far ahead. With each step, and especially around each turn, it grew softly brighter.

It is hard to say which he saw first, the candles or the woman in white. All stood simply before him in a chamber, a widening of the passageway. The candles were ranged in a circle of niches around the walls, and the woman waited in the center. It was the same lady, golden-haired and gently severe, who had beckoned him in the waterfall. Now her hands were serenely clasped about a cup that she held before her. It was not what he would call a cup, but a goblet or a chalice, really. And it was not at all ornamented, but made only of plain wood.

"It is a cedar cup," said the woman. "As old as the oldest tree in the gorge." She gazed at him calmly, her eyes green and clear in the candlelight, her hair suffused with a quiet glow.

Purse looked from her face to the cup and back again. Half ashamed, he quickly put his hands to his lips and found that they were still bleeding.

"You are welcome, Percival," said the woman. "You have striven worthily, and have received an answer for the pride of your words, the only things that kept you from coming. Let me touch those lips, their sand and thorns, with a hand that has held this cup for many a year."

And she did so, reaching out with her right hand as Purse came forward. Immediately his lips were healed. When she removed her hand, he ran his tongue outside his mouth and tasted neither scar nor blood.

"My feet too!" he heard himself cry.

"Your feet will find their wholeness when they are fastened upon the hoofprints of the fawn. That time is not far off, but you must struggle in patience till then."

"Please," said Purse, "who are you, good lady? How is it you know and do these things?"

"I am Stella," she said. "The youngest of the three queens and sisters. The wife of old Villard over the mountains. The stargazer, the keeper of wild and lonely waters. And, for now, the keeper and giver of this cup, given me by the knower and doer of all things."

Purse stood shivering a little, trying to take all of this in. With her left hand she touched him lightly on the shoulder, and suddenly he felt a warmth flow into him like a deep river.

"They killed the fawn," he blurted out, as if it would be news to her.

"They have killed the fawn again and again, since before the foundation of the world. They will keep on killing him, and he will keep on suffering, as long as the gorge and the mountains groan. It is the only way. He dies to interpose a little ease."

"But I don't understand," he protested. "It feels so—barbaric."

"Far worse than barbaric," she said. "*Evil* will do—that word is apt enough. And no one asks you to understand. We are called only to apprehend, not comprehend. It is enough for us to receive an alchemy of good reborn out of evil, of life from death, of salvation out of suffering. We have our little role to play. It is for us to receive the cup, one by one. But none of us could ever fill it."

She held it out and he peered inside. "But it's empty now," he observed quietly.

"Yes," she nodded. "That is your small task. You know where it may be replenished. You also know who most has need to drink of it."

She knelt slowly and held the cup above her head. "Take it," she said. "It is time now."

"I feel so unworthy," Purse said.

"So has and is everyone who has taken the cup. That is what we bring: our unworthiness. But because the fawn is worthy to be slain, you are worthy to receive this cup."

Hearing this, he made no more delay, but simply took the cup in both hands. It was even more plain and coarse than it had looked in hers.

Stella arose and smiled on him. It was a cold smile without being distant. In it there were moon and stars and lake and river, snow-covered trees and meadows buried deep in winter. He felt braced and purified in her presence.

"Now," she said, "there is someone to join you." She gestured behind him and he turned.

Standing a little ways back in the cave whence he had come, and dripping in fragile and quiet amazement, was the forlorn figure of Moraine. She looked from Stella, to Purse, to the cup. "This I thought I would never see," she whispered to them. "The Lady Stella, I presume. I am greatly honored." And here she made an elaborate curtsy in the remains of her green shift.

"You are welcome, child," Stella said.

"Moraine," said Purse, reaching for her hand. "You are safe? However did you make it here?"

Her eyes began to tear, and she shivered. Stella touched her on the shoulder, and the shaking stopped. "You have the cup," Moraine said. There was fear and relief in her voice.

"Yes," said Purse, "but what of you?"

"I was taken," she said. "The ship came back. They seemed to know all about you. Except where you had gone, that is. At first I would not tell. But they threatened me. And it was not just me. It was what they said they would do to my parents—and to you and to Lara."

She broke off and looked about, brow furrowed. "Where is she now? Where's Lara?"

"She's safe beneath the Fawn Wall," Purse said. "I'll tell you soon."

Moraine took a deep breath, not quite satisfied. "They put me on their ship," she continued, "and tied me to the mast on the deck. Their goal was to overtake you on the way to the falls, to keep you from finding the cup." She stopped again.

"Oh, Stella!" she burst out. "Stella, I told them. I told them about the cup. I could not help it."

"No worry, child," Stella said with cool and even graciousness. "They cannot see or take the cup, though someday they may receive it."

Moraine looked dubious but relieved. "They are cruel and strong beyond belief. I did not know what they could not do. But I thank you for that comfort, lady."

She turned to address Purse again. "Over halfway up the gorge, just past the Fawn Wall, we saw you running along the bank when darkness had fallen. Some of the men shot arrows at the shore, but I sensed by their curses that you had escaped. How I wished strength for your legs! The men rowed on and on, into the night, and finally we reached the great pool beneath the falls. Once again they sent their arrows into the water, and I feared that you were swimming there. But the ship began to turn suddenly in many directions. From where I was tied I could see a strong young man at the tiller. He was quite frantic. Suddenly the stern of the ship smashed into a wall of rock, and I saw the young man crushed between splinters and stone. Men began to pour out of the hatch from the rowing benches down below. Some leapt into the water. Others crowded about the mast, where I was, and someone even thought to untie me. I was no sooner free than the ship listed into the water, sending us all overboard. I was underwater a long time, and then I came up near the falls. It seemed to me that some of the men were struggling near me. But then I went down again, for even longer this time. And now, you see, I am here." She held out her arms as if expecting none of them, least of all herself, to believe it.

"Yes, you are here," Stella said. "But here you shall not stay. For with this cup the two of you shall traverse this passage to the tree at the foot of the Fawn Wall—the tree from which this cup was taken, the cup from which this tree was grown. You, Moraine, shall hold a candle in your hand, and Percival shall bear the cup. Go now, you to be reunited with Lara, and you to gain again your parents."

"My parents?" said Moraine hopefully. "Percival, did you see them there, by the Fawn Wall?"

He didn't know quite what to say. "Moraine. Moraine, we—" He looked to Stella for her help.

But Stella was looking down the passage whence they had come. "More visitors," she announced. "Do you know these people?"

Purse and Moraine turned and blanched. Instinctively they clung to each other for comfort. For making their way up the passage were two more refugees from the ship—one in black, another dripping in pink tatters. The first seemed to be Park Savidge, crawling miserably on his hands and knees; the second looked for all the world like Lance Lott. He was walking unsteadily, groping at the walls with his hands. As Purse looked at the man, however, he appeared to be not exactly like his father after all. It seemed in fact that he was only *like* his father, the hollow semblance of what he could be and once had been. The man before him bore some sad and intimate relation to the man he knew—that Purse was sure of. But somehow it did not seem the man himself.

"You apprehend correctly," said Stella. Apparently she had read his thoughts once again. "This is but a shadow of your father, the end result of his worst part. Don't be afraid. Neither of them can see you now."

"Don't walk so damned fast!" shouted Savidge. "You act like we're not together in this."

Lance Lott paused and cursed. "It was you who wanted to bring the ship right into the plunge pool. That was a fine idea!"

"It was the boy's. I was down below."

"Well, a tight ship you run. Letting the help make all the decisions."

Savidge groped about with one hand and caught hold of Lance's ankle. For a moment it seemed he was actually going to gnaw on it.

"Let go of me, you dung-draped marmot! I smell your breath too close on my heels."

By this time they had advanced to within a few paces of the candlelit chamber. Lance looked directly at his son, but Purse could see only wide eyes trying to focus in darkness.

His father stopped and kicked Savidge unmercifully across the teeth. "It's obvious this goes nowhere. I say we go back and risk the water. The idea of believing such a gorbellied fairy tale! Behind the falls! A magic cup!"

Savidge looked up, feeling his mouth and growling with hurt. "We should have knifed her. Just like her reverend parents. She'd have made as good a corpse, she would." With that he laughed drunkenly, spitting blood across the floor of the cavern.

Moraine looked at Purse with alarm, but Stella placed a hand on her shoulder.

Lance sat down against the wall. "We should have," he said convivially. "And she'd no more see the light of day than we in this godforsaken cave. Some fun we had! All my life I wanted to slaughter that poor little innocent fawn, and we get its keepers into the bargain. A saucy dish in three full courses. Something they can remember us by."

"But the girl," said Savidge. "That would have been even better."

"Aye, and the boy too. The one that swam away. He thought he was better than us all, the little flap-mouthed boot-licker. Well, he wouldn't think so if he was here!"

Savidge cackled in agreement, then lapsed into a strange quiet. His eyes wandered over the cave and seemed to come to rest on the cup in Purse's hands. Suddenly his face knotted up, as if he were about to cry. "Lott, I've always wanted to ask you. Why did we want to kill that fawn, anyway?" His voice was halting, sober, earnest.

Lance stiffened. "Like I told you. When we do in the fawn and all of its mammering, milk-livered keepers, the whole valley becomes our stronghold—not until then."

"But it was such a sweet little thing," said Savidge, starting to whine. "I still don't see why we had to kill it."

"If you have to keep asking," said Lance, "you know nothing." He put his arm in a friendly fashion around Savidge's neck, and with his other hand pulled a dagger from his belt.

"Oh! Look out!" Moraine cried.

But Savidge heard nothing. Just as Lance was about to plunge it into his throat, Stella reached over and plucked the knife cleanly away.

Stella turned back to Purse and Moraine. "Have you seen enough?"

They nodded dumbly.

"Then you may go, just as I have charged you. I will see these two back through the falls. Another day they may see and hear, but not now. The blood of the fawn is even for them."

She paused, and they did not move.

"Does this surprise you?" she said. Her face broke into a cold clear smile.

Chapter 15
Full to the Brim

✳

WHEN LARA THREW OFF HER CHILL WET BLANKETS it was still perhaps an hour before sunrise. The moon was hidden, and Lara looked up at the Fawn Wall in the gray light, half expecting to see the eerie, watery climbers from the East who had started up the rock in her dream. But there were only swallows, skimming across the face of the cliff as if their lives depended on a ritual of recklessness. From the cedar tree came morning sounds of chickadees, mingled with the song of red-winged blackbirds down by the river.

She stretched her arms, stiff and cold, and decided to walk along the wall to warm herself and pass the time. Not to the cedar—she could see from here that the bodies still lay undisturbed—but the other way, upriver. To her pleasant surprise she found that her shelf continued along the base of the rock for a good ways, a natural sandy pathway fringed with aster and buttercup, larkspur and lupine, petals folded within themselves but shining under a burden of dew. Green began to emerge from gray, and step-by-step the granite gained its peculiar luster of pearl and rose. The wall rose steep and smooth beside her, unbroken by further cracks. She trailed her fingers along it as if touching hands with an old friend.

After some distance she came to the bulge of a small buttress and hesitated. She did not want to lose sight of the cedar tree, now far behind her, by rounding a corner. For what if Purse came back and found her missing? Or what if the black ship reappeared? And she also felt, for some reason, that she should return to the tree before sunrise. But she was, as ever, curious. She would just traverse to the prow of the buttress and peek around.

The sandy shelf that she had been following now turned into a ledge proper, leaving the meadow and heading across the face of the buttress some distance into the air. She could have kept her feet on the ground and waded through the wet grass, but Lara chose the dry route. It was easy at first—she could practically stroll with her hands in her pockets. Then, when the ledge narrowed, she faced the rock and stepped more cautiously. For the last few moves she held out her hands on tiny holds and shuffled her feet little by little, taking care not to cross them. When she reached the outer edge of the buttress she was forty feet above the meadow.

From her precarious vantage point, she could see another giant cedar growing in the alcove around the corner. Just above it, shielded by the tree from the meadow, a small chimney ascended the face for perhaps two pitches. She found its presence strangely electrifying. Here, just possibly, was an easier and better start to the Fawn Wall. She craned her head to look through the cedar branches. The chimney looked no more difficult than the one just across the river that Lance Lott had fallen out of. Perhaps even Purse could climb it.

She looked up, trying to see where the route might continue. But the rock overhead looked as steep and smooth as elsewhere. Two thousand feet up, the overhanging roof was still there, sluiced by the waterfall that now shone in the first of the sun. Strange how something so beautiful and powerful could be lost to sight by the time it reached the valley floor. The case of the disappearing sublime. Purse would like that.

With unconscious dexterity she reversed her shuffle back to the ledge. Now that she had actually seen the first light of sun overhead, she began to think about Purse in earnest. With dawn really come it was time not just to wait but to worry. She had never been one to worry before. When other guides were late in returning to boat or lodge, Lara always assumed the best—a jammed rappel, a slow client, a small route-finding mistake. And almost always she had been right. But this was different. She had felt the presence of the dragon ship, knew the power of the great falls. And Purse himself was so utterly inept. Why had she ever let him go?

She reached the sandy base of the rock again and began to return to her bivouac, resisting the impulse to scramble around the toe of the buttress to inspect her chimney from below. The line of sun was descending rapidly from the rim. It had now invaded the dank recesses beneath the giant overhangs. She saw not only moss and lichen but entire ferns lit up beneath the skirt of the waterfall high overhead. It would take a gardener, not a climber, to cross that ground. She knew of no one who could ascend such vegetation, wet or dry. How foolish to think that September would have magically opened the route for them.

By the time she reached her blankets the sun was only a thousand feet above her. She spread them out on the sand to dry and walked down through the wet grass to the river to drink. There was no sign of the ship here, or of anyone else. She thought of her dream and wondered if everyone in it had drowned. Perhaps she alone was left. By every law of nature, however, she had been killed at Otium the night before last. Maybe she was dead too. Maybe one just kept dying, time after time, without limit. She wished she could feel confident of this explanation, or of any other. She hated this feeling of confusion. On a climb she liked to stay on route, every move.

The line of sunlight was now close to the top of the tree. She wanted to be there when it hit the base of the wall, if only to dry her feet and legs. Her descent through the meadow had soaked her from the waist down. So she quickly climbed directly to the giant cedar and paused for a moment just below it. For some reason she decided to turn the trunk on the left—not on the right as they had before. To her no small surprise, in a few short steps she found that on this down-canyon side the trunk was opened by a fire-scarred hollow. She had seen this kind of thing before—natural rooms within cedars or sequoias or redwoods. Had she noticed the hollow earlier she might have passed the night here. A lot warmer and drier it would have been, she was sure of that.

She poked in her head to look around—she might yet need a hiding place. But it was much too dark to see. She was just about to step inside to test the floor when it suddenly occurred to her that there was none. Startled, she crouched and stirred the darkness with her hand. There was nothing to touch. She lay on her chest and reached with a stick as far down as possible. Still nothing. Only an empty coolness below.

"Hello!" she called, thrusting her head as far into the hole as she dared.

The echoes came back. "Hello! Hello!"

And then came another. "Lara! Are you there?"

Except, of course, it wasn't an echo. She strained her eyes against the darkness. Nothing. And then she saw a flicker of candlelight, and hands reaching up a tangle of roots.

"Purse!" she called. It had to be Purse. She was overjoyed at the thought that he had returned, and in so unlikely a way.

But the face that first appeared below belonged to a young woman. It was Moraine. She blew out the candle-stub in her hand and passed it to Lara. "Some help if you would," she gently gasped.

Lara set the candle aside and reached down. Moraine firmly took her hand and pulled herself to the lip of the hollow. "Many thanks," she gratefully said, and stooped past her into the morning.

"But where's Purse?" Lara said.

"Right behind. I think he will need your assistance as well."

With the candle gone, Lara could not see his face. But suddenly a wooden cup was thrust before her out of the darkness.

"Can you take this, Lara? Just for a moment?"

The way she felt, she could have taken it for a lifetime. "Sure," she said, trying to sound nonchalant.

For a moment she touched both Purse's hand and the roughness of the stem of the cup. *So this is all it is,* she thought. She quickly withdrew the cup from the hollow and passed it on to Moraine. Then she helped Purse over the lip. When he crawled into the light she saw that his shirt was torn off at the sleeves and that his feet were bandaged and bleeding. She wanted to say, *So, what happened?* But she did not say anything.

His first words were for Moraine. "The cup," he said, panting and holding out his hand.

She handed it to him and quietly said, "Please, where are they?"

Before either of them could tell her—or keep her—she vanished around the trunk by instinct. Lara realized Moraine was in for a terrible shock. Worse, she found she was not so concerned by Moraine's sorrow as she was consumed by a certain creeping jealousy. What nightlong adventures underground had Purse and Moraine been pursuing together? She sensed their bond, the sort built out of dangerous experience. It was precisely the kind of bond she shared with Roper. Or *had* shared until last night, if there were any truth to her dream. But if she had renounced him for Purse, and the fawn, it wasn't quite fair for Purse to go off running about with someone else. No, it wasn't.

Her thoughts were cut short by the sound of weeping from around the tree. Purse, who had been gazing at Lara with a look of relief and happiness (a look she had not bothered to see), now shot to his feet and scrambled around the stolid trunk.

"Moraine," he called. "Moraine! Moraine!"

When Lara reached them Moraine was crying bitterly in the lap of her mother, her arms flung around her waist, and Purse had his arms about Moraine, doing his best to comfort her. Lara stopped short, quiet and aloof.

"Moraine," said Purse. "Take heart. We must try the cup."

Moraine either did not hear him or did not care. She kept weeping bitterly. Then she got up and flung herself upon the body of her father. And wept all the more.

Purse, meanwhile, stepped away from her to the fawn. He touched its neck and looked up at Lara. "Still cold," he whispered. Then he held up his hand, damp with fresh blood. "And still bleeding."

As if driven by promise, he held the cup to a ragged wound in the side of the fawn, and slowly it began to fill. As they waited, the sun broke the rim of the gorge and the fawn shone purest white. The blood in the cup flashed and sparkled.

Lara felt a warmth in her body like the warmth she had felt when she had touched the fawn in the night. She looked at Moraine and suddenly felt real sorrow, untinged by jealousy. She looked at Purse and felt real love. She looked at all of them gathered there, the quick and the dead, and felt real hope.

When the cup was full to the brim, Purse held it in both hands and stepped back to Moraine's side. Feeling it was the right thing to do, Lara pulled her gently away from the body of her father. Moraine resisted, then hung limp in her arms. They both looked to see what Purse would do with the cup.

He was apparently none too sure himself. "I have known where to fill this cup," he said, almost as if he were speaking to himself. "And I also know who most has need to drink of it."

With that he held the cup to the lips of Moraine's mother, and then to the lips of her father, each in turn. "First to you, fair Rosamond. Drink, and live. Now you, noble Colin. Drink, and renew your former vigor." He opened their mouths and tilted the cup so that each one drained half of it. Then he stepped back.

At first nothing happened. Then, slowly, Colin, then Rosamond, opened their eyes. The man looked at his wife and stretched his arms. "Good morning, love. Not terribly restful sleeping against this tree, was it?"

Before Rosamond could begin to reply, Moraine broke from Lara's embrace and flew at them like a swallow to its nest. "Mother! Father!" she shouted at them, and buried herself against their faces, staining them wet with her many tears, if not their own.

Purse and Lara looked shyly on and took each other by the hand. Their eyes were wet, and each was smiling foolishly. "Perhaps we should leave them," Lara whispered. "Family, you know."

"Yes," said Purse, looking at her. "Family."

Taking the cup, they left Moraine with her mother and father by the tree, there under the solemn gaze of the dead fawn, and wandered down to the riverside.

"Was it hard?" asked Lara.

"Filling the cup?"

"No, getting it."

"It was—let me see," said Purse. "Maybe about 5.9? For you, I think, it would have been easy. For me, yes—a little bit of a challenge, I'd say."

Chapter 16
Hoofprints

❋

PURSE AND LARA SAT QUIETLY TALKING next to the river for some time. Still grasping the cup, he told her all his adventures of the night before, and when he was done, Lara expressed great indignation that Roper—or at least some version of Roper—had tried to shoot him with a bow.

"Have you seen him since? Any of them?" Purse asked.

"Only in a dream I had," she said, "while I was sleeping under the wall." Lara tried to explain the dream but got it tangled in her mind. "The thing was, they were very wet. As if they had drowned."

Purse nodded. "Perhaps they did," he said solemnly. He had not told her that Moraine had seen Roper crushed between the ship and the rock face. He saw now that he never could.

As he mused, Lara unwrapped his bandaged feet and exclaimed over the many cuts and welts and bruises. She made him sit on a rock in the river and soak his wounds. Now that the sun shone strong and full, it was not unpleasant to let his feet dangle in the cold water.

Lara was starting to fret over him. "However are we going to get you walking again?" She began to hunt on the riverbank for certain herbs that her mother had once told her about—pleated gentian and wild ginger. Perhaps she could make a healing poultice.

They were thus occupied, Lara snuffling around on the bank, Purse taking his ease on the rock with his feet trailing in the current, when Moraine brought her parents down through the meadow to wash in the river. They all bid each other good morning shyly, and Moraine introduced them to each other with great warmth and courtesy.

"So this is the cup," Colin exclaimed, pointing to where it yet rested in Purse's hand. "To think I have now seen it, and drunk from it even, if what my daughter says be true."

"Mercy," said his wife simply.

Purse modestly held it up to them as if it were a prize or a trophy. Suddenly, almost unaccountably, it slipped from his fingers into the river, making the sort of delicate splash a trout makes when leaping for a fly in the morning. Purse immediately jumped out from his rock to retrieve it, and Colin likewise leapt from the shore. The result was that they collided in a welter of water, and by the time they had disentangled themselves and apologized, the cup was nowhere to be seen.

"It is lost!" said Colin. "What have I done?"

"What have I done, rather?" Purse wailed.

After fruitless search, they waded out onto the bank and stood dripping in great dismay.

"Perhaps it is not lost," said Moraine.

"But we cannot find it," Purse and Colin said almost at once.

"Yes," said Moraine, "but that does not mean it is lost."

They looked at her strangely.

"Don't you see? The cup is never lost to itself. Though you cannot hold it always, that does not mean it cannot be held—at the right time, by those who need it."

Lara and Rosamond both nodded, seeing a truth and comfort in this.

"It is not a weapon, like the ancient ice ax that once belonged to Percival's uncle—and also, Lara, to your father. It is not a talisman or a wishing lamp. The cup came to us in our time of need, and now it goes to the hands of another. I think that it is never kept, always given. Remember the words from the book of the Tower of Otium?

> *Ever full and ever spilled,*
> *The cup is as the fawn hath willed.*

Let us be grateful for its coming, but let us also allow it to go. And let neither of you blame yourself for losing the cup into the river. It is as the fawn hath willed."

Purse and Colin still looked troubled but said nothing.

"Men—" said Rosamond softly to the others, so that Purse and Colin could not hear. "You will learn it is hard for them to relinquish power, to see it slip out of their hands."

"What's that?" said Colin sharply.

"I was just thinking, love, that we should wash these bloodstained clothes of ours and see if Moraine has brought us anything for breakfast."

Moraine smiled and looked at Lara. At the mention of breakfast they realized they were quite famished.

"There is still some bread in my pack," said Lara. "I'll run up and get it. I left it just under the wall."

Purse said he would go, but Lara just looked at his feet and rolled her eyes. "No, all of you need to wash and rest. I'm the one who's been loitering here all night with nothing to do."

That spoken, she set out up the meadow and soon arrived at her sandy ledge under the rock. After some hesitation she packed her blankets, now dry, into the rucksacks, preparing to take them both back down to the river. Nothing had been said, no invitation yet been given, but she assumed they would all be hiking back to Otium. Beyond that, she could not quite imagine. She tried to envision a life for herself—and for Purse—in the quiet cottage under the tower. It felt pleasant enough, yet she somehow wondered if that is what she really wanted.

She strapped the rucksacks one tightly atop the other and hefted them both onto her shoulders. As she turned to leave, her ungainly burden scraped the wall. She jumped back, smiling at her clumsiness, and saw something spring from her feet. The little frog—she had almost stepped on it. In three hops it crossed the sandy shelf from the grass and leapt back onto the wall, where it slipped into the tiny crack. She took a last look up the face and realized she wanted to follow suit and leap onto the rock herself. Then she gazed back down at the river and saw the four small figures there, the people she belonged to now. The Fawn Wall would not be hers.

But the fawn himself—she somehow felt, even though he was quite dead, that he would have her gratitude for a long time. It occurred to her they would come back to bury the fawn after breakfast, before they left, but she wanted to pay her respects again right now. It felt important to do so by herself, to thank him for the warmth in the night that she in particular had been given.

So she turned towards the tree—and suddenly stopped. Though still a little distance away, she was fairly sure there was nothing between the ancient cedar and the wall but a pleasant and open alcove, the sort that is agreeable to belay from while friends sit round about on a spring day, telling tales and laughing at preposterous stories. The sun shone clearly on a strange kind of emptiness. There was no fawn.

She gave a cry, shed her packs, and stumbled to the roots of the cedar. Where before had been all flesh and fur and streaming gore was now clean-washed earth, morning fresh. The fawn had most certainly vanished. She called out again, and saw that the others had heard her cry and were already climbing up the meadow. Then she checked all around the tree, and down into its tomb-like hollow. There was nothing there. She looked every direction into the meadow for footprints—or signs, even, that a carcass had been dragged along through the grass. Still nothing. As the others began to arrive she was standing where the fawn had lain, hand tilted over her eyes and searching far off in every direction, upriver and down.

Moraine reached her first, then Purse, laboring on his wounded feet without the help of his bandages. "The fawn," she told them. "He's disappeared!" It was gratifying in some small way to see their eyes grow very wide.

Just as she had, the two of them searched all about the base of the cedar. Purse even climbed down into the hollow a ways. When Colin and Rosamond finally joined them, no one knew where to look anymore.

It was Rosamond who pointed to the granite face. She didn't have to say anything. For there on the wall, bold and plain, were a series of hoofprints, marked in fresh blood on the rock. The tracks led on, on, and out of sight, as far up the wall as they could see. They found themselves gazing up at the wispy tail of the waterfall, high overhead. A few drops, sailing like swallows, splashed down in their upturned faces.

"To think he would go up there," said Colin, barely breathing.

He stood close to the wall and measured the distance between the first prints with his arm. "They're not terribly far apart," he said. "Just a pleasant romp, for him. You would almost think we could do it ourselves."

"But of course," said Moraine, hardly listening to her father. "He could not bring anyone else alive if he did not come alive himself. The wonder is he was dead so long." Her eyes shone as she spoke, as if she had made the final discovery.

"I'm thinking," said Purse, "of something that Stella said to me." He limped over to Colin's side and stood looking up as if he had not heard what the others had spoken. "*Your feet will find their wholeness when they are fastened upon the prints of the fawn.*"

To everyone's amazement, Lara's most of all, he reached his hands high up on the granite, placed them both directly over a pair of hoofprints, and with no apparent struggle or effort lifted one foot and then the other off the ground. His toes found purchase on a lower set of bloody tracks and rested there, at ease on the rock. For a moment he remained quietly in place. Then, with sure lithe movements that left Lara in perfect wonder, he followed the blood-prints several feet higher. He stopped some distance over their heads, as if only then recollecting that he had left someone behind.

"It's true!" he called down, lifting one foot off the face for inspection and then the other. "My feet—they're fine now!"

"Be careful," said Lara, not quite sharing his enthusiasm. "You don't have a rope up there." She thought of the preferable chimney she had found before sunrise; in her mind she was still every inch the SWAGS guide.

"I don't need a rope!" Purse shouted. "Can't you see? And neither do you. Lara, try it! I never knew that climbing could be so wonderful!"

She looked dubiously at Moraine and her parents and shrugged her shoulders. "Well," she said, "I'd better go keep him from killing himself."

She scanned the face above the tree and saw just the hint of a cling-hold, up and to the right of the tracks. She made a short lunge and locked onto it, working her bare feet up the slab to a tiny nubbin. With her climbing shoes the nubbin would be something she could smear for about four seconds. With just the callous of her big toe, she wasn't so sure she would stick. But there. She was on it. Would it bear her weight? Only one way to find out. Straining, she pulled up on the sharp edge with her fingertips, reaching high with her other hand for something—anything—to hold onto. This was ridiculous, she told herself. Her toe slipped off the little nub and her feet came slapping down in the duff. Fortunately, the landing was soft.

"Sorry," she called up to Purse. "Can't do it." Of course she knew why. But somehow, she liked making her own way. To follow the tracks would be to admit that someone else had already made the first ascent.

"The prints," called Purse. "Use the prints." The way he said it, she thought for a moment that he was talking about *the prince.*

Somewhat reluctantly she put her hands on the same tracks that Purse had touched. Instead of feeling the slipperiness of wet blood she found firm purchase. Just how, she wasn't sure. It was as if there were obvious holds hidden beneath each stain. She lifted her feet easily and felt them attach firmly to the set of hoofprints just below. It was as if there were holds there too. No, she thought, that wasn't quite it. She made a few further moves, tentatively, and realized it felt more as if she were climbing on a low-angle slab, the sort that is so easy you do not even have to look for holds because the sheer friction of hands and feet against the rock is all that is needed to keep you from falling.

Slowly gaining confidence, she reached the spot where Purse had been and realized he had gone on. She looked up. He was waving to her from a small ledge some forty feet higher.

"Wait!" she called. "I'll join you."

In minutes she was there. A little breathless, she took his hand and looked up at the wandering path of prints ahead, shining in the morning sun. Then she looked back down to Moraine and Colin and Rosamond at the base of the tree. The three of them stood there patiently.

"You can do it, Moraine!" she called. "Come on up!" She imagined the five of them climbing the wall, one joyful party together.

But she saw that Moraine was shaking her head.

"Do like we did! Just follow the bloody tracks!" It was the sort of thing Roper would say.

But Moraine was still shaking her head. She cupped her hands around her mouth and called up, "Lara, they are gone!"

Purse and Lara looked at their feet. Where the prints had been, leading in a cloven trail from tree to ledge, the rock was now perfectly clean. As soon as Lara had passed, they had vanished. It took a moment for the import of this to settle.

"I guess they can't come up," said Lara.

Purse took a deep breath. "And I guess that we are not going down."

Chapter 17
Animal Movements

✳

WHEN THE DIVISION BECAME CLEAR TO EVERYONE, Moraine and her father shouldered the rucksacks that Lara had left at the bottom of the cliff and wended their way with Rosamond to the trail by the riverside. In the meadow they turned often to call their goodbyes to Purse and Lara up on the wall. They were sad to part but not overly sad, for their parting was so obviously *as the fawn hath willed*. This was the last word that Moraine had spoken from the base of the cedar tree. They had all believed her.

Still, there was some disappointment. "Why didn't they stay to watch us?" Purse asked. He and Lara were still standing on their small ledge perhaps fifty feet from the ground. The thrill of the climb was starting to wear off for him.

"Well," said Lara, "I suppose they didn't think it would be polite to eat in plain view, since they have the bread and we have nothing. Look, they're unpacking the rucksacks now, down by the river. Perhaps they will stay for a bit. Until afternoon, anyway. That would give them time to walk to Otium by nightfall."

"What about us?" Purse asked. "Do we have time to climb all the way to the rim? Can we possibly make it in just a day?"

Lara shrugged. "I don't know. No one's ever climbed this before. But it's three thousand feet—and that's a lot. More than I've ever done. I suppose we should get on with it."

"What about those overhangs, and that waterfall?" He was gazing upwards, unbelieving.

Lara kept her doubts to herself. "We'll see when we get there, I guess. And you have some experience with waterfalls, don't you? I'll let you lead that part." In spite of herself, she smiled when she said this.

"Lara, don't we have anything to eat?" he whined. "I'm *so* hungry. And tired, too. I've been running and swimming and caving all night, after all, and I'm supposed to top it off with this? It doesn't seem quite fair again. Just when I thought I had earned a rest."

He paused, aware of his petulance. "All those books in the cottage, you know," he sighed quietly.

Lara noticed that the more he moaned, the more confident she herself became in their task. She dug deep in the pockets of her knickers. In one of them she found the tail end of a loaf she had started to gnaw during the night. She gave it to him, and pretended that she wasn't hungry.

He ate it swiftly, wishing for more, but she saw that it gave him some heart. "Would it help if I went first?" she said.

He thought about it. "No," he said. "I like having you right behind me. That way if I do fall—"

"We'll go together," she concluded.

"Whatever."

Decisively he brushed the breadcrumbs from his hands, placed them on the hoofprints above, and set out. Lara followed.

Once more she felt the surprising security of the blood, fastening her hands and feet to the wall as if by gravity. The tracks led where no sane climber would ever pioneer a route, over glacier polish and steep blank sections, seamless dihedrals and holdless space. Each move required a renewal of trust, perhaps more for Lara even than Purse. For she more than he knew the limits of what the human body could accomplish on a smooth rock face, and with every step she exceeded them. As the meadow and then the top of the cedar tree fell away, it came to her that the Fawn Wall was not an achievement but a gift—a gift of glad animal movements, and she accepted each one as it came with a quietly mounting satisfaction.

So they climbed on, and on, and on, stopping merely to admire the valley opening like a park below them, or to stare upward at the roof that only seemed to lengthen and darken as they approached it. They could tell now that the tracks were headed just to the left of the waterfall that split the roof. Beyond that they could not see. By late morning they felt from the fall not small stray drops but swinging sheets of spray that came in little waves by the will and whim of whatever breeze might be breaking on the wall overhead. But the wind was not blowing where they were, and the day had grown fine and hot. The late spring sun felt wonderful on their bare calves. All the same, the longer they climbed the more they felt the ache and sweat of the ascent, and the remnants of the fall bestowed a welcome coolness along the way.

It was some time in the afternoon when they reached the shade of the great roof and decided to rest. By now the waterfall had gathered to a modest great-ness just a short distance away, sparkling in the sunlight as it shot through the rim of the overhang. Here beneath the roof was a commodious and mossy ledge, decked with ferns and bright yellow monkeyflower, and they sat on its cushion gratefully, looking across to the south rim and the rising skirts of the Dark Divide, crowded with fir and mountain hemlock. From where they were seated, the red tracks of the fawn continued across the deep green of their ter-race to the noisy chute of the waterfall. At the edge of the water, a narrow but solid ribbon of white, the tracks disappeared. This gave them much to ponder.

"Is there any other way?" said Purse, leaning over to drink from a small pool in a crevice.

"No," said Lara evenly. "No way that is not overhung. The fall at least is only vertical. We know that we can climb rock, and we haven't slipped on the blood yet, or on any of the water that has come down upon us so far." She paused and swept her arm the length of the roof overhead. "But I don't think we can climb on air."

"But a waterfall," Purse said. "You can't see tracks in a waterfall." He looked down. The cedar at the foot of the wall was no more than a tiny shrub, the Amoenas River a rivulet. Whether Moraine and her parents were still below them next to the river he could not begin to tell. "That's a long way," he said.

She didn't bother to contradict him. They sat in the moss for a long time, looking out. Swallows darted across the cliff and out of sight overhead, and she suddenly found that she envied them. The shade became damp and uncomfort-able, and at last Lara got to her feet, covered with goose bumps. "This is too wet and gloomy for me. I'm going over to that patch of sun by the waterfall."

"You're not stepping into it, are you?" Purse said nervously.

"The sun?"

"The falls."

"I honestly don't know," she said. "I think we should look at it, anyway."

She walked across the spongy moss, feeling the spray billow into her face as she approached the falls. The water poured almost weightlessly through a small channel cut in the roof and continued down past the ledge into thin air, curtain after falling curtain in little jets of accumulation. The moss had left her legs quite wet, but now in the spray the rest of her was soaking through, and strands of hair weighed down with water began to fall across her eyes.

She looked back and saw that Purse was right behind her, stepping exactly where she had. Still she was able to follow the blood-prints, red on the green, shining through the swirl of mist. She crossed into sunlight, out from under the black roof, and soon quite plainly stood at the edge of rushing white. The water did not so much slap the rock as fly past it, a moveable hiss. She was standing on the last of the hoofprints that she could see.

For a long time she did not move. As a guide she knew it was time to set the rappel anchors and go home. (Of course, there were none. She wryly reflected that it would be the famous no-rope rappel.) Purse in fact turned to retreat along the ledge.

"Too wet!" he shouted.

Immediately he slipped on the moss. Like lightning she reached behind herself and grabbed his wrist, slowly pulling him back to his feet. The ledge was spacious, but they were on the outer edge. And the tracks behind them were no longer there.

"Don't move away!" she shouted over the hiss of the falls. "Just do what I do!"

Just what it was she was going to do she had only the faintest idea. But holding his hand, she edged out into the waterfall with one foot, feeling for purchase with her toes. She found none. There were only pellets and streams of water, no rock behind them that she could find. Strangely, however, she was not fighting to keep her balance against the beating of the falls. Her foot was not so much slipping beneath the pounding of the cataract as indeed it seemed to be simply floating, as if in a pool. The sensation was oddly delicious.

"Purse," she shouted, a smile on her face. "It goes!"

Without another moment's hesitation she let go of Purse's hand and lifted her other foot into the water. And she simply stood there, levitating at her ease in the vertical current. With her arms she combed the water above her, creating rooster-tails of spray. Then she pulled against it with her hands, as if stroking across the surface of a lake, and found to her amazement that she was swimming up the face of the falls. It took remarkably little effort. The feeling was one of leisurely exhilaration. She got as high as the notch in the roof and paused to see what Purse was doing.

He was still standing on the ledge, looking up in dumb fear.

"Come on!" she shouted. "It's not too cold or anything."

As if this reassured him, he quite suddenly entered the fall—not bit by bit as Lara had, but all at once, in a desperate lunge. The look of terror on his face was replaced in an instant with a broad smile of pure pleasure. He stood, or floated, or hung in the fall, getting over the first surprise, and then swam a few strokes upward, stopping to wave as she had taught him when he had first learned to rappel from their lunch spot on the Cedar Sidewalk.

A minute more, and he was beside her—the fall was just that broad, and no more. "Let wonder seem familiar!" he shouted, and swam past after touching her cheek.

Thereafter it was a slow but satisfying race. All through the long late afternoon, they breasted the waterfall side by side, first one in the lead and then the other, pausing whenever they had need. And always the fall buoyed them upward, never letting them slip back. Though their progress was not swift, it was steady, and they found the water a bracing delight. Purse lost every feeling of weariness that had come upon him in the morning, and Lara felt a constant refreshment. It was only their arms that needed to rest from time to time—neither of them were practiced swimmers.

Towards evening Lara glimpsed the brink of the waterfall overhead. To their right they could see the entire smoking column of the great falls at the head of the valley, shining in the westering sun, and far to their left the darkening shadows of Otium, the Wall of Early Morning Fright now hidden in a gentle gloom. The rock all around them, the upper shield of the Fawn Wall, was warm and rosy in latening light. It was stone that wanted to be touched, and someday she hoped she would. But not now.

Whether the sun would sink behind the Tower of Otium before they crested the rim of the wall was a question too nice to decide. Whenever they paused to rest their arms, they tried to guess how far it was they had to go and how soon the sun would disappear. As it turned out, sun and swimmers were synchronized. The fall around them had turned to a blaze of liquid fire and the sky about them was burning red when Lara realized her hands were pulling only air. All of a sudden she had to bend to touch the water. She had reached the lip. Purse came over just behind her, and all at once they found themselves crawling on their hands and knees in a narrow, babbling, shallow creek, smooth on the bottom with sand and stone.

Very slowly they stood up, dripping and laughing. There were trees all around them, mountain hemlocks, silhouetted in evening glow. Without even bothering to step from the stream, they joined hands and entertained the notion of a real kiss. But something about getting here had too much joy, too much hilarity, for that. It was just too funny, and all they could do was laugh. Purse started kicking the water to splash her, and Lara splashed back.

"Take that, climber boy!" she shouted, and dished the stream into his face with both hands.

They only stopped when a gray-cloaked figure stepped out from behind a tree. When she put back her hood they saw that she was a beautiful woman with rich brown hair—chestnut, perhaps, though in the unearthly light of the setting sun, one couldn't be sure. She looked at them both and calmly said, "You are welcome, Percival. And you, Lara—you are welcome."

There was a certain merriment in her eye, but Purse and Lara stood shy and still, as if they had been caught playing when they should have been engaged in some serious work.

"Do not wonder at me, children. And feel no shame for yourselves. I have been sent to make you comfortable for the night, before you go on."

"And who—who are you?" asked Purse in a faint voice. Her face and her eyes reminded him of Stella under the great falls.

"Accept my pardon," the woman said graciously. "I am the Lady Demaris."

This took Lara by surprise. Except for the hair—brown, not blonde—she could have sworn the woman standing on the bank was her own mother, the backcountry ranger of the Three Queens Wilderness.

Chapter 18
Among the Living

❋

Lady Demaris took Purse and Lara by the hand and led them through a hemlock twilight. After a day of climbing and swimming on the wall, to walk at will on flat ground held simple pleasure. The space between the trees was soft with wet and flattened cones and needles, covered by an occasional snowbank flanked with flowers—avalanche lilies and coralroot. The snow was pleasant underfoot, and the smell of the trees sharp and spicy. A western wind blew in the branches. Holding the hand of Lady Demaris, Lara remembered her earliest walks in the groves and meadows next to the Demaris Cabin. It seemed curious that this woman bore the name of her home, her birthplace.

When it had grown almost dark, Lady Demaris brought them out of the forest to a sandy prow atop the wall. A small fire burned near the edge of the cliff, tended by a large man.

"We are here, Sir Chambers," the woman said. "Safe and whole."

He squinted out from the firelight, an egg-bald head fringed with white. "Well," he said energetically, "which one's Safe and which one's Whole? Right now I can hardly tell them apart."

Lady Demaris glanced down at Purse and Lara in a way that said they must forgive him. She released them into his company, saying, "I am sure that Lara and Percival are tired and hungry after their long day on the wall—and after other days and nights as well. We owe them our supper and our fire—not, at present, our levity."

The man she called Sir Chambers winced, and shook their hands solemnly. "We've only been married for twenty years," he told them confidentially. "She doesn't know me that well yet."

He seated them on blankets spread across the sand beside the fire while Lady

Demaris checked the contents of a pot that was set alongside the coals. "Dried lentils?" she asked. "Is that what we brought?"

Chambers appeared to take offense. "And what else is there, I might ask, to satisfy the thirst and hunger of the soul?"

"Some salad, perhaps? There was time, I thought. The first greens of the season were out. The staghorn lichen, at least, down in the woods We needn't have been in such a hurry."

"Woman," he said, facing her across the fire, "I am never in a hurry. *Semper lentus*, always slow, that is my motto."

"*Semper* lentils is more like it," Lady Demaris said firmly.

"No," said Chambers obtusely. "*Semper lentus sed numquam certus*. Always slow but never sure. That is the full sentence of my wisdom."

"Always lentils but never lettuce," Lady Demaris pertly replied. "That is the wisdom I have observed."

Lara was beginning to think they were in for an uncomfortable time. She could not tell how serious the argument was. As for Purse, he was hardly aware of the words that passed. As soon as his limbs had touched the blankets he was overcome with weariness. He just wanted whatever happened to be in the pot to be ready soon. That way he could lie down and go to sleep.

Deadlocked, Lady Demaris and her husband looked over at their company in mild and merry embarrassment. "You must excuse us," she said softly. "There are certain things we do not agree upon. Diet is one."

"Place is another," he volunteered. "She's always trying to get us to move down off the pass to her old cabin in the trees."

"Among growing things," his wife added. "One can only live so long on a windswept tundra."

"The only cure for claustrophobia," Chambers protested. "Which is what I'd die of anywhere below timberline. Especially down in a ditch like that," he said, gesturing over the rim with his thumb. "I'd rather be caught in a vice. Not that I don't have a few I'm caught in already. Lentils, for example."

He guffawed in self-deprecating triumph, and spooned the hot lentil soup into four large wooden bowls. Before passing them out, he held one bowl up to the evening star and simply said, "To the fawn."

"To the fawn," Lady Demaris repeated.

"Please," said Lara as she and Purse began to eat, "the fawn—is he the one who sent you to meet us?"

"Perhaps," said Lady Demaris. "As much as he arranges all meetings."

"Perhaps?" said Lara. "Then how did you know to come?"

"The pond, of course," Chambers said with his mouth full.

"What pond?"

"Mine," he said, "so much as it belongs to anyone. Chambers' pond."

"You mean Chambers Lake?" asked Lara. "Between the North and Center Queens? I've been there."

"Precisely," he said. "That's just where I saw you this morning."

"But I was in the gorge this morning. On the Fawn Wall."

"Which you were, to be sure," he said. "That's where I saw you in my pond. We figured you'd be here by nightfall, so that's why we came. A long hike, I can assure you."

Lara paused, taking this in. "So, a magic pond, where you see things that are far away. Is that what you're saying?"

"Not magic," Chambers said. "No tricks. Just—something fawnish. Of course, the ice on the pond has barely melted, and that just on the north shore. I can't say it was very convenient to catch a glimpse of you this morning. No, not convenient at all."

Lara looked at Purse to see what he might think. But after only a few bites of lentil soup, he had lain down on the blankets, eyes closed. Lady Demaris had quickly noticed and come over to cover him.

"Are you tired, dear?" she asked Lara. "We can talk in the morning if you like."

"No," said Lara. "I'm *not* tired." She felt as if she were four years old, the way she said it. Why did this woman keep reminding her of her mother?

"More soup?" asked Chambers helpfully.

"Yes," said Lara.

He spooned her bowl full again and put another log on the fire. He and Lady Demaris settled close together across from her. Lara wrapped herself in a blanket and propped herself against Purse's knees. She figured that he wouldn't mind, being asleep.

"What else did you see?" she asked Chambers suspiciously.

"Nothing by night, but everything that passes by day. We first caught sight of you yesterday morning, at Otium."

"Not before then?"

"Not before then. As I say, the first of the ice has only just melted. Still, that is when the two of you arrived, I believe."

"That's when I fell, you mean. We got here rather violently. Sometimes, to be perfectly honest, I think we are no longer among the living."

"Excuse me?" Chambers said, halting his spoon halfway to his lips.

"Oh, I didn't mean it that way, about you," Lara protested. "It's just that—" She stopped, at a loss for words. In the pause that ensued, sparks flew upward into the stars. The waxing moon came sliding over the horizon, and in its light, the high broad peak of the South Queen rose soft and silver out of the trees.

"Sometimes," said Lady Demaris quietly, "the kingdom of the fawn is taken by violence. There is still an ax, though we did not bring it. From what we saw, you have come by way of the cup."

"Come where?" Lara wailed. She pointed to the moonlit peak behind them, its southern slopes still buried in snow. "I've known that mountain all my life. It's still here, and so am I!"

"What did you expect?" scoffed Chambers. "A city on the hill?"

"I don't know that I expected anything," Lara said petulantly. "It's just that I've felt very confused these last few days."

"That's better," Chambers said. "*Numquam certus.* Join the great chain of being, right in the middle."

"You are still here, yes," said Lady Demaris. "But it may be you are more here than ever. For that I think you may thank the fawn, though you may never know the reason of it."

"Why do you sound—" Lara began, and then thought better of it.

"Yes?" said Lady Demaris quietly. "Like whom?"

"Why do you sound so much like my mother?" Lara blurted. "I do not think you are my mother, and yet you almost are, it seems. Like Moraine and Maureen down in the gorge. They're like twins, almost, yet they have never met each other."

"I know Moraine," said Lady Demaris. "A splendid girl. But I have never met Maureen. Nor your mother, I am sorry to say."

"But I grew up in your cabin," said Lara. "The Demaris Cabin. And my mother lived there years before I was even born. She was the backcountry ranger there, and still is."

"Ah," said Lady Demaris, as if she had just remembered the obvious. "Forgive me. I *have* met your mother once, but she is the one who may not recall. I and my sisters briefly assisted her at your birth, because your father was away at Otium.

So you see, there are times when the two sides meet, in certain moments of great need. Chambers and I have had the delight of knowing your father on more than one cruel occasion—and Percival's mother, Grace, as well. Even Purse's father has come and known my sister Lira in her evil days. I fear he has forgotten, however, or that he has only remembered the worst. But the fawn may bring him back as well. We have even known Maureen's parents, Ronald and Jennifer, if your friend is whom I suspect her to be."

Lara was taken aback. It seemed the entire past generation had been here before her.

"So it is truly a pleasure for us to see the daughter of William, the son of Grace, arriving together. We give you both welcome, Lara. It is two worthy lines that you shall unite."

"But where are we going?" Lara said.

"The same way you have gone all day," said Chambers. "I can answer that one, at least."

"But we can't climb the wall again, or go back to the gorge. The tracks have all disappeared."

"The tracks continue," Chambers corrected her. "As far as I know, they never stop. Though you did not see them in the dusk, they led through the trees from the brink of the waterfall to this fire. And tomorrow they will lead farther still, though where that is I couldn't say. In all these years I have yet to see the fawn alive—even in my own pond. But I'm hoping someday I'll get a proper glimpse of him."

"I'm sure that you will," Lara said wistfully.

"It is my fervent wish, Lara," said Lady Demaris, "that the prints will finally take you back to the place you started. For now that I am bound to this man and his barren lake—"

"I beg your pardon," Chambers said, raising his eyebrows.

"Now that I live in open freedom where the stars never set—"

"That's better," he said. "And we do have a comfortable cottage of our own. Remember that."

"Now that I am gone from my ancestral cabin in the meadows and groves beneath the lap of the Center Queen, it sorely needs a pair such as you to care for it, and to care for the country round about. I hope the fawn will lead you there, and that you will make it a home again—your home, more than ever."

"But my parents," said Lara. "Wouldn't they be there?"

"In a sense," said Lady Demaris, considering. "Yes, they will always be with you there."

They all fell to musing after this, Lara on the strange mixture of hope and fear that rose within her. The fire was fading into embers.

"But it will be as if they've died," she murmured. "Haunted. And I left that cabin. I wanted the gorge. I wanted the rock beneath my fingers." She thought then of the dripping specters of Roper and the climbers from the East in her dream. "At least I thought I did. I used to."

The last of her words began to founder. Lara was sinking farther and farther back against Purse's knees, shivering now and very tired. Lady Demaris quietly rose and covered her with another blanket.

"Sleep," she said. "We cannot discover everything now. But tomorrow you will find out what you truly love."

Chapter 19
Woman in Red

❋

IN THE MORNING PURSE AND LARA AROSE EARLY and stood on the rim, looking down into the unlit gray of the gorge. Swallows were wheeling across the wall, and they heard the echo of waterfalls and empty space. The newly risen sun shone on their bare feet, half-buried in coolness of sand.

"How did you sleep?" Lara asked.

"Like the innocent," Purse said. "Or like the dead."

She looked at him strangely.

"What?" he asked.

"It seems you can't decide between the morbid and the beautiful."

"No," he said. "I mean yes, you're right. Sometimes I can't. Especially with the gorge all dark and hollow at this time of day, and waking up to I don't know what."

"They say we are going on," said Lara. "That the tracks haven't stopped."

"Where do they go?" Purse asked.

"They don't know. But Lady Demaris hopes we end up at her cabin. Purse, she wants us to—" Here she paused and looked down. Her face felt flushed. "She wants us to live there."

"Together?" he asked in a small voice.

"Together," said Lara, and took his hand shyly in hers.

"But doesn't she live there? Or your parents?"

"Lady Demaris now lives with Chambers on a high divide between the North and Center Queens. My parents—well—it's like Maureen's parents, I suppose. They would always be there, just not as much—or in quite the same way—as we would be."

"So I was right," said Purse softly. "From the very first morning we walked upstream from Otium, I was right. We're not in the shadows anymore. Because we've gone into the thisness of things, the true forms, the inscape of the land-scape. Not that it matters that *I* was right. For it wasn't me, really. If it was anyone it was Plato, perhaps. Or Hopkins, maybe."

They were interrupted by Chambers calling that breakfast was ready. "Oatmeal," he said proudly when they arrived next to his fire. Lady Demaris smiled weakly. He dished up their bowls again and this time Purse ate more than his fill.

When breakfast was done there was nothing really to pack up. They no longer had rucksacks, and Lady Demaris and Chambers had brought none to replace the ones they had left in the gorge. Purse inquired if there were some food they might carry with them in their pockets, but Lady Demaris merely said, "The fawn will provide."

Chambers showed them the blood-prints that led from the fire back into the forest, due north. Over the crooked tops of the hemlocks the South Queen rose in morning splendor. They could see the bright and gentle southwest slopes, the sinewy arm of the south ridge, and the lava headwall of a bowl carved into the southeast face. From their campsite on the rim, timberline was far but not too far away.

Even though it did not feel quite necessary, when Purse began to walk from the fire he placed his feet exactly on the hoof marks. They were still fresh and glistening, as if the bleeding fawn had passed only seconds ahead of them. Lara followed, and Lady Demaris and Chambers came alongside them across the sand to the edge of the trees.

"Farewell," said Lady Demaris. "And may your steps find perfect peace." She held both of Lara's hands in hers and then let them go.

"*Semper lentus,*" Chambers called after them. "Take care, Nephew."

Purse wheeled. "Nephew?"

"Well, of course," said Chambers. "Why else would I have come?"

Purse still looked shocked.

"Now don't let the normal pride of such a relation interfere with your task at hand. Come visit at the pond. I will tell you all. Unless, that is, you run into Garth first, and he spills all of the lentils. He is the oldest, and elder brothers love to be the ones to explain, though they are seldom quite as articulate as younger brothers, middle brothers in particular."

Lady Demaris told him to hush. Purse seemed about to speak, but merely waved uncertainly and turned to go, an odd smile on his face.

"That's right," said Chambers. "Until then, *numquam certus.*"

"Do you think we shall visit them often?" asked Lara, once they had walked a few minutes into the trees.

"I'm not sure," Purse said. "It would help if he weren't so—"

"Tedious?" Lara said.

"If that is all it was, I could stand it. But he seeks to be so tedious in an interesting way. Rather like someone blathering on about the sublime and the picturesque."

He turned on a large snowbank and smiled. "The only people we really meet is ourselves," he said. "Divided and distinguished a little, and distributed across the earth, but just ourselves, after all. Bring on all the uncles you want. I think I can begin to take it."

Lara stepped up onto the snowbank and paused beside him. "There's only one decent way that I know of to put a stop to all this talking in your family."

He was about to say, *What's that?* when she put her arms about his neck and sweetly kissed him on the lips. "But in between, I'll listen," she said. "Sometimes." She pulled away and turned him around, and he tottered forward, pleasantly stunned, the music of chickadees in the hemlocks governing his strength of mind.

The snowbank they now crossed was quite long and wide, and they no sooner dismounted it than they found themselves climbing up onto another. Soon the entire forest floor was nothing but snow except for wells about the tree trunks. The surface of it was cool but not cruel on their bare feet, and by and by they forgot to feel surprised about this. After a time the snowslope began to rise more steadily upward. Hour by hour the hemlocks grew shorter and more stubby and gnarled, and islands of grand and noble fir began to appear in shapely krumholz, together with the occasional larch, still bare of new green needles. Highest of all, in ragged outposts, whitebark pine held their own on the mountainside.

For that is what it felt like now—a mountainside. The forest behind them, they found themselves in the open fields of timberline, the rounded keel of the south ridge rising before them as the invitation it was to the summit of the South Queen. The snow and the sky were unbearably bright, but though they had no sunglasses, the splendor did not hurt their eyes. It was hard to bear only in a deeper way. For neither of them could quite get over the feeling that they did not deserve to be here. And yet the tracks led on, meandering up the peak before them through tiny swirls of rosy finches that rose and rested and rose again.

"Have you climbed this before?" asked Lara.

"Partway," said Purse. "With my mother. Just this ridge, in fact—until it got steep near the top. That's where we turned around." He looked about as if expecting to catch a glimpse of her once again, her wheelchair left far behind. "Have you?" he said.

"Lots," she said. "But not this way. Always up the southwest slope, over there on the left. That was closer to home. It's hard to believe, but I never went willingly. I always complained, like a little brat."

"Do you feel that way now?" he asked. "Unwilling to go?"

"No, it is different. I am different, anyway. Or the mountain is, or both of us are. I feel somehow that I have never been here before. Not that I have been—not at the base of this ridge, exactly. But even if I had come this way, it wouldn't have mattered. Something is new."

"Not some thing," Purse said, gently correcting her. "All things."

At the base of the last and highest tree, a wind-beaten whitebark pine, they found two ice axes plunged upright in the snow, one on either side of the hoof-prints. Purse took the taller one. It had a dull gray adze and pick, and the long shaft was dark with age and smooth from use. The one that Lara grasped was shorter, and white like ash. The head gleamed like pure silver.

"How very convenient," Lara said. "Though somehow I think we hardly need them."

Purse was bent over, examining the shaft of his ax. "There are letters here," he said quietly, "carved in the wood."

Lara checked the shaft of her own ice ax and found it plain. "What do the letters say?" she asked.

"Nothing more than what I have done: *TAKE ME UP.*"

"How curious," Lara merely said. "I wonder what you will use it for."

Axes in hand, they continued in the wake of the tracks up onto the ridge proper, stepping in a comfortable rhythm. On their left the curving ridge merged with broad and open slopes, dazzling in sheer extent. On the right they had to be more careful. Here the ridge dropped suddenly and precipitously down into the scissored bowl of a rumpled glacier, tucked into the side of the mountain. To their surprise, the hoofprints followed the very edge of the drop-off, sometimes crossing cornices that overhung the ice below. These were fragile, as a rule, but plunging their axes quietly as they went along, Purse and Lara did not deviate from the path.

As the day grew hot their feet began to sink farther and farther into the softening spring snow. First there was only a slight give, but by noon perhaps, their calves and then their knees began to slip down beneath the surface. The going was slow, though somehow they were not terribly tired or hungry, and sucking on a little snow seemed enough to quench their thirst. The long ridge led them at last to a steep and icy headwall, almost indistinguishable from the cliffs that surmounted the glacier to their right. The crevasses below them were partly in shade, and the gentler slopes on the southwest were now divided from ridge and headwall by a gully.

"This is it," said Purse. "Here's where my mother and I went back. We didn't have a rope and we didn't really know what we were doing in the first place. I suppose we kick steps with our bare toes for the last thousand feet or so?"

"I think," said Lara, "we just keep walking."

He thought about it. Of course she was right. But having been here once before somehow made it more frightening for him. He fixed his eyes on the blood-prints, ascending far over his head in a steady line, and resolved to trust them. Suddenly he felt calm again.

"And Purse?"

"Yes?"

"Have you ever enjoyed a walk like this so much in your life?"

"Yes, I have," he said deliberately.

"What do you mean?" She wanted to see her feeling shared, not contradicted.

"On the trail in the meadow by the Amoenas—I enjoyed that. On the granite of the Fawn Wall—I enjoyed that. On the waterfall, across the rim, through the forest, at timberline, and here on the ridge—I have loved them all, or am learning to, and plan to enjoy them forever."

Lara considered for a moment. "You are quite right," she admitted. "But doesn't this feel like a culmination of all the rest—as if they were all pointing to this ridge, this summit?"

"No," he said. "Each part culminates the other. Whichever part you are touching at the moment, that is best. We enjoy the snow and the mountain now because we happen to be here. No place takes from another; all places give to the rest. To enjoy the whole is to know any particular part."

"You mean—"

"Yes. The best place is always at hand."

"Convenient enough. But then why strive to go anywhere else?"

"Who's striving? We're just walking, as you said."

And that is all it felt like—a walk. They ascended the headwall at a slow and lovely and steady pace, slotting their axes overhead and settling their feet in the blood-red niches left for them by the hoofprints. There was no need to kick steps after all. Near the top the angle began to ease again, and they soon shuffled dreamily, slinging their axes horizontally in hand. The tracks wandered through chutes and ramps of icy crags, silver in the afternoon, and finally led to a flat terrace framed by two great horns of rock all plastered over with snow and ice. There was nowhere left to climb. And just before them, between the horns, the white fawn lay with his head in the lap of a strange and stunning woman in red.

Chapter 20
For Their Kind Sakes

✳

THE WOMAN WAS STRANGE AND STUNNING because of her glossy hair, raven-black. Her face was high-cheeked, but not proud. And even seated as she was, Purse and Lara could tell that she was very tall. The body of the white fawn almost merged with the wind-driven snow on the summit. But the red gown of the woman stood out like all the hoofprints left behind. It was as if all the shed blood of the fawn were concentrated in what she wore. In fact, as Purse and Lara slowly came forward, it seemed to them that the fawn was healed. He was not bleeding anymore. His open eyes rested calmly on their approach, not glassy and dead but infinitely interested.

Purse stopped nearly at the feet of the fawn, and Lara with him. "If you please," he said nervously. "We are here now."

"And you are most welcome, as you always have been," the woman said. "Welcome, in the name of the fawn."

"Is he really alive, then?" Lara asked.

"Here," said the woman. "Touch him if you will."

Lara stepped forward hesitantly and put her hand to the neck of the fawn. It was warm and soft. A pulse beat under her fingertips. Without warning the fawn arose from the lap of the woman and put his nose against Lara's face. She felt his warm wet breath, and it had in it a wonderful smell, like the ferns and meadows of Otium.

"You *are* alive," Lara whispered.

Purse touched the fawn as well, putting an awkward hand on its back. It turned and breathed against his face too. Soon both of them were clasping its neck, realizing why they had come, feeling that the fawn made every place the best place, and now this place best of all. Then, as simply as he had risen to greet them the fawn released himself from their arms and stepped away, taking up a station between the icy horns of rock on the verge, just behind the woman in red. For a moment they both watched him there. He seemed a part of the many-glaciered drapery of the Center Queen rising behind him, of the broadly cratered North Queen floating beyond. The fawn stood perfectly still. Sometimes he appeared to be there, and sometimes not, as if he were fading in and out of the mountains around him.

The raven-haired woman now stood to her full height, and seemed to fill the sky with red.

"May I ask," said Lara, "who you are?" She noticed now that the woman had almost emerald eyes, like Lady Demaris.

"I am the Lady Lira," she said. She might once have announced this with disdain for her hearers, but now it was simply a statement of fact, neither more nor less.

"Like Lady Demaris?" Lara said.

"And Stella?" said Purse.

"Yes, I am the eldest of the three sisters, though not the truest. Were it not for the blood of the fawn I would long ago have remained the prey of the Lava Beast, or a goddess of stone in the desert temple of El Ai. I have done penance for twenty-four years far beyond the Western Sea, and am only now returned by way of Otium." She held out her arm to the west, and they followed it across ridge after ridge of dark fir and cedar and hemlock, falling away to a glimmer of ocean on the horizon.

"You came with my uncle, then?" said Purse. "Garth, I think?"

"Yes, good Percival, with your uncle I have gone and now returned. Garth, the keeper of this great garden, whose ax you now hold well in hand. He who has always loved me well, as once I did and now I do. It is by his urging I meet you here with the risen fawn on the South Queen, by way of reclaiming injury I once intended upon your parents years ago. And Lara, I once bore no good will toward your courageous father as well. I ask you to forgive me all, for their kind sakes."

"Well—of course," said Lara, confused that she must answer for the sufferings of another time.

"Likewise," Purse mumbled.

"It is strange for you," said Lady Lira. "I see your parents have been discreet. The day will come when I will ask their forgiveness in person. But you now are the first fruits of their perseverance, to hold the ax over all this land and to bring the cup when it is needed. It is to you I realized I first must speak."

To their astonishment, they saw now that Lady Lira was kneeling before them. "You must bless me now, even as the fawn has blessed you."

Purse and Lira looked at each other in greater confusion. They saw that the woman had reached out to touch the ice ax in Purse's hand.

"Long ago I would have given anything to possess this instrument of power," she whispered. "And I did. I gave everything I thought I had, even my soul, though I did not know it was not mine to give away. What else I did not know was this—that the power of the ax is only of justice, and the only power of justice is mercy. So in the end, I have possessed it after all. Everything the ax could give me, I have gained."

She retrieved her hand. "There, I have received its blessing once again, now more quietly than before—even as I have been touched by your own ax, Lara, long ago. I thank you both."

With simple dignity she rose.

"Now, turn about, both of you. Look well on your inheritance."

Purse and Lara slowly turned. Blue sky blazed all about them, golden at the edges in the latening hour of afternoon. The arm of the ridge curved simply downward, an almost living reach of silver, and round about the flanks of the mountain the truly living forest gathered strength and sweep against the snow. They saw the trees descend to the brink of a pearl-gray gash in the earth, the smooth sweet granite of the gorge. The Amoenas River fell away into it, foaming green and white from the east. And in the west a slender pinnacle found the air from the gates of the valley. This was the top of the Tower of Otium, small beneath the Dark Divide.

Lara gave Purse a nudge and pointed. She wanted to ask the fawn, or the lady, if now indeed she would ever climb it. For Otium was a good place too.

"Lady Lira," she began, turning around. Then she caught herself. Lady Lira was still standing just behind them, her gown beginning to billow now in a breath of air that was coming with evening from the sea. But the fawn was nowhere. He had vanished.

Or perhaps the fawn was everywhere.

"Purse," she whispered.

He wheeled and saw. "Of course," he said.

Nevertheless he stepped past Lady Lira and looked over the edge of the face between the horns. Lara joined him. An icy runnel fell several thousand feet to a glacier just below the Center Queen. There was no sign of the fawn.

They stepped back and began to look in every direction. Even up.

"Dear children," said Lady Lira, "do not distract yourselves with searching. You will surely see the fawn again, just as before. In the meantime, you have the ax—you have both axes—and you have all that lies before you. And in them you have one another. Keep all well."

It was a long time before they could speak.

"And Garth?" said Purse. "Where is he?"

"Waiting for you just at my sister's cottage below—to unite you as one and to give you his blessing upon your arrival. Go now, and I will follow. It is meet that you should find him first." With that she seated herself again on the wind-packed snow between the horns. "I will see the sun when it sets over the Western Sea. By then your journey may be done—fresh woods and meadows new."

They looked at her dumbly, as if waiting for her to get up.

"Turn. Go. The hour grows late and shadows lengthen while you linger. I shall stay."

In this rebuke Lara felt a small hint of a power of old. Without thinking to bid Lady Lira farewell, she took Purse's hand in her own and turned to the west, where the gentle slopes led golden now to a snow-buried trail at timberline. From there it would be six miles to an old cabin she could not see but well remembered just below the Center Queen. This time, she knew the way. Hand in hand, axes held out to their sides, they took off running down the summit and hit the top of the snowfield heels-first in a tower of spray.

Acknowledgments

✳

HAVING BEGUN DRAFTING THESE TALES ALMOST THIRTY YEARS AGO, I have surely forgotten some of those who have offered suggestions along the way, and thus must begin by laying a wreath at the tomb of the unknown critic. But some names do roll away the stone. First among them is my brother Dave Willis, whose enthusiasm and ready ideas have helped me always. I thank more generally the intrepid staff of Sierra Treks, my lifelong teachers and friends in the mountains. In particular I thank Laurie Vette for illustrating each tale with an exquisitely detailed map.

Speaking of maps, I must also thank Dr. Maynard M. Miller and the many fine scientists of the Juneau Icefield Research Program, who taught me the use of a theodolite for glacier movement surveys—and who also assigned me the task of charting some passages deep within the Lemon Creek Glacier. It was in the nearby meadows that the marmots first had something to say to me.

Those who have offered thoughtful comment on various ones of these manuscripts are very much appreciated. I think of my good colleagues at Houghton College in New York, Jack Leax and Jim Zoller, and of several current and former colleagues (also good) at Westmont College in Santa Barbara: David Downing, Tom Schmidt, Greg Spencer, and Randy VanderMey. Others who have helped with the text include Mark Baker, David Leigh, Judith Markham, Kathy McClymond, David Oates, John Silbersack, Jack Stewart, Dan Taylor, and Loren Wilkinson. In addition, my former editor Jan Dennis and current editor Mark Eddy Smith have been not only encouraging but also punctilious. All have cleansed my doors of perception.

I also want to express my sincere admiration for friends who have no liking for the fantasy genre and would not read a page. Sam Alvord, that includes you.

Thanks as well to Beth Scherfee for permission to print and adapt her "Sierra

Song." All other borrowed poems and poetic fragments are taken from the public domain. Those writers I have borrowed from include Matthew Arnold, St. Augustine, Lewis Carroll, René Daumal, Sir John Davies, John Donne, Thomas Hardy, George Herbert, John Keats, Richard Lovelace, Christopher Marlowe, John Milton, Christina Rossetti, Robert Service, William Shakespeare, Edmund Spenser, Robert Louis Stevenson, William Wordsworth, and William Butler Yeats (and that is not to mention the internally punctuated Alfred, Lord Tennyson). Where would I be without their sustenance?

Westmont College has provided me with generous release time to draft and edit these tales; more importantly, Westmont has given me a community from which I have not sought release. I am especially grateful to John Blondell for adapting *No Clock in the Forest* for the stage and directing a memorable student production in March 1995.

Finally, I thank my now-grown children, Jonathan and Hanna, for listening to various versions of these tales at bedtime and around the campfire. Most of all I thank my wife, Sharon, for her thoroughgoing love and support. To her I have dedicated this book.

Poetry Attributions
by book and chapter

✳

2.17	"... a jewel hung ..."	William Shakespeare, "Sonnet 27" (1609)
	"Thou, Nature, art ..."	adapted from William Shakespeare, *King Lear* (1604)
	"By the waters ..."	adapted from Psalm 137
	"I love El Ai ..."	[original, with a nod to Randy Newman]
2.18	"We lift our eyes ..."	[original]
	"... darkling plain ..."	Matthew Arnold, "Dover Beach" (1867)
2.19	"Sing for love ..."	adapted from Beth Scherfee, "Sierra Song," and Exodus 15
	"This grassy terrace ..."	[original]
	"The tongues of sand..."	[original]
	"Nurture what is ..."	[original]
	"When you wake ..."	[original]
3.1	"But whilst this ..."	William Shakespeare, *The Merchant of Venice* (1598)
	"Things fall apart ..."	William Butler Yeats, "The Second Coming" (1921)
3.5	"Thou has light ..."	John Donne, "Annunciation" (1633)
3.12	"Nor did I wonder ..."	William Shakespeare, "Sonnet 98" (1609)
	"Let me not to ..."	William Shakespeare, "Sonnet 116" (1609)
3.14	"Our hearts are restless ..."	St. Augustine, *The Confessions* (398)
	"... the deadest thing ..."	Thomas Hardy, "Neutral Tones" (1867)
3.16	"There's a divinity ..."	William Shakespeare, *Hamlet* (1600)
	"At sunset of ..."	[original]
3.17	"Another Grace she ..."	Edmund Spenser, *The Faerie Queene* (1596)
3.18	"When she shall die ..."	[original]
3.19	"And we will all ..."	Christopher Marlowe, "The Passionate Shepherd to His Love" (1599)
	"... then wilt thou ..."	John Milton, *Paradise Lost* (1667)
	"There is an art ..."	René Daumal, *Mount Analogue* (1952; translated 1959) [original is prose]
4.3	"If by thy hands ..."	[original]
	"Ne'er saw I ..."	William Wordsworth, "Upon Westminster Bridge" (1802)
4.5	"Little climber ..."	adapted from The Beach Boys, "Surfer Girl" (1963)
4.8	"... daffodils / That ..."	William Shakespeare, *The Winter's Tale* (1610)
4.9	"The fawne, the cvp ..."	[original]
	"Never false and ..."	[original]
4.10	"... a sense sublime ..."	William Wordsworth, "Tintern Abbey" (1798)
4.12	"When by the rout ..."	John Milton, "Lycidas" (1638)

About the Author

✳

PAUL J. WILLIS IS A PROFESSOR OF ENGLISH AT WESTMONT COLLEGE in Santa Barbara, California. He grew up in Oregon, went to Wheaton College in Illinois, worked as a mountain guide in the Cascades and Sierra Nevada, and received his graduate degrees from Washington State University. He first drafted *No Clock in the Forest* while writing a dissertation on *The Forest in Shakespeare: Setting as Character.*

Willis has published two books of poetry, *Visiting Home* (Pecan Grove Press, 2008) and *Rosing from the Dead* (WordFarm, 2009), and with David Starkey has co-edited *In a Fine Frenzy: Poets Respond to Shakespeare* (University of Iowa Press, 2005). He is also the author of *Bright Shoots of Everlastingness: Essays on Faith and the American Wild* (WordFarm, 2005), named by *ForeWord* magazine as the year's best essay collection from an independent press. His poems and essays have appeared in *The Best American Poetry 1996* (Scribner's), *The Best Spiritual Writing 1999* (HarperSanFrancisco), *The Best American Spiritual Writing 2004* (Houghton Mifflin), and *The Best Christian Writing 2006* (Jossey-Bass).